MUSE OF ART

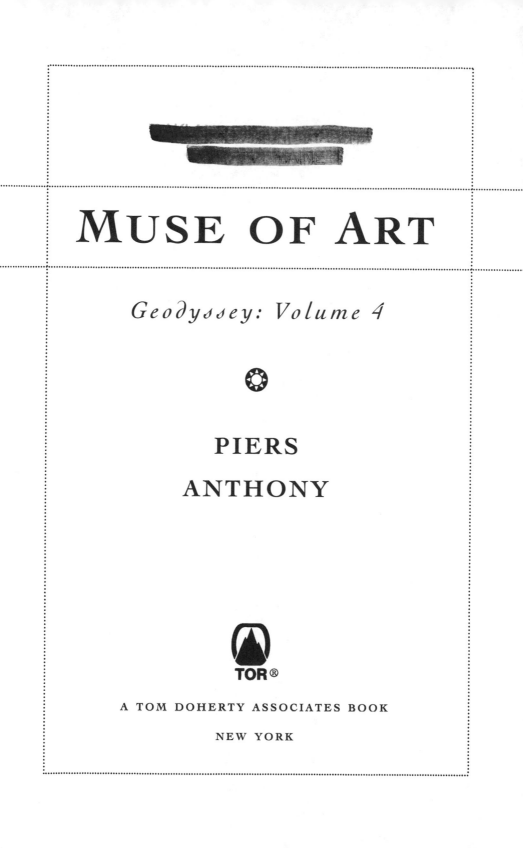

MUSE OF ART

Geodyssey: Volume 4

✦

**PIERS
ANTHONY**

TOR ®

A TOM DOHERTY ASSOCIATES BOOK

NEW YORK

MUSE OF ART

Copyright © 1999 by Piers Anthony Jacob

This book is printed on acid-free paper.

Maps by Ellisa H. Mitchell

A Tor Book
Published by Tom Doherty Associates, Inc.
175 Fifth Avenue
New York, NY 10010

Tor Books on the World Wide Web:
http://www.tor.com

Tor® is a registered trademark of Tom Doherty Associates, Inc.

Library of Congress Cataloging-in-Publication Data

Anthony, Piers.
    Muse of art / Piers Anthony.—1st ed.
        p.   cm. — (Geodyssey ; v. 4)
    "A Tor book"—T.p. verso.
    ISBN 0-312-86896-0
    I. Title. II. Series: Anthony, Piers. Geodyssey ; v. 4.
PS3551.N73M87   1999
813'.54—dc21   99-12905
                                                    CIP

First Edition: May 1999

Printed in the United States of America

0 9 8 7 6 5 4 3 2 1

CONTENTS

MUSE OF ART

A BOUT sixty-five million years ago there was a holocaust on Earth, thought to have been caused by bombardment by meteors and/or monstrous volcanic eruptions, with perhaps attendant rising of gas from the depths of the seas. The mystery has been in the pattern of survivals. There seems to have been considerable randomness. Some reptiles survived, while all the dinosaurs perished. Some mammals survived, though most perished. Some birds survived, similarly, and some fish and other sea life. The survivors hardly seemed better qualified than the species that went extinct. So what was it that set them apart? Sheer luck, or something else?

It may indeed have been something else. The survivors may have been those best protected from the fires and freezes and fumes of air, land, and sea. They were the creatures who dwelt in the deep caves: small insectivores, lichen eaters, and those that preyed on them. The environment of such reaches is constant, even when there are dramatic changes above.

So it may have been that in time the cave dwellers emerged to discover a depleted realm. It was now safe to go beyond the protected depths, and to expand into the larger realm. So they did, radiating into new populations. Among them were the line that became the monkeys, primates, and finally mankind. Of course it wasn't quite that simple, and there can be considerable interest in the nuances.

This is the fourth volume in the GEODYSSEY series—Geo as in geography, Odyssey as in a phenomenal journey—following *Isle of Woman, Shame of Man,* and *Hope of Earth.* The series concerns the evolution and history of our species from the distant past to the near future. Each volume is an independent novel which may be read alone; they all cover the same larger territory, but differ in detail. Each tells the story of a particular family or group of people. Though the total span covered in this volume is half a million years, the main characters are so similar in nature and relationships as to seem continuous, and may be viewed as identical. What changes is their settings, as different aspects of the progress of the human species are explored.

Any creature who deviates too far from his most familiar haunts or customs increases his personal risk. So most who wander, perish. Yet there are rare occasions when the wanderer discovers a better situation, and prospers, while those who remain behind find themselves on a treadmill to extinction. As with mutations, more than 99 percent of deviations may be lethal, but the other 1 percent lead to improved survival, and in the course of time (much time!) the future of the species lies in the 1 percent. Timing counts, too; what is at one time lethal may at another time be the key to survival. So evolution can be devious, and the "correct" decisions may be obscure to the point of denial at the key times of divergence from the norm. One divergence of mankind from all other life forms on Earth is in the realm of the arts. The point in the arts remains obscure to many people (and all animals) even today, yet these arts are vital to the nature of our species. This novel explores a number of them, with the concept defined extremely broadly. Each chapter tackles an art and a historical setting, showing how the two may have interacted in the larger (or smaller) context of the ongoing story.

The major characters of this volume are original to it, but supplementary characters from the three prior volumes do appear on occasion, at the ages and in the situations relevant to the time and geography of the particular settings in which they appear. That is, a person who was young in Roman times in his volume of origin will be young in Roman times in this volume. A person who was a dancer in her own volume will appear as a dancer here. It is, after all, one world.

There is a problem with names, as few single names can properly represent a particular character in time and cultures ranging across half a million years of global history. Accordingly, no particular effort has been made to have realistic names; they are simply convenient identifiers. The real names of such folk would surely have been quite different.

Those who prefer to follow only the story line may skip the italicized material prefacing and concluding each chapter, and the concluding Author's Note. But I hope that most readers will find the nonfictive material intriguing too. It is, after all, the point of the volume and the series. The entertainment value is the sugar coating to make readers who might otherwise be uninterested pay attention. This is, bluntly, a message novel, and the message is that our species has much to recommend it, but is also a threat to the welfare of the natural world and to itself. Those who are turned off by that are welcome to read my funny fantasy instead.

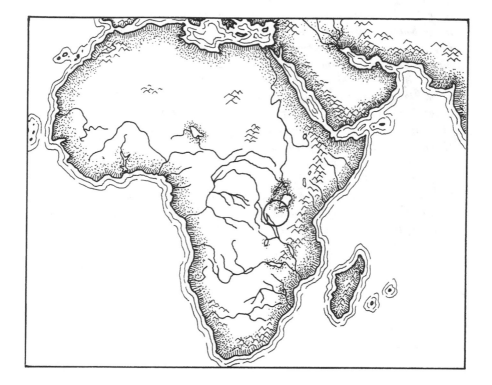

CHAPTER 1

CURIOSITY

Two million years ago, Homo erectus *(henceforth simply* Erectus*) emerged from Africa and conquered the world. As he settled in different regions and climates, he adapted to local conditions, starting the familiar process of speciation. One might suppose that changes would be most extreme in the farthest reaches of the world, but that may not have been the case. The continent of Africa is as varied as any, ranging from the vast Sahara Desert to tropical jungles to snow-covered mountains. One of the most striking features is the Great Rift Valley, which may have been responsible for the distinctive evolution of* Australopithecus, Homo habilis, Homo erectus, *and finally modern mankind. Most of the fossils*

*of early hominids have been found there. This does not necessarily mean that this
was the source; it could be that the species were resident elsewhere, but the conditions were not suitable to preserve their bones. So that only those who happened to
die in the Rift made fossils. But for the purpose of this novel, it is assumed that
the Rift was the source, and this chapter suggests why. The locale is the mountain
range bounding the northeast shore of Lake Tanganyika, not far south of the
equator. Lake Victoria is across the plains to the northeast. Erectus lives both on
the plain and in the mountains, and has a common culture, but the two habitats
are so different that already the transition between them is not easy. This is bound
to lead to relative genetic isolation of the population residing in the geographically
isolated Rift. The time is half a million years before the present era: 500,000 B.P.E.*

*Curiosity might seem like (no pun) a curious art. But just about anything can
become an art if pursued appropriately. In the Introduction the ratio of mutations
is mentioned, wherein more than 99 percent are harmful, but the 1 percent account
for progress necessary to long-range survival. It may be similar, if less extreme, for
character traits. The curious cat may have died, but the curious human being
may have set foot on a path to ultimate satisfaction. For in the dangerous explo-
ration of the unknown lies the key to rare knowledge.*

THE fire mountain struck so suddenly that it caught Od off-guard. He
had watched it warily for days as it rumbled and shook and belched
roiling clouds of smoke. He knew it was dangerous, but his insatiable curiosity had drawn him in anyway. Just what kind of wood did it burn, to
make such smoke? What was going on, down inside the mountain? Could
he find a way inside, to see the source of the mystery? But then it blew out
such fierce smoke, and drooled flowing fire, and suddenly Od could not
go back the way he had come.

He hastily secured his precious bit of fire. He had made a fire-bed in a
large animal skullcap, closing it in with another section of skull so that the
ember would burn very slowly. Right now there was more fire all around
than he could handle, but he had worked so hard to capture some of it
that he was determined to hold on to it. He tucked the closed shell into
his waistband and looked around for the best retreat from this mountain.

A woman screamed. Od looked, and saw her standing still while a monstrous snake of fire twined toward her. He ran to help—and saw another
man running in from the opposite direction.

They arrived almost together. The other man was large and brutish-
looking, so Od gave way; he wasn't keen on fights with bigger men. The
man stopped beside the woman and looked down at her feet. She had
gotten one foot tangled in a mass of vines and couldn't pull it free. Instead
of using her hands to part the vines, she was just standing helplessly and
screaming, girl-fashion.

No, that wasn't a fair assessment. She had simply panicked, because she
was caught just as the fire threatened, as anyone might.

The other man reached down to free her foot, then cursed and pulled
back his hand. Now Od saw that the hand was injured; only the fistful of

green leaves the man grasped stopped the blood from flowing. He couldn't use that hand until it healed.

So Od stepped in and addressed the captive foot. The woman's leg was nicely formed, and so was her body; she was a beauty. The kind who wouldn't smile at Od, ordinarily, because of his slight stature and lack of heavy muscle. But she was too busy screaming to notice his liabilities right now.

He tried to work the vines loose, but she kept yanking her leg, trying to free it, and the vines responded by tightening up. There was no time to waste, because the fire snake was coursing closer; he smelled the burning brush and leaves. So he brought out his chipped stone blade and sawed at the vines. In a moment they parted, and the foot pulled free.

The woman, off-balanced by the sudden release, stepped back, and would have fallen to the ground. But the other man caught her with his uninjured hand and held her upright. His forearm crossed her breast, and his eyes were widening as he realized.

But the fire snake was almost upon them. "Up!" Od cried. "Flee up!" For he had seen that the fire snake flowed downward, in the manner of water. The way to avoid it was to go in the direction it did not.

But the two seemed distracted. The woman didn't seem to realize that she was now free to run, and the man was still appreciating her breast. Both were too concerned with details to appreciate the larger situation.

"Up!" Od repeated. "Fire come!"

Now they looked where he pointed, and realized the immediacy of the danger. They separated and bolted for the slope Od indicated. He ran there too, as the foliage around them burst into flame.

They reached the top of a hillock and could not go farther, because it descended on the far side. Already the fire snake was licking at it, curling around and swelling as it burned everything it touched. Then it divided and coursed along on both sides of the hillock, trying to make it an island.

"Flee here!" Od cried, appreciating the danger.

But already there was fire to either side, and its heat was intense. The stream on one side was thin, but fire was bursting out wherever it touched. They might jump over the fire snake, but how could they avoid the brush burning around it?

But he saw that the streams had not yet flowed far beyond the hillock. The fire snake tended to slow and thicken at the lead edge, and then more liquid fire would flow across it and course on beyond. It was interesting to see, but too deadly to study at the moment.

"Down! Around!" Od cried.

They just stared at the fire, not understanding him.

"Follow!" Od cried, and ran the way he knew it had to be. Then, as they still hesitated, he repeated "Follow!"

At last they acted, following him. He led them down the slope until they were beyond one of the fire snakes, then cut across ahead of it to reach some more rising ground. This time he made sure it led on up into the mountain, so they could not get trapped again.

The way got steep, and they had to slow. But they had left the fire snake behind, and it was not following. It was safe to slow down, for now.

That was just as well, for the woman was panting. Her large breasts rose and fell rapidly, attracting the eye.

"Safe," Od said, slowing to a walk. Then he tapped his chest. "Od."

The man tapped his own chest. "Pul."

The woman did not tap her chest. She cupped a breast. "Avalanche," she said, giving the word for a terrible slide of rocks down a mountain.

"Od—morning sun man," he said, introducing himself further. He meant that he came from the direction of the rising sun.

"Pul—evening sun man." He pointed toward a region beyond the fire mountain.

"Avalanche—plains woman." She pointed toward a region to the south.

So they were from three different tribes. The man must have been hunting, and the woman must have been foraging, and they had gotten caught by the anger of the fire mountain. Just as Od had been caught because he had been too curious about it. Of course that wasn't the whole story, by any means.

Then a large animal charged toward them. It was a beest, huge and shaggy and powerful, with dangerous horns, galloping blindly, crazed by the fires. They were in its way, because this was a region clear of brush.

Avalanche screamed again, and started running directly away from the bull. That was sheer folly. "Run across!" Od cried. He knew that none of them could hope to match the speed of the giant creature. But she wasn't hearing him.

He caught at Pul's good arm. "Across!" he repeated, pointing.

Pul nodded. He surely had had experience dodging such creatures. He sprinted after the woman, caught her around the small waist, and hurled her and himself out of the way as the beest charged through.

"Rescue!" Avalanche exclaimed as they untangled, and managed a smile.

Od caught up to them. "Bad, here," he said. "Animals."

Pul nodded. There could be other crazed creatures fleeing the fires. Ordinarily even large animals avoided people, but this was different.

The mountain rumbled, making the ground shake. Avalanche looked wildly around, plainly terrified, and Pul seemed little better off. Od realized that it was up to him to discover an escape from this dangerous region, because it was clear that they were likely to die if they remained here.

The problem was that the fire rivers kept coming, and the fires they started in the vegetation were spreading. Smoke was clouding upward in several places, marking the carnage. Even if the three people survived the heat, there would be nothing left for them to forage. Survival was more than merely escaping danger; they had to be where they could find food.

He peered up the slope—and saw that it was one of the roots of the fire mountain. There was nothing up there but destruction. But if they went down, they would be joining the fire rivers. Even if they got around one, there would be others. How could they escape them all?

He would have to arrange to see the larger pattern. That meant going up, even if it was the wrong mountain.

He started up. "Where?" Pul asked nervously.

Could he explain? "Up—see down."

Sure enough, both the man and woman were confused. So Od simply moved on, because he feared that there was not much time. The two followed him, though he did not want it. He expected to return this way when he knew better where to go, so there was no need for them to stay close. But how could he explain that? So he continued moving, letting them follow.

He found an outcropping of rock and mounted that. From here there was a fair view of the valley below. There were two rivers of fire, one on either side of this region, and their paths were converging. They would meet near the water river that wound between this mountain and the next one. The next mountain was quiet; its foliage was untouched, and no smoke issued from its summit. It looked safe.

Now he knew his best course. Straight down to the river, across it, and straight up the other mountain. Avoiding the fires along the way. There should be time to do it, if they hurried.

He started down. "Where?" Pul demanded.

"River," Od explained. "Fast."

"Smoke!" Avalanche protested. "Fire!"

Again, how could he explain? But he tried. "Bad," he said, pointing up the slope to the fuming top of the mountain they were on. Then he pointed across to the other mountain. "Good."

They seemed to want to argue, but then the mountain rumbled again, more violently. That convinced them. They started down the slope, as he did.

As they got lower, the smoke spread out to cut them off. Od didn't want to go through it, but didn't want to wait for it to clear, either. The smoke was thinner near the ground. So he bent low, carrying his head below waist level, and ran on down. The others hesitated, then followed similarly. It was awkward, but possible to breathe, and he could see ahead far enough to avoid any open blazes.

Because he knew where he was going, he soon reached the water river. But the fire rivers were closing on them, and the smoke from the burning vegetation was worse. So he plunged in.

Avalanche screamed. Startled, Od looked back—and saw a large shape nearby. Then he realized that it was merely a piece of a tree, not a water predator. He swam on across the river.

After a moment the other two followed. As they reached the farther bank, one of the fire rivers struck the water river, and there was a huge hissing and cloud of steam. It was uncertain which would win the battle between fire and water, but this was no good place for people, regardless. They had made it in time, but not by much.

Now they moved on up the new slope, leaving the raging fires behind.

But the continued hissing of the river indicated that the issue had not been settled; more fire was flowing. They needed to get as far away from it as possible.

"Up," Od decided. Because the fire rivers would not follow them there, and maybe not the big galloping animals.

The others did not question it. They followed him as he picked his way up the slope. Wafts of smoke and steam pursued them, so that they didn't pause, though the steep climb was tiring. They knew it could be death to let the fires catch them.

Pul was the strongest, and soon he was forging ahead. When Avalanche tired, he helped her keep the stiff pace, while Od followed. He saw her clinging close, her body rubbing against the man's body from shoulder to thigh. It was usually thus, with larger, stronger men getting the women. Od wished that he could impress a woman similarly, but of course he could not.

They plunged on until the fire mountain shrank in the distance. The smoke faded, and the air became fresh, with only a tinge of the smell of burning remaining. As evening approached, the day cooled, but they were sweating. Still, how would it be when they stopped for the night?

They converged on a tiny driblet of a stream. Suddenly Od realized how thirsty he had become. The others were the same; they staggered toward the water. But there was nothing there to drink; it was hardly more than a moistening in the soil.

"Water!" Pul cried. "Drink!"

Od considered. Normally streams grew larger as they descended. But it would not be good to follow this one back down the mountain. Maybe there was a pool somewhere above. It seemed the best chance, all things considered.

"Up," he said.

They stared at him. "Water down," Pul said.

"Fire down," Od reminded him.

The man grimaced and nodded. They followed the stream up.

As darkness closed, they found the origin of the stream. It issued from a deep small cave. At the mouth of the cave the water pooled.

Pul threw himself down on his belly and plunged his face into the water, sucking it up noisily. When he was sated, Avalanche took her turn, more delicately drawing in the liquid. Finally Od had his chance—and the pool had been depleted. They had not left any for him. But he knew that it would in time refill; he would just have to endure until it did.

Now Avalanche began digging in the moist dirt of the stream bed, looking for clams to eat. But there were none; this was too high, without enough steady moisture. So she foraged for tubers instead, and soon found some. She was a plains woman, Od remembered, not conversant with this kind of terrain; but maybe she knew where to find food.

But the roots she produced were inedible. "Fire," she said.

Fire—to cook them with. Od remembered his shells. Had his ember survived his swim across the river? He brought it out, opened it, and blew on it. The outside material was soggy, but a faint glow remained in the center. "Fire," he said, satisfied.

Avalanche quickly fetched dry moss and leaves. Od added moss to his ember as he blew on it, and after a moment the bright spot enlarged. Then the moss caught, and he had a small open flame.

After that it was routine. They got a fire going, collecting fallen branches to sustain it, and roasted the tubers. In that period Od checked the cave pool, and found that enough water had seeped in to give him a drink. At last he was able to slake his thirst.

But now the air was becoming cold, and they were inadequately prepared. Pul especially; he was shivering. Od realized that the man's injury was weakening him. He looked cold, but his body was hot. Sometimes wounded men got that way, and they had to rest and be kept warm, or they could become very ill and even die.

How could the man be warmed? The fire wasn't enough, and would be less as it died out. Od considered, and concluded that they needed a way to hold the heat in. "Shelter," he said.

Avalanche nodded. She helped him forage for longer branches, and for leaves. By the light of the fire they made a lean-to and chinked it with small branches, leaves, and dirt. Then Od made a fire inside it, astonishing both Avalanche and Pul. "Burn shelter," the man protested.

"Small," Od said reassuringly. "Warm."

Soon they saw that it was so. His small fire heated the shelter, and when they crawled into it, they were warm.

There was barely enough room for the three of them, however; they were jammed in together behind the fire. There was another problem: the moment Pul was in contact with Avalanche, he desired her. "Avalanche," he said. "Sex."

"Pul," she agreed. "Sex." She had obviously expected this. It was a natural consequence of proximity. A young woman next to a man could not be ignored.

The two had made their contract: they wished to copulate. That meant that Od needed to give them privacy, for as a rule it was not done publicly. Not until a couple was formally established, so that everyone knew; then they could indulge in any sex-play they wished, at any time. It was the first experimental liaisons that were normally hidden. So he crawled out of the shelter and went to forage in the dark for more wood for the fire. It would probably be needed by morning.

He paused a moment to orient on the surroundings, pulling his hide shawl close about him. The air was surprisingly cold, and he thought it must be because the mountain was cold, just as the other mountain was hot. He saw the distant glow of the fires in the valley, and smelled the faint echo of their smoke, which differed from that of his own tame fire.

Now he heard the sounds of the union of Pul and Avalanche. He was a big strong man; she was a beautiful woman, so it made sense. But how Od wished that he could have been someone or done something to deserve the woman!

It was always thus. He simply was not the kind of man who impressed women. Not the good ones. His liaisons had been brief and not wholly satisfactory. The top man always took the prettiest woman, and the second man took the second prettiest, and so on down. Od, at the bottom, got the ugliest woman, or the infirm one. Some of them were willing enough, but were simply not as appealing as the pretty ones.

Still, it had seemed that his luck was turning, recently. But then—

He shook off the thought. What use to dwell on his misfortune?

He found his way by memory and feel, and soon had a good armful of wood. He brought it back and dumped it down just outside the shelter, knowing that the sound would signal his return, if Pul and Avalanche hadn't completed their liaison. He paused a moment, then got down to crawl into the warmth with them.

They were indeed done; it must have been quick. Avalanche, perhaps not quite satisfied, wanted to talk. "Avalanche—leave tribe," she said.

So she wasn't just coincidentally isolated by the sudden action of the fire mountain. She had chosen to leave it, or had been exiled. But why would such a beautiful woman leave on her own—or be sent away?

"Baby no," she explained. And there it was: a girl was not considered to be a woman until she bore her first baby. Then she was suitable for regular association with a man. So girls began having sex as soon as they were able, even before their breasts formed, hoping for an early passage to the estate of maturity. It was all right for any man to indulge himself with such girls, even if he already had a woman, for a girl was not a woman. Indeed, it was an expected diversion for those men whose women were large with child. Only with her passage to maturity did a girl achieve the rights of adulthood.

Avalanche, it turned out, had had sex with every man in her tribe, and many times with some, but after a hand full of years she had not borne a baby. So the mature women had ruled that she must go, because barrenness was not acceptable. Every tribe needed babies, for there were never enough children. That was the official reason. It was also clear that a number of the men were enjoying their diversions with Avalanche too much, for she had a fuller body than some women who had borne babies. Women were not supposed to be jealous of girls, but in this case it seemed they were. They wanted Avalanche committed to one man, or gone. Without a baby, she could not be committed, so she was exiled.

"Baby," she concluded. "Must."

Od nodded in the dark. She had to have a baby, or she would be unable to remain in any tribe. Most girls were small of breast, thin of hip, and inexperienced in the ways of passion, so were no competition to mature women. By the time they filled out fully, and learned how best to please men, becoming fully attractive, they had their first baby. But Avalanche was large of breast, broad of hip, fair of face, and well experienced in passion.

Naturally the mature women were not eager to have her associating with their men. So her beauty was her curse, and had cost her her place in the tribe. She was a pariah, an outcast.

Avalanche nudged Pul. She had spoken her part and made her confession; now it was his turn.

Reluctantly he spoke. "Pul. Leader. Beat."

Oh. Pul had been a tribe leader, finally challenged and beaten by another man. Hence his damaged hand. An ordinary man of a tribe could be beaten and remain; he merely lost his place to the one who had beaten him. But when the leader lost, there was no place for him in the tribe, because the new leader would not want the constant threat of rechallenge. So if he survived, he was exiled. He would then have to find another tribe to join, either challenging its leader, or accepting the lowly status of the bottom man. Some lost leaders preferred to die. Pul evidently preferred to live. But he couldn't fight again until his hand healed, and that could be a long time.

A man could live alone, but it wasn't necessarily easy, especially if he was incapacitated. He would not be able to hunt effectively, and he wouldn't know how to forage effectively, assuming he beat down his pride enough to try it. So Pul was in trouble—unless he stayed with Od and Avalanche. No wonder he had not been eager to speak of his situation. But there was a certain honor among people; if they spoke of things among friends, they had to speak truly. Pul needed friends, so was obliged.

Avalanche nudged Od. It was his turn. He was really no more eager than Pul, or perhaps than Avalanche herself, but he too was obliged. So he started speaking, trying to find the words to convey the nuances, for strangers would not know them automatically.

"Od. Bottom. Ugly women." He felt the other two nodding in the darkness; they knew how it was.

"Band. Hand years. Change women." Again he felt their nods. They knew how a band of young men normally associated with a band of young women, each man taking the best of the women left after the higher men had chosen. Actually this was a sometimes thing, beginning as children formed social bands of their own without yet leaving their parents' bands. Boys associated with boys, and girls with girls. But as they developed their roles, the boys became increasingly proficient as hunters and fighters, and the girls as foragers, so they tended to associate increasingly, trading their wares. As they grew older, the boys became interested in sex, and the girls found it a convenient tool to encourage male attention and assistance. So a boy band would associate with a girl band for several months, trying things out, then move on to a new band. Gradually the individual associations became more serious, and when the girls started getting pregnant, commitments became semi-permanent. New couples could join established adult bands, but some of the youth bands remained, slowly losing members as couples dropped out, and becoming more adult themselves. Such maturing male-female band associations typically lasted three, four, or five

years—the number of fingers on one hand—so that the women had time
to bear their babies, nurse them, and wean them. By then the passion of
love had subsided, and both men and women were ready for new associations. So the male band would move on, leaving the children with the
women. When they found a new female band that was also looking, they
would start the process over, the top men taking the most desirable women.
But women with children tended to lose interest in moving on to new men.
Eventually there would be too few willing to move on, and the male and
female bands might merge and become permanent, or the men might join
the bands of their women's parents. The men were more willing than the
women to move on, but there were constraints, such as not wishing to leave
their children behind. So the old ways passed. But Od's male band had
remained viable, though it had to search ever-farther for suitable female
bands, and to be ready to consider some rather young girls. Pre-nubile girls
were often eager to gain experience, but Od's interest was in mature
women. It was a mixed situation, and time to find a permanent adult band.
If he could. He had not dared leave what he had, until some better opportunity offered.

Then Od's luck had turned, because something unusual happened.
"Woman top man no," Od said. Now there was surprise in his limited
audience. The most desirable woman had turned down the top man? It was
her right; a man was not supposed to take a woman without her acquiescence. But normally any woman wanted the top man, for that conferred
privileges on her. Women knew that they would not remain desirable long,
for much of beauty was in youth. Mating with the top man guaranteed top
status for several years. But if the top man were especially ugly, or brutal,
a woman who was very sure of herself could decline. Then he would pick
the next most desirable, who would thereafter rank the one who had declined. It happened rarely, but it happened.

"Woman next man no," Od continued. "Woman all men no. Woman Od
yes." There was a sigh of romantic appreciation from Avalanche, and a grunt
of disapproval from Pul. The most desirable woman of the band had chosen
to mate with the least desirable man. This was almost unheard of.

"Od love woman," he said. Avalanche reached out in the darkness to
touch him, briefly. Of course he had loved her! What else could he do?
She was desirable. A man hardly had a choice, once she fixed on him. Her
flesh compelled him.

Pul made a sound of disgust. He still didn't like the idea of a desirable
woman turning down the top men.

"Od happy," Od continued. What an understatement! It had been sheer
delight to sleep in her arms. For the first time he was possessing a truly
lovely woman.

Now came the difficult part. "Od make fire." They knew that already,
but he had a special point. "People know. Woman like."

Avalanche touched him again, understanding. A woman liked a competent man, and few men could make a new fire. This woman had liked

smartness rather than physical power. Some women were like that. It was a woman thing.

"Fire burn shelter," he said. "Hurt people. Od blamed. Od banished." And there it was: the reason for his exile from the band. He had been blamed for starting the fire that had hurt the band. He hadn't done it, but everyone knew that he was the fire person, so the blame had fallen naturally to him. He had had no way to refute it.

"Od burn?" Pul asked, verifying.

"No."

"High man take woman," Avalanche said.

Od shrugged. He didn't know what happened to the woman after he left. She had had to stay with her band, and would have had to take one of the other men.

"High man make fire," Pul said.

"Take woman," Avalanche repeated.

Suddenly it connected. They had understood what he had not: one of the bypassed men had set the fire to frame Od, so as to get his woman. So obvious, yet he had never suspected. How neatly he had been displaced!

Then Pul dropped off to sleep. His loud snoring filled the shelter.

Avalanche crawled out, probably needing to urinate. Od remained, hoping to become acclimatized to the snoring so that he could sleep. Then the woman returned, crawling in on his side. He thought she had gotten confused, but then she whispered "Od: sex?"

But she had just had sex with Pul. Why should she want it again? "Why?"

"Find man. Baby," she explained.

Oh. She was trying all men, until she found the one who could give her a baby, so that she could achieve woman status. If that man happened to be one of these two, she could be sure only by having sex with both. It was a practical matter.

"Quiet," she said. That, too, made sense, since it wouldn't be politic to wake Pul. She had no commitment to the man; they were just people thrown together by chance, doing what they could to get along with each other. That was why their actual act of sex had been private. Still, it seemed somewhat like cheating.

But she was extremely desirable. She wasn't the woman he had had, or necessarily one he would want to associate with regularly, but she was good enough for this night. "Avalanche. Sex," he agreed.

But as he put his arms around her, she stiffened. "Avalanche. Band," she said.

So there was after all a price on it. She wanted help in gaining admission to another band. He understood her desire; her life would be far better within a mature band. Even if she bore a baby, she might be required to assume girl status, until she bore a baby for the woman's band, fathered by one of the men of its associated band. But she would not be admitted at all, if it were known that she was barren.

So how could she get in? Od pondered the matter, as Avalanche rubbed the length of her body against him while retaining her token resistance. She was demonstrating what she offered, without yet acquiescing. His body responded eagerly; he did desire her, and she knew it. In fact the places she was rubbing him were excruciatingly well chosen. She had obviously learned a lot during her extended girlhood.

He needed to discover an answer. Actually he needed an answer for himself, too, because he hated being alone. That was why he had tolerated bad treatment in his band for so long. He wanted other men to hunt with, and a woman to sleep with, and only in a band were those things feasible. He could probably join one, but he would start at the bottom again, and have the worst choice of women. But that was the price of his need for continual company. Pul, too, would have to seek another band. At least when his hand healed, he should be able to join one, because he was a large, strong man, an asset, if he didn't challenge the chief. That would be Od's advice to Pul: accept low status, then work his way up later.

But that didn't solve the woman's problem. Women were more closely linked than men, because their daughters remained in the band with them when they became women. The girls formed their girl bands, getting experience with foraging and male relations, but when they got serious, they preferred to bring their men into their parents' bands. Only sons went off to join or form new bands on a permanent basis. So men were often going to new bands, while women seldom did. Their girl bands were more like play, and a majority of girls left them when they became women. The sisterhood of a female band could be extremely intolerant of female intrusions, unless it was too small and needed more members. So Pul could surely find a male band, but Avalanche, lovely as she was, might not readily find a female band. Unless she cared to settle for membership in a girl-child band, and she was plainly getting beyond that.

Then he had it. "Go with man. Sister." For at times brothers were responsible for sisters, and sought to place them in good female bands. The brother would join a male band and his sister would join the associated female band, both taking other partners.

"Baby no," she reminded him. A barren sister would be as unwelcome as any other barren woman.

"Avalanche. Baby. Die." She should say that she had borne a baby, but it had died. That would qualify her as a woman. How could they know otherwise? Women did lose babies. Because such a loss was considered a sign of evil, such women could be exiled from their bands, so that the malady would not spread to others. It would explain her situation perfectly.

She liked it. She relaxed, and gave him immediate entry to her body. He clasped her and finished almost instantly, after the balked arousal. Whether he liked her he wasn't sure, but this was an enormous relief.

Then she withdrew and returned to her side of the shelter. Soon she was sleeping.

Od, satisfied with the conclusion of the day if not with the rest of it, pondered longer before sleeping. He had figured out the way for them to solve their problems, but the three of them could not do it together. So he would go his own way, when he could, and let the two of them join other bands. He believed that there were mature bands in the mountains, because he had heard of them. It would be best if the three fugitives found bands in the mountains, because those bands did not seem to associate much with the bands on the plains. Maybe things would be better there.

He had gotten to sleep late, and slept late. When he woke, he was alone in the shelter. Pul and Avalanche had moved on without him. That was to be expected, yet he was disappointed; he had hoped for an association of at least a few days, and maybe some more secret sex with her. His luck had not changed. Well, at least he would get to do more individual exploring, satisfying his curiosity about the fire mountain. That was a partial consolation.

The three were, inadvertently, entering a new type of life. The temporary youth bands were no longer feasible. The mountains of the Rift were so different from the plains as to represent a distinct habitat where the old modes of hunting, foraging, and sleeping did not fare well. Instead of going in their separate bands by day, and coupling by night, people had to crowd together for warmth. The days were warm enough, but the nights in the heights were chill. It became necessary to make larger shelters where entire bands or tribes could sleep together, and to bring fire inside them to supplement the warmth of the massed bodies. So men and women had to be together in close company with other couples. This was awkward in a number of respects. A woman lying between two men could spark a quarrel between those men, because each desired her exclusively. Some people adapted better than others, and special mental and physical talents developed. Evolution was driven by the habitat of the Rift, and though the adjustments seemed subtle or inconsequential at first, they became significant in time. Curiosity, learning well from unusual experience, the ability to tolerate crowding, to wait one's turn, to practice deception, and to adapt to a changing situation: small but important human traits. Indeed, those bands of Erectus that moved into the Rift were to become a new species: humankind.

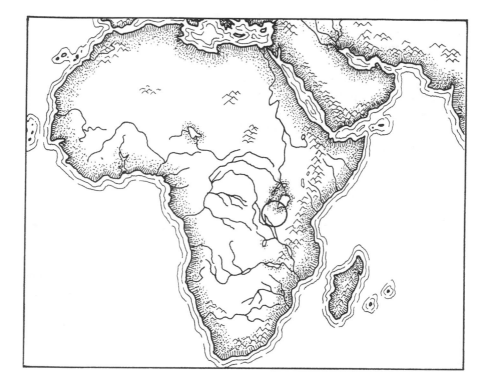

CHAPTER 2

HEALING

Two hundred thousand years of separation in the Rift allowed that portion of Erectus that lived there to deviate from the main portion, and the deviation was driven by the special needs of the mountain habitat. Different forms of hunting and foraging developed, but these were routine. The major change was social, facilitated by the remarkable change in the nature of verbal communication. Man's projecting snout receded to facilitate the production of an enormous range of sounds, weakening its structure, so that his chin had to be braced by an odd external growth of bone lest it be broken in combat or accident. His throat changed, so that it became possible for him to choke while drinking. There had to be a powerful advantage to improved verbalization, to compensate for these potentially lethal liabilities.

There was also advantage in the art of healing, but this was not necessarily apparent to many members of a group. Until a crisis clarified it.

HEATH looked ahead. There was someone coming up the path from the south. He could tell by the outline and motion that it was an unknown male. "Strange man," he said warningly.

The old woman shrugged. "He comes to mate."

"I must challenge him."

She shrugged again, and stood still.

Heath stepped toward the intruder, intercepting him. "Who?" he called.

The man stopped. "Od."

"Why?"

"To join the tribe."

"You will mate with one of our girls?"

"Yes."

"Then stay with the two of us, and I will bring you to the tribe. We are the River Foragers."

Od nodded. He had probably already known it.

"Now we must find your herb," Heath told Bata. He took her elbow again.

The woman resumed motion. Od stood aside, having no rights and no opinions relating to this tribe, until he mated with one of its girls and made her a woman. He turned to follow them at a respectful distance as they walked.

"By the crevice, deep," the old hag said. "There."

Heath was disgusted, but had to take her there. Bata was so feeble that he had to hold her emaciated elbow firmly to keep her from falling, and the walk took forever.

The crevice was a former tributary to the river. A number of useless odd plants took refuge there.

"Small, with a thick stem," Bata said. "Broad leaves. Gray flower buds. It brings down fever, when boiled in water."

Heath refrained from asking her why anyone would want to drink anything to bring down fever, when all the River Foragers were healthy, and in any event, cool water handled fever well enough. He delved into the crevice—and spied the herb she had described. It was half hidden amidst other brush. She would never have found it herself, for she was almost blind. "I have it," he said.

"Is the stem woody?"

It wasn't. He was tempted to tell her it was, but refrained. "No."

"Then it is the one. Take one leaf only," she said. "Do not kill the plant."

He obeyed, and gave her the leaf. She took it as if it were good food, and held it in her withered hand.

They started back to the main camp. "My mate's grandmother," Heath mentioned to Od. The man had probably already caught on to that, too.

"She knows much," Od said with seeming appreciation.

Heath led the old woman to the big shelter. She was so feeble that he had to brace her by the elbow to enable her to climb the steep slope, and he had to guide her constantly because of her excruciatingly weak vision. He resented the time and effort required to attend to her, but she was his mate's grandmother, and so he had to see to her welfare also. He would never voice this, because he loved his lovely mate, but privately he hoped the ancient hag would die soon, and free him of this chore. This business of keeping ancestors alive long past their usefulness to the tribe disgusted him.

They reached the shelter at dusk, where Baya was waiting. He kissed her and squeezed her ample breast, then settled down beside her, with her grandmother on her other side, and her lovely little sister Melee beyond. Baya made it all worthwhile. And of course Grandmother Bata would probably not live much longer.

Men heaped the fire high, and the delightful flames leaped up, illuminating and warming the shelter, driving back the dark chill of night. Heath stared into the dancing pattern of it, loving all that it represented. He had always felt most comfortable when near the fire. Bad animals did not come, and the heat was wonderful. He saw others staring similarly. Fire was inherently fascinating.

Then the humming began. It spread through the group, growing loud. Heath joined in, loving this too. The sound generated real togetherness. The women hummed high, and the men hummed low, and from this combination came a harmony that delighted them all.

After a time the song faded, and the men made their reports. Each got his bragging rights, telling what he had accomplished during the day. When Heath's turn came, he was ashamed to say that he had been occupied mostly with fetching a stupid leaf for a crone, so he focused on the other matter: the arrival of a new man. "I found Od. The girls can choose him, if they wish."

There was a squeal of delight from the girls. Od had to stand up, naked, in the center of the shelter, by the fire, and let the girls explore him. Explore they did, feeling his hair, his arms, and his penis, to make sure it had life. Of course it did, with the soft hand of a nascent woman squeezing it. Heath saw that it was Melee doing it; that mischievous girl was only two hands and two fingers old, but already capable of turning a man on. Others chuckled at Od's embarrassment; this was part of the initiation. It was the main chance the girls had to be forward without reproof, and they gloried in it even if not serious about mating. Soon most lost interest, because Od was not a large or handsome man.

"What do you do?" one of the remaining girls asked him. She was Bevy, well developed, and perhaps tired of the incidental attentions men gave her. If she mated, she would have to put up with only one man. She was also too smart for comfort; others got tired of her difficult questions.

"I make fire," Od said. He brought out a shell, and showed her how he had an ember in it.

"Are you smart or stupid?"

He glanced at her, smiling. "I think you already know."

She liked that. "I will take you."

No other girl spoke, so it was done. Bevy took his hand, then kissed him, then led him to her place in the shelter where they would soon have sex. They were now mates.

It was Bata's turn, as the eldest member of the tribe. Baya and Melee helped her to sit up straight. "Today I found a herb to reduce fever," she said, pleased. "I remember it from when I was a child, and my grandmother showed me."

The tribesfolk accepted that politely, though it was evident that they were no more interested in such arcane things than Heath was.

Then the folk settled down to sleep, each in his or her regular place. Some couples had sex under covers, carefully ignored by their neighbors. The new man, Od, was one of these. He was now accepted by the River Foragers. He would hunt and fish with them, and defend them from enemies, and they would defend him. His admittance to the tribe had been easy, because they were in need of men, but the commitment was serious.

Grandmother Bata lay back to sleep. Baya made her comfortable with extra leaf pillows, then nestled against Heath, not speaking. It was her way of understanding his annoyance, and rewarding him for his patience.

It was sufficient. He clasped her closely, and slept. Baya was the daughter of the chief, but that wasn't why he loved her. She was a good woman. Sometimes he felt guilty because he didn't love her more. But older men said that love took time to deepen and ripen, as new aspects of the relationship were discovered.

He woke to a rumbling or shaking; he wasn't sure what it was. There were muddled shrieks as others woke, confused and frightened. But in a moment the disturbance subsided, and people relaxed. Maybe it was just a buffet by a passing storm. He saw Melee settling back to sleep, her slender bare legs flexing for a moment in the air. That image stayed with him as he closed his eyes.

But then Baya's grandmother started making a clamor, as if the disturbance hadn't been bad enough already.

"Get out!" Bata cried in her thin voice. "Get out! Get out! Get out!"

"But it's gone, Grandmother," Baya said soothingly.

"No it's not!" she shrieked. "I remember! Get out in the open. Now. Now. Now!" Her voice had become unpleasantly piercing, disturbing everyone.

Baya almost sighed. "Yes, Grandmother." She began to climb past the others, to make her way out of the shelter. Melee reluctantly joined her.

Heath went to the old woman and helped her get to her feet. But she ignored him. "Out!" she cried. "All of you! Out out out!"

Reluctantly their immediate neighbors gave up the effort to return to sleep, and got to their feet. But still the old woman wasn't satisfied. "Everyone! Out! Out! Now! Now!"

Heath realized that she would not shut up until she had her way. He grimaced and did his duty. "Let me help you," he said.

"I can help myself," she snapped, shaking off his hand. But he put it back on her elbow, because otherwise she would fall or get knocked over by one of the others. Baya helped from the other side. They guided her to the center aisle, then to the end, where it opened to the night.

Soon most of the tribe was out of the warm shelter and standing in the cold outside air. The moon cast a dim light. Most had their hide blankets over their shoulders, but they weren't comfortable. It was becoming clear that they were not going to humor the old woman much longer. Baya looked cold, and Melee was shivering.

"I think we have had enough of this," the chief, Badu, said. "The fire needs tending." He went back into the shelter.

"No!" Bata cried. But other men were following him.

"Be reasonable, Grandmother," Heath said tightly. "It was just a passing noise."

Then the ground shook with ferocious force, knocking many people off their feet. The water of the nearby river danced as if coming alive. The shelter collapsed. Now women screamed in earnest. This was terrifying!

Men scrambled to help those caught in the jumble of logs and brush that had been the shelter, but it was too late. Several of the men inside were injured, and the chief was unconscious or dead.

Old Bata was still saying something, but it was lost in the commotion. The ground had stopped bucking, but the people were disorganized and frightened.

The new man, Od, was near, with Bevy clinging close. "Bata knows!" he cried. "Listen to her!"

The man was supposed to be smart. What extra understanding did he have? It was better to find out.

Heath put his ear near Bata's mouth. "Get away from the river!" she was screaming. "Get into the open! Now! Worse coming!"

He realized that she had been right to make them leave the shelter. Anyone who might have remained inside could have been hurt by the collapse. Those who had tried to re-enter it *had* been hurt. She did remember when this had happened before.

He amplified her words, calling to the others. "Get away from the river! Get into the open. There is worse coming!"

The others, realizing that someone knew what was happening, began to move. They retreated from the river bank, climbing toward the open section.

The ground shook again, and trees groaned and tumbled. The people fled to the open section, where no trees could fall on them. They huddled together fearfully as trees crashed down and rocks rolled into the river. Children cried, and were comforted, but the terror continued. Baya and her sister helped keep Bata warm by standing close on either side. That meant that Heath could be close to his wife. And there they remained as the dawn came, halfway safe from the fury of the ground.

The shakings became less, and farther apart. But all around the field was desolation. Many trees were down, rendering the forest into a tangle of trunks and branches. Even the mountain slope had changed, becoming alien. All their familiar landmarks were gone.

Men made their way back to the ruined shelter. They returned with grim news: the chief was badly injured, and three others were dying. Their injuries were too great to offer serious hope of recovery. Chief Badu would live, but was in no condition to function for the next few days.

"He spoke your name before he slept," a man told Heath.

Oh, no! That meant that Heath, as the mate of the chief's daughter, was the new chief, for the time until Badu recovered. It was not anything he had sought or desired. Baya's sister Melee was lovely, but still a child, so had no mate yet to assume the burden. And he had been named. Heath had no choice.

"What am I going to do?" he muttered to himself.

"It serves you right," Bata said, overhearing him. She was nearly blind, but not deaf, unfortunately.

But he had little notion what to do. He had hardly assimilated the extent of the disaster; how could he make decisions? Yet decisions were needed immediately, he knew, and good ones, lest the mischief be compounded. He needed expert advice.

At the moment all he could think of was the new man, Od, who had said to listen to Bata. How had Od known that she knew what to do? So, since his own mind wasn't working well, he called to the other. "Od! Here."

Od came immediately, with Bevy following. It was evident that the young woman was frightened, and depended on her new mate for security. "I am here, chief."

"You said Bata knew. Why?"

"Because she is eldest. She lived when it happened before, as my own grandmother did. The old know much. She remembers."

So simple, now that it had been clarified. Bata herself had said she remembered; he hadn't realized the significance, in the chaos of the night. "Help me learn what she knows."

"Gladly. It will be the best information." Od paused. "My grandmother spoke best when she was most comfortable. And when she knew that her words were heeded. She was old and lame, but not stupid."

Heath realized that the man was hinting at something. "Speak your mind plainly."

"I do not wish to give offense, being new to this tribe."

Heath was becoming impatient. "Tell me straight."

Od turned to his mate. "See if you can help Baya make Bata more comfortable. We will return soon."

Then the two men walked away from the milling group. "When I met you yesterday, you seemed annoyed with the old woman."

Heath was embarrassed. "I showed it?"

"Not much. Maybe only my own experience with my own grandmother gave me the hint. But then I learned to respect her knowledge. You must treat her with real respect. Then she will help you enough to earn it."

"I treat her with respect!"

"Not in your heart. You help her only because your mate wishes it. She surely knows that. You must truly crave to listen to her, for yourself. To desire her company above all others."

Heath laughed. "This is nonsense. It is only my wife's company I desire in that manner."

"You asked me to speak my mind."

"You really believe that Bata knows what I should do to be chief?"

"Yes. She has seen more chiefs than anyone else has, and has seen their successes and their mistakes. She can help you more than anyone else can."

Heath shook his head. "If you believe in her so much, you do it, and tell me what she says."

"I will be glad to, if it will not give offense."

"Do it." Heath walked away, going to survey more of their situation though he had little notion what to do about it. He helped others pull things out of the collapsed shelter, but kept an eye on the new man. He was disturbed by what Od had said. How was it possible to stop resenting the inconvenient old woman? It was true that she had gotten them out of the shelter in time, but she could as readily have gotten them into trouble.

Od returned to Bevy and Bata. Soon they were talking. Then Bevy ran to find Heath. "She says not to drink the river water. We must go up to find a clear spring."

Ludicrous! The river was close, and they had always used it. But he had better verify her rationale. "Did she say why?"

"Because there will be dead things in the river, poisoning it. People will sicken. She remembers."

Suddenly her warning made sense. "It will be done," Heath said.

He went from man to man. "Do not drink the river water. There may be dead things in it. Warn your family. We must camp by a fresh spring. Start moving up."

"But Grout already drank," one man told him.

He could hardly blame the man for doing what was natural. Heath himself would have drunk, had he thought of it before learning the danger. "Tell him not to drink again."

There were grumbles, but the men, and therefore the women and children too, made their way up to the nearest high spring. They started constructing a new shelter, knowing it would be colder here at night than it had been below.

Bevy approached him again. "She says there are roots here to feed us, but they must be cooked."

Food! They had been too busy to be concerned with it, but would soon need it. He knew that foraging was not good at this elevation at this season. "Can she tell the women how to find the roots?"

"Yes."

Heath went to the men again. "Have your women go to Bata. She knows the forage here."

A man walked away from the work on the new shelter. Heath walked to intercept him. It was Grout, and he did not look well. Maybe it was coincidence, but Heath remembered the warning about drinking from the river. Suddenly he appreciated the old woman's advice more. She *did* remember. All the things that had happened when she was a child, that no one had encountered since, she knew from experience. She really was enabling them to survive.

"I think the river made you sick," he told the man. Grout was single, so had no wife to care for him. "Lie down in shade, and I will arrange care for you."

Grout nodded, and sought a place behind a tree.

Heath went to Bata himself. "Grout drank from the river. He is sick. Is there anything to help him?"

She smiled. "That herb we found yesterday. That will help. It is for fever, but it does more. Send him here. I will have Melee tend to him."

"Melee? But she's just a child, and he looks bad. He may have— consequences."

She glanced sidelong at him, her dim eyes crinkling with humor. "She's a girl, almost woman. She thinks a penis is a plaything. He'll vomit, and piss, and crap, and she will clean him up. It is time for her innocence to be tempered."

He could not argue. It seemed a shame for such a lovely child to be subjected to work like that, but elder woman had authority over unmarried junior women in their families, so it was Bata's decision. He could only qualify it. "Then let her tend him out of view of others, to spare them both shame."

She nodded. "It is kind of you to think of that."

What did she mean? He decided that he did not want to know. He turned away, going about the business of the tribe. The job was getting easier to do, though no more comfortable to contemplate. He did not like making decisions that affected the welfare of others, but was learning how.

As dusk came, they crowded into the new shelter. It was too small, but that could not be helped; there had been time and material to fashion only a minimal structure. There were roots being boiled and served for the dinner. They did not taste very good, but they were filling.

Heath saw slender Melee come to get a root and a hide cup of water. She took them back to the dark corner where the sick man lay. She did not look happy, but neither did she look miserable. Evidently she was han-

dling Grout's situation, learning as she went, just as Heath was doing with
the tribe. After this, she would surely know all the orifices of a man, and
have no shame in cleaning them. It was a necessary education, for a woman.

The people were tired, and it had been a bad day. The mutterings were
escalating. Even the women were becoming shrill. Something needed to be
done before quarrels and fights erupted. The ordinary ritual would not be
enough to calm these shaken people.

"There will be mischief. What did they do, before?" Heath asked Bata.

"They told stories," she replied. She seemed happy, in contrast to most
of the others. She was feeling useful.

"We tell stories," he said. "Like the day's events? This will only remind
them of our misfortune."

"Funny ones. To make people laugh. Then they didn't fight."

Heath didn't feel like laughing. But Bata had been right so often recently
that she was probably right again, and it did make sense. "Od, tell a funny
story," he said.

Od was up to the occasion. "Before I came here, I had sex with the
prettiest woman of the mountains," he said.

There was a rumble of laughter. Everyone could see that Od was neither
robust nor handsome. How could he ever impress a moderately attractive
woman, let alone the prettiest one?

"Oh, but she was," Od insisted. "A sweet face, and breasts like melons.
I never saw a woman so lovely." He paused, then looked around as if suddenly nervous. "Until Bevy."

This time everyone laughed. It wasn't that Bevy was ugly, for she was not.
Plain, perhaps, not ugly. But it was the nature of men to brag about their
conquests as well as their feats of hunting, and the nature of women to
resent these brags. So Od had played out a familiar scene, in a manner.
Then men enjoyed it, and because of its humor, so did the women.

"But let me tell you about my male cousin," Od continued. That was a
way of saying just another person. "He wasn't too smart." That indicated
that it would be an unkind story. Those were popular. "He saw this beautiful woman, and asked her for sex. She said yes, but only after dark, because she had to finish her foraging and preparation. Then at night she
played her trick: she changed places with her friend. My cousin came to
her bed after dark and clasped her most ardently. She responded similarly,
truly welcoming him in. She waited for him to finish before she spoke.
'That was great! Do it again.' Then he knew by her voice that it wasn't the
girl he thought, but the ugliest girl of the tribe."

There was a roar of laughter. After that other men told their stories, with
similarly unsubtle conclusions. Sexual misadventures were always fun. It was
possible that the laughter of the women had a different quality than that
of the men, as if their perspective differed, but the men neither noticed
nor cared. What did it matter what women thought?

Heath was satisfied. It was working, and they would get through the night
without fights.

Something shifted in his feeling. He had not only discovered what use
an old woman was, he had gained an idea of what he truly wanted to do
in his life. He wanted to be a healer, not just of people, but of the tribe.
Just as he had been this day, thanks to the old woman's advice.

Then he put his arm around Bata and kissed her on the ear. "Grandmother, you have saved the tribe. You alone knew what to do. It does matter
what you think. I want to learn everything you know."

"I will tell you," she said, pleased. "But it will take time."

"The longer the better," he said sincerely. "You know so much. You
know the ways of healing, of the body and the mind. I did not understand
the importance, before, but now I do. The tribe needs your memories. So
do I."

Baya squeezed his other hand. She was glad that he had made up with
her grandmother.

*The rigors of the mountain life required people to crowd together at night, mak-
ing for social awkwardness. Erectus did not have much of a problem in this respect,
because each man could be with his woman separately; there was much less risk
of a neighboring man intruding. Groups of men could get along together, and
groups of women could; the problem was when the groups were mixed. The electricity of sexual appeal and interaction generates strong emotions in all creatures,
mankind no exception. Most animals have female sexual response only at limited
times, so that the mischief is limited. It was probably worse for mankind, because
of women's continual sexual appeal. A young, attractive woman simply can't be
ignored by a neighboring man of any age. So crowding was a formidable challenge.
But this was eased by the development of superior communication, so that people
could talk in the dark and make things clear even without the aid of visible
gestures. The social limits could be precisely defined, linguistically, and this was
vitally important. Even today, most disputes seem to be the results of misunder-
standings, and the worst ones tend to be about male-female relations, so perhaps
the process of refinement is not yet complete. People could divert their minds by
rehearsing the events of the day, giving individuals their chances to tell of their
experiences and receive the appreciation of the group, and sharing laughs. The
stories may have been crude by later standards, but they served their purpose, easing
distress and facilitating camaraderie. This improved communication enabled
larger mixed groups to assemble and get along. The slow developments of the other
arts aided this, but perhaps linguistic communication led the way. These larger,
more integrated groups had more power against their environment and against
other tribes. So over the course of hundreds of thousands of years, this adjustment
of face and brain became the hallmark of mankind. Perhaps because of mixed-
gender crowding.*

*Animals seldom care for their injured companions, other than immediate off-
spring. But human beings do, and the art of healing developed from this need.
This comprised several aspects, ranging from direct support of an injured comrade
to research for obscure medicinal herbs. Those communities who could most effectively treat their ailing members gained strength, for it was more efficient to save*

an existing person than to grow a new one from scratch. From this need came the first crude doctors, and the eventual art and science of medicine, now one of the most vital functions of society. From the need to heal the emotional pains of people and groups came the disciplines of psychology.

Another development was longevity. In terms of heartbeats, mankind is probably the longest-lived animal on Earth. What advantage is conferred by enabling people to live long past their reproductive period? This is another aspect of the improvement in communication. Some crises occur far apart, so that the majority of the members of a given tribe will have had no experience with one until it happens. But if lives are extended, there will be a few old people who remember the prior crisis, and so know what to do to facilitate handling of the current one. This could make a significant difference, perhaps enabling a tribe to survive when it otherwise would have perished. This was buttressed by communication, so that, for example, an old blind feeble woman could still make her information clear to a young man who lacked her experience and memory. Tribes that valued their old members thus gained an advantage over those that did not, and age itself became a survival quality for the species. Age and communication: not much else like this has been seen.

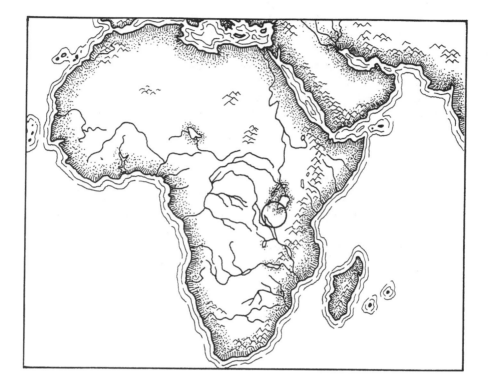

CHAPTER 3

STORY

By 200,000 B.P.E. the Rift folk had become a separate species, or rather several separate species inhabiting the several fragmented sections of the Rift. Erectus, in contrast, remained a relatively unified species in Africa, because he roamed everywhere else. Thus when there were conflicts over border territory, Erectus drew from a larger pool, and had the advantage. This meant that over the millennia the divergent offshoots were marginalized and in danger of being exterminated. But one of the variations of a particular species was in the shape of the mouth and nasal cavities, facilitating the production of a range of vocal sounds beyond the capacity of any other creature, and corollary development of the

brain to process speech sounds. Superior communication had enabled modern man-
kind to survive in the challenging Rift. Now it was to prove its power in inter-
species competition. But the shift wasn't easy, because old ways of thinking were
hard to change.

The ability to communicate effectively is important. But so is the content of that
communication. Sometimes the art of story telling is vital.

TALENA saw them coming from the east: a bedraggled group of men.
She was instantly alert. "Tik—run tell my father that men are coming."
She squinted. "River Foragers, I believe."

A boy took off, silently. He knew that speed and quiet were of the essence
when strangers approached.

"You others—hide." The other children disappeared into the brush, as
silently. Normally they were noisy and active, but they knew when to pipe
down. Strangers were dangerous.

Then Talena walked slowly toward the intruders. She would flee if any
raised a weapon, but she doubted that there was any direct threat. This was
Mountain Slope territory, and the intruders had to know that overwhelming
force would soon be brought to bear. If they committed any hostile act,
they would all be killed. They were coming here as refugees, not raiders.
She hoped.

She calmed her welling pulses. She was young, newly a woman, two hands
and three fingers years, and ordinarily would not be involved in foreign
contact. But she had been the first adult to spy the intruders, so the situation was her responsibility, until her father came.

They saw her coming, and stopped where they were. Their eyes were
downcast, and their hands were low: confirmation of their status. Indeed,
now she saw that several were injured, and their ragged possessions were
slung over their shoulders. There were some four hands of men, three
fingers of women, and one hand and one finger of children. No raiding
party indeed!

"Halt!" Talena cried, though they had already done so; it was a formality,
establishing whose territory governed. "Who are you?"

"We are River Foragers," the lead man said. He was mature, maybe four
hands years, and ruggedly handsome. "I am Heath, the Healer."

A healer! Interesting indeed. "I am Talena, the artist, of the Mountain
Slope tribe. Why do you come here?"

"Our settlement was raided by the Green Feathers. They overran us while
our men were hunting, killing our people. These women and children are
all that survive. When we men returned, it was already too late. They were
gone. Our houses are burned. Nothing is left. We seek refuge."

Talena considered. Her father had not yet arrived, and any real decision
would have to be made by him. It was her duty simply to remain in contact
with the refugees and learn as much as she could, so that she could make
a quick and accurate report to her father. But she had another notion.

"Heath—you alone, walk with me."

He dropped his meager goods and stepped forward. The others remained unmoving, evidently glad to rest, apart from the protocol.

Talena turned to walk beside him, toward the mountain. He was a head taller than she, and far more massive, but she had control of the situation. He kept his eyes focused on the ground, the posture of submission. When they were out of hearing of the others, she spoke again.

"Heath, you know we will not give all of you refuge. The children can be adopted, and the women can in time earn tolerance by our tribe, especially if they are good breeders, but only the men who marry our women can remain with us."

"I know," he said glumly. "But that is better than death for all of us."

"We have only three eligible women at present," she continued. "I am the third. We will choose from among you. I like the look and way of you. Will you mate with me?"

He paused, evidently taken aback. "May I look at you, Talena?"

"You may."

He turned his eyes to her, gazing at her bare feet, her slender legs, her modestly fleshed torso, and finally her somewhat ordinary face. He seemed to be considering what to say, as well he might; her proposal had been somewhat sudden.

At last he spoke. "You are clearly a healthy and apt woman, and worthy of the commitment of any man. I appreciate your courage and directness. I very much wish to avoid offending you, as you are surely worthy of no offense. But I do not wish to mate with you."

Ouch! She had not anticipated this. "You do understand that you must mate with one of our three if you wish to remain with us? That I will select you, before the tribe, if you agree?"

"Yes, and I very much appreciate your offer. But my mate was killed two days ago in the Green Feather raid, and I—" He averted his gaze. "I ask your indulgence. I am not able to be with any other woman."

He loved his mate, though she was dead. Talena reached up to touch his face under one eye. She could look at him, and touch him, without asking, because she was of the home territory tribe. Her finger came away wet. "I understand. I did not mean to hurt you."

"Nor I you," Heath said. "Were it otherwise—"

"I understand," she repeated. Then, distressed by the rejection, though she appreciated its reason, she changed the subject. "My father the chief will be here soon. I will tell him of your situation, except for this personal matter. Is there anything else I should tell him?"

"Just—just that I think it would be better if we all could remain with you."

"But you know that's not—"

"I know. But your tribe will be the next to feel the burden of the Green Feather onslaught, and you may suffer as we have, unless you can muster enough force to oppose them. We can add to your force. This would help you, and would be better for you—and for us."

"Do you mean—merge tribes?" she asked, surprised.

"Only to cooperate, to fight the common enemy, so that we may prevail. I think this would be best, if it could be done."

He was right. It would be best. But she doubted that it was to be. "I will tell my father the chief. But I can not make the decision."

"Thank you. I know my idea is not likely to be adopted, but thank you for hearing it."

They turned and walked back toward the others. Now the men of the Mountain Slope tribe were striding toward them.

Talena lifted her hand in a signal, so that her father would recognize her. Then she made a second signal, and the hiding children emerged, released from their caution.

Her father, Chief Talon, came to join her. The men of the Mountain Slope tribe stood close behind him, their weapons ready. The refugees remained unmoving, their weapons lowered or out of sight. "Who are they?" he asked.

"They are River Foragers," Talena said. "The Green Feathers raided and destroyed their settlement while their men were hunting, and these are all that remain. They seek refuge." She made a small signal, to indicate that there was more.

Talon looked over the refugees. "What else?" he asked gruffly.

"Their leader is a healer. He has a suggestion to make."

Talon knew that his daughter did not do things idly. The decision was his to make, but he wanted full information. "Let him speak, then."

Talena turned to Heath. "Tell the chief your idea."

Surprised, Heath stepped forward. "Our tribe is destroyed. Your tribe may be next. Give us sanctuary, and we will fight the Green Feather beside you, and drive them back. That way both tribes will profit."

Talon was clearly not thrilled with the notion. But rather than reject it outright, he demurred. "We will consider. Meanwhile we will give you a campsite for a day, and our women will choose from your men and your children." He turned. "Pul, take them to the lower river site and let them forage."

Pul nodded. "Follow me," he said gruffly to the River Foragers. A number of men walked with him.

One of the men looked surprised. "Pul," he said.

Pul paused, looking at the speaker. "Od! I did not know you, with your head down."

"I did not know you were here."

"My sister Avalanche and I came here. You lost your woman?"

"Yes."

Talena lost interest. Of course the man had lost his woman. They all had. And the three women had lost their men. But if Pul knew him, that was another source of information about these people.

As the refugees followed Pul, clearing the area, Talon turned to his daughter. "You want that man?"

"Yes."

"Take him then, tomorrow."

This was awkward. "He may not want me."

"He won't have a choice. He looks sound, and he seems smart."

"I would rather that he desire it."

Talon shook his head. "That's not the way it works, Daughter. When I came here, your mother selected me. She was not the prettiest, but I had to take her. It was worth it. She made me chief."

"But didn't you come to love her, in time?"

"You know I did. But that is not the point. If I had not taken her, I would have had to leave the tribe. That is the way it is. Love comes after."

"Yes, of course. And I believe Heath would make a good mate. But—" She broke off, not wanting to give the reason.

Talon glanced shrewdly at her. "You think that man will reject you?"

"It's not that, exactly. I want him, but I don't want to force him."

"If you don't, Avalanche will."

"Bad water!" Talena swore. "I hadn't thought of that."

"In fact she may anyway. She is older than you, so has prior choice. You had better make an agreement with him, or she will take him."

"I tried to. But—" Again she balked.

"Daughter, I want what you want. If you get a good man, I will not have to fear cruelty in my age. You had better tell me, and let me help you."

"But I told him I wouldn't."

"I will not give your secret away."

He was right. She could trust him, and she needed his help. "His wife was killed by the Green Feather, and he mourns her, and wants no other woman. I want a man who is loyal like that. But he will not be loyal if forced; he must accept me."

Talon considered. "Then tell him you will arrange for sanctuary for his tribe, if he accepts you."

She gazed at him wide-eyed. "You would do that?"

"For you, beloved Daughter, I would do anything. You are much like your mother."

They were silent for a moment. Talena's mother had died two years ago. Talon would have had to leave the tribe, were it not for Talena; a wife or a daughter of the tribe gave a man residence. So Talena's choice of mate was doubly important, for though the woman justified residence, the man governed the woman as long as he remained with her. Talena's mate could force her to choose between him and her father, ejecting one or the other from the tribe. She wanted never to face that choice.

Apart from that, both she and her father had loved her mother. The loss had drawn them closer together.

"Suppose I tell him, and he still will not?" she asked.

"He is a man. He is practical. For that, he will accede."

She nodded. "I suppose so. But he will still feel forced."

"This close to the loss of his wife, he will. I did not take another woman, and would have resented her if forced. So give him a compromise: that he may remain free, but will accede to no woman but you."

She liked that. "I will tell him."

They separated. Talon went on about his business of organizing the tribe for this new situation, and Talena walked to the lower river site where the refugee camp was being made.

They were already pulling fish from the water. They were good at that, of course; they had special little barbed hooks they carved from bone that somehow caught and held the fish so they did not escape. Pul and the men stood nearby, making sure no one strayed from the campsite.

Talena spotted Heath, who was tending to one of the injured women. She had been stabbed on the arm, and he was washing it off in the water. The woman was wincing but not making any sound.

Talena came to stand behind him. "When you are done," she murmured.

"There is little more I can do," he said. "She will live, if the bad spirits don't get into her." Then, to the woman: "Rest. Try to sleep. I will bring you food later." She nodded, lay back on the ground, and closed her eyes.

Heath stood and walked with Talena, waiting for her to speak. "You care for people," she said. "I like that."

"Thank you." He did not look at her.

"I know that if you mated with me, you would be loyal to me, as you are to your lost mate. I like that too."

"No other woman could ever replace—"

"I know. But you would be loyal."

"You would settle for loveless loyalty?"

"Yes, at first."

"I can, if you wish, tell you of the qualities of the other men of our tribe, all of whom have suffered similar losses, but a number of whom would surely be glad to mate with you. There is Od, for example; he is small, but very smart, and he knows how to make fire. He—"

"No. You are the one I want."

"Talena, you hardly know me! Even if I were agreeable, I would not necessarily be the best for you."

"But you would be good enough."

He shrugged, not challenging that assessment.

"I think you are an honest man," Talena continued after a pause. "So give me an honest answer. If you had come to our tribe unattached, seeking a mate, would I do?"

"Yes."

"You would not prefer a more mature or beautiful woman?"

"May I look at you again?"

"Yes."

He turned to her, and studied her, this time from the top down. She held herself still, refusing to straighten her posture or inhale or pull in her belly.

"May I touch you?"

"Yes."

He lifted one hand and stroked her hair. His touch was gentle and competent; that was the healer in him. He cupped her small chin, then squeezed one shoulder, not hard. He hefted one breast on his fingers, then reached around her to stroke one buttock, his hand nudging the crevice of her bottom. The caress made her want to embrace him and kiss him, but she resisted, remaining immobile.

He stepped back, turning away. "Yes, you would do," he said. "You are young, and not the loveliest of women, but neither are you ugly, and your flesh is firm. But what is important is your spirit. You are smart and bold and honest, and these qualities are more important to me than appearance or feel. There is also something about you that is appealing."

"I am Chief Talon's daughter."

"So I gathered. But I was not judging by that."

"Then you could love me, were you free to do so."

"I think so."

"And in time you would do so, even if not in the same way as your first mate. Maybe as I grow older and flesh out more."

He smiled. "Yes, I suspect I would." He hesitated then amended himself. "I said I like your spirit. But the feel of your young body arouses me too. When I said you were not the loveliest of women, I meant by conventional standards. You are very appealing for me as you are now. I had to stop touching you because I was reacting."

She felt a flush of pleasure. She had already seen that he did not speak insincerely. He had just allayed her concern that he saw her as too young. "Here is the settlement: mate with me, and all your people will be allowed to remain, as you suggested."

Heath pursed his lips. "You are determined."

She shrugged, masking her further pleasure at the recognition. "Actually, I think your idea makes sense."

"You know that you would always be in the shadow of my first mate."

"I would not have it otherwise."

He shook his head. "You have made a price I can't decline."

She nodded, and walked away. She knew his eyes were on her rear. Victory was in her grasp.

❁

But on the following day, there was opposition. Talon declared that he had decided to allow the refugees to stay, but the tribesmen didn't like it. "There are too many," Pul said. "They might overwhelm us by treachery."

"We will keep them in their separate camp," Talon said. "We will watch them."

But the others were not easy with it. Talon had the authority to declare it, but it was not good to have substantial dissent.

Talena approached him. "The price is too much," she said. "I must give up Heath." She hated saying it, now that she had gained both the man's acquiescence and his sexual interest. Where would she ever find a better prospect?

"Give it time," Talon said. "Let them get used to it." But he was plainly uneasy.

Talena went to Heath. "Our tribe doesn't like it. I may not be able to claim you."

"I am sorry," he said. But she suspected it was the loss of the unity of his remaining tribe he regretted most.

That afternoon they held the ceremony of choosing. The men of the River Foragers lined up in the glade near the river, without any clothing, and the complete Mountain Slope tribe assembled to view the proceedings.

The eldest free woman was Jilana. She had lost her mate to a hunting accident several months before. She was fully mature with ample breasts and one child. She looked over the prospects, then walked along the line, asking questions of several. Soon she selected one, removed the hide from her upper torso to reveal her bosom, and posed the question: "Will you mate with me?"

The men clearly had decided their courses already, knowing that it was far less chancy to mate with one of the women of this tribe than to go to another tribe. "I will," he answered without hesitation.

Jilana took him by the hand and led him to her place on the slope. She would mate with him that evening, and initiate him into the ways of the Mountain Slope tribe.

The next woman was Avalanche. She was six years older than Talena, and a beauty. Her name echoed her appearance: she had a way of making her voluminous hair tumble down and around like the fall of rocks and sand from a shaking mountain. Indeed, her bouncing breasts were like smooth boulders within that avalanche. She had indulged sexually with many men, but had taken none for her mate. This was because she had not been born to the Mountain Slope tribe, so had been assigned the status of girl until she proved her fertility by bearing a baby. Now, however, the established women of the tribe were changing Avalanche's status, despite her lack of a baby, because their men were enjoying this woman too much and she was a distraction. So now Avalanche had the right to choose a man to keep. That would make her unavailable to married men. If any of the men regretted this, as several surely did, they had the wit to keep silent.

Even so, Avalanche seemed to be in no hurry to choose from this wide assortment. Talena wasn't sure what she was waiting for, but feared it was Heath. The woman had seen Talena talking with him, so could guess about her interest; that might be reason enough to take him. And, unfortunately, that was possible now, since Talena's deal to hold Heath was falling through.

Sure enough, Avalanche approached Heath. Her flesh rippled as she walked. Talena knew it was pointless to feel jealousy, but she did. "What is your skill?" she asked.

"I am a healer."

"Will you mate with me?"

"No."

There was a ripple of surprise through both groups of people. "Why not?" Avalanche asked, unpleased.

"I am otherwise committed."

"You can't stay here unless you mate one of us."

"I know."

"I will ask you again, in a moment." Then Avalanche put her arms around him, drew him in close, and flattened herself against him. She pulled his head down for a lingering kiss. He had to accept it; enticement was a legitimate remedy for a balky male. Talena closed her eyes for a moment, fearing that all was lost; she had seen Avalanche embrace men before, and it had always led to prompt sex. If Heath had been even slightly aroused by Talena's slender torso, he would be instantly stiffened by Avalanche's generous one.

The woman drew back only her head. "Now will you mate with me?"

"No."

"But you desire me." She disengaged, to reveal him with an erect penis. There was a subterranean murmur among the males, many of whom were surely now in a similar state. Avalanche could do that.

He didn't answer. His penis slowly fell, now that there was no direct contact. She had made him react, as she could with any man, but had not changed his mind.

There was a faint chuckle in the Mountain Slope tribe. It was the first time anyone had seen this woman balked by a man, since she came to the tribe. The women especially seemed to appreciate it.

Disgruntled, Avalanche shook her hair and moved on along the line. But she asked no more questions. Until she spied Od. "I know you," she said, surprised.

"I met your brother," Od agreed.

"But I think you are not for me."

"I agree."

Then she turned. "I am not ready to choose," she declared. "I don't know any of these men well enough. So I will take them to my bed by turns each night, until I find what I seek."

It was her right. But that had the effect of extending the selection process, because they couldn't send the other men on until they knew which ones had been chosen.

"Beginning with this one," she said, turning back to Od. He nodded, acquiescing to that one night.

"In that case, it is Talena's turn," Talon said. "She may choose now, and you may not take her man, because you have postponed your decision."

Avalanche shrugged, making her breasts ripple. All the men were watching her. She liked that. Then she took Od by the hand and led him to her place on the slope.

Talena approached the line with mixed feelings. The only one she wanted was Heath, but she no longer had the means to make him want to agree. She walked along the row of men, and paused before him, but couldn't make herself ask him, for fear of public rejection. He stood still, giving no sign of anything. She blinked back tears of frustration and grief, and walked on.

Then she turned and spoke. "I, too, am not ready to choose. I will wait until after Avalanche chooses."

The tribesfolk were surprised again. Normally no woman passed up her chance to take her man, unless the choices were few or obviously defective. With four hands of new men, it was unheard of. Avalanche could afford to dally, because it was obvious that she could captivate just about any man she chose. But no such thing was obvious about Talena.

But at least one mating had been settled, so they could celebrate. They brought out sections of antelope meat, tubers, and fermented berry juice. They lit a fire in the center of the glade and piled on dead branches. When all the tribesfolk had been served, children took the extra to the refugees, who remained somewhat isolated at the base of the glade. They carried baked tubers on the ends of sticks, and dipped leaf-cups into the brew pot to take also.

Talena, watching the proceedings, was depressed. Even if she didn't get Heath for a mate, his idea about the tribes cooperating to fight the Green Feather was good, and should be done. But once the mates were chosen, the other men would have to move on, and the opportunity would be lost. All because Pul and others like him were too stupid to appreciate the merit of the proposal.

Then she had a sudden notion. Maybe she could persuade them. Not directly, because the views of a woman had no merit, but indirectly. If she had the courage and wit to manage it.

Well, she had to make the effort, or be shamed forevermore, at least in her own mind. She got up and went to her father. "I have an idea. Will you let me tell the story today?"

"If that is your wish, Daughter."

"But not the usual one? I mean, it doesn't have to be always the same, does it?"

"It doesn't," he agreed. "But if you deviate, it had better be a good one."

"And it doesn't have to be true, does it? I mean, it *is* a story. For fun."

He nodded. "Anything can be forgiven, if it is fun. But what is it you plan?"

"I think you would rather not know."

He eyed her warily. "I saw that look in your mother's eye, before she did something naughty." Then he smiled. "Just don't bring shame on me, Daughter."

"No shame," she agreed. But her pulses were pounding. It was a great gamble she was taking, and if it didn't work, she might never be allowed to be the story teller again.

"It is time. Are you ready?" he asked.

"I hope so."

Talon stood and walked to the fire. The hubbub of chatter faded. "It is time for the story," he said. "But I am getting old, and my tales are well worn. So today my daughter Talena will speak instead." He turned and beckoned to her, then walked back to his place.

Then, as the others ate, Talena took the place of honor beside the fire. She was frightened, for she had never actually spoken before the entire tribe before. On occasion she had sung, so the dancers could dance, but that had been with other girls. But singing was easy, with the familiar melody. Talking was hard.

She opened her mouth, and nothing came out. Her throat was too tight.

"Louder!" Talon called, smiling.

There was laughter. It helped. She tried again, and this time got some sound out. "To-today I have a—will tell a—a different story," she said, making her voice as loud as possible, though to her ears it was almost a scream. "A story of my—my grandmother, Tasia, long ago, when she was as young as I am now."

Talena paused for breath. They were listening! Now all she had to do was tell it well enough to hold their attention, without alerting them to her underlying purpose.

"Tasia was out foraging, and following good berries. She didn't realize how far out she had wandered, until she saw the Green Feather men. Then she ran, but they were between her and home, so she had to flee farther out. They chased her, screaming their awful curses. She ran fleetly, but knew that they would catch her eventually, because they had cut her off. She was afraid she would soon be meat for their fires."

She paused again, for her voice and imagination were straining. She saw the children shuddering; they could picture those brutes roasting a tribeswoman on their hearth. The men and women were listening, paying attention. It was working! She was telling a good story. That was gratifying in itself, but it was only part of what she hoped to accomplish, if only she could.

"She saw the big river. Maybe she could escape across it, for the Green Feather didn't like water as well as our folk do. She ran and plunged in. The current caught her and carried her away, faster than she could swim. She tried to get across, but couldn't. She was drowning! But then a hand caught her arm. She had been caught! But she was too weak to resist, and let herself be hauled out of the water for whatever fate awaited her.

"But it wasn't the Green Feather. It was a man of the River Foragers tribe." Suddenly the River Foragers took close note; this surprised them. "They had seen her flee, and had cut off the Green Feather, and pulled her out, safe. They fed her and let her rest, but she could not stay. She had to earn her keep for the night with one of their young men, but he was gentle and virile and she didn't really mind. Then in the morning they took her to the edge of Mountain Slope territory and let her go, unharmed. She hurried home, and was welcomed; her family had worried about her, for she was just of age to choose a mate." She paused again. Now came the hardest part.

"She did not tell them of the River Foragers, because then they would have known she was not pristine. In her day, as in ours, a girl belonged only to the men of her own tribe, and was spoiled if a foreign man touched her. She said she had escaped the Green Feather and found a place to hide for the night, and returned by daylight next day. That much was true.

"In three hands days some men arrived from another tribe, and she chose one, and they mated, and she became a woman. She bore my mother, Tanela, who in due course took a foreign man to mate, and bore a daughter." She smiled, and there was a general chuckle, because that "foreign man" was Chief Talon, and the daughter was Talena herself.

She saw that all the River Forager folk were paying close attention, and Heath's gaze was fixed on her. Did he know where she was going? She nerved herself and continued. "But what she concealed was the fact that it was not her mate's child she first bore. Her body told her that it was the River Forager's child. Her mate did not know her cycle, so did not know, and anyway, all her other children were his."

She paused, swallowing, though her mouth was dry. She dared not look at her father. The folk of the tribe were absolutely silent. They had never heard this history before, and understood its significance. The offspring of an unmated mother were not entitled to tribal residence. Of course Talena's mother was dead, so it was too late to send her away, and in any event she had been popular and influential in the tribe, so her place was secure. Talena herself was legitimate, and Talon would not lose his position. The secret had been kept long enough.

"So it is that I am blood kin to the River Foragers, via the female line," Talena continued. "The young male who was my grandfather would have gone out to some other tribe to mate, never knowing, but his sisters remained, and perhaps one of these three women is descended from them. Perhaps also one of the children. I do not know. But I am loath to see them sent away in their day of bereavement and need. And the men have lost their women, but remain loyal to their tribe; it seems a shame to destroy that tribe. The River Foragers gave a kindness to my grandmother, and I wish we could return that kindness now."

She was done. Now it was up to the tribe. If they allowed the River Forager men to stay, Heath would mate with her.

Talon stood. "It seems the secret is out. I have said that the River Foragers should stay, but do not wish to generate dissent in the tribe. Are there those who disagree?"

The other elder men of the tribe looked around. They were plainly not entirely satisfied, but were not willing to take the ugly step of contravening their chief and casting out the members of a tribe to which such a connection existed. So the moment passed, and no objection was voiced.

"Then they may remain," Talon said. "We will allow them to fight the Green Feather beside us, and thereafter we will permit young women of other tribes who wish to mate with them to become Mountain Slope residents, so that the imbalance will be alleviated." He paused and looked around, but no women objected.

It had worked! Her father was supporting her, and salvaged the situation. Exhilarated, Talena stood. She walked across the glade to where Heath sat. He did not move, but looked up at her with an inscrutable expression. "Will you mate with me?" she asked him.

He smiled. "Is your young flesh still firm?"

Flush with her victory, she smiled back. "Why don't you feel it and see?"

He got to his feet. He took her two small breasts in his hands and squeezed very lightly. "Yes."

She put her arms around him and kissed him. Then she led him back to her original place, beside her father. She had won it all.

It was time for the dancing. The women, young and old, stepped out into the glade and jumped and whirled, showing off their bodies before beckoning their men to join them. But Talena delayed, for she knew her father would have something to say to her.

Instead, he spoke to Heath. "A woman who will go that far in order to get her man is worth having," he said.

Heath nodded. "It was a good story."

There was a pause, but neither man spoke again. So Talena went out to join the women, then soon turned to beckon Heath. He came out to join her in the dance.

"You knew," she said.

"If your father does not deny it, why should I?"

"You knew," she repeated more firmly.

He nodded. "There was no stray woman. If she was pretty enough to warrant a night with the chief, the tribe would have kept her thereafter."

"The chief? That is not what I said."

"Because you are not conversant with River Forager custom. The chief may treat any guest woman as a girl of the tribe. Then she becomes eligible for the attention of the other men."

So she had made a mistake. But those who knew it had not told, and so the story had worked. The tribe would be strengthened, and would be better able to fend off the Green Feather.

"Yet you agreed to mate with me," she said, inviting his justification for changing his mind.

"We had an understanding. You have saved the remnant of my tribe. I am yours." Then he smiled. "Also, it was clear that if I did not accept you now, any other man would, and I would not have another chance. Though it is not a thing my spirit desires at this time, I could see that you are the most desirable of all women."

"But my body hasn't changed," she protested, pleased.

"Your mind has. No ordinary person would have told that story." He took her in his arms and squeezed her bottom. "And your body is already good enough."

"It is a sensible union," she said. "You are a good man, and we need a healer. But I hope that, in time—" She faltered. "I don't want to displace your lost mate. But if in time you could come to care for me too—"

"I surely will—in time," he agreed.

She relaxed. That was enough. For now.

In such manner, perhaps, the several hard-pressed tribes of modern mankind succeeded in making alliances, so as to bring more force to bear against the larger number of Erectus tribesmen. It was superior communication that did it, enabling them to organize more efficiently and thus to fight more effectively. It was also the arts, notably what was probably the oldest art, story telling, that enabled them to appreciate each other's company, and to enhance the spirit of togetherness. In this case, the telling of something, believably, that is not true, yet still arouses the necessary feelings: the art of fiction. So the slow retreat toward extinction halted, and a slow advance began. It was, in the course of the next hundred thousand years, to lead to the conquest of all of Africa by mankind, eliminating Erectus there.

Because mankind had suffered extreme attrition, its gene pool was at this point small. Those who survived this squeeze spread their genes to all of the descendants of this species. There were a number of them, but the mitochondrial chromosomes of just one woman came to prevail. Thus she is considered the mother of mankind, the common ancestor of us all. She may have been an ordinary woman, not particularly lovely or notable among her associates, but she had what it took to survive and reproduce. In this novel she is called Talena; in science and religion she is called Eve.

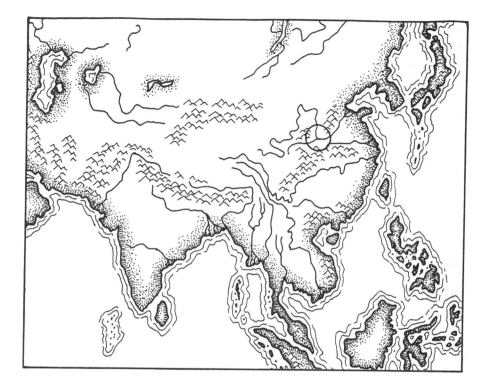

CHAPTER 4

EXPRESSION

The early way of life for mankind was hunter-gatherer, with the men pursuing game for meat, and the women foraging for plant foods. It was a successful mode of existence, requiring only about four hours a day for sustenance, and was healthy. So men and women had time on their hands, during which they could relax, converse, play games, enjoy sex, and develop the various arts. Among these was the art of expression, which was more than mere communication. With it, a man could lead a tribe, or charm a lovely women. Without it he might be considered a dullard.

But in some regions a change occurred. It wasn't swift, and did not seem

significant, but it was in time to change the lifestyle of the species. The region is
a tributary of the Yellow River in China, and the time is about 12,000 years ago.
  Yet some converts to the new order may have come looking for something else.
Some may not even have known what they were looking for.

DILLON paused at the split in the path. Both parts of the fork led
down to a river. Down one he could see a pretty young woman with
a heavy skin bag, standing as if daunted by the challenge of the crossing.
Down the other was an ugly old woman sitting on a rock.

He took the right fork, toward the old woman. Soon he caught up to
her. She seemed to be dozing. "Are you in need, Grandmother?" he inquired politely.

She woke and looked around blankly. "Eh?"

"I saw you sitting, and thought you might need help crossing the river,"
he said.

"Ah. You are right. I am almost blind, and feeble, and fear to misstep
alone, especially with my burden of wine."

"I will help you to cross."

She peered at him cannily, but he saw that her eyes did not properly
focus. "And what do you want for this service to an old hag?"

"Nothing, Grandmother. I just wish to help."

"Maybe you want a sip of this good wine?" She indicated the large skin
at her feet.

"No. No offense, Grandmother, but I don't like wine."

"Why not? Doesn't it make you feel good?"

"I have seen how good it makes people feel. And how sick they feel next
day. I want none of it."

"You are a smart man."

"No, I am dull. But I will carry it across the river for you." He picked
up the skin and waded through the swiftly flowing water.

In a moment he set it down safely and waded back to the woman. "How
may I help you, Grandmother? Do you wish me to carry you across?"

"Yes."

So he picked her up without difficulty and carried her to the other side
of the river. She put a feeble hand on his biceps, feeling his muscle. He
set her down so that she was sitting on a rock there.

"Now I will go on, if you are all right," he said.

"Why didn't you take the other fork?" she asked abruptly.

Startled, he faltered. "There—there was someone there."

"Of course there was someone there! My granddaughter, searching for
a better crossing. Why did you not go to her?"

"She—she looked as if she could have the help of any man she chose.
While you might have more difficulty."

"Is that the truth?" she demanded sharply.

"Yes."

"But is it all of the truth?"

She had him. "No."

"What is the rest of it?"

"I—I don't know how to speak to young women."

"You spoke to this old woman readily enough."

He shrugged.

"We had better introduce ourselves," she said. "I am the old crone Bata."

"I am the young hunter Dillon."

"What brings you here, Dillon?"

"There are too many brothers in my family, so I must seek some other residence."

"Oh, so that's the way of it! No land, no women for you back home."

"Yes. Now if I may, I must go on, to find a place I may stay."

"You're a hunter, you say. Do you also hunt men?"

"Only if they attack me."

"How many men have you killed?"

"Only one. I was sick after I did it."

She nodded wisely. "Killing men is not fun, even when necessary."

"Not fun," he echoed, shuddering.

"Go help my granddaughter cross."

"But—"

"She won't hurt you, Dillon! Just go and do it, so we can resume our travel."

He hesitated, then crossed back through the river and walked to the fork. He went to the girl, who remained where he had first seen her. He had thought her pretty, but now he saw that she was more than that. She was beautiful. "I—I—"

"Who are you?" the girl demanded crossly, turning lovely brown eyes on him.

"I am Dillon." It was easier to answer a question than to initiate speech. "Your grandmother said to help you."

"Oh. Well, take this wineskin across, then."

He lifted the wineskin and carried it to the far side of the river. Then he returned to the girl. "I—"

"What's the matter with you?" she demanded. "Are you dull of wit?"

There it was again. "Yes."

She gazed shrewdly at him, in much the way her grandmother had, but her eyes focused. "Well, help me cross."

He stood there uncertainly.

"Put your arm around me," she snapped. "Steady me, so I can walk across without being washed away by the current."

He put his right arm around her slender waist, thrilling to the touch.

"Tightly," she said. "Do you want me to fall in?"

Embarrassed, he tightened his grip somewhat. Unsatisfied, she put her hand down and jammed his hand against her firm hip.

Then they waded through the river. The current was swifter here than at the higher ford, and it shoved her into him and tried to take her feet out from under her.

"Maybe you should carry me," she said.

He put his right hand around her back and his left behind her knees, and hefted her up above the water. She was so light it was as if he carried a child, but her body was that of a woman. It seemed infinitely precious, yet also far distant, because he could never approach such a creature as a person. Only as a burden to carry for a moment. That made him swallow, feeling the grief of his incapacity.

His mind moved away from that, as it always did. He oriented on his surroundings, and something bothered him. Something wasn't quite right. His hunter's reflexes cast about, trying to isolate the problem, but it was intangible. Everything seemed to be in order.

"If you had thought to carry me at the beginning, I wouldn't have had to get my feet wet," she complained.

"I'm sorry." He always impressed women the wrong way. Nothing he could do with them was ever right. The prettier they were, the worse he blundered.

He reached the bank and set her down. She landed easily. "Thank you," she said curtly. "Now go back to Grandma."

He hesitated.

"What's the matter?" she asked sharply.

"I think we are not alone," he said cautiously. "Something is nearby."

"What are you talking about?"

"I'm a hunter. The birds are too quiet, too far out. Something could be stalking you."

"Ridiculous! I'm in no danger. No go on about your business."

He nodded, and searched out a path leading along the river. But now he was doubly alert. The girl's response had not rung true. What did she know, that he did not?

He reached the grandmother's ford. She remained there, snoozing again, but she woke as he approached. "Well?"

"I got her across. But there's something in the forest between the two fords. I don't know whether it's a predator or a man."

Again there came that canny look. "Did you tell her?"

"Yes. But she dismissed it."

"How do you view her, Dillon?"

"I don't understand."

"Yes you do. How do you see Melee?"

"She is—she is a beautiful girl. But tart."

Bata laughed. "She is that! Lovely and sharp, and only fourteen years of age. She has a thing against young men."

"Oh. But the other thing—I had better find out what it is. There could be danger. To her or you."

"Don't be concerned about it."

Now he was sure there was something. "Grandmother, what is happening here?"

"That is a story for another time. Dillon, if you could have anything you desired, what would it be?"

"Oh, I don't know. I'm just trying to find a new situation."

"Let me guess for you. Would it be the love of a girl like Melee?"

Dillon didn't answer, but he felt the blush spreading across his neck and cheeks.

"But you would never dare approach her, because you don't understand women."

He nodded, ashamed.

"Well, I will tell you how to get such a girl. What you mainly require is felicity of expression. So that you can speak to impress a maiden and make her like you, instead of being contemptuous of you."

"Yes. But I'll never have that."

"I can teach you. I was a girl once myself, incredible as that may seem. I remember what a girl likes to hear. Come to work for me and I will show you the words."

Dillon shook his head. "Even if I knew them, I could never say them. To a girl."

Bata considered. "There are other ways. All you need to do is impress her. Sometimes actions do the job, and you are a man of action. I could show you these."

Dillon was sorely tempted, but he knew better. "I just could not do it. When I get near a woman, my hands shake and my tongue swells up. I become a dull-wit."

"Did that happen just now with Melee?"

"No. Not exactly."

"Why not?"

"I couldn't get the words out, but then she asked me, and I answered. She told me what to do, and I did it."

Bata nodded. "She likes telling folk what to do. Did you carry her across?"

"Yes."

"So you felt her body. And you didn't stumble and pitch her into the river."

"I was just doing what she told me."

"Suppose she told you to embrace her and kiss her?"

Dillon paused, trying to imagine it. "I—I would know she didn't mean it. That she mocked me."

Bata sighed. "You do need help. Well, I have made my offer. Will you work for me, and learn from me? I think it will be an even exchange."

She seemed to be serious. "What is your work?"

"Guarding my garden. Being a farmer."

"But I'm a hunter! I know nothing about farming!"

"Ah, but I do. I am too old and feeble and blind to do much of it myself, but I can tell you everything. It does not exclude hunting; you will bring in animals for food, and drive away those who seek to forage in the garden. You will also guard against hostile men who seek to raid or destroy it. So you will be busy, I promise. In return you will be accepted by my tribe, and I will teach you how to win a woman. Maybe not Melee herself, for her father has another destiny for her. But a pretty and fertile woman, so you can become a family man. You will surely not be disappointed."

"Why should a garden need guarding against men?"

"Because of its nature. We are growing grapes."

"Grapes! The spirit fruit!"

"Good spirits," she said. "Our wine is used only for our annual communion with the spirits of our tribe. We draw our tribal strength from this communion. So the garden must be well cared for and protected. It is an important chore."

Dillon shook his head. "Farming grapes," he said, dismayed.

"You have never drunk wine?"

"Once," he admitted. "It made me crazy. Then it sickened me. I want no more of it."

"Then you don't have to partake of it. But you can not be judge of what others do."

He considered. She was offering him a situation such as he was searching for, in general if not in detail. And she was right: he had no call to interfere with the lives of others, as long as they left him free to live the way he chose. Still, he was uncertain. There was too much he didn't know about this situation. "You are right. I am not here to judge others. But I think I should move on."

She glanced sharply at him again. "What dissuades you?"

"There is too much mystery here. You are too sure of yourself, and so is your granddaughter. You both know something you won't tell me. I prefer to know what is what."

"Dillon, I like you better as I come to know you. You are an honest, forthright man."

"And dull with women," he agreed. "Maybe I can find folk more like me, farther on."

"But you might like us better if you knew us better."

He smiled. "I like you well enough, Grandmother. But I am a simple hunter, while you are complicated."

"What must I do to persuade you to stay with me?"

"I have no right to ask you to do anything."

"If I told you exactly what is going on here?"

"I fear I wouldn't like it anyway."

She patted the stone she sat on. "Sit by me, Dillon, and I will clarify all. Then you may decide."

He wasn't easy about it, but he did as she bade him. She told him a story that opened his eyes.

❂

Bata had been satisfied with her life. She had lived long, and when young had mated with the man who became chief of the River Forager tribe. She was the daughter of a chief, so her mate became chief when her father died. She had borne a daughter who in turn mated with a man, Badu, who became the next chief. They had two daughters, and the elder, Baya, had mated with Heath, who would be the following chief. The younger, Melee, would be mated to a similarly good man, when her father decided on one, so that the line would not finish if something happened to Baya. So there was a good continuity, and the tribe had prospered. Heath had at first seemed diffident, but when he had had to assume the office of chief for a while, he had buckled down to it and done a decent job in a difficult time. From that point on he had devoted himself to learning all that he could of the ancient lore, and he was smart, and learned well.

But the dread Green Feather had pressed them ever more closely. They had fended off the brutes, but there were always more of them. With each defense of their river territory, they lost a few more men. Women, too; they were usually captured rather than killed, and used as playthings for the Green Feather males until ill treatment made them die. Badu had come to the conclusion that the tribe would need help, or in time be overwhelmed. So he had gone to see his tribe of origin, the sedentary Valley Herders, to try to arrange an alliance so that they could beat back the mutual enemy. He had taken his unmarried daughter, Melee, and his wife's mother, Bata, to buttress his case. For though men governed the tribes, the tribal lineages were through the women, and the women had the power of decision in such matters. Only if the women were persuaded would the men make the alliance.

But the Valley Herders had suffered depredations of their own. Their chief had been killed, his wife widowed. Until they resolved that problem, they would not consider any external alliance. So Badu made ready to return to the River Foragers, disappointed. Maybe in another year the Valley Herders would be in condition to consider the matter.

Unfortunately, there was much worse to come. During their absence, the Green Feather had struck again, this time when most of the men had been out hunting, and had slaughtered all the women and children they caught. Badu's wife had been among them, and his elder daughter Baya. Without its women, the tribe was finished. The men had fled to a neighboring tribe for sanctuary; they would have to find new tribes.

It had fallen to Bata to direct the stunned man, for this, too, she had experienced before. "Go back to your origin kin," she told him. "They must take you in. And us." For though she was mortified by the deaths of her daughter and granddaughter, she knew she had to act decisively to save her remaining granddaughter. Her time to grieve had to wait, lest the losses become even worse.

"But I can have no status there," Badu protested.

"Yes you can," she insisted. "Mate with the chief's widow. You are now from another tribe; you are eligible. They need you, and we need them."

And so he had done it. The Valley Herders knew his merit, and needed a chief. Thus he had secured status for Melee, for the daughter of the chief was by definition a ranking member of the tribe, and residence for Bata, because she was blood kin to Melee. Neither Badu nor the tribe had been truly pleased with the compromise, but they did need each other and knew it.

And Badu, experienced as a leader and familiar with all of the elder members of the tribe, was effective. The Valley Herders allied with the Mountain Slope tribe, where many of the lost men had been assimilated, surprisingly, and Heath had made a similar mating of convenience. Together they drove back the Green Feather and acquired dominion over good new territory.

Bata had found a new niche, taking over the grape garden and making it prosper. She could not do much of the work herself, but she was able to direct others. But its security remained precarious, for the Green Feather knew of it and might try to destroy it. So they needed to recruit a competent man to guard and sustain it.

"I can't spare any men to guard a garden!" Badu protested. "We're already short of men; I'm trying to recruit more, for the other widows."

Bata resisted the urge to retort that he just wanted other men to suffer as he did, mating with unattractive women for the sake of the security of status within the tribe. But she knew better. He was a good man, paying the price he had to, to accomplish what he needed to. He could not be blamed for still loving the wife he had lost, who was also Bata's daughter, or for acting like the chief he was. The tribe *was* short of men, and had many priorities; the garden was well down the list.

But the garden was her responsibility, and she needed help. "Suppose I recruit my own man to guard the garden?" she asked.

"And how would you do that, Mother? Who would work with an old woman to do such manual labor? Remember how Heath was."

"Remember how Heath became," she replied. "He was my most devoted disciple. I taught him all about healing and herbs."

He nodded, not caring to pursue that further. When Heath lost Baya, he had found a girl of the Mountain Slope tribe, and talked them into accepting the other remaining River Forager men. Several of those had since mated with Valley Herder widows. So Heath had done what Badu had, and thereby salvaged much. But he differed in that his second mate was as young as Melee, a truly nice and clever girl, and had the potential to win his love, in time. Baya had been good, but so was Talena; Bata saw the potential in her. If only that union had not been precipitated by the death of her beloved granddaughter!

After their mutual pause for thought and grief, Badu spoke again. "What do you have in mind?"

"Lend me Melee for two days, and two men. I will set a snare on the main path for young men, and with luck will obtain what I need."

"Melee! I want no strangers getting at her." Badu loved his remaining daughter with the desperation fostered by the loss of Baya. His indulgence of her could be forgiven, though it was making Melee into an imperious brat. Her beauty would compensate for a lot, but there was likely to be mischief coming, unless she was brought down to address reality. She was getting the notion that she was too good for any man.

"Nor will they, Badu," she said reassuringly. "That's why I need the two men. They will protect her from molestation."

Reluctantly, he agreed. "She will attract men like flies to honey. But they may not wish to settle for you, instead, Mother." He had the grace to smile. It was a rare man who cared to associate with an old woman.

"Especially since I mean to be just as choosy as she is, though in a different manner. I require competence, loyalty, and honesty."

He shrugged. "I want the same. But too many lone men are weak in those respects."

So it was that they set their snare, with Melee as the bait. They had a lookout who reported when men were coming along the path, so that Melee could set up at the one ford, while Bata made sure that none were missed on the other ford.

❂

"But you surprised us," she said to Dillon as she concluded her story. "You came to me even after seeing Melee. Now I am satisfied that you are the man I want. I have explained what is going on; will you reconsider? I offer a billet in my nice round house, and instruction in fair speech as well as the rudiments of caring for the vines. Much of your time will be spent doing what is already familiar to you: hunting for animals and guarding against errant men. And, if you do well, you will be allowed to marry a young woman of the tribe, and be accepted as a member."

"But no young woman would want me."

"You forget our bargain. When I am done with you, you will have the ability to charm a woman. Then there will be no problem."

Dillon reconsidered. It wasn't exactly what he had sought, but it seemed to make sense. Now that he knew the old woman better, he liked her. "Yes. I will try to be a farmer."

"You will be more than that," Bata said approvingly. "Much more, I think."

The great Neolithic Revolution came not with a bang, but in a long slow series of tiny increments. It developed independently in several regions of the world, utilizing what was locally useful. In this region of China, the cultivation of millet was to develop in due course, and mulberry trees seem to have been favored: later used for silk worms. People surely understood the process of seeding and growing long before getting into it commercially. The seeds of favored plants would have been dropped or spat out around the encampments, and so more of the same varieties would have grown there, to be conveniently harvested in due course. They might have planted some, then returned months later for the harvest. But there was little point in going into it seriously, because the existing way of life was sufficient. But in time they evidently found reason to domesticate plants. It probably started with the easiest ones, such as berries, or those with special uses, such as herbs. The domestication of grains seems to have been late; they were troublesome to process and hard to digest. So most likely it was the juicy grape that led the way, because the juice could be stored and fermented, making a brew that when imbibed led to pleasant alteration of mind verging on a religious state. It would have become vital for important ceremonies, especially those invoking the spirits. So grape gardens could have been protected from grazing by herbivores or consumption by birds and bugs, for the sake of their precious juice. The development of crockery facilitated this, enabling the storage of juice until fermentation converted it to wine. The European grape is believed to have originated in the region of the Caspian Sea and spread from there; the ancient Greeks and Egyptians cultivated it. Variants surely spread eastward also, used for similar purpose.

But perhaps the main corollary to agriculture was sedentism: settling in one place, instead of leading a nomadic existence. There had always been camps, but not permanent structures; after a week or a month the tribe would move on to a new location, where the hunting and foraging was fresher. The serious growing of crops required residence in one place for much of the year. So some folk would settle, while others would continue to roam. This may have seemed to be of little consequence, at first.

But those who settled were fundamentally changing their way of life. They could build permanent shelters, instead of the relatively temporary ones used for hundreds of thousands of years, and make walls or other defenses of their region. They domesticated animals for milk, fur, and meat, and broadened the range of their tamed plants. Their supply of food became more dependable. Because they did not need to travel, mothers could care for more than one baby at a time. So the birth rate increased, and the survival rate, leading to an expanding population. Thus there soon came to be more settlers than nomads, and in time the former displaced the latter, and the world came to be as it is today, with the nomads marginalized. It wasn't that settling was superior, just that its incidental effect of increasing the population was to make it dominant.

Agriculture did not necessarily make for a better life. The diet was more limited than the eclectic resources of the hunter-gatherers, leading to poorer health and smaller physical stature. The close concentration of many people facilitated the spread of disease, and epidemics ravaged the population. But now the people were locked in; agriculture enabled the harvesting of more calories per unit of land and unit of time than the hunter-gatherer style did, and mankind now needed those calories. So the seeming blessing had its formidable price.

That price was worse for the land. Every acre converted to cropland was one that no longer existed in the natural state, and the plants and creatures who had lived there were driven out. Their habitat was gone, and they could not endure. As agriculture spread across the planet, the old orders retreated, and in time many

*became extinct. So in terms of the global diversity and abundance of species, ag-
riculture was a disaster. Mankind was dominant, but most other creatures and
plants paid a terrible price. That destruction continues today, and is accelerating.
But because extinctions tend to be quiet, rather than spectacular, they proceed
mostly unnoticed.*

*Of course that may change, once the tapestry of life becomes too thinly spread
to maintain the burgeoning human population of the planet. But by then it will
be very late.*

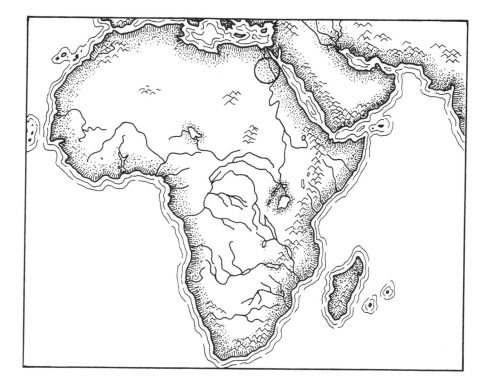

CHAPTER 5

DRAMA

Civilization goes way back in Egypt. The giant pyramids date from the twenty-sixth century B.C., *but they were by no means the beginning of local culture. However, it took enormous effort to build a pyramid, and later kings (not pharaohs at this time) were satisfied with lesser structures. This was probably not modesty—ancient rulers were seldom guilty of that—but the constraints of the budget; if a king does not take care of defense, for example, he may be ousted by a conqueror before he dies naturally. The Middle Kingdom runs from the latter half of the XIth dynasty through the end of the XIIIth: 2066–1650* B.C. *The XIIth dynasty in particular is thought by many scholars to epitomize the nature of the Egyptian*

*culture better than any other period. No wars of conquest were waged in this time,
just sufficient military action to secure the borders from intrusions by the Bedouins
to the west, and the Nubians to the south. During this period the Egyptians traded
amicably with the cultures of Crete, Palestine, and Mesopotamia. Egyptian art
and culture became a catalyst for further development of each of these civilizations,
but Egypt's essentially conservative and Nile-bound nature remained constant.*

*This was also the time when the cult of the god Osiris became a truly powerful
force in politics as well as religion. Egyptian gods and goddesses waxed and waned
in power as the political fortunes of their supporters changed. They took on new
properties as they absorbed, or were absorbed by, the cults of other gods. In this
way they perhaps showed the way for the minor desert mountain deity whom the
Israelites later adopted and carried forward to greatness. Osiris was identified with
the constellation we now call Orion (those three bright stars that are the giant's
belt), and Isis with Sirius, the brightest star in the sky. We now call Sirius the
Dog Star, surely not a comment on the lovely goddess of fertility and motherhood.
The time is 1964 B.C.; the place is the now almost unknown capital fortress-city
of Ith-toui near the Nile delta.*

*One of the most effective of the formal arts is that of the play, and it surely had
great impact on audiences for millennia. There are different types of presentation,
and perhaps one of them utilized one or two announcers together with several
silent actors, as shown here.*

HEATH stepped to the center of the stage. He wore a fine pleated
linen skirt whose cloth was so sheer as to show his legs through it,
and an underskirt provided privacy for his midsection. Above it he wore a
diagonal ribbon extending from the skirt over one shoulder. A colorful
necklet and two bracelets completed his outfit. His feet were bare, as were
the feet of most of the players and audience. His hair was short, but perfumed with a fresh ball of scented oil.

"The world is divided into two parts," he declaimed to the multitude.
"The Black Land of the Nile Valley, whose ruler is Osiris, favored son of
Ra, the great Sun God." He waved his arm, and linen curtains were drawn
aside to show the god-king Osiris seated on his ornate throne. He wore a
fine black skirt and black arm bands, but his body was burnished golden.
He carried a walking stick of black ebony wood the height of a man. Its
upper end was actually a scepter with a finely carved animal head. "And
the Red Land of Outside, whose ruler is his brother Set." He waved to
another section of the stage, and a brooding dark man on a lesser throne
was revealed. "Thus does history begin."

Talena stepped forward. She wore a narrow green dress that hung below
her breasts to the ankles. It conformed perfectly to her body, making her
somewhat slender figure look elegant. She wore a long wig, parted in the
middle so that the hair hung down in two strands. And she wore a necklet,
bracelets, and anklets. Her eyebrows were enhanced by black makeup, and
her eyes were painted green. "The age of Osiris' rule is a golden time,
thanks in considerable part to his sister and wife Isis, ruler of fertility." She

waved her hand, and a third throne was unveiled, whereon sat the splendidly bare-breasted tight-skirted goddess whose wig and makeup enhanced assets that hardly required it. Her perfume was so strong and sensual that it reached out to the audience. The initial unveiling of Isis was always a high moment for the audience, and the actress reveled in it. She knew that she made men desire her, and women envy her, and she wanted the whole of Egypt to join in.

Now Osiris got up from his throne, and Isis joined him. "They taught men to plant crops and reap the harvest," Heath said, as the two mimed the planting and reaping processes. The marvelous breasts of Isis showed to greater advantage as she leaned forward to do the work.

"And to grind grain and make flour," Talena continued. "To cultivate the vine and the fruit tree." The two made grinding and sifting and picking motions. Those breasts flexed and bounced with the activity.

"A father to his people, Osiris taught them to worship the gods and erect temples in their honor," Heath said. Osiris assumed a pose to be admired, spreading his arms and gazing high.

"Peace followed in his footsteps," Talena said. "And wisdom flowed from his lips." Osiris opened his mouth, and it was almost as if honey spilled from it and spread across the stage.

"When Osiris perceived that his work was done," Heath said, "he abandoned his throne and went to travel the world." Osiris turned his back on his throne, as if it were a thing of no consequence.

"Isis lovingly bade him farewell," Talena said. That was somewhat of an understatement; the luscious goddess enfolded the god and kissed him passionately. She twined her fingers in his hair, and set his hands on her bottom, writhing against him. "And in his absence, Isis sat upon the throne and ruled the land." Osiris disengaged as if bored and walked grandly off the stage, while Isis got onto his throne and sat there somewhat pensively. Every so often she moved her feet, shaking her anklets, attracting renewed attention to her fine legs.

"But in Osiris' absence, his evil brother Set plotted against him," Heath said, and Set came to life, dismounting from his throne. His skirt was red, as were his arm bands. "He tried to stir up rebellion against Isis." Set faced the audience and waved his fists as if exhorting them. The audience responded with a roar of negation. Set was eminently dislikable.

"But she was too strong and beloved of the people," Talena said. There followed a pantomime wherein Set, failing to rouse the people against his sister, approached her directly. "He wanted her for himself, for she was beautiful." Set grabbed the goddess and tried to kiss her and fondle her breasts, but she tore away from him and fled the stage. There was a massive grumble of disapproval from the audience. They hated Set.

"So, unable to overcome Osiris and Isis by force or subversion, Set plotted to overthrow them by guile," Heath concluded. Set paced the stage alone, putting his hand to his chin to suggest deep thought. There was somber music, and the beat of distant drums.

Now there was an intermission, so that the stage could be reset. The three actors retreated behind a curtain.

"Listen, Pul!" Avalanche snapped. "You're supposed to let me go right after the failed kiss, not grab for my breasts!"

"Just trying to make it look realistic," Pul said innocently.

"Well, make it realistic without my breasts. They are for Od." She flashed a smile toward Od, who looked stunned. Obviously he hadn't expected any such largess from her at this time.

Actually it had surprised her somewhat, too, for despite his grandiose role, Od was not really a big man. But she had come to appreciate his quickness of mind and inquiring attitude. Pul, in contrast, was a dull thug. A child of Od's might be just as smart as Od, and she liked that notion.

Pul stared at Od. "Well, we'll see," he said ominously.

Then the new set was ready. It was time for the next scene. They left the curtain and walked back out on stage.

"When Osiris returned to Egypt after a long absence," Heath said, "there was great rejoicing." Isis flung herself into Osiris' embrace, kissed him so passionately, and pressed herself so close that it seemed that only their skirts prevented a sexual joining. The audience loved it. The people were well familiar with the play, which was shown often, but could never get enough of Isis in action.

"A royal feast was planned," Talena said. Servants brought out a table loaded with pastries and beverages, as well as perfumes, jewelry, garlands, and lotus flowers. Osiris and Isis approached, stopped near the "entrance," lifted balls of perfume and squeezed them over each other's heads, and decorated each other with colored paints. Then they moved on into the banquet hall and sat at a small individual table. A servant brought beef, goose, chicken, duck, fish, vegetables, and a variety of breads—far more than the couple could eat, but of course this was merely to demonstrate the affluence of the feast. The two picked out token delicacies and ate some of them with dramatic gusto.

"They also quaffed huge amounts of beer and wine," Heath said as servants brought flagons. The two took almost humorously small amounts of these and sipped them. This suggested that the beverages were real, and that they would have trouble performing their roles in the play if they actually imbibed to any degree. "And watched the entertainment." A male singer came on stage, followed by a musician with a lute. He sang briefly but well. He was followed by a female dancer with rather nice hips, which she moved rather well, considering.

"And more," Talena continued. Then Isis led Osiris to a great bed, where they rolled in simulated sex-play, while the singer sang an erotic song and the dancer danced an erotic dance. Isis was, after all, the goddess of fertility; she had to demonstrate her power. It was also fun to work up the man onstage, when it was obvious that he could never complete the seduction. The audience loved it. In due course the singer desisted, and the dancer departed. Isis got up and tiptoed away, while Osiris, evidently bliss-fully worn out, fell into a simulated deep sleep.

"Now Set implemented his foul scheme," Heath said. Set sneaked on-stage bearing a cord of some sort. "While Osiris slept, Set measured his body." The man stretched the cord from head to toe, and from arm to arm, and around the middle.

"He measured everything most carefully," Talena said. Set concluded by miming the lifting and measuring of Osiris' penis. The audience laughed.

"Then he built a great chest along those measurements," Heath said. Set assembled wooden pieces that had been brought onstage, so that they formed a man-sized box. Then he departed, leaving the box on stage.

"Next day," Talena said, "he brought out that box during the feast, and put it on public display so that all could see it." The focus shifted to the side of the stage with the food-laden table. Soon the feasters left it to cluster around the box. "All present admired it greatly, and desired to possess it. As it happened, Isis was away, handling the continuing business of govern-ing, so that everything would be in order for Osiris' resumption of power. Had she been present, Set's cruel trick could not have worked, for a god-dess is difficult to deceive." She frowned, having defended Isis from any possible culpability.

Set then stepped forward and mimed an announcement. "When every-one's heart had been gladdened with beer," Heath continued inexorably, "Set announced that he would make a gift of the chest to the person whose body fitted it most perfectly."

One by one the guests lay in the chest. Some were clearly intoxicated, and needed help getting out. Several gesticulated, as if claiming to have a perfect fit, but others shook their heads. None of them fit closely enough to claim the prize.

Then Osiris rose from his bed and crossed the stage to join the feast, stretching sleepily. Several of the others came to him, indicating the chest, evidently telling him about the offer. They almost hauled him over to try it himself. He shrugged, humoring them, and lay down in it.

"And the fit was perfect," Talena said. "He filled it in every part." The guests stood around, making signals of perfection. All were agreed that Osiris was the one who should have the box.

"But before Osiris could rise again," Heath said, "the seventy-two fol-lowers of Set sprang into action." Several other people swarmed onto the stage. They slammed down the lid of the box, which was now revealed as a coffin, and nailed it into place, while the feasters watched, appalled. But any who tried to protest were menaced by the followers of Set, and re-treated. "Then they poured molten lead through all the openings in the coffin, lest Osiris should breathe and live." The followers brought in a large pot and tipped it to pour water over the box.

"The party dissolved into confusion and bloodshed," Talena said. Some of the feasters drew their weapons and fought with the followers of Set. There were several agonizing deaths scattered around the stage. The actors seemed to enjoy this part. "In the course of this, Set and his followers escaped with the coffin."

The scene shut down, as it would have been too awkward to actually carry the filled coffin offstage. Only Heath remained to tell of it. "Set bade his men to dispose of the coffin secretly. He wanted to know nothing of its whereabouts, and hoped never to see it again. So at night they bore the casket to the Nile and threw it into the current. They watched it float away, sure that it would never be seen again, for in time it would become water-logged and sink to the bottom and be forever lost in the deep muck."

"When Isis learned of Osiris' death," Talena said, "she launched a great mourning. She suspected Set, but he pretended innocence, and no one dared speak of what they had seen, so she had no proof. She cut off a lock of her shining hair and put on the garments of mourning." Isis came on stage, and learned in pantomime what had happened. She gesticulated wildly at Set, who spread his hands in feigned innocence. The audience groaned appreciatively; Set was such a superb liar. So the woman cut a lock from her wig and changed into her mourning outfit. The fact that she did it onstage was not lost on the audience. There were no uncouth exclamations as she stripped away her dress, stood gloriously naked for a moment, then donned the mourning apparel. There was, however, extremely close attention, as befitted a presentation of this importance.

"But her job was not done," Talena continued, once the goddess was suitably garbed. "She knew that the soul of Osiris could not rise from the body and find rest until the funeral rites were performed. The rites could not be done until the body was present, so that their power could have direct effect. So she uttered a solemn vow to discover and recover the body of Osiris." On the stage, Isis gestured bravely, signaling the power of her vow, and there was the roll of drums.

"But Set took advantage of Isis' distraction to imprison her and place himself upon the throne," Heath said. Set marched onstage, came up behind Isis, picked her up, and set her in a section of the stage marked off as a prison. She was so distracted, as described, that she didn't resist at all; it was as though she were a doll. She stood there in her confine, unaware.

"Of course he desired her as well as the throne," Heath said. Set reached into the prison to catch at the goddess. His grasping fingers got a tress.

"But she would have none of it," Talena said. The woman came alive, angrily shaking off the man's too-familiar hand.

"Then she would be confined there until she became more reasonable," Heath said grimly as Set gestured the sentiment with a pair of waving fists. Then, rebuffed, he turned about and stalked to the throne of Osiris. At least he had that half of his desire.

"Isis was not pleased," Talena said, as the goddess stood with hands on her hips, glaring after the false god. "But at the moment there was nothing she could do."

"And so we finish this portion of the history," Heath concluded. "We will resume it tomorrow."

Then both Heath and Talena bowed to the audience, signaling the end of the presentation. There was strong applause. This was the favorite history of Egypt, as well as being highly religious in nature, so any presentation would have been applauded. But this was a very good rendition, so it commanded that much more respect.

Avalanche stepped out of the enclosure and retired to the curtained area, expecting to find Od already there. It had taken her time to realize what a fine man he was, because he was neither large nor strong, but now she did know, and she intended to have an affair with him. Of course in a few months she would find some other intriguing man, for she always did, but for now she really liked Od, and expected to receive almost as much pleasure from him as she intended to give him.

But he wasn't there. She stepped outside the curtains and looked around, wondering what had held him up, for they always gathered at least briefly to review how the presentation had gone and consider small innovations for the next one. She didn't see him.

Pul arrived. "You look great, as usual," he said.

"Where is Od?"

"I don't know."

She glanced sharply at him, knowing by the guilty tone of his voice that he was lying. She could tell when any man was telling the truth; it was women she had trouble judging, as they were cannier liars. "Well, then, I'll just have to find him."

He caught her elbow. "Why bother? I can give you a better time than he ever could."

"I doubt it," she retorted coldly. She jerked her arm away and set off across the stage.

"Hey, you forgot to change," Pul called after her.

Oh, sure—he'd like to have her strip, alone with him and his grabby hands. "No I didn't." She walked away, in her mourning dress.

He ran after her, and caught her before she had taken three steps. "You can't do that. It spoils the play. You must change." He hauled her back into the enclosure.

He had a point, but that was incidental. She did need to change, but she also needed to get away from him so she could look for Od. She knew she could handle Pul if she had to, because, crude as the man was, he *was* a man, and she could handle any man. But she had pride. She didn't want to stoop to sneaky ploys. Unless—

Unless she could trick him into telling about Od. Maybe that was worth some stooping. So she didn't resist as he shoved her inside the curtains. She needed to figure out exactly how to handle this, so as to get maximum benefit from minimum investment. She had had sex with him before, but didn't want it now; could she befuddle him and get without giving? It was a challenge of a sort.

"So I'll change," she decided. "Take my wig." She lifted it from her head and handed it to him. That shifted control of the operation to her;

he was now doing her bidding. That was the prime key, when dealing with men: to gain control, even if the men didn't know it. "Hang it up carefully; I'll need it tomorrow." Of course he knew that; the point was to establish verbal dominance along with the action.

Pul took the wig and hung it on its rack. "Now the dress," he said, licking his lips.

"Now the dress," she agreed. Pul had seen her naked countless times, on stage and off, but he could never get enough of it. That was the ultimate source of her power: her beauty and sex appeal. She had something that every man wanted, and she had it to a degree that made men desperate. The trick was to play it out to maintain control. A woman who lost control got raped. That should never happen, but too many women were stupid.

She loosened her tight waist band, for the form-fitted dress could move neither up nor down otherwise. Then she drew her outer dress slowly up and over her head, in the process completely baring her breasts. They had been pretty well exposed before, but the two dress straps made them seem covered, and now they seemed uncovered. She handed the dress to Pul.

Now she was garbed only in the thicker underskirt. It was designed to cover no more than the essentials; its outline under the translucent outer dress enhanced a focus and allure that would otherwise be diffuse. But the underskirt by itself would soon lose its appeal, being too obvious, so she paused only a moment. She was, in effect, onstage again, acting at precisely that speed that generated the greatest continuing interest. And she did have Pul's interest; he was fascinated, as he had to be. As she had wanted Od to be, at this stage.

She lifted one bare foot to brush off the dirt, facing him so that much of her inner thigh showed briefly. Such a glimpse, she knew from experience, had more impact on a man than an hour of full nakedness. The point of the skirt was to make deep shadows that could not quite be penetrated, so that the male imagination filled in ideal details. Imagination was always better than reality, when it came to sex appeal. The female cleft really wasn't any more esthetic than the male phallus; only when clothed in mystery did it become ultimately compelling.

She set down her foot and lifted the other one, this time spreading her legs to allow more light in. She saw the dilation of his pupils; he had seen so much more than actually existed. His male member would now be governing his head, enhancing his stupidity.

She loosened the waistband and began to draw up the skirt. But she paused just before it uncovered the crotch. "Where did you say Od is?"

"Safely away," he said. Then he caught himself. "Or so I am guessing," he added cannily.

Half a loaf. He had confirmed his complicity. She drew the skirt up another notch. "Tell me."

"Give me your body."

"Tell me first."

"Give, first."

"I think not." She abruptly pulled up the skirt and half flung it at him. Then, while he was putting it with the dress, she grabbed for her regular dress and slipped it on in a smooth practiced motion.

Pul realized that he was losing it. He reacted like the bully he was. "I'll take it!" He reached for her.

She smiled sweetly. "Can you imagine how many people I can summon here, how quickly, if I scream?"

He froze. He knew it was no bluff. So he bargained again. "During." He drew down his own skirt, revealing his erect member.

But she knew that was no good, for several reasons. One was that Od would not be eager to possess her immediately after Pul, and she wanted Od's complete delight. Another was that she wanted to be pristine, by her definition, for Od, which meant no other sex this day. But mainly, it was that once Pul was inside her, he would renege, and what would she be able to do? He would cling to her until he spurted, so she would not be able to disengage halfway.

"No." She stepped quickly outside the enclosure, and this time he did not pursue her, because it took him a key moment to get his skirt back in place, and he did not want to be seen in public with his groin swollen. Everyone would know that the woman he pursued had refused him, and the laughter would be phenomenal. If there was one thing that drove a man more than the sexual urge, it was pride. He could not stand to lose status in the eyes of others.

So she got away. But she didn't know where Od was. Well, maybe she could remedy that.

She approached a man who was watching the next play. His eyes turned on her the moment she came into range, as was the case with the eyes of any man. Men had little or no control over their eyes; a pretty figure drew them like arrows to a target. "Did you see where Osiris went, as the scene ended?"

She was in luck. "Yes. He was drunk. Two friends helped him walk home." He gestured to the street, indicating the direction.

"Thank you," she said, flashing him a smile. He smiled back, pleased to the verge of awe with the reward. Then, before he could progress to the next notion in the male itinerary, she moved on. Timing was everything.

So Od had been taken down the street. He must have been drugged, for he was no drunkard; he imbibed beer or wine only lightly, and she had never seen him intoxicated. But how had he been dosed? He had been all right during the play. She had been close enough to him to verify that. In fact, had there not been a scene to complete, she could have brought him to sex right then. It had been fun, teasing him, knowing that soon it would become real. He had known it too, which meant that the last thing he would have done was to go away without her. So there was definitely foul play.

She had an idea. She went to the wooden box, which had been shoved to the side of the stage. She sniffed it. Yes—there was the odor of the drug that made a person crazy. It must have been in the water (the molten lead) they poured over the coffin. He would have been trapped inside, unable to escape its fumes. The drug normally made a person dazed and confused for several hours, not knowing where he was, or, sometimes, *who* he was. The effect wore off in stages, and it could be several days before the victim was completely himself again. It was normally used by robbers, to daze their victims, or by men to make women amenable. It was rare and expensive, so not used recklessly, which gave another hint about the sophistication of this ploy. So they had taken him from the box and led him away, and he had lacked the wit to resist or even protest.

But what was the point? She suspected that it was to take Od out of the picture so that Pul could have her. Pul was not a good loser. So he must have made a deal with one of the criminals of the street, paying to have his rival removed.

Was Od dead? She suffered a horrible pang, until she realized that probably he wasn't dead, because Pul had said he was "safely away." Pul knew that she would never forgive him if he had Od killed, and that she would soon charm a magistrate to arrest Pul for the murder. So he would play it safe, merely having Od abducted and held, to use as a lever to force her compliance. That was the way Pul thought. But if she reported Od as abducted, and the magistrates got on the case, the abductors well might kill him and bury the body to cover their guilt. So she would have to find Od herself. Then she could act, when she knew the exact situation.

But where could he be? Surely somewhere in the city, but it was a big city. There were countless cells where prisoners could be held, and many brutish families who would hold someone indefinitely for a fee. She wanted to free Od quickly. How could she do that?

She would have to have help. She didn't have money to spare, so couldn't hire any private sleuths. In any event she had not borne three children— or any children at all—so was not entitled to make her own legal or financial decisions. She loved Egypt, but there were details of its law which annoyed her. There was just one approach that was likely to be effective.

She made her way to the temple of Isis, where she was a ranking priestess. That was why she was entitled to play the part of the goddess in the sacred presentation. She had friends there. It was late, but the temples of the gods and goddesses were well patronized during the festival, and there would be women on duty.

She entered the temple. A girl quickly stepped forward to greet her. "Oh—it's you, Avalanche! I thought you weren't coming back tonight."

Avalanche hesitated. This was Lin, barely ten years old, one of the juvenile functionaries who would never be a priestess. She was dawningly beautiful, and would make a truly lovely woman soon, but she had that one liability of the six-fingered left hand that she always had to conceal. She was a nice girl, and trustworthy, but her future was forever clouded by that deformity. Avalanche had interceded for her, so that she could have employment at the temple, and indeed, the girl was doing well. There was a tacit conspiracy of silence in the temple about the hand, and when there was any risk of exposure, a priestess would step in to alleviate it. The temple took care of its own.

Still, Lin would do anything for a friend, and that was what Avalanche needed now. "I need your help, Lin," she said. Quickly she explained about the disappearance of Od, and her suspicion about Pul's complicity. "So I must find him soon, before anything worse happens to him. Spread the word that the man who locates him for me, without alerting the captors, will have that reward which only I can give."

Lin smiled knowingly. Then she faded into the recesses of the temple. She was young and physically innocent, but she understood about the ways of men and beautiful women. She would spread the word, discreetly and rapidly, and others would know it was true, because Lin always spoke the truth.

Suddenly Avalanche felt enormously tired. This situation with Od had really gotten to her. She had anticipated such a glorious evening, and instead encountered this disaster, and she was worn out. But she had done what she could, for now, so it was time to rest. She needed to maintain her appearance of youthful beauty, because that was the primary currency of her life; without it, she was just a barren woman.

She retired to her cell behind the temple, nibbled on figs, performed her evening toiletries, prayed to the goddess Isis, and lay down on her pallet to sleep. She thought of Od, so nice, so smart, always so curious about things. He had not impressed her at first, though she had given him sex a couple of times, but steadily her appreciation of him had grown, and now she was close to loving him. She was, she thought, incapable of true love, but she was beginning to suspect that if it was possible for her, Od was the one with whom it could happen.

And now he was gone. Damn it! That did not diminish her interest, it amplified it. At such time as she found him, and recovered him, she would give him such a good time he would have trouble walking straight for days. Perhaps he supposed that sex with her was always the way it had been before. That was not the case. She could send a man floating toward the moon, when she chose. Now she so chose. And he wasn't there.

At last she slept, wishing she were not alone. Damn Pul and his evil ploy! One day she would settle with him for that, in her own way, and he would not like it at all.

❁

Od woke in squalor. He was lying on a mound of camel dung, and the stuff was all over him. He had an awful headache. What had happened to him? He could not remember. His last memory was of a girl telling a story about her grandmother, and that hardly seemed to connect to his present situation.

He sat up, shedding clods of dung. It was dawn, somewhere, and there was a small chill in the air. He must have gotten drunk at a party, and passed out here in the night, though it was not his way to imbibe heavily. He would have to find the river and wash himself off, then go home. If he could just remember where home was.

"Ho, sleeper!" someone called. An armed man strode toward him.

Od stared blearily at the man. "Who are you?"

"I am your master, whom you will obey implicitly, lest you feel the sting of my lash, like this." The man's arm moved, and a whip struck like a viper, stinging Od's shoulder. The pain was awful. "You may call me Bub. Now go tend your camels."

Od lurched to his feet, lest the whip catch him again. There were five camels grazing nearby. Od hardly knew anything about camels, but if they were what it required to keep the whip from his back, he would quickly learn.

A boy was already working with one of the camels. He glanced across as Od approached. "You're the new camel tender?" he asked.

"It seems I am," Od replied.

"I am Chip," the boy said. "Son of Hue and Ann, working here to help support my family while my parents are on tour."

"I am Od. I don't quite remember my family."

"They drugged you," Chip said wisely. "It will come back."

"Your parents go on tour?"

"They are entertainers," the boy said proudly. "My father plays the flute and my mother dances. She's very pretty."

Od made a connection. "Ann—a dancer," he repeated. "I have seen her. Beautiful woman! But I don't remember where."

"That's her. Folk who can't remember anything else remember Mom." He looked around. "But we had better get to work, or the whip will come."

Od had discovered that. "What am I supposed to do?"

"First get to know them," the boy said. "Camels won't obey strangers. It helps if they like you. So try to make a good impression."

"How do I do that?"

"Feed them. One dipper each." Chip pointed to a wagon loaded with grain.

Od got on it. He was getting steadier as he walked, and his head was clearing. Now he remembered a beautiful woman. But not her name or her connection to him.

When the camels had been fed, they were led to a construction site. Od and the boy were responsible for guiding the camels as they hauled loads for the workers. The camels didn't yet know Od well enough, so were surly, and the boy had to do most of it. "But they'll be better soon," Chip said cheerfully. Evidently he had been having to do the whole job himself, and was glad to have an assistant.

As the day progressed, Od's mind clarified farther. He was an actor in a religious play. They were putting on a series of shows, one each night. He was playing the god Osiris. He played opposite a beautiful woman. That was how he had encountered Chip's mother, when she had been in another play on the same stage. But how had he come here to this camel outfit?

He tried to speak of it. "I don't belong here," he told the boy. "I'm an actor."

"Ssshh, don't let the boss hear you," Chip cautioned him. "He said you were crazy. You don't want to prove it. He'll beat it out of you."

He would be whipped if he spoke of his memories? Od began to understand more. He had been abducted! That was how they recruited men (and sometimes women) for unpleasant duties. There were crews that simply grabbed anyone who was not protected, and sold them into slavery. Od must have been drugged and similarly sold. The foreman, Bub, had to know it. But he would be no help, because he stood only to lose a worker he had paid for. So Od had fallen into the trap, and the boy was right: he would do best not to speak of his other life. It would only alert his captor that he was considering escape.

So he buckled down to the work, cultivating each camel as well as he could. The brutes were surly, but not stupid; it didn't take them long to realize that Od was treating them better than others might. So their constant squeals of outrage were losing force, and they balked slightly less at the tasks he was urging.

Meanwhile he watched for some opportunity to escape. First he had to figure out exactly where he was, and he didn't dare inquire. There were numerous construction sites around the edges of the city. He had once studied a map of the city, for he was interested in maps among other things, and remembered the markings. But he couldn't place this particular site. Maybe the map had been old, and this project had started recently.

Well, in time he would figure it out. Then he would act. In knowledge there was power.

❁

Avalanche slept late, which was just as well. She had routine temple duties, but evidently others had covered for her, and now she was feeling more positive in her despair. Surely someone would find something out, and then she would know what to do. Then, after the play, when her duties for the day were finished, she would act on her own.

She prepared herself and joined the other priestesses. This was a busy time for the temple, because of the extended festival, and because the cult of Osiris was surging in popularity, carrying in its wake the cult of Isis. They had had to train new priestesses and add new chambers. All of which was good, in both the religious and secular senses. The worship of superior gods like Osiris and Isis was certainly an improvement over some of the brutish gods of the past. And it enhanced the positions of women like Avalanche. Women were better treated in Egypt than elsewhere, but still there were only two roles for a wealthy woman, and three for a peasant woman. That was to say, a high-class woman like Avalanche could be a priestess or a wife, or both. A peasant woman could be a servant, a prostitute, or a wife—which often was the same in effect as being both servant and prostitute. The cult of Isis ministered to many women whose lives were wretched. The dominant religion in the land was now the cult of Amun. Amun had been an unimportant local deity of the city of Thebes, but when Amenemhat had assumed the throne thirty years ago, and built this now capital city, he had brought his god with him. The authority of any god varied directly with the influence of its leading worshippers. So now it was Amun-Ra, the Sun God. But Osiris was extremely popular too, and Isis.

Then the time for the play came. Pul was there, of course; she would have to fend him off, in and out of the play. Fortunately her scene with him was brief.

"The evil god Set had imprisoned the goddess Isis," Heath announced as the scene formed. There was Isis, standing within her prison, her hands on her hips, glaring defiantly at him.

"But she would have none of him," Talena said. "So all he had was Osiris' throne." Set sat on the throne, publicly brooding.

"The people had no choice," Heath continued. "They had to serve the one who occupied the throne. But they were not happy." He gestured out over the audience, and the spectators in the front rows bowed their heads, emulating unhappiness. They loved getting into the play, however obliquely.

"But in the night, Isis summoned her protectors the scorpions," Talena said. "They stung the guards to death and opened the door, so that she could escape." An actor garbed as a scorpion, with a huge curving tail, came to open the door. Isis stepped out, and hugged the man-sized creature. That, too, was popular: ugly monster, lovely woman. Avalanche thought it was because men were so much cruder than women, and peasants were so ugly, that they could identify with such monsters. If a giant scorpion could embrace a beautiful woman, maybe a peasant man could too.

"So while Set brooded on the throne," Heath said, "the goddess escaped, and resumed her search for her beloved Osiris."

"Accompanied by her seven loyal scorpions," Talena said. "Three in front, two behind, and one on each side." There was actually only one scorpion onstage with her, but it was understood that the others were there. "Everywhere she went, she asked for word of Osiris' body, but no one could help her."

"Remember," Heath reminded the audience, "Osiris' coffin was put into the Nile, where it floated away. The assassins believed that it would soon sink and be lost in the muck."

"In one village," Talena said, "Isis asked for shelter from a wealthy woman named Glory." Isis walked up to a marked door and knocked, and gestured before the woman who stood there. "But Glory feared her scorpions, so turned her away." The woman closed the door, and Isis faced away. "But a poor marsh woman saw Isis' plight and took pity on her. She invited Isis to spend the night in her poor house. The goddess accepted."

Isis walked to another marked house, where the ragged woman gestured invitingly. Isis entered and joined the woman inside. They shared an invisible meal, and then both lay down.

"In the night," Heath said, "one of her scorpions, named Tefen, crawled away, and under the door of the rich woman's house." The big scorpion walked back to the prior house, got down to hands and feet, and crawled in. "Tefen stung the woman's son, killing him." The scorpion grabbed his tail in his hand and plunged the barbed tip into a boy sleeping there. The audience shuddered; folk well understood the deadliness of scorpions. "Then he set fire to the house." The scorpion produced a torch from somewhere and touched it to some tinder in the house. In a moment there was a blaze onstage. The scorpion scrambled away.

The woman, Glory, had been sleeping. She quickly got up, spied the flames, and tried to beat them out. Then she saw the body of her son. She let out a shriek and gestured wildly, ignoring the continuing blaze. This was a natural reaction. Too many women had suffered similar grief.

"Then Glory's wailing reached Isis," Talena said. Isis sat up, cupping her ear as if straining to hear. Glory shrieked again. Isis nodded, hearing it. "The goddess took pity on the rich woman's suffering. She sent a flood of rain to extinguish the fire." Isis gestured to the heavens, and a man garbed as a black cloud ran across the stage and dumped a bucket of water on the flame.

"She then restored the dead child to life," Heath said, "banishing the poison with a spell." Isis left the marsh woman's house, walked across the stage to the rich woman's house, entered, and made a magical gesture. Suddenly the boy sat up, stretching. Then he put his hands to his head. Evidently the experience had left him with a headache. Little did he know!

"Glory was filled with gratitude for the rescue," Talena said. The rich woman hugged the boy. "And shame for her earlier behavior." Glory made gestures of abject humiliation, even dumping some of the water-sodden ashes on her own head. "She brought all of her wealth and ornaments, her bracelets and necklaces, her gold work and silver work, and laid them at the feet of the marsh woman in repentance." The rich woman carried her armload to the poor woman's house and dumped it inside.

"So it went," Heath said. "But no one knew where the coffin had gone." Isis resumed her walk around the stage, looking hopeless.

"Finally Isis asked the children near the Nile if they had seen the coffin of Osiris," Talena said. Isis came to a place on the stage marked as a river, where two small children played. The children gestured, pointing a direction. "They told her that the body had traveled down the river to the Great Green Sea."

"And so it had," Heath agreed. "All through the night the coffin had floated down the river, refusing to sink, and in the morning it had reached the Great Green Sea and was driven hither and thither, tossed by the large waves. But by this time, several days later, it was no longer floating there. It had reached the shores of Syria, near the city of Byblos."

Now stagehands pushed the coffin across the stage to a spot representing the city of Byblos. "Where it touched the land," Talena said, "a great tamarisk tree sprang forward immediately, and the coffin became hidden in its great trunk." The stagehands placed leafed branches over the coffin.

"The king of Byblos, named Malkander, marveled at the growth of the giant tree," Heath said. A man garbed in the crown and robes of a foreign king marched onto the stage, gazed at the branch-covered coffin, and gestured his amazement. "He had it cut down." The king summoned another, and a man came with an axe and chopped at the branches. "The trunk was then erected in his palace as a scared pillar." The workman carried a branch to another part of the stage and stood it up.

"Meanwhile Isis, not spying the coffin floating on the Great Green Sea, appealed to the Sun God for help," Talena said. Isis put her hand to her brow, peering out across the sea, then shook her head. She lifted her arms high toward the sun.

"The Sun God revealed to her that the waters had carried the body to Byblos," Heath said. A man garbed as the Sun came onstage and pointed to the other set.

"Isis thanked him," Talena said. The goddess made a deep bow. The Sun God took a good look at her bosom and nodded. It was apparent that even a god had to admire that form.

"Then she traveled by ship to that Syrian city," Heath said. Isis got into a boat-shaped box, and was pushed across the stage by two men dressed as Wind and Wave. In due course it came to the Byblos setting, and the goddess disembarked. She waved farewell to the departing ship, and both Wind and Wave waved back.

"Isis went ashore clothed in common raiment. But now she did not know what to do," Talena said. "For Byblos was a big foreign city where Isis knew no one. She did not know in which house the coffin might be, or of whom to inquire. The magnitude of her task overcame her. So she sat beside a well, weeping bitterly." Isis sat on the floor, and put her face in her hands, weeping. At that moment she seemed far more like a woman than a goddess.

"The women of the city came near," Heath said. A woman in foreign garb approached the seated goddess. "They spoke with her with pity, but she would neither answer nor stop grieving." The woman shook her head sadly and went away. "Finally the handmaids of the queen came to her." A richly garbed girl approached. "Isis accepted their gentle words. She stopped crying, adjusted their jewels, and breathed a sweet perfume into each lock of their hair." Isis did that, leaning forward to exhale on the girl's tresses.

"When the maids returned to the palace," Talena said, "Queen Athenais smelled the perfume, and was struck by its beauty." The girl crossed the stage to approach a richly garbed woman wearing a crown. The queen sniffed the girl's hair and made a gesture of delight. "When her handmaids told her of the sad, strange woman by the well, and the lovely perfume that came from her breath, the queen went immediately to the shore." Athenais marched across to Isis, followed by the girl.

"The two women spoke together as women will," Heath said. "They exchanged sorrows. Isis told the queen how she was searching for her lost love, and Athenais told the goddess of her grief for her son, who was sick unto death." The two women gestured at each other, exchanging confidences. Then they hugged each other.

"Hearing of the prince's plight," Talena said, "Isis asked to be taken to the child." The two women walked to the place on the stage designated as the palace of Byblos. "Now the prince of Byblos was a beauteous child, and Isis loved him from the instant she saw him. He was like the child she wished she could have had. She took the child in her arms, and he revived somewhat, hearkening to the ambiance of the goddess." Isis embraced the child, and the child stirred, hugging her back.

"The queen of Byblos was impressed," Heath said. "She saw the good effect the strange woman had on her son. 'What power is it that you have, to make him respond so?' she asked. Isis demurred. 'Just one who knows some healing magic. I can make him strong and well, but I will do it in my own way, and no one must interfere.' 'Then do it!' the queen cried. 'No one will interfere!' "

"And so the prince was given into the goddess's hands for healing," Heath said. "This ends our presentation for today, but we will resume tomorrow." He and Talena bowed to the audience.

Avalanche hurried to the changing enclosure. Pul was there, of course. "Get out of my way," she said irritably. "Unless you're going to tell me exactly where Od is."

"But I don't know where he is," he protested.

She flung off her dress, heedless of his eyes. "Then you are of no use to me." She got into her street clothes and brushed on out. If he had thought to win her by this cruel ploy, he had been even more stupid than usual.

She returned to the temple of Isis, hoping that a lead had been found during her absence. "There is one!" Lin exclaimed. "A wealthy man named Tuho says he has information."

Avalanche suffered a thrill of hope. "Where is he?"

"His servant is waiting in the antechamber."

"I'll go immediately."

"But not alone," Lin protested.

Avalanche nodded. "I'll take Tefen." He was one of the temple guards, nicknamed after the scorpion who guarded the goddess Isis. It was no insult; the guards took their work seriously, and scrupulously protected the priestesses and property of the temple.

She put a light cloak over her dress and set out with Tefen, following the servant. They walked the streets thronged with the folk of the festival. The pastry hawkers were out in force, and the free-lance entertainers doing their little acts for pieces of copper, and the prostitutes. Tefen brushed past them, and Avalanche followed in his wake.

They came to the house. It was a mansion built of mud brick, with a small porter's house guarding the entrance. The windows were small and high, preventing access from the street. They passed through the entrance to the central courtyard, which supported a rich interior garden. This was the source of light and freshness for the house.

The owner stepped forward to meet her. He wore a white knee-length skirt with a pleated front, and a red ribbon. "Thank you for coming, priestess!" he said heartily. "I am Tuho."

"What is your news?" For he might simply be a man who wanted access to her body, pretending to have information.

"I dare not be too specific," he said.

Avalanche started to turn away. "I need to find my friend. Vague news is not enough."

"But I do have information," he said quickly. "I have a friend who works at the king's palace. He overheard some sort of plot against the king. His life—and mine—would be in peril if this were spoken openly. Until he learns more—the identity of the key plotters—he must be silent. But one detail was that one of the plotters abducted an actor yesterday."

Avalanche had been listening somewhat cynically. Palace plots were as common as copper pieces, and few ever amounted to anything, because the king's spies were everywhere. Most were simply talk, as dissatisfied servants vented their frustrations by saying what they wished were true, sowing routine dissent. But if there were a connection of Od's abduction, then she was interested. "Where did they take him?"

"My friend didn't hear. Just that they did it for gold. It seems that someone had a grudge against this man, so paid to have him removed but not killed. The plotters need gold."

So this was mostly conjecture based on part of an overheard conversation. No solid information. The man could have made the whole thing up, just to get her here. "Not enough," she decided. "I must know where."

"I will try to get that information," Tuho said. "My friend may hear more."

"And your friend may not exist," she said. "You are wasting my time." She stepped toward the exit.

"No, it is true!" he protested. "I thought it best not to wait for full information, which may take days."

"You thought I would give you my favor for this mishmash of speculation?"

"I don't want your body."

She paused. This was an unusual ploy. "Then what did you hope to gain by this device?"

"My daughter," he said hurriedly. "She is ill, and the doctor said only a priestess of Isis can help her. But she is too sick to go to the temple, and no priestess would come here. I had hoped—"

"You had hoped to trick me here to see to your child?"

He hung his head. "It was the only way."

"Be thankful I don't have my man burn down your house!" she snapped, and resumed her motion. But then she remembered the play, wherein the rich woman turned away the goddess. In fact that was what had put the notion of burning in her mind. But she was cast in the wrong role, here. So she stopped again. "Show me your sick child." And if that, too, was false, she would put a curse on the girl, making her truly sick.

"This way," Tuho said eagerly. He showed them into a small chamber of the house.

A girl was there, perhaps only five years old. There was no doubt she was seriously ill. She lay on a feather mattress, breathing in gasps. Her hair was matted with sweat, and her eyes were sunken.

All Avalanche's ire melted away. She had so long wished for a child of her own, and been jealous of the children of other women. This girl truly needed help. She had seen similar symptoms before. There was a potion that sometimes helped. "Tefen—fetch the potion, from the temple," she said.

"But Lady, I must not leave you here unprotected," he protested.

"I think I am safe enough here. I must minister to this girl. Go, and return swiftly." Then, another thought: "And bring Heath, if you can." For Heath was more than a historian; he studied the lore of medicines, and knew much about healing.

Tefen turned and left. Avalanche sat beside the child and stroked her forehead. It was burning hot.

The child stirred. "Who?" she asked plaintively.

"The priestess of Isis," her father said. "As I promised."

The eyes opened. Avalanche leaned into the girl's field of vision and smiled, holding up the icon of the goddess. Then she adjusted herself and lifted the small head to her lap. "I will bless you," she murmured.

The girl made a wan smile, and dropped into sleep.

The man shook his head. "So readily, with you," he said. "I could not get her to sleep. She just lay there and suffered."

"The goddess helps whom she chooses," Avalanche said. And that was true. But there was also an effect that a lovely face had, on children as well as on adults. That was why she had smiled at the child. Maybe it was no more than a surface balm, but if it enabled the girl to sleep, it was enough. "What of her mother?"

"The plague."

That could mean anything. Illnesses wracked the city from time to time, but there were also incidental poisonings and infections. But it did mean that the child was motherless. A nurse or servant would be taking care of her, but that was a poor substitute.

Avalanche held the child, humming faintly, stroking her hair with one hand. Half of what this girl needed was a mother. And half of what Avalanche needed was a child. If only—but of course it was a foolish notion. She wasn't looking for an incidental man as a husband, she was looking for Od.

Still, this man had generated this child. Perhaps the gods would bless him again. "Tuho," she murmured.

"I am here, priestess."

"Secure the chamber."

"My house is secure."

She drew on the front of her cloak, baring her breasts. She knew he desired her; every man did. Now she was letting him know that his desire could be realized.

"But I did not ask for—"

She just looked at him.

Tuho stepped out of the chamber. "Do not disturb this room until I give the order," he called to someone. Then he returned.

Avalanche set the sleeping child's head back on the pillow. She stood up, removed cloak and skirt, and stretched. "There should be time before Tefen returns." Then she approached Tuho, putting her hands to his skirt.

"I don't understand," he said, letting her disrobe him, revealing the literal nature of his desire. "You were angry with me."

"Until I saw your daughter. I have no child of my own. Perhaps you will give me one."

"You wish to marry me?" he asked incredulously.

"No. We may not see each other again, after these few days." She stepped into his body, pressing her breasts against his chest.

"Then why?"

"You have partial information. I am paying you for full information. After this, you must deliver it."

"I can't promise that! My friend may not overhear any more."

"I am speaking in terms of fate. I am facilitating your friend's success."

He shook his head. "I am not sure that fate can be coerced, even by a lovely priestess. I do not wish to make a false representation."

She liked his integrity. He wanted her almost unbearably, at this stage, yet he was trying to be fair. "We shall nevertheless make the effort." She put one hand up behind his head and pushed it down for a kiss.

"There is nowhere to lie down," he said after a breathless moment.

"Sit against the wall. I will accommodate."

He sat, and she spread her thighs and straddled his crotch. She could fit any man inside her, in any position, with the seeming ease born of long experience. When he was deep, she squeezed internally. That was another device not all women knew. He was instantly potent, as any man was with her. She leaned forward to kiss him again, then lifted off him.

He stared up at her. "You are amazing, priestess. In an hour I will think this was a dream."

"I am good at dreams." She quickly donned her dress and cloak again and lay down with the child. This both concealed the nature of her recent activity, and held the man's essence within her so that it would have a better chance to make her baby, if it was going to.

Tuho got up and dressed. Then he stepped out of the chamber. She knew this was so that no one would believe there had been time for anything seriously sexual, as indeed would ordinarily have been the case.

"Was it good?" the child inquired. So, womanlike, she had feigned sleep when it suited her.

"Very good," Avalanche agreed. "When you grow to be a woman, you will be able to do it too."

"My father has not smiled since Mother died."

"Tomorrow, when he thinks it was a dream, tell him it was not. Then he will smile."

The girl almost laughed, but was too weak. Avalanche squeezed her shoulder, and she fell back to sleep.

In due course Tefen arrived, with Heath. Heath examined the girl and nodded. "This should help." He gave her a few drops of the potion.

On the way back to the temple, Heath asked "Him, too?"

"Maybe my baby stems from his loin."

"Is there any man you haven't tried with?"

"Aside from you? No. You are interested?"

He laughed. "Let me be, goddess."

Of course he was interested, but he was loyal to his wife. So she did let him be, satisfied with incidental teasing. Perhaps the day would come, but not while he remained with Talena.

Now if only she could be with Od! This lead had proved inadequate, but perhaps it would yield later result. In any event, she had enjoyed helping the child, and trying once more for a baby of her own. How like the play it had been, in general if not in detail. It made her feel closer to the goddess.

❂

It had been a hard day, but Od and the camels had made it through, thanks to the advice and help of Chip. Apparently the boy was here voluntarily, because he liked animals and wanted to help his family. But many other workers were conscripts. Camel duty was the messiest but least physically demanding chore. It seemed that recruits were tried first on this, and if they had any touch at all with the animals, remained. Otherwise they were moved on to stone hauling. Od decided to do his very best with the camels, because the stone work could kill him.

He had finally figured out where they were: at the site where there was preliminary work for a future public building. There was endless preparatory scraping and leveling to do, and measuring of foundation points. Od was interested in this, as he was in everything, so he paid close attention. He hadn't realized that it was necessary for the base of a building to be absolutely level, but now that he thought about it, he understood the truth of it. An unlevel foundation would mean an unlevel structure, and that building would be under strain and perhaps fall.

He had also kept his eyes out for an escape route, but that seemed impossible. The site was away from the main city, so that a man couldn't just walk away; he would be observed long before he got anywhere. At night they loosed the dogs, who ranged the perimeter of the site and alerted their masters to any activity there. He was getting to know the camels, but not the dogs; they were vicious brutes who were bred to be hostile to strangers. Escape by foot was not feasible.

So after the evening meal, and the falling of night, he tried a different ploy. He sneaked up on Foreman Bub's tent. Probably all he would spy would be the man bedding one of the serving girls. But their dialogue might have some useful information. So it was a gamble worth taking. Because Od could not be sure of his fate, if he remained as a camel tender; when this aspect of the construction was done, he might be killed. He still didn't know why he had been drugged and abducted. Certainly the work crews needed workers, and abduction was one of the recruiting methods, but normally the victims were those who were largely unknown. The actor who played Osiris would surely be missed, especially during festival time when the play was being performed. So it seemed likely that there was more to it than mere need for labor. But his mind had not yet completely cleared, so he couldn't be sure of his logic.

He came silently to the partly completed wall against which the foreman's hut was pitched. The wall shielded it from the wind and sand, making it a better location than what was available for the workers and camels. Rank always had its privileges. But this was an advantage for Od, because the wall would conceal him perfectly while allowing him to get quite close.

He found the wall and moved along it, slowly and silently. The dogs should not be ranging here, because it was near the center of the construction site. No one would look for a hiding prisoner here, either; it was the wrong direction. There could be great privacy in doing the unexpected.

He heard the talking before he reached the closest part of the wall. The stone itself was transmitting it. Od crawled low, then lay down with his ear to the wall, listening. It was almost as if he were part of the wall, now, hearing with its ear. The sounds were not loud, but Od was completely silent, so had no trouble picking it up.

"Day after tomorrow?" Bub was asking. "That soon? Are we ready?"

"The question is not whether we are ready, but whether the king is unready," another voice said.

What was this? Bub didn't have a woman in his hut, but a man! And it did not seem to be love they were discussing. What was this about the king being unready? Did they mean King Amenemhat, lord of Upper and Lower Kingdoms? He was hardly a man to be called "unready."

"But even so, what of his son, the co-regent?" Bub asked. "What good to take out the one without the other?"

"That is the point," the stranger said. "Sesostris is even now marching home after a victorious campaign in Nubia. In six days he will be here with his troops. Then it will be impossible to score."

"But to do it now, when Sesostris is so close—will he not simply march in and slay us all?"

"Not if he doesn't know. The key is to do it now, quietly, then let Sesostris disband his troops and enter the city unawares. He can be executed before he suspects. Then the troops will have no rallying point, and will have to serve the new master."

There was a pause, as of someone thinking it through. "Perhaps so, though the timing is closer than I like. What do you want of me?"

"This construction site is south of the city. Sesostris will cross it as he enters. This is where it must be done, before he can discover that the city is in our hands."

"You want me to assassinate the co-regent? I couldn't even get close to him!"

"But one of our serving girls could. You must dress like one of them, and go with their group. When you are close to the regent, spring forth and stab him to death."

"Whereupon his guards will hack me apart! I have little taste for that."

"What better way do you have?"

"An ambush with bows. We could riddle him from behind the wall before he knows anyone is there. Meanwhile the regular workers will be working as usual. His guards will assume they are responsible, and slaughter them. While our bowmen sneak away."

"That sounds efficient. Do it."

Od was stunned. The conspirators planned to assassinate King Amenemhat in two days, and his son Sesostris in six days. This had to be stopped! But what could he do? He couldn't even escape this work site. And if he did, how could he approach the palace? The conspirators would surely kill anyone they suspected of trying to warn the king. Especially since they would know that he had escaped the work site, and they would be watching for him.

Unless he surprised them by doing the unexpected. By stealing a camel and fleeing away from the city, into the desert.

He waited for the stranger to depart, then quietly made his way back to the hut he shared with Chip. Could he trust the boy? He had to, because he needed the lad's help. As far as he knew, Chip was not part of any conspiracy; he was just another conscript stolen or bought from his family. Chip said it was voluntary, but that might just be his way of coping with an uglier reality.

The lad was alert when Od returned. "I hoped you weren't trying to escape," he said. "I didn't want the dogs to get you."

"I wasn't trying to escape," Od agreed. "I was spying on Bub."

"Why? He's just a brute overseer."

Od hesitated, then plunged ahead. "Are you loyal to King Amenemhat?"

"Sure. Why?"

"Bub is not. He is part of a conspiracy to kill the king."

"So that's it! I knew he was a bad one. He promised my father I would not be whipped, but he lied."

"I must warn the king. Will you help me take a camel?"

"Take Lotus. She likes to travel." The boy didn't even question his news about the plot. That helped a lot.

They went to the hobbled camels. Chip got Lotus to get down so Od could mount, then freed her. "Just don't get off her," he warned. "Unless you have someone who knows how to make her mind. She'll walk for you, but she won't let you back on once you're off. There's water and bread in her harness. If you have to pee, just do it from her back; she's used to that. Keep quiet when you pass the dogs and they won't realize it isn't all right. It's folk on foot they watch for."

That was what Od had counted on. "Thanks, Chip," Od said as he took the reins. "If I succeed, I'm sure there will be a reward for you."

"Just don't mention my name if you don't succeed," the boy said, unsmiling.

"Understood." For there would be death for any who tried unsuccessfully to balk the plotters. Chip was acting with trust and courage, helping him like this. "And you had better alert Bub first thing in the morning about how I stole a camel and escaped."

"First thing in the morning. Just as soon as I notice." Chap smiled. "He'll be furious."

"I hope he doesn't beat you."

"I'll yell it to him, then check to make sure nothing else is missing. He'll be too distracted to think of the whip right away."

"You have made this possible. I will remember."

"May the sun go with you, Od." The boy slapped the camel's flank, and Lotus started moving. Her gait was sure. Od had not ridden a camel in years, but could tell that this one did indeed like to travel. She would carry him as far as needed, though it was bound to be a hard journey.

There was a stirring as they crossed out of the construction site. The dogs were investigating. Lotus squealed irritably at them, and they moved away. They knew her, and if there was someone riding her, how could they know it wasn't legitimate? Their prey was any man afoot at night, just as the boy had said. Nothing else.

He turned the camel's nose south. Bub would naturally expect him to flee north, toward the city, where he could return to his own people. With luck, Bub would not realize that Od had spied on him and overheard his treachery. Even if Bub suspected that, he would assume that Od was hurrying to warn King Amenemhat of the assassination. But Od knew that he would not be able to reach the king; the traitors would kill him before he got close. And if somehow he did get the king's ear, why would the king believe him? No, he had to invoke the element of surprise, and go in the opposite direction expected. South, to warn the king's son and co-regent, Sesostris. Hoping that the son was more likely to listen than the father was. If he could do it within one day, then Sesostris would know what to do to foil the plot against his father. If his journey took longer than a day—well, maybe the regent had trained birds to send with warning messages. Or possibly some magical means of communication. Or something. It was all pretty desperate, but there was no alternative except surrender.

Right now, all Od should focus on was traveling south as swiftly as the camel could carry him. Until he intercepted the army of the regent, and delivered his message. The welfare of the kingdom of Egypt depended on it.

❂

"Queen Athenais of Byblos delivered her ill-unto-death son into the hands of the goddess Isis for treatment," Talena said to the audience, "promising that no one would interfere. For this was the requirement Isis made, knowing that others would not understand her methodology. They did not know that she was a goddess, with special powers; they thought she was limited to mortal means.''

Isis walked to the center of the stage, leading a boy by the hand. He looked ill; his head hung and he dragged his feet.

"As soon as the child was given to Isis' care," Heath said, "he began to grow strong and healthy. For the goddess was suckling him from her own finger.''

Isis embraced the boy, and kissed him on the mouth. He began to straighten up, for even the youngest of males had to respond to such treatment. Then she lay on a pallet and had him lie beside her, his head cushioned against her left breast. He smiled, and the audience smiled with him; every man and some women wished they could play that part. She reached across her body and put her right forefinger into his mouth. He pursed his lips around it and sucked. After a moment she withdrew the finger. He sat up and stretched, seeming healthier. But she guided him down again, shifted to his left side, braced his head against her right breast, and put her left forefinger into his mouth. The meaning was clear: she was changing breasts.

Soon she finished nursing him, and the boy got up and ran across the stage, to where Queen Athenais was working at her loom. He hugged her, then went dashing off to play with a ball. "The queen marveled at her son's quick recovery," Talena said. "But she could not contain her female curiosity. So she questioned her handmaids, to see if they knew anything about the visiting lady's method.''

The queen beckoned to a serving girl. The girl gesticulated, evidently speaking animatedly. " 'We know not what she does,' " Heath said for the girl. " 'But we see that she feeds him nothing at all. At night she bars the doors of the Hall of the Pillar and piles the fire high with logs. When we listen at the door we can hear nothing but the titter of a swallow.' ''

As he spoke, Isis enacted the scene in her section of the stage, barring an invisible door and piling invisible logs on a candle that stood in lieu of a fire. When the play called for a burning house, they made a larger fire on the stage, but this was merely a fireplace fire, so a candle sufficed.

"Filled with worry," Talena said, "the queen watched for when Isis was out, and hid herself in the Hall of the Pillar." Isis took a walk around the stage, indicating that she was exploring the palace and its associated gardens. The queen sidled into the chamber and stood behind a small curtain. It did not conceal her at all, but the audience understood that she was well hidden.

"That night," Heath said, "Athenais watched Isis bar the door and pile the fire high with logs." Isis went through the motions again. "When the fire was high, Isis cleared a space in the very center of it. Then she picked up the young prince, who was asleep, and laid him among the flames." Isis did this, putting the boy down beside the candle. He continued sleeping, exactly as if he were not in an inferno.

"Then Isis changed herself into a bird and flew around the pillar," Talena said, "singing a song of lamentation." Isis spread her arms and moved them as if they were wings, circling the pillar.

"The queen shrieked and ran from her place of concealment," Heath said. Athenais ran out, stretching her arms up and opening her mouth. "The queen grabbed her child from the fire, and spun about to face the strange nurse." The queen did this, holding the boy, who was still sleeping.

"But the bird had changed back, and it was the goddess Isis who now stood before her, revealed in all her glory," Talena said as Isis stopped flying and stood straight with her hands on her hips, glaring at the queen. "Foolish mother! Why did you seize the child? In but a few more days all that is mortal would have been burned out of him, and he would have been as the gods are, immortal and forever young."

"The queen was awestruck, for now she knew she looked upon a god," Talena continued. "She set down her son, fell to her knees, and humbled herself before Isis." The queen did these things, becoming most penitent.

"Word was sent to King Malkander," Heath said. "He came to join his wife." The king of Byblos hurried across the stage, and got down beside the queen. "Together they prayed for the goddess to accept a gift. All the wealth of the great city of Byblos was laid at her feet." A servant brought in jars and bags and set them before Isis' toes.

"But the goddess ignored both gold and silver, linen and perfume, and all other riches," Talena said. "Nevertheless, she relented. 'Give me what is in this pillar and I shall be content.' " Isis gestured to the pillar.

"Immediately the workmen were summoned," Heath said. A workman came onstage, bearing his tools. "They took down the pillar and split it open. Inside, the coffin of Osiris was revealed to all." Stagehands carried the coffin to the group and set it down. The sleeping prince woke and watched the proceedings with interest.

"Isis sang a terrible song of lamentation," Talena said. The prince, listening, fell over on his side. The queen quickly covered his ears, and he revived; it was evident that it was the sound of lamentation that affected him, not a relapse of illness. "She spread sweet spices and scented blossoms around the coffin and pillar. She had recovered Osiris' body at last, but she knew she could not revive him. What may work for a mortal does not work for a god. So she did not even open the coffin."

"It was time for the goddess to go home," Heath said. Isis addressed king, queen, and boy, bidding each farewell. The boy clung to her, not wanting her to go. It was clear that he was now healthy, and would live out a normal life. But he had lost the opportunity to become immortal. "She left the pillar in Byblos, where it would forever after be worshipped as having once held the body of a god. She took the coffin back with her to Egypt."

Isis made the long journey by ship, crossing the stage. "When she reached the Black Land," Talena said, "Isis hid the coffin in a solitary place. She opened it only long enough to look on the face of her husband." Isis lifted the lid and peered in. Ordinarily at this point Osiris would have been revealed inside the coffin, but he was missing, so she had to pretend. "Then she left to make arrangements for the funeral."

There was another intermission. Avalanche departed the stage, dispirited. In two more days the play would be done, and there would have to be a substitute for Od in the part of Osiris. None of her leads had been effective in locating him.

But there was always a chance. She returned to the temple—and there was Lin rushing to greet her. "Tuho got it!" the girl cried. "He knows where Od is!"

Hope flared. "I will go see him immediately."

"No need. He's here, with his daughter. I've been playing with her."

So her healing in life had been as effective as it was in the play. That was gratifying. She followed Lin to a meeting chamber where man and child waited.

Tuho greeted her immediately. "You paid me, priestess, and saved my daughter. I had to deliver. My friend learned that your friend is at the construction site south of the city, tending camels."

She grabbed him and kissed him. "I will go there immediately."

He shook his head. "Fetch your guard. In fact, send your guard instead. I have not learned the details of their conspiracy, but if they truly mean to assassinate the king, they will not hesitate to kill a priestess."

Good point. "You don't know who is involved?"

"No. Or the timing. Just that they are planning. So there's nothing to be reported to the king."

"Except the fact of the conspiracy. If the king is warned, he can take precautions."

"Not without knowing the identity of the plotters. In fact, anyone at the palace I might report to could be an assassin, who would promptly kill me to prevent me from telling the king. We need to know the identities before we can report. Otherwise we merely alert them."

Another good point. "So we must be silent, until more is known. But I can still go to rescue my friend, without saying anything about a conspiracy, because he's just the victim of an abduction and enslavement."

He nodded. "Yes. I wish you success." He looked around. "Now my daughter and I will give thanks and gifts to the Temple of Isis for her salvation."

How like her scene in the play, she thought. The saved child, the grateful parent. And the delivery of what she most craved: the information about her beloved. She was, in a manner, living the role of Isis. Maybe the goddess chose to animate her with some of Isis' grief and power.

She got Tefen and set out for the construction site. "I have learned where Od was taken," she explained to the man. "He is tending camels. But there may be danger, so be prepared."

The man nodded and touched his sword. He would not act unless the need arose, but then the chief danger would be to whoever threatened her. The Temple of Isis hired few males, but those were good ones.

They reached the site. Work was proceeding on the foundation for a new public building. She saw camels, but not Od.

So she marched up to the foreman. "I have news that my friend was abducted and brought here," she said boldly. "Where is he?"

The man turned an insultingly direct gaze on her. "Who wants to know?"

"A priestess of Isis. Are you looking for a curse?"

He glanced past her at Tefen, perhaps appreciating how literally a curse could be applied. "Who is your friend?"

"A man named Od."

The man spat into the dust. "He stole a camel night before last and left."

Could she believe that? "Where did he go?"

"If I knew that, I'd have brought him back before now and hacked him to pieces. That's a good camel! There's no news of him. For all I know he rode straight into the desert."

So it was still like the play, for there was a scene about Osiris being hacked apart. "Let me talk with your camel tender."

"It's a stupid boy. He doesn't know anything."

"Except whether you're telling the truth."

The man put his hand on his whip, scowling. But Tefen put his hand on his sword, and the man reconsidered. "That way," he said, pointing.

They walked across the site to intercept the boy. "Was there a man named Od here?" Avalanche asked him, after seeing that he recognized her Isis icon.

"He was," the lad agreed. "But he was gone yesterday morning."

"So the foreman is telling the truth?"

"Some of it."

"What is the rest of it?"

"I can't tell you, priestess."

Tefen put his hand on his sword again, but Avalanche stayed him. Instead she leaned down, took the boy's head in her hands, and kissed him firmly on the mouth. She hoped he was old enough to feel the impact of her beauty.

"He rode to warn the regent of the plot against the king," the boy said, his eyes staring fixedly ahead, pupils dilated.

It had to be the truth, for the boy was too stunned to dissemble. "What plot is this?"

"They mean to kill the king tonight. The foreman is in on it. Od found out and said he had to do the surprising thing, so the assassins wouldn't catch him. That's all I know."

That was Od, all right. "Thank you." She stroked her hand over the boy's face, interrupting his blank stare, and he recovered somewhat. He had proved to be old enough. She turned away, with mixed emotions. She had hoped to rescue Od, but he had already rescued himself, and was surely well beyond reach by now. But at least he was doing something about the plot.

"Priestess!" the boy cried. "Please don't tell I told! He'll beat me to death."

He meant the foreman, for revealing the plot. "Not a word," she agreed.

They walked back toward the city. "You amaze me," Tefen remarked.

"The goddess aids me," she said smugly.

"That she does." Tefen was an old, tough hand, but her manner of interrogating the boy had evidently impressed him.

Unfortunately Isis hadn't aided her enough to recover Od. Not only would they have to finish the play without him, she still couldn't give him the rapture she longed to. But if he made it safely to the regent, and returned to the city, ah, then she would have a reckoning he would never forget.

But meanwhile, what about this assassination plot against the king? There had seemed to be no point in trying to warn the king when the details were nebulous, but now she knew it was tonight. She had to act, if she was going to.

But how was she to get past the assassins? They would be alert for anyone on an urgent mission to the king. Was there any way she could gain a private audience with the king, without arousing suspicion? It seemed impossible.

Unless she used her position as a priestess of Isis. If she went to the palace to plead for more support for the temple, garbed in a manner that suggested her plea would take a most intimate form—who would suspect that? They might even think the plea was a cover for some of the king's incidental entertainment. She would do her best to give them exactly that impression.

Yes, that would do. So she returned to the temple and girded her loins most appealingly. She perfumed her hair and breasts. She would pretend that she had an appointment, and show enough flesh to make officials disinclined to doubt her. If she got close enough to have any word with the king, she could whisper her warning, and that might be enough.

It was night by the time she could get quietly away. Tefen took her to the palace, understanding her mission. She knew she would have to get through a series of functionaries, but she was experienced at negotiating such obstacles. Just as long as they thought she sought a liaison with the king, rather than delivery of a key message.

But when she arrived at the palace, there were no challenges. People were running around, shouting. There was chaos.

"What's happening?" she asked the nearest guard who wasn't running.

"The king has been killed," he said. "He was assassinated moments ago."

Avalanche's heart sank. She was too late. All she could do was get away from the palace before any indiscriminate vengeance killing started.

❁

Od had little notion how long it had been, for he had faded in and out as he rode the indefatigable camel. He had used up his water and hung on, unable to stop and dismount by the river. His thighs were raw and blistered from the constant abrasion against the animal's hide. But now it was the evening of what he hoped was the first day after the first night, and there was the vanguard of what had to be Sesostris' returning army.

In a moment he was surrounded by soldiers. "The regent!" he rasped. "Message—only for him."

They must have decided that he was legitimate, because they helped him dismount and half carried him to the command tent. A warrior stood there. "I am Sesostris."

Od looked at him, but his eyes were so bleary that he couldn't make out the details. But the straightness of the stance and the authority of the voice satisfied him. "A plot to kill your father," he blurted. "And to kill you as you enter the city unawares. You must act before they strike!"

"Who?"

"I know the name of only one. I overheard him talking with another plotter in the night."

"When?"

"Tomorrow night."

"What day? Say the day."

Od said the day.

"That is today," the regent snapped.

Od sagged. He must have ridden two days instead of one. He stared at the man, appalled. "Then I am too late," he said, dismayed.

Sesostris studied him. Od realized that the regent had to be a good judge of men, in order to be competent in command. He was deciding whether to trust the information Od had brought.

The regent snapped his fingers. A man appeared. "Summon and equip my elite guard for immediate foray. Do not tell my staff."

"Sir—"

"Immediately." The officer left the tent.

Sesostris spoke to Od. "Speak to no one else of this. If there are traitors around my father, there may be traitors around me. So I must act before they know. Without others knowing I know."

Od nodded. It made sense.

The regent snapped his fingers again. Another officer appeared. "Care for this man and convey him in a wagon with the main force. He is to do no work and is not to be questioned before arrival at the city."

The officer stepped forward to take Od by the arm. His touch was firm yet gentle. "This way, traveler."

Od let himself be guided out. He had come too late, yet the regent was taking action. Maybe he hoped that there would be a delay in the assassination plans, so that he could still get there in time to thwart it. Od hoped the regent succeeded.

Time became indistinct again. A male nurse tended to him as he rode in a bumpy wagon. "You are dehydrated, sunburned, and raw," the man said. "But otherwise healthy. These salves will ease your sores, this water will restore your fluids, and the canopy on this wagon will protect you from the sun. But you will look like one risen from the dead for a while, until your sores heal."

"I got through," Od said. "That is what matters."

"Yes. The regent has confirmed your news, and is on his way to handle his business."

Od wasn't sure how much the man knew, so he was noncommittal. It could be a ruse to make him blurt out what he should not. "That is good." He slept.

It seemed like forever, but the nurse informed him that it was only four days, as the army traveled at its regular pace to the city, arriving on schedule. That was important, for whatever spies the plotters had in the army believed that nothing had changed. But the regent had arrived two days ahead of schedule.

Od, walking but still wincing from his healing thigh sores, was ushered into the regent's presence again. "Because of you, I was able to surprise and rout the conspirators and secure my throne," he said. "Those who are not yet dead are wishing for death." That meant that the torturers were extracting the last information about the rebellion. "Name your reward."

"Lord, did you save your father?"

"No. I have only his letter to me, composed by his adviser from the remnants of his fate. It says that the killers came upon him in the night, bypassing the guards by the treachery of courtiers and junior wives. He leaped from his bed like a desert snake to battle unarmed against his attackers. 'But no one is strong at night; no one can fight alone; no success is possible without you.' I was not there in time, and so he died."

"Then I failed," Od said. "I deserve no reward."

The new king considered. "Ask of me some minor immediate boon, and I will decide later how else you will be rewarded for the effort you made on my behalf."

Od considered, for to decline such a request could be taken as an insult. "There is a boy named Chip who helped me get on my way. He works at the construction site south of the city. I fear the foreman, Bub, who is the conspirator I overheard, will harm him."

"That foreman has already fled to Syria," the king said. "The lad will be rewarded. But this is not a boon for *you*."

He had to try again. "I wish only to be rejoined with my associates, and to resume my part on the Osiris play, when I am able."

"Ah, yes. Isis is lovely, is she not?"

"Lovely," Od agreed. He had dreamed many times of the way Avalanche had suggested that she was interested in having more of a fling with him than she had in the past. Her attention was fickle, and of course in his present state of ugliness she would not touch him, but the dream remained fond.

"I believe I am ready for a moment of diversion," Sesostris said. "It has been a wearing four days. I will bring the players here. I believe the events of recent days disrupted the schedule, and the final act may not yet have been performed."

Od hadn't thought of that. "My part is merely to lie in a coffin as if dead. I think I can handle that much."

The king laughed. Then he made a small signal with one hand. Servants came to lead Od away. They garbed him appropriately, which meant stripping him naked, and put him in a curtained alcove. There he remained, covered by a drape, as the players assembled for the command performance. He heard their hurried comments; they were thrilled to have this chance to play for the king, but surprised that he should ask for only the last act. They hauled the coffin onstage. Od knew that it contained fourteen pieces of rather bloody meat. The shock value of the scene was considerable. After the play was done, the meat would be roasted for a feast.

The king and his favored advisers and courtiers and servants entered the chamber and settled themselves; Od heard their murmurings. The play commenced. "Isis has rescued the body of her beloved Osiris," Talena said. "She has now gone to make arrangements for the funeral which will free Osiris' soul and allow him to go to the underworld, where he will become the god of judgment over the dead and weigh the souls of men."

"But in her absence, the god Set came upon the coffin," Heath said. "He had been suspicious, and his spies had alerted him when Isis returned to Egypt. So he opened the coffin and spied the body of his enemy therein." The pipes squealed angrily and the drums beat like thunder. Od could not see the stage, but he knew from countless performances what was happening there, and could see it clearly in his mind's eye: Set stalked up to the coffin and flung it open and glared down into it.

"His rage at this spectacle was unbounded," Talena said. "The very sight of Osiris caused black clouds to form around him." For this effect, an assistant waved a black sheet around Set; the audience understood.

"He tore the body into fourteen pieces," Heath said, as the music made awful ripping sounds. "And scattered them all through the land of Egypt." Now came the gore: Set reached into the coffin and hauled out a dripping chunk of meat. There was an appreciative gasp from one of the servants. He flung it across the stage. It landed with a thud. He took out another, and threw it in another direction. He continued, until thirteen chunks littered the stage. Then he fished around in the coffin for one more: a huge phallus. There was a murmur of laughter in the court; this was so grisly it was funny. Set hurled that right off the stage, into the audience, where a man dressed as a fish caught it. Then Set stalked off the stage.

"When Isis returned," Talena said, "she was appalled to discover what had happened. The body of her lover had been despoiled again, and lost. But she refused to be dissuaded. She set out in a papyrus boat to recover all the parts of Osiris." Now Isis got into a small boat-form and scooted around the stage, picking up the grisly pieces one by one and returning them to the coffin.

"Wherever she located a piece," Heath said, "she built a temple to Osiris." Stagehands set small model temples at the site of each meat fragment.

"Until at last she had them all," Talena said. "Except one. The phallus had been swallowed by a Nile Carp and was beyond recovery." The fish actor held up his prize, then made swimming motions as he departed. Everyone knew what a tough fish the Nile Carp was; it bred well, could drive out other fish, and survive for weeks in drought by burrowing into the mud. Now they knew why: it possessed the most prized flesh of a god.

"So Isis had an artificial phallus made," Heath said. "The god Thoth helped." The god Thoth came onstage, carrying a wooden phallus. "Isis took it and set it carefully in the coffin, in just the right place." There was another murmur in the audience as the goddess reached down into the coffin, adjusting it. Isis set great store by that particular part of a god.

"Then they had the funeral ceremony," Talena said. Stagehands enclosed the coffin with curtains. This was the point at which the meat was removed and the actor entered the coffin. Od got up and intercepted the actor who was supposed to substitute for him in this scene. The man stared, surprised, then backed away. He surely had not been sure whether Od still lived, so this was like seeing a man return from the dead, appropriately. Od climbed into the smelly box and pulled the drape over himself, as a shroud.

"But before they put Osiris' corpse in the vault," Heath said, "Isis had one more thing to do. She had to bid parting to the body of the god she loved, in her own way." The goddess drew away the curtains to reveal the coffin, which was now propped up at an angle so that the audience could see inside. All that was visible was the shroud; the audience did not yet know about the substitution.

"She lay with the mummy," Talena said. Isis drew off the shroud and stood there looking down at the restored naked figure. Her mouth dropped open in surprise. The audience was surprised too, seeing that there was now a real man inside; they assumed that the surprise of the actress was feigned. He was fairly realistic for a dead man, with his wild hair, flaking skin, and sores on the inner thighs.

Then Isis made an expression the audience couldn't see, and drew off her dress. She turned, showing off her perfect body as she always did, then climbed onto the corpse so as to simulate copulation, as she had done so many times before. Od had always enjoyed this part, pretending in his fancy that it was real. The audiences always responded well, too.

But this time her simulation was remarkably realistic. She kissed him hard on the mouth, and whispered endearments in his ear. "So, my love, you return from the dead for me! I will make you glad." She shifted her body, so that her smooth scented breasts caressed his chest. "But you dare not move, lest you disrupt the play." He knew that; the point of it was that the god was dead. Still, her warmth and contact made him react. Oh, how he desired her!

"And so great was the potency of Osiris," Heath said, pausing to allow the action to continue.

"And so great the fertility of Isis," Talena continued, pausing similarly.

"That even dead, even with a phallus made of wood, the god was able to impregnate the goddess," Heath said.

Isis reached down and found his stiffening member. She fitted it into her warm slick avenue with the delightful expertise she had, then slid down so as to entirely surround that supposedly wooden phallus. Surely to the audience it looked like a very fine emulation. She rocked on him, causing the connection to slide in and out somewhat, and clenched and released with her internal muscles. Even wood might have produced some sap for that! "Come, my love," she whispered, nibbling on his ear. "Give me your gift of love. I long for your godly essence." She pressed her breasts even more tightly against him, and inhaled. At the same time she caught his wrists with her hands and drew them around her sleek torso so that his hands fell on the hot mounds of her buttocks, his fingers sliding into the artistically curving crevice between them. She flexed her bottom encouragingly.

Od couldn't help it. He geysered into her, his body still but his member spurting recklessly. She had made the emulation turn powerfully real. She kissed him as the pulses came, surge after surge, drawing from him everything he had to give. It seemed like eternity, compressed into a moment.

"In this manner the goddess conceived her son Horus," Talena said. Her voice had a slight quaver, as if she had just realized something extraordinary. The awed murmur from the audience suggested a spreading similar awareness. Od even heard a chuckle from the direction of the king.

"Who was destined to grow up to avenge his father," Heath said. Od realized that this could be taken as Sesostris avenging his treacherously slain father. How well it fit together!

"She left the body, carrying her new child within," Talena said. Isis kissed him once more, and disengaged. But, in a final act of naughtiness, she picked up his now-limp penis and aligned it so as to be quite straight. Then she spread the shroud over him again.

"And Osiris' spirit traveled to the underworld," Heath said. "Where he governs today. Thus concludes the history of Osiris and Isis."

The two narrators bowed. There was enthusiastic applause. Od knew that the king had found the play more relevant and diverting than anticipated. So had Od himself.

Sesostris took the name Kheperkare and ruled thereafter for thirty-five years. His capital city of Ith-toui was south of present-day Cairo, but no longer exists. It was a time of general well-being in Egypt, and the arts flourished, including, perhaps, staged dramas of the sagas of the gods. It is not known who actually got word to Sesostris about the assassination of his father, but someone did, and his quick reaction enabled him to squelch the rebellion at its outset. Thus the Twelfth Dynasty continued, and so did the Middle Kingdom. And the cult of Osiris flourished.

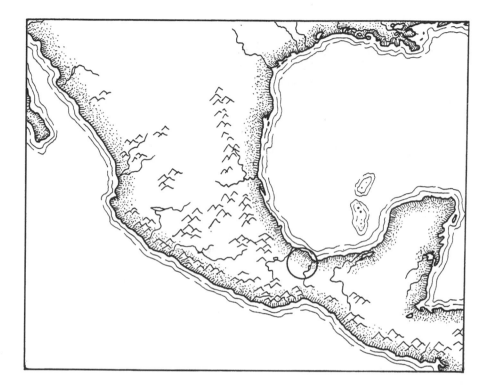

CHAPTER 6

SEDUCTION

*Opinions differ about how long mankind has been in the Western Hemisphere.
Certainly for the past 12,000 years, perhaps longer. Most of that time the cultures
were hunter-gatherer, which in terms of longevity must be mankind's most successful mode. It may even have defined the human genders, with man hunting
and fighting, woman gathering and caring for the children. Some men, however,
prefer peace, and some women are militant. Then sedentism developed, first in
central America and later spreading. It seems to have been more recent in the
Western Hemisphere than in the Eastern, but followed a similar pattern. Men still
hunted and fought, but began to turn their efforts also to building and trading*

and the arts. Women still gathered, but also gardened and wove. The earliest and perhaps most influential known sedentary culture was that of the Olmec, at the southern edge of the Gulf of Mexico, where the Sierra Madre mountain ranges enclose a large lowland area. Their development must have been long and slow, but it peaked between 1200–300 B.C. There is a conjecture that there was influence from China, as some Olmec writing resembles Chinese characters, but this is suspect and is not accepted for this book. The setting is southern Mexico, circa 900 B.C.

The art is seduction. There are ways in which the human male and female really do seem to be separate species. The male tends to think in terms of straightforward power, while the female tends to accommodate while establishing her own understandings. The man normally looks first for beauty in a woman, while a woman normally looks first for power in a man. When a special situation limits or nullifies their respective attributes and desires, so that neither strategy can readily prevail, the game can become interesting, or even bizarre. We know little of the romantic and sexual conventions of the Olmec, but a beautiful and strong-willed young woman could surely mock them and make a man suffer.

DILLON was a hunter, but today he hunted wild fruit, because it was easier on Old Bata's teeth. He carried a brimming basket of prickly pears to the house and set it down in the main chamber. He had been lucky enough to spy a region where the cactus was fruiting and the animals and birds hadn't yet eaten the fruit.

The old woman heard him, and came from the back room. She moved slowly, for she was feeble, and almost blind, but her hearing remained sharp, as did her mind. Dillon removed his leather helmet so as to stand before her with his shorn head, as a mark of respect. His two years with her had taught him both the protocol and the reality of respect; she knew more, and understood more, than he had dreamed of.

"My son the chief has summoned you," Bata said. She meant her son-in-law, the man who had married her daughter. "I suspect he has a good mission for you to perform, that will bring you favor in the kingdom."

"But I have not asked for any such mission," Dillon protested. "I still have much to learn from you." Again, his politeness mirrored his reality: he truly valued his association with her.

"Perhaps. But the chief's summons may not be denied. You must go immediately. You know the way to the capital city?"

"I will find it," Dillon said. "Down one river and up another. But I hope the mission is not long. I would prefer to return here, where I have useful work, and can profit from your wisdom."

The old woman smiled. "You are a delight, Dillon. Were I sixty years younger, I would marry you and make you a prince. But who knows what the future holds? Go."

"Were you sixty years younger, you could enslave me without marrying me," he replied with a smile. He didn't mention that the royal women of Olmec did not make princes, but only gave existing princes a claim on the lineage. He, as a commoner, would only have caused her to waste her opportunity to wield significant power. But they enjoyed their game of flirtation, despite the overwhelming differences in status and age. Bata, in her youth, had surely been alluring. "Even, perhaps, were you only fifty-nine years younger. But then you would have to give me more than a smile." He squinted, almost managing to see her as she must have been, full breasted and full hipped and lovely in her canny intellect. That was one of the things she had taught him: that there was ever so much more to a woman than her face and body, and that what did not show could be as important as what did.

She glanced down at her skirt, twitched the hem, then shook her head as if giving up a tempting notion. "I promised to teach you finesse of expression, you handsome rogue. I succeeded."

She had taught him far more than that. He had come to love her as a grandmother, and did not like leaving her. But she did have a male slave for brutework and a maidservant for personal details. They would see to her needs during his absence. "May I see you again, soon," he said sincerely as he set his bow and spear in the canoe. There was also a package of dried snook and hard bread, together with a ceramic brazier for cooking, so that he would not have to take time to hunt or forage for food on the way.

"The spirits know," she said as a benediction. Then she remembered something else. "Here is a royal tassel. Show it when challenged, and they will let you through."

He took the tassel, stepped into the canoe, and shoved off. Usually he canoed on the broad lake, but now he was traveling down the river to the sea. There would be no problem finding the way down, and once he reached the sea he could watch for signs, or inquire. It wasn't as if the capital city were unknown territory; everyone would know its location.

"And if you should encounter one like me when young, remember all I have taught you," she called after him.

"There can be none like that," he called back, laughing.

The stream was small and rocky in places, but he was traveling light and managed to avoid portaging. Soon he intercepted the river, and its flow facilitated his motion. He used his paddle to keep in the swiftest currents, but didn't try to outrace it. He wanted to move swiftly, in answer to his summons, but was conserving his strength for the time he would need it.

The river joined a larger river. This one he knew would carry him to the sea. He chewed on the tough fish without pausing, and by dusk was well along.

He was familiar with the river to this point, and knew that it was clear for the next few hours' travel. So he did not pause. He sat with the paddle in his hands, trailing in the water behind, and slept. The motion of the canoe and the feel of the water coursing by the paddle kept him in touch with the river. He would wake immediately if anything unusual occurred.

He dreamed. A beautiful young woman approached him, saying "I am Bata when young. Kiss me." He saw that it was indeed she, and yearned for her. But her old self had warned him to remember her lessons, and chief among them was to take nothing at face value. So he demurred. "If you are she, repeat the ritual of trust." At that the figure screamed in rage, and became an ugly bird, and flew away. She had tried to deceive him with her simulated beauty, but an evil spirit could not speak that ritual. His caution had saved him from being consumed.

He woke in the darkness, and smiled. Bata had saved him, for surly the evil spirit had thought him an easy target, alone at night on the river and asleep. Without the old woman's advice, he would have been lost. Yet there was that in him that regretted part of it, for it would have been life's greatest experience to possess a woman like that. Of course that was how the bad spirits worked; they preyed on a person's secret desires, which were also his vulnerabilities. A man alone had to be ever watchful against their artifices.

In the morning he was well downstream. He saw a rabbit by the bank, and was tempted to bring it down with an arrow or a dart, but preparing it would take time, and he wanted to keep moving. So he brought the canoe to the bank instead, so that he could stretch on land and catch up on natural functions. Then he moved on downstream, chewing on more dried snook.

By dusk the second day the river was broadening and slowing, and he knew it was getting ready to debouch into the sea. This was beyond familiar territory, so he was more cautious. Instead of sleeping while the boat moved, he pulled to the side and made a quick hidden bed for the night.

He resumed travel before dawn, and as the sun appeared he was at the edge of the sea. It was so vast he was awed; the water stretched out beyond the sight of land. So he remained close to the shore, turning southeast. The next big river should be the one to take.

As he stroked along the edge of that monstrous body of water, he fancied that it was watching him, ready to swallow him if he had the temerity to go far out across its surface. But he had done nothing to annoy it, and so it let him be. The spirits of nature generally had better things to do than discipline individual people, so proper respect was usually enough to avoid trouble. In due course he spied the indentation that marked the next large river. That must be the one.

He made his way up the river, making much slower progress. He passed many rich green fields of maize, and wondered who could possibly eat all that was produced. At one point he saw the smoke of a burning field, and knew it was being prepared for a new crop after a fallow period; ashes made rich soil. On occasion he saw whole packs of dogs, which he knew were being raised for their excellent meat. Here in the civilized section, they needed to raise more of their food, of whatever type, instead of depending on the forest and lake.

The river fought him as it narrowed. Rivers did not like to be contravened. They preferred to carry everything down to the sea and dump it there. But he had saved his strength for this effort, and made fair progress, day by day. The ugly bird spirit did not try to trick him again when he slept at the bank. That was just as well, for now he was tired, and needed good sleep for recovery.

On the eighth day of his journey he reached the capital city. This was bustling, in contrast to much of the route here; people were everywhere. The first thing he noticed was the colossal stone heads. They were all around the center, staring out from under their helmets, each one higher than a man could reach. He knew that each head represented an Olmec chief, remaining after the chief died to keep his memory and greatness alive. He had heard that the heads were awesome, but never actually seen one before—and here were at least six. There were also standing and seated figures, stele, columns, animal-figure altars, and baths. Men were working on the huge drainage channel leading from one of the elite baths; the ditch was lined with basalt rock, rather than just being dug in dirt. He had never imagined so much construction and art; his mind balked at the assimilation of it all.

But he couldn't dally; he had to report to the chief. He showed his tassel and got directions to the royal residence. This was a stone-and-mud brick castle of huge size, with two guards at its terraced entrance. Somewhat diffidently, he presented his tassel again. "I am to see the chief."

To his surprise, they nodded and showed him inside. He tried not to stare at the huge chambers he passed; he would only reveal himself to be the country hick he was. But he was highly impressed by the religious icons lining the inner halls: representations of the sacred jaguar, serpent, ancient woman, frog, and the dread were-jaguar, which was a cross between human and jaguar. There were also wooden human masks encrusted with jade. It must have taken many artisans many years to craft all these fine representations. This was certainly a holy place.

Chief Badu met him immediately. Dillon recognized him by his bearing, his brightly colored kilt, his fine cloth cape, and his sturdy head gear. "You met my daughter Melee two years ago. Do you remember her?"

The question surprised him. "Yes. A lovely, spirited girl."

"Who held you in contempt."

Dillon spread his hands. "Perhaps I warranted it."

"Perhaps not. I am banishing her."

This was so startling that Dillon could think of no response to make. So he waited.

"She has grown willful. I have valued her perhaps too much, since losing her mother and her sister. She refuses to marry the man I choose for her. This has become politically embarrassing, and so I need to curb it."

Dillon waited, not understanding why the chief should tell a country hunter this. It was hardly his business to know the private embarrassments of royalty.

"I can't simply send her away," the chief continued. "She is royal, and must be protected. Neither can I confine her here; her status does not allow it. The matter is awkward. So I am banishing her to the care of her grandmother, who will perhaps accomplish what I am unable to, and bring a proper sense of discipline and familial obligation to her."

Now it began to make sense. Dillon would have to convey the princess to Bata, keeping her safe along the way. But wouldn't it have been easier to send her there under competent guard?

"But Mother Bata will need help. She will require you to do much of it, as she can no longer see well and is physically weak. You will obey her strictures, even if they sometimes seem strange."

"Yes, always," Dillon agreed. "I have the deepest respect for her." That was no understatement.

"Until you bring Melee to Bata, you may be considered Melee's elder brother. She must obey you in the incidental details of travel. If she flees you, you must lay your hands on her and bring her back, albeit without harming her."

This was astonishing. "But she is a princess! A common man may not touch her! And if she fought me, and was bruised, I would be subject to execution."

"As her brother you may be considered a prince. For this purpose a bruise on the arm will not be considered harm. You will hold her if necessary, to the extent required to ensure that she completes the trip with you. If she attacks you, you must defend yourself, nullifying her. If she remains unmanageable, you will bind her. Do not let her prevail."

"This is impossible! I would never—"

"You would never abuse a royal woman who was put in your charge, nor would you willfully cause distress to any woman. I believe that. That is why you have this assignment. You must treat her as you would your own woman, without forgetting that she is not."

"My woman!"

"Your sister. She will perform the household chores. She will forage for you both, and clean your clothes as well as her own. You will protect her from molestation by any man, and help her in whatever way she requires. But you will neither give her orders, other than when necessary for her safety or captivity, nor take orders from her."

"My lord, you give me too hard a task. She has no respect for me, and will not listen to me."

"Could you handle it with a regular woman?"

"I think so. But Princess Melee is not that."

"You will have the advice and support of her grandmother. When you are in doubt, ask Bata. You know how much she knows. She also knows my desire in this respect."

Dillon saw that this was to be the way of it. "I will do my best, lord."

"You will succeed. You understand the consequences of success and failure."

Dillon understood. Success would mean significant reward. Failure would be death. "I will succeed," he said grimly. If it was humanly possible.

"You will keep her there one year, and bring her back here at its conclusion. If, after this experience of exile, she still refuses to do my will, I will send her back with you for another year. So it will be, until she accedes.''

Dillon had to ask one more question. "If I succeed, and return her to you safe, she may nevertheless be angry. If she should accuse me of mistreating her—"

"You will tell me the truth, and I will accept it. I expect her to make just such a charge. See that you are not guilty."

"Yes, lord."

Badu frowned. "Understand this, as a man: Melee is beautiful, and knows it, and plays upon it. She can sway any man to her will. Even me, which is why I am foolishly lenient with her. But she is also wild. She may defy you, and when that is ineffective, she may tempt you. She may invite you to have sex with her, then claim you raped her. Since her word may not be questioned by others, this would normally be your death."

Dillon felt a chill. "Lord, I will not touch her."

Badu shook his head. "I speak to you as a man: if she chooses to be touched, you will not be able to avoid it. You have never encountered a woman like her." He paused, thoughtfully. "Not at that age, at any rate. So I am realistic. I lay on you these strictures: never touch her sexually unless she wills it, and even then you must obtain her word that she will not tell. Only then are you safe. She will not break her given word, but she can be extremely cunning about the giving of it. She must look into your face and say she desires it and will not tell. She remains sufficiently pristine as long as she does not deny it. If there is any doubt at all, do not accede."

"But lord, a woman can not make a man—"

"That is illusion. You have been warned. If she tells me you touched her, and you can not deny it, you are lost. You must avoid her as long as you can, and obtain her word before you succumb. Your life depends on it."

Dillon felt dizzy. He could not accept the implications, but also could not tell the chief that he was speaking nonsense. "Yes, lord."

"Melee plays games with men, but she follows her own rules, and the stakes can be high. If you can beat her in a game, she will respect you for it. But never forget that it *is* a game to her. Do not play a game with her if you can possibly avoid it. Her mind is not like yours or mine, or like that of any other young woman. She can be as winsome as she chooses, but she is dangerous too. Never forget."

"I will not forget." But neither did he believe. The man was describing not a human woman, but a phantasm. Games were agreeable pastimes played by two or more people on a voluntary basis; they could not be forced.

"I will turn her over to you now." Badu stood, and Dillon stood with him. The private interview was over.

The chief led the way to a small chamber of the palace. There was a young woman, beautiful and angry. Her forehead was shaved, while the back of her hair trailed into glossy braids. She wore a fine closed shawl over a dark knee-length skirt, small bird-claw earrings, and bright shell anklets above her bare feet. It was Melee.

"Go with this man, for a year," Badu told her. "I will speak again with you then."

Melee turned a cold gaze on Dillon. "This won't work," she muttered.

The chief shrugged and turned away. Dillon waited, but so did the girl. He realized that he would have to take the initiative. "Please follow me, Princess."

She made no motion. But he was pretty sure she wouldn't refuse in the presence of her father, so he turned and walked away. Sure enough, after a moment she followed. "Do you show me your back, peasant?" she demanded.

"You are welcome to walk beside me." He paused so she could catch up.

"I'm not your woman, peasant!"

Dillon didn't know what to say to that, so he said nothing. He resumed walking.

She caught up and walked beside him. He saw that she now carried a finely woven large handbag. "You will not enjoy this, peasant."

Again, he had no answer. He was in awe of Melee's status and her beauty, but knew he must not show it.

"I know you from somewhere."

Now he could answer. "I helped you cross the river, two years ago."

"The dull-wit!" she exclaimed. "I should have known."

Again, he had no ready answer. All that Bata had taught him about finesse of expression was gone as if it had never been. This sullen, lovely creature banished wit.

"Grandmother Bata said you were diffident about women, and lacked the wit ever to dissemble."

Bata would have said that, but intended it as a compliment. "True."

This time Melee didn't answer, so perhaps he had withstood that attack. That pleased him.

The folk of the city ignored them, probably because they recognized the princess. It was death to address such a person other than in response to a query or command. That was part of what made his position so awkward; had he not been given the specific directive of the chief, treating this woman this way would have gotten him quickly cut down by the chief's guards. But he had been told to treat her like a sister, which meant no sex but also no special respect.

They came to his canoe. "I won't ride in that!" Melee protested. "It's small and dirty."

Dillon shrugged. "Perhaps you can walk along the bank, then, while I use it."

"Don't try to be clever, you bumpkin," she snapped. "The crocodiles don't hunt just in the water." She climbed into the canoe and took the front place, facing forward. She kneeled, for the only seat was at the rear. She set her bag before her.

Dillon got into the back, took up his paddle, and pushed off into the water. The canoe sat lower, with her added weight, and was clumsier to handle, but could be managed. He stroked it forward. She was right about the crocodiles: they tended to congregate in favorite spots, but could be anywhere along the river. It was safer in the canoe.

They passed near a tree that leaned out over the river. Melee had to duck her head. "Steer it to the center of the stream, bumpkin," she said.

Dillon considered. He didn't like her name for him, but decided not to make an issue. But he felt free to make an issue about the canoe. "Pick up your paddle and guide it as you will."

"I'm not your servant!"

He ignored that and continued to stroke with his paddle. She opened her bag and took out a small polished stone mirror, glancing at her own face. If she sought to impress him with her affluence, she was succeeding, for hardly anyone had such a possession. Then she shrugged and put it away.

After a moment she picked up the front paddle and began stroking in time with him, balancing the forward thrust. She did know how to do it, as any woman should. So the princess had not been completely spoiled. The canoe moved more smartly, and stayed in the center of the stream.

"Are you wondering why I'm helping?" she asked.

"Yes. I presume it's not just to stay clear of the crocodiles."

"So I won't look too obviously like your prisoner."

Was she taunting him? First she had shown a precious mirror, then she had settled down to menial work. Was he supposed to agree that she was his prisoner, or to deny it? Either way seemed like mischief, so he kept silent.

They moved smoothly downstream. After a while she removed her shawl, evidently growing hot from the exertion, and continued paddling with her upper section only lightly covered by her trailing black braids. Dillon had to admire it. She was sixteen, and had the perfect supple figure of a young woman. Her waist was as slender as any he had seen, and her hips full. Her body flexed with each stroke, enhancing the effect, and showing occasional glimpses of the sides of her breasts. He had remembered her as pretty, two years ago, but now she was more than that. She was perfect.

"Stop looking at me," she said without turning her head.

Dillon found his face heating. She had set him back, as she had meant to. He averted his gaze, glancing to either side of the river. But her lovely back drew his gaze like the iridescent plumage of a sacred bird. Perfection was difficult to ignore.

"Are you deaf as well as stupid?" she demanded, still without turning.

Then he knew she expected him to be looking at her. He decided to assert himself. "I will look where I choose."

"I could have your eyes put out for that."

"Not this year."

"Are you trying to play a game with me, lout?"

"Your father told me to treat you like a sister. A man can look at his sister."

"Some do more than that."

It was true, but not something he cared to dwell on. "I will not touch you, or play a game with you."

"No game? But anything can be a game or contest."

"Not if there is no betting on it."

She turned part way, showing more of a breast. "Name one thing that can never be a contest."

She was challenging him, forcing him to answer, or to look stupid in his own eyes. So he cast about for some example that would shut her up. "Urine."

Apparently he had won that small encounter, for she was silent. But the day was late, and soon they would have to camp for the night. He wanted time to prepare a safe site, for he could afford no danger to the princess.

When he saw a suitable spot for a camp, he turned the canoe toward the bank.

"What are you doing?" Melee demanded.

"We must camp for the night. This seems to be a good place. The bank rises high, and there is brush for enough of a fire to keep predator animals away."

"Why not just float downstream and sleep in the canoe?"

He was surprised. "Alone, I would do that. But I assume that you would not care for that."

"You assume too much. I want to get where we are going, and be done with it."

"But if you need to—"

"I'll piss off the side."

She was trying to set him back, because of his use of urine as a counter-example. But she had overshot the mark, so he was amused more than abashed. He had been in awe of a princess, but she had just reduced herself to the level of a crude peasant woman. That made him considerably more comfortable. He could argue with a peasant. "In a canoe? You'd fall into the river."

"No I wouldn't. Want to see?"

She was daring him. "Yes."

"Oh, you'd like that, for sure!" she said witheringly. "Men are really set off by the sight of a woman urinating."

She had scored, but not perfectly. He would indeed have been excited to see her do it, but there was another aspect. He wanted to secure his verbal victory. "You can't lean out of a canoe, so you'd have to stand in the center, and it still wouldn't clear the edge."

"No. I'd brace on hands and feet and arc out behind. I've done it be-fore."

He hadn't thought of that. If it really was feasible, it was no occasion for banter. "Then tell me when you wish to do it, and I'll face away."

"What, not watch? What happened to your interest?"

"It is my duty to take you to exile, not to humiliate you. You are not a common woman, however commonly you may choose to talk. I will observe the bounds of propriety to the extent possible."

Now she lifted her paddle and turned to face him, for the first time showing her breasts fully. He had of course seen breasts all his life, as common women did not normally wear shawls. These were the best formed ones he could remember, neither small nor pendulous. "I assumed that humiliation was part of the exile."

"No. I will treat you like the princess you are, as long as you act like one."

After a moment she shrugged, and those perfect breasts shook, sending a thrill through him. "Well, we'll see." Then she turned back and resumed paddling.

Yes, they would see. He would much prefer it if she behaved, but if she didn't, he would have to make her, by binding her if necessary. He strongly suspected that she would put him to the test soon enough. If she had the will to resist the wish of her father, she would have much more will to resist captivity by a common man. He did not trust her at all.

But she was beautiful and smart and spirited. He couldn't help liking those qualities. For the first time in his life he wished he could have been born a prince instead of a hunter, if only to have even a hope of touching a creature like Melee.

Then he realized something else. Melee was like Bata—sixty years younger! Bata must have known that this would be his mission, so she had warned him. Badu had seen the parallel too, for she had said that Dillon had never encountered a woman like Melee, at that age. He had encountered her at *Bata's* age. Badu respected Bata's knowledge and nature as much as Dillon did. So he, too, had warned Dillon, expecting him to succumb. But Dillon did not intend to be defeated. He had been well trained, and twice warned. That was enough.

The dusk closed in. There was no other traffic on the river at this hour; they were alone. The sounds of the night creatures came.

"What have you to eat?" she asked.

"Dried snook and bread."

She made a little shrug of resignation. "They will do."

He shipped his paddle and brought out his staples. He realized that they would not last the whole trip, for he had planned for one, not two. But he could hunt for meat when he needed to.

Melee turned to face him, barely visible in the darkness, and took what he handed her. For this purpose she sat with her legs crossed, shadows covering what the skirt did not. It was pleasant, eating together while drifting gently downstream. They each dipped a pottery jar into the river to get drinking water. His was a crude baked clay effort of the type peasants used; hers was a finely crafted vase decorated with stylized images of hawk's claws.

"Now I will do it," she said abruptly as she licked off her fingers.

He was blank for a moment, then remembered: she needed to urinate. "I will turn."

"Don't bother. I'll use the jar."

Oh. Of course that would work best for her. At any rate, he couldn't see anything in the darkness, other than her vague outline. Somehow that didn't help much; his imagination filled in the lifted skirt, the parted thighs, the jar held close-in. This vision made his member swell. He heard the faint swish of the flow, and pictured it issuing in a stream and filling the jar. Never before had he been so fascinated with this aspect of a woman's existence. In fact he had hardly thought about it, apart from a session he had once had with a cooperative young girl. Now he wished Melee were not a princess, but a country girl who would welcome his attention. But she was not, and he would never allow himself to forget it.

After a moment she poured the jar out into the river, then rinsed it, so that she wouldn't have the taste of urine next time she drank water from it. He realized that this was probably the way she had always planned to do it; she had been teasing or baiting him before. In fact she was still teasing him, because she had done it while facing in his direction. Had it been daylight, he would have seen everything.

"But you can do it your way," she said.

He did need to urinate, but now he wasn't satisfied to do it the usual way, in her presence. The gathering darkness might conceal his action, but not the sound. Yet what alternative was there? Use his jar, as she had? This did not appeal.

"Or would you like me to hold the jar for you?" she asked, knowing his thought.

It had to be done, lest he be subject to more of her contempt. He stood carefully, faced the side, drew aside his loincloth, and made ready to urinate into the river. It might be awkward, because—

"Shall I turn my back?" she asked softly.

Something about her voice made him react. It had somehow been suggestive of what must never happen. His member became fully erect, preventing him from urinating. He had to give up the effort and take his seat again.

"Whatever is the matter?" she inquired with mock solicitude.

"I'll do it later," he said, feeling the heat of his face.

"By daylight, maybe."

And of course it would be worse then. The very thought of her seeing his member would stiffen it instantly, as perhaps she knew. She was young, but had probably had experience teasing men. So he would have to do it in the dark, preferably when she was sleeping.

"Do you yield the contest?" she asked.

"What contest?"

"The contest of urine. Remember, you named it."

"But I didn't mean—"

"You challenged me to make a contest of urine. I am doing so. I urinated in your presence; now you must do it in mine, or lose the game."

He started to protest, but realized that he had indeed named urine in connection with a contest, and had not otherwise defined the terms. She had tricked him into it, and succeeded in making her game of it.

He had been warned about her games. He would be more careful hereafter. He was not one to be taken twice by the same ruse.

They moved on down the river. "We can take turns sleeping," she said. "Do you wish to sleep first?"

With this pressure of urine inside him? "No. You may sleep first."

"Thank you." She adjusted herself, her silhouette dropping low and disappearing into the deeper shadow of the canoe.

He took the paddle and used it to steer without paddling, keeping to the center of the current. Fireflies were flashing along the shores and out across the water, defining the channel of the river.

When he was satisfied that she was asleep, he shipped his paddle and stood again. But as he was about to relieve himself, she spoke: "Do you want me to hold it for you?"

That had exactly the effect she wanted. He became too stiff to do it, and had to sit down again.

"I'm sure I could help you get it out," she said. She knew what had happened, from the absence of sound.

Was this going to continue all night? How long was he going to let her torment him? He had to find a counter to her power over him. So he rose to the bait. "How?"

"I could ram you hard in the belly with this paddle. After that, the water will flow."

And leave him bruised or incapacitated. Her teasing was becoming cruel. "No."

"Then do it your way."

He steered the canoe toward land.

"You can't do it!" she exclaimed.

"If you and I were lovers, I could do it after," he said. For after the sexual act, a man lost erection and relaxed. That put the matter on a footing she could not challenge, for surely the last thing she wanted was to have sex with a common man. "But we are not, and will not be. Therefore what is private will remain private." He was rather pleased with the way he had put it; Bata had taught him to find different twists to problems, and to turn them over so that they became soluble. Age had brought her enormous wisdom. She had taught him far more than finesse of expression, though that followed naturally from inverted thinking.

"Well put. But you have nevertheless lost the game."

"I lost the game," he agreed.

He turned the canoe toward the bank. Once he got away from her, he would be all right.

"If you leave me alone in the canoe, I will take it and leave you stranded on land." Melee was trying to find a way to interfere. But he had her at a disadvantage now, having taken the initiative. That was another of Bata's lessons: don't let your enemy set the agenda. Gain control, and keep it, until victory. He had come to understand why Chief Badu respected her so much. She had an answer for every question.

He brought the canoe to the bank, and wedged it onto land enough to secure it. "I am taking the paddles." He reached forward and got her paddle as well as his. He stepped to shore and walked into the night. She made no comment, which suggested that he had won this aspect of their encounter.

He was not familiar with this region, but his long experience in the wilderness, tracking intruders in the night, made it easy. He got far enough away from the canoe so that he could not be heard, and paused to urinate. He was right: he could do it readily enough, when Melee wasn't near.

He returned. The canoe had not moved, and she remained in it. She had realized that without a paddle she would have very little control over the canoe, and might even be carried out into the great sea and death beyond its horizon. So he had beaten her, this time.

He got back in, and returned the second paddle to her. He shoved off.

After a while, she spoke. "There will be other engagements. It is only fair to give you a chance to win a return contest."

He shrugged in the darkness. "Get your sleep."

"No. It's your turn. I will guide the canoe."

He didn't quite trust this, but he did need rest and sleep. Maybe it was better to find out what further mischief she had in mind early rather than late. "As you wish. Wake me when you tire." He slumped in his seat.

"You must give me the rear seat," she said. "Where I can control the canoe."

She was right. They would have to exchange places. But that could be tricky, in a canoe. One man normally hunched down while the other stepped over him. "Then crawl this way, and I will go over you."

"*You* crawl; I'll go over you."

She was still being the princess. He put his hands down and went on hands and knees toward the center of the canoe. Then he felt her small hands on his back. Her skirt brushed his head as she passed across him, her legs briefly straddling him. There was a musky feminine smell about her he found tantalizing. For a moment he wished he had lain on his back, so as to be able to peer up as she crossed. But to what purpose? She was not a woman to be touched, so there was no point in teasing himself with such visions.

She made it to the rear seat. "Just think what you would have seen, on your back in daylight," she said.

He laughed ruefully. "You fathom my thoughts so well."

"You're a man. What other thoughts would you have?"

If she was guessing, she was guessing well. "None," he agreed. He moved farther forward, found a comfortable place, and stretched out prone. He rested his head against his crossed arms and relaxed.

"Maybe in the morning, when we cross back," she said.

That jolted him awake. She would walk over him face-up in daylight? But in a moment he realized that she was just trying to interfere with his sleep, as she had with his urination. She knew she was a phenomenally appealing figure of a young woman, and that he was not allowed to touch her sexually, so she could get away with teasing him. It was her way for getting back at him for being her captor. She wouldn't actually show him anything, and even if she did, he shouldn't look. "If this is another game, I am not playing."

"You will play the game I choose, for you chose the first one."

"I did not—" But that argument would not prevail. "I lost. That ends it. No more games."

"We shall see."

He did not reply, and she was silent. Still, the suggestion that she might allow him to peer under her skirt disrupted his relaxation, and delayed his sleep. Normally, when alone, he could sleep immediately; it was part of his expertise as a hunter. Now he was not hunting, but being tricked or beguiled into treacherous contests with this unnervingly perceptive young woman.

He woke several times, expecting Melee to ask him to resume his seat before dawn, but she did not. He knew by the sound of her breathing that she was awake and alert. She must be tiring. But as long as she did not ask him to exchange, he would continue to sleep; it might be long before he had another chance.

Then it was morning, and the pre-dawn light was brightening. He had turned over, sleeping on his back to vary the cramped posture.

"Now we will exchange," she said. "I will cross over you." She was moving as she spoke, not giving him time to object.

He lay there as she moved, her hands on the two sides of the canoe, her legs spread so her feet treaded on either side of him. Was she actually going to cross over his face?

She did. He knew he should close his eyes, but they were locked open. He saw up into the cone of her skirt. Her legs were slender, but above there was darkness, obscuring all detail. As she surely knew.

She paused, with her body directly above him. "Would you like me to lift my skirt to let in more light?"

She would win another aspect of their tacit contest if he agreed, and he wasn't going to lie about it. "What I would like has no bearing. You may do as you wish."

"No, there is no harm in pleasing you, in little ways. Tell me the truth, and I may surprise you."

He realized that he might as well, since she knew the answer anyway. "I think it would be the most inspiring sight of my life." So how would she tease him now?

She balanced carefully, lifted her hands, and used them to lift her skirt high, revealing everything below the waist.

Dillon was stunned. He had been sure she wouldn't do it, yet she was showing him her private parts. He stared up, unable to speak. It was indeed awesome, for her legs were perfectly formed, and so were her belly and buttocks, and the crevice above him was exquisite.

Then she removed the dress entirely. "If you will take your seat, I will wash," she said. Then, after a pause, "Move, if you haven't been stricken blind."

Oh. He scooted toward the back seat, getting out from under her, then turned over and backed the rest of the way. He got into the seat and took up the paddle. He remained dazed. Badu had said she would tease him and tempt him; now it was clear how forthrightly she was doing so.

They were on a broader section of the river now, still in the center current. Melee had done well. Soon they would reach the great sea, and the settlement there.

She squatted naked, facing forward. She dipped water with her jug, poured it across a cloth, and used the cloth to wash herself. He couldn't help wishing she were facing back toward him.

"Of course," she said, divining his thought again. She turned and gave him full view of her breasts and thighs. Everything he had imagined about her figure remained true. She was the most beautiful creature he had seen. She used the cloth to wash her breasts, belly, and legs, and the slight motions of the glistening flesh thrilled him.

"Why are you doing this?" he asked, fascinated. "You know I would have turned away, if you had asked. Instead you have shown me—" He paused, for a moment at a loss for words. "Utter perfection."

She smiled, appreciating his sincerity. "You are my captor. You will know all my secrets, in time. So you may as well know them now." She rinsed out the cloth, then used it to wash her genital region, carefully.

"I would have treated you with respect throughout," he said.

"As you are doing now." She paused, as if considering. "I'm sorry I teased you yesterday. I will not do so again." She stood, carefully, and wrapped her dress about her again.

He tried to recover his equilibrium, though still somewhat dazed. "You may do as you wish."

"I teased you. Now that I regret it, I am showing you whatever I might have withheld. If you wish to look at me again, at any time, just say so, and I will oblige." She brought out a bone comb and began doing her hair. She had unbraided it during the night, and now it flowed lustrously.

"I don't understand."

"I am a princess. It is not my way to act beneath my station. I am expected to treat others fairly."

This was a change. But he didn't trust it. "You are still teasing me."

"By showing you my body? Then don't ask to see it again."

If only it were that simple! "Your very nearness is a temptation. Your manner, too. It would be easier if you were ugly."

She shrugged. "That I can't arrange. But now I have shown you all I have, so you need not be concerned about looking." She looked around. "Now I am tired. I think I have earned my rest."

"You have," he agreed. "You should have called me during the night."

"No, I had some thinking to do. Then I decided to wait until dawn, so as to do what I needed to do."

"You didn't need to keep paddling all that time."

"Yes I did." She spread her shawl on the floor of the canoe, then lay down on her back and covered her face with the cloth. "Wake me when anything interesting happens."

What could happen, more interesting than what had just happened? He steered the canoe, reflecting on that. She had teased him, causing him embarrassment, then abruptly turned about and showed him her body, and spoken sensibly. Was it just another phase, that would pass as suddenly as the prior one had? Did he need to brace for another unsettling attack? He rather feared that he did. He had been warned that she was wild, and she was proving it.

Still, the way she had shown him her body suggested more than just a reversal of teasing. She knew he couldn't touch her. Maybe when the lesser teasing didn't disrupt him sufficiently, she had decided to advance another step by offering him unlimited sight of her body. That certainly intrigued him, but didn't change his mission. He could see her but not touch her. Maybe she hoped that he would become maddened by the sight of her, and be unable to stop from touching her.

Yes! That would compromise him, and make him unworthy of the mission, even if she didn't immediately report him. In fact, she could then dismiss him as her guardian. Of course she would still be subject to her grandmother Bata, who would be proof against any such tricks. But Bata was feeble and nearly blind; it would be much easier to get around her.

So all he had to do was avoid touching her, and that ploy would fail. What could she do, if he held his course steady despite her blandishments? He gazed at her softly rising and falling breasts, which were somewhat flattened in this position but still quite appealing. She had made a tacit issue of them by covering them at first with the shawl, so that now they seemed even more interesting than they would have been.

Melee shifted position, lifting one knee. That showed her shapely inner thigh, immediately compelling his study. She had, as she said, shown him everything. Then why did that sight of what he had already seen send such a guilty thrill of excitement through him? Maybe she thought that one complete view ended the mystery and made subsequent views irrelevant.

No—more likely she knew that she had merely whetted his appetite for more. So now she was besieging him, even in her sleep. She no longer had to work at it.

Well, he would look. But he would not touch. Once he delivered her to Bata, the siege would be lifted, for Bata would be in control.

Satisfied that he knew his proper course, he watched the land pass behind. In due course they would come to the settlement at the river's mouth. Then there would be the sea. Meanwhile there was Melee's other leg, now raised, and the gentle heaving of her bosom. Since all he could do was look, he might as well get his fill of that.

When the town came into sight, he considered, then concluded that Melee might be interested. So he spoke to her. "Princess."

After a moment she stirred. "Yes."

"We are passing the town. Are you interested?"

"Yes." She sat up, shaking her hair into place. "Let's go shopping."

"We have what we need." They would run out, but spot hunting would give them fresh meat. He had meant for her to view the town, not enter it.

"Maybe what *you* need. I need some variety of food. Pull in, and I will buy something good."

Of course she had trade items. But the last thing he wanted was to have her get loose in a town. "No."

"I will scream and say you abducted me. They have little way of knowing otherwise."

"You have no future here!" he protested. "Your father would soon know."

"But too late for you, I think." She cocked her head and looked him in the eye. "Look, Dillon—I know I don't want to be in this town. I could escape my father only by pretending to be a peasant woman, and doing the drudgery they do. When a warrior decided he wanted me, he would take me, for I am beautiful, and I could stop it only by stabbing him or revealing my identity. So I would be lost either way, being married to a man not of my choice. There is no escape for me here. Indeed, I am better off with you, for you are charged with keeping me pristine. So I will not attempt to flee you in this town. All I want is to buy some decent food. You can trust me in this respect because you know I have no better alternative. So don't make me make it unpleasant for you. Let me do my shopping."

She was making uncomfortable sense. She could indeed bring mayhem on his head, because she was a lovely young woman and folk would readily believe that he had desired her so much he had tried to capture her. And she did have no future in this town. So the lesser risk was to allow her to do as she asked. He hoped that was not after all a mistake.

He turned the canoe and headed to the town. But then he reconsidered. "This is but a village. There is a major town not far beyond, where there will be a far better array of foods. That is the one for you."

She glanced back at him in surprise. "Why do you tell me this?"

"Because if we are to stop, it is better that we do so at a competent place, so as to get everything you might desire. Then there will be no need to stop again."

"And no excuse," she said. "You are limiting the risk to a single stop."

"Yes. But what I say is true. You will prefer the larger town."

She nodded. "You are learning to manage me, as I manage you. I can not decline your offer, though I know it serves your purpose better than mine." She smiled, briefly. "I like it when you fight back."

That gave him a foolish thrill of pleasure. He distrusted her flattery as much as he did her nakedness, but he enjoyed both better than was wise.

The major town was on a small island in the swamp. It was not possible to miss it, because the channels were well marked and used; canoes were thick.

Melee paused in her paddling to rearrange her dress and disarray her hair. Aware of Dillon's curiosity, she explained: "I am not ignorant of politics. This town has aspirations of rivaling my own in influence. It is better that I be no princess, here. You understand?"

They just might take her hostage, a lever against her father, if they knew her identity. They would find some other term for it, but that would be the reality. And, as she had pointed out before, she might be forcibly married to a local noble. Then what followed would not be rape, but her value as a liaison for some political alliance would be ruined. That was not in her interest, or in Dillon's. Not only would it represent the failure of his mission, he might well be killed to prevent interference. "Yes."

She turned her shawl so that the stitched side was out, making it look cheap, and put it around her shoulders, closing it in front. She hunched her shoulders forward slightly, so that her breasts hardly pushed out the material. Now she looked less well endowed, and considerably more common. She must have had some experience sneaking out.

As they came to the main docking area, a sharp-eyed official challenged them. "Who are you?"

Dillon hadn't thought of a story to tell; that wasn't his way. But Melee spoke immediately. "Dillon the hunter, and maiden. We come to trade."

The man glanced at Dillon, then back at Melee. She had put herself in some slight disarray, but her beauty could not be concealed. Why would a lovely girl travel with a hunter? Probably an association of courtship, possibly one not fully approved by the girl's family. Such things happened.

"Shop with what?" the official asked.

"I have stones," Melee said, showing a sufficient but not large amount.

"Shop, and be gone by noon," the official said, and turned away. Dillon knew he would be alert for them, to see that they did move on.

They got out and drew the canoe to shore beside others. No one would disturb it; that was why there was an official on duty. They walked along the road leading into the town.

They passed a major work site, where a clay pyramid in the shape of a volcano was being constructed. The monument was vast in scope, and would surely take a long time to complete. "Father had better watch this town," Melee murmured. "It has too much ambition." Dillon was inclined to agree.

There was a central bazaar, with farmers and merchants standing by their wares. There were common and rare cloths, leather helmets and belts, bows, arrows, dart throwers, darts, spears, atlatls, and an array of stone knives. Dillon's eye lingered, for weapons of all types intrigued him, though he already had what he needed.

Melee went to the food section. The major wares were maize, beans, chili peppers, squash, and sweet potato, with some nice honeycombs, but she wasn't interested in vegetables. There were snook from the sea, catfish and turtle meat from the river, and dog, venison, and even some rare turkey from the forest, but she ignored these and went for the more solid layouts. She looked at a slaughtered peccary, then at the dismembered body of a man nested in sea salt for preservation. It was laid out in rough order, except for the missing head, which the priests normally saved for their own obscure purposes: disjointed arms at the sides, gutted torso in the center, disjointed legs below. Human sacrifice was important for ceremonies, but the spirits valued the life and heart rather than the meat, and there was no point in wasting it. A human torso could feed a family for some time, so was valuable, especially when fresh. "This," she said, indicating the left upper leg, where the best meat was. "And this." She pointed to the phallus and scrotum, which had been cut off and set tastefully between the legs.

"What do you have?" the merchant demanded.

She reached into her bag without looking and brought out a small necklace of brightly polished stones of many colors. Some were jadeite or serpentine, the most precious of all stones, normally reserved for items of ritual or status. She handed it to the man.

He inspected it closely, pursing his lips. "How came a maiden by jewelry like this?" he demanded.

"I smiled at a hunter," she said, glancing meaningfully at Dillon. "He gave up his most prized booty, from the farthest region." Then she smiled at the merchant. "I will repay him in due course, in my fashion." She opened her shawl briefly to show her breasts. Even with her slightly hunched posture, that glimpse was compelling.

The man shook his head in wonder. "That would do it. Fair trade." Which meant that he was sure he had a bargain. He thought the necklace had been taken in battle, and that the hunter had not properly understood its value, so had given it away for the favor of a pretty girl.

The merchant took a cattail-fiber section of cloth and wrapped the thigh in it, together with the genitals and enough salt to keep them fresh for several days. He handed the package to Dillon.

"Wait," Melee said. "We will want some of that today. Cut off a portion and cook it separately."

The merchant shrugged, drew a knife, and sliced off a layer of meat from the top of the package. He set it in his ceramic brazier and blew up the fire below. They had one in the canoe, but of course it couldn't be used there.

"The delicacies too," Melee said.

The merchant reached into the package, drew out the penis and scrotum, and added them to the cooking chamber. This was more than a merchant normally did to oblige a customer, but Melee was a very pretty woman, and she had paid well; he clearly did not want to imperil the trade.

While that was happening, Melee went on to another booth, where she bought a large jug of fruit wine and some condiments, which she carried herself. At a third booth she bought a jug of chocolate. Then they took their purchases, returned to the canoe and paddled out. Once they were safely alone downriver, she poured out small jars of wine for them both, then opened the package. She handed the cooked thigh meat to Dillon, and took the genitals herself.

Dillon was impressed. Human flesh was a major staple for the wealthy, but he had seldom tasted it. Normally the poor folk had little meat, and subsisted mainly on maize and fish, but as a hunter he had tasted most types of meat. The princess treated it as if it were routine—as evidently it was, for her. It was delicious.

"Now admit it," Melee said as she cut open the scrotum and nibbled delicately on a testicle. "You like this better than dried fish."

She had him there. "I do. But I think it was a foolish risk for us both to go into that city, and for you to show such value in stones."

"Of course it was," she agreed amicably. "But you couldn't stop it, and I am a risky woman."

He nodded. Actually she had behaved well enough, not trying to embarrass him or make any trouble while they were on land. She had posed as his spoiled girlfriend. It had indeed been as if they were courting. That aspect had been fun, though he knew that he must never let himself believe that she cared for him as a person.

She lifted the penis. "It seems a shame to put this in here," she indicated her mouth, "when it should go in here." She lifted her skirt.

Dillon shrugged. She was baiting him again, symbolically consuming his masculinity. "You can have it both ways, in turn." Would she actually put the thing into herself?

She considered a moment, touching her cleft with the tip of it. The sight made Dillon react, as she surely knew. "No, it isn't hard enough." She put the end in her mouth and bit down hard. "Maybe soon I'll find a better one."

Badu had warned him, but it hadn't done much good; Dillon was shaken by her implication, despite knowing that she was trying to unnerve him. He had never before encountered a woman as alarmingly suggestive as Melee.

"Let's finish with some chocolate," she said, bringing out the other jug. That was another rare delicacy. She poured out a small amount and gave it to him, then poured a similar one for herself.

The chocolate drink was bitter, but nevertheless a great experience. It was flavored with spices and vanilla, leaving a rich aftertaste. Melee was indeed showing him how a princess lived. She could have been ugly, and he would still have been impressed. As it was, he knew she was doubly dangerous. Her beauty and her generosity were twin arrows aimed at his self-control.

After eating she brought out her jar, the one she had used for urination the evening before. "Shall I do this facing toward you or away from you?"

And now this. "You said you would not bait me any more."

She turned to face him. "I said I would not tease you. I said I would show you anything you wished to see. Now I am asking whether you wish to see this."

He wasn't sure whether she was simply teasing him on another level, but surely she did need to urinate, and he did too. They were in the middle of the broadest part of the river, near the sea; it would not be convenient to go to land again. Neither was it feasible to wait until darkness. So he would have to address this again. He decided that complete candor was best.

"You are a bold and beautiful young woman, and I am a man. The sight of your body excites me, though I will not touch you. You may use the jar as you wish, and show me what you wish. But how am I to do what I must do, when your presence affects me in a way that my presence does not affect you?"

She laughed. "You think I lack an answer."

"You have an answer that does not involve getting jammed by a paddle?"

"Yes. It may not be easy for you at first, but it will solve the problem."

"How can a girl barely nubile know of the problems of a man?" Actually she was fully nubile despite her youth; it was mostly a figure of speech.

"You have asked, and I will answer," she said seriously. "When I was young, there was an emergency, and a man of my father's work force named Grout was very sick. So I was assigned to tend to him. My father said it would be good experience. I was disgusted, but I had to do it. And it did turn out to be good training. I gave him bread and water when he was able to eat. I had to clean him up when he vomited, and when he had diarrhea. I got to see and handle all his parts. When he recovered enough to realize that it was no man and no woman who tended him, but a girl child, twelve and barely breasted, he was embarrassed. He would eat and drink what I gave him, but would not urinate or defecate any more in my presence. He was too weak even to sit up, but he struggled to hold it in. Since I was not allowed to leave his side, it was a problem."

"I should think so," Dillon agreed. He was coming to understand how she had fathomed his own embarrassment so accurately.

"But it brought its own solution. When the water inside him became too much, it burst forth. He used a jar, lest he spray on the bed, and I had to hold it for him. It overflowed, but once started, he could not stop, and I had to grab a second jar and fit him to it. After that he did not protest any more; he knew I had seen everything. Then he mended, and my duty was over. But I remembered."

This was a revelation. Her father truly had seen to her education. "So when you teased me about holding a jar for me, it was a thing you knew."

"Yes. And I know there will come a time when my presence does not inhibit you, and you are able to do what you need to do. After the first time, it will be easier the second time, and the third, until you have no trouble at all."

"But it will be really uncomfortable."

"Yes, the first time, until you let go. But I will help you, if you wish. Hold the jar for me."

"But—"

"You will know I have no secrets from you. Then you need keep none from me. Also, you should drink more water, or wine if you prefer, to make it happen faster."

He wasn't sure whether she meant the wine as added fluid, or as a way to diminish his resistance to urination in her presence. Both, probably. "But how can you be sure I won't—" He broke off, unwilling to say it.

"That you won't get so excited that you lose control and rape me? I have already tested you on that; you look but you don't touch. Your mind does not dissuade your penis, but it does control your action. You may be crazy with desire, but you will not act on it."

She was right. He had discipline over his voluntary actions, if not his involuntary ones. And probably the fewer secrets she had from him, the less they would affect him. "Then—I will try to follow the course you suggest," he said, hoping he wasn't blushing. "Though I think it makes you my captor, rather than leaving you mine."

"Yes," she agreed, smiling. "But you never had a chance to remain my captor. No man other than my father has ever been able to control my actions, and his control is imperfect. That is why I am being exiled."

"But I will die if I do not keep you safe in that exile!"

"No. I will not put you in that position. I am merely coming to an understanding with you. You will remain my captor, as far as all others are concerned. But now you know that it is by my sufferance."

"Now I know," he agreed ruefully.

"One other thing. Take off your clothing."

"But—"

"I took off mine for you—and will do so again." She stood, and removed her skirt. "We must be even, for this first time. I am giving you a fair chance to even the score in the contest of urine."

She was still playing that game! "But I am—a man is—"

"I know. You will have to show yourself to me when you do it; this will make it faster. It was with Grout." Then, when he still hesitated, she poured him more wine. "This will help."

He gulped it down, and soon felt it spreading out from his stomach. Then, reluctantly, he disrobed, revealing himself with an erection as stiff as the phallus on a stone statue. "No secrets," he said, definitely blushing.

Yet at the same time there was a certain illicit pleasure in this contest, if that was what it was, because it gave him an excuse to reveal his full masculinity to her.

She eyed his member, evincing no concern. "Now come help me." She held up the jar.

He put his hands to the sides of the canoe and moved toward her. Then he kneeled before her, and accepted the jar. She spread her thighs. "Hold it up close, here." She guided his hands. He wasn't sure how much of his dizziness was the wine and how much was Melee.

Then, without pause, she was urinating. His face was close; he saw the stream coming from her body, and felt its impact inside the jar. He willed his eyes not to close; he understood that this was something she wanted him to see in detail. It was fascinating and almost frightening, this view of the secret nature of a woman. What could be more intimately personal than this?

The stream stopped. "Now dump it," she said.

Oh. That jogged him back to the larger awareness. He lowered the jar and glanced inside. The smell of warm urine came up. A moment ago it had been inside her. He had seen it come out. That made it somehow precious. But he could not afford to be overcome by foolishness. He poured it over the edge, then rinsed the jar.

"Now I will hold it for you," she said, taking the jar.

"But I can't—" He glanced down at his clearly unready state. Unready for what it was he had to do, because too obviously ready for what he had not to do.

"When you are ready." She had the grace not to smile. "Go and paddle; I will come to you when I see that you can do it."

And when would that be? If his member ever relaxed, her mere approach would stiffen it again. "Whatever game you are playing with me, you have won it already."

She shook her head. "Not yet. To win, I must enable you to do what you think impossible."

He backed away, then sat on the seat and took up the paddle. His mind was whirling. He had never been this sexually excited before, and part of it was because he knew there was no chance of satisfying his desire. His erection remained rocklike. The wine had not had any effect on that aspect.

Melee kneeled, facing back toward him, and paddled with reverse motion. Her bare breasts shifted with her motions.

"I will never be able," he said.

"Yes you will. After a while this nakedness will grow dull, and tiring. And after today, it won't have much effect at all."

He hoped she was right. He could not urinate, but the pressure was already uncomfortable.

"And drink," she reminded him.

He had had enough wine. He dipped his jar and drank a good amount of water.

They moved on out of the river and to the sea. Melee looked around in awe. "It's so large!"

Had she intended a personal jibe, she could have said it long ago. So it was clearly the sea she referred to. But his mind had a bit of doubt.

"It is the great sea," he said. "We must follow the shore. We don't want to go too far out, lest there be a storm."

She shivered, though the day remained hot. "It frightens me."

He laughed. "I thought you were afraid of nothing."

"I never said that."

"I was teasing."

She flashed him a smile. "Thank you."

She thanked him for teasing her back? "I don't understand."

"I told you, I like it when you fight back. A game with no opponent is no fun. But it is more than that. We must associate for a long time. I thought you would be angry because I have achieved an even basis with you."

She had referred to it as a game, just as Badu had warned. That insight helped considerably. She had gotten him naked and stiff, as part of her game—and would respect him if he played it through. So he tried. "How can I be angry, exposed like this before a beautiful woman?" He glanced again at his erect member. His embarrassment was fading, becoming humor. This situation hardly seemed real. But as a game, it could be handled, even if the game was weird.

"Oh, you could be. But I think your teasing was not malign. Therefore it was friendly. You are accepting me."

"It is not my place to accept you, Princess."

"That is why I am pleased to have you do it."

She was right. He was accepting her as a person. There was something about their mutual nakedness that made acceptance easier. The mysteries were gone, and they were simply two people who were sharing an experience, though it was one of embarrassing exposure. "I am accepting you," he agreed.

"But the sea does scare me. It's too much. Can we move faster?"

Sex did not scare her, public urination did not scare her, but the great sea did? Maybe so, for it was physical rather than social. "Yes, if you care to turn around and paddle."

"Not yet. I must see you, and you must see me. I think soon it will be all right."

He doubted it. But he needed a distraction, because the water he had drunk was filling his belly, and he really needed to release it. This aspect of the game was growing uncomfortable to the verge of pain.

They paddled vigorously. Melee was doing so backwards, yet was doing well. Her body flexed and her breasts sometimes bounced with her effort. He closed his eyes.

"No, keep watching," she told him. "When everything I have to show you has no further power to excite you, then it will be time."

"It will never be time—until I burst," he said.

"You will see."

He stroked as hard as he could—and as he sweated with the effort, his erection finally began to fade. She was right: her body remained as exciting as ever, with her parted thighs and moving breasts, but he had seen these things for a significant part of the day, and they were losing their novelty and potency. It simply wasn't possible to remain sexually excited when the stimulus remained the same and he was working so hard. Also, when his need to urinate was becoming excruciating.

"Keep paddling," she said. Then she shipped her paddle and came toward him. She took the jar and put it to his crotch, cupping his penis. "Now let go."

But the touch of the jar made his member surge back upright. "I knew this would happen," he said, disappointed.

"Some day you will make a woman supremely satisfied," she said, briefly grasping his penis. That, too, surprised him, and worsened his condition. But he reminded himself that he wasn't touching her, she was touching him. That was a vital aspect of the game. "But once the first weakening occurs, the next is not far behind. Keep paddling."

"The last limp penis you touched, you ate," he reminded her.

She laughed. "Next time I'll buy vulva meat, and let you eat it. Paddle!"

He continued, putting all his strength into it. She squatted before him. And sure enough, soon his member softened again, bored by the sameness and overwhelmed with the need to release the pressure. This time she took hold of it and put it to the mouth of the jar before it dropped all the way. "Let go," she said. "Squeeze your belly. Piss will come." Then, as he hesitated: "Keep paddling."

He tried, knowing it would not flow. But his member stiffened only a little, and soon subsided, and then the urine did begin to leak through. A thin stream issued, and then a stronger one, until it was surging unhindered, into the jar. He was amazed; his penis was only half down, yet was working.

She grasped his member and squeezed, gently, then more firmly, cutting off the flow. What was she doing? He wasn't nearly through. With her other hand she put the full jar over the edge and poured it out. Then she brought it back, nudged his penis inside, and released her compression. The flow resumed. This time it went to the end, giving blessed relief to his distended belly.

She dumped the jar a second time. "You had a lot to give," she said, satisfied. "Now you have done it once. You can do it again, when you need to."

He was amazed, yet doubtful. "I am not sure of that."

"Then I will come help you again. We will get it done. But now we can dress, if you wish."

The sun was hot on his back and shoulders. "Yes."

They dressed, then resumed paddling. She faced forward. "Once a po-

tent man has pissed with a woman's hand on his penis, he can do anything," she remarked. "But I would prefer this to remain our secret."

"Our secret," he agreed. "We have pissed together." Who would believe
it, if he ever told? Best to leave it as a feature of the game, not much
relevant to real life.

She turned her head and glanced sidelong at him. "When you reckon
up your life experiences with women, what is more remarkable? Having
sex, or pissing?"

"Pissing," he agreed, bemused. "I have done more with you than sex
could have been."

"So Grout said when he did it. Of course your achievement is greater
than his, because you are not sick, and I am not a child now."

She certainly wasn't! It would take him days to assimilate what she had
shown him and taught him. "I think, after this, I will never again be afraid
of a woman," he said. "Other than you." It was better to show respect for
her works, as well as for the game.

"Yes. You are a strong, handsome man. You should be good with
women." She glanced at him again. "Next time I wish to play a game, will
you agree?"

"What can I do? If I try to deny you, you prevail anyway. And your games
are—interesting."

"Of course. I have an aversion to dull games."

"But I will play only if the contest or the stakes are not dangerous." He
hoped he could enforce that much.

"We shall see." She stretched. "Now I must get the rest of my sleep."
She settled down in the bottom of the canoe.

He watched her, as he continued paddling with less vigor. Her body
remained shapely, and her thighs as they were exposed remained engaging.
But now he had a more solid understanding, and the urgency of his interest
was diminished. It was as if they had had sex. And maybe they had, in a
way.

Melee was one remarkable young woman. First she had teased him, then
she had required him to go into town, and then she had made him urinate.
This could have seemed like utter humiliation, but because of the way she
had done it, showing him her body first, and urinating for him first, she
had made it instead an experience to remember all his life. In the process
she had indeed shown him that she was only nominally his captive, and
remained so only while she acquiesced. So far she had not caused him to
do anything that would get him executed, but her father's cautions now
seemed well taken: she could make him do whatever she chose, in time.
He just had to be sure that when she did, he made her give her word. That
would be his only protection. That was the one game rule he must never
forget. He had neglected to get her commitment not to start a contest, and
that had led to complications he had never imagined. So he was learning.
He was lucky that this particular game had been harmless. Or at least secret.
The next one might not be.

Later she woke, and resumed paddling. She said nothing about what they had done.

They had to pause as evening approached to eat some more. The meat was good, and gave him renewed strength, as did the wine. Dillon did need to urinate again, because of the extra water he had taken, but again he was unable.

Melee smiled, ready for another demonstration of the game. "Take off your clothes," she said, drawing her own off. "Paddle." When he hesitated, she added "You know that resistance is pointless. This issue has been settled. Strip. Give me the pleasure of seeing your virility."

He did so and watched while she took the jar and held it to her own body. She made sure he could see the urine flowing, then emptied it. He realized that she had not really had to do it; there was not much in her. She had done it merely to show him. So that it was an experience they shared. But he wondered whether it was also because she liked having a captive man she could do this before, safe from either molestation or exposure to others. Wild as she was, she couldn't have made a habit of peeing with virile men. Did she enjoy showing him as much as he enjoyed being shown? She had hinted that it was so. That could be another aspect of her game.

She approached him with the jar and waited. And, soon, she was able to draw his water from him. His body had learned the way of it, and knew how to relieve the pressure in the familiar nakedness. What point was there in torturing himself, when it would make no difference in the end? It was her victory, and perhaps his. *Their* victory, as they did what perhaps no other man and woman did.

He laughed. "And when I am with a woman, some day, and she takes off her clothes and spreads her legs, suddenly I will piss instead!"

She laughed too. "I think not. Because she will not be me. She will not share the secret. You will not have seen her piss. You will not know her well enough."

It was odd logic, but probably correct. "I suppose so. I knew from the outset that I would never have sex with you. With her I will know it is possible."

"Yes. And she will not be as beautiful as I."

"She could never be that," he agreed.

"How are we to handle this night, without the river to carry and guide us?"

"We must put ashore, or take turns paddling."

"I would rather keep paddling. Tell me the way, and I will do it while you sleep."

"You can't do that. It takes strength and endurance."

"I do have some muscle, under these breasts," she said, pausing to cup them with her hands. That, too, enhanced her beauty and suggestion. He wished he could cup her breasts similarly. "I can not come close to matching you, but at least I can keep the canoe oriented, and make some slight progress. Let me do what I can."

Again, she had a point. "Just keep moving along the way we are going. There will be a river, but that is not the one. Go on across it."

She nodded. "We must change places. Shall I go over you?"

"Will it annoy you if I say yes?"

She smiled. "No."

So he lay down, facing up, and she crossed over him, swishing her skirt over his face. That gave him another erection, but it soon faded. This was just part of the ritual they had. He realized that she had teased him, and then shown him everything so as to get him used to it, but that she *did* value his attention. His intense and continuing interest was a constant and sincere flattery. Which was of course why she continued doing it: not so much for him, but for her. She liked seeing his penis react to her provocations. She surely did get as much from it as he did. But in a different way. The sight of his ready body probably did not drive her to the same pitch of sexual desire. It was her mind set, her need to make and win a contest. It was her constant proof of power. She would grow tired of that game only when his member did. That was unlikely to be soon. She would see to that.

She took the rear seat and began paddling. He turned over and put his head on his arms. Suddenly he slept.

It was night when he woke. The stars were shining down, with their familiar constellations. He sat up. "Melee! Why didn't you wake me before this?"

"And lose the sight of your member growing large by itself?" she asked.

He realized that he had forgotten to put his loincloth back on, so had slept naked. There it was again: her fascination with his reactions. But now he could handle it. His growing understanding of her nature helped. "It was surely dreaming of you."

She laughed. "My grandmother has been teaching you how to turn insults into compliments."

"Yes." But it was significant that he had thought of the clever response before doubt clouded his ability to deliver it.

He found his clothing and put it on. He was no longer bothered by her remarks; they had seen each other too intimately for any such references to have impact. That was the lesson of the urine.

"Grandmother is a great woman. How is she now?"

"Old, feeble, and nearly blind. But she knows more than the Grandmother of Creation."

"I think she *is* the Grandmother of Creation."

"Or her representative," he agreed. "Now you must be tired. I will paddle."

"I am tired," she agreed. "Now I truly appreciate your strength and endurance."

She was deliberately flattering him—and he liked it as well as she liked the flattery of his erections. But while his flattery of her was involuntary, hers of him was calculated. He reminded himself not to forget that. "I thank you for the effort you made."

"I am ready for sleep."

"Get down and I will step over you."

"A common man does not go over a princess."

"As you prefer," he agreed, chuckling. He got down low, lying on his back.

She passed over him. "If you had awakened earlier, you could have seen me again in daylight."

"I know. It is a loss I must survive."

"Give me your hand."

Perplexed, he lifted his right hand. She caught it and put it up under her skirt, against her firm inner thigh. "This is what you would have seen."

"I am not supposed to touch you!" he protested, alarmed, though his member stiffened instantly.

"And you are not. I am touching you." She slid his hand up slightly, so that the tips of his fingers touched her projecting buttock.

She was right; he had not tried to touch her. She provided the motion of his hand, guiding it where she chose. "I am truly disappointed to have missed that sight," he said. But his banter covered a wild excitement. She continued to surprise him with her nerve and novelty. She had given him as gifts sights and touches that could have gotten him executed if he had taken them on his own initiative.

"You should be," she agreed. "But perhaps there will be another time." She leaned forward and found his loincloth with her free hand, and slipped her fingers inside to verify his erection. Then, satisfied, she dropped his hand and moved on beyond.

He sat up and got into the rear seat. He took the paddle and stroked. He could see the slight luminescence of the shoreline to the left, so knew that they remained on course. She had not taken advantage of his sleep to put to shore and try to escape.

"I used to think I did not understand women," he said. "Now I am sure of it."

"You grow smarter by the hour," she agreed. He could tell by the shifting of the balance of the canoe that she was lying down.

Then there was a long quiet period, as he stroked the craft forward. As dawn approached, he found the river mouth, and turned to enter it. Progress would be slower against the current; what had taken him hardly more than a day to cover before would take three or four days returning. But he no longer dreaded it, for he knew there would be no tedium. Melee would make sure of that.

She woke. "We must eat," she said. "Then I must paddle."

"You will not be able to make much headway upstream," he said.

She nodded. "But here where the current is slow, I can make some, so as to let you rest."

"Why are you so cooperative?" he demanded. "You know you will not be able to manipulate your grandmother the way you do me."

"I suppose you are right. We had better put to shore."

"And will you try to flee?"

She glanced back at him. "Why do you think I would do that?"

"Because you haven't promised not to."

"Haven't I satisfied you that I don't intend to flee?"

"You have amazed me and spoken reason and given me illicit pleasure, but you haven't ever said you won't flee."

"The man continues to grow smarter," she commented. "Very well: put to shore, and I will not flee."

There was the specific commitment, given only after she had tried to evade it with questions. He turned the canoe toward shore.

"You accept my word?" she asked.

"Yes. If the word of a princess is not good, what else could be?" And of course her father had said that her given word was good. So far, Badu had been completely correct—which suggested that the contest with Melee was not nearly over. For that he was perversely grateful.

"*Too* smart," she muttered darkly. But she smiled.

They ate, and went to separate bushes to defecate, and then Dillon lay down in the banked canoe and composed himself for sleep.

"Way too smart," Melee said, and kissed the back of his neck. Her breasts touched his back, surely by no accident.

When he woke later in the day, she had the ceramic brazier going, and the smell of stewed cactus and agave leaves was wafting out.

"You foraged!" he exclaimed. "You cooked!"

"I foraged, and did not flee," she agreed. "I cooked, and did not put your penis in the stew. Is that so amazing?"

He realized that it would not be politic to agree too readily. "I did not ask you to do these things."

"Therefore I did them," she agreed. "Now eat, and restore yourself for the work ahead."

He ate. She had augmented the stew with some of the dried meat, and used some condiments to flavor it. It was not the best he had eaten, but it was good enough.

"Thank you for doing this," he said sincerely. "It makes my work easier."

"How do you know I did not put toad skins in the stew?"

"Because that would be an effort to escape, and you agreed not to." He shrugged. "Besides, I know the taste of toad skin; there is none here."

She shook her head. "Were you not my abominable captor, I could almost get to like you."

"You may like my body, not my mind—as I do yours."

"I like your animal cunning—as you do mine."

He laughed, and she laughed with him. "Agreed."

Then they got back into the canoe, and proceeded upstream. Dillon felt better; the rest had done him good, and so had Melee's demonstration of integrity. He had not been quite sure, despite her given word, that she wouldn't flee. He had risked it, in part, because he knew he could quickly track her down. He had also needed the sleep.

The remainder of the journey was slow but pleasant. Melee did her share of work, and even flattered him into demonstrating his skill with the dart thrower when hunting pocket gophers at dusk. She charmed him into showing her how to do it, and he, conscious of her closeness as he guided her body and hands, was happy to oblige.

"But why do you wish to learn a manly art?" he inquired. For even common women did not try to hunt; foraging was their limit.

"If I am to be exiled for a year, I might as well profit from it any way I can," she replied. She lifted her hand with the dart thrower, trying to get the correct stance, and yielding to his corrections. "No one will know if I step outside my role, if no one tells."

"There is already much not to tell," he said. He brushed her hip with his wrist, in this manner guiding her without technically touching her, for touching was normally done by hands. "I see no reason to tell this."

She turned suddenly and kissed him on the mouth. Then she adjusted her stance, and threw the dart. It struck the edge of the tree-trunk designated as the quarry. That was not a good shot, but neither was it a bad one, for a first try.

"I must try another," she said. "Dart." For Dillon had frozen in place, half stunned by the kiss. She had surprised him yet again. She kept looking for ways, and kept succeeding.

"Dart," he agreed, giving her another. In all her prior demonstrations in the canoe, she had not directly touched him with anything but her hands, and seldom then. Except for that brief brush of her breasts. To do it with her mouth—to kiss him—was something else entirely.

She glanced at him. "You did not touch me; I touched you," she reminded him.

"You touched me," he agreed. "But you play a dangerous game."

"These are dangerous times." She threw the dart. It struck the center of the trunk. It was sheer luck, but he did not care to point that out.

Her third dart missed the trunk, but the fourth and fifth were reasonably close to the center. She was improving.

It was now too dark to do more. They gathered up the gopher he had gotten, and cooked it for supper.

"May I practice again tomorrow night?" Melee asked.

"There may not be gophers."

"I would not get one anyway. A tree will serve me well." She glanced sidelong at him, as she did when having more on her mind than was proper. "You will have to correct my stance again."

Meaning that she would let him touch her body, in that coincidental way. That she would stand almost within his embrace. Perhaps she was teasing him, but the delight of her nearness made him acquiesce. Not all of their games were openly stated. "If you wish."

"You are my captor," she said, reminding him of another aspect of the game. "I am your prisoner. But that doesn't mean we can't help each other."

And that help took the form of his teaching her a skill she could not otherwise learn, and her rewarding him with her seeming friendliness. It seemed to be a fair bargain. "And not tell others," he said.

Her white teeth flashed in the faint light from the fire. "Let them believe that we fought constantly."

"I think we are." For behind this seeming camaraderie they were indeed captor and prisoner. If she fled him, he would hunt her down. If he touched her—in any way she did not want—she would report it when they arrived, and he would be in trouble. So their cooperation had an edge that heightened its seeming sweetness.

They resumed the journey up the river, now traveling by day and sleeping on land by night. There was room in the beached canoe for them both, if each took one end, but their feet overlapped. Melee took delight in using her toes to tickle his calves. There was something sensual about her delicate, seemingly intimate touch. Once he woke to discover that she had slid down, so that her feet were well beyond his knees, and his soles were wedged against her inner thighs. That was not merely sensual, it was erotic. He suspected that had he slept with his legs apart, he would have found her toes massaging his crotch. She relished stimulating him, making him erect, knowing that he would not approach her sexually. She still liked to constantly verify her power in this respect. She had enabled him to get past an erection and urinate, but that was by no means the end of her interest. To make him erect, then not erect, by her choosing: she had control.

"Why?" he finally asked, when she had once again managed to interfere with his urination, and had used her way then to enable it. "Why do this again, when you have made your point?"

She answered him seriously. "At home, I am a princess. I have not had such opportunity before to play openly with a man. Either I had to remain aloof, as befitted my station, or take a man secretly. In the latter case, sex had to be swift, and parting swift, for I would not have cared to risk being caught with him. Of course I had sex; every girl does. But princes like to think they are marrying virgins, so the pretense is maintained. With you I can safely have my fun."

"By constantly arousing my desire, and never satisfying it."

"Exactly. Isn't it fun?"

Actually, it was. But it was also highly frustrating.

She understood. "If you wish, I will desist all temptation. Tell me that you wish it."

And he couldn't do that. Because though he could never indulge in the culmination, the temptation itself was far more delight than he was ever likely to experience elsewhere. Melee was highborn, beautiful, and mischievous, and it was a joy to be close to her, by whatever pretext. It made

it seem as if they were lovers, and that seeming had its own devious satisfaction. So he was silent, yielding yet another victory to her.

She nodded. "We understand each other. And it is true that if I were
not sure you would never break your oath to my father, I would not tease
you at all. With you I can be utterly free, and when you are gone I will
never have such freedom again. So let us enjoy each other, in what fashion
we may, and after this we can both say that you never touched me."

"You have shown me new definitions of non-touching," he said ruefully.

"And I do appreciate your appreciation. Sometimes I have wondered
whether the desire of men is for my body or my position. Now I know that
if I were a peasant girl, I could still arouse a man."

"You would have difficulty *not* arousing a man!"

She considered that. "Yes, I ought to learn that art too. How may I become unattractive?"

"You are serious?"

"Yes. What would make me be homely in your eyes?"

Dillon thought about it. "If you turned old and fat."

"No. Now, as I am."

He tried again. "If you had a bad disease."

"Yes!" She cast about. "The pox. Boils on my body." She was paddling,
but became impatient with it. "Go to shore. I need markings."

He looked for crocodiles, and saw none, so it was safe for the moment.
He steered to the bank. She jumped out, and scrounged for mud and
decayed wood. She plastered her torso with brown sludge, and dotted her
arms and face with spots of black. "How am I?"

"Still appealing. You look like a lovely girl caked in mud."

"Maybe if I aged. Paint lines on me."

"I can't—"

"Oh, forget it! I won't tell."

So he coated his finger with dark mud and carefully stroked her face,
making age lines. He put crows' feet around her eyes. She brought out her
stone mirror and studied her reflection. "Yes. I'm starting to look like
Grandma. Now do my breasts."

"But lines won't—"

"Shading. Make them look pendulous and leathery."

"I suppose I could. But—"

"Don't be finicky." She grabbed his dirty hand and jammed it against
her breast. "You haven't touched me."

She had abated that particular objection, and of course roused his penis
again. He tried, patting shades of mud on the upper surfaces and making
dark rings around the nipples. The effect wasn't perfect, but did make them
look at least somewhat baggy.

"And my hair," she said. "If I make it wild and gray."

"Yes. But it would be uncomfortable, and hard to clean up."

"You're right. So I won't do that right now." She gazed at herself in the
mirror again, then at her reflection in a clear pool of water. "You are good

at this, Dillon. If I ever want to convince a prince he doesn't want to marry me, I will have you paint me.''

"Maybe with age lines and disease spots," he agreed. "But even so, you may not fool him. You really don't look much like your grandmother."

"But I know how to try. Now we must wash." She doffed her skirt and squatted to splash water on herself. "You too; you're almost as muddy as I am."

So he stripped, and they splashed water over themselves and each other. Soon it became a splashing match, until she ended it by stepping into him and hugging him closely, not seeming to care about his continuing erection. Or perhaps that was why she did it. She kept finding ways to touch him with her body, and to have him touch her with his own. For a moment, under the surface of the water, his hard penis brushed against her groin and slid between her legs. They both pretended not to notice.

Then they dressed, got back into the canoe, and resumed paddling. "Nothing happened," she reminded him.

"Nothing," he agreed. What else could he do?

Melee continued to help paddle, becoming more useful as she developed better stamina and skill. Dillon was surprised and pleased by this, and glad to instruct her in the intricacies of such work. The labor tired her, so that at night she slept as soundly as he. But when he announced that one more day would bring them to Bata's lakeside residence, Melee became more playful.

"What would you do if I teased you at night, like this?" she asked, joining him when he lay down under his blanket. She was of course naked, and of course he reacted.

"I would tell you that I have already urinated," he replied.

She laughed. "So there is no point in softening you. Suppose I kissed you, like this?" She found his mouth with hers.

"You have kissed me before." He could not admit how much he liked it.

"And if I pressed against you, like this?" She hugged him closely, putting her thigh over his thigh and her breasts against his chest, squeezing his hard member against her soft belly. Each time she played with him, she took it farther. She evidently needed this kind of interaction, teasing herself as much as him. But the difference between their present contact and full sexual entry was becoming awesomely slight.

He decided that candor was best. "Melee, if I touch you, I die. You can destroy me just by telling me to enter you, for I think I could not hold back. Do you hate me so much that you want this?"

She paused. Then she answered. "No. You are a decent man. I will let you be." She got up and went to wrap herself in her own blanket.

She had surprised him once more, not by her approach, but by her abrupt cessation. It was almost as if she cared. "Thank you."

"Don't thank me," she replied. "You will curse me soon enough."

What did she mean by that? Was she going to accuse him, when they arrived? He would have difficulty denying it, considering the types of experiences they had shared. But it would be his word against hers, and Bata knew his word was good. Yet he had spoken truth when he told Melee that she could make him touch her by asking him to. He could save himself only by requiring her to give her word first, but if she refused, she could still make him do it. She would not have to accuse him falsely; she could make him guilty. So he was truly at her mercy.

But what was this about cursing her? "I hope not," he said. "I bear you no ill will, and it has been a rare experience being with you. You have shown me much."

"We'll see." And that was all. He would just have to find out, in due course.

They arrived the following afternoon. Bata heard them coming, and met them by the river bank. "Am I dreaming?" she asked.

"No, Grandmother," Melee said cheerily. "This brute has forced me to paddle. He said if I didn't want to feel the paddle against my bare bottom, I'd better hold it in my hands."

"I'm sure," the old woman agreed. "And you made sure to show him your bare bottom, calling his bluff."

"Several times." She got out as the canoe went aground, and hugged the old woman. "How are you doing, Grandmother?"

"As ever. Are you going to behave?"

"Of course not." Melee walked toward the house.

"Beware," Bata said to Dillon as he got out. "She is up to something."
What an understatement! "She said I would soon curse her."

"And how was she on the journey?"

"I learned almost as much from her as I did from you."

"You did not touch her?"

He hesitated, knowing she would fathom the reason. "She touched me."

"Then it was not an easy time."

"Not easy," he agreed. "But not unpleasant. She—she is like you, sixty years younger. I tried to heed your warning." He started to unload the canoe.

"Don't bother with that," Bata said. "I know you are tired in more than the physical sense. Go sleep; Melee is in my charge now."

"Thank you, Grandmother." He went to the bushes to relieve himself, drank same water, ate some fruit, retired to his chamber and lay down. The accumulated tension of the journey sloughed off his shoulders, and he slept quickly and soundly.

He woke much refreshed. He got up and sought Bata and Melee, but they were not in the house. He found Bata packing supplies in a canoe. "Grandmother—surely you aren't going to travel!"

"Dillon, it's my fault. I didn't think she'd break this soon. You will have to go after her. I'm sorry."

"Melee fled?" he asked, realizing it was true.

"She took your canoe. I didn't think we needed to unload it immediately. My mistake. She must have gotten in after we were both asleep, and started downstream. She will know the route; she surely paid attention on the way in."

"She did," he agreed. "And she worked to improve her paddling. And she got me to teach her how to hunt with darts. I thought she was just flattering me."

"Never trust a woman," Bata said matter-of-factly. "She always has another agenda."

"She made a fool of me. I thought she just liked to toy with me, making pretexts to have me see her and be touched by her. She could so readily have compromised me." As Bata surely knew. The girl had probably learned some of those arts from her grandmother.

"You fathomed only the level she wished you to fathom." And of course he understood that, now, too late.

He nodded ruefully. "Now I know why she said I would curse her. She planned this."

"Of course she did. I am chagrined that she fooled me too. I am getting dull-witted in my dotage."

"Sometimes the rabbit makes an odd jump, and the hunter misses. It does not mean he is losing his ability." He was speaking of her, not himself. His own idiocy had been established.

"Thank you, Dillon," she said curtly. "Now go and rectify my mistake. You can catch her long before she reaches a town. This time, if you are in doubt, bind her."

Dillon hesitated. "Grandmother, I don't think I can. She—she was in charge of me, more than I of her."

She nodded. "Women are deadly. Do what you must."

"But she can master me. I am a fool, but not fool enough not to know when I am overmatched."

She turned her dim yet penetrating gaze on him. "She likes you, Dillon. Otherwise she would indeed have compromised you, and been rid of you. Instead she left you innocent, by fleeing after she was in my charge. When you catch her, make her swear not to flee you. If she will not swear, then bind her. She will let you do it."

"How can you know that, Grandmother?"

"Because I would let you. Now go."

This was beyond his understanding, so he didn't challenge it. He got in the canoe and took up the paddle. "I am sorry to leave you alone again so soon, Grandmother."

"I'll get by, dear boy." There was something in the way she said it that reminded him suddenly of Melee. Both of them flirted with him, but with Bata it indicated genuine affection rather than any exercise of power. It was endearing.

He shoved off, then paddled briskly downstream. He knew, as Bata did, that the girl would not have tried to paddle upstream, because the current was swift and the mountains close. She would be better off on foot than in a canoe, that way. But downstream she could go fast and far with minimal effort. He just had to make sure she didn't try to hide the canoe and wait for him to go by; he would never find her, if he got ahead of her. That meant he would have to limit his travel to daylight, so he could scan the banks.

As he moved, he pondered how she had deceived him. Bata was right: he should not have trusted her even partially. Melee had said she would not try to flee him, and she had not; she had indeed waited until she was in her grandmother's charge. But she had prepared for it throughout. Even when she had foraged while he slept, and made him a good meal, she had been rehearsing for the time when she would forage and cook for herself. Why hadn't he been suspicious? Because she had kept him distracted with her sex appeal, giving him so much else to think about that only an obvious break would have alerted him. Even the last night, when she had joined him under the blanket, tempting him: that had prevented him from pondering anything other than her desirability. She had let him think she was behaving, lulling him into fatuous complacency.

"Oh, Melee, you have taught me so much," he muttered. "But I learn readily, and you will not fool me that way again." Yet at the same time he had to admire the finesse of it. She had planned well and acted with dispatch to achieve her objective. Though why she should want to go to another town was perplexing; they had already discussed how pointless that would be for her. Obviously she did want to escape, but the reason for it was not clear to him. So he still did not understand women, her in particular.

And what Bata had said: Melee had spared him because she liked him. She would not destroy him, though she could. She would let him bind her. Because Bata herself would let him, were she in that situation. And Bata knew her granddaughter's nature. He had to trust the old woman's judgment in such a respect. But he was flattered too. When he and Bata teased each other, he had always assumed that were she really young again, she would toy with him exactly as Melee had, but never actually give herself to him. Because her intellect dwarfed his own. Now it seemed that her concern for him was more than that of mentor for student. He hardly deserved it, but he was enormously honored.

Meanwhile he watched the banks of the river, seeing no sign of departure there. He could readily read the indications; it was his skill as a hunter. So, as expected, Melee had fled straight down the river. What town did she have in mind? She surely would not return to her father's town, and the others hardly seemed worth her while. The mystery of her motive was as great as that of her location. He wondered whether she would tell him, after he caught her. Probably she would just tease him, making up obviously false reasons that would further tantalize him.

Yet he looked forward to that. He liked her company, though her behavior masked her contempt for him. Maybe she did like him, as Bata said, but probably it was like the affection a person felt for a pet puppy. Catching her, bringing her back again—would she play the stiff-penis game with him again, pretending solicitude for his incapacity? It was such sweet torture. Whatever sport she wanted to make of him, was welcome. Being tormented by her was better fare than compatible association with anyone else. And so, indeed, he could recapture her only if she let him, for whatever reason she let him. For teasing a cute but stupid puppy whose devotion was unshakable.

Toward the end of the day he spied something ahead. It was the canoe! But as he stroked toward it, he saw that it was empty. She was gone. What had happened to her? She couldn't have been so foolish as to swim in this water, for there were crocodiles.

He caught it and peered in. The paddles were there, and his spear and bow, but the food and darts were gone. That meant that she had taken what she could carry and use, and gone overland. But where? He had seen no trace of a landing by the banks.

Slowly it penetrated: *she had never used the canoe.* This whole thing had been another clever diversion, to lead him astray. She must have gone afoot, upstream. And by the time he could get back to the starting point, she would have a three-day head start on him.

Melee just kept making a fool of him, over and over. It was maddening, yet admirable. She was no pampered princess; she was as canny as any peasant girl.

He used a length of cord to tie the vacant canoe behind his current one, and started paddling upstream. Soon it was growing dark, and he had to pause to eat and relieve himself. The very thought of urination made his penis swell, because of his memories of Melee. So he pretended that she was there watching him, and after a time was able to do it. Then he chewed on dog meat, imagining her there with him. Finally he lay in the canoe to sleep, bunching part of the blanket as if it were one of her limbs touching him. He had never needed company before, but now he needed hers. What would he do, when she finally realized that she would be better off with a prince of her father's choosing, than languishing in exile? He would have to deliver her back to her hometown, and then return alone with his memories.

Would another girl ever replace his interest in Melee? He suspected not. Oh, he would find one, and marry, in due course; Bata had said he would, and she knew. But she would be a shadow of the sheer excitement Melee represented. Melee had forever spoiled him for any ordinary woman. That was surely deliberate on her part, but nevertheless true.

However, there were other things he could see and appreciate, but never possess, like the sun and the moon. And maybe, when he embraced that other woman, he could close his eyes and pretend it was Melee. So he would have a piece of her, in his fashion.

In the morning he resumed travel, and continued as rapidly as he could. But going upstream was twice as hard as going downstream, at this level, and there was no way to gain appreciably on its inexorable schedule.

He arrived at Bata's lake on the evening of the third day. "She tricked me," he said ruefully. "She sent the empty canoe downstream."

"Yes, I realized that after you were gone," Bata agreed. "That girl is cannier than I credited. As canny as I am. She must have gone for Oaxaca."

"Yes." He had made the trek over the mountain ridge on occasion, to trade with the folk of Oaxaca. They spoke a different dialect, but sign language sufficed. "That makes more sense. She could marry a prince."

"It's idiocy. She refused that prince, before."

Dillon was astonished. "She refused him? He was her father's choice?"

"Yes. So why should she seek him now? She is playing some deeper game."

"She practiced changing her appearance. Making herself look old, or ill. Maybe she plans to conceal her identity there."

"To what point? A woman alone is subject to any man who fancies her. An old, ugly, or ill woman would be fancied only by a similarly unappealing man. She will not like that. She is better off here, where we will treat her with respect."

"She knows it," he said. "She said as much to me."

Bata shook her head. "I must be suffering an erosion of wit in my dotage. Her strategy is too subtle for me."

"Could she be crazy?"

"Unlikely. Well, I will figure it out in due course." She shrugged. "Meanwhile, you must fetch her back. She has a three-day start on you, but you can travel twice as fast as she can. You can catch her before she reaches Oaxaca."

He nodded. "My arms are tired, but not my legs. I will go immediately."

"No, stay here the night. I will feed you and prepare a competent pack for you."

"Grandmother, you don't need to do such things for me."

"When it is my error, I must do all I can to correct it. Rest, Dillon; you will travel better tomorrow."

So he ate and retired to the floor of the chamber reserved for him. Bata was right; good rest and a good morning start were best. He was familiar with the trail, and should indeed catch Melee within three days. She must have assumed it would take him longer to catch the empty canoe and return, so that she would have time to lose herself in the town across the mountains.

Still there was the mystery: why should she seek a town outside the Olmec realm? Why either marry a prince she had refused, or hide as a commoner? Neither alternative should appeal to an imperious princess.

He heard voices and activity elsewhere in the house. Bata was instructing her maidservant in the preparations for his trip. The servant was a homely, dull-witted girl. Dillon had thought that Bata employed her from compassion, but now it occurred to him that the old woman had wanted no attractive young woman in the house. Because of Dillon's presence. That had worked; he had never had interest in the servant. But it had also left him inexperienced with respect to a woman like Melee. He had been like a deer before the hunter.

In the morning he set off, carrying bow, arrows, darts, knife, and the dry meat in his pack. He would have liked to bring his spear and atlatl, but their added weight would have impeded his progress. He was not on a hunt, but on a pursuit; speed was of the essence.

He followed the path upstream, moving well. He liked the exercise, and he liked being in the wild forest. He would have liked to bring Melee here, to give her another dart-throwing lesson, or whatever else she might want. Now he was pursuing her, a distinctly less delightful matter. Would she express her withering contempt for him when he caught her? Probably. But it was his duty.

The way soon became steep. This slowed him, but would have slowed her more, so it was good. She was a fine figure of a woman, but by that token lacked his lean physical power. He could see the signs of her passage; she had definitely come this way. She hadn't even tried to mask her bare footprints, though an intervening rain had washed out most of them. She knew that he would know where she was going; the trail led only that way, and there was no point in leaving the trail, for the jungle terrain became impenetrable to anyone in a hurry. Still, he watched to make sure her signs continued, lest she try some other trickery.

The river bore west, then south, then east, then south again, wending its way up the mountain. Dillon was sweating, though the air became cool. He wondered how Melee had managed; she was of much slighter build than he, with less muscle, and would have found this arduous indeed. Yet obviously she had done it; her signs remained.

He stopped at darkness, ate and drank, and chose a good tree to sleep in. Of course a tree was no protection from a panther, but his weapons were. He hoped Melee had not been stalked by any such animal, for with only darts and a knife she would have been in trouble.

He resumed next day, departing from the river to crest the mountain pass and start down the other side. The ground was bare and bleak, and there was a cold wind cutting across, making him shiver. But Melee had been here, braving it all for the sake of her escape. She was some woman!

The path followed the river on the far side, down into the new valley. On the third day he moved well, going downhill. There was an art to it, though it actually took more energy than traveling on the level did. He should be catching up to Melee soon; her traces showed how tired she had become. Perhaps she had underestimated the rigor of the trip over the mountains, where the very air thinned, making a person pant for no seeming reason, and the cold could be wearing.

And at dusk he found her, hobbling along, evidently in pain. "Melee!" he called.

She turned to see him. "So you caught me," she said dully. "Much good may it do you. I am worn and ugly."

"You will never be ugly."

"Thank you."

"Melee, there is nothing for you here. At least your grandmother and I will treat you with respect. Will you return with me voluntarily?"

"You will have to carry me."

"If that is the way of it, I will do it. But I don't want to force you."

"I mean I am lame. I will come with you, if you help me."

Oh. He got down to look at her feet. They were bruised and bleeding, the nails cracked from repeated contacts with stones. Her legs were scratched and somewhat swollen. "I will carry you to a better path," he said.

He put his arms out before her, and she turned and fell into them, so that he could lift her without technically touching her. As she came up, she caught his head with her hands and brought her face in close, and kissed him on the lips. "Thank you," she repeated. For a moment he felt as if the mountain were turning upside down, for her kiss was phenomenally sweet.

He carried her to a smoother section of the path, then set her down. "I will fetch a medicinal plant, and bind your feet. Then you will be able to walk."

"You are kind to me."

She sounded as if she meant it, but he wasn't sure. Certainly her feet pained her, so she would not run away. "I give you my pack. There is food in it. Eat and rest."

He moved into the forest, searching for the key herb; it normally grew not far from a river. Bata had made him fetch many such herbs for her, and had explained the use of each. It had actually helped his hunting, for particular animals sought specific herbs in certain seasons. Soon he found it, and cut out the part he needed, and brought it back. "This will ease your pain," he said, making a paste of it in his hands. "If you will put your feet on it—"

She lifted one foot and set it in his hands, thus nominally preserving the notion that she was touching him, rather than he her. He rubbed the salve around her foot, especially the toes and bruises. Then she lifted the other foot for similar treatment.

After the feet were covered, he looked up—and her knees were parted, opening the view under her skirt. "Gaze where you will," she murmured. "Go where you will."

"Aren't you angry that I caught you before you reached the Oaxaca town?"

"No. I like being with you."

There did not seem to be irony in her tone. "I don't understand."

"I know you will take care of me. It is better than walking alone. Take what you want of me, and I will say nothing."

He stared at her. "You know I can't do that!"

She returned his gaze. "I know you are not supposed to. If I accuse you, and you can not deny it, your life could be forfeit. But if I do not accuse you, no other person will. You will be safe."

"This is a cruel temptation."

"If I swear you my oath, by the Jaguar and the Serpent, and the Grandmother of all Things, that I will not accuse you of touching me—"

"No!" For he had experienced the way her games affected him. He had to balk at the outset, or inevitably be lost.

"And I do so swear. Take me, Dillon."

"You are trying to destroy me. When I am trying only to salve your hurts and bring you back to safety."

"I am trying to reward you for constancy and kindness. Take me. I have sworn."

"I can not trust you. You have deceived me at every turn, and made a fool of me."

"You can trust me now, Dillon. Take me. I desire you."

He laughed, bitterly. "And what would be the cost of believing you?"

"You have asked, and I am answering," she said evenly. "Before, I was playing with you, and I enjoyed it, knowing you could not touch me, however much your desire welled. Now I am not playing. I am tired, and hurting, and in much need of comfort. But first I want to pay for it. Kiss me, and plunge me, and I will give you such joy as no other can provide. My desire is to please you, and I will do that in full measure until you deliver me back to Grandmother Bata. Then I will not accuse you. She will know, for no secrets can be kept from her, but she will know also that I asked to be touched, and she will be silent. You will never be held to account. Nothing will be changed, except that you will have had your will of me with impunity. I do not see how I can make a better offer."

"No. I do not trust this." For he had seen how a seeming immediate victory over her could lead to a larger deception and loss. He still did not comprehend her real motive, and it was perilous to accede to any of her ploys without knowing where it might lead.

"Then I will have my will of you, in my own time. You will not escape me."

"You can make me desire you, but you can't make me take you." But he was bluffing.

"We shall see."

Almost, he capitulated then. But he had spoken truth when he said he did not trust her. He did not know what web she wove, but believed it would be disaster to become ensnared in it. Maybe if he kept reminding himself of that, it would stiffen his resolve.

She looked at him, half smiling, surely fathoming his thought. "As I said, I like it when you fight back."

"There is a better place to camp, farther up the slope. I will take you there." He put his pack back on.

"I think I can walk now. Your balm is helping."

"No need. I will carry you." He put out his arms.

But now she balked. "Why should I let you carry me, when you will not let me oblige you?"

That set him back. "Melee, I am trying to help you. Please let me do it."

"I could say the same to you." She grimaced. "But I will yield, for now." She put herself into his arms.

He carried her uphill. She was light, but her weight added to that of the solid pack was a considerable strain, and soon he was breathing hard.

"I will give you extra strength," she said, and kissed him again. The odd thing was that it worked; new power surged into his arms and legs, and he carried her the rest of the way before his arms gave out.

"You are tired too," she said, as he set her down. "Rest; I will fix a meal."

"You are the one who needs rest," he protested. "I am accustomed to hard work."

"So I see. But if you do not let me do something, you leave me no alternative but to reward you by seducing you."

He shook his head. "You are the princess. I am the guardian. You have no need to reward me for anything."

"No impersonal need. But you have made me *want* to reward you. That is a different matter."

"I preferred it when you were merely showing me things. Then you made no claim to desire. You were satisfied to give me partial pleasures, teasing me."

"The teasing is done. I will show you all those things." She parted her knees toward him. "But the pleasures need no longer be partial."

He ignored her and worked on the meal. He made a small open fire, lacking the brazier, and cooked meat and leaves together. They ate. Then she said, "I can stand on my feet only with pain. I would be more comfortable sitting and using the jar."

Was it really that bad for her? Or was she trying to tempt him with her sights, as before? Did it matter? He had to be proof against anything she might try. He fetched the jar and held it for her so she could urinate. As always, the sight excited him, as she intended it to. After all, she could have held the jar for herself. Instead she was treating him to the full view of her parted legs and the action between them, as she leaned back and streamed into the close orifice. In fact this position was even more arousing than the standing one had been, because it resembled the pose she might assume for sex. It was so easy to picture himself pressing in instead of the bottle, finding the place so close, disappearing into her.

"And I would welcome you," she said. "Now let me do you."

"There is no need. We are not on a canoe."

"There is a need of a different kind." She reached to his loincloth. "Free that serpent."

"Still you tease me."

"I do not tease you. Take your will of me, and thereafter you will be able to urinate."

"No."

"I do not understand, Dillon. I have given my word."

He smiled, somewhat grimly. "For once, it is *you* who do not understand *me*."

"Then let me help you with the jar, as before."

There was no real logic there, but it was easier to acquiesce than to continue fighting. So he removed his loincloth, exposing his solid erection, and sat beside her as she handled him. Only by letting her touch him as she wished, and remaining proof against it, could he get her to desist. Or was it that he wanted her to have her will of him, in whatever partial manner, and this was the only way he could justify it?

"You are doomed to lose," she said. "It is my will to have you inside me, and your desire to be inside me. Why must you fight so long?"

"I just must," he said.

In time he did urinate, though by no means flaccid. Then he stood, put on his loincloth and got out his blanket. They had now done what they had on the canoe trip, and his control over his desire was not weakening. But neither was it strengthening.

"It is too cold," she said. "I am not used to it. It was awful, alone, even with a fire. Give me your warmth."

She had a point. Normally the nights were warm, but up on the mountain it got cold. So he spread both their blankets, and they lay under them, close together. She opened her cloak so as to press her breasts against him, and her skirt hardly masked the firm warmth of her thighs as she slid one leg between his. They might as well have been naked, but he intended to sleep regardless.

"I will do with you as the great mother did with the Jaguar God," she said.

"No you won't."

"For back in the early days, when the six directions of the world were new, the jaguars and the humans did not associate," she said, starting the ritual narration.

"Melee, must we review this now? I want to sleep." But his words belied his emotion. He wanted to possess her.

"The Grandmother of All Things was then a young woman, more lovely than any since. She had borne many human children, and would bear many more, for from her infinitely fertile cleft issued all the tribes of mankind. But she realized that without liaison with the jaguars, there would always be strife between the species, and that was not good. So she sought a way to relate better."

Dillon realized that she was going to review the celebrated were-jaguar history regardless. So he joined in, so as to get it done with so he could try to sleep. "But the Jaguar God did not care to associate with the human folk," he said. "Because his kind were creatures of the forest, while the humans were moving into houses and villages and towns where jaguars weren't welcome. 'Come back to the jungle,' he said. 'Return to the state of your origin. Then we can get along well enough.' For it was not the distinction of species he was concerned about, but that of lifestyle. He felt the humans were going wrong."

Then they were in the story, assuming the parts: he the jaguar, she the grandmother.

But the Grandmother Goddess replied, "You must not judge us without understanding us. We are learning to love maize, and it feeds us so much better. Now we have strength and time to play our wonderful ball game."

"What ball game is this?" the Jaguar God asked. "I know of no such thing."

"Then you must come to play the game with us," she replied. "Only then will you properly appreciate its wonder."

So the Jaguar God, partly from curiosity and partly to see what he could do to get the humans to return to what he felt was the proper way of life, agreed to go to the ball court and play a game of ball with her. "But what are the stakes?" he asked. "For no game is worthwhile without significant stakes."

"Why, the issue we were discussing," she replied. "If you win, we humans will give up our square houses and villages and return to the jungle. If I win, you jaguars will give up the forest and come to live in houses and villages. What could be higher stakes than these?"

"None," the Jaguar God agreed with a shudder. "How many games shall we play to decide the issue?"

"Three," she decided. "For a single game may be decided by chance as much as skill, while three games are more likely to establish the superior player."

"Agreed. I will meet you at the game court tomorrow."

"Come today, for then we can spend the night there and be ready to start early in the morning before the heat of day."

So the Jaguar God accompanied her to the game court. When the people saw them, they were amazed, for no jaguar had come there before. But the Grandmother said to them "We are here to decide the residence of humans and jaguars. Go tell the jaguars, so that they may come and watch too."

At once the people ran out into the forest and notified all the jaguars they saw, and those jaguars notified their brethren, and they all ran toward the game court to watch the big game.

Meanwhile the people prepared a great feast for themselves and the jaguars, and enjoyed it tremendously. Then the Grandmother thought of something. "Do you know how to play the ball game?" she inquired.

"I will learn," the Jaguar replied.

"I will explain the rules to you tonight," she said. "Come join me in my house."

So the Jaguar went to her house. "Come lie down with me," she said. "Make yourself comfortable, and I will describe the game."

So he lay with her, and she said "There are four hoops set high on the walls, two at the ends and two at the sides. There is a big heavy ball. You

must put that ball through one of the hoops, but you may not touch it with
your hands or your feet or your legs or your arms or your head. Just your
torso. Each time you succeed, you score a point. The one who scores the
most points wins."

"That seems simple enough," the Jaguar said. "I have no hands or arms.
But how do I move the ball?"

"You must strike it with your hip or your belly or your chest or your
back."

"I can do that. But suppose it flies out of the court, or falls on the ground
and lies there?"

"Then the judge will throw it toward the one who did not touch it last."

"That seems fair." Then the Jaguar, being full with the meat and wine
of the feast, put down his head and slept.

The Grandmother tried to get around or under him, but he was curled
up tightly with his belly down, and she could not budge him. So she kissed
his ear and settled down to sleep leaning against his spotted back, and was
comfortable.

In the morning they got up and went out to the arena. The judge threw
the ball into the middle of the court, and the Grandmother ran to intercept
it and bumped it so well with her hip that it flew through the nearest hoop.
She was ahead by one point. The people cheered, but the jaguars were
silent.

The next time the ball was thrown in, the Jaguar ran for it. But he was
unused to the game, and did not bump the ball through the hoop. So he
concentrated on preventing the woman from doing it again. When the
game ended, the Grandmother was ahead by that point, and she won
the game.

"I will do better tomorrow," the Jaguar said. Then they retired to the
feast, and had a wonderful time, and so did all the other people and jaguars.

That night the Jaguar shared the Grandmother's house again, and they
talked of incidentals, and then he laid his head on his paws and slept. She
got around to his front, and tried to roll him over, but could not budge
him, so she kissed his nose, put her head against his spotted side, and slept.

The second day they went out again to play. This time the Jaguar
bounded for the first ball so swiftly that the Grandmother was left standing,
and bumped it right through a hoop. The jaguars cheered, but the people
were silent. They played longer, but he kept the lead, and won the game.

Again they feasted with much relish. Grandmother urged more and more
wine on the Jaguar, for the third day would have the deciding game. He
staggered as he walked to her house, fell on the floor, rolled over with his
feet in the air and slept soundly. This was what she wanted. She got on him
and kissed him and rubbed her body against him, so that he dreamed of
endless mating. When his penis became hard, she lay on it and closed about
it so that his seed shot into her. In that manner she conceived by him, as
she had wanted to do, but he did not know it.

In the morning, refreshed, they went out for the third game. They fought hard, but were evenly matched, and neither was able to score. So in the end it was a tie, and the issue was unsettled. So the jaguars returned to the forest, and the people returned to their houses, and that was the way it remained ever since.

But the Grandmother of All Things birthed a were-jaguar, and it spoke the languages of both the people and the jaguars, and was worshipped by both, and many statues of it were made, and many altars were raised to it. It became a god in its own right, and was associated with rebirth and fertility. The Grandmother raised it among the people, so it associated more with them, and their luck was greater, and they prevailed over the field and forest and became great. All because the Grandmother had obtained the seed of the Jaguar. She had not won the ball game, but by her cunning she had won everything else.

At last they had finished the legend, and Dillon had the chance to relax. He succeeded. But in the night he woke and found her on him, her body pressing hard against his. "What is this?" he demanded.

"I am around you," she said. "I am having my will of you, as I said I would. As the Grandmother of All Things did with the Jaguar God."

He suddenly realized that it was almost true. He must have been erect in his sleep, and she had drawn his loincloth aside and was trying to set herself on him. Emulating the role of the Grandmother, as she said. Now he understood why she had insisted on reviewing that story. She had given him fair warning.

He put his hands on her shoulders and lifted her with brute strength, hauling her body off his and breaking the connection. Then he let her drop down again.

"I think no other man could have done that," she said. She was not referring to his physical strength.

"I knew you were not to be trusted."

"But I *am* to be trusted. I have said I desire you. I have said I will have my will of you. I have said I will not accuse you. All these things are true. What must I do to persuade you?"

This time he answered. "You would not need to accuse me. I would accuse myself."

"But if you will just lie there, you need do nothing. I will touch you, as I was doing. Had you not awakened too soon, it would have been complete."

"You will destroy me."

"No. I will make you happy."

He shook his head in the darkness. "Melee, I beg you: do not take me like this."

She sighed. "You have asked me, and I must agree: I will not do it by stealth. I will make you touch me."

"And I will not." He closed his eyes, her body against his. This time, for once, he had won. But there were still several days' travel ahead. Was he going to be able to make it? With each of her sieges, his resistance weakened.

"You will," she murmured, snuggling against him.

Then he slept. He woke briefly several times thereafter, but she was not doing anything. She did seem to be keeping her word. For now.

In the morning he found her kissing him. "You said you would not," he protested after a moment.

"I said I would not do it by stealth. This is not stealth. This is open solicitation."

"It is a pretense of affection. That is stealth."

"By the Great Jaguar!" she swore. "Must you ruin all my fun?"

"Retreat to showing me, instead of touching me. That should be fun enough."

She grimaced. "Then let's go to the river and wash."

"Can you walk today?"

"I think so. The night in your arms has healed me much."

"It is your touch that is magic, not mine."

She laughed. "I thought you a dullard, but you have left that behind without footprints."

"Experience is an effective teacher."

"So is Grandmother Bata."

He had to agree. "She warned me about you."

He stood and waited while she got up. She winced, but stood unaided. "Show the way, Jaguar."

"I think I should carry you, old woman."

"I think you should not, but I would like it if you did." She took a step forward, biting her lip.

"Does it embarrass you to be helped?" he asked.

"Yes, when it is because of weakness."

"Then I will help you." He stepped to her and put out his arms.

"You are getting good." She fell back into them. "But I will make you regret it." She stroked his ear with her fingers, then leaned her head in and sucked on the lobe. The effect was seductive.

He carried her to the small stream, where it pooled briefly. "This is cold."

"I know. Let me drink first."

He set her down, and she flopped on her belly and put her face to the water. Then she drew back, getting on hands and knees, making way for him to drink. He lay beside her, seeing her breasts elongating below her chest, forming globes, and put his mouth to the pool. The drink was good; his thirst had developed during the night.

He lifted his head, and felt her body on his. "Why did you not lie on me like this?" she inquired, stretching out on him. He realized that she had slipped off her skirt. "You could have taken me from behind."

"Fortunately you can't take me from behind."

"I can't? Let me see." She lifted her hips somewhat and reached back and down, sliding her hands around his buttocks and down between them inside his loincloth until her fingers touched his testicles. She tickled.

It was excruciating pleasure. "You can," he gasped. "Now let me up."

"Oh, go on into the water. It's time to wash." She rolled off him.

Dillon pulled off his loincloth, crawled forward, and splashed into the pool, which was about waist deep. The water was numbingly chill, but that was what he needed. He turned over and looked back at Melee. She was squatting at the edge, her knees toward him and parted, as usual. He stared, compelled to look though he knew it was what she wanted. Every new view of her was intriguing.

"I'll splash your face," she threatened, putting her hands down to the surface.

He put up his crossed wrists to fend off the mock attack. She grabbed them in both hands. He jerked his arms back, hauling her with him. She made an exclamation and fell into the water. She shrieked as her body hit the cold liquid. Then she wrapped arms and legs around him, trying to dunk his head. He was at a disadvantage because he couldn't touch her, and found his face being squeezed against and between her slick wet breasts. He opened his mouth to breathe, and she shoved a nipple in and fastened her arms around his head to lock him in. He tried to speak, but his tongue was depressed by that nipple.

"Do you yield?" she demanded.

He stretched both arms upward in surrender.

She pressed in closely for another moment, then drew back. "Now lick off the other one," she said, proffering the other breast.

"But then I would be touching—"

She jammed it into his mouth. Obediently he licked that nipple too. "Think how much fun this would be if you agreed to touch me," she said. "Now let's wash, before we freeze."

He nodded. She ran her hands over his body, scrubbing away supposed dirt, then took his wrists and made his hands stroke her face, breasts, legs, and buttocks. "Now we are clean," she decided, shivering. "Lift me out."

He extended his arms, and she laid herself into them. He put his feet down and stood, carefully, lifting her out. He stepped around, finding firm footing, and carried her up the bank and back to their blankets. He set her down on one, then picked up the other. He hesitated.

"Wrap your hands in the blanket," she said. "Then you are not touching me."

He did as she bade, and rubbed and patted her body dry. Then he left her swathed in the blanket and went back to fetch their clothing. She had made the simple act of washing into a memorable occasion. He knew that next time he washed, he would remember her breast in his mouth. She was right: he longed to do it of his own volition.

They dressed, ate, and resumed the trek. Melee's feet did seem improved; she walked slowly, but without obvious difficulty.

They spent the next night high on the mountain. There was no question of separation; the air was cold, and there was a wind. They snuggled into a sheltered crevice, wrapped themselves in the two blankets, and clung close for shared warmth.

"Tonight is too cold for games," Melee said. "But if you should change your mind, I am ready."

"Just sleep and let me sleep."

She stroked his buttock and pressed her face into his shoulder. "As you wish."

He woke several times, but this night she was behaving, as she had promised. She did keep her word, once given; he just had to be wary of the words she didn't give. Meanwhile, it was extremely nice being with her like this.

"Oh, come on," she murmured in his ear. Somehow she always knew what he was thinking, perhaps because any man this close to her had to be ruled by passion. She maneuvered her hand until she caught his wrist, and hauled his hand down inside her skirt so that it cupped her rounded buttock. "How would I know whether you touched me, when I'm asleep?"

"I wish I could," he replied, giving her a squeeze. Her muscle twitched in response. His desire surged, and then faded into sleep. He had become used to living with unsated desire; it was a chronic state in her company. It had its own odd comfort.

In the morning they were still clasping each other's bottoms. "Maybe you are right to wait," she said. "If you ever sate your desire, you will not be as warm at night."

"I am burning," he agreed.

"But when the nights are warm, you will succumb."

"When the nights are warm, you will be able to sleep by yourself."

Her mouth quirked prettily. "Able; not willing."

They crested the chill pass, walking together, their arms around each others' midriffs, wrapped in the blankets. "This is much better than when I did it alone," she said. "Your warmth and strength make all the difference."

"Your warmth and softness make all the difference," he agreed.

"Anyone seeing us will know us for lovers."

"They will be mistaken."

"No they won't."

He didn't argue. She was fixed on seduction, and refutation seemed only to encourage it.

"We have done everything except one detail," she said. "And that is only a few days away."

He still didn't debate the matter. It was more fun to share her fantasy than to refute it.

They started down the other side of the mountain. It was a relief to reach the cover of some trees. Then Dillon spied the traces of peccary, the wild pigs. "We need fresh food," he said. "I will get it." He set up his bow.

"Aren't you afraid I will flee, if you leave me?"

"With those feet?" Her feet were healing, but remained tender. "And how will you seduce me, if you are gone?"

She sighed. "Not to mention where I would go. What do you want me to do?"

"Sit here and rest. Make a fire, if you wish. I will return soon."

She nodded and sat. They had been walking at her pace rather than his, but it was clear that she was tired. The trip over the mountain had depleted her, and though she didn't complain, she was weak.

Dillon tracked the spoor of the pig. He did not want to take time to lie in ambush; he wanted to get the meat and resume the trek to the warmer region below. So he followed swiftly, holding his bow ready. And soon he caught up to a sow and several small ones. They squealed and scattered, but his arrow caught the shoat he sought, impaling its hind leg and crippling it. He ran up and cut its throat with his stone knife. He picked it up and carried it back.

Melee had made the fire. Dillon butchered the piglet and laid the pieces around the fire to roast.

"I never even tried to use the darts," she remarked. "I thought I could hunt my own food, but I couldn't. Nothing came near."

"Animals are wary of the hunter," he agreed.

"I couldn't even forage much. So I went hungry."

"You will have all you want, now."

She nodded. "There is something about a man. He always has what he needs."

"No. The woman has what he needs." He glanced at her. "You are forgetting to show it to me."

"Oh!" she said, mockingly appalled. She turned sitting to face him, and spread her lifted knees so that he could see under her skirt. Despite the humor, the sight was compelling, as always.

"I suppose I am foolish to think that you have grown accustomed to my presence, so forgot that you never want me to relax."

"That would be foolish to think," she agreed. "I just wanted to make you ask."

"I didn't ask. I merely commented."

"In much the way you haven't touched me."

He considered that. "True. I should not have mentioned it."

"And I should not have forgotten."

They smiled at each other. They were both enjoying the contest, on this level. But it remained serious.

The smaller sections were ready. Dillon sharpened a stick and speared a roasted piece for her. She chewed on it avidly. He should have realized how hungry she had gotten. He had shared his rations with her, and she had never asked for more, but she needed more.

"Your hunger," he said, as he fetched his own fragment. "Why didn't you say?"

"I was ashamed."

"But you made a good escape. You tricked Bata and me."

"I couldn't make it on my own."

"Well, you're a woman."

"I wanted to be free."

"What is the point in a free woman?"

"None. But I dreamed."

He shook his head. "If I thought you could survive, if your father hadn't charged me to keep you safe, I would let you go."

"You tease me cruelly."

"No! I would. And pay the price. But you would perish alone."

"I almost did." She finished her piece, and he gave her another. "Do you really mean it?"

"I would let you go," he repeated. "But I can't."

She set down her piece, wiped her mouth, stood, and circled the fire to join him. She got down on her knees and took hold of his shoulders. She kissed him, and kissed him again, pushing him to the rear. When he fell back on the ground she pursued him, kissing steadily. She fell across him, still kissing.

After a time she relaxed, pinning him to the ground, but her passion remained. "Why?" he asked.

"Because you would," she said. "Because you can't." Then she kissed him some more.

"I still don't understand women."

"You would grant me my dream, if you could," she explained. "But you can't, because you know I couldn't survive, and because you honor your duty to my father."

"Yes. Why the kissing?"

"You are the first who has cared what I might want. And who cared whether I survive."

"Your father cares."

"No. He wants only the political advantage my marriage to a prince would bring him. Because no prince could stand me if I didn't agree, he has exiled me to the wilderness to make me agree."

Dillon was taken aback, realizing that she was right. "Your grandmother cares."

"Does she? Or is she merely doing the will of my father? Do you know her secret thought?"

She had set him back again. "Bata knows more than anyone. But I do not know her secret thought."

"Think how crafty and guileful I would be, at her age."

"I do not know your thought now."

"Well, you are a man." She kissed him again.

"Yet I have the feeling that for a moment you acted without calculation. That you were really pleased."

"For a moment," she agreed. "But you are right: I should be seducing you." She rubbed her body against him suggestively.

"Why do you want to seduce me? I doubt that you have much real interest in my welfare or my passion."

"Because then you will be in my power. Once you touch me, you will exist at my sufferance. You will know that if I tell, you are dead."

"But you promised not to tell."

"And you believed me?"

"Yes."

She smiled. "Here is the trap: once you have touched me, you will hunger eternally for more. I promised not to tell the first, but I will not promise the second. Or the third. So you will possess me physically, and I will possess you emotionally. There will come a time when I can tell, without breaking my word, and you will know it. Then you will do my bidding, which will not be arduous. But the power will be mine."

"The power is already yours."

"No. You still honor your duty over my convenience. When I make you compromise that duty, my convenience will govern. We will continue much as before, but I will no longer be your captive."

"You made me *your* captive in the canoe."

"But didn't free myself of your honor. So it was an empty victory. To truly prevail, I must not only compromise you physically, but also bind you eternally to my will."

"I appreciate the logic," he said. "And if those kisses were true feeling, I value them."

"You should. Here is one more." She kissed him again, lingeringly. "Now can I seduce you at this point, or would the effort be wasted?"

"It would be wasted, on the level you wish. I know better than to let you become my eternal captor. For one thing, then all the teasing and closeness would stop."

She cocked her head, considering. "Not necessarily."

"If you took away your desire to make me subject to your will, how much passion for me would remain?"

She thought about it some more. "This is a good question. Some would remain, but perhaps not a lot. On occasion I do crave entertainment. You know we are not talking about love."

"I know. So if I like your closeness, it behooves me never to touch you."

"But you are as cynical as I. You do not love me; you merely desire satiation in my body."

"And to fulfill my duty."

She nodded. "I liked it better when we understood each other less well."

"So did I. I think I will see less of you, and feel less of you, now that you know I will not yield."

"But you *will* yield."

"So you think. You can seduce my body when you choose, but not my honor."

"Suppose I promised to let you see and feel as much after, as before?"

"Your heart would not be in it. Your attention would wander."

"True. But you would have only to remind me. You could say 'Melee, lift your skirt, open your legs,' and I would do it."

"It would not be the same."

"Why not? You know it is all calculated now."

"Now you pretend you want it. Then you could show me, but scowl and revile me, dropping the pretense. The sight would be the same, but the feeling would be worse."

"Would it? Suppose I screamed, not loudly, and protested, not strongly, and cursed you while opening my legs for you? Have you never taken an unwilling woman?"

"Never. And I never will. I would hate even the pretense of unwillingness."

She made a small fist and pounded him gently on the chest. "You drive a hard bargain. I will ponder some other promise, that may be better for you."

"It doesn't matter. I will not yield to you."

"It does matter, because your resolve will weaken if you know the cost is diminished. When you are weak enough, you will succumb." Then she kissed him once more, and got off him.

They ate heartily, while the remaining pieces cooked slowly and dried over the fire. They would be carried for future meals.

They did not travel much farther that day, but did find the beginning of the river. They drank, and made camp. It was warmer here, but still cool enough to warrant sharing the blankets.

"Suppose I guaranteed pretense?" she inquired as she snuggled close.

"I would know it for what it is."

"But you know it for what it is now."

"No. I have the faint hope that some of it is actual desire. Maybe the knowledge that you truly need something from me makes it better. Once you no longer need it, the effort will become more apparent. Anyway, it is not to be."

She kissed him savagely. "Stop saying that! It only delays the inevitable."

"I wish I could kiss you as you kiss me."

"That's it!" she exclaimed. "I will let you kiss me like that. Then you will generate the passion. You will become willing."

"No." But he spoke with less force than before.

"I am gaining on the prey," she said, and closed her eyes.

She was indeed gaining on the prey. He had every intention of holding out, but what if she found something that really did make a difference? He had to hope they would get back to the lake before that happened.

He slept, but dreamed of her. He was trying to fight it, but her constant attention was tiring his resistance.

And she knew it. "One more day? Two? Surely not three."

"We'll be back in three."

"So my victory must be in two."

They got moving. He thought she might try to delay things, to give herself more time, but she didn't.

Down the slope he spied new traces. "Jaguar," he said, feeling a chill.

"I don't see any footprints."

"They don't necessarily leave prints. But one passed this way."

"Anyway, the jaguar is sacred. We should have nothing to fear from it, should we?" She paused, sobering. "Unless it's a ghost."

"This one is real. And hungry. They don't stalk men, but if we surprise it there could be trouble." He made sure of his knife, and strung his bow, ready to use it quickly.

"You speak as if it's an animal."

"It *is* an animal. Priests may worship it, but it's a beast, like the others, only more dangerous. Stay alert."

She looked around, shuddering. "You may be sure of that."

As they proceeded, the traces disappeared. "The jaguar is elsewhere," Dillon said, relieved.

"How do you know? I mean, couldn't it be lurking, watching us?"

"No."

"But they do lurk, don't they? And they're cunning? Even the physical ones?"

"Yes. But I know their signs. It's not here."

"You are so sure."

He was sure, for he had hunted all his life, and knew the ambiance of different creatures of the wild. He could wind them, and hear them, and see their days-old traces. He knew their habits. But how could he persuade Melee, who knew none of these things? "I am as sure as you are that you will seduce me willingly in two days."

She looked at him, assessingly. Then she walked on down the trail.

It was warmer that evening, but Melee insisted on sharing the blankets with him. "It's not the cold," she explained. "Or the seduction. It's the jaguar."

"But it's far from here."

"So you say."

And why should he object? After this trip, there would be no delightful maiden in his arms. So he acquiesced, and they embraced, as usual.

She kissed him. "I'm not fooling you, but you accept it."

"Yes."

"Never again will you have a girl this pretty, this eager to have sex with you."

"Never again," he agreed.

"Suppose I let you possess me, at will, for a set period of time? A month, two months—how many do you want?"

"Ten years."

"That's too much. After this year you must return me to my father, and it will be over."

"Unless you still refuse to marry a prince."

"True. But he may ship me off to some other wilderness, in the care of someone else. Then you will have lost your opportunity."

"It won't matter, because if I make that deal, I will be dead."

"No, I won't report you, if you obey my whim. You will be free."

"No. I will be the ultimate captive."

"Your head is made of wood," she said in exasperation, kissing him.

"No. With you here like this, it is my penis made of wood."

"I know. I would have more room against you if we softened it."

"Go to sleep, maiden."

She rubbed her loin against his, and closed her eyes. Still he wondered: what made her so sure that tomorrow would finish his resistance?

Next day they moved farther on down, getting into the thick jungle. For the first time in days they were hot. "Let's bathe," Melee suggested. "We're dirty, and you know you like me wet against you."

"There is a pool below. We'll be there later in the day."

"I want to be there now. I'm burning up."

"We can reach it quickly, if you have the courage."

"Courage?"

"We would have to jump in from above."

She shrugged. "That sounds like fun."

So he led the way to the overhanging hammock. The roots of a giant tree held it secure, but below it dropped an awesome distance. The sound of the river's falls was loud.

Dillon took off his pack and the blankets and set them against the tree. They would only get in the way. "Hold on to a branch," he suggested as they circled the tree.

"Why? I have good balance." Then she saw the drop-off, and screamed. She reeled, starting to step forward.

Dillon caught her arm and hauled her back to the trunk of the tree. She clung to him, terrified, not even noticing that he had touched her. "It's the edge of the world!" she cried.

Actually it was only several man-heights, but that was awesome enough. He had first spied this place years before, and had been overwhelmed by its grandeur. Melee, coming upon it suddenly, was suffering that dizziness of height.

He put her hand on a low branch. "Hold on. After a moment, it passes, and you can enjoy the sight."

She nodded, clinging to the branch with both hands. Dillon let her go and turned to peer down. Yes, the pool was still there, its deepest section just beyond the plunging water of the falls. It was important to jump into that portion, where there was room to plunge well below the surface without colliding with the bottom. He had explored the pool carefully before making his first leap. It had been an exhilarating experience, that brief fall through the air and sudden immersion in deep water. Melee should love it, once she got up the nerve to do it.

Melee screamed again, piercingly. Dillon turned quickly, afraid she had lost her grip. If she fell, she would land in the wrong part of the river, and suffer serious injury. But she was hanging on tightly, facing the tree, staring upward.

His eye followed her gaze. Then he saw the serpent. It was a large anaconda, coiling its way down along the branch. Melee's pull must have shaken the branch, disturbing the snake. It was simply seeking a more secure repose, but the girl didn't realize that. She let go of the branch and pushed herself violently away. She was about to fall backwards off the edge.

Dillon leaped to intercept her. He put one arm around her and grabbed the branch with the other. He wasn't trying to stop the fall, just to direct it, so that they would drop into the deepest pool. He swept her in toward him, and leaped.

She screamed and screamed as they plummeted. He held her until they struck and plunged under the surface; then he pushed her up, and followed. In a moment they were both there, before the falls, bobbing in the frothy water.

But she had swallowed water, perhaps unsurprisingly, as she had been screaming as they struck. He put one arm around her again, and stroked one handed for the bank. In a moment his feet found it, and he hauled her out and laid her down on the grassy slope. He turned her over onto her belly and pounded her back, encouraging her to cough out the water.

Soon she recovered, and sat up. He was relieved; now he realized how afraid he had been for her. She flung her arms around him and kissed him with wet passion. He kissed her back; he couldn't help it. The relief was overpowering. It was just so good to have her all right.

Then she was tugging at his soaking loincloth, and he was tugging at her skirt. Part of him thought they just needed to get dry, but part of him knew better. Naked, he hung back.

"This you have to do yourself," she said, spreading her legs. "You must possess me." She smiled encouragingly.

He desired her overwhelmingly. She could so readily have fallen and been grievously injured, and it would have been his fault. How much better to embrace her, than to hurt her! But it was his honor and his life at stake.

Tears showed at her eyes. "Please."

The tears did it. He embraced her and kissed her, and she kissed him back, avidly. He sought her cleft with his member, and she moved to accommodate him. In a moment it lodged in slickness, drove on in, and spurted with all the power of the extended seduction of their association. He was touching her, jetting inside, and it didn't matter. Nothing mattered, other than this precipitous culmination.

She was still kissing him and moving with him, her arms and legs clasping him. "Give me everything!" she gasped, thrusting her tongue into his mouth.

But all too soon the pulses ebbed, and sanity returned. "I touched you!" he cried in horror.

"You touched me," she agreed. "And what a touch it was. I think you would have burst if you had waited any longer."

"Now I am dead," he said.

"Now you are alive." She kissed him again. "Wonderfully."

"But this was what—I knew I shouldn't have—"

"I promised not to tell, and I will not. Rest, and soon you can do it again, more slowly. I want to savor your virility. You saved me from horror, and I am grateful."

Almost irrelevantly, he remembered. "The supplies—they are up there. I was going to throw them down before we jumped, but—"

"We shall have to go back up for them. That will extend our time together. Does it matter? You have no need to hurry back, now."

She was right. "There is no hurry," he agreed. "You rest here; I will go up and get the equipment."

"Shouldn't I remain with you?"

"You are tired, and recovering from near injury or death. I prefer to have you rest."

"And you can do it much faster without me."

"Yes."

She kissed him again. "You are uncompromisingly truthful."

He shrugged. "What other way is there to be?"

"Conniving, calculating, and sneaky, like me. You are hopelessly naïve."

He looked at her, knowing that she was correct about this too. Yet she had also treated him honorably, in her fashion, giving him warning. "I am just a country hunter."

"And I am a city schemer. We are well matched."

"Well matched? I don't understand." Or perhaps he just didn't want to.

"Of course you don't." She kissed him once more. "Go fetch our things. I promise to wait."

Unsettled, he left her there and made his way swiftly up the steep mountain slope. She called him naïve, and herself a schemer. That far, he understood. But how were they well matched? He was a man, and she was a beautiful woman; apart from that, they were no match at all. And she had, by her wiles, destroyed him.

In due course he reached the tree. He thought about tossing down the supplies, but concluded it would be safer to carry them down.

He circled the tree and peered down to see whether he could spy Melee. And she was there, standing at the edge of the pool, waving to him. Then she cupped her breasts with her hands and spread her knees, leaning back, inviting him to clasp her again.

And suddenly he wanted to. He had done it once; another time would make no difference to his fate, and she was infinitely desirable. So he fetched the pack, made sure it was tight, and flung it down to the brush on the other side of the pool. He did the same with his bow and arrows. Then he leaped, aiming for the center of the pool.

He heard her scream as he fell. Then he struck the water and went under.

As he swam to the surface, he saw her body there. She was swimming out to meet him, her breasts and belly showing from below, her legs spreading and coming together. She was lovely.

He came up beside her. She came in close and kissed him. "Take me here," she said. "You reckless show-off."

"You beckoned me. I had to hurry."

She laughed. "I thought I was teasing you." She wrapped her arms around his body. "Do it now."

"How can I, when I must swim or drown?"

"In the shallows, then, where your feet can stand."

They moved there. She jumped high and clasped him with her legs around his waist. Her breasts nudged his face, begging to be kissed. "But this time I am not promising to keep silence."

"It doesn't matter." He put his hands on her hips and drew her down onto him. It had been not much more than an hour since they had had sex, but his eagerness was almost as strong as before. She seemed as ardent, holding his head between her hands, kissing him throughout. He thrust deep within her, and she met him with her own push down, and clenched herself around him so as to heighten the pleasure of his release.

"You seem to be good at this," he remarked as the passion subsided.

"I told you I had experience. I made sure to learn how to make a man finish swiftly."

"It was wonderful. But next time, make me finish slowly."

"You are thinking of next time already?"

"You have destroyed me. I might as well enjoy my last day."

"But this is not your last day!" she protested. "I did not promise to be silent, this time, but neither did I say I would speak. I want only your knowledge that I *can* speak, when I choose."

"It doesn't matter."

"So you said. But it does matter. The distinction is important. I am not breaking my word to you."

"You have no need to." Then he lifted her out of the pool and set her on her feet on the bank.

"I don't understand."

He smiled. "The schemer doesn't understand the bumpkin?"

"That's right. *Why* doesn't it matter?"

"Because when we return, I will tell Bata, who will tell me to kill myself, and I will do it."

Melee was appalled. "I never intended this!"

"You knew it was death for me to touch you."

"Only if I told! I never intended to tell, only to have the power of the threat of it."

"No one ever had the power of a threat against me."

"But this makes no sense! It is only a struggle for dominance. I meant to abuse it no more than you did."

"What you meant does not matter. The penalty for violating my trust is death."

"Dillon, no!" she cried.

"You pretend you didn't know?"

"I knew, but thought—" She moved her hand in a gesture of incapacity. "I think I don't understand honor as you define it. No one asks for his own death."

"A warrior does."

She grabbed him by the shoulders. "This is a power ploy, isn't it? To take back your authority? What do you want? I will give you my promise, and my body."

"It doesn't matter," he said a third time.

She stared into his face. "Dillon, I beg you! My tears are real. What can I do?" Indeed, her tears were flowing. She was beautiful that way, too.

He felt awful, for making her cry. But there was nothing he could say. It seemed that she had after all meant the seduction innocently, but the damage was done. He turned away.

"Dillon." There was a new tone.

He turned. She was holding her knife to her throat. "While you remain with me, you must protect me," she said. "But you can't protect me from myself. Promise not to tell Grandmother."

He thought she was bluffing, but wasn't sure, for she was capable of high emotion. So he hung his head, and spread his hands—and as she relaxed, he swept the knife out of her hand. "Must I bind you to keep you safe?" he asked.

"Yes!" She dived for the knife.

He caught her before she got close to it. She struggled, then collapsed. But he was not so stupid as to let down his guard. "Promise not to harm yourself, or I will bind you."

"No!"

"Melee, I don't want to tie you."

"You will have to," she said with bitter satisfaction. "Unless you promise not to tell."

"No."

"Then I won't promise either. Bind me."

Dismayed, he let her go. The pack with its cord was on the far side of the pool. He picked up her knife and tucked it into his belt. He looked around, making sure there was nothing else she might readily use to harm herself. Then he dived into the water and swam across.

He thought she might run, but she stood unmoving. He fetched the pack and bow, walked downstream to avoid the pool, and waded through the river. He returned to her, opened the pack, and brought out the cord. She held out her hands before her, her wrists crossed, her eyes closed. She was, indeed, submitting herself to be bound, as Bata had said she would.

"No. Behind you."

She put her hands behind her. He made a loop of cord, circled her crossed wrists, knotted it, and drew it just tight enough to be snug without chafing. He knew how to make a knot that would hold. Then he addressed her feet.

"What are you doing?" she demanded, surprised.

"I am hobbling you, so you can't run and throw yourself into danger." He paused. "Unless you promise not to."

"Hobble me," she said grimly.

He made loops connected by a cord long enough to enable her to walk normally, but not to take long steps. He knotted the loops carefully, so that they rested lightly on her ankles but could not readily be untied. It was done.

"Suppose I jump into the river, and can't swim?" she asked.

"I will pull you out."

"Suppose I trip and fall into a tree, breaking my neck?"

He nodded. "You could do that. So I must control your movement." He made one more loop, and put it around her neck. "This is not tight," he explained. "I will hold the end. If you move suddenly, the cord will go taut, and the noose will tighten around your neck, cutting off your breath. You will suffocate, losing consciousness, if it remains too long. I will release it, but it will be uncomfortable and will leave a mark around your neck. So it is better not to move in such a way as to tighten it."

She eyed him with a new appraisal. "You are good at this."

"I have had to lead balky animals."

She chuckled bitterly. "And I am that." Then, in sudden appeal: "Dillon, promise me, and all this is unnecessary. It is your life I am trying to save, not mine."

"I know. I appreciate it. But I must do what I must do."

"I thought I knew you. I did not know you at all. You are twice the man I thought you to be, and I curse you for it."

"I deserve your curse," he said. "I hate putting you through this humiliation. But I must deliver you safely to Bata, and talk with her myself. After that you will be free."

"I will not be free!" she exclaimed in tearful anger. "I will be responsible for your death, when I never wanted it."

She spoke the truth, and there was no answer to be made. He picked up the pack and his bow and arrows, and took the end of the cord around her neck. "We must go on to a good camping site. Tomorrow we will be there."

She walked before him, unbidden. She stepped carefully, so as not to run afoul of the hobble and trip and fall. He walked behind her, and from that vantage watched her flexing buttocks. He desired her more than ever, but knew that that aspect was now hopeless.

Before long they reached his selected campsite. "I will untie you, if—"

"No. Unless you promise."

He sighed, and went about the business of making a fire and preparing a meal. He was afraid she might refuse to eat, but she squatted and sat on the ground, leaning back against a tree trunk, and when he brought her a piece of meat and held it up, she bit into it. "I will free your hands, if—"

"No."

So he fed her, and held a jar of water for her to drink, and ate and drank himself. Then, feeling the fullness, he needed to urinate, and realized that she would need to also. "I can free you for—"

"Just hold the jar."

So he held the jar close between her parted thighs, up under her skirt, and she streamed into it. The sight had the usual effect on him, so that he couldn't urinate immediately.

She glanced up at him mischievously. "I can't hold a jar for you, but I can enable you to piss. Take off your loincloth."

"The only way I could do it soon is not—"

"Yes it is." She parted her knees farther. "Do it."

"But you are tied!"

"And must remain so. But you can hold me, and get into me."

"Melee, I am trying to preserve your life, not rape you!"

"There is no rape. I want you."

"But I thought—"

"That I would be angry, and refuse your desire?"

"Yes."

"I am angry, but not at you. At myself, for so misjudging you, and putting your life in peril. I would not have done this for all the world, had I realized the mischief I was making."

"You acted as you thought appropriate," he said. "I am the one who did not."

"Dillon, I set out to seduce you from the start. How could you resist?"

"I should have, nevertheless."

"Do you know why I fled over the mountain, when there was nothing there for me?"

"It seemed strange to me, and Bata did not understand either."

"Because I wanted to be with you again, alone. I knew you would pursue me and catch me. And it worked. Here I am, traveling with you."

Dillon's jaw dropped. "You did it—to be caught?"

"To have more time to seduce you. As I did. I desired you, Dillon. I still do. I love you."

He thought he had misheard. "What?"

"I love you."

"You can't! You are a princess."

"And you are a good man."

But he was catching on to her ways. "And you are a schemer. You think I will bow to your will if I think you love me."

"No. I think you will bow to my will if *you* love *me*."

"So you are trying to—" He paused, and tackled it more sensibly. "Promise me the truth, Melee."

She sighed, and laughed. "I should never have taught you smartness about women. The truth is I do not love you, but I do want your love. I thought seduction would give me power over you. I was terribly mistaken. But now I think love may do it. Could you kill me if you loved me?"

"I can't kill you anyway."

"But if you knew that your death would precipitate my own, because though my feeling fell short of love, my remorse would leave me no other way out? I do have some honor. It is more devious than yours, but it exists."

"I must do what I must do," he said seriously. "My personal feelings do not matter."

"I am sick of that phrase!" she exclaimed. "Feelings matter most of all."

He looked at her, and felt unmanly tears at his own eyes. "Melee, I care, but—"

"Then take me! Take me now. I give you the gift of myself, and of the love I could feel for you, if you live."

All that was beyond his competence of the moment. "I will take you," he agreed, removing his loincloth to expose his taut erection.

"Yes! Do not wait."

He approached her, and she spread her knees wide and lay back. He got on her, and she kissed him avidly. He drove into her and erupted, kissing her, feeling her tongue against his, her breasts pushing up against his chest. It was as intense as the first time had been.

As he faded, he realized that her position had to be quite uncomfortable. "Your hands are bound under you!"

"Yes, they hurt now. But there was no other way. I had to have your love."

He got off her and drew her to a sitting posture. "I must free you." He reached for her hands.

"No! You must not."

"But Melee—"

"Give me your promise."

That stopped him. "I hate this."

She smiled sardonically. "And here I thought it was great passion."

"It *is* passion. You have given me experience that would fulfill a full lifetime. But to possess you like this, bound and hobbled—"

"It is different," she agreed. "But since I can not be trusted, so it must be. Only, if you would, this last night—"

"Anything within my power, as you understand it."

"Stay with me. Now, close. Your arms around me."

"Gladly." He embraced her, and kissed her.

"You asked for it slowly, but this was not," she said.

"I forgot," he agreed, embarrassed.

"But I will give it to you. If you enter me now, it will be slow."

"Yes," he said, realizing.

"But one favor, first."

"What?"

"Go piss. That was after all the point of this."

He laughed, covering his embarrassment. Then he stood, walked to the bush, and relieved himself. After he had done it, he realized that he had not even thought to do it away from her sight. Her hand had guided his urination; there was no secret to keep from her.

But there was one thing to establish. "It was a pretext, not the point," he said as he returned to her.

"Of course. After this you will need no pretext."

"And with you, the distinction between pissing and passion becomes indistinct." They both laughed, for it was true in ways others would not understand.

"Now turn me away from you, on my side, and cup me," she said. "I think I can be comfortable, that way."

"But your hands—"

"Just don't press them hard."

So he set her up as she asked, on her right side, and lay behind her, his legs against her bent legs, his belly against her crossed wrists. He was becoming erect again, but without full force, so was not ready to enter.

"Take my breasts," she said. So he reached over her side with his left arm and took her left breast in his hand and stroked it. That strengthened his erection.

Then she moved her hands, and took his penis, surprising him. Her wrists remained bound, but one hand was in position to find him there. She gently massaged him.

He kissed her shoulder and the back of her neck, where her hair fell away. "That feels almost like love," she murmured.

"I must not love you."

"Why not? If you live, you will enjoy it, and if you die, it won't matter."

It took him a moment to fathom the flaw. "You want me to love you, so I won't anger you by telling. So I will live a lie."

"You won't anger me by telling. You will grieve me. I beg you again—"

"No." He hesitated, feeling her body stiffen. "Should I withdraw?"

She relaxed. "No! If I must see you die, I want as much of you as I can have, now while you live." She squeezed his member again. "And I think you are coming to life."

"Slowly," he agreed. "Remember, I have possessed you three times already today."

"Not really."

"Not?"

"*I* have possessed *you*. You never had true self-will. You couldn't help yourself."

"That could be true. I have never been so mad for any woman before."

"And so it was I who did it. You were merely the chip on the surface of the river."

She had interesting ways of seeing things. Meanwhile, her hand on his member was making it increasingly difficult for him to think clearly. "I suppose."

"So you agree," she said, inhaling so that her breast filled his hand more perfectly. That, too, was compelling more attention.

"Yes."

"Then you have not touched me," she said victoriously. "I touched you—more intimately, more forcefully, but it was my doing."

Oops. "I didn't mean—"

"Therefore you have nothing to tell Grandmother."

But his attention had not yet wandered that far afield. "You told me that this I had to do for myself, and I did it. The blame is mine."

"And when we fell off the high bank into the pool, unnerving me so that I had to have you, the blame was yours?"

"Yes. I should have been more careful."

"You are determined to die."

"I can't blame you for being angry. Had I been stronger and more careful, this would not have happened."

"Not angry!" she repeated. "Desperate. You are surely the finest lover I have had, and I am losing you."

That sparked a curiosity. "How many lovers have you had?"

"Does it matter?"

"No, if you do not wish to tell."

"Three. Two, perhaps."

That further piqued his interest. "There is doubt?"

"Three if I count Grout."

"Who?"

"The man I tended, four years ago."

He remembered. "But you were a child."

"I was twelve. My breasts were budding. I already dreamed of embracing my big sister's husband, not that he ever noticed me. I used to try to show him my legs, which were better than my little breasts, wishing he would be tempted and come to me in the night. But of course I knew that would never happen. He was a completely honorable man. Even if he noticed me, he would never betray his wife. That's what made such dreaming safe. So I was ready to discover sex. And here was this other man I could play with."

"But he was a sick man."

"Whom I got to urinate. But I was curious, so when he couldn't sleep I calmed him by massaging his member, like this." She squeezed more authoritatively. "And in time it spouted, sending out several pulses of slippery whitish fluid with an interesting smell. I was much intrigued. Did that count?"

"I think not. It did not spout in you."

"Two, then. What of you?"

"I would rather not."

"I told you. You must tell me."

In his distracted state, the logic seemed valid. "Two."

"What of the first?"

"I was twelve. She was grown, the mother of many. I had delivered a turkey I had hunted, repayment for chili peppers she had given us. Her family was out, and she was bored, so she paused from her work and asked me if I would like to learn something. I thought it would be some funny story, so I agreed. Instead she said she would show me what my penis was for. I thought I already knew, but my ambition had been limited. She held it as you are doing, and licked it with her tongue. In a moment it was large, and then she had me lie on her and put it in the opening in her cleft. I was amazed; I had not known there was such a place for it. She had to take it in her hand and steer it, and then it sank down inside most readily. When it was as deep as it would go, she had me pull it back some, then thrust again, several times, until it—you know."

"I know." Melee guided his member down and into her, then caught at his hips with her fingers.

"She wasn't even pretty," he continued. "She was fat. But ever after, that was where my penis most wanted to be. And she knew it. It was just so nice, deep inside her. I made pretexts to deliver other things to her, and she always took me in. I think she enjoyed playing with an innocent stripling."

"So do I."

He laughed. "And you have been doing it since we met."

"My second was much more straightforward," she said. "I was thirteen, and for a time was coincidentally alone with a priest of the region. He was looking at me, and I realized that he was seeing me as a woman. Flattered, I asked him if he wanted me. He said no one was allowed to touch me. I asked if that meant that I would die untouched, and he said no, I would one day marry. I asked what about if I didn't marry, and he said I could still touch others. That was how I learned. I said I wanted to try it. So he sat on the floor, with his loincloth pulled aside and his penis pointing up, and I didn't even lift my skirt; I sat on him. We both knew that we could be discovered at any time, which added to the excitement. I was dry, and didn't know exactly how to guide him, so there was some fumbling before we found the place. He spouted almost before I got him in, and he wasn't in far. That was just as well, because it was uncomfortable. Then he left quickly, and I washed. It wasn't much, but it had satisfied my curiosity of the moment, and whetted my appetite for more. At least at that point I knew exactly what went where, and what it did there. Later I got a young man, who had no status and did not dare tell me no, so I could tell him to stop at any point and he did, so I never needed to suffer discomfort, and with him I learned the mechanics of full penetration and male fulfillment, as well as how to gain better satisfaction myself. I found that when he had spouted once, he could not do so again immediately, though soon he could get hard. So if I got him in me then, I could in time gain my own rapture. That was a marvelous discovery."

Dillon found her narration fascinating. He was ready to climax at any time, but not so urgent that he had to, so he remained inside her without moving. "My second was a girl. She was ten, and curious, and when we were alone she asked me. She had no breasts and wasn't beautiful, but the thought of showing someone else excited me. The woman had shown me about oil, when a woman wasn't ready, to make it slippery, so I put some on her clean little cleft and on my member, and went in slowly so it wouldn't hurt her. She was much smaller and tighter and I had to push hard, and I kept asking if it pained her, and she kept saying no, and then I gushed in that taut crevice and it had a power and sharpness lacking in what I had done before. I think it did hurt her, but she wouldn't admit it. She said she liked it, and maybe she did, because she kept coming back on other days, just as I had with the older woman."

"She had a crush on you," Melee said. "She wanted you to like her, and that was how. A woman expects pain, the first time; it is part of the initiation experience."

"But she was a child."

"She was a woman child. Women learn these things younger than men do, because they want to conceive."

"Maybe so. I wouldn't have looked at her, but for that. But under her skirt it was great. I would close my eyes and pretend she had breasts. She came back for a year, being my lover. We never spoke of it elsewhere, but we liked being lovers. And she did get better, learning how to make it easy. She became looser, and I think larger, but was always firm. She kept asking me to kiss her. Then she was sold in marriage elsewhere, and I never saw her again."

"You had surely taught her how to make her marriage work."

"Actually she taught me as much as I taught her, after the first time. I liked being inside her—I would have liked being inside any woman—so I asked her what pleased her, and she told me as she discovered things. It was mostly the kissing; I think nobody else ever kissed her. She preferred it slow, with a lot of hugging first. And she liked words, like 'love' and 'need.' She wanted me to talk love to her before I went in, and when I did, she was warmer and wetter and it was better."

"Yes. She was definitely a woman. You were fortunate. Talk to me, Dillon."

"But I can't say those words to you."

"Why not?"

"Because they might be—" He stalled, not able to say what most readily came to mind.

"Because they might be true?"

"Yes," he agreed, abashed.

"Since what hour do you refuse to speak the truth?"

She had him there. "I can't love you, Melee. You want to corrupt me."

"I want you to *live*. I will do anything to make you agree to live. Say the words."

"But you are not saying them."

"Because I can't be trusted. You would know they were false. I don't want to be false to you."

"So you do care, some." As Bata had said.

"More than some. Dillon, if I truly love you, will you live?"

"You mean, if I knew your love wasn't pretense? I don't know."

"If I love you, and you die, then you will have hurt me more cruelly than any other way you could have. You are pledged to safeguard me from harm. So will you live?"

She was shaking his resolve. But she had not won the case. "I can not believe that you love me. You just want me to live, so that you need feel no guilt."

"The two are connected. How can you be sure my love isn't true?"

He thought about it. "I don't know."

"I will promise."

"Not to kill yourself? But I haven't promised not to tell."

"Take me, Dillon. Then free me. I will not harm myself. I love you."

The need to finish, barely quiescent, became too strong to resist. The words did have power, and they heated his head and his loin. He thrust, and his seed drove into her as she nudged her soft bottom back to meet it. He felt her reacting, inside, and her breathing quickened. This was the third, no the fourth time he had possessed her this day, and though all were different, this one was special. Slow was better than fast, because of the words and the feeling. "Oh Melee," he gasped. "I love you!"

"I love you," she echoed. Then she echoed his unexpressed thought. "You took me on the bank, and in the water, and bound, and slow, and the first was memorable because it was the first, after my fright, and the second because of the novelty of the water, and the third because of the innovation of being bound, but this is the one I will most remember, though we did not kiss."

"I kissed you."

"On my neck and shoulder, and that was nice. But I did not kiss you. Normally I need the kiss to truly feel it, as your little girl did. But the words, and the shared experiences gave meaning. We know each other better now."

He lay for a while longer, holding her breast, subsiding deliciously. Then, without quite disengaging, he reached down to untie her hands. She moved them clear, flexing her wrists, and he hugged her closely.

When he was ready, she rolled over and kissed him. "Take the rope from my neck," she said.

"But your hands are free now."

"You must do it. You must free me."

She took her symbolism seriously. So he removed it, then undid the hobble. "Remember, you promised," he reminded her.

"And I keep my promises. May I have my knife back too?"

"Yes."

She fetched it. "You know, if I killed myself, it would not have changed anything for you, since you already plan to die."

"But I do not matter. It is you who must live."

"I will live," she agreed. "But so must you."

He shrugged.

"I love you," she repeated.

"You are making me hurt."

"I will make you hurt worse. How can I prove my love?"

"I don't think you can. You will lie to me, to make me live."

She sighed. "Yes, I am lying. But I can lie more. I will tell Grandmother it is all a lie. That you never touched me."

"She will know the truth."

She sighed. "She will know the truth," she agreed.

He looked around, realizing that it was now completely dark. "We must sleep."

"Together."

"Together," he agreed. He got the blankets, then picked up his loin-cloth.

"Naked, tonight," she said. "If you wake and find me on you and around you, do not push me off. That issue is settled."

"But how can you want more, after all this?"

"I want your love."

Without giving him her own. He let that be. They lay down, and she pressed herself against him. He stroked her hair. "I think I am glad you destroyed me," he said. "All I knew before was a fat woman and a child. I think I would never have known one like you."

"Surely so," she agreed. She reached down and took hold of his penis, gently retaining it. Then she slept.

He lay thinking for a while. He knew he would die, but it didn't bother him intensely. It was the price of Melee, and he had known it when he first took her. "I love you," he whispered into her soft hair, thinking she could not hear. But she must have, because she squeezed his penis in response.

He woke later, and she was indeed on top of him, fitting him into her and kissing him. This time he let it be, and she settled back to sleep, connected. Apparently this was a closeness she desired. Certainly it was pleasant enough.

In the morning she was on her stomach and his hand was on her bottom. Was it chance, or had he put it there—or had *she* put it there? It hardly mattered. He squeezed the mound, and felt her answering flex.

"Oh, Melee, I wish I could live," he said.

She shifted her head. "I have prayed to the Jaguar, and been answered. It will intercede. You will live."

Could it be true? Dillon did not have experience with prayers, but she was of a class far removed from his. Maybe she could solicit the Jaguar's intercession.

"Do you desire me?" she asked.

"Always."

"I possessed you in the night."

"I know."

"Lie there. I will do it again."

He lay there, and she mounted him. "Lie still and I will have my will of you."

"It is my will."

She fitted herself to him and began to move, not strongly, but enough. Her breasts slid slightly, tantalizingly. They tickled him exquisitely. He brought up his hands to touch them, and she did not object. She kissed him. "There are so many ways to do it, and we will try them all."

"Now?"

She laughed. "In the coming year. I love you."

They had been over the business of the lie. There was no point in rehearsing it. "I love you."

She gradually increased her pace, until he swelled and burst inside her again, in the midst of a kiss. Once again it was different, this ecstasy in stillness.

She shuddered, and then lay still. "This way, I feel the joy too," she said. "I am glad to make you thrill, but sometimes I like it for myself."

"Teach me how, and I will always do it for you."

"Already you are resigned to living."

"But I will tell Bata."

"You will tell, but the Jaguar will change it."

He doubted that, but he much preferred to have her believe it. He was finishing out his life in the most pleasant way possible.

At last they got up, washed, dressed, ate, and resumed their trek. The closer they got to the lake, the tighter Dillon's chest became. Finally he stopped walking. "Melee, I don't believe. I think I do love you, but I must tell. Please forgive me."

She kissed him. "I forgive you. I love you. You will see."

He embraced her closely. "And if I die, it will be loving you."

Suddenly she melted. "Dillon! I beg of you—don't tell! Don't tell! Take my body, take my tears, take anything, but don't tell."

So she did not truly believe. "All I need is your love."

"You have it! Dillon, I will run away with you!"

Yet again, she had astonished him. "But that can't be."

"Yes it can! We can run and hide. I will be a peasant girl for you. I don't want to be a princess, if it means your death. No one will be able to find us."

"I will not deny you your heritage. You can never be a peasant," he said sadly. Then he resumed walking.

"Dillon—" But she saw it was useless. After a moment she firmed her jaw and walked beside him.

They reached the house together. Bata stood at her door. "Speak," she said. "I can't see you."

"We have returned," he said.

"Returned," Melee echoed brokenly.

Bata turned to her. "My dear, what happened?"

"Spare him, Grandmother! I love him."

The old woman turned to Dillon.

He nodded. "I touched her."

Bata's expression grew grim. "I must talk to you."

"I know. I betrayed my trust."

"Grandmother! Please! Anything. Only let him live." Melee was openly crying, a rarity for her.

"Alone," the old woman said firmly. She turned and entered the house.

"I love you," Dillon whispered. Her profession of love might be a lie, but his was not. Then he followed Bata inside.

Bata took her favorite chair. "Sit down, Dillon."

He sat at her feet.

"What have you to say?"

"I touched her. I must die."

"You couldn't just run away with her." It was a bitter statement.

"I love her. But I must die."

"And does she love you?"

"I think she feels a little of it. But it is because she fears for me."

"It is because you are worthy. You mastered her."

"She beat me every time. She mastered me."

"But she could not break your honor. So you won."

"I should not have touched her."

"She set out to seduce you. No man living could withstand that, if she had time with him. Remember, I taught her, though I pretended ignorance of her dalliances with the priest and slave youth. I made sure she knew how to handle a man. Any man. It isn't sex so much as continual suggestion. When did it finally happen?"

"Yesterday, at the falls pool."

She shook her head. "I thought she'd have you before you crossed the mountain pass. You are truly heroic."

"One more day, and I would have made it."

"You fool! She would have had at you for a year! You never had a chance."

"But you would have stopped her."

"No. I would have let her."

He stared at her. "Bata—did you want me dead?"

"No, dear boy. I wanted you married. And now it shall be.".

He continued to stare, baffled. "Married?"

"Swear secrecy."

He raised his hand. "I swear."

"You are the man we chose for Melee to marry. But we could not tell her. Or you, for she would worm it out of you."

"But I am common!"

"Listen closely. Badu is my son-in-law. He married my daughter, and became chief. The line goes through the females, not the males. That is why Melee is so valuable. Her refusal to marry a prince has put the kingdom into deep jeopardy, for her father is dying."

"Dying!"

"She had either to marry a prince who could bring power to support the kingdom, or a peasant who could hide her in anonymity. For the new powers will seek to kill her, to be sure of their line. Since she would not marry, we had to go the second route. I recommended you, and Badu trusted my judgment and made the priests issue the writ. But Melee must not know. If she learns—"

"She will refuse," he said.

"Therefore I charge you not to tell her. When she demands to marry you, you must go with her to the capital and obtain her father's reluctant agreement. Then you can marry her. But if she learns, all will be lost—including her life as well as yours."

"I will not tell," he agreed, awed.

"Now I will tell her that I have postponed judgment until my old mind can come to a conclusion. That will give her time to dazzle you into submission. Do not yield too easily, or she will suspect. Do you understand?"

"I understand, Grandmother."

"Enough. Now we must go to her."

Melee was waiting. "Girl, you have done much irresponsible mischief," Bata told her severely. "You may have destroyed my favorite young man. But there may be a way out. I am postponing my decision until I know whether it is possible to save him."

Melee looked up with sudden hope. "Grandmother—what way?"

Bata snorted. "Nothing I would tell you, you disreputable gamine! Now go away while I ponder."

"But what of Dillon, while you decide?"

"He has plenty of work to do, thanks to the loss of time chasing after you." Bata turned and reentered her house.

Melee turned to Dillon. "She didn't tell me to stay away from you."

"I do have work," he said gruffly, walking away.

She pursued him. "Is she sparing you just long enough to catch up on that work?"

He paused. Could it be? Could Bata have told him a story, to give him hope, so that she could have his help until she could get a replacement? No, he couldn't believe that. Bata had never lied to him. "No."

"But you aren't sure. Dillon, I know she likes you, and wants to spare you. She is giving you opportunity to run away."

"She knows I will not."

"You're impossible!"

He walked to the storage shed and picked up a covered basket and a pair of gloves. "The toads are coming into season. I must forage for them."

"The magic toads? I will help you."

He shrugged, and walked toward the canoes.

She grabbed another pair of gloves and followed. "Dillon, this morning you said you loved me. Now you won't talk to me. What did she say to you? Did she forbid you to be near me?"

"No." What could he tell her?

"So it makes no difference now. You have touched me. You can touch me again a hundred times, or never. It is all the same."

"It is all the same," he agreed. "As far as others are concerned."

"So touch me! There may be little time remaining."

He wanted to, but was mindful of Bata's warning: not to accede readily. He had to make her pursue him. "This morning I thought I was going to die. Now I don't know."

She nodded. "I thought so too. Now it is changed. So maybe we spoke love under the goad of fear. But I do like you, Dillon, and respect you, and want you to survive. You have made me cry. I don't do that often. Not when it's real. What can I do to help you?"

So her passion for him had abated after the crisis passed. His interest in her remained high, but the decision was not his to make. He had to win her true love. He doubted he could do that by indulging in constant sexual passion with her. Probably good hard work was best; she would be impressed, or bored, and that would bring her to him or drive her away. His future was in her hands, or rather, her feeling. "If you are good at spying toads, that will help."

"I will try."

They got in the canoe, and he paddled out onto the lake. The best place for the toads was some distance from the farther bank, at dusk.

"We are back in the canoe," she said, paddling in the center. "I like it."

So did he. But did he dare admit it?

She took his silence for negation. "Dillon, I'm sorry! I wanted to seduce you, but I had no idea of the cost. I can't blame you for being angry. But I don't know how I can undo it."

She could marry him. But he couldn't tell her that. "If I had been stronger, I would have resisted you."

"If there is a way to save you, I will find it," she said. "But until I do— can't we be friends?"

He didn't answer, though his silence hurt him.

"Would it make you feel better to hit me?" she asked. "Punish me, Dillon! Do what you must. But don't deny me."

This was becoming too painful. He had to speak. "Melee, I am not angry with you. I don't want to punish you. I would rather love you."

"Then love me!" She shipped her paddle and turned to face him. "Here, now! Take me. Anything you want." She lay down in the center, spreading her legs toward him.

Desire surged, but he resisted. "I spoke of love, not sex."

"But sex is love's most ardent expression. Dillon, please!" She gazed pleadingly at him.

Should he do it? Or would that merely ease her guilt?

"Dillon, please!" she repeated. Her eyes were wet again. "I have no more to offer." That was surely the truth: sex was as close as she could come to love.

He could not resist her. He shipped his own paddle and moved toward her. He got on top of her, and she clasped him and kissed him eagerly.

And so they did it in the rocking canoe, and it was different yet again. She clung to him after he subsided. But she did not say she loved him. It seemed she was done with lying to him.

"Dillon, I have your penis but not your mind. What more can I do for you?"

"You can love me!" he exclaimed before he thought.

"But I am a fickle creature who loves no one. And what if you die?"

"I would rather die after being loved by you, than after not being loved." She sighed. "You want too much."

"I know." He got off her and returned to his place.

"But I will try," she decided. "If my love is the penalty for destroying you, I will try to pay it."

That was hardly the way he wanted it. But he couldn't say so. So he resumed paddling, and after a moment, so did she.

It took about three hours to cross the broad lake, and they were tired. Dillon knew that they both should simply have rested after their arduous trips across the mountain pass, but he had been unable to think simply. Maybe getting tired, and sleeping well, were what he needed.

"We won't find them at night," he said. "Tomorrow will do."

"Here we are, camping again," she remarked, smiling. When he did not respond with a smile, she came to him. "Please, Dillon. Tell me what will please you. I will even sleep by myself, if you prefer; it's warm enough. I can't stand to have you aloof."

He was living a lie, and he hated it. So he decided to abate it to the extent he could. "Melee, Bata told me something, and swore me to secrecy. I know why she spared me, and I can't tell you. If I am diffident, it is not because I find any fault in you. I wish I could please *you*, and I don't know how."

Her eyes narrowed. "You know? And won't tell me?"

He nodded. "So I have no anger at you. But you may have it for me."

She came to him and put her arms around him. "You know I will worm it out of you, in time, for I can't abide defiance."

"You must not, lest you destroy us."

"Again." She squeezed him. "I should not have seduced you physically. Now I must not do it mentally." She smiled. "But with that assurance, can we be as before?"

"We were opposing each other!"

"Yes! It was glorious. The thrill of the chase—I love it. Let us make this another chase. You know something. I want to learn it. So I will try to get it from you, and you will resist. So we have reason to fight. Only this time you must hold out longer."

"Melee, this is no game! You put my life in jeopardy once; must you do it again?"

"It is the way I am. I am not your passive dull peasant woman; I must thrill to the chase. Would you have me otherwise?"

And once again she had surprised him. She was indeed no peasant woman, and she excited him because of it. "No. You are more like a jaguar than a sloth. But your embrace is deadly."

"What is more beautiful than a deadly jaguar?"

"Nothing," he admitted. "But I would not sleep in the embrace of one."

"Nor would one embrace you without disemboweling you. But on the mental level, these are the stakes."

"These are the stakes," he agreed. She was right: the idea of engaging in another contest with her was powerfully alluring.

She stepped back two paces, and caught her skirt in both hands, lifting it only a little. "Tell me, and I will show you this."

"No."

She lifted the skirt part way. "Here is part of what you will see. Tell me."

"No."

She lifted it the rest of the way. "Tell me, and you can have this." She moved her knees, opening her thighs.

"No."

She frowned. "I see you are proof against my charms. But suppose I make you love me?"

"I already love you."

She shook her head. "Not enough, for you will not tell me." She dropped her skirt. "You have missed your chance, and may you long regret it. We must eat."

It was foolish, but he did feel real regret. He had possessed her so many times in the past day and night, yet desired more. Still, he had said what he had to, and given her a basis to relate to him. He realized that he had loved the temptations she had offered on the river trip, and on the mountain trip; now they had a similar framework. She would never give over as long as she lacked the secret. All he had to do was keep it.

He made a fire, and she used the supplies in the canoe to make a meal. She sat cross-legged opposite him, her skirt lifted by her knees so that the flickering firelight illuminated her inner thighs not quite far enough. The sight gave him an erection.

"Be fair," she said. "Take off your loincloth so I can be as tempted by you as you are by me."

He didn't argue. He stood, removed it, and sat again. She nodded approvingly. "I wonder how long I can prevent you from pissing?"

"Be fair," he said. "You must not piss before I do."

"That's fair," she agreed. "Who pisses first loses." She paused, considering. "But that means I must make you flaccid instead of hard."

"So I must not let you make me flaccid before you piss."

"This will be a hard night," she said with mock resignation. Dillon agreed, for he was already uncomfortably bloated.

When the meal was done, they brought out the blankets. She removed her skirt. "Naked, together, and touching," she decided.

What was she up to? "That will keep me safe."

"But the other can't stop what one does."

"But you could hit me with a paddle!"

She reconsidered. "Then the other can say no."

That seemed safe. "Agreed."

She took hold of his penis and began to massage it. He started to say no, for she could quickly make him jet, but thought of an alternative. There was a game he had played with the young girl that had had a special effect. He reached down and tickled her cleft with a finger.

She laughed and squirmed, squeezing her legs closed, pinning his hand. "Don't do that! I can't stand to be tickled there."

"Are you saying no?"

"No! I mean, I'm not saying no." For then he would say it too.

"Then don't close your legs."

She sighed and parted them again, giving him access. She increased her effort on his member, plainly knowing what she was doing. She was laughing, and not from mirth, as his fingers tickled her mercilessly. But she kept her legs apart, and squeezed his member with almost painful vigor.

But he had the advantage, and in a moment the tickling compelled her performance. "You toad!" she cried as she threw off the blankets and urinated on him.

He laughed, and thrust his member into her before she finished. Bathed by a puddle of hot urine, he climaxed within her. It was one more quite different experience.

"So you won," she said, kissing him. "That time." She grabbed his member as it subsided, and rubbed it, forcing his own urination, which splattered on her.

Then they went to the lake and immersed themselves, laughing. Piss and love: it was their way. They set up the blankets at a new site and lay down together, now craving neither urination nor sex.

"Dillon, you're good," she murmured as she closed her eyes. "But I won't play that game again unless you tell me."

"I love your games," he replied. "I wish I could play them all my life."

"You may well do that, if you don't survive long."

"Then we must play them all quickly."

"After we get some sleep."

He was more than ready. "I love you, though I die for it," he whispered.

Her body stiffened. "You say this, with neither piss nor passion driving you. But will you tell?"

"No."

"Then you lie about love."

He wasn't sure about that, for his definitions differed from hers. "Will you say you love me?"

"Dillon, if I loved you, I would make no demands of you."

"So it will be true love only when you don't ask my secret and I do answer."

"That must be it."

She took hold of his penis—it seemed to be her mode of possession—and he put a hand on one breast. They slept.

In the morning they searched for the toads. There were frogs all over, but not the toads they sought: the ones whose skin yielded the substance that gave men bright visions. "I thought the season was right," Dillon said. "But it must be still too early for them."

"Maybe our game annoyed them, and they hid."

"Toads urinate all the time when handled," he said. "They should understand."

"Maybe we forgot to pray to the Frog Goddess."

"I did forget!" he said, appalled. "No wonder they hid."

"It is my fault. I distracted you."

"I don't think so. I never thought of it at all."

"How could you think of anything but me?"

She had a point, again. He remained obsessed with her.

They returned to the canoe and paddled back across the lake.

So the time passed. Melee helped him in all his chores, and played games with him, and seduced him so often that there was no counting the times, and it seemed impossible that any time in his life could have been happier. She seemed to feel that every sexual act brought him closer to love, and therefore her victory, and it was possible she was right. But it was her love that was needed for the final settlement.

Without warning one night she woke and sat up. "That's it!" she exclaimed.

"What, do you love me?" he asked sleepily.

"I must, for I have your baby in my belly."

"What?" Suddenly he was wide awake.

"You don't understand how it happened?" she inquired archly.

"I never thought of it. Melee, you can't have my baby!"

"Yes I can. And that is the answer. Now I must marry you."

She had thought of it! But he dared not accept it immediately. "Melee, you are a princess. You must marry a prince. I am just a diversion."

"But I love you. For I have conceived by you."

That was her definition? "But I am common."

"If I marry you," she said firmly, "you must live. For a married woman can be touched by her husband. And you will be common no longer. That is what Grandmother was hoping for."

"Bata wanted this?" He knew she did, but acted confused.

"Yes. If you touched me, you had to die—unless I married you. And I will marry you, for I have your baby. You will live."

"I will live," he agreed, feeling a great relief. She never questioned his acquiescence, nor did she need to.

"But Grandmother could not tell me to do it, for that would implicate her. It had to be my decision. And it is. I will tell Father that I have chosen, and it must be you. He will have to accede, lest I humiliate him by bearing a bastard baby."

She had come so close to the truth, without quite getting the whole of it. "I love you, Melee."

"And I love you." She lay down and kissed him. Then, hesitantly: "Is it all right if we don't have sex, right now?"

"Whatever you want is all right," he agreed.

"I'm afraid the baby might change its mind. I don't want to lose it." Then she settled back to sleep.

Dillon lay awake for some time. Thus unexpectedly had Bata's ploy worked! Melee would marry him, preserving his life—and she had not caught on to the rest of it. But she might think to ask tomorrow, and he could not afford to answer. That could make her angry.

In the morning they went to Bata. "Grandmother, I have figured out the way. I will marry Dillon."

"But child, he is a commoner!" the old woman protested.

"And I never wanted a prince. I think I was saving myself for him. I have his child within me, and I will bear it, with him or without him. Give me your blessing."

Bata nodded. "It is not me you must persuade, but your father. You may not marry without his consent."

"I know it. But he will more likely give it if you support it."

"You are sure you want this?"

"Yes."

Bata glanced at Dillon. "And does he agree?"

"Of course he agrees! How could he not?"

The old woman smiled. "But did you ask him?"

Melee paused, surprised. "I suppose I should. She turned to Dillon. "Can you stand to marry me?"

Dillon laughed. "How could I decline so eloquently phrased a proposal?"

"You couldn't. See, Grandmother—he agrees."

"So I see. Then you have my blessing. I know he is a good man. Were I fifty years younger, I would never let you have him."

"Fifty?"

Bata grimaced. "Sixty, then. To make me your age."

"If you had wanted him, you would have seduced him yourself."

"And ruined him for you? I think not."

Then they all laughed. But Bata shot Dillon a warning look: it wasn't over yet. He had to keep the secret.

"Now that you have decided, do not delay," Bata warned. "Your father is ill. He suffers sieges of the fever, and they are getting worse."

"I know. But Father always gets through. He's tough."

They packed the canoe and set off for the capital city. Melee remained diffident about sex. "But there are other ways, Dillon. I can satisfy you without disturbing the baby."

"That baby makes you love me. I don't want to disturb him either."

"I think she will be beautiful, like me."

They camped at night on the bank, for Melee no longer wanted to play games with urine. She remained demure, showing him nothing special. But she did share the blanket with him, and did alleviate his ardor in an alternate manner, using her mouth. She was acting much more like a prospective mother than a wild woman, and he appreciated this side of her too.

In the morning, Dillon studied the banks of the river. "Someone has passed, going upstream."

"You can see traces on the water?"

"Under it. There's a gouge in the bottom, where a paddle wielded too strongly struck. He must have been in a hurry, to be moving before dawn."

"Some message for Grandmother, maybe. She will handle it."

"Yes." But he wondered what could be so urgent. However, they had an urgent mission of their own, and couldn't delay to check on something else. So they resumed their travel downstream.

They reached the great sea, and in due course the proper river. Then the paddling became harder, though Melee did her share. They took their time, because he did not want her to strain herself.

In several more days they were close to the capital city. "I hope Father doesn't give me trouble," Melee said pensively. "He did want me to marry a prince."

"Maybe he was resigned to your refusal."

"Resigned," she agreed. "In fact, he might even—" She froze. "Why, that treacherous lizard! He set this up!"

Dillon was afraid to comment. But he could not get away with silence. She turned on her seat, facing him. *"What is your secret?"*

"I can't—"

"If you love me, Dillon—"

"Melee, I do! But—"

"If you will not speak it, neither will you lie about it. I challenge you to deny it. Did my father arrange for me to marry you?"

Dillon did not answer.

"If you don't deny it, you admit it," she said ominously. "That is the secret Grandmother told you. That is why she spared you. Not just in the hope, but in the knowledge. You knew all along!"

"Not all along," he said lamely.

"But when she talked to you, after our return, when you told her you had touched me."

"Yes," he said faintly.

"And you wouldn't tell me!"

"I couldn't."

"Because then I wouldn't marry you."

"Oh, Melee—"

She lifted the paddle. "I will knock you into the water! May there be a crocodile close!"

Dillon set down his paddle, letting the canoe drift backward, and spread his arms, inviting the blow.

She hesitated. "No, a crocodile is too good for you. I will have you executed instead. My father will have to do it, when I tell him you touched me. Then I'll shame him in turn by bearing the bastard baby. I will make him pay for his scheming."

The horror of it was that she wasn't joking. She was in such a fury about being deceived that vengeance was the only thing on her mind. She would destroy Dillon, her father, and herself, rather than accept the course others had planned for her. She was beyond reason. She was a wild panther.

"Pick up your paddle," she said grimly. "Take me into town." There was no trace of compassion.

He took the paddle and moved the canoe forward. Melee sat in the front, facing forward, absolutely still. She would not relent. Nothing he could say would sway her. He was doomed.

They reached the dock. Melee got out. She turned briefly to face him. "If you are smart, you will flee now. That will give you a head start before my father's men come after you."

"I will see you safely to your father," he said.

"Please yourself." She turned and marched toward the palace.

Dillon followed. Maybe there had never been a real chance for happiness with her. She would have found out some time, and would have been as angry then, even if already married. She valued her independence more than her welfare. More, even, than love itself.

They came to the palace. A guard met them. "I will see my father," Melee said curtly. "Now."

"Lady, you can not."

"What?"

"Lady, he is dead."

Melee fell back as if struck, her face blank, her eyes staring.

Dillon spoke. "When? How?"

"Ten days ago. He was ill with the fever, and this time he could not overcome it. Did the messenger not summon you for his funeral?"

"The canoe!" Dillon said. "That was the messenger we missed!"

"Well, you are here in time. It is scheduled for tomorrow."

Dillon glanced at Melee, who remained blank and silent. "The princess will be there." He faced her. "Where will you stay the night?"

She turned and shuffled to another building. He stopped at the door, but she reached back and caught his arm, drawing him in with her.

Inside, she stepped into his embrace and wept. Then she drew back and gazed into his face. "It is all meaningless without him. There is no game any more. I will marry you. It was his will." Then she put her head against his shoulder and cried some more.

Dillon held her, not speaking. He did not understand her abrupt shifts of mood, but it seemed he had been redeemed by her father's death. She had been playing a game with her father, too, trying to establish her will over his. Now that Badu was gone, she couldn't fight him or shame him, so she was apologizing by doing his will.

She lay down on the bed, and he lay with her. There was no sex. She cried a while, then drifted into troubled sleep. He held her, unable to assuage her grief. Yet he wondered: she had been ready to shame her father in the worst way, and now she wept for his memory. She had seduced Dillon, and spoken love to him, then been ready to destroy him, and now was accepting his comfort. What was he to make of this?

Yet perhaps there was an answer. Melee did not understand why he put his honor before convenience or love. He did not understand the way she put her games before family or love. Maybe one day they would each come to understand each other's oddities. Until then—it could be a most interesting experience.

After an hour Melee woke. She went to a small chamber where there was a pot for natural functions, used it, then gestured to him. He wasn't used to doing it inside a house, but realized that it was no worse than doing it in a canoe.

There was food in another chamber. They ate cooked beans and sweet potato with honey, and drank berry wine. Then Melee lay down again, requiring Dillon to be with her, and slept with fewer tears.

She was up before dawn. She stripped naked and washed. As the first light came, she got a sharp stone knife and brought it to her head. Dillon watched, alarmed but not speaking. She beckoned him, gave him the knife, and indicated her hair.

Oh. She would sacrifice her loveliness for grief. He took a hank of hair and cut it off. He laid it on the floor, then cut another. In time he had cut it all off, leaving her with a patchwork of oddly cut fur across her head.

Then she took the knife and cut his hair similarly. Normally he wore his head shaved under his headgear, as was the custom among men, but he had never thought of it during his distraction with Melee, and it had grown somewhat. So her cutting of his hair was symbolic rather than significant, and the result would be concealed under his helmet anyway. But by that token he knew that she intended him to be with her at the funeral. He would go along with whatever she wanted, in the hope that she was serious about marrying him.

She donned an elegant dress and shawl, and found a robe for him. Then she got ashes and painted both their faces in streaks. They were ready for the funeral.

They went together. The ceremony was simple: the people of the city gathered, and stood in a great circle around a huge pyre. Most of them had hair similarly cut off. The priest set fire to it, and they all watched as the wrapped body was bathed in flames. Badu had been sent to the other realm.

After that they proceeded with the ritual defacements of the things of Badu's reign, which was now over. Under the supervision of the priests, the craftsmen set about cracking altars from the corners, beheading statues, and scouring steles. No other ruler would use these things; they would join Badu in the other realm.

Then Melee brought Dillon to stand before the huge head statue of Badu. This one was not to be defaced, as it was plainly Badu himself, resplendent in his leather helmet. A number of the other folk followed. A priest came too.

She addressed the statue. "Father, your daughter bows to your will. I, Melee, hereby marry this man Dillon. I will remain with him in this life, and bear his children."

The priest stepped forward with a jug of oil. Dillon and Melee linked fingers, and the priest poured the oil over their hands.

Melee kissed him. "I will make you glad for your patience," she murmured.

"You already have," he said. But he suspected that their relationship had by no means settled down.

The chief town of the Olmec for the years 1200–900 B.C. was at the site now called San Lorenzo. Its name and exact layout are unknown, but it was obviously a ceremonial center with a population of up to one thousand people. The nature of Olmec government is unknown, so what is described here is conjectural. It was probably somewhere between a chiefdom and a kingdom. Thus the ambiguity here: the ruler is a chief, and his daughter a princess. The huge heads were mostly at San Lorenzo, probably representing its succession of chiefs, but some were also in other towns, perhaps indicating their allegiance to the chiefs of San Lorenzo. What is known is that circa 900 B.C. the monuments of San Lorenzo were destroyed or defaced in a ritual manner, and the town was abandoned. The most influential Olmec town then became the one at the site now called La Venta, shown in passing here. Between 400 and 300 B.C. La Venta was similarly defaced and abandoned, and the primacy of the Olmec was over. Most scholars believe that these towns were raided and destroyed by the conquerors, but there is no real evidence of conquest from outside. There could have been a plague that took out the chief and leading officials. So it may be that San Lorenzo faded in power and lost its artisans when its dynasty of chiefs ended, and La Venta assumed the leadership without actual conquest. We just don't know. The defacement of ritual objects could have been an act of respect, sending them "killed" to join the leaders in the other realm. They might also have been treated to take away their spiritual power, which otherwise could be dangerously uncontrolled after the death of the figure to which they were attuned. We of the science age lack proper understanding and respect for the ancient forces of magic, no longer being subject to its rigors. Think of a nuclear power plant being deserted without being properly shut down, to get a notion of the magnitude of their concern.

Human sacrifice was established in all the great central American cultures, beginning, it seems, with the Olmec. Other parts of the world generated meat for human consumption by raising herds of cattle or other large creatures, but in the Americas only dogs were raised commercially for meat. Thus there was a need for more, and so the most prolific and accessible source was utilized: mankind itself. It may have been second only to snook as a source of animal protein for the Olmecs, and would have been much in demand, as it continued to be through the Maya and Aztec cultures.

The Olmec culture was the first approaching our definition of civilization in central America, and its influence extended to Oaxaca to the south, the valley of Mexico to the west, and the Maya to the east. Its actual level of organization is doubtful, but it seems to be the origin of all the great central American civilizations. So while it was no empire, and perhaps not even a kingdom, its significance in this region makes it the mother culture. Yet today the main memory of it is probably its nine-foot-tall statues of human heads.

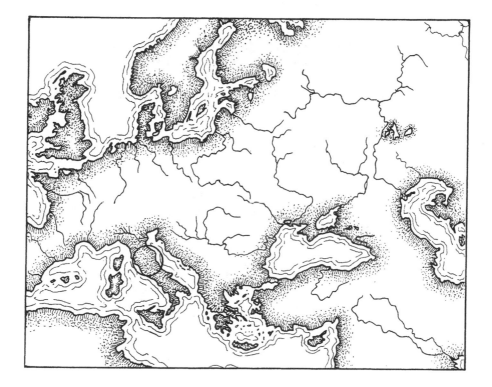

CHAPTER 7

ARROGANCE

Circa 1000 B.C.E. the archaeological bronze age Urnfield complex was becoming the historical Celtic or Keltic culture. (Pronunciation seems to have been "Selt" among the Romans and "Kelt" among the Greeks; either seems correct today, but for convenience, this narrative will use the latter, with matching spelling, thus distinguishing it from the celt "selt" which is a small axelike implement.) It was centered in eastern France and expanded to include most of Europe, with thrusts extending into England, Spain, Greece, and Italy. In the British Isles these peoples became known as the Scots, Picts, Irish, Welsh, and Bretons. There was a similar diversity throughout Europe. They were early ironworkers, and were fierce in war.

Some went into battle naked except for helmets, horrifying their opponents, and some painted their bodies entirely in blue, with faces on abdomen and thighs, and wild decorations everywhere else. They were not politically unified, but consisted of a number of tribes looking for new lands to settle. Thus, in due course, the Kelts encountered the Romans in central Italy. This led to a perhaps surprising interaction in 390 B.C.E.

One might not think of arrogance as an art, but the Romans seem to have made it so throughout their history. They repeatedly got embroiled in what should have been unnecessary complications because of it. This is an early and forceful example. They thought of the Kelts as barbarians, and did not take them seriously. That was a mistake.

PUL spied the three oddly armed strangers and sounded the alarm. He lifted his spear and shield, signaling his men to fall in around him, and went to challenge the party. "Notify the Crow," he snapped to a slave. "The enemy party is here." That was not an insulting reference; "Crow" was the meaning of the name of their leader, and the brash bird was associated with the Keltic war goddess.

The three men came to a halt before Pul's troop. They were garbed in short metal skirts, helmets, breastplates, and greaves, and carried short swords. They were short; none of them came up beyond Pul's nose in height. Their hair was cropped short, and they had no mustaches, in contrast to Pul's own long, braided hair and huge mustache. Overall they did not look very impressive.

"Who are you?" Pul demanded, though of course he knew. They were the officials from the southern city of Rome, coming to sue for peace. They had been expected. Who else would be leaving the gate of the besieged city of Clusium and approaching the Keltic camp?

A translator spoke to the men. In a moment one of them responded, and the translator turned to face Pul. "We are Roman ambassadors. Conduct us to your leader."

Pul didn't like the tone, even translated, but since what they asked was exactly what he was supposed to do anyway, he complied. "Follow me." He shook his bracelets, turned briskly, and marched toward the main Senones camp.

Meanwhile the slave's message had been delivered, and the chief was coming out to meet the party. He wore a robe, as befitted a formal occasion, but warriors stood behind him with their hands on their swords. Beside him stood his own translator, a Kelt who had been enslaved by the Romans and learned their language before escaping.

Pul stood aside and let the ambassadors approach the chief. He assumed a position of attention with his own hand on his sword. One wasn't supposed to actually draw a weapon during negotiations, but to appear to be ready to do so instantly.

"Who are you?" Chief Brennos demanded. His words needed no translation, but the Roman translator nevertheless did so.

The Roman spoke. "Ambassador Quintus Fabius of Rome," the translator said. "Who are you, and what is your business here?"

There was a small stir among the Kelt warriors, for the question was insulting. Who else could it be but the chief? But the chief answered politely enough. "I am Chief Brennos of the Senones tribe, otherwise known as the Crow, here to conquer and plunder the city of Clusium and settle the lands around it with my people."

"Why do you leave your own land and try to settle elsewhere?" the Roman demanded, as if he had any right to know.

Brennos refrained from taking offense at this repeated affront. He replied by repeating the tale every Keltic child knew. The Romans were too dull to realize that he was talking down to them, as one would a child. "Our great King Ambicatos discovered that our people had done so well, and increased their populations so much, that he devised a way to deal with it. He sent each of his sister's sons, along with enough men to make their passage unstoppable, away to whatever country the gods should indicate with omens. Thus Sigoevesis was sent to the Hercynian Forests, while Bellovesos was set upon the road to Italy. We are of the latter people, and we have settled the fertile river valley in the north, and now seek to try suitable regions to the south. It is our destiny."

"There should be peace between the barbarians and the blameless people of Clusium," the Roman replied, seeming not to have heard this reasonable explanation. "Thus peace between the Kelts and the city of Rome. This is the will of the Senate. But if you attack Clusium, then Rome will retaliate in kind, and drive you out of Italy."

There was further restlessness among the Kelts, and Pul's hand tightened on his sword. What arrogance! This stupid Roman was begging for a whipping. But Brennos responded moderately. "We assume that the Romans must be courageous people, because it is to them that the Clusians have turned in their hour of need. Since the Romans have tried to help with an embassy rather than with arms, we Kelts can not reject this offer of peace." Then he came to the essence: "Provided the Clusians cede a part of their superfluous agricultural land for our use."

There was a pause for the translation. Pul would rather simply have fought the city, but realized that if the land the Kelts wanted could be had without a fight, that was easier. There were plenty of good fights to be had elsewhere, after all.

Then the Romans responded. "And what right do the barbarians have to ask such a condition?" the translator demanded. "And what are you doing in Etruria anyway? This is not your territory."

Pul's grip tightened again. Indeed, Brennos had clearly had enough of this attitude. "Our right is in our arms: to the brave belong all things."

"Then you have chosen war," the Romans said, and marched haughtily away. Pul would have liked to cut them down, but they were noncombatants and had to be spared. So he marched with them, through the Keltic forces, treating them like guests rather than enemies. It was the way of honor. Pul did not fully understand it, but knew the protocol. So he and other chiefs surrounded the ambassadors, pushing back the warriors.

The Kelts had formed their lines and prepared to attack the city. They were waiting only for the ambassadors to reach safety within it, before starting the action. But as the gate opened and a column of Etruscans emerged to escort the Romans inside, Quintus Fabius paused and turned back. He shouted at the Kelts, who were in the process of opening their small formation to let the Romans enter that of the Clusians. Evidently he didn't think the Romans were being given enough room. But it was hard to give them very much, because of the press of Kelt warriors who didn't want to be shoved back. In any event, the transfer was almost complete. After that, they could get down to the serious business of fighting.

Then, before they could accede to the ambassador's foolish demand, Quintus suddenly drew his short sword and thrust it at the nearest chieftain, who wasn't even facing him at the moment. The sword plunged into the chief's side, felling him. The Roman yanked it out and stepped into the Clusian formation before Pul or the others could react.

Then a roar of outrage went up from the Keltic ranks. Often disputes could be settled by individual combat, and it was an honorable way. But there had been no challenge, and in any event, ambassadors were not supposed to fight. This was a grievous breach of protocol, as well as a cowardly sneak attack. The warriors surged forward, but the Romans were already in the gate, and the gate was closing.

In a moment the recall horn sounded. What, they were calling off the attack on the city? Right when they should be laying it waste? But Pul and the others had to obey the summons. They retreated from the city and returned to form around the chief.

Brennos was grim. "Clusium did not breach its honor," he said. "The Etruscans did not breach theirs. It was those arrogant Romans. It is Rome we must lay waste."

Then a cheer went up. He was right: the Romans had to pay for this outrage. They would march south that very day.

But now an Elder interceded. "No. The Romans may be uncivilized, but we are not. We must send envoys there first to protest their ambassadors' conduct and demand that Quintus Fabius be surrendered to justice. This is the proper course."

Brennos grimaced, but could not oppose the will of the Elders. So he acted forthrightly. "We will send envoys." He glanced around. "You, Blaze. And you, Grout." He glanced again, his eye falling on Pul. "And you, Pul, to guard them. Go now." He looked at the Elder, in case the man should object, but the Elder simply nodded.

Thus, within the hour, they were on their way, marching south. Blaze was an old man of about fifty, with a huge burn on his forehead, but still spry enough; he had tended fires for the metalsmiths for years, and was known and trusted by all. Grout was younger, but not in as good health; he had suffered an illness years ago and never fully recovered. Still, he was able to move along well enough, so they made reasonable time. They also had an interpreter and guide.

In four days they reached Rome. It was a huge city; Pul had never imagined there could be such an expanse of dwellings in one place. It was across a broad river where there were many craft.

The guide spoke to the guards at the gate, and their party was admitted to the city. Pul tried not to gawk at the throngs of people in togas on the streets, or at the huge stone buildings. There was a constant babble in their weird language of Latin. Pul was glad he couldn't understand any of it; that kept things simple.

In due course they were given a building to stay in, and slaves brought halfway decent food. The guide explained that in two days the Roman Senate would consider their petition. There was nothing to do but wait.

"At least they could have provided a pretty female slave to make the time pass," Pul griped, and the others laughed.

They whiled away the time exchanging stories. It was understood that these would not be repeated to others; this was private man talk. Pul told of the night he had spent with a breathlessly lovely woman who had traveled with him for a while pretending to be his sister, then moved on. "But maybe sometime I'll meet her again," he concluded. "I still dream of her."

Blaze told of the night he had spent with a lovely girl of fourteen he had bought for his son to marry. "And she did marry him," he said. "But she wanted that one night with me, though I was twice her age. I could not resist her. Ever since, I remember the feel of her glorious body against mine, though I shouldn't; my wife is a good woman."

The others nodded. Who, indeed, married or not, could resist a lovely young woman? Then Grout told of his experience with the daughter of a chief he served. "She was just a girl of twelve, but already turning lovely. She was evidently curious about male matters, and no demure flower. She tended me in my bad illness, and when I was too weak to get off the bed, she held my penis so I could urinate into a jar. Then another day she held it tighter, and worked on it, until she made it spout again. I couldn't stop her."

"How hard did you try?" Pul asked.

"Not nearly as hard as my member was," Grout admitted, and they all laughed understandingly. "She surely became a beauty in the next year or two, and any man she fancied would have been lost."

After that they moved on to stories of other men and women, though some were too fantastic to believe. It was amazing how swiftly the time passed.

The time came. They were admitted to the enormous fancy building where the Senate was, and Blaze stated their case for translation: Quintus Fabius had broken international law, treacherously killed a Keltic chief, and should be delivered for justice.

There was some hemming and hawing, and then the translator explained that the Senate was passing the Kelts' appeal to the popular assembly for consideration. That meant more delay.

On another day the popular assembly made its decision: not only were the Fabians not punished for Quintus's action, they were appointed to military tribunes with consular powers for the following year. That was, it seemed, the highest honor that it was possible for Rome to grant to them.

Blaze and Grout were fairly easygoing men, but even they were outraged by this. It was apparent that the Romans cared nothing at all for justice. "This means war," Blaze said. But he counseled them to make no strong protest, but rather to seem to accept it. "Our first duty is to get home alive."

Then Pul understood. There were indeed times when discretion was the better part of valor. The dishonorable Romans might not hesitate to do some more treacherous killing, if they thought they could get away with it.

They departed the city and marched north. Their shared wrath was such that the return trip took only three days.

Brennos seemed not completely surprised. Indeed, he had been marshaling the tribe for the new campaign. Now that he had confirmation of the atrocious bad faith of the Romans, the Elders could no longer balk him. One old man's word they might have doubted, or one sick man's word, or one dull warrior's word, but the three of them, and the interpreter and guide, all unified in outrage—no one could question that. Indeed, as the news spread, the entire army became melded into righteous rage. It would be impossible to stop them from smiting Rome.

Still, the forms had to be honored. The Druids were summoned for a divination. Pul, Blaze, Grout, and the healer Heath were present for it, as well as other chiefs and of course the Elders. Heath was an apprentice Druid, quite knowledgeable, but not of sufficient rank to qualify for something important, like divination.

"Do you really believe that entrails can foretell the future?" Blaze asked Heath. "I mean, you have seen many wounds, so have experience."

Pul had wondered the same, but never dared to express his doubt openly. But both Blaze and Heath had important positions, so would not be required to become the subjects for such work. The Druids had the authority to expel any man from all religious ceremonies. Any man who defied a Druid's power, or refused to abide by a Druid's ruling, could be excommunicated. Thus he would be cut off from all contact with the gods. It would be for him as if the gods didn't exist. That thought terrified Pul. Almost as bad, other members of the community would shun that banned man, fearful of contamination. So questions could be dangerous. Still, it was possible to wonder. Pul kept his mouth shut and listened closely.

"While I am not in a position to say by what mechanisms the gods may choose to express themselves to mortal men," Heath replied in the cautious manner he had, "I admit to a certain sentiment that entrails serve best when they remain inside their hosts, enabling them to function. I should think that the gods would prefer more direct methods of communication, such as blasting a wrongdoing person with thunder. However, it is not my business to know such things. It is the business of the qualified Druids, who spend their lives perfecting their skills in such matters. I am a mere dilettante, beneath notice."

"Artfully answered," Blaze said.

Pul didn't see what was so artful about it. What Heath said made perfect sense to him. Who could doubt a Druid?

"What about spasm reading?" Grout asked.

Pul had wondered about that too. Such divinations were fascinating to watch, but how the Druids figured out their meanings was beyond him. They would put a bound, gagged man, the sacrificial victim, on an altar face down, and slowly drive the point of a knife into his spine. Of course he would twitch something awful, sometimes even managing to fall right off the altar before he fainted or died. Then they would study his position carefully, and consult among themselves, and announce the message of the gods.

"Again, it may be that the Druids have avenues of information that ordinary folk lack," Heath replied. "But it seems to me that a person who has no knowledge of a situation and could not clarify it if asked directly, could not be expected to do so when under the influence of the agony of death. The same goes for sacrificial burnings in man-shaped wicker frames. It is my theory that it is the agony of such deaths that appeals to the gods, who may then put their information directly into the minds of the Druids."

"The minds of the Druids," Blaze echoed. "There may be the key. Why bother with sacrifices, when it is the minds that count?"

Heath smiled. "But sacrifices are such a good show."

There seemed to be an undercurrent of grim humor, but Pul could not fathom its cause. Sacrifices *were* a good show; what was funny about that?

But now it was time. The Druids brought out a cow. They tied its legs, pushed it down, and cut open its belly so that its guts welled out while it screamed. They poked and prodded, making additional cuts.

"And they will announce that the omens favor marching on Rome," Blaze said.

How could he know that?

"The Druids know which way the wind blows," Heath agreed.

What did the wind have to do with it?

But sure enough, after due deliberation the chief Druid made the announcement: the gods said that the mission would be victorious.

Brennos nodded, vindicated. The Kelts were on the march to Rome, with forty thousand fighting men.

Of course this meant that their campaign was extended, because Rome was several days' march to the south. Pul missed his family's nice rectangular house with its peaked roof and the women who could be depended on to come to a warrior with adequate spoils of war.

He also missed his nice home village, for its double oval walls and ditch were permanent defenses, along with the fierce local pigs, who roamed the alleys between houses and attacked strangers. Here on the march they had to build their own rude temporary shelters, and assign guards throughout the nights. It was uncomfortable in many ways.

Of course they received word that the Romans were scrambling to muster a defense. It hardly mattered; the city folk were plainly not much for honest battle. What would happen, would happen. The Druids had pronounced victory, so there was no question of the outcome.

In due course the Keltic army approached the big river, which the Romans called the Tiber. Just north of there, by a small tributary river, the Romans made their stand.

The Kelts saw the enemy arrayed for battle, and lined up their own forces. But they did not attack immediately. Instead, Brennos summoned subchiefs from the ranks. Pul was among them. He left his troops in place and reported to the command tent. Was the chief going to try to negotiate again, even at this stage?

Pul arrived at the same time as other commanders from across the army formation. They went in to see the chief.

"Pul, what do you see?" Brennos asked.

Surprised, Pul answered somewhat haltingly. "Chief, I am on our left flank, at the base of a slight rise. Ahead of us is the enemy's right flank, awaiting our onslaught."

"And what is on the hill?"

"Just some trees."

"Are you sure?"

Nonplused, Pul admitted that he wasn't. "I suppose there could be a few Roman stragglers there. We can't check directly, because the hill is beyond the enemy line."

"And if there were more than a few stragglers, what effect would this have on your campaign?"

Pul was baffled. "Chief, I don't understand. We'll kill any Romans we find there; they won't affect the battle."

"Suppose there are ten thousand troops there?"

This was weird! "Why—why it could be bad, chief, if they came down on our flank. So we should be wary of those trees, and guard against possible surprise."

Brennos addressed the main group. "I have had experience with massed warfare, and I have heard of the tactics of these Romans. They don't fight fair. Here is how it works: they invite direct attack against their center, then they retreat somewhat. Then their flanks sweep in to enclose the enemy, routing it. Since I don't see extra Roman troops on our right flank, they must be on the left. They expect us to walk foolishly into their trap." There was surprise on the faces of the other subchiefs; suddenly the complexion of the battle had changed.

Brennos turned back to Pul. "But of course we shall not be deceived by such a simple ruse."

"No, sir," Pul agreed, abashed. Obviously he would have been deceived.

"We shall make a little surprise of our own. Grout—you will direct your forces to the left, to engage the Romans on the flank."

"But—" Grout protested.

"Ignore the center. Go left."

"Yes, sir," Grout agreed dubiously.

Brennos returned to Pul. "You attack the forest with your full strength. Circle left; come at it from *their* flank, swiftly. Do not try to slaughter them all, and do not pause for booty; drive them toward the center."

"But—" Pul started.

"Strike with all your strength. Crush them. Make them retreat toward their own main force, and keep the pressure on."

"Yes, sir," Pul agreed, much as Grout had.

Brennos gave instructions to the other subchiefs, and dismissed them. Pul returned to his formation, dazed. Now he understood far better than before why Brennos was chief. But what was the use in driving enemy troops into their main strength, instead of slaughtering them on the spot? Then there would be twice as many enemies to fight.

But he instructed his lieutenants as directed. "There may be massed troops hidden in the trees on that hill. Circle left and rout them into the main enemy force. Strike hard. Do not pause for booty. Drive them before you." They nodded.

The horns sounded. The Kelts attacked. Grout's troops moved left, engaging the Romans Pul would ordinarily have tackled. Pul's forces circled left and charged up the hill toward the trees, screaming villainously, as was their wont in battle.

And there were indeed enemy troops there—thousands of them. They weren't even looking outward; they were arrayed to charge down on the Keltic flank. Pul's men piled into them, screaming and flailing with their swords.

There wasn't even a decent battle. The Romans, completely surprised, broke and fled. Some jumped into the river; most ran down the hill into the position of their own center. Pul's men encouraged them, charging hard upon their rears. The ones in the river were in immediate trouble, because their armor weighed them down, encouraging them to drown, and those who tried to wade back out were easy targets for the Kelts on shore. But the ones who fled to the center were in just as much trouble.

And now the nature of Brennos's strategy became apparent. For instead of the enemy contingents supporting each other and turning to fight, the fear and disorder of the flank spread to the center, and all of them turned and fled the field, harried mercilessly by the Kelts. It was an utter rout.

Now the subchiefs sounded the cease-attack horns. They allowed the remaining Romans to flee back toward their city. It was time for the spoils. The Kelts set about collecting the heads of their fallen victims, according to their custom, and stripping the nice Roman armor. The head was the house of the soul, and any Keltic warrior attached much prestige to the skull of an honored enemy. Of course these Romans weren't much, but still, their heads were better than nothing. The skulls would be cleaned and preserved, and later displayed; the best ones would not be sold even for large sums. They worked into the evening, and all next day. What a haul!

And of course there were the prisoners, who would be duly ransomed back to their city or family, or sold as slaves if no ransom was forthcoming. So an enemy soldier was valuable either dead or alive. That was the beauty of war. There was a good business in slaves, and they were one of the main Kelt exports, along with mercenaries, amber, salt, and tin.

"We might have done even better, had we given them no respite," Grout remarked. "But the spoils are great."

"There's much more in the city," Pul reminded him.

"Yes, I saw. This is only the beginning."

On the third day after the battle, the Keltic army arrived at the gates of Rome, though it was less than one day's march south. Pul appreciated what Grout had said; the Roman walls were formidable, and it might have been better to give the enemy no chance to set up for defense.

But the favor of the gods was with them, for the Romans were not even defending the outer walls. The gates were left open. The Kelts passed without challenge and entered the city. It was deserted. All the people had retreated to the fortified center of the city, up on the main hill, or fled to the neighboring cities. It was strange, passing through this giant metropolis, with all its streets and buildings and temples, and seeing no people. The throngs Pul had seen before had vanished.

There was clearly enormous loot to be had for the taking. But Brennos did not allow it yet. He was wary of a surprise counterattack by the Romans, and wanted to be sure of the city before sacking it. After seeing how readily the prior battle could have gone the other way, Pul appreciated that caution. So they moved slowly through the empty streets, working toward the heart of the city.

Finally they reached the Forum, which was the political, religious, and commercial center, lying between the Palatine and Capitoline hills Pul had visited before. Here they found a group of gray-bearded senators sitting silently on ivory chairs, wearing purple-trimmed togas. Pul almost thought he recognized some of them, though he couldn't be sure, because all Romans looked alike to him. What were they doing out here?

"They look like Druid holy men," Grout murmured, awed. "Maybe they have divine powers."

"If they did, they would have used them to defend the city," Pul pointed out, though he too was amazed by this sight.

"I think they are simply too old to be of use in the defense of the inner city," Blaze said. "So they were put out here. The Romans don't want extra mouths to feed."

That was probably it. Pul approached one of the senators, who took no notice of him. The man certainly didn't seem as high-and-mighty now, as when the senators had refused to do justice for the envoys. So Pul reached out and tweaked the man's beard.

The senator reacted by lifting his long staff and hitting Pul over the head.

Well, now. It didn't hurt, because of his stout helmet, but it was an affront. Pul drew his sword and struck off the old man's head.

Then the spell of awe was broken. The other Kelts slaughtered all the old Romans. The Roman arrogance, even in the face of overwhelming power, was simply too much to tolerate.

Now Brennos organized for the attack on the Capitoline Hill. But this was a more difficult target than the Roman army had been. The wall was higher and stronger than the city's outer ramparts, and the steepness of the hill made it hard to charge up. In addition, this wall was defended. The Roman archers had a downhill field of fire, and were well protected by battlements. They showed their heads only when firing, and were gone before return fire could be effective.

But the Kelts gave it a try. Pul was among those who led his troops in a frontal assault. They could not use their two-man chariots on the hill, so did it afoot. Pul wore a breastplate of iron rings, while his men were naked except for their weapons, shields, and body paint. But it turned out that bronze helmets and rectangular shields were not sufficient protection from bowmen who could take careful aim from cover.

Still, these were the same Romans who had been routed from the battle-field, and who had not even tried to defend their city. Now they were holed up like rats in their central fortress, and their nerve should break at any time. So Pul kept charging—until a stone struck one of the horns of his helmet, knocking it askew and making him see stars. He lowered his shield so as to use both hands to reset his helmet—and an arrow struck his side where the breastplate left off. He fell to the ground in agony, and found himself helplessly rolling down the hill, his side flashing new pain every time he passed over the wound.

He must have faded out, for then he found himself in a building with Heath the Healer tending to him. "It is not mortal," Heath said. "I have cut out the arrowhead and stanched the flow of blood. You will recover if you don't get the fever." Then he went on to the next patient.

"But my men!" Pul said, wincing as the effort of speaking brought another surge of pain. "I must lead them."

Talena appeared. Wherever the healer was, she was too, even in battle, and her presence was always welcome. She wasn't any great beauty, but her touch was gentle and competent, and she often gave verbal comfort, which counted for a lot. She helped prop him up so that he hurt less, and brought him beer to ease his thirst. But more important, she gave him information. "Your men are half wiped out. We are tending to the survivors. Brennos has called off the attack; that hill can't be taken by storm. We will have to lay siege to it."

"Besiege it!" Pul repeated, wincing again. "I hate that kind of war."

"We all do," she agreed. "But we have no choice, for the alternative is to let them go without punishment."

Pul nodded. "Brennos knows best," he agreed. "How fast will I recover?"

"Rest two days. Then if there is no fever, you can see to the sacking of the city."

That delightful prospect made him feel much better. As usual, she had known exactly what to say. He relaxed as Talena went on to the next patient.

He did have some fever, but Heath had done a good job with him, and it wasn't bad. In two days he was on his feet, unsteadily, and in three he was able to rejoin his less battered men and organize for sacking.

In the following month Pul and his companions gave themselves over to an orgy of sacking and burning. There was an amazing amount of loot in this giant city. The Romans might be uncivilized fools, and stupid in battle, but they had acquired many good things.

Meanwhile the siege of the central hill was established, and it continued. It wasn't very effective. Kelts were matchless on the battlefield, but sitting around and waiting for the other side to starve was no fun at all.

Then Brennos summoned Pul. "Something is going on," he said darkly. "The Romans managed to sneak a man out to summon help. We must stop that from happening again."

"Through my section?" Pul asked, alarmed.

Brennos smiled. "No, I am not blaming you. We don't know how they got out. We know only that one Roman soldier from their garrison at the Etruscan city of Veii up the Tiber River came down, swam the river, and passed through our lines to bring them a promise of aid once their general Camillus is recalled from his exile. Why they were so foolish as to exile a winning general I don't know; obviously they lack the wit of Kelts. We know about the soldier only because one of our Roman-speaking men listened close to a parapet at night and overheard their men talking about it." He focused his gaze on Pul. "And here is the key: those same soldiers said that the Roman commander, Marcus Manilius, planned to send the soldier back by his secret route to beg that the relief force come as quickly as possible. Do you know what that means?"

"It means that the Romans are hard up and we'll take them soon," Pul said promptly.

"Perhaps, were it not for their impenetrable wall. No, I am thinking of a useful action we might take."

"You want me to intercept that soldier and kill him so he can't deliver the message!"

Brennos shook his head in the way that hinted that Pul had said something foolish. "No, I want you to watch that man without disturbing him."

"But sir—!"

"And mark his secret route into the Roman ramparts, so that we can use it to gain entry."

Pul's jaw dropped. "Sir, you are a genius!"

"No, merely a warrior with some experience. It often helps to consider a thing more than one way. Once we spy the Roman spy, we will follow him and dispatch him safely away from the city, so his message will not get through. But meanwhile we will need a picked force to sneak into the Roman Capitol and secure it for our larger forces. With luck we can finish this siege within days. I remember how you turned the Roman flank in the battle, so I thought you would be a good man to tackle this dangerous chore."

"I'm your man!" Pul agreed proudly.

Brennos nodded. "Assemble your men, brief them, and be ready for action tonight. We are watching closely; if that Roman comes out, we will see him. A man will show you the route. Go in silently. Don't kill anyone unless you can do so silently. Get all the way in, then space your men out and kill all guards there. When we hear that commotion, we will charge the wall with a larger force, and funnel them in by your route. Can you handle that?"

"Yes, sir!"

"May the gods be with you."

Of course the gods would be with him. The Elders had said that the campaign would be victorious.

Pul returned to his men, and soon had them briefed and ready. They went to the rendezvous point at dusk, eager for action.

The word came about a third of the way through the night. A warrior woke Pul. "The spy came out. We traced his route. Follow me."

Pul rallied his picked men and they followed the warrior. They sneaked along a devious route up the hill. The Roman spy had taken advantage of cover, but also had known of certain covered cisterns and low ridges. There was a big drain hole some distance out from the wall that turned out to be large enough for a man to crawl through. Pul felt claustrophobic, going on hands and knees through this completely dark tight tunnel, splashing in waste water. But it had to be done. He followed the guide, and his men followed him, single file.

After what seemed like an interminable distance, the way opened out, and they were able to stand. They were inside the wall! They heard the stupid sentries snoring, and marked their places for slaughter, when the time came. Pul assigned his men, one to each snorer, awaiting the signal of destruction. They were able to distinguish the animal sounds of sleeping guard dogs. That was something, when even the Roman animals were criminally stupid!

"Temple of Juno," the guide whispered, taking Pul's hand in the darkness and pointing it to indicate the direction. "Secure that, and it is done."

Good. Pul had four men remaining unassigned. He touched them, indicating the direction, then started forward. Their mission was on the verge of success.

But as they drew near to the temple, a horrible noise broke out. "The sacred geese!" the guide exclaimed, appalled. "No way to shut them up!"

So they had to act immediately. "Do it!" Pul cried to his men, and headed back. There was no chance to take the temple, because of those cursed birds.

His men struck, each his assigned target. But the geese had alerted the whole area, and the Romans and dogs were lighting lamps and fighting back. There were shouts from farther within the compound, and it was clear that overwhelming force would soon concentrate. "Get out!" Pul cried, setting the example by plunging into the drain channel. He scrambled through and emerged outside the wall, where the Keltic forces were already gathered. "Don't strike!" he cried. "We're Kelts! Their asinine geese woke them! They are alert and ready for us."

In the end, Pul lost five men, and the Romans plugged up the drain. The attempt to breach the wall by stealth had failed. The dreary siege continued.

No rebuke came to Pul for the failure of his mission, but neither was he in any favor. The suspicion circulated that a better commander could have prevented the geese from clamoring, and thus cut short the siege. All he could do was lay low and hope the notoriety wore off in time.

No relief column came to the rescue of the Romans; at least that detail had been covered. But neither could the Kelts storm the walls. It was an impasse. Word was that the Romans were suffering from hunger and disease—but so were the Kelts. Heath tried to say that they should at least bury their dead, and the Roman dead too (!) to abate illness, but since this made no sense at all, they ignored him. Who cared how ill the dead were? How about doing something about the disease the living folk were suffering?

Also, the Kelts were hungry too. They did not have secure lines of supply to their farms in the Po valley in the north, and the plunder they had taken was mostly things rather than food. They ranged out into the countryside, but the Roman farmers were no longer farming, having fled, and those fields that hadn't been burned were plundered out.

But mainly, it was that Kelts were warriors, not campers, and had better things to do than sit outside a wall counting their fleas. Only Brennos's strong leadership was holding the army together. Pul and the others were sick of this whole mess.

After half a year, the Romans sued for peace. Brennos was glad to accept their surrender. "We will depart," he said, "in exchange for one thousand pounds of gold." That would be enough to give every Kelt a nice bonus.

The Romans agreed to the terms, though they complained that they would have a difficult time trying to arise such a ransom. "Would you prefer us to continue the siege?" Brennos demanded. That silenced them.

Finally they had the gold ready. They met in the Forum to weigh out the amount. Pul was there to help keep order. The Romans didn't like the process. "You are using false weights!" one complained.

Brennos didn't bother to refute the notion. Instead he threw his sword onto the balance as well. "Woe to the conquered!" That shut them up again.

And so at last the Kelts headed back north, for home, leaving Rome to the Romans. It wasn't as if there was anything left worth having. Pul knew that this sprawling wreck of a city would never amount to anything. The Romans simply didn't know how to fight or how to negotiate. Their supreme arrogance was based on nothing.

Actually, the potential of Rome was greater than the Kelts judged, and in time that was to become apparent. This particular sequence did little to support the honor or valor of Rome. Unfortunately, the lesson did not accomplish the eradication of Rome's worst fault, arrogance. Had the Romans treated the Kelts with proper international courtesy at the outset, or granted the justice of their case, or even respected their prowess as warriors, considerable mischief and embarrassment could have been avoided. But the Romans went right on antagonizing others, and having to fight unnecessary battles because of it. It was the Roman Way.

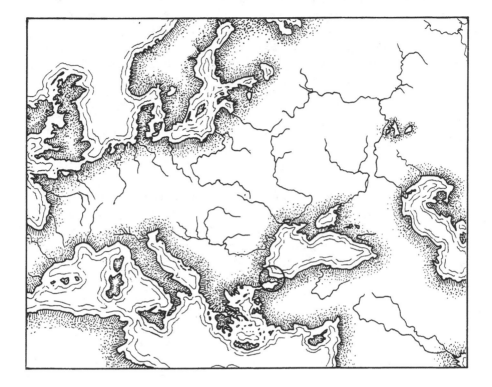

CHAPTER 8

PLOY

The arrogance of Rome continued, and in the end sundered it. Beset by "bar-barian" tribes, Rome was forced to negotiate and compromise, and even so was getting overrun. Goths, Franks, Vandals, and Burgundians occupied major seg-ments of what had been the Roman Empire. The empire itself was in the process of dividing into eastern and western sections, each with its own emperor. But the greatest threat to both halves was the growing empire of the Huns, whose king Attila (properly accented on the first syllable) was a fearsomely effective warrior and leader. It had been established by his father, and the Huns were fairly settled;

*they were no longer the same slash-and-burn terrors of prior decades. But Attila
had further ambitions.*

*Sometimes when a situation seems hopelessly confused and blocked in, it is
possible to find a single move that transforms the entire picture. It is seen notably
in chess, where a seemingly losing game can become a winning one with a brilliant
move that the opposition never anticipated, but it applies elsewhere too. Such as
in politics. Such a ploy by an ambitious young woman may have seriously affected
the destiny of Rome, though it is possible that the device is a myth. The art of the
ploy is something to be admired, regardless. The setting is the Eastern Roman
Empire capital of Constantinople, A.D. 447.*

MELEE woke to a terrible shaking. The whole world seemed to be
moving under her bed. She heard the screams of her older sisters,
and so knew that it wasn't just a bad dream. Something awful was happening.

She leaped out of bed, flinging on her wool tunic. She knew she had to
get outside; the building was trying to collapse around her. But she paused
to slide her bare feet into her sandals, because she was afraid of what her
toes would encounter outside. She wished Dillon were here to help her,
but she couldn't even cry his name. Their marriage was secret, on pain of
terrible consequences. So he was a soldier and she was a favored damsel
serving the emperor's sisters. If they ever learned of her marriage or her
lost baby, she would be summarily cast out, if not killed.

In moments she was crowding out the door along with the other damsels,
who were just as frightened as she was. In fact they were more frightened,
being truly innocent damsels in a way she definitely was not. Melee herself
was more like a prisoner here, locked in to the fasting and praying and
supposed virginity dictated by the matron Pulcheria, the emperor's elder
sister. It was almost impossible to sneak out.

Suddenly she realized that this was her chance. In the terrible confusion
of the shaking of the building, it would be hours before things got settled
back in. She would not be missed. So instead of joining the huddling group
of maidens, she faded back behind a column, then fled the palace.

She ducked into an alley, going against the flow of folk who were streaming
from the nether complex of kitchens, storerooms, stables, and servant's
quarters. All of them were wild-eyed in the early morning chill, partially
dressed, heedless of anything other than their need to get away. They had
not yet noticed what she had: that the shaking had stopped.

She made her way quickly to the palace guard barracks, hoping that it
remained disorganized. She was in luck; the men were milling about just
as uncertainly as the servants. But she knew that Dillon was no man to
panic in an emergency. Maybe he had the same idea she had.

He did. "Melee," he murmured, stepping into sight as she approached
the rear of the barracks.

"Where's a private place?" she whispered, not looking at him. It was as
if they were simply passing each other.

"There is a nook in the public bath that should be vacant this hour."

"Meet me there. Where is it?"

He described the section so she could find it. She brushed on, gratified to have arranged the liaison so readily. She made her way toward the Hippodrome, where the chariot races occurred. There would be no races there today! She circled it, going to the great bath house. Sure enough, its attendants had fled, though it wasn't much damaged. The warm water remained in the basins and pools, not having had time to chill.

She found the nook. It was indeed nicely sheltered, normally reserved for private parties by wealthy citizens. Dillon was already there, naked, pouring steaming water into the pool.

She stripped away her tunic and plunged in. The water was cool but not cold; the hot addition helped. Normally servants heated the bathing pools almost to body temperature, but that wasn't necessary for her purpose. She swam across, put her feet down, and opened her arms. "Come and get me!"

He did. He slipped into the water and came to embrace her nakedness. They kissed avidly. She wrapped her arms and legs around him and got herself up to facilitate his entry. It wasn't ideal, this fast, for water was actually "dry" on the tender surfaces, but she didn't care; she wanted him close and fast.

In a moment he was in her and jetting. Then, the edge off, he relaxed. "The gods know how I love you, Melee!" he breathed between kisses.

"Well, I worked hard enough to win you," she retorted. "If my father had lived, our marriage would have been recognized."

"I know. Pulcheria thought she was saving you from a fate worse than peonage."

"Actually, it's not a bad life in the palace. We are well treated and adequately fed. But all those prayers and fasts—"

"And all that virginity! How can you stand it?"

"Only because you are always in my mind, and sometimes in my body," she said, squeezing him. "When can we get away from this stifling city?"

"Where would we go? To Rome?"

"Can it be as bad as Constantinople?"

"It could be worse. The Goths have just about taken it over."

"I know. But are Goths so bad? I hear they are lusty folk."

"Who lack the sophistication of the civilized people. But if you really want to go there—"

She sighed. "Not yet, my love. When my inheritance is cleared, I'll be able to afford a villa of my own. Then, perhaps, we can have it all."

"I don't care about a villa. Only about you. I would go among the Huns, if you went with me."

"So would I, if that were the only choice. But I like the comforts of wealth, and would like to teach them to you. Have patience, love."

He laughed, somewhat bitterly. "When did you ever have patience?"

"Never! That's why you must have it all, to make up for me. I want everything: you and the villa."

"I suppose I could suffer through the rigors of wealth," he said. "Especially if you bought me a nice lovely slave girl."

"Dillon!" she exclaimed with mock affront. "I wouldn't do that!"

"Of course you wouldn't. You are never stingy. Make it two lovely slave girls."

"No. No."

"Well, then, three: morning, noon, and night."

"That is more like it," she agreed. "And you wouldn't be interested in any of them, as long as I was near."

"True. None of them could ever approach you in beauty or passion."

"None could," she agreed. "Now we must return to our stations, lest we be missed. Don't forget me in the interim."

"Never." They kissed once more, then separated and climbed out of the pool. Their pleasures had to be efficient, lest they be discovered and pay a hideous price.

She shook herself dry, satisfied that Dillon was watching, then donned her tunic and sandals and left the chamber. Just in time, for the bath servants were now returning, realizing that the immediate danger was over. They took her for one of them, and that was fine. She had learned to value safety beyond pride.

She got back in time to integrate with the other maidens, who had finally come to realize that the shaking was over. It hadn't been long, and no one realized that Melee had not been simply wandering the street in a confused state.

The matron Pulcheria arrived. She was forty-nine years old and severe of aspect, as was the case with her two younger sisters; only the damsels, being of lower status, had pleasant faces and bodies. Not that their dull woolen tunics let much of that show; none of them were supposed to be attractive to men. "It was an earthquake," Pulcheria said. "Very bad, but it is over. Surely a warning sent by benevolent Jesus that we are sinning and must reform."

Melee felt a flare of fear, but then realized that her sin had come after the quake, not before. So if Jesus was speaking to her, it was to encourage her to have a better life rather than to punish her for anything done before.

"It should be safe inside now," Pulcheria continued. "But there may be damage. Offer a prayer of thanks for being spared, and start cleaning up."

There was a joint murmuring as the damsels spoke their prayers of thanks. Then they grouped behind the matron, who led the way toward the main entrance.

They re-entered the palace. Some columns had fallen, but overall the structure remained solid. There was choking dust, but it was settling out. They got to work cleaning surfaces and floor, and checking for damage. It had been the worst shaking in living memory, and they learned later that other sections of the city had suffered worse, but they were all right. The gods had indeed spared the beloved of Jesus, Melee thought irreverently.

Melee overheard one of Pulcheria's sisters talking to the other as they worked. "Have we really been sinning? I have been trying so hard to be perfect for Jesus, but sometimes I do miss the life I had before."

"She meant the city, and the others in it," the other sister reassured her. "The common folk sin all the time. Look at the number of babies they produce!"

Melee wondered. If enjoying sex was sinful, then she was guilty. But how else did Jesus expect people to be fruitful and multiply?

Then the rain came. It was heavy and continuous. The streets flooded, driving people indoors and preventing supplies from arriving at the markets. Fortunately the palace storerooms had supplies, but it did cut down on fresh vegetables.

Another damsel came to stand beside Melee as she gazed out the window. "If the quake means a warning, is the rain another warning? It's pretty heavy."

Melee knew better than to betray her true thoughts. "It could be. But surely it is intended for those who have been sinning, rather than those who have been striving for perfection." She was borrowing from what Pulcheria's sister had said.

"Yes, it must be," the girl agreed, evidently relieved. She interpreted Melee's ambiguous statement in the way an innocent person would.

Suppose Jesus were to return to life, as it was said he would one day do, and visit this palace? Would he really prefer the company of austere virgins to that of full-bodied and willing women? Melee's own beauty was reserved for just one man, but if she ever met Jesus in person, she might almost be tempted to tempt him, just to find out whether he was truly man or eunuch. She suspected that he would prove to be a man. She could not recall anything in the scriptures that indicated that Jesus thought the enjoyment of sex was wrong. Hadn't he even welcomed a prostitute into his camp, and praised her above others? Melee would think better of him if he were fully human.

The rain kept coming. Water coursed in rivers through the city and washed out the foundations of a number of buildings, which had already been weakened by the shaking. They were all right in the palace, but the word was that many other people were getting driven from their homes and accumulating in makeshift shelters. This seemed to be proof that the sinful were being not merely warned but punished. Would they learn from the experience? Melee doubted it.

The deluge continued for four days and nights, and seemed to be doing more damage than the shaking had. Impromptu crews were routed out to shore up the major buildings, but the work was makeshift. At one point Melee saw Dillon on one of the crews around the palace, and didn't dare signal him, lest her interest be noted.

"Do you think it will continue for forty days?" a damsel asked Pulcheria.

"No!" the matron snapped. Then, realizing that she was hurting the damsel's feelings, she relented somewhat. "It is surely not God's purpose to destroy the good with the evil. It will pass when the time is proper. When enough of the evil has been washed from the city."

About all Melee could say for it was that it was a break in the deadly routine of prayer, psalmody, and embroidery that was the standard Pulcheria enforced. Pulcheria had taken over the palace early in her life, soon after her brother Theodosius became emperor. She was a devout Christian, a religion that happened to believe in just one god and resented the other gods. This Christian god evidently didn't like the pleasures of the flesh, for Pulcheria, her two sisters, and the favored damsels were supposed to be austere and virginal throughout. Their clothing was simple, for this god didn't like the vanity of dress, and their diet frugal. Worse, all men were scrupulously excluded from the palace, except for occasional saints who had no use for the distinction of genders. Seclusion was the order of the day—and the month and year.

Meanwhile, Pulcheria pretty much controlled the affairs of state, acting through her brother Theodosius, who even as an adult remained somewhat in awe of her. He was actually a rather decent man, learned and friendly to all, not given to violence. It was Pulcheria who had decided what woman he would marry. Fortunately for him, she had chosen a girl of exceptional beauty, Athenais, who was the daughter of a university professor and spoke perfect Greek. But in this perhaps Pulcheria made a mistake, for Theodosius fell in love with his lovely wife, and she slowly assumed greater power, at Pulcheria's expense. Still, Pulcheria ruled the palace, and was able to channel money to build many splendid Christian churches in different parts of the empire.

But that didn't help Melee, whose profession of Christianity was a matter of survival rather than conviction. All this austerity was foreign to her nature. So she welcomed this break in the regimen, and not just because it had given her the chance to snatch brief pleasure with Dillon.

The rain finally stopped. God had finished with washing the sin from the city. Only then did the full extent of the mischief become apparent. Not only had the city suffered severe structural damage, a siege of plague broke out, spreading rapidly through the crowded shelters. This must be the third stage of the warning to the sinners. Worse yet, more than half the towers of the city's defensive wall had been destroyed. There were gaping holes in the wall, through which an enemy could readily advance. Constantinople was virtually defenseless.

Suppose the Huns invaded? They were ferocious fighters, who could surely take the city, if they struck while the wall was down. Could that be the fourth part of the warning? If so, it would be a savage one, for little was left after the Huns sacked a city. No gold and no virgins. Already the common folk were gathering up their meager possessions and fleeing the city, though this might have been as much to escape the plague as from fear of the invader.

The fear of the Hun continued to build. Wild stories spread of the terrible things the Huns did to captives. "I have heard that they line up maidens against a wall, and rape them in public before they kill them," one of the maidens said. "We must flee before they come."

Melee had her doubts about whether the Huns were any more brutal than Roman soldiers, but she wasn't easy about the fate of the city if the Huns came. The hysteria was spreading.

"We can't have this," Pulcheria said firmly. She talked to her brother, and the emperor set out to repair the wall before anything else.

The effort was so desperate, and so important, that even some of the favorite damsels were allowed to help. Melee put aside her embroidery and went out to help bring food and comfort to the crews laboring diligently on the wall. The damsels were supposed not to soil their delicate hands with any physical labor, but in the throes of the effort Melee was able to escape observation and rendezvous with one of the construction supervisors: Dillon. So she did not soil her hands, and the part of her that might be considered soiled did not show. But she was doing her best to facilitate the work, in her fashion. Dillon agreed emphatically.

The crews were organized along the color lines. This derived from the supporters of different factions of the chariot races: Blues, Whites, Greens, and Reds. This followed the patterns of Rome. But the colors were not equal. The Blues and Greens had become dominant. The factions, called demes, were so powerful that they were organized along political lines, with a strict chain of command. The Blues and Greens had private boxes on the side of the Hippodrome closest to the palace, flanking the emperor's own box. So it was to this existing structure the city turned when something needed to be done in a hurry. The Blues competed against the Greens in repairing the wall. The Reds and Whites worked too, but their sections were comparatively small. The work went quickly, because each deme wanted to prove itself.

Dillon was a Blue. Melee helped make him be proud of it. Now if only the terrible Huns would delay their invasion until the wall and towers were repaired!

But Attila was not immediately threatening Constantinople. He normally raided the rich lands in the summer campaigning season, having other business in winter. The earthquake and heavy rain occurred in January 447; it wasn't until about three months later that Attila's campaign started, by which time the repairs to the wall had been completed. Actually Attila wasn't much interested in sacking Constantinople, because it was out of his way and there were far easier spoils to be had in the smaller cities whose defenses were less formidable. Also, he was still consolidating his control over a very large and somewhat sprawling empire in which some of the subject tribes, such as the Scythians, had certain notions of autonomy. His forces included a core of fine Hun cavalry, Gepids under their king Ardaric, Goths led by Valamer, and contingents of Sciri, Rugi, Suebi, and other subject tribes. The Romans fought bravely, but Attila won, and raided Greece

freely, plundering as many as a hundred cities. This was the point of such cam-
paigns: to gain plunder that sustained the Hun empire. Naturally Attila did not
plunder his own domains, and in any event, the economy of the Huns had little
to export other than horses, slaves, furs, and mercenary troops. So the influx of
wealth from these routine campaigns was vital to the stability and growth of the
kingdom. Finally the Romans had to sue for peace, and agreed to pay an annual
tribute of 2,100 pounds of gold and evacuate significant territory south of the
Danube River. So it was a successful campaign, for Attila, yielding plunder,
tribute, and land. Who needed Constantinople?

In 448 Attila's attentions were taken to another area. A nomadic tribe known
as the Acatziri, or Forest People, lived independently north of the Black Sea. Em-
peror Theodosius solicited them, hoping to gain an ally at Attila's rear. This
provoked Attila's attention, and in a succession of battles he reduced most of these
tribes to subject status. His eldest son, Ellac, was sent to govern them. Perhaps
there would have been peace, then, for a while, except for continued Roman med-
dling. Relations between the empires were at best somewhat strained, but the Ro-
mans went beyond acceptable limits. Again. The time is A.D. 449.

Od arrived at Queen Kreka's quarters and stood silently, waiting for his
presence to be recognized. There were several buildings, some fashioned
of intricately meshed carved boards, others on round wooden blocks so
that they were clear of the ground. All of them were for the use of the
queen and her servants. As Attila's first wife and mother of his three eldest
sons, she was an important figure, and no one questioned it. Attila had
several lesser wives, and it was the younger, fresher ones who normally
shared his bed, but Kreka had power. Attila listened to her, if she chose to
make a point.

After a moment Avalanche came out, as beautiful as ever. She was a body
servant to the queen, but often enough she came to spend an hour with Od,
with the queen's blessing. The queen could have prevented any such liaisons,
but preferred to maintain good relations with Od's employer, Orestes. This
was one of the little ways: letting her servant keep his servant satisfied.

Avalanche stopped before him, assuming a formal pose. She wore a standard rough wool robe underlaid with precious silk to eliminate chafing,
and looked lovely. "What is your business with the queen?" she inquired.

"Orestes has news to convey to her."

"And why does not Orestes come himself?"

"Orestes needs to make no accounting to you," he said with mock
haughtiness. They both knew that they had to stall long enough to allow
the queen to compose herself and her servants for a semi-formal reception.

"In that case I won't show you this." She put her hand on the lapel of
her robe.

It was a game they played, but it had a real effect on him. If any woman
had a finer body than she, he did not know of it. Od lowered his voice.
"He's going to make a special journey to Constantinople."

"Thank you." She drew open her robe, and her silken undergarment, showing her full left breast. Then she stepped into him and kissed him. "I'll be free tonight."

He patted her firm bottom. He was a little surprised that she remained interested in him, as her attention normally was fleeting. But though she had affairs freely with others, she did not seem to want to let Od go. She was so beautiful that he was unable to deny her, though he knew that in time she would tire of whatever it was she saw in him. After all, he was nothing but a poor Roman servant serving a Roman noble, who in turn served a barbarian king, making himself useful in whatever ways were feasible. He understood the technology of Roman catapults and aqueducts, but such things were not to be found here in the hinterlands. "I will be ready."

Enough time had passed. "This way," she said, disengaging. She took his arm and guided him up the wooden steps and through the thick curtains of the entrance.

The floor inside was covered with woolen mats. Od paused to remove his leather shoes, and stepped barefooted on the nearest mat.

Queen Kreka reclined on a couch at the far side of the chamber. She was a woman of about forty, no longer pretty, but impressive in a splendid red gown. A number of female servants stood around her, some of them comely, and maids sat on the floor in front of her, embroidering linen cloths. These would be sewn onto the queen's dresses for ornament. It was a pretty scene, carefully crafted to be so.

He walked to the appropriate spot and stopped, bowing his head.

"What brings the emissary of the Roman here?" Kreka inquired after a moment. "The Roman" was Orestes, who had been prominent in the Western Roman Empire before coming to offer his services to Attila. The Hun king had surrounded himself with prominent men from many lands, in this way elevating his court to a level beyond what was normal among the so-called barbarians. Attila did not pretend to be cultured or educated, and was personally frugal, but he was no fool. He commanded a loyalty among his supporters that went beyond his generosity to them; all of them respected his qualities of leadership.

Od lifted his head. "High Lady, the Roman wishes you to be the first to know that he must travel to Constantinople on business for the king. He inquires whether there is anything he might acquire there for you."

Kreka smiled, genuinely pleased. "How thoughtful of him! Yes, I would like fine silk for a dress, and a necklace of amber to wear with it. Would that be within his means?"

"I believe it would," Od said.

"Must you return to your master immediately?"

"We depart in two days. My only mission today is to bring this message to you, High Lady."

"Two days," she said thoughtfully. "Then Orestes must have a bit of time free, too. Do you suppose he could join us tonight for a banquet? We would like to talk to him about the gossip of Rome.''

The gossip of Rome was a very popular subject for the wives of the nobles of Attila's court. Rome was the acme of dissolute wealth, and therefore endlessly fascinating to those who had to labor in the real world. It might seem frivolous, but the wish of the queen was something any lower person took extremely seriously. ''I shall ask him, High Lady.'' That, in the code of courtly behavior, meant that Od would convey the queen's order for a command appearance to Orestes, who would adjust his schedule to oblige. It would not be a complete loss, for the queen could arrange an extremely nice table.

''Then the two of you must join us for a banquet. My maid Avalanche will make you comfortable.''

Od saw a possible problem. ''Is the Roman's wife to be included?''

Kreka laughed. ''You don't trust your master near Avalanche? Of course his wife is invited. She knows more gossip than he does.''

Od bowed. ''Your courtesy and kindness are remarkable, High Lady.'' It was no less than the truth. The queen, despite being a native Hun, was a pleasant and generous person, and not stupid about the relationships of those around her. Like her husband, she liked to learn the ways of culture, choosing which aspects to adopt. She had a sharp eye for what was fashionable among the civilized upper classes.

Avalanche saw him out. ''Od, about what she said: you know that if Orestes wanted me, I would have to oblige him.''

''I know. And I know that he has no intention of being indiscreet with anyone. He is an honest man. But I also know that his wife does not like being left out of things. Especially royal events.''

''Especially all-female events,'' she said. ''Where some of the girls like to see how far they can make a man's pupils dilate, just by chance.'' She opened her robe again, demonstrating on Od's own pupils.

''That, too,'' he agreed.

She kissed him. ''Od, I like you because you know my nature, yet still associate with me as an equal.''

He shrugged. ''You are the only beautiful woman who pays any attention to me.''

''Because I know *your* nature. You are the smartest man I have encountered. You know everything about everything, though you pretend to be ignorant. One day you will be prominent.''

Her faith in him was pleasant, if probably unrealistic. He could live with her flattery, especially when she followed it up with close contact with her body, as now. But he couldn't dally long. Od returned to Orestes and delivered the message.

The Roman sighed. ''I will oblige. There is nothing as potent as a woman's thirst for news of scandal.''

There followed a very nice meal, with Od seated at the table between Avalanche and Orestes, while the Roman was next to the queen. They were the only males present, and all the women treated them as if they were royal, though all knew Od was not. It was a charade he found pleasant enough. Once a mischievous Hun girl, encountering Orestes and Od together, had shown the highborn Roman a flash of her higher torso, and the lowborn Roman a similar flash of her lower torso, implying that each was entitled only to its own level. Orestes had laughed and remarked that it might be pleasant to exchange roles some day.

It seemed that the queen had heard of a prominent Roman lady, Galla Placidia, and wished to know more about her. Orestes, as a prominent former resident in the Western Roman Empire, had thorough background information on its most notorious figures. Placidia was certainly one of them.

"Is it true that she was a Goth?" Kreka asked. "And that she seduced kings?"

"Not exactly, High Lady," Orestes said cautiously. "But she is nevertheless a remarkable woman."

"Tell me all about her. Every detail."

So Orestes evidently dredged his memory for what he knew of that particular lady, and recounted her history for the benefit of the queen and her handmaidens. It was apparent that this fine banquet was his reward for this vital information, and he did not want to disappoint anyone.

Od glanced at Orestes' wife. She was happily eating. She had no doubt primed her husband, knowing what Roman ladies had made the foreign news recently. She knew that the favor of the queen had significant bearing on the favor of Attila, and that the queen really did not abuse her position.

Galla Placidia was the sister of the rather weak former emperor of the Western Roman Empire, Honorius. While he was largely ineffective as a leader, his sister was in contrast strong-minded, imaginative, and determined. But of course she was a woman, so could not assume power on her own. Not directly.

The ladies of the court nodded understandingly. It was this way among the Huns, too. A proper lady exerted her influence on politics by affecting the men she was close to. Women could be quite adept at this subtle continuing process.

When Honorius' disastrous policies resulted in the siege of Rome by the forces of Alaric the Visigoth, most Roman nobles fled the city. But Galla Placidia, then aged twenty-two and beautiful, had been too proud to flee. Perhaps she had supposed that Rome would not fall. Alaric had needed reinforcements to take the city, and his wife's brother Athaulf brought a contingent of Gothic and Hun troops, and these prevailed. Thus when Rome fell, Placidia was taken prisoner by the Goths.

"Of course," Kreka agreed, and her women applauded. Naturally they favored the Huns, the most effective fighters in the world. Naturally they captured the prettiest royal women.

Then Alaric became ill, and died, leaving Athaulf as the leader of all the Goths in Italy. But he wanted legitimacy as well as power, so he decided to marry Placidia, whom he well knew was the emperor's sister. The fact that she was perhaps Rome's most beautiful woman might have had something to do with it.

There was laughter around the table. They all knew that men had little judgment of women, other than their appearance. A man's weapon was his sword; a woman's weapon was her beauty.

So Athaulf sent emissaries to Emperor Honorius with this proposal: unify their empires with a royal marriage. But Honorius, with the arrogance for which Rome had always been known, scornfully rejected it and demanded his sister back.

Athaulf would not let Placidia go. She was too valuable and too lovely. Instead he kept her with him, nominally as a hostage. The truth was that he had fallen in love with her, and treated her as well as any lady could wish. He even took her with him on his next campaign. This was in Gaul, two years later. He led a large army over the Alps. Then he formally demanded from the emperor a land where his people could settle.

Honorius, realizing that the Visigoths were going to take Gaul anyway, ceded a large region, and suggested that Placidia be sent back now. Athaulf agreed to the first and rejected the second. After he established the Gothic kingdom in Gaul, he married Placidia. She was by no means an unwilling bride. She had come to love Athaulf, and he was after all the king of a powerful people. It was a splendid occasion, and even the Romans realized that this was not after all a bad conclusion to the affair.

Kreka and her ladies nodded knowingly. Placidia had gone from hostage to queen, and was in control of the situation. She was even accepted by Athaulf's six children by a prior marriage.

A year later they celebrated their anniversary in a spectacular manner. Placidia was garbed as a Roman empress, seated on a throne. Athaulf had a subordinate position beside her. Fifty young men approached, each carrying a bowl filled with silver and another filled with precious stones, and presented them to Placidia. A noble named Attalus, who had once briefly been named as a puppet emperor of Rome, led the singing. Thus, symbolically, Placidia was the ruler of them all.

"Symbolically, my sore toe!" Kreka snorted, and the others laughed. Their sympathy for the bold woman was overriding their identification with the "barbarian" kingdom. Placidia was doing her gender proud.

Then disaster struck. Athaulf was murdered by a turncoat servant who was definitely not enamored of Placidia. He forced her and Athaulf's children to walk in a procession through the streets in front of his horse, for several hours. He didn't kill them, but was determined to humiliate them.

Fortunately a new ruler soon came into power. He realized that Placidia was a valuable property, so he ransomed her back to Rome for a substantial shipment of wheat. So, after five years among the Goths, Placidia finally came home to the Roman Empire. It might have seemed that her days of notorious glory were over.

The Hunnic women shook their heads. They knew better.

Emperor Honorius arranged for his sister's second marriage. She was still a beautiful woman, and still well connected. He married her to a former consul, by whom she had a son and a daughter. But in five years he died, leaving her a widow a second time.

Placidia decided that she and her children would be better off in the Eastern Roman Empire, which was by then more secure than the Western Roman Empire. So she traveled to Constantinople. But the ship in which she sailed was struck by a storm, and seemed about to founder in the high winds and heavy seas. Placidia was a devout Christian, so she prayed to her god: "If I survive this crossing, I will build a suitable church!" In due course the winds abated and the ship completed the crossing safely. So she arranged for a fine church to be built in the provisional Western Roman capital of Ravenna.

Placidia had satisfactory relationships with the Eastern Roman Emperor Theodosius and his sisters, notably Pulcheria, who was an even more devout Christian. But she kept in touch with the west, and her influence there was strengthening. Her brother Honorius died in two years, and she then arranged to have her six-year-old son proclaimed emperor in the west, as Valentinian III. She of course became his guardian and regent, the most powerful figure in the Western Empire. "From that time to this, some twenty-five years," Orestes concluded, "she has essentially run the empire. It has been a generally beneficial influence. In that period much of its deterioration has been reversed, and it has become a formidable power again."

The maidens smiled, pleased with the accomplishment of the bold woman.

Kreka nodded. "So when my husband invades the Western Roman Empire, it will be this woman who organizes the opposition."

"Indeed," Orestes agreed. "Of course she will defer to her son's military advisers in matters of strategy and tactics. Her power is not complete; no person's is. But as long as she lives, Rome will be formidable."

"But she is getting old," the queen remarked.

"Sixty or sixty-one," he agreed. "And not in the firmest health. She has built her mausoleum in Ravenna. It is an exquisite monument. The walls are partly faced with yellow marble. Light is filtered through paper-thin alabaster. Figures of St. Peter and St. Paul are in the mosaics, dressed in white togas like Roman senators, with doves. In the cupola there are concentric gold stars set against a dark blue background, like the night sky, and the figure of the cross dominates the whole. It suggests abiding faith and character. When one stands therein, as I have, one knows that it was designed by a person of rare artistic appreciation tempered with a clear understanding of the ways of the world."

"I would like to meet that woman," Kreka said. "Meanwhile, I will ask my husband to spare the Western Empire while Placidia is there."

He glanced at her in surprise. "But campaigning for spoils is the Hunnic way."

"Spoils can be had in Persia."

Od realized that his homeland might just have been spared a devastating invasion. Because a royal Roman had had the courtesy to satisfy a woman's curiosity about another woman.

❁

Two days later they started on their embassy to Constantinople. Its purpose was to demand major territorial changes, so as to keep the peace. The mission was headed by Orestes and the Hun chief Edeco. Though Orestes was a noble Roman, Od suspected that he was the one Attila most trusted. That trust was not misplaced; Orestes was a thoroughly honorable man.

The Hun guards were armored in leather, and wore conical caps, with the captains possessing metal helmets with noseguards. They carried bows, lances, lassos, and straight-bladed swords, and bore shields of hide stretched over wicker frames. Edeco wore bone armor handed down from his father, and had a metal scale tunic. Od, who knew about metal-working, had helped craft such armor, though there was little raw metal to work with.

When they arrived at Constantinople, they met with the Bishop of Smyrna, a eunuch named Chrysaphius. Orestes could speak with him directly, for he spoke Greek, but Edeco needed an interpreter. The bishop provided one, a former Hun named Bigilas. After the official business had been discussed, Orestes took a walk in the gardens. Since he did not signal Od to accompany him, Od remained where he was, standing on the fringe.

"These royal apartments are splendid!" Edeco exclaimed, awed. As a Hun he had not before seen such affluence.

"You might also be the lord of a golden-roofed house, and of similar wealth," Chrysaphius replied, when the statement was interpreted. "If you care to disregard Scythian matters and take up Roman ways." Od knew that the term "Scythian" was a euphemism for "barbarian." He was saying that the Hun should renounce his people and join the Romans. It was interesting listening to both parts of the dialogue, understanding both. It was like watching a chariot race: first one chariot led, then another led. Od saw that the bishop did not realize that Od, in common Hun clothing, was a Roman.

Edeco was plainly intrigued. But he answered properly "But it is not right for the servant of another master to do such a thing without his lord's permission." And Edeco was not aware of Od's origin either; the matter had not come up. Thus he was listening in more directly than either man knew. Not that it mattered.

The bishop seemed to change the subject. "Do you have easy access to King Attila's presence?"

"Oh, yes. I am on intimate terms with him."

"How much influence do you wield at his court?"

"Much. I am entrusted with his bodyguard, along with other men chosen for this duty. Each of us in turn guards Attila with arms on specified days."

"This is very interesting," the bishop said. "You must come to dinner at my house, and we can talk more."

"I shall be glad to!"

"But do not bring Orestes or any of the other envoys with you," the bishop said. The interpreter then approached Edeco and spoke privately to him, so that others could not hear.

But Od had heard the Greek version. Why this privacy? But it wasn't his business, so he kept his face neutral.

However, later when he was alone with Orestes, he mentioned it. Orestes shrugged. "Perhaps it would be too expensive to entertain the whole embassy."

Od dropped the matter, but he didn't forget it.

Orestes gave him time off to explore the city, knowing how fascinated Od was with the advanced architecture. Od walked along the huge defensive wall, staring up at its turrets and towers. It was three times his height, and the towers were taller. No wonder Attila wasn't eager to attack this city!

But actually he was looking for a person he had known years ago, who was said to live out by the wall. This might be his only chance to see her, as he might never see this great city again. He had only a crude description of her address, which was on a street near the south gate.

A guard walking from his post spied him. "Ho, stranger, you look lost."

"I am," Od agreed. "I am looking for a house on Mese Street."

The guard laughed. "The Mese runs through the entire city! In fact there are two Mese streets. You will be all year looking."

"By the Golden Gate," Od amended.

"That helps. That's the main gate to the south. Just keep walking. You can't miss it."

"My thanks," Od said, and headed south.

In due course he found it. The Hun party had entered by the Gate of Charisus in the northwest section; this was well to the southwest. It was massive, with a supplementary wall enclosing it so that any attackers would have to fight through a second barrier after breaching the first. Now where was the house? There were so many tightly squeezed little houses that he did not know where to begin.

Another guard hailed him. "What's your business, stranger?"

"I am looking for the house of the matron Bata."

"Wait an hour, and a man will take you there."

Od wasn't sure why he had to wait, but he had no choice. So he studied the gate complex, analyzing its structures. The builders had certainly known what they were doing.

"What is your business with Bata?" a man suddenly asked him.

Od jumped. The hour had passed so quickly! Before him stood a tall and powerful-looking Roman man wearing a soldier's tunic and sword, and military boots. "I knew her, years ago, and wanted to remake her acquaintance."

"Oh, seeking more hot flesh?"

Od stared at him. "It must be a coincidence of names. The woman I seek is ancient and almost blind. I can not be sure she still lives."

The man smiled. "Just testing. I am Dillon, come from the palace to bring her food for the evening."

"I am Od. I learned much from her. She knows everything."

"That she does! She will surely be glad to meet you."

They went to a shack no better, and probably somewhat worse, than the others of the vicinity. Dillon knocked, in a set pattern, then pushed open the door. "Grandmother!" he called into the interior gloom. "I bring you a visitor named Od."

"Od!" she exclaimed from her chair. "We met at the time of the disaster."

"Two years ago, when the walls were felled?" Dillon asked as he set down his bundle of bread and fruit.

"Six, in another region," Od said. He went to the old woman and took her hand. "I met you, and your son, and granddaughters."

"Only the younger granddaughter lives," Bata said.

"I know. The aliens wiped out the city and slaughtered most of its people. We had to flee to another."

"I heard that a woman borrowed you."

"Yes. Avalanche. She is still borrowing me. She is a beautiful woman."

"But not as lovely as Melee."

"Melee is a child."

Dillon laughed. "Not any more."

Od caught himself. "Of course. Six years—she must be a woman now."

"Yes. A woman of eighteen."

"What is your business here?" Bata asked.

"I am with a Hunnic embassy, here to demand territory. I took the opportunity to see you, as there may not be another chance."

"With whom have you dealt?"

"The Bishop of Smyrna."

Bata frowned. "He is a mean man. They should have cut off his head instead of his testicles. Corrupt, power-hungry, and widely detested."

"That's strange. He invited one of our leaders to dinner at his house."

"He is surely up to no good. Maybe you should ask Melee; she keeps up with the current gossip."

"But I came to see *you*, Grandmother!"

Bata waved him away. "And see me you have. Now go with Dillon. There may be a mystery to fathom."

Od realized that the woman was probably tired, and this was her way of dismissing him. "Then I will go, Grandmother. I am glad to have seen you again."

"Kiss your Avalanche for me when you see her." The old woman smiled. "But don't tell her that you met one lovelier than she."

"I will see you tomorrow, Grandmother," Dillon said as they left.

"You are good to me, dear boy. If I were sixty years younger—"

"Fortunately for Melee, you are not."

They left the hut and walked down the street. "I see you have learned from her," Od said.

"Everything. Sometimes I think it is because Melee resembles what Bata must have been that I love her."

"I remember Melee's elder sister, Baya. She was a lovely, competent woman. I remember only that Melee was pretty."

"You will see how pretty. But the meeting must be private. I would not do it, if Bata had not said to."

"I really don't need to—"

"Bata said. That is enough."

Od nodded. "That is enough." The old woman had always had good reasons for her demands.

They were walking along the covered street. The Mese, it turned out, ran from the gate to the center of the city, and was covered by a stone roof supported by stone columns on either side. The porticos were decorated with classical statues, and the sidewalks were lined with shops. Some merchants had built small booths between the columns. At intervals, staircases led up to the roof of the colonnades. It was, taken as a whole, as impressive as the outer wall.

"Here is where the two Mese streets join," Dillon said as they came to a juncture. "The other fork goes to the Gate of Charisus."

"That is where we entered," Od said. "But we did not stay on the main street. I didn't realize that it was covered its whole length."

"Oh, that's standard in many larger Roman cities."

"I'm a small-town man," Od said, with a laugh.

"So am I. But when I married Melee, I came to know her life."

"You married her!"

Dillon looked abashed. "I didn't mean to say that. It is a secret marriage."

"I will keep your secret. It is no business of mine. But why marry secretly?"

"She is of royal descent. I am of common descent. Her father meant for us to marry, but he died before that was known, and her family, except for Bata, didn't know. So to protect us both—her from shame, me from death—we made it secret. Maybe one day we will be able to make it public."

"I understand. The woman I love will not marry me. She values her freedom to have sex with any man she chooses. I tolerate that, because otherwise I would lose her entirely."

"Melee is supposed to be virginal. But your situation and mine seem similar."

"Yes."

They followed the merged Mese streets to the palace complex. "I will try to signal her," Dillon said. "She will come out if she can."

They went to the rear of the palace, where there was an alley used for service personnel. Carts of food were being rolled in, and carts of garbage rolled out. Od saw that sometimes the two jostled each other in passing. They went to a section where the servants' quarters connected to the main palace, and Dillon looked around to be sure no one else was in sight, then tossed light gravel at an arched window.

In a moment a head appeared in the window, and a hand came up in a small wave. "She will come down," Dillon murmured. "Hide yourself, because she won't approach if she sees anyone besides me."

Od ducked down behind a parked garbage cart, and watched. Soon a cloaked figure appeared, evidently a young woman. She kissed Dillon, who murmured something in her ear. Then his hand came up, beckoning Od.

Od rose and approached them. "This is Od," Dillon said. "He knows Bata."

The woman turned to face him. Her face under the hood and scarf was a thing of rare beauty. "I—I met you when you were twelve," Od said. "With your sister Baya, Heath's first wife."

"I remember," she said. Her voice was soft. "You married Bevy."

That memory hurt. "She died in an enemy raid. She was a good woman."

"Why do you come here?"

"I am with the embassy of the Huns. I overheard something curious, and Bata said you might know more about it."

She smiled, briefly, and it was like a flash of sunshine. "We do survive on gossip in the palace. Tell me."

He told her of the meeting between Edeco and the Bishop of Smyrna. "Orestes says it is probably nothing," he concluded.

"The bishop has no use for anyone he can't squeeze for power or profit," Melee said. "I have heard nothing of this, but will be alert."

"He says his companion Avalanche is a beautiful woman," Dillon said.

Melee opened her cloak, showing them a flash of her almost naked body within. Then she turned and departed, knowing that she had made Dillon's point. Avalanche was solidly endowed and well proportioned, but Melee had a slender perfection that seemed matchless. She was indeed the most beautiful woman Od had seen. "You are the most fortunate of men," he said.

"I know it."

They moved away from the palace. "If she learns something, how will I know it?" Od asked.

"If you are still in the city, I will find you." Then Dillon reconsidered. "But I may not be free then. So do this: check with Bata. I will make sure she has the news."

"Thank you." Then they parted, their business together done.

The rest of the mission was uneventful. The Byzantines agreed to send an embassy to Attila with their answer, in due course. So the work of the Hun embassy was done, and they were free to relax. They would return with the Roman embassy, showing the way.

But Orestes wanted Attila kept current. So he sent Od back privately. "Tell the king where we stand, then return to me with his word."

There was no word from Melee. Od visited with Bata, but she could say only that though there was a smell in the air, there was nothing they had been able to identify. "But keep alert, Od," she concluded. "There may be something there."

Thus Od made his way alone back to the land of the Huns. Orestes had arranged for him to have a good gelding, and that helped considerably. The horses of the Huns had come with them from the east, and were short, skinny, long bodied, crooked nosed, and small hoofed. But they were re- nowned for their intelligence, trainability, spirit, endurance, and hardiness. This one had a wooden saddle and leather loop stirrups. The animal was well trained, so that Od did not need to use the reins or whip; the pressure of his legs alone guided it. As far as he was concerned, the Huns were superior to the Romans in animal training.

The return trip was uneventful. He was familiar with the route, and had silver to purchase food and feed along the way. He looked like a Hun, so was treated courteously by the villagers he encountered. He went directly to Attila's court, and petitioned to speak with the king.

Attila received him promptly. The king was short and square, with a large head, swarthy complexion, flat nose, deep-seated eyes, and a beard so sparse it shouldn't have bothered. In fact he reminded Od of a Hunnic horse, but he would never say that. Attila was of the Black Hun tribe; the White Huns, to the east, had lighter complexions and resembled Romans to a greater degree. But Od knew better than to judge by appearances, for that was the way others judged him. Attila lived a plain life, despite being sur- rounded by the wealth of his conquests. His clothing was simple, without jewelry. He was, everyone understood, faithful to his wives, to whom he was a loving husband, and he was a good father. And his mind was always there.

"What is your news?"

"The Romans will send an embassy with their response. Their city is rich beyond the imagination of Huns." Od hesitated.

"There is something else?"

"I do not wish to waste my lord's time in inconsequentials."

"Waste just a bit of it," Attila said with a smile.

So Od described the curious dialogue he had overheard. "It probably means nothing, yet I wonder."

Attila nodded. "It is in the little details that kingdoms can be made and unmade. Keep your ears open. Did they say anything about a bride for my secretary?"

"Lord, if they did, I was not privy to it."

Attila made a negligent wave. "The matter will be resolved in due course. Rest three days, then return to the embassy."

"Thank you, lord." Od knew that Attila would treat him well. Sure enough, as Od departed the palace, the chief of guards intercepted him and gave him a gold coin. No more was said; the king was satisfied with his performance.

Avalanche soon caught up to Od, and relieved him of his coin. "What's this I hear about you making out with the women of Byzantine?'' she demanded as they lay together on his bed.

"I had dealings with only two women," he replied. "One was older than Rome. The other was sequestered in the palace, sworn to perpetual virginity."

"That one. She was beautiful?"

This could be awkward. "How can I answer, without making you angry, so that you never dilate my pupils again?"

She took him by the ears and hauled his head into her ample bosom. "Speak, or I smother you."

"I dare not."

She put her arms around his head, locking it in, and indeed her breasts covered his mouth. She could make him dizzy just by breathing. "Speak!"

He surrendered. "She was Melee, and I think she must be the most beautiful woman in Rome."

"She can't be. Honoria is."

"Who?"

"Galla Placidia's daughter, sister of the Emperor of the West. You do not know of her?" She gave another squeeze.

"Oh. *That* Honoria. I misspoke. I meant Constantinople. Melee is there."

"And she is lovelier than I?"

He hesitated, but she squeezed his head again, and he spoke. "Yes."

She pushed him away. "You never learned when to lie."

"True," he said, ashamed.

"Come into me." She was never annoyed when he told her the truth. He suspected it was because every other man lied to her, trying to win her favor. She preferred truth to flattery.

Later in the evening he remembered Attila's comment about a bride for his secretary, and asked her about it.

"You didn't know? That man was promised a rich and noble bride from the court of Constantinople. They selected a bride, but she was reluctant. They tried to encourage her, but she fled. So they confiscated her family's fortune, but she remained unreasonable. So they promised Attila's secretary a widow of exceptional beauty and wealth, but have not yet delivered. Attila is irked, because it makes it seem as if he has not been able to deliver for a loyal associate."

Od had a horrible thought. "Could it have been Melee? The one who refused?"

She laughed. "No. I misremember the name, but it was not that."

Od was relieved. He had seen Melee only very briefly, and remembered that he had told no one about her marital status, but that encounter had impressed him deeply. It wasn't just her beauty. There was a fond tension about her, a seeming capacity for wildness, that was fascinating. She loved Dillon, which spoke long scrolls about the potentials of that man.

He rode back to Constantinople on schedule, and rejoined the embassy.

He did not seem to have been missed. "The king asked about his secretary's promised bride," he reported.

"That is high on the agenda," Orestes said. "Imagine a woman turning down the chance to marry a noble of Attila's court."

"The Romans don't really know the Huns," Od said. "They think them barbarians."

"And the Romans are fools. Attila may be uncultured by Roman court standards, but he is as worthy a king as any on the horizon, and his secretary is a good man, hardly a barbarian."

When Od visited old Bata, she had news: "Watch the interpreter, Bigilas. He has been given fifty pounds of gold, and it surely is not for incidentals. That is bribe money."

"Bribe money? To bribe whom? For what?"

But that was the extent of what she knew. He would have to find out for himself. But he made sure to tell Orestes about it.

"I agree," Orestes said. "There should be no need for that kind of money on a trip like this. So it could indeed be bribe money. But surely they don't expect to bribe Attila out of demanding a wife for his secretary."

Early in the summer, the Byzantine party assembled. It was headed by Maximus, a noble of proven integrity and distinction. He was known as a soldier and a diplomat, and had played an important part in negotiating a treaty with the Persians a quarter century before. He was also noted for his eloquence. He in turn invited a noted man of letters, Priscus, to accompany him on the mission. Priscus was not eager to journey for an extended period into the barbarian hinterland, but Maximus' entreaties moved him, and finally he agreed.

Orestes seemed mildly surprised by the quality of these people. "There is a smell, but it can not associate with men like these," he remarked privately to Od.

Attila sent word that he would be willing to come as far as the city of Sofia, north of Greece, to meet the mission, as its members were sufficiently high ranking to warrant this courtesy.

They set out in early summer, with Edeco and the translator Bigilas in the group. Under Edeco were a number of Hun warriors. There were also seventeen Hun fugitives being returned to Attila; he did not like deserters.

They moved slowly but well, for the Romans traveled in style. The trip to Sofia took thirteen days. The city was ruined and deserted, having been sacked by the Huns eight years before, and again more thoroughly two years before. But Maximus felt obliged to entertain Orestes and Edeco with a good dinner. They managed to get some cattle and sheep, which they duly slaughtered for the main entree. What the meal lacked in variety it made up for in wine, and it was going well—until certain disharmonies developed.

The Huns toasted the health of Attila, their leader. Maximus raised his cup in a toast: "To Theodosius, Emperor of the East!"

"But it is not proper to speak the name of a god such as Theodosius in the same breath as that of a mere man such as Attila," the translator Bigilas protested.

The Huns grew hot. "You, a Hun yourself, say this?" one demanded.

"By birth a Hun," Bigilas retorted. "By choice, a Roman."

"By choice a pig!" another said.

The man of letters, Priscus, quickly intervened. "It is a matter of interpretation, of no account among friends. Mere humor, in fact. No affront was intended to Attila, who is among the most prominent of leaders and perhaps of divine descent himself." Od was beginning to appreciate why he had been brought along; he was good at making peace.

"Without doubt," Maximus agreed quickly, with a warning glance to Bigilas. Bigilas, half drunk but clearly stung by the implied reproof, staggered out of the house.

Things settled down. However, the Huns were not as relaxed as they had been, and it was clear that the interpreter's intemperate words had not been forgotten. Od wondered just how loyal the man was to his employers. Bata had warned him to beware of the interpreter. And what did he propose to do with all that gold?

Then Maximus presented Orestes and Edeco with some fine pears from the far country of India, and some colorful silks. This was exactly the kind of thing that Orestes had bought for Kreka; now there would be some for Orestes' own wife. Orestes was plainly pleased.

At the end of the meal the others left. As Orestes was gathering up his things to go to his own quarters, he paused to speak in Greek. "Congratulations, Consul Maximus, on your cleverness in not following the example of some court officials by inviting Edeco to dine alone with you." Both Maximus and Priscus seemed puzzled, but Orestes did not elaborate.

"So you do suspect Edeco," Od murmured as they departed.

"Edeco is a good man," Orestes said. "And I think Maximus and Priscus are good men too. But perhaps we can stir up some hidden currents."

Od didn't argue, but he was in doubt about Edeco, and certainly about Bigilas. He wondered whether Orestes was too honest a man to be ready to believe in the treacherous nature of some others.

As it turned out, Attila did not come to Sofia, so they marched on northwest to Nish. This city, too, was a desolate scene. Its splendid buildings were broken hulks, and the able-bodied people had fled. Only those too sick or weak to travel remained, eking out their tortured livelihoods amid the ruins. Od realized that war was in the nature of things, but he hated to see its leavings.

They halted by a river, where white bones of those slain in the war were lying all around on the banks and in the flow. They needed water, and the water here was probably clean, but they elected to find another place from which to draw it.

At last they reached the great river Danube. There they were met by Hun ferrymen in homemade single-log boats. In these hollowed-out trees their party was ferried across.

But Attila still wasn't meeting them, though he was said to be in the vicinity. So Edeco with some of his followers went ahead to announce the mission's arrival. Orestes also went, but he told Od to remain with the Romans. "Help them out as you can, but keep your mouth shut," he said. "Let them forget your presence."

"Are you asking me to spy on them?"

"On someone, perhaps."

Oh. So Orestes wasn't satisfied with Bigilas. This must be his way of keeping an eye on Edeco without leaving Bigilas unwatched. "Eyes open, mouth shut," Od agreed.

A few hours later two Hun horsemen appeared. "Follow us to Attila," they called, and led the way to the king's camp.

When they reached the area, Maximus decided to pitch his tents on a hill. But one of the horsemen said that this would not be allowed, because Attila's tents were on lower ground. Maximus shrugged and directed his men to lower ground.

Then Edeco returned, with Orestes and another noble of Attila's court named Scotta. "I must speak with Maximus," he told the Roman sentinel. So they went to the general. "The king wishes to know what you intend to achieve by your embassy?"

The translator Bigilas looked uneasy, but Maximus had no hesitation. "I will speak only directly to Attila, as is proper for an embassy."

Scotta spoke. "The king already knows your mission."

"Perhaps so," Maximus said stiffly. "But he must also know that I am trying to implement it in the prescribed manner."

Scotta spoke to Edeco. Bigilas did not translate, but it was evidently some kind of directive.

Edeco and Orestes departed. But soon another party of Huns returned. One stood, and then recited what sounded like an official letter. Maximus' jaw dropped. "That is the exact contents of the letter I carry," he said.

Od was similarly surprised. How had they found that out?

Scotta nodded. "So you have no need to deliver it. Now break camp and leave."

Maximus was clearly annoyed, but like the good diplomat he was, he didn't argue. He gave orders to his men to prepare to depart.

"You shouldn't be doing that!" Bigalas told Maximus. "You came here as an embassy, a representative of Constantinople. You should have pressed your position."

Maximus didn't answer, though Od marveled at the temerity of a mere translator to berate the leader of an official delegation. Bigilas didn't know his place.

Scotta merely stood and watched. Apparently he was here to make sure that the Romans did depart.

As night fell, and they were ready to move, another group of Huns arrived. They spoke to Scotta, who then turned to Maximus. "The king bids you wait, because the hour is late."

Maximus, ever accommodating, reversed course again, and they pitched the camp they had just unpitched. The man was a marvel of patience.

Then more Huns arrived, bringing food for the evening. It was an ox, and river fish. "The king bids you eat," Scotta said. Then he departed.

So it was not a complete loss. They ate, and slept.

But in the morning Scotta returned. "Depart, unless you have something to say beyond what the king already knows."

Maximus was plainly nettled, but maintained his poise. "As you know, it is not proper for me to reveal my mission to anyone other than King Attila himself. I can't promise any new information beyond what he seems already to know."

"In that case, depart." Scotta folded his arms, his business completed.

"You idiot!" the translator Bigilas exclaimed to Maximus. "You should have promised him something new, to get the audience!"

Maximus had had enough. "Listen, you slimy slug! If the man does not desire an audience, it is not for the likes of you to second-guess those of us who seek a dialogue. He asks us to depart, so we shall depart."

Priscus quickly stepped between them. "I'm sure it will all work out." Then he turned to Scotta, beckoning another member of their party who spoke the Hun language. "General Maximus will give you considerable gifts if you can arrange an audience with Attila. So if you really have the influence with him that the stories claim—"

The translation got no farther before Scotta responded, angered by the implied slur. "No one has more influence with Attila than I! I will prove it." He stalked to his horse and rode away.

Maximus turned to Priscus. "He was looking for a bribe? That never occurred to me."

"You are painfully honest," Priscus said. "I wondered why he stood around after delivering his messages, and finally realized that he might be hoping for that which he would not ask."

Soon Scotta returned. "The king summons you to an audience."

Just like that, after all the delays! But Od was mystified too, for though Attila knew the ways of bribery, he had little but contempt for them. He preferred straight power. Scotta was loyal; it was unlike him to act in any way contrary to Attila's wish.

Maximus, Priscus, Bigilas, and their attendants followed him to the impressive royal tent. Od tagged along, unnoticed.

When they entered, they found Attila seated on a wooden stool, his nobles standing behind him. There was a brief exchange of courtesies. Maximus was about to make the official presentation of his mission, but Attila suddenly turned on Bigilas.

"How dare you come into my presence when you know that the Hun fugitives have not been returned!"

"But they have been," Bigilas protested, with some justice. "Some were turned over yesterday, and the others—"

Attila turned red with anger. "You filthy toad! I would have you impaled and given to the birds for food, were it not for the law of embassies. Now get out of my sight!'' He made a gesture that included the whole party. ''All of you!''

Disturbed, Maximus led his party out. Od hesitated, knowing that Attila recognized him, but received no signal, so he followed. The Hun king could throw a fit with the best of them, but this was strange. It would have been easier to listen to Maximus' formal presentation, then dismiss him politely. Attila was being deliberately difficult. Why?

When they were safely away from the tent, Bigilas spoke to Priscus. ''I am amazed that Attila spoke to me like that.'' The man was clearly chastened.

''Maybe he learned of your injudicious comparison between Attila the man and Theodosius the god,'' Priscus replied.

But Od wondered. Attila professed no religion, though he was tolerant of the faiths of others, so long as they did not get in his way. He more likely would have laughed, seeing it as Attila the man and Theodosius the fool.

They returned to the Roman camp and waited, as they had not been ordered again to depart. That night, when the others were settling down to sleep, Edeco arrived, alone. Od, alert, in the next tent, listened closely. ''It is time to bring the promised gold,'' Edeco said. Then he left, without speaking to the others.

Then Priscus approached Bigilas. ''What was your discussion about?'' he inquired.

''He said I need to return to check on the remaining fugitives.''

''But they are in safe hands, and will soon be turned over anyway.''

''Still, it seems I must check.'' Bigilas sounded evasive.

So Priscus was suspicious too! Something certainly seemed to be going on, and Edeco and Bigilas were at the heart of it. But it seemed that Priscus and Maximus knew nothing of it.

In the morning Bigilas announced that he had to go to see about the return of the remaining fugitives. He might have to use some of the gold he had brought.

But before the interpreter could leave, Scotta rode up. ''The king decrees that the Romans are not to purchase anything in the Hun domains, except for food.''

Maximus had no problem with that, but Bigilas looked stricken. Obviously his fifty pounds of gold was a far greater sum than any food purchases would require. What was that gold for? But he rode off on his expressed mission, carrying the gold with him.

Scotta spied Od. ''It seems you must translate, now. The king has a special mission. He will meet with you in a few days. Proceed north, and he will rejoin you in due course.''

Od repeated that to the Romans.

''Another mission?'' Maximus said. ''I had understood that we were the only one.''

Scotta smiled. "This is not political. He is making a detour to marry the daughter of Eksam."

"That is surely worth a detour," Maximus agreed. "I trust she is lovely."

"Indeed. And well connected. He should be in a mellow mood in a week." He departed.

Maximus turned to Priscus. "Did you note how much mellower the Hun noble became after Bigilas left?"

"Yes. I have the feeling that the Huns don't like Bigilas any better than we do. And I don't understand what he means to do with all that gold."

They traveled north. The Huns traveled with them, and supplied them generously with food and mead, so that they did not need to spend any gold even for that. The representatives of Attila were uniformly polite, in contrast to the way they had been before. This was more like the Attila Od knew.

One night there was a heavy storm that blew over their tents. Soaking wet and disheveled, Maximus and Priscus were in a foul mood. But Scotta approached. "I see you are in difficulty. These things happen. Please come to the nearby village, where you will be suitably entertained."

"Entertained!" Priscus exclaimed.

"Hun hospitality is not to be derided," Od said privately to him. "They will treat you well."

Priscus looked at Maximus, who nodded. "Then we most gratefully accept," Priscus said.

They followed Scotta to the village. It was not impressive, consisting of huts. But the village was, it turned out, ruled by one of the former wives of Attila's deceased brother Bleda, and she was an excellent host. Not only were the huts well lighted by burning reeds, attractive young women soon arrived, bearing plates of good food and skins of mead.

The women did not leave after delivering their goods. "Why do they remain?" Priscus asked Od.

"The girls, too, are for your use," Od explained. "They are here to comfort you in your misfortune. It is called a Scythian complement."

Maximus and Priscus tried to mask their astonishment. "We have severely underestimated barbarian hospitality," Maximus said. "But we can't touch these women. We are married men." But his attitude suggested that the greater constraint might have been his distrust of the situation. Was this some kind of a test? Od couldn't blame him, having had similar doubts until Avalanche had educated him.

Od spoke to the women. "The Romans greatly appreciate your beauty and kindness, and hope you will not be affronted if they lack the fortitude, after the terrible storm, to take you to bed. They are afraid they will only embarrass themselves by the effort. They deeply regret their incapacity."

The girls were not at all affronted. They selected tidbits and fed them to the men, smiling, and when the food was gone, they departed with the remnants. Od suspected that though they had been quite prepared to indulge their guests to the fullest extent, they much preferred to spend the night in the arms of their regular lovers.

In the morning, refreshed, the men presented Bleda's widow, who had shown them such kindness, with three silver goblets, and with furs, dates, and pepper from India. The woman was thrilled, for these were things seldom seen in remote villages like this.

They repaired their tents and continued north for several more days. As they approached the village to which their Hun guide was directing them, Scotta appeared again. "King Attila will be arriving soon. You must wait for him to enter the village first. It is a matter of protocol."

"Of course," Maximus said graciously.

They waited outside the village, resting, as Attila's party came up along the trail they had used. It was an impressive entrance. A select band of women came out to meet the king, then marched ahead of him in separate files. The spaces between the files were traversed by long white linen veils. The women carried these above their heads, stretched out, and they formed a canopy for a group of young girls, who sang laudatory hymns in chorus.

Once Attila had been suitably ushered in, the Romans were allowed to enter the village and make their camp. They pitched their tents and waited for what came next. This surprised them, for they discovered that there were a number of West Romans there, some of them prominent. Among them was Romulus, who was Orestes' father-in-law, and the commander of the military forces in the Roman province of Noricum, north of Italy. There was also Promotus, the governor of Noricum. Maximus was amazed. Here in what he had thought was a backwater were people of known power and reputation in Rome.

Maximus and Priscus were sitting in their tent when an elder Roman man arrived. "I am Tatulus, Orestes' father," he said by way of introduction. "Attila invites you to a banquet at the ninth hour of the day." That was mid-afternoon.

It turned out to be several days of banquets, and they were as fancy as anything in Byzantium. The West Romans, who were part of an embassy from Rome, attended also. As they entered, cup-bearers gave them cups of wine, so that they might pray before sitting down. After they had done so, and tasted from the cups, they went to their seats. All the chairs were set along the walls of the house on either side. In the middle was a couch, and Attila sat on it. Behind that was a set of steps leading up to his bed, covered with white linens and embroideries. Beside Attila were some of his honored nobles, and two of his sons.

A servant brought in Attila's food first. Then other servants brought the provisions for the guests.

"Now that's interesting," Priscus murmured. "We are served sumptuous food on silver plates—but Attila himself has nothing but meat on a wooden platter. We have gold and silver goblets, but he has a mug of wood."

"Yes, he lives simply," Od explained. "He entertains well because it is expected, but he has no use for such things himself."

"And his clothing is plain," Priscus continued. "His boots, his sword—unadorned. There is no flash, no embellishment in the man at all."

"Well, he is a barbarian," Od said, smiling.

But Priscus did not smile. "No, he is not." He turned to Maximus. "That man is dangerous, because he is without personal vanity. Flattery is not going to move him."

"I haven't tried to flatter him!" Maximus said, irritated.

"Precisely. I think he likes you."

Priscus was catching on.

After the banquet there was entertainment. There was singing, which rehearsed Attila's victories in war. Some of the Hun nobles were moved to tears, but Attila himself looked politely bored. Then a dwarf appeared. He was a short humpback with distorted feet. His nose was so flat it was indicated only by the nostrils. He made jokes in a mixture of the languages of the Huns, Goths, and Latins, and soon had the entire company laughing uproariously.

Od glanced at Priscus, who was watching Attila. Attila was completely unmoved.

"There is no laughter in him," Priscus said.

But when Attila's youngest son went and stood before him, then Attila pinched the boy's cheeks and laughed.

"So he does have feelings, seldom as they may show," Priscus remarked. "But why does he view that boy with such favor?"

"It is because of a prophecy," Od said. "It says that Attila's race will fail, but be restored by this son."

"He believes in prophecy?"

"So it is said," Od said.

"Or does he merely profess to believe, because it is proper?"

Od shrugged. "Perhaps."

During the next few days the Romans were treated to several more banquets, and tours of the grounds. Priscus was especially interested in the palace, which was made of wood, but contained baths of marble like those of Rome. There were no quarries in this region, so the stone had been brought in from afar. The baths had been built by a captive Greek architect, who now had to keep them in running order.

Finally the Romans had their formal audience with Attila, and agreed that they would arrange for a wealthy, lovely, and noble Roman widow to marry Attila's secretary, to make up for the woman he had been treacherously denied. It was apparent that Attila was as loyal to his supporters as they were to him.

That done, they commenced their long journey back to Constantinople. They still needed translators, and Bigilas had not returned, so Od remained with them. "This matter is not yet done," Orestes told him. "If you learn anything, get back to us forthwith." Orestes himself was not going on this trip.

They traveled south without special event. Then, on the road between the Greek towns of Philippopolis and Adrianople, they encountered Bigilas, who was returning from points farther south. He had his son with him, and still had the gold. They briefed him on their meetings with Attila. "And have you made arrangements for the return of more Hun fugitives?" Maximus asked.

"I am still working on it, but it is complicated," Bigilas said evasively.

"That man is lying," Priscus muttered to Od. "I don't know what he is up to, but I think it doesn't concern us."

"Then who would it concern?" Od asked.

They exchanged a glance, and suddenly it came. "Attila!" Priscus whispered. "All that gold—it must be some kind of plot against his king!"

"Against Attila himself," Od echoed. "That must be what Edeco plotted with the evil Bishop of Smyrna."

"Who must have arranged for the gold," Priscus agreed. "And Attila suspects, but thought that we were part of it. No wonder he delayed meeting us."

After Bigilas went on northward, they talked with Maximus. "This is mere conjecture," the general said. "Where is the proof?"

"There is no proof," Priscus said. "But nevertheless, it seems best that Attila be warned about Edeco, a man he evidently trusts. Once he and Bigilas get together, who knows what could happen? It should not be risked."

"We can't be involved in anything like this, on mere suspicion," Maximus said.

"But suppose Od returns, to speak privately with his liege?" Priscus said. "Leaving us out of it?"

Maximus nodded. "I think we can proceed from here without an interpreter."

So it was that Od parted company with folk he had come to respect and like, and rode swiftly by a different route back to the Hun capital.

He arrived a day before Bigilas was due. "You must speak with the king," he said to Orestes. "We met Bigilas on the road, and think he is plotting against Attila himself. With Edeco."

"Do you have proof?"

"No proof. But if it is so, and we do not warn Attila—"

"I will take you there."

They went to the palace, where Orestes quickly obtained a private audience with the king. "Tell our liege what you believe," Orestes said.

"Lord, the Romans think Bigilas and Edeco are conspiring to do you some harm," Od said. "There is no proof, but we feared that you might be trusting someone unworthy of it."

Attila frowned. "You accuse Edeco? This is serious business. I trust this man."

"Lord, please, at least get him away from you until you can resolve this question."

"I think not." Attila lifted one hand and snapped his fingers.

In a moment Edeco stepped out from behind some curtains. Od's heart sank. He had heard everything!

"This is a clever man," Edeco said, looking at Od. "Without evidence, he has fathomed the essence of the plot."

"The plot?" Od asked numbly.

"When I met privately with the Bishop of Smyrna, he bribed me to assassinate Attila. Bigilas carries the money to pay the assassins. I agreed, in order to learn as much as possible, and to discover any other traitors in our midst. It is apparent that you and Orestes are not among them."

"Of course we aren't!" Orestes said. "We were under suspicion?"

"No. But we can not be too careful. If I could be suspected, why not you?"

"So you told Attila," Orestes said, clearly relieved.

"And I told him to keep his mouth shut, and learn all he could," Attila said. "Now I say the same to you. Stand by and watch me deal with Bigilas."

"Yes, Lord," Od said, weak kneed. For a moment he had feared for his own life.

"Thank you, Attila," Orestes said, in much the same tone.

"Bigilas arrives tomorrow," Edeco said. "I have primed him to be ready to act. I myself will be absent from this particular encounter, so as not to influence it, but the two of you will be present and silent."

Orestes nodded. He bowed to Attila, who nodded, and Orestes stepped back and away. Od followed.

"Attila is pleased with you," Orestes said. "I suspect that henceforth he will allow you to enter his presence armed."

That was a rare compliment. Orestes and Edeco had such a privilege, but Od and others had always been subject to a search for weapons before entering the presence. Should a surprise attack ever be launched against the king, his armed associates would immediately leap to his defense.

"Of course," Od agreed.

Next day he was indeed admitted armed, though his weapon, a dagger, did not show. He stood behind Orestes and other courtiers as the translator and his son, a quiet young man, were led into Attila's presence.

"Why do you carry so much gold?" Orestes asked, speaking for the king.

Bigilas assumed an air of righteous innocence. "It is for provisioning myself and those accompanying me, so that I may not stray from my zeal for the embassy because of lack of supplies or scarcity of horses or baggage animals."

Orestes nodded as if satisfied. "And is that all?"

"The gold is also to purchase fugitives, for many in the Roman territory have begged me to liberate their kinsmen." That had the ring of truth, because the Huns had captured many Romans, and commonly did ransom them back to their relatives when the price was enough.

Attila had had enough. "No longer, you worthless beast!" he cried. "No longer will you escape justice by deception. Nor will there be any excuse sufficient for you to avoid punishment. Now tell me all the details. Who else is in this plot with you?"

Bigilas realized that he had been found out. But he tried to maintain some secrecy. "No one, Lord. It is all my own doing."

"None of this lying!" Attila shouted. "Make a complete confession, or I will have your son struck down this instant!"

The boy's mouth dropped open in surprise and fright. Bigilas looked appalled. The king had certainly found the key to reducing all equivocation, in the classic Hun manner.

Scotta stepped forward, drawing his sword. He was plainly ready to implement the threat.

Bigilas lost all semblance of resistance. "Oh, my lord, spare my son, who knows nothing of this and has done no wrong. Kill me, the guilty one." He prostrated himself, tears flowing from his eyes. The man truly loved his son. "I beg of you, let my son go! Take the gold, take everything, only spare him."

Scotta paused, but did not step back. Now Orestes spoke. "Your accomplices. The details. Now. Who hired you? For exactly what purpose?"

"The eunuch who is Bishop of Smyrna arranged it," Bigilas babbled. "He bribed Edeco with promises of rich living in Constantinople. Please let my son go. The emperor Theodosius agreed and provided the gold to hire assassins. I agreed to handle it. Put me to death, but set my son free."

Orestes scowled. "You accuse a loyal Hun noble like Edeco of betrayal?"

"It is true! It is true! He is your traitor. He agreed to the bishop's proposal, and ordered me to use the gold to pay the hirelings for the assassination." Bigilas looked wildly around. "He must have fled! Capture him. Torture him. He will confirm. But let my innocent son go."

Attila nodded. Scotta finally stepped back, sheathing his sword. By this token he indicated that the son would be spared.

But not Bigilas. Men stepped forward with chains. They chained him and led him away, his frightened son following.

"What shall we do with this trash?" Attila inquired of his court.

"Slay him, of course," Scotta said. "But the son does seem to be innocent, and should be spared."

Attila glanced at Orestes. Orestes nodded. "Scotta is of course correct. But it occurs to me that more can be gained from this than the death of one traitorous Hun. It is the arrogance of the Eastern Roman Empire that needs to be curbed. An embarrassment and warning to it may be worth more than the gold."

Attila looked at Scotta, prompting his response. "Now I am just a simple barbarian," Scotta said, with a hint of a smile. "It seems to me that the best embarrassment and warning is to publicly execute the assassin. Do you have something more devious and effective in mind?" There was of course some rivalry between the chosen people of the court, though all were completely loyal to Attila and never questioned each other's loyalty. This was a challenge.

"I may have," Orestes said. "To a Roman, honor is not simply a matter of vindication or vengeance. He must not allow himself to be ridiculed or treated with open scorn. Now consider the case of Emperor Theodosius, heir to what the Romans believe is the greatest empire on earth. He has acted in a reprehensible manner, and deserves to be made the object of righteous scorn. But simply killing the lowly assassin will not accomplish that; the Romans will pretend it was his own idea entirely. Bigilas may be more important as a symbol that can't be ignored."

"What are you talking about?" Scotta demanded.

"Suppose we don't kill him," Orestes said. "Instead, we send him back with the bag of fifty pounds of gold hung around his neck? Make him be brought into the presence of the emperor, that nominal god whose name is not to be uttered in the same breath as real kings, with the evidence of his faithlessness weighting down his body. How will the Romans explain that away?"

Suddenly Scotta saw it. "Absolute scorn for the traitor *and* the money—and the one who hired him. Spit in the face of the treacherous god. Beautiful! But make it a hundred pounds."

Orestes nodded. "Send the son back for fifty more pounds of gold. The ransom of his father. Then send it all back, contemptuously."

"Done!" Scotta agreed.

Then both men looked at Attila. "Done," Attila agreed, satisfied.

It was done. The son went back to Constantinople for another fifty pounds of gold, brought it back, and then Orestes conducted Bigilas, burdened by that hundred pounds of gold, into the presence of Emperor Theodosius. As a gesture it was in one sense magnanimous, for it spared the life of the assassin and returned all of the tainted money. But it was also such a magnificent gesture of scorn that it became widely known. Possibly this dramatic ploy accounts in part for the fury with which Christian historians were to savage the reputation of the injured party, Attila, King of the Huns, for fifteen centuries thereafter. Far from being a scoundrel, he had demonstrated superior ethics, embarrassing the supposedly more civilized emperor. That could never be forgiven. Thus his name was to become almost a synonym for viciousness. Attila was no saint, but neither was he a devil; he was simply a king who showed up the faithlessness of Byzantium. Hell has no fury like that of a culture unmasked.

Yet this was not the end. There was to be an even more remarkable incident that was to shake up the other half of the fading Roman colossus, the Western Roman Empire. Like the assassination plot, this originated with the Romans, but finished with Attila. The setting is Constantinople, the spring of A.D. 450.

NOTE: the standard unit of measurement in this context was the cubit, approximately the length of a man's arm from elbow to fingertip. The Greek cubit was just over eighteen inches, and the Roman cubit just under eighteen inches. Perhaps the Romans had shorter arms.

"Melee." It was Pulcheria, as grim as usual.

Melee hurried to attend her. Had her latest tryst with Dillon been found out? "Yes, Lady."

"We are to have a new sister. I fear she will be somewhat wild, and in need of considerable guidance. You will attend to her."

Now this was interesting. Another woman was coming to join the devout sisters? "I am unworthy," Melee said with proper humility.

"No doubt." Pulcheria's lip almost twitched with a trace of humor. She surely knew of Melee's indecorous past. "She is young, about thirty, and has behaved injudiciously. She may not readily adjust, but it is important that she consider herself to be well treated here. You must be her friend."

Melee had to make at least a token protest. "Lady, my friendship is not given frivolously or falsely. And if she is royal, it would be presumptuous." Actually Melee was royal too, but that counted for next to nothing here.

"Then treat her as a friend would, advising her so that she seeks no mischief. But I believe you will like her. There may be a certain affinity."

"Yes, Lady." This was getting intriguing.

"She is Honoria, sister of Valentinian, Emperor of the West." Pulcheria paused, waiting for Melee's jaw to drop.

It did. "Galla Placidia's daughter? The one who—?"

"The same. It seems that her life is not secure in the West, so her mother is sending her here for a time. It is a matter of safety rather than devotion, but the forms must be followed. Do you suppose this will fall within your compass?"

This was a shrewd assignment. Melee had considerable sympathy and admiration for Honoria, who struck her as a woman of her own type. The descendants of Theodosius I were unusual in that the men were weak and vacillating, while the women were lovely, strong, and imperious. Galla Placidia was the most powerful woman in either empire, and her daughter favored her in spirit. Had women been allowed to become emperors, Honoria would have been in line to command the West. But as it was, her ambition had nearly gotten her killed. Melee would be delighted to make her acquaintance. "Yes, Lady."

"She is destined to arrive this afternoon. Take a coach and meet her at the Golden Gate."

"Yes, Lady." Melee tried to mask her thrill at this assignment, but it surely showed. Pulcheria was old and devout, but she was no fool.

A brightly painted wooden carriage was waiting when she went down to the stables, with its driver and guard. It was drawn by two mules in ornate harnesses. And the guard was Dillon! She knew by his expression that he was surprised to see her; he must have expected Pulcheria herself to be traveling.

Did Pulcheria know? Was this the reward for special service? If Melee kept Honoria in line, would she be granted tacit access to her love? For as long as she succeeded in making the West Emperor's sister behave? She rather suspected it was. Pulcheria could connive as well as any royal Roman, and she had considerable power.

"To the Golden Gate," Melee told the driver. "See that we are not delayed."

The driver started the horse, and the carriage moved out. It would stay on the main street, for it would not fit on the narrow smaller streets. Melee drew the curtain closed so that she could ride in privacy. Then she spoke to Dillon. "Guard, attend me."

Dillon silently entered the closed compartment. She beckoned him with a twitch of fingers, and touched her lips. He needed no other invitation. He embraced her and kissed her. Then she hoisted her skirt and sat on his lap, lifting her weight so that he could draw his tunic aside to bare his midsection with its erect spike. She let her bottom down on him, guiding his connection, delighting in their slow merging. When he was secure, she opened her upper tunic and gave her breasts to his hands. They made love, silently, with very little motion, so that there was no shaking of the carriage. Actually, the bumping of the carriage over the obstructions of the road did most of what was required; she had to hold on to him closely so that she did not on occasion bounce off. She kissed him, feeling his urgency within her as his fingers caressed her taut nipples.

"Oh, Melee, Melee," he murmured in her ear. "How did you arrange this?"

"Pulcheria arranged it. She must know."

"But then she should have me reassigned, or worse!" His alarm could be felt all the way from his mouth to his member.

"I have an assignment. I must succeed. I think this is my payment for being sure I succeed. If I fail, then it could be severe mischief for us both. She is letting me know, by this token."

"You must succeed," he agreed. "What is the assignment?"

She waited for his urgency to build to the climax, tightening her bottom to encourage it. Just as it occurred, she told him. "I must attend Honoria, the West Emperor's sister."

"You sow!" he swore, unable to halt his explosion despite his amazement. He knew she had timed it deliberately, to tease him.

"You boar," she said, kissing him again. She flexed her buttocks and tensed her abdomen, clenching around him, squeezing the last pulse from him.

"There will never be a woman as maddeningly desirable as you," he said.

"Well, Honoria may be."

"And if I ever look at her, you will cut off anything I have that has ever been inside you."

"True. What goes inside me is mine forever. I hope you can remember that when you see her."

"I shall make a valiant effort."

"I think you just made one." She kissed him again, feeling him diminish within her, his fuel spent.

They disengaged, carefully, used handkerchiefs for spot cleaning, and reassembled themselves. Then Melee explained as much as she knew about her assignment.

As the carriage drew near the Golden Gate, Dillon resumed his post riding beside the enclosed portion of the carriage. They entered the walled postern and came to a halt.

Melee drew the curtain aside and stepped down, quickly assisted by Dillon, who was now a mere guard again. She was always impressed by the great outer wall, and its massive guard towers. The postern was like the central court of a huge house, a virtual castle in itself. Its arches reached up into the facing of a building ten times as tall as a man, dwarfing the gateway itself. Woe betide any intruder who tried to storm this edifice! He would find himself in a rain of boiling pitch before he got halfway through.

But she wasn't here to gawk. She walked to the postern commander. "We are here to meet an incoming party."

"Who?"

"A woman from Italy." Melee doubted that it was prudent to identify the person.

"Overland?" he demanded. "Why not by ship?"

That set Melee back. Of course Honoria would travel by ship! It would be a long, wearing, and dangerous ride by land. The harbor was close by the palace. So why had she been sent here?

Dillon spoke up. "It is not for the likes of you or us to say. The lady is traveling incognito, and would have no privacy at the crowded harbor. She will have debarked at Perinthus and ridden here."

The commander nodded. "She'll have to show her authorization, same as anyone else."

"We will check back in an hour." She glanced at the driver. "If anyone asks to go to the palace, she's the one." He nodded.

They walked to Grandma Bata's house, nearby. Melee seldom got to visit her, so grabbed the opportunity.

"Melee!" the old woman exclaimed when they got there. "And Dillon. But you two shouldn't be here, wasting your time with me. You should be making love."

"Already done, Grandma," Melee said.

The old woman laughed. She really appreciated any company she could get.

They told her of their mission to meet Honoria. "Oh, that one!" Bata chortled. "I knew she wasn't safe in Italy, with her jealous brother. He would have killed her, if it hadn't been for Galla Placidia."

"Why?" Dillon asked. He was not as current on such events as were the women of the palace.

"Because she conspired to have him replaced as Emperor of the West. He tortured and slaughtered everything connected. So Placidia had to get her daughter to where Valentinian couldn't reach her, which is here in the East."

"And now I am to be her companion in the palace," Melee said. "And keep her out of mischief."

Bata laughed again. "As if you have any expertise in that, you wild honeybee!"

"Am I to blame if the gods stuffed me with wildness?"

"They just wanted me to be happy," Dillon said.

But there was a serious side. "Do you think Pulcheria knows? About me and Dillon?"

"Of course she knows, child! And now she's using that information. She has a perfect hold on you. She can reward you or punish you in ways you can't resist, and she knows you know it. Mind you prevent Honoria from embarrassing her."

"I'll try, Grandma."

But soon they had to return to the postern, lest they miss Honoria.

As it turned out, they needn't have rushed. They waited for another hour. Melee was glad just to be with Dillon, however unacknowledged as her husband. So much of their marriage had been apart, even if nearby.

Then a carriage was admitted to the postern. A swathed woman stepped down.

Melee went forth to meet her. "Let me see your face," the woman said in Latin.

Melee spoke Latin, as she had lived in Rome before coming east. "As you wish, Lady." She drew aside her hood and showed her face. She knew she was beautiful, even to a woman.

"We shall get along," the other said, and walked on to Melee's carriage.

Melee realized that Honoria, whose life was in danger, wanted to be sure she was not stepping into the hands of an assassin. Here in Constantinople few spoke Latin, but the royal figures were bilingual. So she had tested by speaking in that language, and Melee had thus vindicated her origin. A Latin-speaking woman was unlikely to be a hired assassin.

They entered the carriage, and it started moving. Melee started to close the curtain, but Honoria stayed her hand. "Let me see the city. My mother was here, and spoke often of it, but I have never been here before." She drew down her hood, so that her face showed. She was indeed an attractive woman, whose age hardly showed.

"You want a tour?" Melee asked. "I will be glad to show you everything." She gestured outward. "This is the Mese, or Middle Street, or at least one fork of it. It leads directly in to the palace. It is really the main shopping mart, because of all the merchant stalls along it."

Honoria seemed less than excited. "First show me yourself. Why were you assigned to me?"

Melee had expected to like this woman, and did. "I suspect it is because I was the daughter of a lesser Latin noble. Then my father died, and I was guilty of an indiscretion. So I was sent to be sequestered as a Chosen Damsel. I think Pulcheria saw points of similarity between us. I am supposed to keep you out of mischief."

"Indiscretion? What happened to the baby?"

"Stillborn. But the pregnancy was enough to damn me."

"And your man?"

"I would rather not say."

Honoria turned a direct gaze on her. "What you tell me in confidence, I will maintain in confidence. What I learn on my own has no such restriction."

That was a threat, and by no means an empty one. "It could mean his death."

"Of course it could! I loved Eugenius, who was the chamberlain managing my establishment in the palace precincts in Ravenna. But when I became with child by him, the secret was no more. So I tried to have him made Emperor in the West, so I could marry him and have power in the manner of my mother. But my jealous brother had him promptly put to death. They took my baby away, for adoption they said. I do not even know whether it was male or female."

Thus Honoria had told Melee of her humiliation, making it confidential material, though Melee had already known it. Honoria certainly knew the way of such things, by savage experience. It was surely safer to trust her. "We were married, secretly. He took work as a guard in order to be near me. We get together when we can."

"Who?"

"His name is Dillon. He is this guard." Melee flicked her eyes in the direction of Dillon, who rode just out of earshot.

"And Pulcheria knows?"

"I think she does. If you embarrass her, she will make me hurt. Terribly."

"Even as my brother made me hurt," Honoria agreed grimly. "Then if I should need to be guarded, he is the one I can trust. For you are hostage for his behavior, even as he is hostage for yours."

"Yes." This woman had wasted no time establishing her dominance.

"I will be discreet. More than discreet. If you wish to bring him inside, I will protect you from intrusions."

Melee stared at her. "Why would you do this?"

"When I have secrets, you will protect them similarly."

So it was a quid pro quo. Honoria would not cause mischief for Melee, but Melee would have to work hard to support Honoria's projects. The reward matched the danger. "You will want to—to bring in a man?"

"Not necessarily. But I want no adverse reports on my activities to be bruited about."

"No reports," Melee agreed. "But if there is trouble, what am I to do?"

"I know what trouble means. I will do my best to see that there is none, if no one tells. I think we understand each other."

"Yes, Lady." Evidently the gods had had wildness enough for more than one woman.

"They tried to force me into a betrothal to a rich senator, Flavius Bassus Herculanus, who has no imperial ambitions. But the man is fat and dull, and has little respect for women. I promised to make him rue the day. He lost interest in the match, though I believe he found me physically appealing." She opened her cloak to show a well-formed breast, in much the way Melee herself had done on occasion. A good body was a thing to be savored and appreciated, in the proper setting. "Mother concluded that the only place where I could be kept safe without disturbing the peace was Constantinople. So here I am, and I can't say I am pleased."

"I understand."

"And so does Pulcheria. What is she like? I have heard she is a determined virgin and religious zealot."

"Definitely. I will have to acquaint you with her daily regimen of prayers and fasting."

"Prayers and fasting! How can you stand it?"

"I sneak out to be with my man."

"Tell him to find one for me."

"There are none here we can trust."

"Then import one! He doesn't have to be noble, just handsome, virile, and discreet."

"It's that final requirement that sticks. The last discreet man I met was a Roman who was an emissary of the Huns, and he is small and smart rather than handsome."

"Virile?"

Melee considered Od, the man she had known peripherally when she was twelve. "Probably. I knew his wife, once, and she didn't complain, and now he has a beautiful mistress. But he is far away, at the court of Attila. I saw him last year, briefly, when he was part of the barbarian embassy."

"Barbarians are not necessarily bad folk. My mother married a Visigoth, and he treated her well. They are more straightforward than civilized folk are, and often more lusty."

They were approaching a wall that was visible on either side beyond the stone roof of the Mese. "This is the Wall of Constantine," Melee said. "The second of the city's three walls. The first is the Wall of Byzantium, enclosing the original city when it was small. The palace is there. But we depend mainly on the Theodosian Wall, where I met you."

They passed through the gate and continued into the central city. "And here is the Forum of Arcadius," Melee said as the street widened into a plaza with a monument in the center.

Now Honoria paid attention. "This is impressive," she said.

Indeed it was. It was perhaps the most impressive monumental column in the city. It towered more than ninety cubits high, crowned with a statue of Emperor Arcadius, who had ruled fifty years before. It was striking against the skyline of hills and valleys that was the city.

"The interior has a spiral staircase of two hundred and thirty-three steps," Melee said. "They lead up to an observation platform just below the statue. From there is the best view of the city and the sea."

"I don't think even Rome has an edifice like this," Honoria said. "We had better visit it."

"Now?" Melee asked, surprised.

"When there are men to be had. We will arrange a coach, perhaps in the evening. Then who knows what sights we will see."

Melee doubted that any such thing could be arranged. But Honoria was royal and bold, so might be able to wangle it.

They passed on northward, and soon came to the Forum of the Ox. Then they reached the intersection of the two Mese streets, at the Amastrianum Forum, and turned east.

"This is the Forum of Theodosius," Melee said. In its center was a statue of Theodosius on a forty-cubit column. "Near it you can see the Capitolium, designed after the one in Rome. This holds the University of Constantinople. Theodosius founded it a quarter century ago, and it teaches Greek and Latin grammar, rhetoric, philosophy, and jurisprudence."

"Maybe I can take a class," Honoria said, grimacing.

They rode on. "And here is the Forum of Constantine." Within this oval plaza was a column of porphyry, the reddish purple stone from Egypt, reserved for the use of emperors. Above an eighty-cubit column was a statue of Apollo, with the head of Constantine substituted for that of the pagan god. "There are Christian relics in the base, as well as an ancient image of Pallas Athena that was supposed to insure the safety of Rome."

Honoria laughed. "Tell that to my mother, when the Visigoths took Rome. Do you believe in any of this religious nonsense?"

Melee felt a surge of alarm. "Don't speak that way before Pulcheria!"

"Don't be concerned. I will try to be suitably devout in her presence. My mother is devout, and officially so am I. But it's all a pack of superstition that no sensible person could credit." She paused, smiling. "Now you have one of my secrets, and you know its danger. If I had been inclined to believe before, that belief suffered when Merciful Jesus allowed my lover to be murdered and me to be shamed for being a natural woman."

Melee looked at her, nodding. There was savage emotion under the lovely surface of this highborn creature. They were indeed two of a kind.

They passed through the Wall of Byzantium. They were now in the oldest section of the city. They passed the Praetorium, which was the office of the governor of the city. Then they reached the Augustaeum, the heart of the city, where the Mese originated.

"This is the heart of the heart of the Empire of the East," Melee said. "Here is the Hippodrome, and here is the Church of St. Sophia, the Shrine of Christ the Holy Wisdom of God. This is the strength of this God-Guarded City."

"I think I'm going to vomit," Honoria muttered.

"And at last the palace," Melee said, keeping a straight face. "The core of it was built by Constantine along the lines of Diocletian's palace at Spalato, which was in turn based on the square plan of a Roman army camp. But subsequent emperors added onto the base structure, building south and east toward the sea. They had to build brick substructures out from the hillside to provide enough new space. Today it is a vast and complicated compound of gardens, leveled terraces, detached summer pavilions, churches, reception halls, and now they are working on an indoor riding school."

"That I will visit."

"And beneath it all are the servants' quarters and other necessary functions," Melee concluded.

"So it should be possible to get lost in the labyrinth," Honoria said, perking up.

"If one is careful," Melee agreed. "I have done it."

"You will find me a quick learner."

They stepped out of the coach. Dillon came forward to assist them, while the driver took the coach away. Honoria made an appraising look at the guard. "You're a handsome one," she remarked. "Suppose I asked you for a kiss?"

Dillon looked surprised. "I do not understand, Lady."

"She knows," Melee told him. "She may want to go outside the palace, in secret."

He nodded. "Secrecy, yes; kiss no."

Then they entered the palace, ready to be welcomed by Pulcheria and the other devout Sisters. Melee hoped Honoria was as good an actress as she claimed.

❖

"I can't stand it!" Honoria cried, literally tearing at her hair. "I don't know which is worse, the prayers or the fasting or the virginity. At least the old gods have human feelings and failings. I've got to get out of here."

Melee well understood. The saintly regimen was deadly for red-blooded women. She was almost ready to ask Dillon to take the woman to bed, just to stave off the disastrous explosion that was building. It wasn't that she was open-minded about sex; it was that she was afraid that Honoria would throw a fit that brought an investigation of all of them, and possible death to Dillon. It would be better to free him to ease the problem, than to suffer the alternative.

The situation was serious. Honoria had already let slip some remarks that had caused some Damsels to blush and made Pulcheria stare thoughtfully at Melee. It was up to Melee to curb the trend, lest she pay the price of failure.

When she got out to meet Dillon, while Honoria covered for her, she brought the matter up before they made love. "That woman is going to be the death of us. I love her like a sister, but she is going to bring Pulcheria down on our heads. I can't abate the prayers, but I have been sneaking food in during the fasting. But it isn't enough. She needs a man—and the only one we can trust isn't a man, it's that eunuch Hyacinth. He'd do anything for Honoria, but he can't do that."

"There just isn't any man she might like who can be trusted," he agreed. "Isn't there?"

"You know of one?"

She set herself and said it. "How about you?"

He laughed. "I'm taken. You ought to know."

"I'm serious. She likes you. She gives no sign, because she is honoring her pact with me. But she would enjoy sex with you. Would you like it with her?"

"Melee, you don't need to test me! I never desired anyone but you, since I met you."

"You are evading the question."

"Are you determined to pick a quarrel with me? I love you, Melee!"

"You are still not answering."

He sighed. "She is a beautiful woman. Not as lovely or young as you, but a fine piece of flesh withal. Yes, I could enjoy her. But you know I would never—"

"I know you are faithful, Dillon. But I fear for your life. If I don't settle Honoria down somehow, Pulcheria may have you arrested and killed, just to punish me. I can't stand the thought. I would rather share you than lose you." There, she had said it all. There were tears in her eyes.

He stared at her. "You're serious."

"I am serious. Let me take you in to her, and I will stand guard while you do it."

"Let me have you first."

"No! You're trying to get out of it. You know you couldn't do it with her right after me. Not so you would satisfy her. She's not naïve about sex."

"I know," he confessed. "Melee, there must be some other way!"

"I wish there were. But there isn't. You can have me after her."

"No, you'll be angry with me then. You know you will. Even though it's your idea."

"I'll be furious," she agreed. "But it *is* my idea. So I'll understand. Tomorrow I will thank you for saving your life."

"It's a man's dream," he said. "Two beautiful women. Why does it feel like doom?"

She kissed him. "Wait for my signal, then climb in the window." She hurried back into the palace.

When she was safely back in the chamber she shared with Honoria, she spied the woman on her knees, facing the entrance, her hands uplifted in the position of prayer, her eyes closed.

"You are praying voluntarily?" she asked, amazed.

Honoria cracked open an eye. "Praying for relief from this virgin hell." She smiled. "And it is an excellent guard position, in case a Sister enters unexpectedly. She will not seek to pass me or question me. It would be sacrilege."

"This is very clever," Melee agreed. "I will do the same. But your prayer has been answered. Dillon will come in, for you."

Honoria did not pretend to misunderstand. "I never asked this of you."

"You must be eased, or you will burst. Then we all are lost. I love him. So I make this sacrifice. He finds you attractive; he will do it."

"Melee, I would turn this down. But you are right. You survive because you have him. I could survive with a share of him. But only till we find a better way."

"Till we find a better way," Melee agreed, feeling the tears flowing again. Then she went to the window and summoned Dillon.

In a moment he was inside. Melee set a cushion on the floor and went to her knees, facing the door. An intruder would take her tears for special religious devotion.

"You know what we are about?" Honoria asked him softly.

"I know."

"I have a passion that will not be denied."

"I know."

"Do you mind if we kiss?"

"May I close my eyes?" He sounded plaintive, and Melee loved him for that. He wanted to pretend that Honoria was Melee.

"Yes, for that. And for the rest, if you wish. But you must touch."

"I will touch."

"Then come to the alcove, and I will show you my secrets, in darkness, and learn yours." There was the rustle of clothing.

"I feel like Attila the Hun," he said.

"He has several lovely wives," Honoria agreed. "But the first one reigns supreme, and will never be displaced."

"Never," he agreed.

They were playing it out for her benefit, Melee knew. To abate her natural jealousy. But it just made her feel worse. She knew that Dillon would know it was Honoria he embraced, and secretly delight in the possession of two women, whatever he told her. It was the nature of his gender. If only her prayer for a better solution could be answered!

Then it was as if a blinding flash of lightning struck down without hurting her. Suddenly she had the answer. "Attila!" she cried.

The other two paused. "You are saying no?" Honoria asked her. "It is your right."

"I have the answer," Melee said, turning. "It is Attila. He has many wives. He could take one more. For a political union. If you cared to do it. And it would free you in more than one sense." She was thinking of the attempt to marry Honoria against her will to a Roman senator, as well as of the power of such an association with the Hun king.

"Great gods!" Honoria whispered. "I believe you're right. We must consider this." She gathered together her robe, which had fallen open rather far by no coincidence. Dillon had evidently been trying to look away, and not succeeding; his eyes were locked onto the woman's lush torso, until the robe closed. "My mother married a barbarian, and she was happiest then, as far as men went. My father was a good man, but he was old. Had Placidia not been beautiful and apt, my brother and I would have had a hard time getting started."

"He would marry you," Melee said. "Because of your lineage. It would give him a claim to the empire. You wouldn't even have to bed him, probably, after the first night."

"But I'd love to bed him! He's a small, knobby, old man, but consider his power. And our son would have a claim to the empire of the Huns."

"Does this mean I can go?" Dillon asked, sounding both relieved and disappointed.

The two women exchanged a glance. Then they turned as one and leaped on him. Honoria grabbed his head and thrust her bosom at his face, while Melee grabbed his waist and thrust her nether section at his crotch. He was surprised, but did not resist. In fact, after an instant, he cooperated. In hardly more than a moment they had their mutual will of him, top and bottom.

Then they disengaged. "Yes, you have come; now you may go," Melee said, patting him on the thigh.

Bemused, he went. Honoria looked after him. "I almost wish you had had your bright notion a short time later," she said.

Melee was taken aback. "I didn't think of it to—I wasn't trying to deny you."

The woman laughed. "I know it. But he is a good man."

"He is a good man," Melee agreed.

They settled back down to their dialogue. "I'll send Attila my gold ring," Honoria said, twisting it off her finger. "That will constitute a proposal of marriage between us."

"But we must arrange to get it to him, with identification as to whose ring it is," Melee said. "Maybe Hyacinth can carry it. He would do anything for you."

"Almost anything," Honoria agreed with half a smile. "Yes, I will give him money, a message, and the ring. Attila will know how to get in touch." Then she leaned forward and kissed Melee on the mouth. "You have found the answer. I will be free, and I can exploit the marriage to great advantage."

They spent much of the night working out the details. Not the least of it, by Melee's reckoning, was that when Honoria married the king of the Huns, she would arrange for Melee and Dillon to assume honored places in Attila's court. They would all be free.

❄

"Have you heard the latest?" Avalanche inquired as she stretched luxuriously.

Od tried to pretend that he wasn't interested in court gossip, but he was interested in everything. "Not yet."

"A eunuch named Hyacinth has arrived from Constantinople with a message for the king. It has everyone agog, but no one is telling what the message is."

"That *is* interesting," he agreed. "Could it be news of another assassination plot?"

"Why would anyone send a lowly eunuch with such news?"

"Eunuchs know everything," he said. "They overhear what their masters are talking about. Still, it does seem unlikely. They can't be bribed by promise of fair women. So it must be for money. What would Attila pay handsomely for?"

"That's another thing," she said, remembering. "It is said that the eunuch isn't asking for anything except an answer to his message." Then she came and embraced him. "I'm glad you're not a eunuch."

She was warm and soft and very female. "I'm glad too," he agreed, kissing her.

One thing led to another, but before that process was fairly under way, a messenger came to their door. Od disengaged reluctantly and closed his cloak to conceal his state. "What?"

"King Attila summons Od and Avalanche to court immediately."

"Both of us?" he asked, surprised. Attila generally wanted Od when there was some technical device to be explained, and Avalanche when there was a problem with a wife. Not for sexual purpose, but to clarify the female view. Only last month a young wife had been furious with Attila, mystifying him. So he had interrupted their liaison, donned a concealing cloak, and gone to Avalanche's house, which was Od's house. This was unusual, for normally people were summoned, as was the case now. Od, learning on that occasion that it was Avalanche and not him the king wished to see, was about to depart, but Attila bade him stay with a curt gesture. So he faded back, and overheard an interesting dialogue:

"My lord," Avalanche said, alarmed. "Have I committed some offense?"

"No, dear woman. I need your private advice."

"Of course, lord." They sat on cushions, his higher than hers, closely facing each other.

"Tonight I am with the daughter of Eksam." That was the woman Attila had married last year, in a union both political and pleasant, for the girl was lovely.

"Yes, it is her night."

"She is angry with me. I can tell. I dare not ask her why."

Because it would be extremely impolitic for a lesser wife to express discontent of any nature with the king. If he asked her, she would have to deny it. Also, Attila was known as a good husband to all his wives, and it would be an embarrassment for him to be seen as otherwise. So if he had a problem, he would not publicize it. He would handle it quietly. But first he had to know what the problem was.

"Let me be sure I understand the situation," Avalanche said. "You perceived her muted ire, and broke off the liaison to come here for information?"

He nodded.

"So you must return to her soon, lest you complicate what is already difficult."

Attila nodded again.

"Then I must question you closely, and perhaps embarrassingly." She paused, but he did not react, so she took that as permission. "Were you impotent?"

"No. We have not gotten to that yet. I do not want to embrace an angry woman." That was understandable, even though she would not resist him in any way.

"Were you late? Ill garbed? Inattentive?" Avalanche paused slightly after each part, giving him a chance to express negation. "Did you notice what she wore?"

"Fine blue silk I gave her last month. She looks lovely, and I told her so."

"Is it possible she is suffering some passing malady, perhaps the time of the month, which discomfort you mistake for anger?"

"No."

Avalanche shook her head. "This is a mystery. That girl is not unduly temperamental. If she is angry, she has reason."

Attila nodded wanly.

"Did you bring her a suitable gift?"

"A figurine of silver from Byzantium."

"And what did you bring your youngest wife, last night?" By youngest, she meant most recent; age had little to do with it.

"A medallion of gold."

Avalanche pursed her lips. "Oh, my lord! You have done it. Even Od would see that."

"But it is a very fine figurine!" the king protested. "Of superb artistry. Worth more than the medallion."

"But of silver rather than gold. The symbolism is that you value her less than a more recent wife. She will be shamed before the other wives."

Attila looked stricken. "I never thought of that!"

"Men don't think of such things. She thinks she is being degraded."

"What must I do?" the king asked humbly.

"Get a statuette of jade." Jade was more precious than gold, to the Huns. "Do not delay at all. Tell her that you suddenly realized you had brought the wrong gift, so had to fetch the right one immediately. Apologize abjectly for the error. She will forgive you. In fact, you may even have a better night than you expected."

Attila leaned forward and kissed her on the mouth. It was his greatest mark of favor, because it was spontaneous rather than rehearsed. Then he rose and hurried out.

"You are a genius," Od said admiringly.

"No, just a woman. Now come to me, but do not kiss me on the mouth. Anywhere but there. I don't want to erase his mark."

Od understood. He embraced her, and found her flushed with passion. She gave him many fine other places to kiss. It wasn't merely the kiss of the king. It was that she had tackled a serious and touchy problem and successfully solved it, on short notice. She loved that.

Later that night, as they lay ready for sleep, a messenger came. "For Avalanche," he said, handing her an object wrapped in silk. Then he was gone.

She unwrapped it. There was a fine jade figurine. "Oh, lovely!" she breathed.

"But it was supposed to be for his wife," Od protested.

"This is another. It is his appreciation for good advice. It means he had a good evening."

Evidently so. They had kept their mouths shut about the matter, so that no one else ever knew. The king had trusted their discretion, and knew his trust was justified. Now Attila was summoning them both, but it couldn't be for a wifely problem. It had to relate to the arrival of that eunuch. Od was really curious.

Attila was alone when they were admitted to his presence. Before him was a small box, and in it was a gold ring. "The eunuch brought me this ring from Honoria, the sister of the Roman Emperor of the West," he said. "It appears to be genuine, with her unique seal. What do you suppose it means?"

"It's a proposal of marriage!" Avalanche said, amazed.

"Yes. But is it genuine, or is this another nasty Roman trick, like the assassination plot last year?" He looked at Od.

"Orestes would be the better one to say," Od started. But he knew that Orestes was away on other business, which was surely why Od had been summoned instead. It was up to him to answer. "If the ring is authentic, so is the proposal. Royal Roman ladies do not jest about such things."

"Tell me about her."

"She is the daughter of Galla Placidia, Rome's most powerful woman," Od said. "In her youth Placidia was captured by the Visigoths, and she married their prince Athaulf. When he was killed she was ransomed back to Rome, and married a consul. Her son is Emperor Valentinian, and her daughter is Honoria. Of the two, the daughter is far more strong willed. It is said that Honoria is much like her mother: beautiful, intelligent, spirited, and passionate. But she got pregnant by her chamberlain, and was sent to Constantinople lest her brother have her killed."

Attila nodded. "And it is from there this ring came. But why would she pass up the chance to marry a leading Roman man?"

Od remembered what he had learned of life in the East Roman palace. "Honoria would be under the wing of Pulcheria, sister of Emperor Theodosius of the East. She is a devout Christian, whose life is said to be fixed on fasting and prayer and perpetual virginity."

"And a red-blooded woman like Honoria would feel horribly stifled there," Avalanche said. "Both her natural passion and her political aspiration would be denied. I think she would do anything to break free of that cage."

"And her mother did marry a 'barbarian,' " Od said. "So she knows it can be a good life."

Attila nodded. "Would she be a good match for me?"

"Yes!" Od and Avalanche said together.

Attila looked at them, inviting clarification.

"She would represent a valid claim to the throne of West Rome," Od said.

"And she would probably give you a moderate son or a marvelous daughter," Avalanche said. "She is old—thirty—but surely as spirited in bed as any Hun."

"But of course what she most desires is power," Od said. "A regency over Rome, in the manner of her mother."

"And she would be loyal as long as you were the source of that power," Avalanche said. "I believe you could trust her."

"So you recommend that I accept her proposal?"

"Yes," they said, again together.

"This is what my advisers said. I wanted confirmation from someone who knew Rome better, and from a woman who understands women." Attila nodded. "I will marry her. And claim half the Empire of the West as her dowry. She will govern it as my vassal-wife, and have the life she desires. But I will want a woman I trust to be near her." He looked at Avalanche.

"As my lord wishes," Avalanche agreed, blushing with pleasure.

"And a man I trust as liaison, for I shall not care to dwell in Rome." He looked at Od.

"As my lord wishes," Od echoed, as deeply pleased.

"Now we shall publish the news of the betrothal," Attila said. He clapped his hands, and several of his picked men entered. Things were under way.

Thus the beautifully crafted ploy that seemed to give both Honoria and Attila what they most wanted: power over Rome. Had it been effective, it would have changed history as we know it. For Rome's strongest rival would have had reason to defend Rome from all other intrusions, and the West Roman Empire might have survived, as did the East Roman Empire.

But it was not to be, because of the jealousy of others. When Theodosius, Emperor of the East, discovered what Honoria had done, he was appalled. He could not simply hand Honoria over to the Huns, for she was the sister of the Emperor of the West. But if he did not, he was afraid that Attila would march on Constantinople, demanding Honoria as his bride. And that Honoria would raise a disturbance within the city, demanding to be given as the Hun's bride. This was, to use an anachronistic term, a potato too hot to handle. So he packed Honoria and the eunuch Hyacinth off back to Italy, with a recommendation that Honoria be handed over to the Huns, and allowed to marry Attila and give him the dowry of half of that empire. This was sensible advice, because there was no army in Rome capable of withstanding a serious Hun invasion.

But Valentinian had a different view. He realized that his own position was threatened, if not by Attila, then by his sister, who was really more competent than he was. So he had Hyacinth tortured for all the details of his mission, then executed. He was going to have Honoria killed too, but their mother Placidia interceded, and she was spared. However, Valentinian did not allow her to marry the Hun. He rejected Attila's demands for bride and dowry.

Attila then chose war. He made peace with the Empire of the East, which had really done its best to appease him after the embarrassment of the assassination plot. (The situation was a good deal more complicated, and was changing, but this was the essence of the moment.) Then he focused on the West, which had foolishly annoyed him. In 451 he invaded what is now Germany, and France (Gaul). City after city was devastated by the terrible thrust. The Empire of the West had to scramble to raise an army capable of balking him, and that wasn't easy.

The Roman general was Aetius. He had had a long and good relationship with the Huns. In 433 Aetius had been in danger for his life, and had fled to the Huns for safety. They had given him troops, enabling him to win many battles and become perhaps the most powerful figure in the West, apart from Placidia and the emperor. But recently relations between them had soured, and now Aetius would oppose Attila in the battle for Gaul. The Visigoths might well have joined Attila, but Aetius managed to persuade them to join him instead. He thus assembled an army that matched the Hun forces in size and power. In June 451 came the battle of the Catalaunian Fields, near Orléans in France. It is considered to be one of the definitive battles of history, not for what it accomplished but for what it might have accomplished. If Attila won, the West Roman Empire was probably finished as such; if Aetius won, the Huns were probably finished.

It was brutal. The Huns—actually their army was a melange of many allies— used their cavalry to break through the center. Then they wheeled and attacked the Visigoths on the left wing. The hand fighting was described as "fierce, confused, monstrous, unrelenting." A stream was said to become a torrent because of the flow of human blood, and those whose wounds made them thirsty drank water mingled with gore. Theodoric, King of the Visigoths, was killed, but his son Thorismund rallied the troops and drove back the Ostrogoths on the Hun side. By the end of the day the Huns were on the defensive. Attila faced the prospect of defeat, for the first time in his career.

But then something remarkable happened. The Visigoths departed. They abandoned their allies and went home. Without this formidable contingent, Aetius could not afford to risk pursuing the battle. So it was called off, and the opposing parties went home. Thus what could have been a victory over the Huns, and the likely end of the Hun Empire, became a draw, deciding nothing. Instead of getting killed in battle, Attila remained with his power balked but hardly diminished. In 452 he invaded and devastated Italy. In 453 he died of natural causes on his wedding night, and the Hun Empire fell apart.

One of Attila's close associates, his secretary Orestes, returned to the West Roman Empire and in time achieved considerable power. In 475 he had his son Romulus *proclaimed emperor, evidently intending to rule through the child. But his Gothic mercenaries demanded a third of Italy as a sub-kingdom. He refused, and they turned against him, rebelled, and killed him. Then they required the harmless boy Romulus to abdicate, gave him a pension, and let him go to live with his family. They formed the Ostrogothic Kingdom of Italy. The Empire of the West was no more. One can only wonder whether if Honoria's ploy had been effective, and the Huns and West Romans had united, instead of dissipating their strength with continued fighting, they both might have prospered instead of perishing.*

Back to the Battle of the Catalaunian Fields. Historians have struggled with the mystery of why the Visigoths deserted Rome in the hour of incipient victory, and there are several persuasive theories. But for the purpose of this narrative, there is a more personal conjecture. Beware; this is not recorded historically.

Placidia managed to save Honoria's life, but Placidia was sixty-two years old, and failing. Indeed, she died in 450, so her protection was gone. So she did what she could for her willful daughter, and secured her future safety by arranging a marriage for her to a Roman general serving in Gaul as a nominal adviser to the nominally subject Visigoths—a position of tacit impotence. Placidia knew and respected the Visigoths well, because her sole love-marriage had been to Athaulf the Visigoth. Valentinian would not be able to threaten Honoria in Gaul, but would have prevented any marriage to a Visigothic chief for the same reason he had opposed her marriage to Attila: it would lend far too much support to the competition. But a Roman who could be kept far from the centers of power—that was tolerable. The general chosen was named Pul, who was strong in battle but not bright enough to be politically ambitious. In short, safe. Honoria was hardly keen on the union to such a dull man, but realized that the alternative was almost certainly death, so she reluctantly acceded and went to Gaul. Rumors that she was bound and carried there slung over the back of a mule are surely not true. She yielded with a certain sullen grace to what had to be. More on this in a moment.

One of the other mysteries of history is why Attila invaded Gaul instead of Italy, if Honoria was in Italy. The unromantic answer is that Attila was more interested in the rich loot to be had from Gaul than in any woman; the Hunnic way of life was to invade, pillage, and return with economy-boosting booty. For such excursions it was best to vary the locale from season to season, for harvests were poor in too recently devastated regions. Attila had a good sense of resource management. The romantic answer is perhaps that Honoria was now in Gaul. Attila would probably not have cared to marry her, once she had been married to another man, but his pride was involved. At least he could free her to join the Huns, and her presence in his camp would have been awkward for the Romans. She represented another chance to shame the arrogant civilized empire. He might marry her to one of his lieutenants and put the man in charge of Italy, once it was conquered, thus giving Honoria a good situation. Or perhaps he would after all have married her himself, for the sake of their usefulness to each other. Certainly he was intrigued by this nervy and appealing woman. So, like a bold white knight, this Black Hun came, as it were, for his lady love.

His interest was returned. Honoria wanted more than ever to be rescued from the dullness of her impotence. But when it seemed that her savior was about to lose the key battle, costing her the remnant of her dream, Honoria had to act. Her Visigoth husband was not bright, which made him easy to manage, but he was well connected. Through him she schemed to get the Visigothic contingent to disengage. She managed to get her husband to spread a rumor that the younger brothers of Thorismund, who with the death of his father was in line to be king of the Visigoths, were conspiring to seize their father's possessions and gain control themselves. That meant that Thorismund might have to return to another battle at home, after a wearing campaign against Attila. That prospect did not appeal to the Visigothic heir. So, to secure his rightful heritage, Thorismund marched hastily for home. And it is quite possible that the rumor was true, for his younger brothers were ambitious types. Indeed, two years later Thorismund was assassinated and replaced by his brother Theodoric II.

In this manner Honoria may have saved her savior. But because the battle was inconclusive, Attila was not able to rescue her. Thus their merged ambitions were muted, and Honoria disappeared from history, much to her regret. But perhaps, if due credit were given, her impact on history would be recognized. This bold woman's ploy had certainly generated considerable mischief, and changed much. But for the arrogant ambitions of others, it might have changed everything.

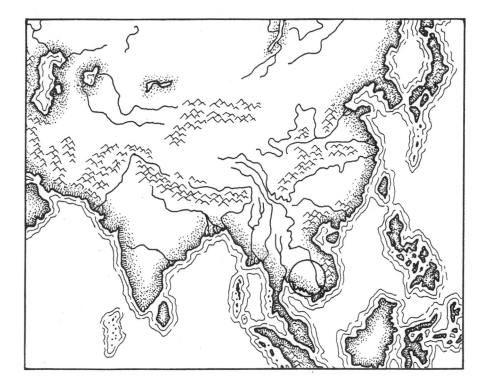

CHAPTER 9

JUSTICE

One of the fabled ancient and splendid cities is Angkor, in southeast Asia. The name is from the Sanskrit word for "city." It was the capital of the Khmer culture, which is dated from A.D. 802 to 1431. It was known at the time as Kambuja-desa, from which derives the present name for the land, Cambodia. Originally there were several regions ruled by generally independent chiefs or princes, and there was no sense of national identity. But Javarman II managed through po-litical, familial, and military maneuvering to dominate the other princes and become the "universal monarch." His successors maintained the kingdom, notably Yasovarman (889–912), who founded the capital which was later to be called

*Angkor. This kingdom was heavily flavored by both Indian and Chinese influ-
ences, being very roughly between the two massive cultures, but had a unique
character that has survived to the present day.*

*Khmer society was highly stratified from the king at the apex to the slaves at
the nadir. It had a form of caste system, with the Brahmans as a noble priestly
class, and the Kshatriya as noble warriors. These represented the upper tier, the
equivalent of nobility, and the lines between them were not firmly fixed. The second
tier had Sudra as servants and artisans, and Vaisya as farmers. Beneath these
were what were called mountain savages, which perhaps were simply the outlying
country folk who did not take the caste system seriously, and slaves. There were
many distinctions between slaves, with perhaps as many as fourteen separate cat-
egories. Some were hereditary; some were indentured for set periods; some were
captives. Some were attached to particular masters or institutions; others were
bound to specific pieces of land. Field slaves were reviled, with names like "Dog"
and "Foul Smelling," and had to prostrate themselves and beg permission to enter
a farmer's hut. Temple slaves might be addressed by polite titles, and some even
owned land and had slaves of their own.*

*An orderly society is vital to any kingdom, and there were mechanisms to settle
disputes and ensure fairness. But what about cases in which there was no clear
resolution to be had by ordinary channels? Here there could be a special art to
justice. The place is just north of the Great Lake of Cambodia; time is A.D. 890.*

H EATH was a healer, and a good one, so that he was in demand by
princes despite being only of the artisan caste himself. He had been
well rewarded for his services, and now owned choice land near the capital
city. He had a comely, fertile, and devoted wife who supported him absolutely. Yet he was uncomfortable, and the problem was with his wife. He
dreaded his sessions with her, though she was in no way at fault.

It was their agreed night for sex. Talena had borne him four daughters
in the course of their six years of marriage, and was eager to get started on
a son. She was nineteen, and still in the prime of her femininity. Her breasts
and buttocks had fleshed out well with childbearing, but she remained
slender overall, and pleasant of face. Sex with her was certainly no chore.

As usual, she had arranged to have the children cared for by the slaves
in another chamber. As usual, she brought him his evening meal herself,
prepared by her own right hand. The left hand, of course, was impure,
being used exclusively for lowly chores such as admonishing slaves and
washing the bottom after defecation.

She entered, bearing the wooden platter. She wore her simple sarong,
stretching from her waist to her ankles, with her feet and breasts bare. Her
hair was pulled back and knotted into a tight conical bun, but after the
meal she would loosen it for his pleasure.

She smiled at him, and set the platter before him. It bore cooked rice,
with crayfish, bananas, onions, pomegranate, milk curd, and several spices.
Sauce was in leaf cups, and sweet berry drink was in clay cups.

They ate, dipping their fingers into the rice, adding sauce or spice, eating it, and rinsing their fingers in the water bowls. The food was good, as it always was. Heath wished the meal could last longer, because he knew what was coming after it was done.

But it finished in the usual time. Talena set this spent platter aside and returned to kneel before him. "How may I please you best, my husband?" She smiled with assumed hope and expectation.

Suddenly it was too much. "You know you can't ever please me enough," he said, feeling the sting at his eyes. He had avoided the truth for all of their marriage, hoping it would fade, but it hadn't faded enough. "We have always seemed to be the perfect couple; others have remarked on it. But it has always been hollow."

"But I must always try," she said bravely. "I must banish my faults and hope at last to meet your expectation."

"Talena, Talena, you have no faults! You are in all ways the perfect wife, and I know there is no better one. The fault is in me."

"No!" she protested. "There is no fault in you. Only in my failure to properly address your needs."

"I have not been fair to you from the outset. I should not have married you."

"But you were more than fair. You told me that you were not ready. I didn't heed."

"I didn't tell you that I would never be ready," he said. "I thought that in time my memory of Baya would dwindle, and finally go entirely, and then I would be able to turn wholeheartedly to you. But now I know that will never happen."

Her eyes were brightening with her own tears. "I never sought to displace your wife! Only to win a place beside her, in your esteem."

"Baya is dead. You are my wife. I do you the dishonor of placing you second to a ghost. You never deserved that."

"I consider it an honor to accept whatever you have to give me."

"I should free you while you are yet young enough to find a man who can truly love you."

"No!" she cried in alarm. "I love you, only you, Heath."

"I know you do. That makes my guilt into a mountain. You love so perfectly, and I am unworthy of it."

"I love perfectly because you are perfect! If your feeling for me is less, it is because I am less than—"

He reached forward and put his hand over her mouth, stopping her speech. "I have failed you, and I know it. I must try to make it up some other way. This is only justice. But what way can I find?"

She spoke against his hand. "Just clasp me, and maybe this time I will give you a boy."

"You haven't failed me that way either. Those girls will all grow up to be fine women like you. I don't care if we never have a boy."

"Still—"

He drew her down to the cushion with him. "And you have been a delight to embrace, from the first. But answer me: what can I do to make up, in some degree, for my failure?"

"I don't consider it a—"

"But I do. I owe you so much, Talena, and maybe I can repay you with some other satisfaction. What is there?"

"There isn't any—"

"Tell me."

She yielded. "There is something. But I have no right to ask."

"Ask."

"And it probably isn't possible to fix it, anyway."

He stroked his hand along her back. "Describe it."

"Our neighbor, Pul, has a slave wife. She is the sister of a noble who supported the wrong prince."

"Yes. That prince's estate was dissolved, and his assets distributed to the supporters of Yasovarman. That is how we got this nice property."

"I have interacted with her in the market place, and in the temple. She is dying of sadness."

"Well, she was a virtual princess, and is now an ordinary wife. It must be a considerable adjustment."

"She remains a slave. Pul takes her to bed, but the moment he tires of her, she will be a slave again, bound to the land until she dies. He hasn't freed her."

"Well, that would be expensive."

"She is a lovely, spirited woman, capable of so much more. If she could be transferred to the temple, she could surely prosper."

"Surely," he agreed. "I have seen her. But Pul would never do that."

"Yes, he would never. But if you were to obtain her—"

"I seek no woman for my bed but you!"

"Even for your bed, as a second wife, she would be better off than she is now. But the temple would be better. If you could—"

"I would never interfere in my neighbor's business."

"Of course," she agreed, hurt.

"By the great lingam of Shiva!" he swore. "How would you have me do it?"

She brightened. "There is a question of title to the land to which she is bound. I researched it in the temple records."

She was good at such things. She knew all the old stories, and the nuances of law. "A question of title?"

"Pul was to receive the land north of the stream that passes us. You received the land west of the mountain. That property is in both areas."

"It is? It never seemed so to me."

"Because perfect as you are in every other way, your sense of direction is, dare I say it, imperfect."

He had on occasion gotten lost. "So?"

"I verified the direction west of the mountain, and it is confusing because of the lay of the land. But I am sure that that piece of land is there. So you have a claim to it."

"But it is also north of the stream."

"Yes. So the issue is confused. But your claim is as good as his. You might take that piece from him. And Honoria is bound to that land. She would become yours."

This was amazing. She had found a way. "And you want me to make the issue, take the land, and transfer it and the woman to the temple."

"There are legal precedents. If the land is declared unusable, its bound slaves can be moved. It could be done, if you got the land."

"All because she is dissatisfied as the wife of Pul?"

"Wouldn't you be?"

He laughed. Pul was a dull brute. Of course she was unhappy. But for him to go to such trouble to free her was ridiculous. "Do you realize that this may require a celestial judgment?"

"Yes. I am confident that you could prevail."

Her confidence was touching, but not necessarily justified. The average person dreaded such a judgment, for good reason.

Then he looked at Talena. He owed her, for the love he was unable to give her. He had asked her a price, and she had named it. She wanted Honoria freed, if not from bondage, at least from unkind sex. Was he going to renege on his offer?

He sighed. "I will try."

"Thank you, Heath." Then she clasped him with such ardor that it was almost possible to forget that he didn't quite love her.

In the morning he went to the temple with her and verified the records. The description of the land grants was indeed ambiguous, if the direction was as she said. He was sure it would be.

Now came the unpleasant part. Heath didn't like quarreling with his neighbors, and Pul was an ugly neighbor. But if this was what it took to square his conscience about Talena, it would be worth it.

Pul's house, like Heath's own, was supported by tall posts of hard timber that reached up to brace the curved roof. The floor was attached to these posts about head-high from the ground. Below that floor were the animal stalls, chicken coops, storage space, and pallets for the field slaves: the only place where they were allowed to sit or lie down. There was an open veranda with curtains that could be raised when the day was cool.

Heath stood near the house and called to alert its inhabitants. "Ho, neighbor!"

In a moment Pul's close-cropped head showed. "Ho, neighbor," he echoed. "What's your concern?"

"I have a matter of property to discuss."

"Then come on up."

Heath put his hands and feet on the ladder leading to the veranda. It had an odd number of rungs, for evil spirits could use only even numbers. He pushed aside a curtain and stepped onto the veranda.

There were two bamboo chairs. Pul had one, and Heath took the other. Pul was a large muscular man wearing the common male skirt, the sampot, which was a rectangle of cloth wrapped around the waist and knotted in front. Heath's own apparel differed only in that he also wore a thick scarf twisted into a rope and draped over his chest and neck. This was because as a healer he often had to travel to remote dwellings and could return late, so the scarf could be unwound to form an additional wrap.

"So what's this property business?" Pul demanded. He was a wealthy farmer with a number of fertile plots, and an equivalent number of slaves to work them. The agricultural caste was parallel to the artisans caste to which Heath and Talena belonged, but there was a world of difference in outlooks. Pul was rough and crude and not overly smart. He had been a warrior, but injury had caused him to retire to less arduous work.

"It has come to my attention that one piece of land was distributed to you, but should have been given to me," Heath said.

Pul's low brow furrowed. "*What* piece?"

"The piece west of the mountain. That was to be part of my dispensation from the king. But it seems that it is also north of the stream, so it was given to you. It is good land, and I believe I should take possession of it."

"It's *my* land!" Pul snapped.

"I can have the temple surveyors establish the direction from the mountain."

"And I can have them do it for the direction from the river. I want that land."

"But you aren't even farming it."

"You wouldn't either. You're no farmer."

"True. But the land has something I want."

Suddenly Pul caught on. "The woman! You want the land-slave!"

"I want Honoria," Heath agreed. "She is attractive, talented, and smart."

"Well, she's royal. That's how they are."

Heath nodded. "Yasovarman couldn't enslave her as a captive, because she was related to him, but he needed to nullify her. So he bound her to that plot of land. That greatly enhances the value of that land. I think he meant for me to have her."

"She's mine! I married her."

Heath raised an eyebrow. "Oh? Did she consent?"

"She doesn't need to consent. She's a slave."

"And she wouldn't need to consent if I took her with the land. As you point out, she has no rights in that respect."

"She's a beautiful woman. I won't let her go. My claim on the land is as good as yours."

"Then I fear we have a difference that can't readily be settled. I shall apply to the king for a judgment."

"You do that," Pul said angrily. "Now get out of my house."

Heath made haste to comply, lest the man's temper get the better of him and he throw Heath from the veranda. The irony was that Heath had considerable sympathy for the man's position. He had gotten a wonderful break, obtaining land with a lovely female bound slave; Honoria was a higher class of wife than such a farmer could ever obtain by normal channels. Now that situation was being threatened. By Pul's reckoning the feelings of the woman concerned had no relevance; she was there simply for his use. His marriage to her was simply a declaration that he was using her in the manner of a wife, and would recognize any children she bore him. She had farmer-caste status as long as the marriage continued, so was not considered a slave. But the moment she lost the marriage, she would be a slave again. So naturally she had not protested the marriage, but neither had she consented to it; she simply accepted it as her lot.

When Heath returned home, and entered the wooden-walled interior of his elevated house, there was Honoria. Talena had brought her home from the market. "I told her what we are trying to do," Talena said.

Heath looked at Honoria. She was thirty-one years old, nominally past her prime, but her face and bare breasts remained full and smooth. Her royal heritage showed in bearing and form. "If I get the land, I will donate it to the temple in your name," Heath said. "Is this what you want?"

She stepped forward and kissed him. Then she left the house. In this manner she indicated her agreement without actually saying anything inappropriate for one whose status remained slave; she was bound to another man.

"Of course you could get the land, and simply keep her as a sex slave," Talena murmured with a smile.

"I already have one of those." They both laughed, but there was an awkward tinge, because of the imperfection of their marriage.

Heath entered the capital city. Its market street was really the center of life. Goods were on sale from China, India, Viet Nam and Siam. There were precious stones on sale, and pearls, silver, gold, cotton cloth, fine silks, slaves, livestock, household goods, incense, spices, and ceramics. The local traders had aromatic woods, elephant ivory, rhinoceros parts, kingfisher feathers, resins, lacquer, pepper, vegetable oils, and beeswax. In villages, women did the marketing, laying out their mats from morning to noon, but here in the big city the foreign merchants held sway. It was a region of endless fascination.

But today Heath had special business. He passed through the market and went to the capitol hill. This was a scene of just as much activity, but of different nature: a grandiose temple to Shiva was being constructed. There had been damage to the prior capital city during the war of succession, so the king had moved the site of government and worship here and was in the process of making it the splendor of the world. On the summit of the hill they were building a five tiered sandstone pyramid, and making a middle square with four corner temples and a central shrine, mirroring the five peaks of Mount Meru. Stairways were climbing the center of each side of the pyramid, and small chapels would adorn each corner. Forty-four brick towers surrounded the base, decorated in stucco. From the foot of any of the staircases, thirty-three temples would be visible, representing the thirty-three gods residing on Mount Meru. At the top of the stairs, looking straight at the central shrine, there would be only three temples in the field of vision, representing Shiva, Vishnu, and Brahma. But Shiva would loom above the others. Every temple would house a lingam, the stone phallus symbol of Shiva's creative potency. Each lingam actually included the three major gods, with the square base representing Brahma, the middle octagonal section Vishnu, and the circular section at the top being Shiva himself. Since all was Shiva, the lingam actually represented all other deities. Taken as a whole, it would be the greatest religious complex ever known, when finally completed. Heath found himself awed simply by the scale of the artistic vision, and was sorry that he probably would not live long enough to see the final system.

Meanwhile, the court system was housed in lesser buildings. Much of its business was the disciplining of criminals. Thieves might have one of their hands cut off, or if their thievery were great and incorrigible, a hand and a foot, and would also be branded on the chest. Adulterers might have their feet placed in a wooden vise and squeezed by the cuckolded man until the pain made them agree to give all their property to the plaintiff. Heath had had to attend a number of such cases, to provide medical treatment after the decisions were made. After all, there was no point in letting a recent amputee bleed messily all over the law offices. But the mere threat of such punishments sufficed to dissuade many criminals, and others would promptly flee the city when caught. So the general population was fairly law abiding.

He came to the civil court. There were a number of cases waiting to be settled, but because Heath was a person in favor here—he had tended the ailments of several of the judges—he was given a prompt hearing.

The judge was sympathetic, but reluctant. "The claim seems to have equal merit by both directions," he said. "It is a confusion of definition. I can not arbitrarily give the land to one party or the other."

Heath had suspected that would be the case. The title to this property was ambiguous. "Then how can this be settled?" he asked, knowing the answer.

"You will have to submit the matter to celestial judgment."

Heath nodded. "I am ready."

The notice went out. Pul was summoned to present his side of the case, and then a day was set for the judgment.

They each reported to the palace on the morning of the set day. Pul had several slaves from his household, including Honoria, to provide support during the ordeal. Heath was accompanied by Talena and a couple of child slaves to run errands. What the support crews could do was limited, in the physical sense, but essential in the social sense. This was a duel, not of weapons, but of conscience.

There were six small stone towers standing in front of the palace, with sites being prepared for several more. They were hardly comfortable as residences; indeed they had been designed to be uncomfortable. Each had a small door in the base, and a ladder up the inner wall, and an open top. Each had a rope tied to a bucket that could be lowered from the turret to the ground outside: this would suffice for all supplies and waste disposal.

No supplies could be taken inside. The men had to enter their towers naked. They were allowed no diversions and no food—only water or wine. Their time in the towers was to be deadeningly solitary. Apart from that, they were free to say or do whatever they wished. That was the problem.

"Enter," the official said. Heath and Pul stripped and squeezed into their separate towers, and the official barred the doors behind them. They were in the towers—for as long as it took.

It was dark inside the close confine of the circular wall, and it stank of stale sweat. A disk of light showed at the top. Heath spread his arms, and found that there was not enough room for that; in fact there was barely room to sit down, and not enough to lie down. He felt the stone wall, and realized that it angled slightly inward; the tower was narrower at the top than at the bottom.

Heath found the wooden rungs of the ladder, tested them carefully, and started up. The slight slope meant that he was pulling inward, as if hanging; that was not comfortable. Of course the ladder could not fall; it would merely fetch up against the other rim. But it still felt insecure.

The tower was about three times the height of a man, so it was probably possible to escape it by jumping to the ground from the top, but even if there was no injury, it would forfeit the decision. The confinement was social more than literal.

He tested each rung before trusting his weight to it, just in case, and continued to the top. The air improved as he got there, and the light brightened. At last he poked his head out over the top, reveling in the fresh air and light, though he had not been at all long in the depth.

The top of the tower was jagged, with stones pointing up irregularly. It would not be possible to sit on it or lie across it. The ladder was the only place to be. Or down below. Heath thought he knew the reason for that.

There was a rope knotted to the top rung of the ladder. It dangled down to a bucket on the ground. Ah yes, the supply system; it seemed inadequate from up here, but it would have to do.

"Hello, Heath!" Talena called, waving. There she stood, really not all that far away, but seeming to be in another realm.

He waved back. "All is well."

He looked across to the next tower. Pul's head was just appearing. His slaves applauded as if he had accomplished a victory. But Honoria stood silent. She was, after all, the object of this contest. She could not afford to shame her husband, but neither did she have to pretend devotion. She looked quite pretty, from this distance, with her demure aspect, as if it were sheer poise that motivated her.

"Who are you really interested in?" Talena inquired teasingly, noting his glance. She wasn't worried; she knew that if Heath's love for her was imperfect, it was nonexistent for any other woman. In fact, if he were able to orient fully on any woman other than his first wife, there would not be any problem between them.

"She does seem worth acquiring," he said. It was easier to let others think that it was his desire for a royal woman that motivated him, rather than his wife's desire to free that woman. For one thing, that made it his challenge, rather than hers.

"Well, while I'm here I expect you to look at me. Are you ready for water?"

"Yes." He wasn't thirsty yet, but would be in time, and it was better to get his supplies in at the outset.

She put a gourd of water in the basket, and he hauled it up hand over hand. She had wanted to put sugar palm wine in, but he had insisted on straight water. He wanted his mind fully functional, for that was the key to victory. He unloaded the gourd and perched it somewhat precariously on the wall. Then he let the basket drop down again.

He looked across the city. Dark clouds were building. They were not yet properly in the monsoon season, but it was incipient, and there could be heavy storms at any time. "Go on home," he called to Talena. "You have chores."

She glanced at the sky, knowing his reason. She blew him a kiss, and departed.

He watched her go. She was such a good wife, a perfect wife. He was idiotic not to love her. But his objective mind did not govern his deep feeling. She was not Baya, and never could be.

"Some support you're getting!" Pul called, taunting him.

"That is all right," Heath called back. "I will look at your slave, who will soon be mine."

Honoria turned her face to him, but did not smile. She had to remain neutral.

"So look at her," Pul said. "I'll help you. Slave! Take off your skirt."

Honoria looked at him, hesitating. If he was serious, she would have to do it; he owned her. He nodded, showing that he meant it. She untied her skirt and stood naked.

Heath looked. Pul looked. The court representative looked. And so did a growing collection of passers-by. Naked slave women were nothing special, though they normally covered their bifurcations with their hands or concealed them behind packages or bundles being carried, but other men's naked women were, and well-formed ones more so.

It was Pul who broke. "Cover it up, woman," he said, disgusted. He had thought to shame Heath, but it hadn't worked.

Heath's feet were tiring on the narrow rung of the ladder, so he took his water in the crook of one arm and moved down the ladder. He hated the depths, but he was not a robust man like Pul, and needed to rest his feet.

He sat on the stone floor and took a sip from his gourd. He would have to go back to the top soon, because the litigants were required to present themselves to view for anyone interested; this was a public spectacle. But for the moment he could relax.

But it was uncomfortable here, as indeed it was meant to be. He needed to divert his mind. So he pretended that his water was but the fringe of a nice meal. Suppose Talena had put in crocodile belly meat and onions with the rice, giving him a treat? It was the kind of thing she would do. She took such good care of him, in so many little ways. Any other man would be thrilled. Actually he was grateful, but still lacking. He wished he could get that off his mind, but it pressed in more closely now that he was alone. He had a guilt that would not abate, and that, in large part, had brought him here.

So much for his effort to divert his mind: the imagined meal had led inevitably to its provider, and his related guilt. Better not to think of food.

The storm came. Sudden wind buffeted the tower, making it creak. Suppose it collapsed? But of course it wouldn't; it had survived many prior monsoon seasons. He was better off in here than in the open.

Then the rain came. It sluiced down inside the tower, soaking him. He had no escape, and neither did his imagined food. He tried to close his mind to it, but his unruly fancy insisted that he had to gobble the rest of his rice before it swelled with rainwater. Even in unwanted imagination, he could not let what Talena had prepared for him go to waste. It was ironic. The pretended onion, at least, would hold.

The water continued. He scrambled to his feet. It felt as if he were standing below a waterfall. It pooled around his legs, rising to the ankles. The stone contained it, not letting it flow freely away to the river. Would it fill the tower?

No, that was a false alarm. The water was seeping out around the closed door, which did not fit its frame perfectly. It was deep enough to prevent him from sitting, unless he wanted a dirty bath, but would not remain long.

He let the fancied onion float—it really wasn't going anywhere, unfortunately—and climbed the ladder. The rungs were slippery, but he was careful and was in no danger of slipping. He reached the top and put his head into the blast of the storm. Now it was cleaning him, and that was good, because he normally washed several times a day, as did all people of respectable castes. Being unclean was part of what made the tower trials unpleasant.

The rain eased. He looked down and around, and saw his two errand slaves huddled against the base of the tower. "Go home," he called to them. "Tell my wife I told you to."

They got up, bowed to him, and ran gratefully off.

"You fool," Pul called. "Now you have nothing."

For answer, Heath looked meaningfully at Honoria, who stood bedraggled but unbowed where she had been. She had not yielded to the storm. The more he saw of her, the more she impressed him. She *was* a woman worth contesting for, even if he wasn't going to use or keep her. Pul, of course, thought Heath wanted her for her body. Heath's real purpose was beyond the man's understanding.

Shamed, Pul called down to her. "Go home, slave!"

Honoria bowed acknowledgment, turned, and walked away with dignity, her hips swinging with a natural and appealing cadence. She glanced quickly again at Heath, expressionless, but that was enough. She appreciated his intercession. Then she was gone.

The storm had passed. Heath's feet were fatiguing on the rung again, so he went back below. He knew that nothing would be settled on the first day, and probably not on the second. But by the third or fourth day there could be action, as hunger became urgent. Few litigants cared to starve in order to prove their point.

One thing about the rain: it had cooled the tower. But what about tomorrow? Heath wished he could stay at the top, to catch the breezes there, but unless he found some way to support his tender feet, he couldn't.

He had a notion. He felt around, looking for loose stones. He found one in the floor; the water had washed out some of its support, and it was small enough to lift out. He balanced it on the bottom rung, then put one foot on it. It was flat on top and irregular on the bottom, so tended to hold its place as long as there was weight on it. He put both feet on it, and they were crowded, but it was possible. This spread his weight out across a much wider area, making it more comfortable for him to stand.

He put the stone in the crook of his left arm, and climbed using his right hand. The stone was heavy, and he was breathing hard, but he made it. Awkwardly he set it down on the rung his feet used, and held it there with first one foot, then both feet. He stood, and was comfortable at last.

The towers were in front of the palace, which meant that they commanded a good view of palace activities. Oxen were hauling covered wagons to the back area, and several elephants were being walked around the grounds. There were squawking sounds from the wagons, and Heath realized that the palace was preparing for an entertainment, bringing in crates of fighting cocks. He wasn't sorry that he would miss that; he enjoyed seeing the wrestling matches between burly guards, and the clever acrobats and tightrope walkers and jugglers, but watching animals kill each other was not to his taste. Watching human beings kill each other was not to his taste either; it was too hard to save their lives when they were badly injured. He thought that things might be better if competitive kite flying were substituted for physical combat. It could be done; some kites had barbed strings that could sever the strings of other kites, if maneuvered into position. But that was not considered royal sport.

"I'm not going to let you have her," Pul said.

Heath shrugged. "That remains to be seen."

"Why do you want her? You have a good wife of your own."

That was actually a fair question, so Heath tried to give a fair answer. "I don't want her for myself. I want to free her for temple service."

"Ludicrous! You want a buxom mistress to supplement your thin wife."

"Have it your way. Yours is buxom."

Satisfied that he had exposed a motive, Pul was silent. He simply could not think in terms of generosity, or of doing a favor for one's wife. At least Heath had tried to explain.

The afternoon passed, and his feet did not hurt. He had solved that problem. But he could not remain here indefinitely. The curious folk had moved on; no one would care if he disappeared for a while. So he carefully lifted the stone, held it, and made his way back down to the bottom. He drank the rest of the gourd of water. He sat on the floor, getting drowsy.

There was a tapping against the tower. "Heath!" It was Talena's voice, faint through the stone.

He roused himself and climbed the ladder. Talena had brought him more water, and was putting it in the basket.

"Are you all right?" she asked.

"Very well," he said. "Thank you for coming again."

"I will stay here through the night, if you wish."

"No. I want you to rest, and the children need your care. I have no problems here."

"I hope not," she said, sounding worried.

He hauled up the basket. "I will see you in the morning," he said.

"It will be lonely without you in my bed."

"Go, woman," he said gruffly. "Before you weaken my resolve."

Talena went, and suddenly he felt regretful, almost grief stricken. He had meant the comment half-humorously; had she taken it seriously, and thought he was rejecting her? Sending her away because he didn't like to look at her? That wasn't what he had said, but considering their imperfect relationship, she might have heard it that way. She was a good woman, such a good woman, and it wasn't her fault that he had lost Baya. She had done everything a good wife could do, and he really should have loved her.

"So is it true that you don't take your wife to bed?" Pull asked nastily. "And that's why you want mine?"

Word was getting out about his problem with Talena? Heath felt a surge of embarrassed anger. But then he realized that the man was guessing, thinking that he must want Honoria for sexual purpose and therefore must have a deficiency at home. So he went along with it, mockingly.

"I wonder who sired my daughters?" he asked. "While I was out about my business?"

"Not me!" Pul said quickly. He wasn't sharp enough to realize exactly how the insult had been turned around, or to know how to counter it.

Honoria reappeared, bringing water or wine to Pul. She looked clean and elegant. She was indeed an attractive woman, and seemed wasted on a man like Pul. But was what Heath was doing right? Taking her away from a neighbor who really had not done him harm? This whole business was less than perfect.

The woman squatted, transferring the gourd to the basket. Her breasts touched her thighs. She did not look at Heath, but he knew she was aware of him. Did she think he was only pretending to honor his wife's request, and that he actually wanted her for himself? Did she care?

He went down his ladder, removing himself from illicit notions. He settled in the dark base and sipped from the gourd. The water was cool, indicating that she had drawn it from the spring just before coming here. She was infinitely thoughtful.

Unbidden, the thought of food returned. His stomach was empty, and was making its hunger known. So he diverted it again with the thought of what food there would be, if Talena had brought any. This time it was freshly baked fish and sapodilla berries along with the rice. But it didn't assuage his hunger; it worsened it.

Now he needed to urinate. He could do it in the tower, and that must have been what prior occupants had done. The smell lingered. But his sense of cleanliness objected. Why surround himself with the stench of his own waste, breathing it? So he used the empty water gourd, then took it up the ladder to the top. He was about to pour it out, but there were people passing by. So he simply set it in the basket and lowered the basket to the ground. Talena would know what to do with it.

He returned to the base, and sat on the floor with his knees drawn up. The circle of light above faded, and the darkness became complete. It was night, and there was nothing to do but sleep. So he rested his head against the stone wall and let himself drift. Right now Talena would be putting the girls to bed, telling them one of her stories. She was good with those stories, very good; she could entertain one child or a whole community, retelling the great tales of their people. If only he could be as entranced by her narrative and person as the children were! What was the matter with him, that he clung to what could never be recovered, while not properly appreciating what was there for the taking?

He woke, feeling stifled, and realized that the air was getting bad. As a healer he understood the importance of fresh air for health. It wasn't a matter of bad spirits; there just seemed to be a quality to new air that got used up in close quarters. But how could he freshen the air? If he climbed to the top of the tower there would be plenty, but he couldn't perch there while sleeping.

He pondered, and then felt the small wooden door. Sure enough, it did not fit quite tightly; there was the faint coolness of incoming air leaking around the edges, especially the bottom. He scraped away the dirt and grime, widening the bottom crevice as well as he could. Then he curled up on his side with his head against the door, his mouth down as close to the bottom crevice as possible. The fresh air was like a diffuse stream of water, and he sucked it in avidly.

He woke several times to change his position, for he could not simply stretch and turn over in the cramped tower. But always he got his head low, down where the air was best, and that sufficed. By morning he was somewhat cramped, but well enough, considering how much worse it could have been. He wondered whether Pul had had the wit to seek fresh air, and doubted it.

He climbed the ladder. Dawn was in the east, spreading its lovely red tents across the clouds and sky. The palace guard had changed; the new one was just as stiff and distant as the other. A guard would be present throughout the ordeal, to make sure that neither man left his tower or remained out of sight too long. But the guards were under orders to interfere in no way, and to speak to none of the participants.

And there was Talena arriving with more water. No—it was Honoria, for Pul. Pul was evidently not yet up; his head did not show above his tower. The woman came to the base of the tower, set down her basket, and waited for a moment. No one was around; the guard did not count. Satisfied, she turned her face toward Heath, and smiled. Then she turned back, and knocked on the door. That would rouse her master.

Such a small gesture, that fleeting signal of gratitude, but Heath really appreciated it. Maybe what he was doing was of doubtful validity, but at least the one most concerned acknowledged it.

Now he saw Talena arriving—and she had their children with her. The eldest daughter, Lita, was five, and the next was four, and the next three. She was carrying the one-year-old. And the basket.

"Hello, Daddy!" the eldest called. "Did the *nak ta* get you?" She referred to the spirits that were associated with ancestors, or rivers, or trees—or towers. They were not necessarily hostile, but it was best not to offend them.

"We got along well enough," Heath replied. "The spirit of the tower must know I am right." Though he himself was not sure. Between the awkwardness of challenging a neighbor, and the attractiveness of the neighbor's wife, the doubt was significant and growing.

Talena checked the tower basket, and noted the content of its gourd, sniffing. She nodded, and exchanged it for the new gourd.

Meanwhile, Pul had appeared atop his tower. He hauled roughly on his rope—and the gourd with his water slopped. The woman quickly caught and righted it, but the lost water could not be restored. "You stupid slave!" he cried at Honoria. "You spilled it!"

Honoria nodded apologetically, not deigning to argue. The guard glanced in her direction, expressionless.

Talena, about to depart, hefted the gourd she carried. "I have extra—but I think it would not be right to give you this."

The guard almost cracked a smile. It seemed he knew what was in the gourd.

"But I will walk with you, if you wish to borrow it to refill yourself."

"Thank you," Honoria said.

"Stay here," Talena told the children. "And don't tease the guard." Then the two women walked away.

Pul stared after them, then angrily took his partially filled gourd below. Heath stayed high, to keep an eye on his children. He had almost laughed when Talena pretended to consider giving her gourd to Honoria. It was full of his piss! Pul didn't even know he was the butt of the joke. And the guard would have a story to tell when he was relieved.

Soon the women returned, and Honoria was carrying the gourd. They had evidently filled it at the nearest public pool. Honoria was smiling; she must have come to understand the joke, too, as Talena emptied the gourd and rinsed it.

"Pul!" Honoria called. "More water."

After a while Pul's head showed. He didn't like taking water from one of Heath's gourds, but knew he needed it. So with bad grace he hauled it up. He did not thank anyone. He disappeared into his tower.

Talena waved to Heath. Then she and the girls departed.

Honoria remained, for Pul had not dismissed her. She sat and leaned against the tower, her knees lifted, awaiting his convenience. Heath watched her, for there was not much else to do. The morning sunlight was striking at an angle, illuminating her. Her eyes were closed, thus giving Heath leave to inspect her as closely as he wished. Her hair was loose and thick and lustrous, in the fashion of the upper castes, and it half masked her breasts, enhancing their interest. Her ankles showed below her skirt, decorous but suggestive. What might lie beyond such ankles? Surely nothing he had not seen yesterday, yet now it seemed that it must be special. She was certainly an interesting woman.

But his feet were getting tender, for he had not brought up his standing stone. So, reluctantly, he descended, letting go of the view.

He drank and rested, for there was not much else to do. Already the heat of the day was rising. If it did not rain, it would become unbearably hot. Then he would have to take his rock up and stand at the top until rain or nightfall. In fact he ought to go up now, for it was a better location than the depths. But he was lethargic. He slumped down and slept, though he didn't need it.

He woke at midday, to Talena's knock at the door. He climbed the ladder and hauled up the new basket. This time she had provided two gourds of water, so that he would not run dry in the heat. She was always thoughtful in such ways. He thanked her, and looked around before going down. Honoria was gone. He was almost disappointed.

"She will return," Talena said. "I told her to wear a shorter skirt."

"Thank you." But he had to marvel at his wife's attitude. She had no jealousy at all. She knew he would look at what was offered, but also knew that he would never do more than look.

She departed, and he went down to rest some more. He drank one gourd of water and saved the other for the worse heat coming. There was no sign of rain on this day.

It was becoming very hot. It was time for him to go to the top. But he felt weak and dizzy, and lacked the initiative to get moving. He was no longer hungry, and knew that was a bad sign; his digestive system had given up and shut down. He should at least get his head down by the crack under the door, for fresh air, but he didn't. It was just too hot to let him move at all.

His mind drifted. He stared into the opposite wall, which was really the wall he leaned against. So how was it to be defined? Was it a separate thing when across from him, though there was no break between it and the one he leaned against? He pictured the tower unwinding, its wall becoming a flat wall: all one piece. Yet surely what was opposite could not be the same.

The wall re-formed before him, dark and impenetrable. But he did not need to be confined. He concentrated, and the wall became transparent. Now he could see the palace beyond it, and part of the city, with people on the streets.

One of the people left the street and walked toward him. It was Honoria, in a shorter skirt. She sat down outside the tower and drew up her knees. This time her ankles and calves showed, and her thighs behind them, under the skirt. There was a shadowed region between the thighs, gradually coming clearer. "Do you want it?" she inquired.

It looked very interesting. "I should not," he said. "I am married."

"To whom?"

"To Baya. I have always been married to her."

"But she died."

"She died," he agreed, wincing as he saw that scene of destruction. "And I remarried." He saw young Talena, really too young to marry, but so eager to have him, and there were social and economic constraints that made it well worth his while to do it. So he had done it, but never really done it sufficiently. Because he couldn't let go of Baya.

"That is not true," Honoria said.

"How can you know that?"

"I will prove it." She got up and walked through the wall. She kneeled and embraced him. There was no room, yet it didn't matter; they were in each other's arms.

"But my wife—"

"Not true." She kissed him.

His desire flared. He returned her kiss, and embraced her, and entered her, and spent himself in her, endlessly, for the release was never quite complete.

"You always desired me, not your wife," she said. "But you couldn't have me."

"But I never knew you, before this—"

"Not true. Here is my true identity." Her face fuzzed, and became Baya. No, not Baya; a younger woman. A girl. In fact—

"Melee!" he gasped, astonished. "Baya's little sister."

"Now you know your true desire," she agreed, and faded away.

The ancient woman Bata, Baya's grandmother, appeared. He had learned the essential art of healing from her, and it had changed his attitude and his life. She wasted no words. "Get your head straight before you go mad," she said.

Heath woke from his reverie, horrified. He was covered in sweat. The heat and hunger and the bad air had made him hallucinate.

He grasped the rungs of the ladder and hauled himself up. His head seemed to be floating, yet his feet were heavy. He struggled to get higher, rung by rung, concentrating to make sure each hand held on tightly.

At last his head broke out the top, and he sucked in fresh air. His mind began to clear. He had fallen afoul of the heat and stale air, but he could avoid that somewhat up here. He would have to bring up his stone and settle here until nightfall.

But the relief couldn't clear his mind completely. The hallucination had uncovered certain appalling truths. He did desire Honoria, simply because she was an attractive woman; in control of his faculties he would never act on that. But Baya—could he have been to her as he was to Talena, because his actual passion was for her sister? Melee had been a child when he had known her, eleven, twelve, thirteen, but a winsome one with fine features and intriguing manner. He had never paid her much attention. Because she was a child, and was his wife's sister.

By now Melee would be nineteen. He had not seen her since the tragedy that killed Baya, but if she lived, that would be her age. Somehow she had remained in his mind, not openly, but in the deep recesses that governed his secret passion. And he feared it was true: she had balked his love for Baya too. He had not truly loved Baya, though he had thought he did; he had loved that aspect of her that most resembled her sister. When she had died, he had thought it was her loss he most suffered, but it had been Melee, who had disappeared with her father and Bata, leaving him with nothing.

And Talena was another victim of that emotional balking. Now he knew its true nature. And knew that he was not rid of it. He could not tell her. Why torture her with the knowledge that she competed not with a dead woman, but a living one?

And what would happen if he ever encountered the adult Melee?

He had entered this contest to oblige his wife. He had hoped to win what she desired. Now he knew that he had only confirmed what she least desired. There seemed to be little point in going on; there was nothing pleasant to be had from this ordeal.

Still, he didn't call out to the guard. Pointless as this had become, it wasn't in him simply to capitulate. Pul remained in his tower, and the idea of yielding to that man did not appeal.

He climbed back down, fetched his stone, and brought it up. His lack of sustenance made him weak and faint, but he took his time and got to the top. He braced the stone in place and stood on it. He waited.

After a while he became aware of a sound. It was a series of dull thuds. It seemed to be coming from the other tower. What was Pul doing?

In due course Talena and Honoria arrived, walking together, carrying their baskets. Heath felt guilty, looking at them. He had dreamed of passion with one, and discovered the nature of his problem with the other. He could not tell either.

They stopped at the towers. "What is that?" Honoria asked.

"He must be pounding the door," Heath said, glad for the chance to shift from his thoughts.

Honoria went to the door. "Pul! What is it?"

The pounding increased in volume. Now there was an indecipherable yelling.

Suddenly Heath realized what should have been obvious. Pul had not had the wit to get fresh air, or to get out of the worst heat. He was hallucinating. Who could know what evil spirits lurked in his mind? Surely worse ones than Heath had encountered. "Let him out."

"But then he will lose," Talena protested.

"I think so," Heath agreed, realizing that he had after all won the contest. Not the way he had expected; normally it took three or four days for one party or the other to break out in boils or demonstrate his guilt for his wrongness in some other way. But this was a very hot day, and so the towers had been worse. Pul could die if not released.

Honoria was silent, realizing that the issue had been so suddenly settled. She would be donated to the temple with the land, and have a far better life.

The two women went to the guard. The guard went to Pul's tower door and unbarred it, lifting it out of the way. Suddenly Pul's screaming was louder. Then he fell through the door and lay on the ground, twitching.

Heath recognized the symptom. "Douse him with water!" he called. "Use the gourds!"

The two women poured their gourds over Pul's body and head. The one Honoria used had colored fluid. The idiot had been drinking wine! It was allowed, but foolish, without food. That would have made things that much worse.

The guard faced the palace and waved. Soon several men came, leading a horse bearing water skins. They poured more water on Pul, and soon he quieted. "You have lost the issue," the palace official told him. "The judgment of heaven has been rendered." He turned to Heath's tower. "Release that man. He must come and approve the transfer of property."

A man opened Heath's door. Heath climbed down, replaced his stone in the floor, and crawled out.

Talena met him there, and hugged him as he stood up. "I knew you could do it!" she cried. "You can do anything."

How little she knew.

The city that Yasovarman founded became a model of elegance that remains remarkable to this day. But when he died his sons soon dissipated the power and security he had made. However, the culture continued, and over the course of five centuries the Khmer kingdom became quite wealthy. Visiting Chinese were im-

pressed, though they considered the people of this region to be barbarians. Eventually it faded, and the jungle grew over the city, and the grandeur that was Angkor was almost forgotten. Today most of what we know of it comes from Chinese reports, preserved stone inscriptions, and the phenomenal architecture. But it was great while it lasted.

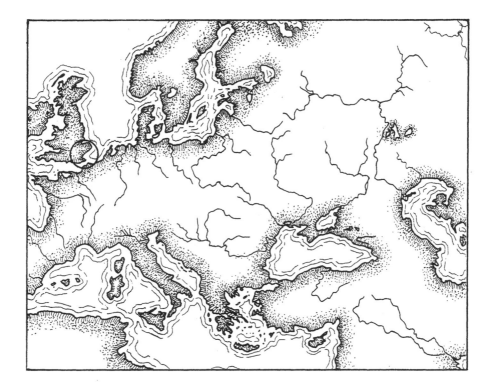

CHAPTER 10

POLITICS

Some of the greatest historical moments are not phenomenal battles like Hastings in 1066 or significant decrees like the Magna Carta in 1215. Some pass almost unnoticed, yet their impact can be felt worldwide. Such as the development of a superior clock that would work on a ship. The art of politics came into play here, as elsewhere, in both positive and negative ways. The place is London, England; the time is 1772.

OD saw the king's messenger coming, and hastily straightened out his sloppy clothing. He was working on a mechanical music box, trying to get its tiny innards to work reliably, and it wasn't going well. He had the principle down well; the devil, as was said, was in the details.

"The king requests your attendance at a private audience at your convenience within the hour."

"I am ready now," Od said. He wasn't; he had been about to break for lunch, for the last hour, delaying for just one more adjustment, and another. But the king's stipend sustained his endeavors, and King George's whim was his command.

He went with the messenger. One advantage of doing that was that the messenger had a coach, so that Od could ride to the palace instead of walking the dirty crowded streets of London. The coach was bumpy, but it commanded the right of way, and that made a big difference.

The messenger guided him to one of the king's private audience chambers. George was already there, evidently having expected Od's prompt attendance. He was a relatively young man, for a monarch, thirty-four years old, and a king for twelve. He was also amiable in private, as long as his prerogatives were not crossed, and it was easy to forget his status.

Od reviewed the nature of the king quickly as he approached, because it was important to remain on George's good side if at all possible. As a boy, George had been described by his tutor as shy, backward, and lazy at his books. He was conscious of his future mission as a monarch, but diffident about his ability to fulfill it. He was known for his "censorious chastity" and sobriety, and "unforgiving piety." In short, the nobles of his court couldn't stand him. His father, George II, had been a weak king, who had lost much of his power to the nobles. George III was uncompromising in his determination to reclaim for the crown all the powers constitutionally allotted to it. This change from lazy student to rigorous persistence mystified others. But Od believed that the king had simply found his mission in life, and now applied himself to it. He was not unduly smart, and tended to take a head-on, opposition-be-damned approach to things, which could be counterproductive. Od believed that George had been neither lazy as a child nor pigheaded as an adult; he simply was not intelligent enough to finesse things, so came across poorly. But he did mean well, and did try his best. And it was Od's job to help him succeed in whatever he wished to. By being an unofficial, compatible, and competent adviser. For the king did not much like looking like a fool, and forewarning about difficult situations could help a lot.

"Ah, Od, my friend!" he said, rising to greet Od. "Just the man I need to help me with a problem." The king was royally garbed, of course, with a white powdered wig, ornate layered robe, knee stockings, and white shoes. Od suspected that George didn't really like the fancy clothing, but regarded it as protocol. Appearances were vital, for royalty. But for this private meeting, the king was dispensing with some of the protocol. He knew Od wouldn't tell.

"Whatever I can do, Your Majesty," Od said. He hoped he would be up to it, for the king's problems could be complicated.

"I have a received a letter from one William Harrison. It seems his father has made a clock, and has a problem with the Board of Longitude. This gets rather technical. I would like to know whether this matter is worthy of my attention. Could you advise me within two days?"

"I will do my best," Od agreed.

"Here is the letter. Anything you can ascertain to verify the nature of the case, and the rights of this man, and its importance to England will be appreciated."

Od accepted the letter. "In two days," he said, bowing and backing away. The messenger remained, to give him a ride home.

Back at home he found Avalanche. She was an expensive prostitute who seemed to admire his knowledge of technical things. She liked to talk to him, and she never charged him for her favors. That was just as well, because he could not have afforded their price. "The news on the street is that you went to see the king," she said.

"Yes. He pays me a modest retainer to be available when he needs me. It's the main thing that enables me to survive without giving up my diversions."

"And by diversion you don't mean women," she said. "You have the best mind I know. I don't know why you aren't famous."

"Science doesn't make people famous." They had been over this before. "What did the king want?"

He had read much of the letter on the ride home. He already knew it was important. But he would have some quick research to do, to ascertain exactly how important. "A man has made a good clock. He wants recognition for it, but the appropriate board is putting him off."

"A clock!" she exclaimed. "What does a clock have to do with anything?"

"It could save uncountable lives, and magnify the British Empire."

She laughed. "Convince me of that, and I will give you something nice." She lifted the hem of her skirt just enough to provide a tempting flash of thigh.

He did desire her. He always desired her. She was a beautiful woman, the kind that normally paid him no attention. She was also a nice person, when not stressed. But her intellect was not technical. How could he make the point, in a way she could appreciate? It would be no good to talk about parallels of latitude and meridians of longitude as essential elements in the geographic definition of the globe; her eyes would glaze over. He cast about—and had it. An episode of history that had its drama and its irony. She should like it.

"About sixty-five years ago, Admiral Sir Clowdisley Shovell led a fleet of five gallant British warships on a victorious engagement with the French at Gibraltar, at the mouth of the Mediterranean Sea."

"Is there a woman in this story?"

He pondered a moment, and remembered. "Yes." He knew she would picture herself as the woman. It was nonsensical but that made him think of himself as the main character, the admiral. He resumed his narrative, feeling increasingly as if he were in it. He assumed the mantle of the fifty-seven-year-old admiral.

The small fleet made its way back toward England, skirting the coasts of Spain and France. For twelve days fog shrouded the region, leaving his navigators without visible bearings. That made the admiral uneasy; he did not like sailing blind. As they approached England the heavy autumn overcast became worse. So he summoned all his navigators to a conference aboard the flagship, the *Association.*

"This dirty weather hides everything," he said. "We dare not misjudge our position. I need not remind you of the peril of foundering if we run aground in untimely fashion. I want all of you to put your heads together and come to a consensus as to our precise location."

The navigators consulted and argued, but in due course a consensus opinion emerged: the English fleet was safely west of Ile d'Ouessant, an island outpost of the Brittany peninsula of France. That meant a clear sea to the north, crossing the English Channel.

Satisfied, the admiral ordered the fleet to proceed due north. But as they moved, a member of the *Association*'s crew approached the admiral.

"Sir, if I may speak—"

It was highly irregular for a simple crewman to address an admiral. But Sir Clowdisley bore with it. "What is it, man?"

"Sir, I know this is forbidden in the Royal Navy. But I fear the peril is so great that I must risk it."

"What are you talking about?"

"Sir, I fear we are significantly off course, and there is great danger."

"Off course? How could a mere sailor possibly have an opinion on such a matter?"

"Sir, I have kept my own reckoning of the fleet's location during this whole cloudy passage. I believe that we are not where we think we are."

Admiral Shovell stared at the sailor. "What?"

"Sir, the danger appears so enormous that I am risking my neck to make my concern known. I believe we are near the coast of England, and will run aground if we proceed much farther north."

"You kept your own reckoning?" the admiral repeated, appalled.

"Yes, sir. I would not have spoken, but for the fear of destruction to the fleet."

"And you have the temerity to question the judgment of qualified navigators?"

"Yes, sir," the sailor said, ashamed. "I beg you, turn the fleet, lest we founder."

"This is beyond tolerance," the admiral snapped. He turned to the ship's captain, who was listening with similar outrage. "Hang this man on the spot for mutiny."

"Yes, sir!" And at the captain's gesture, other crewmen laid hands on the luckless sailor and strung him up from the mast. In a few minutes he was dead, a lesson to all others who might seek to breach the regulations of the Royal Navy so egregiously.

The fleet continued north. Until, to the admiral's horror, they suddenly sighted land. The stiff wind was blowing them right upon it; it was too late to turn aside, for the fog had allowed them no clearance.

They had, in fact, been not near the west coast of France, but near the south coast of England. They had steered north onto the chain of Scilly Isles, that projected about twenty miles west from the southwest tip of England. It was the very calamity the admiral had tried so hard to avoid. His navigators had been collectively wrong by a fatal amount.

The *Association* was in the lead, and struck the submerged rocks off the isle first. The men screamed, knowing doom was upon them. In just a few minutes the ship sank, casting all hands into the sea. But not before the admiral was aware that two other ships, the *Eagle* and the *Romney,* were being similarly holed by the rocks and were going down too. His fleet was being destroyed—and all because he hadn't listened to the crewman who tried to warn him.

Then Sir Clowdisley himself dived into the water, rather than be sucked down with the ship. He was a strong swimmer, unlike most of the crewmen, and knew how to handle rough waters. He got his bearings and stroked for the nearest land.

The swim was terrible. He was hampered by his clothing, and the water was chill. He was fatiguing rapidly. There came a time when he thought that he, too, would drown. But somehow he kept on, and in the end managed to drag himself out onto a beach and collapse on dry sand. He had made it!

As he lay there, too tired to do more than pant, a woman came along the beach. "Oh, a man!" she exclaimed.

He couldn't even identify himself. But at least he had been found. Help would soon come.

The woman took hold of his arm and raised his hand. "Look at that gem!" she exclaimed, staring at the precious emerald ring on his finger. "I must have it!" She grabbed his finger and twisted the ring, trying to get it off.

This roused the admiral somewhat. "Here, here!" he protested.

She was taken aback. "I thought you were dead!"

"No," he said, and lapsed into semi-consciousness.

"I must have that ring," she repeated. Then she put her hands on his feet and hauled with surprising strength. He was dragged the short distance to the water. She rolled him the last bit, until his head splashed in the surging sea.

"Woman, desist!" the admiral commanded, realizing that she was up to little if any good.

"And you'll never tell," she said. Then she took two handfuls of his hair and plunged his face under the water. She held it there until his faint struggles ceased. Then she grabbed his hand again, and wrenched the ring off.

She shoved the body the rest of the way into the sea and departed with the wonderful emerald ring. Thus did the admiral's misjudgment of his fleet's position cost him his life and the lives of two thousand of his men. Only one ship escaped, and only one other man managed to get to shore and survive.

"And so," Od concluded, "in seeking to avoid the Charibdis of the coast of France, they had blundered into the Scilla of the coast of England: the Scilly Isles. They paid the awful penalty, with the lady monster finishing off the admiral personally."

Avalanche shuddered. "But if she murdered him, and they thought he drowned naturally, how did anyone ever find out?"

"Thirty years later, on her deathbed, she confessed her crime to her clergyman," Od explained. "She even produced the admiral's emerald ring as proof of her guilt."

"And what does this have to do with clocks?"

"Everything. The latitude is easy enough to get; a simple sighting of the elevation of the sun suffices. But the longitude is a challenge akin to the mystery of perpetual motion. One of the methods of calculating it is to compare the time of the home port with the ship time; since one degree of longitude spans sixty nautical miles at the equator, an accurate comparison can theoretically enable—"

"Od, you lost me back at the word 'latitude.' I still don't see how a clock can tell you anything but time. And why should a clock on a ship tell a different time from one back at home?"

Od realized that what was a simple matter for him was not for her. She lacked his scientific training and interest. Then he realized something else: "The king! He may have the same trouble comprehending."

"Of course. That's why he asked you to explain it. But you better do a better job than this. I understand about the admiral getting lost; he should have listened to his crewman. But how a good clock would have saved him is beyond me."

"Avalanche, you may have spared me a horrible embarrassment. I must find a way to clarify the science of sea location in a way the king can readily comprehend. I don't want him to have any confusion. If I can explain it to you, then I can explain it to the king."

She assumed a pose. "Does that make me a queen?"

He laughed. "Close enough. This may take some time, but it's important."

"If you treat me like a queen, I will treat you like a king." She hoisted her skirts and sat on his lap. "The closer you get to my understanding, the closer you will get to my body. See if you can rise to the challenge."

With that inducement, Od managed to find a way. It was a remarkable and satisfying experience, in two respects.

❂

Next morning Od tried to obtain a meeting with a man named the Reverend Nevil Maskelyne, of the Board of Longitude, the leading exponent of the Lunar Distance method of determining longitude. But he was rebuffed at the door; the reverend did not care to speak to strangers off the street.

"But I am on a mission for King George," Od protested.

"So you say." The door closed in his face.

Od did his best to control his anger. He had tried to be fair, and to obtain both sides of the issue from authorities in their fields. He would still try to be fair, but now he had sympathy for a particular side.

A day later Od was back with King George. "I believe Mr. Harrison has a case, and that this matter is worth your while," he said. "While I don't wish to bore you with material with which you may already be familiar, the matter is somewhat technical, so I thought I should review it in as simple a manner as possible."

"By all means," the king agreed, not at all deceived. "Simplicity is a virtue we do well to practice."

"Ascertaining the ship's time is easy," Od said. "Any sun dial can do it, so long as it is level and correctly oriented. A good compass and suspended platform can accomplish both, even if the ship is swaying in the waves. But the ship's time tells nothing about its location."

"For sure," George agreed. "The time changes as the ship moves. It may be morning in America while it is noon here."

"Exactly, sir. Now the ship's location has two components, latitude and longitude. The first is how far from the equator it is, and the second is how far around the world it is. I have brought a model of our globe," Od said, taking out an orange. "With the equator already marked."

"Delicious model," George said, with a bit of a smile.

"The parallels of latitude circle the globe above and below the equator," Od said, making circling motions with his finger. "Each aligns exactly with the equator. But their circles grow smaller toward the poles, until they disappear." He made smaller circles until his finger stopped at the north pole. "The farther north a ship goes, the lower in the sky the sun looks, because we must peer around the curve of the Earth to see it. Since we know how high above the horizon it should look for a given day and time, this means that a ship can tell its latitude simply by sighting accurately on the sun and reading his chart. So a ship always knows its north-south position, assuming that its navigator is competent."

"Of course," George agreed.

"But that is only the first component of its position. It must also know its east-west position, and for that the sun won't help. It would be possible to ascertain it from the moon and certain stars, comparing their precise positions with respect to each other, but as yet we have no sufficiently accurate charts of their positions for given times ahead. Also, cloudy weather interferes with celestial observations, and the phases of the moon aren't always good." Actually, such obstacles could be overcome, to an extent, by a combination of techniques. But Od was still smarting from the rudeness of the Lunar Distance man, and preferred not to go into this at this time. "So another solution is an accurate clock."

"Now we come to it," George said.

Od held up his orange. He brought out a toothpick. "Suppose the ship's home port is here in Africa," he said, sticking the pick into the equator. "And let's assume that it is noon at that home port. But the ship has sailed west until it is here." He stuck in another toothpick not far from the first. "The ship's time is eleven o'clock in the morning. So it is one hour different from the home port time."

"To be sure."

"Now we know that there are 360 degrees in a full circle, and 24 hours in a full day and night. So one hour difference must be 15 degrees west. Since we also know that there are 60 nautical miles to a degree on the equator, the ship must be 900 miles west of its port. The comparison of times provides the location. The farther west the ship goes, the greater will be the difference in times. If it goes east, the same principle applies, only the ship's time will be earlier than the port time. But no matter how far it goes, a comparison of the two times will yield the distance."

"Of course."

Od breathed a silent sigh of relief. He had clarified it so that the king remembered the basics. "So by ascertaining accurate latitude and longitude, the ship's navigator can locate the position of the ship. Of course he must calculate the miles per degree differently, the farther from the equator the ship is, because of the smaller circles. But his tables tell him that. So he has only one problem: accurate home port time."

"And there is the crux," George said.

"There it is, indeed. Because we have no clocks that can tell time reliably at sea. The constant irregular rocking of the ship disrupts any pendulum clock, and the changing temperatures play havoc with lubricating oils, and the combination of heat, cold, moisture, and salt air destroys the integrity of metal springs. All this is hell on clocks."

"I know."

"So we can't set a clock at home, and carry it on the ship, and use it. It simply will not remain accurate, if it works at all. So we can't travel far into the unknown with confidence. Thus our ships must travel through relatively narrow corridors that are known to be free of obstacles. All the other nations know this, and so do the pirates. So anyone who wants to ambush our ships or fleets knows just where to do it. The wealth carried by some merchant ships is enormous, so unless they are guarded by warships they will risk predation by hostile forces. All because they can't set their own courses with confidence."

"And a terrible burden it has been," the king agreed. "But you say this man Harrison has a clock that will remain accurate at sea?"

"I believe he does. John Harrison has a long history of making excellent clocks." Now Od's spot research came into play. He had not known of the man until given the name. "He seems to have had no formal training in clock making, and was never apprenticed to any watchmaker. He simply educated himself, and he must have had an immense thirst for knowledge. He built his first clock at the age of twenty, almost entirely of wood."

"Of wood!" the king exclaimed. "Was it a toy?"

"No, it was a fully competent clock. He went on to build others, and achieved a local reputation. In 1720 he was commissioned to build a tower clock, and in two years he completed it. From that date to this—fifty years—that clock has run continuously, without oil."

"Without oil! All clocks need oil."

"They do. But Harrison had done away with the need for additional lubricants by carving the friction-bearing parts from a tropical hardwood called lignum vitae that exudes its own grease. There is no iron or steel anywhere in the clock, since the damp climate would make it rust; the only metal he used was brass. He invented a new kind of wheel, shaped like a child's drawing of the sun, whose teeth are carved of different types of oak so as to have exceptional strength where needed, and lightness where needed. Sir, the thing is said to be a marvel of innovation and precision."

"I should think so. My knowledge of clocks is slight, but even I am impressed."

"Since then he and his brother have built other clocks, and they, too, are marvels of precision and innovation. The finest quality watches being produced anywhere in the world drift from true time by as much as a minute a day. The Harrison clocks never erred during tests by more than one second a month."

"One second a month! This is sheer genius!"

Od nodded. "I examined the design of one of them, and I think 'genius' is a suitable term. These self-taught clockmakers are the best in the world at their trade."

"Why haven't we heard more of them?"

"That is an unfortunate story, and the reason William Harrison has written to you, Your Majesty. I believe you should summon him for a personal interview."

"That I expect to do. But tell me something of the situation."

"As you know, the need for a truly accurate method of computing the position of ships is so great that in 1714, in response to a disaster of Admiral Shovell, who lost four ships and his life because of an error in calculating the location of his fleet, Parliament passed the Longitude Act. It offered a prize of twenty thousand pounds for a practical and useful means of determining longitude at sea, for accuracy to within half a degree of longitude. Many folk have struggled to win that prize, for it represents wealth beyond the means of any ordinary person, but in almost sixty years none have claimed it. The problem is simply too challenging. The clock method is only one of hundreds of approaches, and I think the most promising."

"But why didn't this man Harrison try for it?"

"He did, sir. In 1727 he decided to tackle the longitude problem. He realized that the pendulum that was so vital for maintaining the cadence of landbound clocks would have to go. It just couldn't work well on rolling seas. So he pondered an alternate mechanism, a springing set of seesaws, self-contained and counterbalanced to withstand the wildest waves. He worked with this notion for almost four years, until he was satisfied with it.

"Then in 1730 he approached Dr. Edmund Halley, the Astronomer Royal, and a member of the Board of Longitude." As he spoke, Od found himself getting into the scene, as he tended to do, identifying with the clever clockmaker.

London was a huge city, vast beyond John's home village of Barrow or the major nearby port city of Kingston upon Hull. He made his way to the Royal Observatory in Greenwich, just south of the great Thames River.

Dr. Halley was an affable man, disliked by some because he drank brandy and could swear like a sea captain, but he was well liked by most. There was a story that one night he and Peter the Great, the exiled king of Yugoslavia, had cavorted like a couple of schoolboys and took turns pushing each other through hedges in a wheelbarrow. But there was no sign of such frivolity now; he was a man in his seventies and sedate.

He received John politely, and listened intently to his concept for the sea clock. When John spread out his drawings, the astronomer was impressed, and said so. "You well may have the answer to the question of the age," he said. "But there is a problem. I fear the Board of Longitude, which is heavy with astronomers, mathematicians and navigators, will not welcome a mechanical answer to what it sees as an astronomical question. I can understand its likely skepticism, for I myself spend most of my days and nights working out the moon's motion in an effort to further the Lunar Distance method of finding longitude. But I do try to keep an open mind."

"I am glad of that," John said sincerely.

"I feel that your notion deserves serious consideration, but I am loath to send you into the lion's den that will be the skeptical Board without some additional armor. I lack sufficient knowledge of clocks to make a judgment. Suppose I send you to my friend George Graham, who is a well-known watchmaker? He is an honest man, and he will certainly be competent to judge the merit of your proposal. If he endorses it, then I will be free to give my recommendation to the Board."

John felt an ugly chill. Yes, a watchmaker would be competent to judge—but he might also be inclined to steal the notion for himself. After all, the prize was enough to make any man as rich as a baron. But what could he do? John needed Halley's support. "I will be glad to meet Mr. Graham," he said bravely.

"Excellent! I will arrange an appointment."

Graham was about twenty years older than John, in his late fifties, and he was not polite. "You suppose you have a notion for a clock that can operate efficiently at sea? Have you any notion of the difficulties?"

"Yes I do!" John retorted. He needed this man's good opinion of his clock, but he was not about to be belittled for ignorance of his profession. He then described those difficulties in fair detail.

Graham remained skeptical. "And do you similarly suppose that you have the solution?" But the edge was off; at least the man was satisfied that John was not a complete novice.

"Yes." Then John took the plunge and described his major innovation, the counterbalancing seesaw springs. He was trying to navigate the twin horrors of Scylla and Charybdis, the sea monsters who threatened ships on either side of a narrow passage. Scylla was rejection of his ideas; Charybdis was theft of them.

Graham's eyes widened. "I never dreamed of such a mechanism," he said. "I think it could actually work."

"It does work. I have made a working model at home, Mr. Graham."

"Call me George. I think you and I are going to be friends. This mechanism strikes me as genius. Tell me more about it."

So the ice was broken. But what of the man's honesty? It was a risk that had to be taken. John spread out his drawings.

The two men had met at ten in the morning. They were still talking at eight that evening. "You must stay to dinner, John. I can't get enough of your brilliance."

John was flattered. "Oh, I would not presume—I am just a village carpenter."

"And a genius. John, your notions are so brilliant, I want to become part of them."

This was the dread moment. Was he going to ask to keep the drawings, so he could pirate them? "Part of them?"

"You will need considerable support to develop your mechanism. Your genius goes well beyond mine. So I will do what I can. I will make you a generous loan, to be repaid at no interest and in no great haste. You shall have your day, John."

John was overwhelmed. He had feared rejection or theft; instead he had found crucial support. Graham was so impressed that he was becoming Harrison's patron, giving him more than mere encouragement.

In five years, Harrison completed the clock, which became known as Harrison's Number One, or H-1 for short. It was like none other ever seen. It was made of brass with two dumbbell-shaped bar balances and four helical balance springs sticking out at odd angles. It looked like some weird model of a ship. Its four dials marked the seconds, minutes, hours, and days of the month. It rested in a wood cabinet four feet on a side, and it weighed seventy-five pounds.

The Harrison brothers tested it on the river Humber. Then John took it to London in 1735 and delivered it to Graham. Graham displayed it to the Royal Society. A number of authorities wrote glowing reports and urged the Board of Longitude to give it a formal trial. This was supposed to be a passage from Great Britain to any port in the West Indies. But the Admiralty hesitated for a year, then took the clock on a ship bound for Lisbon, Portugal. Harrison spent most of the trip hanging over the rail, desperately seasick, but the clock performed well. Unfortunately the captain died suddenly, before recording the account of the voyage in his ship's log. So they tried again on the return trip, which was a month-long ordeal through mixed gales and calms. The captain's reckoning, when they finally neared land, was that they were at the Start, near Dartmouth.

"But not according to the calculation done from the clock's time," Harrison protested. "That indicates that we must be more than sixty miles west of the Start."

The captain was skeptical. "Hmpf. That clock has never been to sea before."

But when they verified their position, the clock turned out to be correct. It had done its job. The captain was impressed, admitting his error and praising the clock. He added his recommendation for it.

And so the following week the Board of Longitude convened for the first time, to consider John's device. His supporters were impressive, and the general consensus was that he had every right to demand a West Indies trial, to prove H-1 deserving of the £20,000 prize. Then came a surprise.

"It is not good enough," John said. "There are defects I want to correct. And I believe I can make it smaller. With another two years' work, I could produce a better timekeeper, if the Board can see its way clear to advancing me funds for further development."

The members of the Board were amazed, but it was an offer they could hardly refuse. They agreed to pay him £500, half now, half on delivery, with certain other conditions.

But by the time John completed H-2 and presented it to the Board in January 1741, he was already disgusted with it. It just wasn't good enough.

The Board disagreed. Though H-2 never went to sea, it was subjected to rigorous tests. It was a design as innovative and competent as the first, and it passed the tests, converted critics, and won full backing from the Royal Society.

But John disappeared into his workshop, which was now in London, for sixteen years, to work on H-3. This was another remarkable innovation. It used combinations of metals, whose expansion and contraction in varying temperatures canceled each other out, and a revolutionary new anti-friction device: caged ball bearings. It was two feet high, one foot wide, and weighed sixty pounds.

Yet even this did not satisfy him. He was already considering a precision watch, the H-4, which he completed in 1759. It was about five inches in diameter and weighed three pounds. Unfortunately, it was not perfect: miniaturization sacrificed the frictionless aspect, and it needed oil. If run continuously, it would lose a significant amount of precision—in three or four hundred years.

He presented H-4 to the Board of Longitude in 1760. The Board decided to test H-3 and H-4 on the same voyage. But it delayed. It seemed that a proponent of the Lunar Distance method of determining longitude wanted the prize, so was interfering with the testing of the timepieces.

Fed up, John withdrew the H-3 from the test, allowing the Watch to handle the challenge alone.

In 1762 the Watch crossed the Atlantic Ocean. John's son William accompanied it. After eighty-one days at sea, the Watch had lost only five seconds. On the return trip the weather was worse, and rough seas washed over the sides, at times swamping the deck with two feet of water, and six inches seeped into the captain's cabin where the Watch was kept. William had to keep the Watch wrapped in a blanket to keep it dry, because actual immersion would be beyond the delicate mechanism's tolerance. When the blanket soaked through, he held the cloth against his body to dry it. This protected the Watch, but not William; he had a raging fever by the time they reached England. But the Watch was healthy, and its cumulative gross error for the round trip was just under five minutes.

H-4 had passed the trial. Now at last John Harrison could claim the prize money. Or so he thought.

When the Board met to evaluate the trial it was unsatisfied. It called for three mathematicians to recheck the data for the whole trip, though the measurements had been performed by the Board's own astronomers. The Board complained that William had failed to follow certain rules set down by the Royal Society by using the moons of Jupiter. How was that, again? Why hadn't this been mentioned before? The Board concluded that the trial had not been sufficient. The Watch would have to be subjected to a new trial, under stricter scrutiny. After all, the first trial might have been a fluke, a mere chance occurrence.

So instead of the £20,000 prize, John Harrison received £1,500, with another £1,000 promised if it passed the second trial.

What was going on? Well, the composition of the Board had changed, and those now on it were not as interested in timekeeping as prior members had been. Also, the Reverend Nevil Maskelyne was an advocate of the Lunar Distance method of determining longitude. In fact, he was soon to be appointed to the Board itself. Meanwhile, the Board wanted to give his method a trial. Since Maskelyne boasted that he was certain he had clinched the prize and proven the superiority of his method, William and others challenged his fitness to judge H-4 impartially. Outraged, Maskelyne botched his own trial despite good conditions. The prize remained unclaimed.

In 1764, H-4 was retested. The mathematicians took months to compare their computations with the astronomers' observations. At last they gave their unanimous report: the Watch had passed. It had predicted the longitude to within three miles, which was three times as accurate as the Longitude Act required.

But now the Board made new demands. It offered half the money, on condition that John Harrison turn over to them all the sea clocks, plus a full disclosure of the working of H-4. To receive the full award, John would have to supervise the creation of two duplicates for H-4. In 1765 the Board made more new requirements. John was furious, but in the end agreed, and cooperated fully. And so at last he received the £10,000 half prize.

The secrets of his device began to be spread about. That was exactly what he had feared. He was losing control of his life's work. In addition, in 1766 the Board, under Maskelyne, decided to test H-4 once again, more strenuously than ever. And, perhaps unsurprisingly, he announced that it failed. Thus the Watch's actual success at sea was set aside.

John was enraged by this bad faith, and published a two-penny book attacking the trial. Maskelyne never responded; how could he?

A copy of H-4 was completed in 1770 by another watchmaker, and it was good; John praised it. Meanwhile John had been working on his own copy, the H-5. By the time it satisfied him, the year was 1772. John was seventy-nine years old, and did not see how he could build another new clock. The Board, under hostile auspices, seemed determined to delay indefinitely, so that John would be dead before achieving his proper recognition for his achievement.

"And so William wrote this letter to you," Od concluded. "He believes that his father is not being fairly treated, and he asks that H-5 be tested at the Observatory in Richmond. This would remove it from the authority of the hostile Board. If you care to intercede on John Harrison's behalf, this can be accomplished."

"I shall certainly meet with William Harrison," the king said. He now had a good understanding of the man and his works, so would be able to converse knowledgeably on the subject of the Clock.

In a few days William reported to the palace. Od was in the background as King George interviewed him at length, learning new details of the history of the timepieces. The king was well informed, and did not have any embarrassing confusions. William was surely impressed.

"These people have been cruelly treated," George muttered. Then, to William: "By God, Harrison, I will see you righted!"

The king arranged for a trial of H-5 at Richmond, with three witnesses: the observatory director, William, and the king himself. But the Watch fared poorly. It gained and lost time with abandon. Could Maskelyne have been right? Harrison's hopes were crushed.

Then Od remembered something. "Your Majesty," he whispered to the king. "What about those lodestones you have stored in the closet?"

George was surprised. "That makes a difference?"

"It could. Lodestone is magnetic, and the watch has metal parts."

George went to the closet. "We must move these lodestones away," he said.

William stared. Lodestones! No wonder!

Now H-5 performed admirably. The king extended the trial for ten weeks, anticipating objections from Harrison's enemies. At the end of that period the Watch had proven itself accurate to within one third of a second per day.

King George was satisfied. He put pressure on the Board of Longitude, and it convened before two witnesses from Parliament. This time it reexamined the entire affair of the Clocks and Watches, from beginning to end.

"And this time," George told Od, "we'll go in there and beat those bigots down. It's high time they got what's coming to them."

Oops. There was the king's doggedly blunt approach again. "Sir, while it is certain that you yourself could accomplish this, the one going on trial, as it were, is not you but the old ornery clockmaker. I think this is a case in which discretion is the better part of valor. Finesse may be more effective than force."

George was perplexed. "Eh? How so?"

Carefully, with infinite delicacy, Od explained. "If you can get this across to him," Od concluded, "he should have a better chance."

George considered. "It's a novel approach, but I'll try it. I will talk to the man."

Od hoped this worked. If it didn't, not only would the clockmaker lose his case, Od himself could be out of a job.

Three days later, clockmaker John Harrison appeared before Parliament. George himself counseled the old man in the politics of the situation. "You have a strong case, but as you have seen with the Board, that does not necessarily win the day. Drop any legal blustering; it will only make them get their backs up. Simply appeal to the hearts of the ministers. You are an old man who has devoted his life to the cause, and been denied your full reward. This is the most promising approach."

Od's knees felt weak. The king had made the correct diagnosis. Now would it succeed?

John Harrison heeded George's advice, and made his case. The members of Parliament were favorably inclined, and awarded him £8,750. The amount was almost equal to the remainder of the Longitude Prize. But it was not the prize; it was a separate sum given in spite of the Board, not because of it. It was really a slap in the face of the Board.

"And so justice has at last been done," Od told Avalanche later. "And when more copies of that Watch are made, it will transform navigation in the world."

"I'm sure it will," she agreed, kissing him.

And so it was, though the change took time. The astronomical sighting method was a good deal cheaper than the Watches, and in many cases was as effective. But as the marvel of mass production brought the price of good timepieces down, more chronometers were used on ships, and it ushered in a new standard of accuracy that was to enable far greater safety on the seas. A fair portion of Great Britain's vast global empire was surely owed to this new precision of navigation. The innovations in timekeeping made by John Harrison spread through the watchmaking industry, and his principles profoundly affected the technology that obtains today. As the clocks enabled this method of navigation to prevail, the Greenwich Meridian of Longitude became the standard by which the time of the globe is measured. Seven miles from the heart of London, it is the Prime Meridian. Today the most authoritative global maps use this standard. It might not have happened, but for John Harrison.

But though the art of science and technology was supremely important here, so was the art of politics. As long as John Harrison fought the system, his progress was mixed. The ambitions of others thwarted him despite the perfection of his clocks and the merit of his cause. When he worked with the system, by invoking the support of the king himself, he finally won his case. The king knew that even when injustice had been done, the soft approach was apt to prove more successful. So the king's sensible advice, unusual for him, may have been just as important as his royal influence in bringing the case before Parliament. In the end the king enabled justice to prevail, and his nation to profit greatly, not by fiat but by political art.

It is an irony of history that this sincere if imperfect statesman, whose under-standing and fairness were in this case so appropriate, and under whose reign the kingdom of England was becoming arguably the greatest global empire ever seen, was reviled as a crazy and evil man in one quarter. He reigned for sixty years, and while it is true that he lost his sanity in the last decade, during the 1770s he was generally sensible and effective. But in the western hemisphere upstart colonists revolted, doing stupid things like throwing tea into the harbor. Yet by a combination of boldness and luck they managed to make it stick, declaring them-selves the United States of America. So they ridiculed "Bad King George" and made his reputation in America somewhat akin to that of Attila the Hun, for no better reason.

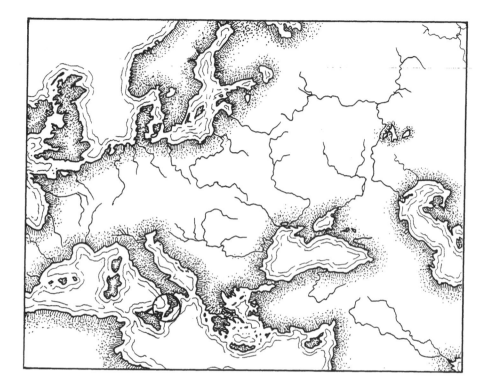

CHAPTER 11

SURVIVAL

One of the major figures of history is Napoleon Bonaparte of France, who brought his nation from the verge of disaster to European dominance, then lost it. One thinks of the invasion of Russia, and of Waterloo. But there was another side of it: the drudgery of forming and maintaining an empire over scattered unwilling territories.

The notorious French Revolution occurred in 1789, remembered for the storming of the Bastille and the Reign of Terror that guillotined thousands. Napoleon was then serving in Italy, opposing the territorial ambitions of the Austro-Hungarian Empire. Italy was not then a unified country, and held strategic importance as a

*staging ground for that conflict. He showed great competence, but the political
situation in France was fluid, and as power changed, Napoleon was even arrested
briefly.*

*Thereafter his fortunes rose, and in 1796, at age twenty-seven, he was given
command of the Army of Italy. His genius as a military campaigner enabled France
to drive back the Austrians and take over northern Italy. The Austrians used
armies to protect terrain; Napoleon used terrain to protect armies. Thus even when
outnumbered, he managed to concentrate his forces to overwhelm the enemy at key
points.*

*But Napoleon had business elsewhere, as he maneuvered his way to supreme
power in France, and during his inattention to the periphery, southern Italy was
recaptured by its former rulers, Ferdinand and Marie Caroline. They were assisted
by the British, who were suspicious of France's global designs. In due course,
annoyed, Napoleon decided that it was time for France to secure this region once
more. So one of his most able commanders, Marshal Masséna, concentrated a force
of 35,000 men in the vicinity of Rome. Early in February 1806, Masséna marched
south.*

*The arts are not necessarily pretty. During warfare in a backward region, sub-
jugating a hostile population can make survival itself become an ugly art, and
results are uncertain.*

"**B**UT you're not a combatant," Talena protested. "You shouldn't have
to march with the troops."

"I'm a doctor," Heath said. "I must go where France needs me. I can't
stay forever in a soft location like Rome."

He was a good man, a perfect husband, and she knew she had nothing
to complain about. But she couldn't help wondering whether he hadn't
accepted this difficult position of military doctor because it tended to take
him often out to the field, away from her. He didn't truly love her, and
never had, though he never said this. They had six children, and she knew
it wasn't the fact that they were all girls that bothered him; he was wonderful with them, when he was home. It was just that he had loved his first
wife, and never could quite let go of her.

Still, he had a good position, and it paid well, and he was a hero figure
to the girls. So she kept her thoughts to herself. "Well, stay out of harm's
way," she said. "Your daughters and I need you."

"I'll try."

"Need you now," she murmured, glancing toward the bedroom.

"But the others—" He glanced nervously at Melee, who was cooking at
the hearth, and Avalanche, who was reading a story to the children.

"Understand," she said. "We have just one private room. Whoever has
a man home gets to use it. I want you, before Od gets here, or Dillon."

He laughed. "You women have things all worked out!"

"We do. We have to. We don't have much space, here in this foreign
city, or time with our men. So we cover for each other."

Still he hesitated, until Avalanche looked up from her book. "Get in there, you fool!" she called. "She'll never be more ardent."

The girls burst out laughing. The eldest, Telita, was seven years old, and knew the score. The others were catching on.

Heath, discomfited, moved hastily into the bedroom. Talena shut the door. Then she met his gaze. "If you would rather not—"

"Of course not," he said quickly, meaning that he was ready.

"Because we can just stay here a while, and they won't know the difference."

"Nonsense." He took hold of her and kissed her.

She met him eagerly. It was an irony that after eight years of marriage, and six healthy children, she still knew he didn't really want her. She had done everything she could to be the best wife she could be, to fill his every need. She had eaten carefully, and exercised, struggling to restore her early figure after each pregnancy, and succeeded well enough, she thought; she really did not look older than her age of twenty-one. But she couldn't compete with a dead woman, whose image in his mind was forever pristine. As a result, most of the passion of their relationship was hers. She wished—but that was pointless.

Heath came alive as she did what was required to make him react. He did like sex, and he did like closeness; she just had to make him forget that she was not Baya. For a little while.

They were naked on the bed, and he was forgetting. He kissed her mouth, her breasts; she kissed his mouth, his neck. Soon he was into her, trying for another baby. She hoped this time it would be a boy.

Soon it was done. She stroked his hair as he relaxed.

"You are a good woman," he said. He always said that, right after. Never that he loved her.

"Thank you." She wished she had some better response, but her imagination always failed her.

Soon they were out with the others—and just in time, because Od arrived. He was no better suited to the military life than was Heath, but he was a patriot, and very intelligent, and though he was listed as a mechanic for the heavy weapons, he was actually a strategic adviser. Avalanche hustled him into the bedroom, and Talena took over the reading. Heath hesitated, glanced at Melee, and evidently decided not to stay for the meal she was preparing, because food was scarce and he could get fed at the officer's mess.

They were an unusual group. Talena and Heath knew Od and Avalanche of old; they had even once performed a play together. Od knew Dillon and Melee, who was the little sister of Heath's first wife, so when he had encountered Dillon as a musketeer captain, he had invited them to join the group. It was compatible, because the three men were all intermediate-grade officers, and the three women were nice. Actually Avalanche and Melee were beautiful, making Talena feel plain despite her hard-earned trimness of figure. Melee liked to cook, and she was an artist with food.

She could convert the veriest scraps into a delectable dish. They generally did have enough food, here in Rome, but much of it wasn't very palatable in its natural state. Horse meat from animals who had been injured; wheat from commandeered peasant fields, with manure admixed; milk from sick cows.

In due course Od and Avalanche emerged. Talena knew the woman had given him a phenomenal time. She always did. Talena envied her fullness of body; she was voluptuous without being fat, and men noticed. When the three of them ran short of money, Avalanche would go out for a few hours, and return with enough to tide them through. The others did not inquire how she did it; there was really only one way. With her body, it was surely easy.

Od, too, elected to return to the officer's mess, though it was plain that he would have liked to spend more time with Avalanche. But the army was marching in the morning, and the men had to be ready. So this was adieu, for now. They were used to such temporary separations; it was the military way. They were never quite comfortable with them, though, because there was always the chance that one or more of the men would be injured or killed.

In the evening they had dinner, the three women and six girls. The children went to the their shrouded corner to sleep as it got dark, but the women stayed up a while, though they did not waste a valuable candle to make it light. Instead they just talked a while.

"I have a secret," Avalanche announced. "You must promise not to tell the men."

"We promise," Talena and Melee said almost together. Secrets were great diversion.

"I am with child."

Talena was thrilled. "You have been trying for that for ten years. Congratulations!" For Avalanche was older; Talena and Melee were both twenty-one, but Avalanche was twenty-eight, the same age as Od. She had seemed to be barren, and had wanted more than anything else to have a baby.

But Melee was sharper on a key detail. "Is it Od's?"

"I'm not sure."

Oh. Of course. Avalanche had sex with so many men, it could be difficult to know. She was with Od for preference, but had never concealed her business.

"But it could be," Melee said.

"It could be. I was with him in December. But it may not be. That's why I didn't tell him."

"But you want it to be his," Talena said.

"Yes. But I won't lie to him. I'll lie to any man but him. Our relationship—"

"Yes, of course," Talena agreed. "Love is like that."

"I can't even tell him I love him," Avalanche said sadly. "I like him, I love being with him, I wish I could marry him, but I don't think I can give my love wholly to any one man. Now—"

"Now you had better marry him," Melee said. "For the child."

"But if it isn't his—"

They saw the problem. "Tell him," Talena said. "He's a good man. I have known him almost as long as you have. He'll marry you."

"But it wouldn't be right, if—"

"It will be right if he says it is," Melee said firmly, and Talena nodded agreement. "And he will."

Avalanche gazed at them. Then the tears started flowing. They had given her a way to fulfill her dream: a baby—and a secure home for it.

Talena felt awkward, so she said something she suspected she would regret tomorrow. "I have a secret too. If—"

"We promise!" the others said together.

"My husband doesn't love me." Now it was out, and the emergence had not been as painful as that of a baby, perhaps because she had done it without giving herself time to reflect.

"But he's the most caring, decent man!" Avalanche protested. "He treats you so well."

"Indeed he does," Melee said. "He knows you are the best woman he could have. You have given him six fine children."

"But no sons," Talena said.

"He doesn't care about that!" Avalanche said. "He loves them all. He says they remind him of their mother."

"For whom he has no real desire."

Both of them laughed. "No desire," Melee said. "Then how did those babies come about? Magic?"

"He loves his first wife," Talena said, feeling her own tears starting. She had never before told this, and it was good to get it out at last, but it hurt too.

"Baya," Melee said.

"But she is dead," Avalanche said.

Talena shook her head. "He still loves her. He told me when we met that he was not ready for another love. Because of her. I thought it would pass, but it didn't. He will never let go of her."

"That's like me and Od," Avalanche said. "I know he loves me, but I can't love him. Not completely. I feel so guilty."

"I don't want his guilt," Talena said. "I want his love."

"Then we are sisters," Avalanche said. "In a way we wish we were not. Neither of us can make a perfect union."

"Sisters," Melee echoed. "I have a secret too."

"We promise!" Talena and Avalanche said together.

"Mine is similar to yours, Talena. I have a muted passion for Heath, of course never requited."

The other two stared at her. It was dark, so only the faintest shadow of her outline showed, but Talena was doing it, and she knew Avalanche was too.

"You long for your sister's husband?" Avalanche asked, as if not quite believing what she had heard.

"In my fashion. He married her, and I was only eleven, but I knew he was a good man. I had a crush on him. But of course I never let him know, and Baya wasn't concerned. He didn't know I existed, anyway. Not that way. I was a child. He was always nice to me, but it was his innate courtesy. The one he noticed, aside from Baya, was our grandmother, Bata. He studied constantly with her, for she knew so much. Later, when I met another man who respected Bata like that—" She shrugged in the darkness. "I married him."

"Dillon," Talena said, amazed by the connection.

"He was only a shadow of the image I had of Heath. But by then I knew that it was only an image spawned of the imagination of innocent youth. No one could be that wonderful. And Dillon—has merits of his own. I do love him. But I remember Heath, from that childhood image. And do you know, he is not that far from it." She turned to Talena; the sound of the voice shifted. "That is why I know how good you are, Talena. Heath would not have married you at all if he had not recognized in you the potential to replace Baya. And I know it, if he does not: you are more than her equal. You are worthy of him. In time he might have become disenchanted with her; I saw the little signs. But her death prevented that, and left him forever in love with her image."

Talena's amazement continued. "He did not truly love her, either?"

"I think not. In my juvenile fancy I thought perhaps I could take her place some day. So maybe I imagined it."

"But Baya—" Talena said, faltering. "If he did not truly love her, then why—?"

"Because he loved her little sister," Avalanche said.

"No, that's not possible," Melee said. "He did not notice me. It was all in my fancy. He never—"

"I know men," Avalanche said firmly. "They like women. Especially pretty ones. Especially young ones. You were prettier than your sister, even then, weren't you."

"I suppose I was. But—"

"You were the one he wanted. But you were too young, and you were his wife's sister. So he suppressed it. But it remained. Maybe he didn't realize it himself. But it was there."

"It was there," Talena said, an awful light dawning.

"But I never—never even indicated—and he never—"

"He is a good man," Avalanche said. "He would never cheat on his wife. But neither did he care to cheat on his true love, though he did not admit she existed. So he never touched you, Melee, or gave any open sign. But I saw the way he looked at you, before he left. I thought it was just because you are beautiful; men can't help but look. But now I know it was more. He wants you, and can't acknowledge it. Especially not in the presence of his wife. Especially not right after having sex with his wife. So he had to leave; the two of you together is too much for him to handle.''

Melee looked at Talena, the outline of her head turning. ''My secret was mine alone. I never—''

''I know you didn't,'' Talena said, glad that the darkness concealed her own troubled flush. ''We all have young fancies. Mine was to find a good man and bear him many children. Maybe I tried too hard, too early.''

''The two of you are the same age,'' Avalanche said. ''When Heath lost Baya, and encountered you, the same age as his suppressed interest—''

''He married me for my age!'' Talena cried, appalled.

''You have other qualities,'' Avalanche said. ''I'm sure he had legitimate reason to marry you. But also the hidden one—the same one that ironically prevents him from fully accepting you.''

''I will leave,'' Melee said. ''I never meant for anything like this to happen.''

''No,'' Talena said. ''Your presence here is incidental. He was never mine.''

''But now—we can't be together. Heath is yours, to whatever degree he can be, and I am Dillon's. There is nothing but mischief to have Heath and me in the same room any longer.''

''The men are going out on the campaign,'' Avalanche reminded them. ''So there is no problem there, for now.''

''Stay,'' Talena said. ''You need a place, and we need you. Now that we know the mischief, we can avoid it when we have to.''

''Thank you.'' Melee was crying too; there was the sound of it in her voice.

''And we shall keep the secrets,'' Avalanche said. ''We women are good at secrets.''

Then there was a knock at the door. ''Dillon!'' Melee cried, jumping up. In a moment he was inside and embracing her, and in another they were in the bedroom, and the sounds of their union could not be ignored.

''She really has no designs on Heath,'' Avalanche said. ''She told her secret to reassure you, not realizing the other side of it.''

''I know. But how can anyone fight hidden passion?''

''No one can. Except to work around it, and keep it confined, in the way of a hearth with fire. Even if you didn't exist, Heath would not go to Melee, nor she to him; she's married, and both are honorable.''

Talena shook her head. ''I almost wish that I had a passion for Dillon. Then maybe we could exchange partners.''

''He's not your type. And he absolutely loves Melee.'' Avalanche lay down, ready to sleep. ''No, this is a secret that simply has to be kept. It has no solution other than silence. At least now we recognize it.''

Talena nodded. ''I am glad to have an answer to the mystery. And I can see how Heath can love her. Her beauty is matchless.''

''Yet if no one else existed, in all the world, except you and Melee and

Heath, and he had free choice between you, I don't think it would be easy for him."

"He'd take both," Talena said.

"Of course. He's a man. But my point is that though you are not Melee's equal in beauty—no woman is—you are more than her equal in other respects, and he recognizes that. He would not want to give you up. He is one man who is driven by more than sexual interest. So if he had to choose between you, I think he would remain with you."

"But still desire her."

"Yes." Avalanche lay still a moment. "But if, somehow, there were the two of you and him—I know you do not see things as I do—but you might be well advised to let him *have* the two of you."

Talena was repelled. "Her to sleep with, me to take care of the children."

"No, I think he would have sex with you too, and she would cook for the children. A man—once the edge is off his lust—he becomes more sensible. It might be a way to have his true passion, having sated the other side of it."

"You're right: you do not see things as I do."

"I apologize. It was a bad notion."

"No, just not right for me. I could never share a man. I want—I want *all* of him. That's my problem."

"It's hard to have all of any man. They aren't like us; they don't commit completely."

"None do?" Talena asked, appalled again.

"Oh, some can. I spoke generically. But in a general way, total commitment to one woman is as foreign to their nature as multiple commitments are to ours. I am rather like a man in that respect; I can't settle long with any one."

"What about Od?"

"I love him, I truly do, and he loves me. But I have had sex with several hundred other men since I met him, and he knows it. I suppose I love him because he still does love me, despite knowing my nature. He can commit, and so when I return to him, he always accepts me. So he seems more like a woman in that respect, always accepting, always forgiving. He is perfect for me; I wish I were perfect for him. Now he will have me completely, for I am loath to let other men plumb me when I have the baby inside. But once it is birthed, I will be returning to my wandering ways, and we both know that. I wish I could be like you; he deserves a loyal woman like you."

"What an irony," Talena said. "We are all mismatched." As women, the two of them were as different as they could be, yet they were friends and would remain so. They complemented each other, the wanderer and the homemaker. And also the passionate beauty, whose passion extended to the culinary arts. No, she did not want Melee to leave. They all made a team, helping each other endure emotionally as well as physically.

"We are all mismatched," Avalanche agreed. "But together, maybe we can survive. We can love each other."

The bonding of women. "Yes." It was commonly believed that men bonded in some special way that women didn't understand. That belief was mistaken.

Then Dillon and Melee emerged. "I must go," he said. "May all be well with all of you."

"And with you," Talena answered.

He departed. "Now we can take over the bedroom," Melee said. "I think we are done for the day." Then, after a pause: "But I still think it would be better if I—"

"No!" Talena and Avalanche said together.

"You are very generous." Melee was crying again.

"No," Avalanche said. "We just understand. We have been talking, and we just finished wishing that I were more like Talena, and that Talena could have a passion for Dillon."

"That must have been some discussion."

"It was. Come; we'll catch you up on it as we clasp each other for warmth."

And so they did, sleeping together under a common blanket. But Talena remained uneasy in her mind. The revelations had been overwhelmingly significant to her perspective on life and love. How could she resolve the conflicts within her?

❁

There was little resistance, for the French force of 30,000 troops was overwhelming. They marched rapidly, and Dillon appreciated that. He liked exploring new territory, and he liked hunting, whether of animals or men. Of course he would rather be back in Rome with Melee, but first he had to earn his stake or get some plunder, so that they could afford to retire together to some country estate well stocked with game. They had been scrambling too long in minor roles, serving others. He had joined the army in the hope of gaining quick riches or land, and now with the march into southern Italy, it could be happening. Those who served well would be rewarded with land grants. He hoped to serve very well.

Dillon was an advance scout, accustomed to ranging far ahead and making sure that there were no ugly surprises awaiting the main force. He tried to report to General Masséna each day, before going out again.

"We are coming to a village of about eight thousand called Gaeta, on the road from Rome to Naples," the general said. He spoke in French, but knew that Dillon also spoke Italian. "We shall be there tomorrow. Scout its defenses, then see what else you can do. Go there under truce and tell their commander that if they surrender immediately, they will not be sacked, and their people will be well treated, just as has been the case with the other villages we have taken. I'd like to let my men sleep indoors for a night, if it can be arranged."

"Understood, sir." Dillon accepted the paper identifying him as a representative of Emperor Napoleon, and headed out.

He often traveled by night, because that was when others were not around, and he could spy on possible opposition. This time he went to the woods, chewed on some rations from his pack, and napped for three hours. Then, refreshed, he loped along the road, completely alone. He loved the cool of night, with the bright stars overhead and the songs of the nocturnal insects. He smelled the nearby sea, and felt the occasional caress of a breeze. He was a creature of the wilderness, and this was a reminder of it.

Well before dawn he reached Gaeta, for a man traveling alone could readily outpace an army; a day's march for the troops was just a couple of hours for him. He studied it as he approached, his eyes well adapted to the darkness. It sat on a hilly peninsula whose highest point faced the mainland. That made it readily defensible from attack by land. The neck was about thirteen hundred paces wide; he could judge such things at a glance. He saw the dark outlines of two, perhaps three lines of walls. Just beyond the neck the promontory expanded to almost twice the width. That meant that the defending forces could train twice the width of cannon on the neck as an attacking force could. They could also fire generally downward, increasing their sight and range. But every advantage had its liability; the base of the walls were exposed to cannon fire, and if the base gave way, so did the wall above it. Still, it was a remarkably good region to defend, and if it had to be taken by siege, it could be a rough campaign.

Of course it had to be taken, one way or another, because of its strategic location. Troops from Gaeta could cut off any lines of supply and communication between Rome and Naples. There was no way that such a site could safely be left in enemy hands.

He found himself a nook, and curled up like a wolf for another nap. He could use a bed readily enough, especially when Melee shared it, but the forest ground was his true home. He could hear approaching danger in his sleep. Then at dawn he got up, brushed himself off, urinated—that, too, made him think of Melee—and walked openly down to the isthmus.

"Who are you?" a guard demanded as Dillon approached the first wall.

"I am a scout for Emperor Napoleon. I come to talk with your leader."

There was a dialogue in the sentry booth. Then the guard came out again. "Under truce?"

"Yes."

"You'll have to leave your weapons here."

Dillon was traveling light, as this was not combat duty. He drew his wicked hunting knife from its sheath, flipped it over, and offered the hilt.

"The hidden dirk too."

He reached into his shirt and fetched out the little knife. He knew it wasn't any great perception on the part of the guard, just experience; no one depended on a single obvious weapon.

"I have to search you."

Dillon raised his hands and stood still for the search. Should he need a weapon inside, he would simply take it from one of the guards; he could move much more quickly and accurately than most folk suspected. Sometimes he played a game with Melee: she would blindfold him, then try to touch him somewhere on the body without having him catch her arm. If he caught her three times, he could have his will of her, pinning her to the mat without removing the blindfold. He would pretend she was an enemy princess never before plumbed by man, and she had to play along, making token resistance, begging for mercy as she spread her legs. Not that she was ever truly unwilling; she loved such games. If she touched and escaped him three times, she could have her will of him, while he remained blindfolded. Then he would be an enemy prince in need of humiliation, forced to strip naked and remain unmoving during torture, which took the form of tickling in private parts. She had an exquisitely sensitive touch, so that it could indeed become sexual torture. There were variants; the winner could choose the rules. He almost liked those sessions better, because she was an ardent lass with considerable imagination. Sometimes she pretended she was someone else, such as a scorned former lover. "You must plumb me three times in an hour, three different ways, or I'll chop it off in the guillotine," she would threaten. The guillotine was a new execution device that had recently replaced the sword for lopping the heads off royalty. Somehow he always managed to avoid the penalty, just in time. She was absolute fun, and could be very quick with her hands, but usually he won, unless he let her win, for the sake of her punishment. He would do that by grabbing her knee or hair instead of her arm, pretending confusion about the exact location of her body. So he could get a man's weapon without having to look directly, and on occasion that made a key difference.

A guard conducted him to the local commander, who turned out to be a German soldier of fortune, Lieutenant-General the Prince of Hesse-Phillipsthal. Naturally he lived in the largest house in the village, but this was a hovel compared to the buildings of Rome. He was a short man with a red face and aquiline nose, and he carried a bottle with him.

"So you're from Napoleon!" he said. "Have a drink!" He proffered the bottle.

Dillon wasn't much for drink, but this was a matter of hospitality. The informality surprised him; in fact the prince's willingness to see him surprised him. The man was evidently unconventional. He accepted the bottle and took a fair swig. It was good, strong wine. He gave it back. "I see you have good taste, sir." He knew it was best to treat this man with utmost respect, for it would be just about impossible for Dillon to fight his way out of here. He could do some damage and kill some soldiers, but here in the heart of the enemy stronghold they would soon overwhelm him. Only if they broke the truce and tried to make him captive would he fight. So he was utilizing the aptness of expression he had struggled to master.

"I've got a good wine cellar. Now what does the upstart emperor want?"

"Sir, his Marshal Masséna is marching south with a formidable force. He wants you to surrender the town without hostilities."

"Oh, he does, does he?" Prince Hesse took another swig. He proffered it again to Dillon.

"No offense, sir, but I'm not used to good wine, and I need to be able to make it back to report to my commander."

The prince laughed with seeming good nature. "Well spoken, Frenchman! If I must fight your marshal, I'll have to give up my pleasures for the duration. I'll station myself on the Breach Battery and stay there until the siege ends. I'll give the key to my wine cellar to the Bishop of Gaeta and tell him to allow me only one bottle a day. Oh, I hope I don't have to do that!"

"Sir, I am not clear as to your answer."

The prince frowned. "What does your marshal offer?"

"Sir, he will refrain from looting the town, and will treat the people with courtesy. You will retain your command, but under his overseer. This is what he is doing with the villages that don't give him trouble, as your spies may have told you. He will also want housing for his troops for one or two nights before they move on to Naples."

"And what if we resist?"

"Then he will lay siege and take the town, sir, and will not treat it kindly."

The prince sobered. "Listen, I have four thousand men to defend the fort. I admit that many of them are recruits dredged from the prisons of Naples and Sicily. But they'll fight, because they'll have to. Your marshal will not be able to bring enough force to bear in the isthmus to breach my defenses, no matter how many men he has. But even if he does, it will take a long time and there will be heavy losses. I doubt it's worth it to him."

"It might not be, sir, except for its strategic location. He can't afford to have it along his supply line from Rome."

The prince nodded. "I suppose so. But neither can we afford to relinquish it. So tell your leader that we will fight to defend our town."

"He will be sorry to hear it, sir."

"He will be sorrier when he tries to attack."

That was it. "Thank you for your courtesy, sir." Dillon bowed and retreated.

"I like you," the prince called after him. "Come back for a visit, after you give up the siege."

"If my commander allows it, sir."

The guard was impressed. "He really does seem to like you."

Dillon suspected that it was his careful obsequiousness that was responsible for that. "He seems a jolly sort."

"He is. We all like him. But he will fight your marshal."

"We expect no less."

The wall crew returned his knives, and he went on his way. He was relieved; going into an enemy camp was never a sure thing, even under truce. In this case the enemy had been honorable, but that was never guaranteed. He had given as much information as he had received; now both sides knew where they stood.

By noon he met the army, marching south. He reported to Marshal Masséna. "Prince Hesse won't surrender. He says he has four thousand men from the prisons of Naples and Sicily who will have to fight."

The marshal nodded, unsurprised. "Yes, they will have to. Even scum will fight well to save their sorry lives. Well, I can't let him delay my advance on Naples; speed is of the essence, before they have a chance to organize any resistance. I'll detach a unit to handle the siege. But I'll give them one more chance, just in case the sight of my force impresses them."

He did just that. As soon as his force reached the first wall, he sent an officer to formally demand surrender.

The answer was a cannon shot.

Masséna nodded, having again confirmed his diagnosis. He had given the prince two chances. "I will detach a force to see to this business, under General Lacour. Dillon, I know you would prefer to be with the vanguard, but I want you to stay here and scout out the coast, to make sure we know if the British send any help to the defense. You will serve as liaison with me or my deputy in Naples. I doubt the reduction of Gaeta will take long; then you will rejoin my force."

"Yes, sir." Dillon was indeed disappointed, but it was not his place to choose where he would serve. At any rate, the reduction of the fortress should be interesting. Certainly it would be a challenge.

❂

Od was kept busy maintaining the equipment, for the army was moving quite rapidly. Marshal Masséna had reached Naples just one day after Gaeta, and the day after that Napoleon's older brother Joseph Bonaparte had made his official entry into the city, to be the new king of Naples. Joseph was a decent man, fair minded but not strong willed, evidently content to exist in the shadow of his little brother, and well rewarded for that loyalty.

But the invasion had not stopped there. Marshal Masséna had detached two independent forces to go after the remaining territory. One went east toward the Adriatic, while the other went south toward Sicily. Od was with the southern thrust, under General Reynier. He was bunking with Pul. It wasn't that he particularly liked Pul, but he had known the man off and on for a decade, and they shared an interest in Avalanche. Od knew that the woman still slept with Pul on occasion, but it was clear that she preferred Od. She had sex with any man she chose, whenever she chose, and usually got paid for it, so it wasn't as if there were any commitment. So the two men got along, with the tacit agreement that if one of them should die, the other would let Avalanche know, in due course. Meanwhile, it was easier to associate with a familiar person than with a stranger.

They were heading for the mountains of Calabria, in south-central Italy. On the map it was in the upper portion of the toe of the Italian boot. Their route lay along a mule track that served as the "major artery" between Naples and that remote province. This was the desolate backwoods region of the country, surely no fun in any season, and worse in winter. Od was constantly directing the repair of wagons and mobile artillery pieces whose wheels got wrenched in the mud. This was the military idea of science.

The opposition, under Comte de Damas, had about 14,000 men, half of them irregulars. This was a larger force than Reynier's 10,000, but Od knew they had been recruited from local brigands and wouldn't have much discipline. So the French force was superior, and the enemy knew it. That was why the enemy was retreating. But it wouldn't retreat forever, so the French force—and its equipment—had to be ready for battle at any time.

On March 6 the French vanguard caught up with the Sicilian rearguard, at Lagonegro. The French light infantry, with Pul participating, maneuvered rapidly and skillfully, and prevailed. They inflicted losses of 300 dead, wounded, and captured, and captured four big guns. Suddenly Od was very busy. He had to convert those guns to French use, educating French artillerymen. While still traveling along the mule trail at speed.

Three days later the main forces met, at Campotanese. It was in the Apennine Mountains, and the Sicilians had had time to dig in defensively. The mountains were the best place to stop an advancing force, because they were natural walls, difficult to navigate and impossible to march around. So this was to be *the* battle.

Od studied the region, making small sketches. He could tell by the wind that a storm was coming. It would be brutal weather tomorrow—the day of the battle.

"God, I don't like this," Pul complained. "I've got the left flank, and there's snow up there. Worse, they're dug in. They'll mow us down as we try to charge up that slope."

"Not necessarily," Od said.

"You've got a scheme?"

"Maybe. At least, I've got a crude model of the terrain, which may be as good."

"Yeah, sure: Napoleon uses terrain to protect troops. But this time we're on the wrong side of the slope."

"Maybe not. I've been studying the lay of the land. It's not an even slope; there are ridges and defiles and cliffs. Tomorrow there may be a snowstorm."

"Are you trying to make me feel worse?"

"I'm trying to show you how to save your hide. Suppose you were a Sicilian defender?"

"I'd be safe behind those breastworks, with my jug of wine and my musket, waiting for the fools to charge in to get shot."

"Precisely. You would know that your front was completely protected by those breastworks, and your flanks by the steep mountain sides. And you'd swig a lot, to alleviate boredom and warm your toes."

"For sure. So what's your point?"

"I told you. There are ridges. Suppose you infiltrate those cliffs and narrow passages, going single file, and get behind the Sicilians?"

"Get behind them? But they'd see."

"In a snow storm?"

Pul gazed at him. Then, slowly, he smiled. He had had prior experience with surprise flanking.

Od watched it happen, next morning. There had been a heavy snowfall, and gusting winds blew toward the defenders. He knew that Pul's force was advancing only when the flying snow veiled their movements. They were sneaking up the left side, working their way along the snow-covered cliffs, silently.

Meanwhile, there was a distraction: the main French column was advancing frontally with a bayonet charge. Actually it was a walking pace, treading across the slippery snow. All enemy eyes should be on that seemingly foolish ploy. Because the moment the column came within range, it would be gunned down. Some might get through, but not in enough numbers to prevail. The losses would be formidable. The Sicilians should be smirking.

But the snow was joined by fog, masking the progress of the charge. So the Sicilians had to be tracking it mostly by sound—and the snow muffled that. So there would not be a lot of time between the clear emergence of the charge and contact with the defenders. That made the French cause seem possible.

Then Pul's detachment struck, advancing in skirmish lines from behind the Sicilian right flank. Now they made noise, shouting as they moved, deliberately attracting attention. The surprised Sicilians tried to turn their lines, but their dug-in nature made this awkward.

Now the bayonet column broke into a run, suddenly bearing down on the breastworks. There were one or two sporadic volleys as the enemy tried to re-orient, flustered. Then the undisciplined troops broke ranks, making a confused rush to escape. This was absolute foolishness on their part, because they had nowhere to go.

They fled into the constricted defile that was their only retreat, presenting their backs to the bayonets. It was a setup for slaughter. But the French called for surrender, and the rearmost Sicilians did so in masses, raising their hands, and were spared. Those farther away continued running, no threat at present—but they could become so, if allowed to escape. So the pursuit continued.

As the battle site cleared, Od and his workers moved in. The French had captured about two thousand men, including two generals and many lesser officers—and *all* of Damas's artillery. What a haul!

Od checked the big guns. They were in good condition, as the enemy had not had time to disable them. They would soon be serviceable in the cause of France.

Od went on, following the trail of the troops, as Reynier would want an early report. The army had evidently kept pushing through rain, snow, and mud, driving the hapless Sicilians before them.

By dusk he caught up. They had reached the small village of Morano, and the general had surely set up a temporary headquarters in a suitable building there. The village itself was an awful sight, as the French troops ravaged and pillaged it; fires were burning, women were screaming, and children were trying to hide. This was of course what many soldiers signed up for: the license to do anything they wanted, to anyone, without limit. It wasn't mere greed; it was sheer brutality.

Od was sickened, but he knew that this was part of war, where the best and worst in the species of man could be closely juxtaposed. If only men could leave each other in peace! But there was always one more band leader to grasp for more power, in turn taken by one more king, in turn defeated by one more emperor, until perhaps at last all the world would be subject to a single man. Perhaps Napoleon. Then when he died, his lieutenants would fight among themselves, each trying to take more power than he could handle, and it would all fall apart. Until the next leader amassed his burgeoning power, rising until he fell.

A man lurched out of a house, hauling a woman by her long dark hair. Her blouse was torn, revealing much of one breast, and her skirt was askew. He was familiar. "Pul!" Od called.

Pul paused. "Od! You looking for some of this?"

"No. I'm here to report to the general, when I can find him. Where is he?"

"I'll take you there." Pul yanked on the woman. "Come on, you!"

Od showed his distaste. "Must you do that? You know she's just an innocent civilian."

"There *are* no innocent civilians! She's booty. I'll plunge her again, soon as my soldier stiffens."

So he had raped her. What else, in war? Yet Od wanted to ease her pain if he could. "Maybe if you simply told her not to flee, on pain of death, she would behave."

"Can't. She doesn't know French."

Od addressed the woman in Italian. "You are this man's prisoner. Will you stop screaming and trying to escape, if he lets your hair go?"

The woman stared at him a moment. Then she hung her head and wept.

Pul let go of her hair. She stood there, unresisting. "Here, you take her," he said gruffly. "I'm done with her anyway; I can grab another anytime."

Od spoke to the woman again. "This man is releasing you. But it would be better if you remained with me for a while, because I can protect you from further molestation."

She nodded. She thought him another rapist, but realized that what he offered was better than the alternative. She sidled around to put Od between herself and Pul.

"You sure have a touch with women," Pul said with brutish humor. "The command post is this way." He set off through the village streets.

Od followed, and the woman followed him, adjusting her clothing. She might have been lovely, once, but now was a bit beyond youth and more than a bit beyond equilibrium. A bruise showed on her right cheek, and her eyes were puffy from crying. Od didn't even ask her name; what was the point?

They came to the command post. This was a pillaged house beside another that was still burning. There were two naked corpses at the door, and something like a dead man on the staircase inside. At least Od hoped he was dead, because the body lacked an arm and a face. "Upstairs," Pul said.

"Thank you."

"Got to be about my business. There's got to be some gold around, and some food." With that explanation, Pul departed.

Od took the woman's elbow. She made a stifled cry, drawing away.

"I am trying to help you, not molest you," Od explained in her language. "You will be safer upstairs with me."

She nodded with resignation and suffered his hand to steady her as they went up the stairs.

General Reynier was sitting in a bare room, dictating orders to exhausted staff officers who were lying on the floor. Several were making notes, though Od wasn't sure whether these records were genuine or for show.

Reynier spied him. "You brought a woman here?"

"I've been raped!" she screamed, realizing that she was being noticed.

"Well, you will not die of it, lady," one of the officers muttered, fortunately in French.

"I wanted to protect her from further brutality," Od said, somewhat stiffly.

"Put her in that corner," the general said tiredly, gesturing. "That's your bunk space."

"Yes, sir." Od spoke to the woman. "You may lie there in the corner. These men will not bother you; they are officers. I will try to get you some food and a blanket, soon."

There was ironic laughter from the officers who spoke Italian. "I would plunder too, by Jove, if I knew where to find something to eat," one said. "There is not a morsel here."

"But there is a blanket," another said, lifting one.

"My apology," Od said to the woman. "There is no food here. But there is a blanket." He accepted the proffered one. "Thank you."

He settled the woman in the corner, where she covered herself and settled down to subsiding sobs. Then he reported to the general. "All the enemy artillery pieces are undamaged and serviceable. We captured their ammunition too."

Reynier smiled. "Good. We shall surely have use for them. Now get yourself some rest."

"Thank you, sir." Od suddenly realized how tired he was; he had not been in the combat, but it had been a busy day and a long walk.

He went to join the woman, not attempting to touch her, though he would have liked a share of the blanket. He sat down and leaned his back against the wall. "Sleep," he murmured. "Tomorrow we will be moving on, and I'll release you. It should be safe for you, once we are gone."

After a moment she stirred. She looked up at him from under the blanket. "You are not going to take me?"

"I seek only to protect you from further mischief. I—I have a woman of my own, in Rome. I don't like to see women mistreated."

She seemed to have recovered some poise. "I know where some food is."

"Then you will eat tomorrow," Od said. "Don't tell anyone."

"No. I will give it to you."

Od was surprised. "Why?"

"You have saved me from some of hell." She got to her feet. "I will show you."

"Any food I get, I will share with the other officers," Od said.

She wrapped the blanket more closely about herself and walked to the door. Od followed, bemused.

She led him to a cache concealed under the floor of her house. There were several loaves of bread, and a jug of milk. "I hid it when I heard the troops coming," she explained. "Take it. Take it all."

"But you will need it yourself, when we go," Od protested.

"I know where to find more." She dug out the loaves and put them in his hands. She carried the milk herself.

"Thank you," Od said, touched.

"You are a kind man."

They returned to the general's office. There they passed out the food, distributing it to all the officers.

The one who had first spoken stood. "What a reward there may be in innocent courtesy," he remarked in French. Then he approached the woman. "Madame, on behalf of the general and his officers, I thank you for this bounty," he said in Italian. "I am called Tree, and I too appreciate decency." He caught her limp hand, bent forward in a kind of bow, and kissed it. "In the morning you must show us your home; I believe we can guarantee that you will not be bothered by French troops again." He glanced at Réynier, who nodded.

"But I just wanted to repay the man who helped me," she said.

"But you helped all of us, and so now we repay you," Tree said. "We apologize for the brutality with which you have been treated, but we cannot undo it. This is war."

It was war. Od settled down beside the woman, sharing her warmth, careful not to make any gesture of desire for her. She was by no means recovered from her victimization. But the night had become less horrible than it had been.

❖

By mid-March it was clear that the city of Naples and the surrounding region were secure, so some of the families of officers were allowed to go there. Personnel were rotated when feasible, so that it was possible to have some pleasant breaks despite the continuing campaign.

Melee was relieved. She wanted to see Dillon again, and not just because he was her husband. The discussion the three of them had had on the night of the army's departure from Rome still disturbed her at odd moments. The idea that her big sister's man had somehow fantasized about her in much the way she had fantasized about him—that left her with split emotions. On the one hand it was stupid; there was nothing between them, and never could have been. She had been a child, and he an honorable man. But on the other hand, there was a forbidden longing, a wish that went back before Melee was married, so that it didn't count, for these things were different for women—a wish that he might have come to her room, confessed his passion, and stroked her oh-so-delicately on breast and thigh, and kissed her willing lips, and gently entered her willing body, and jetted that divine essence so deep within her, its radiance completely suffusing her being. Then he might have departed, leaving her fulfilled, the glow slowly fading so as not to betray their illicit passion, and the secret would never be known, for neither wished to hurt Baya. One quiet liaison, known to no other living thing, yet a love fulfilled.

Now it was too late. Both of them were too old, and knew too much, and had other commitments. So the chance was gone forever, if it had ever existed. It had never existed, really, for his honor and her state of childhood prevented it. Yet again, was twelve a child? She had had nascent breasts, and feelings that, could they have been plotted on some universal cosmic scale of amplitude, should have registered well within the range of adult desire. She had discovered what it was all about, and was learning the power of her beauty. And he—suppose he had come to her before he married Baya? So that she was just another available woman, young perhaps, but able to do what maturity could. Then could their liaison have been? She knew it could not, yet her inner fancy claimed it could. And so her dream persisted, never quite letting her go.

That was why she needed Dillon, because in his arms there was no room for illicit fancies. Anything she wanted to do, she could do with him. They had had some phenomenal sessions. Maybe she could even play the game with him, of a secret liaison, he the tempted husband of another woman, she the wife's willing little sister. No, because that could make him suspect. And it was nothing, really; just a naughty thought she had no right to have.

Naples was the only true city in southern Italy. It had been a metropolis of great contrasts for centuries. It had a fine harbor that was regularly visited by ships of the world, bringing exotic wares. Its central Toledo Street was famous throughout Europe for its wealthy shops and aristocratic entertainments. Yet the carriages of the wealthy had rolled past naked and starving masses, the "lazzaroni," a huge army of paupers and beggars. They were still there, though King Joseph was trying to establish policies that helped the poor. He wanted to abolish the oppressive feudal system, and foster economic growth, and curb the excessive influence of the church, and make the system of justice equitable. Some thought this showed weakness, but she thought it showed decency. He was at least trying to establish reforms, and to enforce the Napoleonic Code, though the population was resisting change, even for the better. It was hard to do things for people who refused to understand.

They were given a house near the palace, protected from the worst of the persistent underworld. This was just as well, for Avalanche was beginning to show. She could mask it when she went out, but not for much longer. So they kept her mostly inside. They had money from their men, enough to sustain them economically. Many were not so fortunate, but they were pooling their resources, and they were after all officers' wives or (in Avalanche's case) mistresses.

Meanwhile they had learned that both Heath and Dillon were actually at Gaeta, north of the city, with the contingent that was besieging it. If only they had known when they passed by! But military secrecy had shrouded the information, and maybe that was just as well. A battle site was no place for women. But the moment Gaeta fell, both men would be here in Naples, ready to be with their women. And how did Talena feel about that? It was her man whose hidden passion was in question. Melee could not reassure her about that, for it was nothing that could be spoken of. They had not mentioned it, after that one surprising night. But no matter how properly each person behaved, there was bound to be that emotional tension, like lodestone pulling against iron, between Heath and Melee. That must tear Talena up! So that incipient arrival was a thing to be feared as well as desired. At least the men would be together, so that each would be suitably occupied by the right woman.

Melee had no idea how it would all work out in the end. With luck, the campaign would finish, and the men would be sent to separate other locations, and the women, too, would have to separate. That would be sad, for she did like Avalanche and Talena, but perhaps for the best, because it would eliminate any problem of illicit lust.

Meanwhile, there was Avalanche to take care of. If only Od would return, so that Avalanche could talk to him, tell him, and make him marry her. At least that part of the problem could be solved.

○

On the twenty-first of March, General Lacour called again for the surrender of the fortress. Prince Hesse replied that his answer would be found in the breach. That meant combat.

The French had taken over the nearby fishing village of Mola di Gaeta, and moved in artillery pieces from Naples and Capua. The prince would soon enough discover the price of his recalcitrance.

"I don't know," Dillon said. "That's one solidly defensible site."

They were bunking together in the village, as officers who knew each other socially. Heath suppressed his too-persistent awareness of the woman who was now Dillon's wife. He had realized, during a siege of another nature, that it was not his dead wife Baya, but her sister who had secret hold of his passion. He had thought never to see that woman again, and certainly he would never tell his own wife Talena, who deserved nothing like this. But fate had somehow brought Melee right into their camp, stirring ancient fancies. The proper thing to do was to bury those fancies so deep they would disappear, but somehow he hadn't been able to do that.

Meanwhile, Dillon was a good man and a fine scout and soldier. Heath had developed a high respect for him. He was a good match for Melee, and there was every sign that she loved him. Heath wished them every success.

But they were talking about something else. "Our cannon should break down their walls fairly readily," Heath said.

"Not from this distance. And they have more cannon than we do. It's that narrow isthmus: we can't get around it, and they can concentrate all their pieces on it. Even if we take out the walls, they can blast us into oblivion if we try to cross. We'll just have to hope they run out of ammunition—which they won't, if they keep getting supplied by sea."

"I hope it doesn't come to that. Bullets can on occasion be survived; cannonballs are worse." As a military doctor he had seen both types more often than he cared to.

"For sure," Dillon agreed.

Lacour's artillery opened fire. But the return fire from some eighty pieces along the walls was devastating. It was just as Dillon had said: the defense had better concentration. The breastworks were blasted, and the supports for the cannon were undermined. The men had to retreat from the rain of fire.

Lacour was grim but undaunted. "This is just the first day."

Even as the dust cleared, Heath got down there with his bandages and medicines. Some of the men were shell-shocked; others had suffered shrapnel injuries. Crews were already hauling away the dead.

One man was uninjured, but was burning with fever. He screamed with hallucinations. "He was bad two days ago," a comrade said. "But yesterday he was okay."

Dillon helped hold him down while Heath examined him. "What is it?"

"It looks like malaria. It has forty-eight-or seventy-two-hour cycles of fever and chills, answering the patient's description. He should recover, but will suffer later sieges of it. I have some bark he can chew on; it should help."

"Bark?"

"From a South American tree, the cinchona. It contains juices that seem to oppose the infection. We call that essence quinine. Nothing else works."

"What causes malaria? I didn't see it in France."

"I believe it is mosquitoes. They carry it in their bites. Near the coast, near swamps, at night, there are more mosquitoes, and on a campaign like this, more men get bitten. There will be other cases."

Dillon slammed his palm against his arm, flattening a mosquito. "Suddenly I am very nervous about this region."

Heath nodded. "When you are outside, stay active, so they don't land on you. Sleep under cover, so they don't get you then. That's your best protection."

The French repaired the damage to their works, and dug trenches along the hill slopes, so as to bring their guns closer to the neck of land connecting Gaeta to the mainland. More cannon were set up and trained on the walls. The enemy did not fire on the workers. Heath wasn't sure whether that was decency, or that it wasn't worth it to take out individual men. It was beyond accurate rifle range, and shells were after all valuable.

On April 5 they tried again. They opened fire—and again the return fire overpowered them. Heath had more work to do.

"We just don't have enough force," Dillon said as he helped. He had other business during the actual fighting, but not in the aftermath. "Men, guns, and ammunition are in short supply. We can't mount a siege operation on anything like the scale required to take Gaeta by force. In other sections a mere show of force has been enough, but Prince Hesse is tough. He won't yield to a bluff. We need a different strategy."

And so it happened. General Campedon, one of the best engineers in the French army, took charge of the siege works. He decided to push the trenches all the way forward to the neck.

"This is good," Dillon said. "But it means crossing the six hundred yards from the crest of the hills to the first fortress wall. That's open ground, exposed to enemy fire. It's rocky ground, that will require heavy equipment to dig. They'll have to cover the workers by constant fire from the batteries. It can be done, but it will be slow."

It was indeed slow. But Heath found himself busy regardless. There were more cases of malaria, and he did not have a big supply of the key tree bark. He tried to educate the men about the danger of mosquitoes, but they didn't credit it. They didn't see what connection there could be between a tiny pest and a horrendous recurring fever.

There were also deserters from Gaeta. The French held them in contempt, and simply returned them to prison, where most had come from. But the ill ones were funneled to Heath for treatment.

Dillon handled this aspect. He addressed a motley crew of three deserters. "You are sick. This is our medic, the best in the region. He can help you, or he can hurt you. Which is it to be?"

They got the message. "What do you want to know?"

So while Heath treated them for abrasions and fungus infections, and gave them good hot broth—guaranteed to improve their condition most rapidly—Dillon questioned them, making notes.

The news was interesting. Prince Hesse had problems of his own. He was more concerned about trouble from within than from without. His troops were so poor that he did not dare launch a sortie to disrupt the slow enemy advance toward his outer wall. Desertions were a constant problem. (Heath found this eminently believable, considering the source.) The prince feared that he would lose too many men to man the walls effectively. He had repeatedly asked for resupply and reinforcements from Sicily, but none had come. His situation was growing desperate.

This was good news for the French. Perhaps by the time they were ready to mount the third attack, the defense would be ready to crumble. But a premature attack would suffer the same fate as the first two, because the erosion of the defensive force had not yet gone far enough.

Then news of another nature came, from a combination of sources. A British fleet appeared in the waters off Naples. The British were supreme on the sea, ever since their breakthrough in navigation; they no longer feared getting lost and foundering on unsuspected rocks. On occasion they might lose a battle at sea, but overall they dominated it. If they interfered with the siege of Gaeta, the situation could become more difficult.

It seemed that Lord Collingwood had dispatched Sir Sidney Smith, with four men-of-war, to the area. Smith had been instructed to stay out of local politics, but had allowed himself to be caught up in the schemes of the fanatical Marie Caroline, Ferdinand's wife. She wanted desperately to maintain a foothold on the mainland of Italy, and Gaeta was it. So Sir Sidney had found himself carrying four guerrilla chiefs, whose purpose was to land and rouse the populace to rebel activity.

Among these brigands, the most notorious was Fra Diavolo: Brother Devil. He had come from humble birth a few miles north of Gaeta. He had spent his youth in various criminal enterprises, and had phenomenal luck. However desperate his deeds and infamous his escapades, he had always somehow escaped capture. In the popular imagination only a monk or the devil could be so gifted. Hence his nickname. In 1799, under a promise of amnesty, he had led one of the free companies whose revolutionary activity had for a time dislodged the French control of the region. He had achieved fame as leading the most undisciplined, insubordinate, and monstrously cruel band extant. As a reward, he had been made a colonel, calling himself Colonel Michele Pezza.

France was now recovering southern Italy, so Fra Diavolo had made himself scarce. He had been petitioning Sicily for money he claimed he was owed, and becoming involved in the occasional homicidal fray to terrorize the countryside. He had received instructions to form a flying corps, but like the coward he was he had fled with the others. But now, with his three brothers, and the active support of the British fleet, he was back in action. He would be landed on shore, stir up the locals, make a raid, and then be picked up again by Sir Sidney's ships. It was an ideal situation for him, because he had the perfect retreat to the one place he could not be pursued: the sea.

And he had come at last to Gaeta. He had been landed there with his squadron, and the British were unloading provisions for the besieged fortress: four heavy ship's guns, several English gunners, and stray supplies. This was bad news for the French.

Mischief was not long in coming. Dillon, ranging out as usual, spied a landing at a nearby river mouth. They were raiding the French lines of communications. News came of promises of pay and amnesty to any local folk who would join him and harry the French outside the walls. Such promises might be worthless, but some folk were enticed.

Of course in a few days the French responded with sufficient force to handle the matter. But Fra Diavolo was already retreating back to the fortress, leaving his dupes to face the consequence of their folly in believing him. After that Dillon was especially vigilant, and Fra Diavolo was unable to land without the French closing in on him within hours. So he was unable to practice his primary occupation of banditry; the locals knew that he represented nothing but trouble for them.

In early May there came another surprise. "Something for you," Dillon said. "An emissary from Fra Diavolo approached me under flag of truce, out in the field. Diavolo wants to meet you."

"Me!" Heath exclaimed, astonished and not pleased. "What have I to do with a sewer rat like that?"

Dillon smiled. "You are indeed his opposite. He is a complete scoundrel; you are a man of integrity. He is a killer; you are a doctor. He is a disciple of no nationality other than his own short-term self-interest; you are a loyal Frenchman. Why should he approach you?"

"You have a notion," Heath said, catching on. "Has he been injured, and needs medical attention without betrayal?"

"I think not. They do have medics there."

"Is he an emissary of the prince, coming to offer terms?"

"Why negotiate with a healer, instead of a siege officer?"

"I give up. What does this trash want with me?"

"I think he means to betray his master."

"And he thinks I would cooperate in that?"

"Be realistic, Heath. If you could find a way to end this siege tomorrow and get home to Talena this week, would you do it?"

"I hate realism! I see too much of it on the field after a battle." But Dillon had gotten to him. "If so, why me?"

"Because you are one officer who can go afield, especially in my company, without attracting attention. My guess is that he wants a private meeting, with someone trustworthy, that will not be bruited about."

"Then why not you?"

"I know Prince Hesse personally, from my brief meeting with him. That probably makes me suspect; I just might be his double agent."

"You are nothing of the kind!"

"I merely conjecture what a dishonest man might think."

Heath mulled the matter over. "So he wants an honest, invisible officer who can go privately to our leader. And who won't arrange an ambush at the meeting. So that he can propose treachery to his side."

"That is my assessment."

"Well, I'm not the man for this betrayal. Prince Hesse has fought a fair fight, and deserves to finish it on the open field."

"I agree. But would our commander?"

"I don't know."

"Maybe you should ask him."

Heath sighed. "I hate the position you put me in."

"I hate it myself. But I was approached, and I felt I lacked the authority to decline it on my own initiative."

"So do I." Heath got up and marched to General Campedon's office.

"So the scoundrel wants to scuttle his own ship," the general said, disgusted. "Yet I am mindful of the lives on both sides to be saved by a quick ending to this business, not to mention the time. The man surely wants gold. I will authorize twenty pounds, and safe passage to a region of his choice, if he has information leading to a rapid resolution of the siege."

"You wish me to meet him, then?" Heath did not want to believe it.

"Yes. Go now."

Then Heath thought of something else. "I would not presume to imply that you would do anything dishonorable, sir, but in a case like this—"

"You will not be followed!" the general snapped. "There will be no betrayal of this man's confidence, little as he understands honor. We are French officers."

"Yes, sir," Heath said, relieved.

"Besides, he will have scouts out. He will know if we try anything like that."

Heath did not respond. He returned to Dillon. "Take me there."

Dillon took him. They walked out of the village. No one paid attention.

"There's one," Dillon said.

"One what?"

"One enemy spy, watching to ensure we are alone." He lifted his hand in a salute to the forest.

"I saw nothing."

"You are not a scout. I would not know what to do with a wounded man. We each have our specialties."

That was true. They walked on.

Soon Dillon saluted again. "You spied another? Why do you let them know you see them?"

Dillon shrugged. "I can't resist telling them that I'm a better scout than they are. But I'm not a complete fool. I did not salute the third one. So he thinks I missed him."

"And only the fourth one was truly unobserved."

Dillon laughed. "If there was a fourth, yes."

They came to an isolated shed. "He will be in there. You must go alone; he will not trust me that close."

"But suppose he just wants to kill me, so we'll be short a doctor?"

"He doesn't. But if he did, he knows that his scouts could not catch me before I killed him in retribution. He will behave. Now I will fade from the scene, until you emerge."

"Fade from the scene?"

There was no answer. He looked around. Dillon was gone. There was no sign of him.

They seemed to have thought of everything. Heath was not comfortable with it, but he walked on to the shed. He hesitated, then knocked on its door.

"Come in, healer."

He pushed open the door and stepped into the interior gloom. A grizzly man, somewhat short and fat, stood there: not at all what he had expected. "Fra—I mean, Colonel Pezza?"

"The same," the other replied in Italian. "The devil."

"I am Heath, health officer for the French detachment. I was told you wished to speak with me."

"I will open one of the gates at night, so that your men can go through. That will give you the victory with little loss."

As expected. Heath masked his disgust. "What do you want?"

"A hundred pounds of gold, and safe passage to the hinterland."

"A hundred pounds!" Heath exclaimed, outraged.

"Seventy, then."

"I'll not bargain with you, you piece of filth!"

"Fifty, then. My final offer."

Heath realized that he would have to convey this offer to the general. How much was even one life saved worth? "I will tell my leader. I can't promise his response. We shall have to meet again."

"Your scout will be told where. Bring the gold with you. Don't bother coming if he won't pay fifty. I know what it's worth."

Heath opened the door and stepped out. He walked away from the shed. Dillon was not in sight. But after a time Dillon appeared beside him. "What news?"

"He wants fifty."

"He'll probably get it."

"He says you will be told where to meet again."

"No doubt. I'll be around."

They returned to the village. Heath reported to the general. "He will open a gate at night, for safe passage and fifty pounds of gold."

Campedon nodded. "It's cheaper than another month's siege. Half in advance, half on delivery. Greed will keep him honest."

"He is sewer scum. Selling out his own side for money."

"The world requires all types. Fortunately he knows that we will keep our word, detestable as we find the necessity. I will give you the gold now, so that there need be no delay when the meeting is arranged."

"But sir!"

The general smiled. "I trust you, Heath. This way."

And so Heath found himself with a small but heavy bag of gold coins: the price of betrayal. Twenty-five pounds of filthy lucre. He remained disgusted by the whole business, but had to follow through. He reminded himself of the lives that would be saved by a quick conclusion to the siege. But still he felt dirty.

In three days Dillon received word. "Tomorrow, early. Another location. I know where."

Before dawn Heath roused himself and donned a knapsack holding the gold. Dillon led him to an empty peasant house by the sea. "This time they haven't posted scouts," he remarked, surprised. "Fra Diavolo must trust us better than his own henchmen, when there's gold being handled." He faded out.

Heath knocked on the door. There was no answer. He pushed it open. The house was empty. Fra Diavolo had stood him up.

Well, he wasn't going to leave the gold here untended. He needed proof that it was delivered to the right party. He left the house and walked back toward the village.

Dillon reappeared. "Not there? Maybe he's testing us."

"Maybe," Heath agreed shortly. He knew better than to hope the devil had changed his mind and decided to be loyal to his own side. There would just have to me another rendezvous.

But there wasn't. There was no word at all. After three days, Heath returned the gold to the general, not comfortable with it in his possession.

Then another deserter brought the answer. Fra Diavolo had been discovered and arrested. The prince was having him shipped back to Sicily in chains.

"How did they know?" Heath asked, relieved.

"Probably one of his henchmen betrayed him," Dillon said. "When he didn't agree to share enough of the gold. There is no honor among thieves. That's why they have to deal with honest men."

"Honest men!" Heath exploded. "I feel like a whore."

"This is war," Dillon reminded him. "But this increases my respect for Prince Hesse. The man is not a dullwit, and he knows what to do with traitors. Now the siege will continue. We'll have to do it the hard way."

"The siege will continue," Heath agreed, thinking of the slaughter that would mean.

✪

By the third week of March, Reynier's lightning marches had brought him victoriously to the toe-tip of Italy. It was declared that the "comic" defense of Calabria was at an end, and some of the troops were rotated back to Naples for needed rest and recovery. The wildest province in Italy had been pacified.

Well, not quite. They had moved so swiftly that they had not had time to capture and police the hordes of deserters from the Sicilian ranks, and many of these reorganized into bandit groups that raided French-held villages. For a time Reynier's lines of communication were severed by mountain guerrillas. But it hardly mattered; a supporting column from Naples rendezvoused with them, and they gained important supplies.

But for a time their soldiers had been without rations, and they had looted without conscience. The young officers chased women, and the old officers chased money. A detachment of fifty men was left in charge of one village, and they behaved poorly, raping a woman. That wasn't supposed to happen once the fighting was done. The village rose up in fury and slaughtered most of the soldiers. Then the French had to retaliate, sacking and burning the village. Unfortunately, that led to increased bad feeling among the natives.

But now they were away from that. They learned that the women had come to Naples, so there was a warm welcome there. Pul would have liked to have had that welcome from Avalanche, but it turned out that she was pregnant, and that ended his interest. Od, the fool, was eager to marry her despite her condition. So Pul stood up for him at the quick ceremony, witnessing the occasion. Actually it wasn't so bad; she wasn't showing much yet, so would probably be good for a number of nights in bed.

King Joseph tried to enforce discipline among the troops. He insisted on shooting French soldiers when they performed criminal acts. He had made a trip to Calabria, where he ordered two commissary officials held over for courts-martial for stealing from villagers.

But then King Joseph made a mistake. Pul didn't care much about it, but Od did, and so did the three women, so Pul agreed with their outrage. That kept him welcome at their house, as long as he didn't try to make a move on any of them, and of course he didn't. There were plenty of native women in Naples who would do just about anything for some extra food, and it was his policy not to mess with a friend's woman. That accepted, he found he rather liked their company, because Heath's woman Talena was a trim item despite having borne six children, and Dillon's woman Melee was a rare piece indeed, as sultry and sexy as any he knew, and she cooked very well. He couldn't touch them, but he could revel in their company, enjoying a kind of companionship that was uncommon for him. Women did have other qualities than sex appeal; he hadn't appreciated that before. So during this time of relative idleness before they would be sent out on another punitive mission, he spent much of his time with the three women, even when Od wasn't there.

The Sicilian military leader Rodio had surrendered early in the campaign, finding himself in an untenable situation. Normally such an officer was given a token penalty and let go once the campaign had been settled. But a letter came from Napoleon ordering Joseph to make an example of Rodio, as a show of strength to the populace. So Joseph had Rodio tried by a military commission, on charges of rebellion and insurrection.

"But all he was doing was fighting for his country," Talena said as they relaxed inside on a rainy day. "That's not rebellion, is it?" She glanced at Pul.

Pul liked being consulted, and he knew the preferred answer. "No," he agreed. "He's a good officer. I'd have been satisfied to serve under him, if I'd been on that side."

"So why are they trying him, then?" Avalanche demanded rhetorically, showing some of the flair he had always liked in her. She was with child, but sitting the way she was now, swathed in a blanket that let much of her legs show, she looked good enough.

"It's because there are so many spot insurrections," Pul explained. "Just about every day there's something going on somewhere, and we have to put it down. So if we put away a top man, maybe they'll give it up."

"That's what Dillon says," Melee said. "Sometimes a show of strength makes the battle unnecessary."

"But Rodio surrendered," Talena said hotly. "And he hasn't done anything since."

"He is nevertheless a figure of respect for the other side," Pul painted out. "If anything happened here, and he got free, the people would follow him."

"So don't free him," Melee said. "But don't put him on trial for doing his duty either."

The commission did not take long to make the decision. Pul carried the news to the women as soon as he heard it. "They acquitted Rodio!"

"That's wonderful!" Talena said, clapping her hands.

"Have some bread," Melee said, bringing a freshly baked roll. "Your reward for good news." She pushed it into his mouth.

Oh, it was nice having a woman like that do something like that! It was all he could do to keep his hands idle. He hoped he would have more good news for them. Meanwhile, he chewed.

But another commission was immediately formed. "They are trying him again, and this one's stacked," Pul reported.

"Can they do that?" Talena demanded. "Trying him twice for the same thing?"

"They can do anything they decide to do," Pul said. "The winner makes the laws. Napoleon wants Rodio dead."

This time the commission understood what was expected of it, and convicted Rodio. There was a public outcry, and Pul discovered that many of the French officers felt exactly as the women did. Rodio was an honorable enemy who deserved to be treated fairly.

Nevertheless, he was shot the following day, March 30.

"This is a barbarous breach of military etiquette!" an officer muttered to Pul, who soon repeated it to the women. They were duly furious, but their fury was not at him. "I thought King Joseph was better than this," Talena said tersely through her tears.

"Joseph does what his brother decides," Avalanche said. "Joseph by himself is a weak man."

"There will be mischief because of this," Melee said.

Indeed there was. There were demonstrations in the streets, and though the French troops were sent out to quell it, many officers did not push very hard. Pul's own men hardly threatened the people, merely herding them off the main thoroughfare, and he did not reprimand them. The attitude of the three women had infected him, and he was sorry Rodio was dead.

❁

By the end of May, considerable reinforcements arrived at the French force at Gaeta, and the siegework progressed much more quickly. Dillon was glad. He was a man of action, and he did not like being tied to one location for months. True, he had been allowed a rotation of leave, so that he had been able to spend a few days with Melee. She had been unusually ardent, even for her; it seemed that absence made the heart grow fonder. The other two women had been very good about giving up their bedroom for hours and even whole nights at a time. Heath's wife Talena was especially nice. That was odd, because once Heath had mentioned that there were times when he wished he had married elsewhere. He had the perfect wife, and wasn't satisfied? Of course she was his second wife, and it seemed he had never fully gotten over the death of the first one. Still. Meanwhile Od's wife Avalanche was fattening in the tummy, thrilled to have baby and husband. She had a reputation going way back, but she was a changed woman now.

Early in June the trenches approached to within 200 yards of the neck. More than 70 guns were in position to open fire. The defenders' guns rained down constant fire, costing the French a continual drain of casualties—but reinforcements came in even greater numbers, so the force actually gained. It was an ugly equation, but the French position was improving.

The original siege had been established by 4,000 men, but in June it swelled to 8,000. On June 28, Marshal Masséna himself arrived from Naples to take personal charge. He was fed up with the delay in taking Gaeta; it neutralized a considerable portion of his troops and artillery.

Masséna called a staff meeting, where he was blunt. "It is time for the artillery to carry the day. It has been silent for several months, while the enemy has been punishing our trench workers constantly. I believe a good barrage will break down their wall and silence enough of their pieces so that our infantry can carry the day."

That meant that Dillon's troop would finally see action. He was glad.

"Any questions?" Masséna asked.

"Sir, our ammunition is limited," the head of the gunnery said. "We were supposed to receive more, but it hasn't reached us yet. If the assault is not effective soon, we could run out."

Masséna frowned. "I will see about that. How long can we maintain a full barrage with our present supplies?"

"Perhaps a week, sir. After that it gets chancy."

"But if we prevail within that week, it won't matter. So we shall operate on that assumption, not holding back. The fortress must be ours."

"Yes, sir!" the officers agreed. They were all sick of the siege and its attrition.

Next day it began. Fifty heavy guns and 20 mortars opened fire. Dillon watched it with Heath, as neither of them had immediate jobs until there was infantry action or injuries.

It was impressive. There was a special thrill to the booming of the guns, the wafting of black smoke, and the sight of the blasts at the enemy position. It was almost like having good sex, experiencing the fury of the full barrage. Each big gun was like a spouting penis, with fire and smoke and an unstoppable discharge that blasted into the laid-out target. Boom! Boom! Boom! What a climax! And there was progress. The enemy guns returned fire, but several of them were dismounted. The walls began to crumble in places. There was a constant stream of dead and dying men falling from the ramparts. "It must be like hell, on that wall," Dillon breathed.

"I wish we had been able to end it before it came to this," Heath said.

"But we're tearing them up!"

"They are taking horrible injuries. They are doing an honorable job of their defense."

Naturally the doctor had a different perspective. But he was right. "Yes, they are doing a good job, especially considering their tight situation and losses by desertion. Prince Hesse is a good leader."

But though the defenses were severely battered, the enemy guns still answered the French barrage. As long as that was the case, they could not risk an infantry charge.

By July 1 the fortress had lost three magazines; the spectacular explosions had been visible. But the wall held.

"Damn it," Masséna swore. "We have run them through the grinder, and still they won't quit."

Dillon's respect for the prince grew. The man had to be a strong and capable leader, to wage such good war with such poor troops. But this siege was grinding to its close, and Gaeta would soon fall.

The French barrage slowed, so they could move their pieces even closer. Also because they were starting to run short of shells; half of their ammunition had been expended. But they hoped that the enemy would understand only the first reason.

Masséna offered a reward of 450 centimes for every unexploded enemy shell that was found and delivered to a French battery. That got some volunteers out on the field, braving the diminished enemy fire, and some did bring in some items. This also brought newly wounded men to Heath's infirmary, because unexploded shells were touchy things, apt to detonate whimsically. Still, the effort helped. With the guns close enough, and the salvaged ammunition, they might make it on the next push.

But on July 3 the enemy received reinforcements by sea. Then English gunboats shelled the French position. The result was indecisive, but this surely gave a boost to the morale of Prince Hesse's troops. "Damn," Dillon muttered, echoing Masséna's comment. "Every time we get close to victory, something happens to snatch it away."

The French resumed working their guns closer to the walls. The last barrage had come so close to success that the next one should do it, even with reduced ammunition.

But Dillon wasn't feeling good. He felt hot, then cold. Nursing a dreadful suspicion, he sought his friend Heath. "I want your promise to keep silent," he said.

"I don't like such promises," Heath said. "I already have more secrets than I like."

"This is important. I must have your word."

Heath spread his hands. "You have it, of course. I hope I don't regret this."

"Tell me whether I have malaria."

"Oh, no!" Heath examined him, and asked questions. "Yes, you do seem to have it. Fortunately it's not a bad case. I'll give you a medical pass for immediate layoff to Naples. That should enable you to handle it with minimal discomfort, though it won't necessarily be pleasant, regardless."

"No. I mean to remain on duty."

"But malaria is nothing to fool with! Out here, with inadequate facilities, the danger is heightened. For your own safety—"

"No. I want no report. Treat me as you can, and have me in shape to command my men for the final assault. I will see this siege through to victory."

Heath was appalled. "You are asking me to put your life unnecessarily at risk. My medical ethics—"

"You gave your word."

Heath was silent a moment. "I do regret it," he said seriously. "But I will keep it. But answer one question: If you die because of this, what should I tell Melee?"

That set Dillon back. Almost, he relented, as he knew Heath wanted him to do. But the lure of incipient victory was too great. "Tell her I love her, and I want her to get on with her life. To find another man. To be happy."

"She will blame me for your death. With justice."

"No. You will not tell her of this aspect."

"So I must lie to your widow. Damn it, man—"

"Tell her that I went the way I chose to go. She will understand."

Heath shook his head. "There is only one solution. You must not die. Now I have some medication. Get yourself to bed. I will give you a pass for a passing indisposition. The food's bad enough to account for that. You should be able to be on your feet for brief periods without betraying your condition, and with luck that will be all that will be necessary."

"That's all the luck I need." Dillon looked him in the eye. "Thank you, friend."

"This is not the act of a friend," Heath said sourly, and turned away.

But Dillon was satisfied. He didn't care how bad the illness got, after the victory was won. Just so long as he could participate.

❁

Reynier was angry. "Just when we get the region pacified, and can think about crossing the Straits of Messina so as to wipe out the source of the Sicilian problem, the damned British interfere."

"Crossing from Scilla to Charibdis," Od remarked, with a sense of *déjà vu.*

"What?"

"Mere humor," he said quickly. "In ancient Greece, the legend was that in that region ships had to pass a narrow strait with the monster Scilla on one side, who would gobble seven men from the deck, and the whirlpool Charibdis on the other side, who would swallow the entire ship. So it was a region of fear that one might think it better to avoid."

"Well, stifle it. This is serious business. My sources have it that Sir John Stuart has been thinking of warding off our advance to Sicily by a preemptive strike. He is nominally in charge of six thousand Sicilian infantry, but while the officers for his regiment are in place, the actual recruits don't exist. It does take time to recruit, equip, and train a regiment. So I thought we could cross before he generated a more formidable force. But he does have a British garrison stationed on Sicily, and the advantage of sea maneuver. So he must be using those special troops to strike while we are stretched thin between these scattered local uprisings and the siege of Gaeta. The brigands we have been dealing with are as nothing to seasoned British troops. We'll have trouble, especially if he lands in a bad place for us. As he will do his best to do. What do you recommend?"

Od unrolled his map. "Where is the British fleet now, sir?"

"On the Gulf of Sant Eufemia, sailing north."

"I suspect that's a feint, sir. North of the gulf there are a hundred miles of nearly unbroken cliffs. The villages there are accessible mainly by sea, and the British control the sea, so that coast remains in a state of chronic insurrection."

"Tell me something I don't know."

"If Sir John wants to make a preemptive strike, there's little point in going to a region already friendly to him. He's more likely to land by the gulf itself, where our communications lines and supply route pass close to the coast. He may hope to cut us off between there and Sicily."

Reynier nodded. "So as you see it, he will make a significant landing there."

"Yes, sir."

"That is my sentiment. With what kind of force?"

"With his whole force, sir. His purpose would be to cut us off and destroy us. If we can destroy that force, the lion's fangs will be pulled. But it may take some doing."

"My thought again. I have already sent word to assemble every available man we have, even though it means abandoning all but two or three indispensable posts in the region. You will go and establish suitable sites for our artillery. Just as soon as we know exactly where he is landing."

The next few days were hectic. Sir John did land on the coast of the Gulf of Eufemia, near the village of Eufemia. The estimate of the spies was that there were almost 4,800 British Infantry, and sixteen guns. This was a formidable force, considering that none of it was native. The British would have excellent discipline and precise maneuvering. They were already throwing up entrenchments to the north and south of their landing site, and stirring up a popular uprising in the dense mountain forests farther north. The small French garrisons and flying columns had all they could do to contain that swell of revolt. Their main lines faced a little east of south, where they expected the main French force to appear. They were correct: that was where Reynier would have to go, if he wanted to engage them soon. And he did want to do that, before they could arouse the whole countryside against him. Calabrese were already closing in from all sides to watch the fray, and some had already marched into Sir John's camp to join the British. Time was of the essence.

And so on July 3, Reynier pitched his bivouac close by the village of Maida: 5,150 men, including a battery of horse artillery. Was this enough to do the job? It had to be, because there were no more.

The French were strongly positioned on the hill of Maida, and Od had made sure that the guns were well placed and oriented. Sir John was unlikely to force that hill, but the surrounding Calabrese would pounce if any significant weakness showed in the French.

On the morning of July 4 the two armies were camped about nine miles apart. The British were to the north of the swampy lowlands of the mouth of the Amato River, and the French were to the south of them. Sir John was well entrenched, and supported by the artillery of the ships. But the spies brought some good news: not only was the area unsuitable for any long occupation, malaria had already broken out. The British weren't used to the rigors of the open wetlands, and so were more vulnerable to an illness that had largely completed its business with the French. That is, Reynier's troops had become relatively immune to the awful malady. So now, suddenly, it was the British who had the best reason to complete the battle quickly, so they could get away from the swamp.

Od was not a direct combatant, but he needed to be on hand to handle any enemy artillery that got overrun. So he and several of his technicians got as close to the likely action as they dared, and remained hidden in the brush. As it happened they were near Reynier's left wing, commanded by General Compère, and Pul's contingent was there. It was a scrub-covered plain just north of the mouth of the Amato River.

Sir John was the first to move, advancing one column along the line of the beach. Was this a feint? To what point? There was nothing but the river ahead. So when it appeared that this was a real advance, designed to march on the French encampment, Reynier moved. For this was a chance to literally drive the British into the sea, finishing the battle almost before it started. Sir John had been foolish to allow himself to be caught in such an exposed position, with no easy retreat.

As the French approached the coastline, the British column halted and faced inland. Then it advanced to meet the French. The British right wing led—the one toward the river. The French left wing led—also the one toward the river. So the two wings met beside the river while the other units were still far apart.

This certainly seemed favorable for the French, who were seasoned and quick in maneuvers. If the leading French echelon either outflanked or broke through the British front, a rapid turning movement might roll up the entire British line. But it seemed that Sir John wasn't entirely stupid. He had protected against flanking maneuvers by anchoring the wing on the river, and further shielded it with a detachment of riflemen who had crossed to the opposite bank. If the French had realized that the rifles would be there, they could have sent their own detachment to take them out. As it was, Reynier's best chance of success depended on a breakthrough at the collision point.

Od heard the orders being bawled. The men made a rapid advance in a solid column, then broke into a bayonet charge. The British halted, awaiting the French charge. They formed the long drawn-out line that was their fashion.

Reynier used a screen of cavalry pickets to raise a cloud of dust that marked his troop movements. Only when the dust cleared would the exact location of the charge become clear. It was a lovely spectacle. A general on horseback led the way. Drums beat the rhythm for the pounding feet. Unit flags waved proudly in the wind. Surely that gallant charge would carry everything before it!

The British light infantry had no drums, no horses, no flag bearers. The men waited coolly and with unflinching discipline, muskets at the carry. Od had to admire them, for all that they were about to be swept into the sea. They were carrying through their folly without cringing at all. They certainly had discipline.

Then came the British commands for battle. With marked precision, the troops aimed and fired in a volley. The effect was devastating. Gaps opened in the French formation. General Compère and two colonels fell. Naturally the British had made sure of the enemy leaders first.

But the advance was not checked. "Charge!" Pul bawled, and his men broke into a full charge, bayonets raised for close combat. They were intent on overrunning the British position before the enemy could reload.

The British maintained their drill and discipline. They reloaded as the French bore down on them, just as if no one were threatening. The French were within thirty yards when the second volley was fired.

At that range, the entire French front disintegrated. The ground was covered with the fallen. A few brave men continued the charge, and Pul was one of them. They got within fifteen yards—and were mowed down. The French left wing had been utterly destroyed.

Now the British broke ranks to swarm over the fallen enemy and loot anything of value. That was undisciplined, and surely against orders. So the British weren't perfect. But what did it matter? They had won the battle.

Od heard a moan he recognized. Pul! He wasn't dead!

He ran out from his hiding place. The scene was now so disorganized that no one paid him any attention. Most of the British had gone well out across the French position, scrambling to loot the bodies that had fallen in the first volley.

Od dropped down beside Pul. "I've got you," he said. "I'll haul you to safety." He took hold of the man's arms.

"No," Pul groaned. "I'm done for." He paused to draw another breath. "I feel my guts leaking out." He breathed again. "Just tell them—" But then he stiffened, and his eyes opened wide.

After a moment Od realized that Pul was dead. The man's dying statement had been lost. Nothing of value remained on his body; everything had been taken.

Od had seen death before, and become somewhat inured to it. But this was, if not actually a friend, a close acquaintance. Od had known him for a long time—almost, it seemed, for millennia. Pul's courage under fire had not been enough to enable him to survive. "I'll tell them that you died with honor," he promised the corpse.

He walked away, not caring if anyone challenged him. Therefore no one did. He did not even care that he was walking back into the battle. He seemed separated from it all, as if a ghost, passing through it without being affected. He saw that the British looting had given Reynier precious time to re-form his line, and he was doing it with admirable swiftness. He wasn't willing to admit defeat, and was trying to take further advantage of the chance to outflank Sir John's left. But the wind was blowing the smoke from the battlefield directly into his troops' eyes, making their firing generally ineffective. He was clearly unwilling to make another direct charge; the British fire was too devastating. Still, he was making some progress.

Then a fresh British regiment came up to support Sir John. It advanced, covering the British left flank. That ended the last chance of the French to save the day. Reynier retreated, covering his infantry with cavalry and artillery fire. The British, evidently tired, did not pursue.

But Od knew that the craven Calabrese would crowd in like maggots to leach what they could from the retreating French. The bold British had given them the opportunity. Soon the British would depart, and the Calabrese, left to their own devices, would fade before the reorganizing French. But this day was a loss. July fourth: a day of infamy.

✿

On July 9 the French opened fire again, with ninety guns trained at shorter range on the neck of Gaeta. Heath watched it with mixed feelings. He hoped that this time the barrage would be successful, but also that Dillon would not feel the need to get up and participate. The man was recovering, but he needed more rest before the malaria was fully beaten back.

Most of the shells were directed at the Queen's Battery, whose return fire was soon reduced. But the four heavy ship's guns continued to fire throughout that day and the next, and the French ammunition was rapidly becoming exhausted.

On July 10 there was furious fighting. The French trenches were close to the walls, and they attempted to establish a breaching battery close to the shore. And of course Dillon had to be there. Heath tried to restrain him, but Dillon was determined to be in for the kill.

Actually, the man seemed fit, for the day. Malaria was like that; one day it was incapacitating, and the next it was gone. But it always returned. A victim who did too much when feeling better was begging for worse trouble. But Dillon led his men in toward the wall.

The defenders concentrated their fire, raining shot and shell down on the French position. A French shell made a lucky score, bursting inside the Breach Battery. But the defense held out, and finally the advance was repulsed.

And Dillon had been wounded. He had concealed its severity from his men, lending them his courage, but when he returned Heath found him bleeding from the gut. He rushed to attend to the awful wound, but Dillon waved him away. "Go tend my men! They are in a bad way."

"There are other medics," Heath said. "I must tend to the officer first."

"Forget it! See to my men."

"And," Heath said carefully, "if others see you, they will realize that you were sick before you went to fight, and will soon fathom how, and you will be shipped directly to Naples for recovery."

That got him. Dillon ceased protesting, and Heath escorted him from the field. Back in their quarters, he addressed the gut wound. "This is bad," he said.

"I know it. Fix it."

"It's a shrapnel hit, and the fragment is still in you. I must take it out and sew up your intestine. This will be painful. Dillon, it really would be better to have this done quickly, in Naples. Your life is in danger."

"I must see the siege through."

"I can do it," Heath said grimly. "But here your danger of infection is much greater. You will survive the wound, but not necessarily the infection. Not on top of malaria. I judge your chances here to be less than fifty per cent."

"Do it."

Heath tried once more. "At Naples, Melee can come and hold your hand and encourage you."

Dillon was clenching his teeth to fight back the pain, but this made him pause. Then he dismissed it. "She can do that after the siege is won. Do what you have to do. Now."

Heath wasted no more time on argument. "Here is strong wine. Drink it, to dull the pain."

"No. I'll get by. Just give me the bullet."

"Drink it, damn you!" Heath snapped. "Or I'll have to bring in men to hold you down while I operate, so that your involuntary struggles don't exacerbate the injury."

Dillon finally relented. He gulped the wine while Heath used cloths to clean the wound, and prepared his instruments. Then Dillon took the bullet, and bit down on it, determined not to scream.

Heath dug into the wound. The shrapnel was small, and seemed to have stopped before doing more than penetrating the skin and lodging in the intestine. He peeled back the flesh and used forceps to take hold of the metal and work it out. Dillon tensed, and his breath whistled around the bullet, but he did not scream. Oh, the man had self control—but that was not enough.

The ragged piece came out. Heath waved it before Dillon's face, so that his glazing eyes could see this success. Then he drew out the injured segment of intestine, and used stout needle and thread to sew it together. He squeezed it back into the abdominal cavity, closed the wound, and made additional stitches. He wrapped a bandage around the lower torso. It was over, for now.

"Done," he said.

Dillon heard, spat out the bullet, and lapsed into unconsciousness.

Heath summoned a man, one not of Dillon's complement. "Stand by this officer," he said. "When he wakes, give him water or wine, as he prefers. If he hallucinates and says wild things, repeat them nowhere else. If he asks for me, fetch me immediately."

"Yes, sir."

Now Heath went out to see to others. He hoped he had been able to do enough for Dillon. He had seen such injuries before; they were terrible, but could be survived. Except for the infection that so often followed.

One of his medics spied him. "Sir! Did you hear? Prince Hesse was mortally wounded by that explosion in the Breach Battery!"

That was news indeed. Without the iron nerve of the prince, the resistance would soon collapse. Yet Heath was sad, in a way, for Prince Hesse had proved to be a worthy opponent.

The prince did not die, but he was incapacitated, and command of Gaeta devolved to his second, Colonel Hotz. The word was that the colonel had moderate ability, but little prestige or leadership. This was certainly the time to push ahead with full force.

Masséna ordered his batteries to double their fire, regardless of the state of their supplies of ammunition. All could be won with a single all-out push. He issued another demand for surrender.

On July 12, Hotz responded: he refused to surrender. That meant that the prince was still alert enough to make the decision.

Four more days of shelling followed. The supply of ammunition dwindled dangerously, but still the fortress did not capitulate.

Dillon was not doing any better. The infection did come, and added to the malaria it had him burning up. He couldn't eat, and was becoming gaunt. Still he held on, refusing to be shipped out until he saw the victory.

Heath had severely mixed emotions. The man's loyalty to his cause and courage when in awful pain were amazing, but he was dying. Never had

Heath so much regretted giving his word; he had to protect Dillon from discovery, knowing that he was helping the man to kill himself through neglect. He was tempted to break his word and get the man to better care, but could not do it. For one thing, he was afraid that it was already too late: Dillon well might die on the road to Naples, knowing that he had been betrayed. That would be worse than nothing.

On the night of the fifteenth, a French engineer reported that a passage could be waded from one of the trenches to the lowest of the two breaches the shells had made in the walls. It was now possible to set up a storming party.

Heath brought the news to Dillon. All he had now was information; there was nothing more he could do for his friend medically. Dillon would win or lose the battle within his own body on his own—and encouraging news about the external siege was perhaps his best medicine. Heath had been tempted to lie to him, to tell him that the victory was being had, but he couldn't make himself do that either. Dillon trusted him to bring the truth, and he had to do it. The truth was that an opening was in the making, but it had not yet been completed.

This avenue was just in time. On the morning of the sixteenth the French had only two days' worth of ammunition for sustained fire. Then the guns would fall silent, win or lose. Worse, news had come of a disastrous setback that Reynier had suffered in Calabria. The British had landed a force and defeated him and sent him into an extended retreat with heavy losses. The natives had snatched the opportunity to rebel, and were crowding in, committing atrocities. So there would be no reinforcements for the siege of Gaeta; all the available reserves were being rushed to help Reynier in the south. Worse yet, Napoleon was pulling troops out of the Kingdom of Italy to support the French forces in Germany.

So the issue here had to be decided quickly. They were so close; they just had to wedge through that last inch and finish it, so that some of the troops here could be sent down to join Reynier.

Masséna decided to risk everything on victory. The French guns would expend all their ammunition, and then the infantry would storm the fort with bayonets, if necessary.

"I must be in that charge!" Dillon gasped.

"It's not for two days," Heath said. "You must eat, drink, get your strength back."

Dillon tried, but the food would not stay down. The only nourishment he could get was from the wine, in tiny sips. It did not go to his head; apparently the terrible fever burned out the spirits. But he was not improving; his eyes glowed in gaunt sockets.

For two days the guns blasted the wall, targeting and enlarging the breaches. Then, as the last of the ammunition loomed, the French made their preparations for storming both of those breaches.

"I must be there!" Dillon rasped.

What was there to do? Heath got him dressed, and with the help of an aide walked him to the front. His men cheered when they saw him; they had known he would not let them down.

But the charge was not yet. Normally a besieging general would attempt to hide his preparations from the defenders, so as to gain the maximum advantage of surprise. But Masséna had given orders that the preparations be ostentatious, so that the defenders could not possibly miss them. He knew that Prince Hesse was down, if not dead, so that the defense would lack the courage of that leadership. They were being given full opportunity to lose their nerve. With luck, this demonstration would break their will.

The French forces made ready. Dillon wanted to join his men, but Heath held him back. "The order has not yet been given. We may win without charging."

"Maybe just as well," Dillon murmured. He knew that he would be lucky just to keep his feet, let alone charge. But if there was no charge, his mere presence lent support.

Then at three in the afternoon, as the columns were forming, a white flag appeared over the wall. "They are capitulating!" Heath cried. "You have seen the victory."

"It could be a ruse," Dillon said.

"If it is, we'll soon know. Meanwhile, back to bed with you." He hauled the man off the field.

It was no ruse. Within three hours the conditions of surrender were agreed. The French would take over the fortress, together with its guns and munitions, but the entire defensive garrison would be allowed to retire to Sicily. The defenders had been adamant and honorable, worthy of respect, so were to be treated with honor. The only condition was that they not raise arms against the French Empire or its allies for a period of one year.

"And so they are moving into the fortress now," Heath told Dillon. "The defenders know that General Masséna can be trusted. Tomorrow morning a portion of these forces will be sent south to assist Reynier. The tide is turning. And you can go to Naples. You have seen the victory."

Dillon nodded, smiling. "Give me your word, again," he said.

"What?" But he saw that the man was about to lose consciousness, or worse. He had another request, and very little time. "Given."

"See to Melee." Then, before Heath could answer, Dillon fell back on the bed.

Heath leaped to help him, but there was nothing he could do. Dillon's labored breathing had stopped. He was dead.

He pushed the man's eyes closed. "I will see to Melee," he promised. Then he turned away and let his tears flow.

❂

It was the ninth month, but Avalanche knew that all was not well. She had never been this far with child before, but there was pain that should not be. The baby within her seemed well, but she herself was not. She wouldn't tell the others; there was nothing they could do anyway. She had sent Od away, on the pretext she wanted to sleep; it was actually so that she could wince and writhe without attracting attention. She had been able to mask it well enough so far, but she felt the incipient birth pangs, and knew that it was about to get much worse.

As she lay alone in the bedroom, she reflected on recent events. The French were winning Italy; the tide had turned with the capture of Gaeta, and the enemy forces and brigand bands were in general retreat. But at what price? Her old friend Pul had died in Calabria, shot down by the British. Od had returned to report that Pul had died with honor, leading the charge. But he was nevertheless dead. She had slept with Pul many times, in the early days before she oriented on Od, and sometimes more recently. She had never charged him, but she had asked him not to tell Od, and apparently he had died without telling. That was indeed honor, for Pul normally liked to brag. She had never loved him, or ever really liked him, but now a piece of her seemed to be gone.

Then, almost two months ago, Dillon had also been killed. He had taken a gut wound, and it got infected, and he had died on the day Gaeta fell. Heath had returned with the grim news. Heath had had to tell Melee, and she had screamed and torn her hair, reacting with flair, but her emotion was real. Avalanche and Talena had known better than to try to console her; there was no consolation to be had.

Worse, was what else Heath said: Dillon had made him promise to "see to Melee." Dillon's last thought had been for his lovely wife. He hadn't known how Heath felt about Melee. None of the men had known. And of course he hadn't meant for Heath to do anything with her personally, and Heath would not. He simply had to see that she was well taken care of. But how? Their group was short a man.

But now Avalanche had the answer. If she could just convince the others. It made perfect sense, but she feared they would not be willing to see it.

This was the time, and not just because both Heath and Od were here with the three women today, on separate leaves from their units.

"We must talk," she said, as Talena entered the bedroom. "All of us."

Talena glanced at her. "Is this serious?"

"Yes."

"Then we will join you here in the bedroom while we eat. I hope we can work it out." She had the grace not to inquire what. Talena was always good at not prying.

In due course they assembled, with their food on wooden plates. Avalanche had very little to eat, because she knew she couldn't keep it down. That was all right; it was talking, not eating, she had to do.

"We have had a problem," she said as they listened. "Melee is a widow, and Heath promised to see to her welfare, but the only thing he or anyone could do was to keep her here with us, as before. But we all know that she will need a man, long term."

"Dillon was all I wanted," Melee said darkly. She had lost weight during her grief, but remained lovely in a haunting way.

"I am not speaking romantically, but practically," Avalanche said. "I have Od, Talena has Heath, and if their units get sent far from each other, our group will disintegrate, but they will still take care of us. But with whom will you go?"

Melee was silent, appreciating the point. She could stay with the two women, because they formed a compatible group, but she would be a disruptive influence if she stayed with a single couple. She couldn't help it.

"Fortunately, I have a solution," Avalanche continued. "But I think the rest of you will not like it."

"The solution is for me to leave," Melee said. "I came here because of Dillon's friendship for the two other men. Now he is gone, and there is no obligation."

"But I promised Dillon," Heath said, anguished.

"Be quiet, both of you," Avalanche said. The other women knew why she could not speak of the reason for his anguish. He had a double commitment to Melee, only part of which could he confess. "There will be a man for Melee. Maybe not a love match, but a reliable, good-hearted, good provider. If we can agree."

Talena was looking at her quizzically. So was Heath.

"But first I must make you understand something else," Avalanche said after a moment. "I am very soon to birth my baby. But I think I will not survive the birthing."

Suddenly all of them focused sharply on her. "What?" Od demanded.

"I have been hiding it, but can do so no longer. There is something wrong. That baby is not going to come out peacefully. I think my evil prior life has given me illness, or scar tissue, or something. Heath, you are going to have to cut the baby from me. I think you can save it, but you can't save me."

"But I wouldn't—" Heath started.

"It's not the cutting that will kill me. It's the ailment. I don't know what it is, but I know its nature. I have been hanging on, to see the baby through, but then it will be over for me. You will cut me open to save the baby; otherwise it, too, will perish. You don't want that."

Heath got up and came over to her. He put his hand on her forehead, then on her belly. Then she spread her legs so that he could reach in past her underclothing and probe her pained cleft. He was after all a doctor, and he needed to know. His fingers nudged inside her, while the others watched. Grimly, he nodded. "Why didn't you say something before? You can't birth this baby."

"Could you have fixed it before?"

"No. You are right; I will have to cut you open. We must take you to the hospital immediately." He withdrew his hand.

"No. That will only prolong the agony. I want to die quickly. It is kinder to bleed to death." She stared directly at him. "Isn't that so?"

He spread his hands. "It is so."

"It can't be so!" Talena protested. "This isn't a battlefield. There is no need to die without attention."

But Heath shook his head. "She has a condition that makes pregnancy lethal. If I had known early, I could have arranged to abort it—"

"No! I have longed for this baby all my life. It is my fulfillment as a woman. It must survive. Nothing else in my life has been worthwhile, except this. Save the baby; let me go."

"So it must be," Heath agreed. "You cling to your mission as adamantly as Dillon did, though your life be forfeit."

"And that is the rest of it," Avalanche said. "My life has never been worth much, but I can give this baby life—and I can help my friends. Od, you will need a woman, because what you know about babies is little. Take Melee."

Od looked astonished. So did Melee.

"You both know that you represent one very good man and one very lovely woman. The man needs a woman to care for his baby; the woman needs a man to support her. You don't need to speak of love, though perhaps it will come. You need each other, and you are both good people. You can work it out."

Heath looked at them. "Can you?" he asked Od.

Od, nonplused, looked at Melee. "I never dreamed of—but if she were willing—"

Talena looked at Melee. "Can you?"

"Yes."

"Just like that?" Od asked her, surprised again.

Melee nodded. "It is, as Avalanche suggests, a practical decision. I'll never have Dillon back, but I still need economic and social support. You are an unexciting but good man who can provide both. I believe I can give you what you desire. But I would do it regardless, because Avalanche asked. As she says, we are not speaking of love, merely of need."

"But a baby who is not yours—"

"It is Avalanche's—and yours. That's enough."

"But still—"

Avalanche smiled, though her pain was strengthening. "He does protest too much. Melee, I think you should kiss him."

"By your leave," Melee agreed. Then she got up, kneeled beside Od, took his head in her hands, and kissed him firmly on the mouth. After a moment she disengaged and returned to her own place.

Od did not move or speak. Melee had done what Avalanche had once been able to do to man or boy, stunning them.

"I wish I could do that," Talena said, laughing a bit self-consciously.

"You can do something more important," Avalanche told her. "Wet-nurse my baby, until it can eat."

"Yes, of course. I haven't yet weaned my last." Talena touched her bosom, as if hefting a breast for content.

"And so my man and my baby will be secure," Avalanche said. "And, you, Heath, will have seen to Melee. You know she could not be better situated than this."

"I know," Heath agreed. He looked relieved, and she suspected why: he retained his illicit passion for Melee, but knew he could never fulfill it. This way, there would be no temptation, and he honored Dillon's stricture. He had seen Melee given what she needed, and had no further obligation.

"Yes," Talena said. The danger to her own marriage had been abated. "But to sacrifice your life—"

"I made the choice when I first felt the quickening," Avalanche said. "My only regret was inflicting my death on Od. But now I think it won't be so bad, for I leave him to one more beautiful than I ever was."

"I am not sure about that," Melee murmured.

Heath nodded. "It is a beautiful, if necessary thing you are doing. I see you are in pain. Do you wish me to do what must be done?"

"Yes. My time has come." Indeed it had; her belly was writhing with the contractions that would destroy her. "I think you will need help. Maybe if Talena will stay—"

"I'll stay," Od said quickly.

"No! I don't want you to see me as I will be. I want you to remember me as beautiful. Get well away from me, until I am gone."

He stared at her a moment. Then he got up and approached her. He kneeled before her. "I love you—and your baby." He kissed her, and she fought back her rising agony to kiss him back.

"I love you," she echoed. "Now go. With Melee. See to the children."

He got up and left the room. Melee got up also. Her eyes were bright. "I love you too," she said, and followed Od out.

Avalanche waited until she heard them leaving the building with the children. Talena peeked out the shrouded window. "They are beyond hearing," she said after a pause.

Then Avalanche felt free to let go. She groaned, and it was half a scream.

"Take this," Heath said, giving her a cup of wine into which he had added something. "It is tincture of opium, for the pain."

"But it will harm the baby!"

"I'll have the baby out of you before it can be harmed. Take it."

Gratefully, she accepted the drink. And while the wine warmed her throat, and the opium reached for her brain, Heath and Talena stripped her and laid her out on the bed belly-up.

Heath readied the knife. "I can try to save you," he said. "I can sew you up, stanch the flow of blood. I judge you have a one-in-three chance to survive."

"No. I would not be as I would want. I would be scarred and of weak health. My body would no longer appeal to men. Let me die."

"This will hurt. The drug can't stop the pain entirely. But you can bear it, especially if you direct your mind elsewhere. You will know it's over when you hear the baby cry."

"I'll think of birthing it normally." The room was wavering; the opium had reached her eyes.

Heath leaned close, with the knife.

But she had one more thing to do. "In my drawer—my jade figurine—"

"Your one most precious possession will go with your baby," Talena said quickly. "In memory of you."

Then she was in a turmoil of pain and struggle, but she didn't fight hard because she knew it was Talena holding her down so her thrashing wouldn't harm the baby, and Heath's knife cutting it out of her. At the same time she felt as if she were floating, her body laid open like a gutted fish. An instant passed, as it were an eternity, and she saw the baby. It was a boy! Talena had always wanted to nurse a boy, and now she could. But was it all right?

Then she heard the cry. She relaxed, gladdened, and ebbed away.

The French reduced the remaining resistance, but had some difficult campaigns. The last set battle was in 1807, when Prince Hesse, now recovered from his wound, landed at the tip of the Italian toe with five thousand men. He took up a strong position at Mileto. Reynier attacked before dawn. Most of the Sicilian regiments bolted at the first sight of French bayonets, leaving only one regiment to make an honorable defense. Thereafter, the resistance was mainly a matter of brigandage and guerrilla attacks. The lawlessness continued through 1808, and grew worse in 1809. In 1810 a new military commander issued special decrees: every insurrectionist who surrendered would be pardoned and placed on the government's payroll. A price was put on the head of every guerrilla chief. Every village was to live under military guard, with herd animals kept under watch or within the walls. No food was to be taken outside the towns or villages, and no person was to have any contact with any brigand. The penalty for violation was death. These harsh measures were executed to the letter. Even innocent violations resulted in action, such as when women and boys went out to pick olives and took bread with them: they were shot. When a woman cared for a newborn baby given her by a girl who followed the brigands, she was shot. Millers who sold flour to outlaws were shot. And by the summer of 1811 every major brigand chief had been captured or killed.

So Italy was taken and held by Napoleon's forces, protecting the southern flank of his empire. Otherwise it was a distinct historical backwater of no particular significance. When Napoleon lost power in 1815, King Ferdinand recovered southern Italy, forming the Kingdom of the Two Sicilies, and ruled as autocratically as ever. So this campaign serves mainly as a precursor of the guerrilla warfare that was to hurt Napoleon in Spain, and other strong kingdoms in other times. And as an indication of the costly and often pointless brutality of war, when mere survival was victory. History does run rampant over the common man.

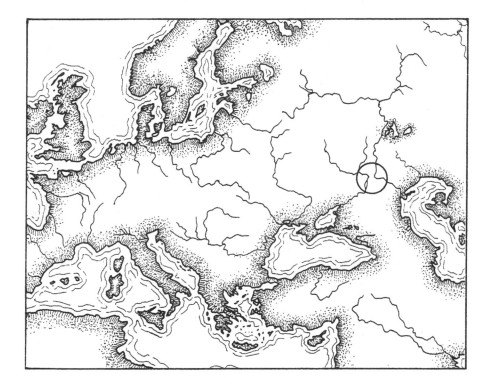

CHAPTER 12

IRONY

Appreciation of the magnitude of the conflict that was World War Two may be fading, but there are still a fair number of us who lived through that period and were significantly affected by it. The war had more than one theater, and a number of aspects, each of which was significant enough to represent a major historical event by itself. There was the war between America and Japan in the Pacific, and the conquest of Europe by the Axis powers, mainly Germany, and the subsequent reconquest of Europe by the Allies. One aspect of the European theater was Germany's eastern front, as it advanced into the Soviet Union, stalled, and was finally turned back. This front, by itself, could be reckoned as one of the largest and most savage wars our planet has seen.

Nazi Germany made a non-aggression pact with the Soviet Union, and when the war started, the two invaded Poland from opposite sides and partitioned it. Then later, suddenly, Germany attacked the Soviet Union. The attack occurred in June 1941 and the German troops made rapid initial progress. But they were slowed subsequently by the harsh Russian winters and by increasing resistance as the Soviets got their forces together.

On June 28, 1942, the Germans launched another offensive. Its object was the oil fields and refineries of the Caucasus region of southwest Russia. But the German leader, Adolf Hitler, sought to direct things personally, and wreaked a fair amount of mischief thereby. For example, he suddenly ordered the Fourth Panzer Army to veer south and push to the Caucasus. This took it across the path of the Sixth Army, which was advancing east. The two armies became horribly entangled as their supply and support lines crossed, and both were slowed by the confusion. The Fourth Panzer wound up with most of the fuel intended for both armies, leaving the Sixth somewhat isolated and unprotected by the heavy armor. But Hitler ordered it to drive deeper into Russian territory anyway, because he was certain that the Communist forces were on the brink of collapse.

The German chief of staff managed to convince Hitler to support the Sixth Army more strongly, and the Fourth Panzer changed course again. It approached Stalingrad from the southwest, while the Sixth Army came at the city from the west. For now Hitler had decided that Stalingrad must fall. This was to lead to the art of irony, for the siege of Stalingrad was to become a turning point in more than one sense. The time is August 4, 1942; the place is Stalingrad, Russia.

"**G**ENERAL Yeremenko is arriving today!" Melee said as she burst in the door. "I must see that his things are in order."

Talena looked up. "Doesn't he have his own staff?"

"Not here. Not yet. So I have been assigned to cater the first meal for him. In a few days his staff will catch up, and I'll be through." She hesitated. "Do you mind if—"

Talena laughed. "Of course I'll take care of Avan. We get along just fine."

"You are a better mother than I am," Melee said.

"I have had more experience. But really, I like having a little boy with my girls. The girls like it too; they think of him as a little brother." Her six girls were ages nine down to two, while Avan was one. Melee hadn't borne him, but she had adopted him, for the sake of her friend Avalanche, who had died giving him life.

She rushed around the kitchen, preparing what they had for a meal. "I don't know when I'll be back. The general may be late."

"Phone, and I will come to pick you up," Od said.

"I had in mind your taking me there," she said. "Maybe you can meet the general."

He nodded. "I'd like that."

"Heath and I can handle this," Talena said, looking up from a diaper. Heath was getting the other children organized. "You two go ahead now."

"Thanks." Melee dashed to the bedroom and flung herself out of her clothing. She laid out her prettiest dress. She unbound her hair and shook it out. She wanted to look her best for the general. She had gotten lean a year ago, when her tragedy came, but had recovered her form this year. She could thank her three truly fine and supportive friends for that.

She stuck her head out the door. "Od, wear your dress uniform, just in case. Come change now."

He came to the bedroom. "You know, the chances of me actually meeting the general are remote."

She closed the door behind him. "I know. But God knows how late I'll be finished there, and what assignment you'll be on tomorrow. I thought I'd better see to you now." She unfastened his belt and guided his trousers down.

"Melee, you know I don't require—"

"I know you don't. We are ill matched, and it's no fault of yours. You're the perfect husband. I'm the wild one. But at least I can do this for you." She drew down his shorts, then stripped away her own underwear. "Quickly." She spat into her hand, then stroked her fingers through her cleft, wetting it well. She couldn't afford to wait on nature.

"I like your wildness. But—"

She stepped into him and kissed him. That ended his objection. His hands came around her, stroking down her back and across her bare bottom. He did like her body. He should; it was an excellent one, that she had done her best to preserve and restore. She pressed it ardently against him.

In a moment they were on the bed, and she was moving in the way she knew, parting her legs just enough and guiding him into her. There was no pretense of foreplay or love, only sudden passion. They had married when his wife and her husband had died a year ago, to keep their small group together and make a family for Avan, but it had been a marriage of necessity rather than love. He had made sure to provide for her economically, and she had made sure to provide for him sexually, and they did respect each other. But both knew that it fell substantially short of love. They were friends, very good friends, rather than true marriage partners. But sex was a significant aspect of their relationship, and actually she liked doing it well enough. They had agreed that when they clasped each other he could pretend she was Avalanche, and she could pretend he was Dillon. Thus in their moments of passion they could forget their separate griefs, somewhat. It was something they both needed.

"Oh, Melee—" he whispered as his urgency erupted, fostered by her swift competence. And of course he didn't *have* to pretend. Neither did she.

"It's good," she said, squeezing him close, giving him the most sensation. She had no climax, of course, but hadn't sought one, and he knew it. He always wanted her to, and sometimes she did, but right now there wasn't time.

"I wish—"

"So do I." She disengaged as he released her, and went to the bathroom for a fast efficient cleanup with a narrow sponge. She wet it, wedged it in, drew it out, rinsed it, and wiped off her external cleft.

"But—"

"After the war, we can take time," she said. "I promise."

"It's not that. I—"

"I know it isn't. But then we can get to know each other without the horrible tension of war. It will be different."

"Oh, I hope so! It's not that you are in any way deficient; far from it."

She emerged from the bathroom, brought out the washcloth and cleaned up his groin for him, because his distraction was diverting him from the need to be efficient. "I know." She squeezed his penis gently, then kissed it. "Now go piss. You don't want to ooze on your good clothing any more than I do."

He gave up the dialogue, and went into the bathroom while she laid out his uniform.

When he emerged, she was well into her own outfit. He got to work on his own. "You are amazing," he said. "If only—"

She leaned forward and kissed him, then straightened his collar. "After the war. I promise," she repeated. Yet she wondered. Od was a good man, a perfect man, but he wasn't Dillon. Or Heath. And would never be.

They were ready. Melee opened the door and stepped out. Talena looked up. "I don't know how you manage to change so fast," she said. "And you got him changed too."

"She took care of me," Od agreed halfway ruefully.

"I'm glad it worked out so well between you," Heath said.

Was he jealous? Melee hoped so. There had never been anything between them, but in her fancy she would have preferred to have him in bed instead of Od. If it had just been Talena who died, instead of Avalanche— but that was an unkind thought she had to suppress. Talena was her friend, and she would never do anything to breach that friendship. Her private passion was all in her mind, and would remain there.

She picked up the sandwiches she had made before. "We'll eat on the way. See you this evening." She waved as they exited.

Od drove, and she gave him a sandwich. "I'm sorry about rushing you like that. But I didn't want you to be deprived, if our duties separate us for long."

"I have no complaint about that aspect," he said. "You can seduce me any time you choose. But how much better it would be if we were in love."

"You're not Dillon, and I'm not Avalanche. We know that. Our relationship still feels more like an illicit affair to me."

"And to me. I admit that lends excitement, but also guilt. If there were any way I could undo what happened—"

"If I could take up a rifle and go back in time to assassinate Adolf Hitler before he took over Germany, I would." She lifted her right hand and sighted along it, as if firing a gun. "Then we would be six or seven friends instead of four. But that's just one of the foolish dreams I have, that have no reality. Our union made sense, and still does, and I have no complaint of you. I think that in time we can make it real, and I mean to do that, when the time comes. We are two pieces of a broken pot, and while the original can never be restored, at least we can make something of what remains."

"I suppose so. And at least we are honoring promises made."

The dialogue lapsed. Melee gazed out the car window as the streets of Stalingrad passed by. There was not much traffic, and much of that was military, as this was a major staging area for the defense of southwest Russia. Military horse carts moved easily through the wide boulevards. Theirs was one of the few cars, and it was of course connected to the government. The civilians would come out in the evening as pedestrians, filling the streets, whistling tunes from *Rose Marie,* which had recently played here. Many of the young people would have copies of books by Jack London, who was popular among the city's youth.

Their house was in the western residential section, near the downtown shopping district and theater. It was a nice city and she wouldn't have minded living here even if the military requirements hadn't brought them. But today it was a mere shadow of its civilian self.

"How did it come to be named after our leader?" she asked. Od would know, for he knew everything. He was a very intelligent man, and she did appreciate that.

"Originally it was called Tsaritsyn, or 'Yellow water' in the Tartar language," he replied. "Actually, the narrow region between the two great rivers, the Don and the Volga, has been settled since ancient times. The Cimmerians were here for over a thousand years, beginning before 1800 B.C. The Scythians took over in the seventh century B.C., giving way to the Sarmatians about 200 B.C. They fragmented, and that portion known as the Alani or Alans assumed power in this region about 150 B.C. This was to remain Alan territory for more than fifteen hundred years, though they were overridden temporarily by the Huns in A.D. 400, the Avars in 550, the Khazars in 650, and so on until the Mongols or Tartars in the thirteenth century and finally the Russians in the sixteenth century." He broke off, realizing that she was staring at him. "Sorry. I'm somewhat of a scholar of the region, which I find fascinating."

"No, go on. I find your knowledge as fascinating as you find my body. But maybe it is time to penetrate to the sweet core." She smiled, having no embarrassment at all in sexual analogy.

He glanced at her, well appreciating the metaphor. "In 1920, during the Bolshevik Revolution, Joseph Stalin won a great victory over the White army here. So the city renamed itself in his honor. Perhaps flattered, he rebuilt his namesake into a model industrial city for the modern Soviet Union. More than half a million people live here now."

She smiled. "And all of them like to shop the same time I do! Now here's another question for you: why is it so hot?"

"It is August," he reminded her. "The hot season. The daily highs are rising well above a hundred degrees Fahrenheit, but it won't last, for fall will come, making the temperature fall."

"Don't give me that humor, Od! The concrete sidewalks are warping and cracking under the heat, and the asphalt roads are making waves of heat mirages. I can even see reflections in some of them. No rain has fallen in two months, and yet the humidity is stifling. Explain *that*."

He sighed. "You are a hard taskmistress. The humidity can be accounted for by the fact that the city lies along the steep west bank of the Volga River, so is bathed by the rising water vapor. The heat is worsened by several factors. It *is* the hot season, aggravated by the fact that the wind has been from the west, hot and dusty. Buildings and streets absorb the sun's heat, and there are not enough trees to alleviate it; it's a phenomenon common to many cities. But I think we also owe much to the industrial northern sector of the city. Clouds of smoke and soot belch forth from hundreds of smokestacks. That's the other face of modernization. That holds the heat in, intensifying the effect."

She sighed. "So the industry that makes the city rich enough to have broad streets, spacious parks, and gleaming white buildings in the residential sections, also makes it unlivably hot. How can we win?"

"We wait for winter."

"The Germans will be here first!"

"Not if our defenses are good."

"Well, I hope General Yeremenko sees to that."

"I hope so too."

They passed the beer factory and turned on Pushkinskaya Street. Here they were flagged down by military police. "What is your business here?" an officer demanded gruffly as they stopped.

Od showed his papers. The man looked at them, compared the picture to Od's face, and saluted. "What is your business here, sir?"

"I am conducting my wife to the general's bunker. She is to cater it, until the general's regular staff arrives."

The man looked at Melee. She smiled and handed forth her papers. "Yes, ma'am," he said after a moment, swayed by her beauty. "Park there, and a man will admit you." He gestured to a controlled parking lot.

"Thank *you*," Melee said, smiling again. He smiled and made another salute. It was not serious, as she was a civilian, but she knew it came from the heart. She had that effect on men, and took pride in it.

They parked and got out. Od walked beside her, and she took his elbow. The guide did not challenge this, so they continued to the heavy door of the bunker. If they let him in with her, so much the better; she knew he really wanted to meet General Andrei Yeremenko.

But they were not admitted immediately. The matter was being called in to headquarters, to be absolutely sure. When the security of a general was involved, it required more than papers. Personal recognition was better.

Soon an official vehicle screeched to a nearby stop. A driver jumped out and hurried around to open the passenger door. The officer with Od and Melee snapped to attention. So did Od. Both saluted as the senior officer approached. It was a lieutenant-general.

"Ah, so it *is* you, Od," the general said, returning the salute. "I did not realize that you had business here."

"My wife is to cater to General Yeremenko," Od explained. "She brought me along." Then, as General Khrushchev glanced at her: "General, this is my wife, Melee."

"So glad to meet you at last," the general said graciously. "I had heard you were beautiful; it seems the case was severely understated."

"Thank you, general." Despite herself, she was flattered and a bit flustered; Khrushchev was the man Od worked for.

The general nodded to the officer. "I'll take it from here."

"Yes, sir!" The officer saluted again, then opened the door and stood at attention beside it. Khrushchev gestured Melee in first, and followed, with Od bringing up the rear.

It led to an antechamber, and another solid door. Beyond that was a series of staggered reinforcement partitions. "The Germans will not blithely walk in here, sir," Od remarked, impressed.

"We do mean to protect the general," the officer agreed.

Steep stairs led down and down, flight after flight. "What a job it must have been to excavate this!" Melee remarked.

"It is dug into the Tsaritsa Gorge," Od explained. "Which is a two-hundred-foot-deep dried riverbed about five hundred yards from the Volga's west bank. Formidable reinforced concrete surrounds the structure. There is another entrance below, similarly protected."

"You have done your homework," Khrushchev remarked.

"As a political officer, it is my job to know such things. I am as concerned about the general's security as you are, sir. Not to mention my wife's safety."

Khrushchev laughed. "Of course."

They reached the residential portion. The interior was lavish by Russian military standards. The walls were paneled with oaken plywood, and Melee quickly ascertained that it had a kitchen and a flush toilet.

"I'll need supplies, so I can greet the general with a good meal," she said, checking the cupboards, which were bare. "And there are no sheets on the bed. No one thought he would sleep here?"

General Khrushchev opened his mouth, but didn't manage to speak. He looked amused. Obviously these details had slipped by some underling.

"This is why a woman is catering," Od murmured confidentially to him. "Women think of these details. I believe there is an errand vehicle, and a chauffeur, at the disposal of the general's aide, with adequate funds and rationing coupons, of course."

"Of course," Khrushchev agreed.

Melee smiled brilliantly, rewarding the man. This was why she had wanted Od along: he knew how to open doors without fuss. "I must go shopping immediately, while my husband verifies the security features."

Khrushchev went to the telephone. "The Lady Melee will require a vehicle and driver for a mission for our visitor, in ten minutes," he said, and hung up without waiting for an answer. Then, to her: "I shall be glad to escort you to the surface, if—"

She smiled again. "By no means. You must show my husband the features, so he can verify the security. It is his job. I can find my own way." She started up the long stairs.

Od and the general stood politely as she climbed. She knew they were admiring the increasing exposure of her legs as the angle of view shifted. This was another reward for the general's cooperation, as Od had explained to her beforehand: let them look. Nothing need ever be said, but it facilitated things marvelously. It was grease for the axles. Even when the interim officer was much higher than anticipated. She was glad to do it; she liked being admired, and it *did* make her job easier.

A lesser officer was waiting for her at the top landing, and a car with a driver was at the curb outside. They had probably drawn straws to decide who had the privilege. Oh, yes, this was the way to run a war.

They drove past Railroad Station Number One, which was near the city center. For months trains had passed through there, carrying refugees from other battlegrounds: Leningrad, Odessa, Kharkov, and who knew where else. The official news was that Soviet forces were winning impressive victories west of the Don, but Melee knew better because Od, as an officer in the know, knew better. Naturally she kept her pretty mouth shut, and officers assumed that no woman as lovely as she was could have any sense about the realities of warfare, so she didn't get into trouble with the censors. But she wondered whether other civilians didn't catch on, when they saw the trains coming through, with soldiers crammed into cattle cars. They would jump gratefully off as soon as the trains hit the station, hoping to barter food and water from the merchants lining the platform. She knew that many stole what they could not afford to buy: a loaf of bread or a piece of fruit. Now there were additional hordes of Stalingrad's natives, ordered with little warning to evacuate eastward. They couldn't guess that the war was not going well? Surely they suspected, but knew as well as she did when to be silent.

They passed the five story office building where officials responsible for the evacuation of the city operated. It was on one side of Red Square, lined by shrubs. Across the square was the huge post office, and the headquarters of the local edition of the newspaper *Pravda*, or "Truth." Truth was hardly its business, however; political correctness was. But at least it still published a daily edition, just about the only source of official news. It ran information about air raid drills, rationing, and of course the fake battle reports from the front.

Close by was the squat bulk of the University Department Store. It had once been a showplace for the latest fashions from Moscow, but now the store shelves and counters held only essential items: boots, trousers, socks, underwear, and so on. "Here, first," she said. "For sheets for that bed, and a good blanket. Maybe the general will bring his own, but I wouldn't care to gamble on that."

"Of course," the officer agreed. She had the feeling that he was enjoying this, and not just because he was getting to be seen in public with a strikingly pretty woman. Maybe he liked seeing someone do what no military man could do: second-guess the arrangements of a general.

There was a delay in getting a suitable blanket. It seemed that the reserve stocks in the basement warehouse had sunk to an alarming level. She had to settle for a slightly discolored army blanket. So she got a flower-pattern bedspread to cover it. The officer kept a straight face.

She also bought a pair of furry bedroom slippers. The only ones available had daisies painted on the toes. "His feet will be tired, and no one will be seeing him there," she explained. The officer nodded. Oh, he would have a story to tell his comrades, in the privacy of the barracks.

They returned to the car with their booty, and drove on past the Gorki Theater at the south end of the square. The theater was a bastion of culture for those residents who resented the city's reputation as a manufacturing town. She had been inside its Corinthian-columned hall where the philharmonic orchestra played. The seats had velvet backs, and there were crystal chandeliers. In there, one could almost forget what the real world was like.

They shopped for groceries. The assortment wasn't much, but she knew how to make do. She bought potatoes, cabbage, lettuce, chicken, peppers, some canned fruits, dark bread, butter, and a small jug of quality wine. She would have a good meal for the general. She did not know his tastes, but he would surely appreciate the civilian flavor of it.

They returned to the bunker, and the officer carried in her purchases. "I can handle it," she offered.

"By no means, lady. It is my pleasure." And she was sure it was. For an hour he could imagine himself married to a woman like her. It would be a high point in his grim tour of duty, and the envy of his comrades.

Od and General Khrushchev had evidently completed their review of the security measures. She got busy in the bunker's kitchen, while Od unpacked cans and vegetables and put them in the cupboards and refrigerator. "Oh, I almost forgot!" she exclaimed. "I must make the bed."

Od made no move, remaining purposely busy.

"I shall be glad to assist," the general said.

"Thank you so much."

They went to the bedroom together. She stood across the bed from him, and leaned forward to tuck in the sheets. Of course her décolletage dropped, showing her breasts. The general pretended not to notice, but he, too, would have a fond memory for his evening fancies. It was another reward for his continued cooperation. She knew he was married, but his wife was surely far from the front.

They completed the bed, and she set the slippers at its foot. "His feet will be tired," she repeated for the benefit of this man. "This was the only pair I could get. At least they match the bedspread."

"Of course." Again that tacit amusement. Yes, he was enjoying this.

She returned to the kitchen and resumed activity. Khrushchev took his leave and mounted the stairs. He surely had pressing business elsewhere, and could dally no longer. He had after all seen as much as he was going to.

"Very nice," Od remarked when they were safely alone. "I got an excellent briefing, and he—" He glanced at her.

"Yes, I bent low to make the bed," she said.

"I thought you might. General Khrushchev is by far better as a friend than as an enemy, even for those not in his command. His attendance here was a fortunate break."

"We work well together," she said. "You open some doors, I open others."

"Yes. General Yeremenko will be here within the hour. He is flying in, and will be met by a car sent by General Khrushchev. I will be allowed to meet him. Then I will probably be dismissed. I will return for you when the call comes."

"That will do." She continued working. "Set the table for the general. There is genuine silverware in the drawer by the sink."

"Yes, sir," he muttered, smiling, getting on it.

Within the hour, the generals arrived. Melee and Od, warned by the phone, went up to meet them. Everyone was standing at rigid attention as the command car drew to a halt by the street door.

The generals emerged: Khrushchev and Yeremenko. They came to stand before Od and Melee. "This is my man Major Od," Khrushchev said. "Thoroughly versed in the political situation. And his lovely wife, Melee, who is catering until your household staff arrives."

Yeremenko nodded. "A pleasure. Now we must get to work. I need a thorough and rapid briefing, and a bite to eat."

"My staff is at your command."

Yeremenko's eyes narrowed slightly. "Staff? Major Od?"

"No, sir. He is here only to—"

"He and his wife will suffice, for this hour. I will call you."

Melee knew that Od was startled. This was an unexpected development.

"Yes, sir." Khrushchev saluted, perhaps disgruntled, and returned to the limousine.

"I never liked arranged presentations," Yeremenko said. "They tend to tell me what I want to hear, which is *not* what I want to hear. I hope you are competent, major."

"He is, sir," Melee said before Od could speak. "He knows everything."

"Sir, I never—"

"Show the way," the general said gruffly to Od. He did look tired. Melee had heard that he had been wounded, and was still recovering. He had been pressed back into service because he was one of Russia's most competent commanders, and the situation was desperate.

Od opened the bunker door and stepped inside, holding it for the general. Yeremenko entered. When he was out of sight of the street, he wavered a bit on his feet. Yes, he had been hiding physical weakness, and needed to rest.

Melee stepped up to his side. "There are long steps," she murmured. "If you will brace against me, sir—"

"No need." But as he passed the baffles and saw the endless stairs, he changed his mind. "Perhaps so."

She stood close, and guided his arm around her body. She knew it was her proximity as much as her steadiness that gave him strength. It was one of the effects she had on men, learned from her friend Avalanche. She could not have supported him if he had put any real weight on her. She matched him step for step, and they followed Od down.

"Thank you," the general said as he eased onto the chair at the table. He glanced at Od. "Now what do we have to work with, major?"

"Not enough, sir. As you know, the command is divided between the Southeast Front and the Stalingrad Front."

"I know." He glanced up. "Is your wife discreet?"

"She will repeat nothing she may overhear," Od assured him.

"Good, because I am too tired to maintain the protocol at the moment. If some of what I say sounds radical, blame it on fatigue. We are all loyal Communists."

"Yes, sir."

"You have a map?"

Od brought a map and spread it across the table. "The Stalingrad Front, commanded this week by General Gordov, extends from the town of Kalach, by the Don river basin forty miles west, to this command post. The new Southeast Front runs south of that line."

"Divided fronts? This is idiocy!"

"Sir?"

"It's an impossible situation, created by Stalin's meddling, instead of letting professionals handle it. No wonder we're losing the war!"

Melee brought a steaming platter and set it before the general. "You must eat, sir."

"Bless you, maiden! I'm famished."

"And wine," she said, bringing a full glass.

"Your wife is an angel," Yeremenko said to Od.

"I know, sir. Now the Germans have taken Kotelnikovo, here, seventy-three miles to the south, two days ago. That city controls the main road to Stalingrad, and the German line of approach is obvious: through Chileko, where the Siberian 208th Division has just been decimated by the Luftwaffe. Then on to Krugliakov and Abganerovo, here."

"These contour lines are interesting. They indicate hills rising two hundred to three hundred feet, following the road for twenty miles until it reaches the suburbs of Stalingrad. And they are cut across by deep ravines running from east to west. Here perhaps we can slow the German advance, though I suspect it will not be enough. Eventually we shall have to defend the city block by block."

"I fear so, sir."

They continued to discuss the prospects for defense, and Od provided positions and figures for the available troops for this purpose. Melee was silent, but she heard everything. The Germans were much closer than the official pronouncements claimed, and the city was in dire peril.

The general finished his meal and stood. "I must find the bathroom," he said, and walked into the bedroom. From there his voice came back. "Soft slippers! Just what my worn-out feet need. Let me get these damn tight boots off."

Melee breathed a silent sigh of relief. She had guessed right.

❂

Early in the morning, Heath was up and ready to go. Talena got up with him, making sure of everything. It hurt him to see her eagerness to please him, her quiet pain. She was afraid he would die on the front, and he couldn't honestly reassure her that he wouldn't.

She drove him to Railroad Station Number One, for she and the others needed the car. He kissed her as they parted, and she clung to him. "I love you," she said.

And he couldn't say it back. He did love her, but more in the manner of a sister, for all that she had borne him six daughters. "If the evacuation order comes—obey it," he said. "I want you and the girls safe."

She nodded bravely. He kissed her again, got out, and waved her off. He felt a lump in his throat. Why hadn't he said he loved her? He would be devastated if anything happened to her. Now she was gone, disappointed, and he would regret it until he saw her again.

He swung his duffel bag to his shoulder and marched into the station. The train was there, and the men were already being loaded. They were being returned to their units in the sixty-second Army beyond the river Don. In July the order had been to save men first and equipment second, in the face of the threat of encirclement. But on July 28, Premier Stalin had made a radio broadcast ordering the armies to hold at all costs. "Not one step back!" So they had to try to hold, and there were likely to be heavy casualties. That's why Heath was needed at the front. With limited medical supplies and a desperate strategic situation, this was likely to be ugly.

As an officer, he rated seating in a passenger car instead of a cattle car. So few were going west that he had the car almost to himself. This was not reassuring. A massive transfusion of men and equipment might save the front, but it was apparent that most men had managed to avoid getting sent back. There were stringent measures against desertion, but when even the officers were trying to escape apparent doom, enforcement was mixed.

He rode to Chir Station across the Don, then was trucked north to Kalach. This was where the road crossed the river and bore east to Stalingrad; it had to be held, or the Germans would have easy access to the city.

He reported to the makeshift field hospital west of Kalach. It was jammed with the wounded and dying. He was put in charge of triage for the incoming casualties: to determine almost instantly which had minor injuries and could be returned to their units after spot treatment; which had serious injuries that could be expeditiously treated; and which were too serious to merit treatment, as they would soon die anyway. The men were not to be told which category they fell into, but directed into one of three tents. Heath hated the process, but understood its necessity. This was war.

He worked until the light was insufficient. They could not use artificial lights, because fuel was scarce and they served as a magnet for German attention. He had dutifully classified all the cases, and was by then doing spot surgery to remove bullets and shrapnel. There was no proper anesthetic; vodka was it.

He ate at the officer's field mess and dropped onto his assigned bunk in a house in the town. His uniform was blood spattered, but there was little point in trying to clean it. Tomorrow would just make it worse.

The next day was August 6. When he reported to the field hospital, he learned that he was assigned to another hospital farther west. A supply truck took him there. It was worse; there were more wounded, worse off, and fewer medics. Many could have been saved, in better circumstances, but as it was, there was no hope.

Heath got to work. For some victims, water and vodka was the best he could offer. They knew they were in the dying tent. But there were difficult choices even between those who could be saved. Should he take an hour to shore up one salvageable case, when in that time he could save three others with simpler conditions? He had to try for the greatest good for the greatest number, cruel as the decision was. At least he was gaining on the backlog, for the front was for the moment quiet. Maybe the Germans had supply problems, so were resting.

In the evening, dead tired, he ate and dropped onto a bunk in the hospital. He slept amidst the groans of the suffering.

Next morning was trouble. They heard the sound of aircraft, and from the west, which meant the dread Luftwaffe. Stukas and JU-88's attacked the forward emplacements and the artillery positions of the Sixty-second Army. The blasts shook the ground, and dark smoke coiled up into the sky. Close behind came shells from German tanks. It was a major attack.

Heath sent a man to the local HQ to find out what the instructions were for the field hospital. The man returned with grim news: "Sir, the line is dead. The officers have fled to Stalingrad. No one is in command."

"The officers deserted their posts?" Heath asked, unwilling to credit it.

"Yes, sir. You are the ranking remaining officer at this site. You will have to make the decision."

"I am an officer only by courtesy. I'm a doctor. I know nothing of command."

The man just stood there. Heath realized that he didn't feel free to contradict an officer, but still needed an answer. "Fetch the ranking noncommissioned officer."

"Yes, sir." The man saluted and left.

Heath stared across the hospital tent. He could see that several of his patients had died overnight, and several more were getting there. A number could not be moved without severe threat to their lives. But with the Germans attacking, they could not remain here. What was he to do?

A sergeant approached. He saluted. "Sir."

Heath returned the salute. "Are you the ranking noncom here?"

"Yes, sir."

"And am I the ranking officer here?"

"Yes, sir."

"In your opinion, is our situation salvageable?"

"No, sir."

"Then I think we shall have to surrender to the Germans."

"Sir?"

"It is my understanding that they treat prisoners reasonably well, sending them back to work camps in Germany. My patients here can't flee, so may have a chance. Spread the word that this hospital will surrender when the Germans come, and that those associated will be part of that decision. Since this is not in accordance with our directives, any who wish to go to join other units toward the rear will be allowed to go." He paused. "This includes you, sergeant. Spread the word, then do as you decide."

The man swallowed. "Yes, sir." He saluted again and departed. Heath had just given him and the other men leave to retreat without being charged with desertion.

The sound of the enemy shells seemed to become loud.

Heath saw to his patients as well as he could, bringing them water and vodka. The food had run out, and no more would be coming in. His directive had seen to that.

An hour later, the sergeant returned with a number of men. "How can we help, sir?"

Heath was surprised. "I thought not to see you again, sergeant."

"Leaving you alone here felt more like desertion than staying with you to surrender, sir. You know you face court-martial if ever returned to Russia."

"I know. But I will be the only one. The rest of you will be obeying my orders. You may disagree with them, but must nevertheless obey. This is the way it will be recorded. So you will not be punished."

"We understand, sir. It is a brave thing you do."

"It is a desperate thing I do. I can't leave my patients."

"We approve your decision, sir."

That was gratifying. "Distribute our remaining supplies to those patients who can best use them. Raise a white flag over the tent. Stack your weapons and raise your hands when you see the advance enemy units."

"Yes, sir."

"This is a gamble. We know the Germans are capable of atrocities." Heath raised his voice. "Any of you who wish to depart now, to rejoin units farther back, are free to do so. It is a course I recommend."

Several men did reconsider and depart. The rest kept working.

Too soon, the supplies were gone. There was nothing to do but wait. "I think it is still possible for you to escape," Heath said to the men. "There are risks in remaining here."

No one answered.

"I treated some partisans who had fought behind enemy lines last year during the German drive on Moscow," Heath said. "They had seen first-hand the brutality of which the Nazis are capable. One saw a young school-teacher who tried to resist rape cut limb from limb, and then her torso was ripped open from crotch to naval with a bayonet." He looked around. "If any of you were partisans who might be identified by the Germans, you had better leave."

"We have heard the stories, too, sir," the sergeant said. "Russian prisoners and civilians were shot, stabbed, burned by flame throwers, or marched across minefields. The Gestapo tortured some to death on racks or with wires run into their orifices. One had his hands tied to the tail of a horse, and then they spooked the horse, so that he was dragged through the snow of a forest. But regular German army troops are better. They are more likely to treat us fairly."

Heath nodded. "I hope so."

By day's end, the German advance guard appeared. Heath stood outside the tent, carrying a white flag. Several rifles were trained on him, and a German beckoned him forward. He obeyed, his hands raised.

"*Sprechen sie Deutsch?*" the German soldier demanded.

"Yes, I speak German," Heath said in that language. "I am Major Heath, and this is my field hospital. Our situation is hopeless, and we are surrendering."

In a moment a German officer came. "Tell your men to put their hands on their heads and sit on the ground."

Heath walked back to the tent and relayed the directive in Russian. The men did it.

The Germans quickly checked the tent. There was no doubt of its nature. "We will do what we can for your wounded," the officer said. "But we must tend to our own casualties first. You understand."

"I understand," Heath agreed.

"Your men will be shipped to work camps in the Fatherland."

"Yes."

"But you are an officer. You must be sent back to headquarters for interrogation."

"I understand."

"Will you give your word as an officer to obey all directives and take no hostile action against Germans?"

Heath nodded. "I give my word."

The officer in turn nodded. The guns that had been trained on him were put away. This was a good sign, and not merely because they had ceased threatening him with instant death. It meant that these were indeed regular military units, with normal standards of honor. The men and the patients would be treated according to the international protocols of war. There would be no unwarranted brutality.

He was taken to a truck. He rode in back with several injured German soldiers. "I am a doctor," he said to the sergeant in charge. "Do you wish me to look at your men's wounds?"

The man considered. Then he nodded. But he kept his hand close to his pistol.

Heath lifted the stained arm of the nearest man. He peeled away the material of the shredded shirt. "It is a clean wound," he said. "The bullet passed through. But loss of blood is a danger. Is there material for a bandage?"

The sergeant indicated a blanket. That wasn't good, but it was better than nothing. "Are there heavy scissors?"

The sergeant shook his head.

"A knife, then. A bayonet will do."

The sergeant brought out his bayonet blade.

"Cut a length of a meter, eight centimeters broad," Heath said.

The sergeant sliced a section of approximately those dimensions. Heath wrapped it carefully and snugly around the man's arm. "That will stanch the bleeding, and allow clotting," he said. "Until you reach a hospital."

He turned to the next. This one had a head wound. Blood was streaking down his face. "I must clean this, to see what it is," he said. "Is there water?"

The sergeant lifted his canteen. Following Heath's directions, he cut a section of blanket about the size of a washcloth and wet it down. Then Heath used it to wipe the blood away from the matted scalp. "You are lucky," he said as he bandaged it. "It is superficial. Get rest and sleep, and it will mend."

But the next case was more serious. "There is shrapnel in your gut. You must get to a hospital promptly, before it poisons you."

"Take it out!" the man gasped.

"Even if I had surgical equipment with me, it would be dangerous, in a bouncing truck, in septic conditions. And you will need anesthetic."

"Take it out!" the man repeated.

The sergeant spoke. "We are six hours from a hospital. Are you competent?"

"In a hospital, with proper equipment, I would be. I am a surgeon. But even were I not an enemy captive, this is dangerous."

"Will he live six hours untreated?"

"I can't answer that. It depends on many factors."

"What chances?"

"Perhaps fifty per cent. It's a serious injury."

"Then take it out," the sergeant said.

"But I could kill him!"

"And I could kill you," the sergeant said, touching his pistol.

And they would call it an attempt to fight or escape, and there would be no investigation. Also, the man did need prompt attention. "Then I will need strong spirits," Heath said. "For my hands, to sterilize them, and for him to drink, in lieu of anesthetic. Also a knife. Cloth. A man to assist me. Two more to hold his arms, and one his legs. This will not be pretty."

"We know," the sergeant said grimly. He gave orders, and the men Heath had already treated were drafted as his assistant and "holder," along with others who could manage.

They produced a bottle of vodka someone had liberated from Russian territory. The sergeant handed over his bayonet, then withdrew and drew his pistol. He did not point it at Heath, but his meaning was plain. That bayonet would be used only on the patient, or there would be a bullet through the doctor's head.

The patient drank vodka while Heath cleaned the wound. He thought it was operable, but couldn't be sure until he tried.

"The truck must stop moving," he said. "If it swerves or bounces while I use the bayonet—"

They understood. The sergeant pounded on the back of the cab. The truck pulled over and stopped. "He *what?*" the driver demanded.

"This man will die," the sergeant said. "I have seen it before. The shrapnel must come out. The doctor can do it."

And so Heath operated with the point of a bayonet, while others held the half-drunk soldier down. He probed with the point, and found the shrapnel. It was not too deep. He had done similar work before, successfully.

"Your hands," he said to the designated assistant. The man held them out, and Heath poured vodka on them. "Now hold his belly open, like this," he said, demonstrating. The man gulped, and did so.

The patient writhed, then fainted. Several of the other soldiers looked squeamish. They had seen wounds before, but not surgery.

Carefully Heath worked the metal loose, while the man writhed. It was not too ragged, another blessing. The internal damage was not as bad as it could have been.

He got it out, then closed the wound and bound layers of blanket over it. "There will be internal bleeding," he said. "But he should live until he reaches the hospital. Keep him flat and quiet. Give him more vodka if he wants it."

Grimly, they nodded.

He wiped off the bayonet and returned it to the sergeant. The sergeant accepted it, then holstered his pistol. The men returned to their places in the truck, and it resumed its journey.

The patient woke. "Is it out?"

"It is out," Heath reassured him. "But you must rest. You are not out of danger, because of sepsis and bleeding."

"I will make it," the man said, and lapsed back into unconsciousness.

"Now I will see to the others," Heath said. He got busy, doing minor repairs, until all had been treated to the extent possible. In several cases it was mainly reassurance that their wounds were not lethal.

After that, the Germans were more affable. They shared their rations with Heath, and chatted about civilian life. Heath relaxed, and caught up on sleep. He had been short of it for the past couple of days.

They finally reached the German hospital facility, and the serious case was unloaded on a stretcher. The others went afoot. Heath was taken to a detainment area for interrogation. He did not look forward to it; the Gestapo and SS had some cynical notions about the rights of prisoners of war. But he had done what he had to do, to protect the welfare of the patients in the field hospital. It was possible that the Germans would kill them, but he hoped that they would merely intern them and let them recover.

For several days he waited, one of several officers who had been captured. They were treated reasonably well, considering. Their accommodations were Spartan, but they were fed regularly, and there were no cruel games, such as pretending to execute one of them. From the others, and from jubilant guards, he learned that the Russian attempt to hold the line at the river Don had been a disaster. In four days the Germans overran it, taking more than 50,000 prisoners and 1,000 tanks. The only bright spot was that the Germans halted their advance west of the Don, pausing to secure their lines and prepare for the river crossing. Heath knew that every day of the delay was crucial for the defensive preparations of Stalingrad.

Then they came for him. He went with his chin high, but he feared what he was about to encounter. He was not supposed to give military information, but was not at all sure how he would stand up to torture.

He was surprised to be ushered to an office with a lone thin man whose uniform showed him to be a doctor. What was this?

"You are Dr. Heath," the man said briskly.

"Yes, sir."

"I am Dr. Ottmar Kohler, of the Reich sixtieth Motorized Division. I have been associated with it since its formation in 1939. Have you heard of me?"

"No, sir."

"Then allow me to provide you with a capsule summary culled from the gossip of associates. I am notorious for my brilliance, acerbic attitude, and occasional wildness. I care little for the chain of command or the niceties of regulations. My first priority is the effectiveness of my medical treatment, and I spare no effort to enhance it." He gave Heath a straight look. "Do you have a problem with any of this?"

"Only with the freeness with which you describe yourself to an enemy prisoner, sir. If you are warning me that you are a dangerous man to oppose, I can believe it. But I don't see why you bother, since I have no power to interfere with you anyway."

Kohler did not answer directly. "Is it true that you did abdominal surgery on a German soldier, with a bayonet, in a moving truck, thereby saving his life?"

"Approximately, sir. They had to stop the truck while I extracted shrapnel. I am glad to learn that he survived."

"An enemy national? Are you not loyal to your country?"

"Of course, sir. But he was a man in need. Actually, I tried to demur, as it was a very chancy operation, but the sergeant insisted."

"You could have killed him without anyone suspecting."

"I was afraid he might die," Heath agreed. Then he caught the thrust of the remark. "Sir, I would never deliberately harm a person medically. I am a doctor."

"Precisely. And it seems a good one." Kohler considered. "Heath, I want you with me."

"Sir?"

"For months I have been preparing a plan for medical personnel to treat the wounded within minutes of their being hit, rather than waiting hours for them to be evacuated to rear echelon hospitals. But I am balked by the inanities of regulation and the shortage of competent personnel. Men are dying while I struggle with the bureaucrats. I need a competent doctor who answers only to me. I believe you are that man, Heath."

"But I am a prisoner being routed to a work camp. A Russian."

"And an excellent surgeon and honest man. I can take you from that routing to the work camp, which I assure you, you would not enjoy. I want you to swear loyalty to my purpose, treating German casualties promptly and well. In return I will allow you to treat Russian prisoners also, as the occasion permits. You will thus save lives of your countrymen who would otherwise die."

"But the German authorities would never allow—"

"They need not know. You will be my private aide. You will have to wear a German uniform, but that is only for your own protection. You will have freedom of the unit, and will be well cared for. It will be a far, far better life than the alternative that awaits you."

"But to labor in the support of Germany—"

"And what were you doing when you treated German soldiers on the truck?"

"They were people in need."

"As will be all future cases. It is not Germany you will labor for, but the lives of individual men who are caught up in the endless folly of war. Germans must serve just as Russians must, and give their lives, however point-lessly."

It was a fair case. Yet Heath was doubtful. "I don't see how I can agree to such service, kind as the offer is."

"I will sweeten the offer. Serve me, and I will serve you."

"Sir?"

"When we get to Stalingrad, where I believe your family is, I will release you. You will not serve in a work camp, and you will be free. To save your daughters."

The man had done his homework! Heath had to return to save his wife and children if he possibly could. Dr. Kohler had made an offer he could not decline.

"Then I must agree to serve you," Heath said. "Until Stalingrad."

"Excellent." Kohler stood and came around the desk, proffering his hand. They shook hands, sealing the deal.

✪

The two women gazed at him with wary expectation as he set down the phone. "Yes," Od said heavily. "It has been confirmed that Heath was captured by the Germans. He refused to leave the wounded men in a field hospital, who couldn't be moved. All the other officers of the region fell back, but he remained. He sent all available men back to rear units, and waited with his patients."

"He would," Talena said, turning away to hide her tears.

"But that doesn't mean he's dead, does it?" Melee asked quickly. "Just that he's being sent back to Germany."

"That's right. He is probably well, but we are unlikely to see him again until after the war is over."

"That will have to do," Talena said. "As long as he's alive."

"What do we tell the children?" Melee asked.

"That their father is away at war." He smiled a trifle grimly. "That will satisfy their need to know."

"For a while," Talena said.

"Who will take me to the office?" he asked.

There was a pause. The two women exchanged glances. Then they seemed to come to a silent understanding.

"I have to shop," Talena said. "I'll do it."

"Get more potatoes," Melee told her. "And some peppers."

"Yes, dear." Talena kissed her on the mouth, patted her rear, and took the keys.

Od had to smile. They were acting as if they were the couple, making a joke of it. In the building tension of the threat to the city, humor helped. He was glad the women got along so well. They were the same age, but their underlying temperaments differed like day and night.

It was the morning of August 13, 1942. The German advance seemed inexorable, but so far the city of Stalingrad didn't know it. Children and dogs were out on the streets, running errands and enjoying the air before the daily heat became unbearable.

Talena drove, so they wouldn't have to exchange places when he got off. "Is there any other news on Heath?" she asked, her voice artificially light.

"No. I wish there were. But the Germans treat officers more carefully, just as we do, so he should be all right."

"I hope so. The girls adore him."

"As if you don't?"

She was silent, and he realized that he had said something inappropriate. "I didn't mean to imply—"

"You don't know, do you, Od."

Something was amiss. "I apologize for any offense I may have given. I thought I was speaking humorously."

"Heath doesn't love me."

Od was caught flat-footed by the statement. Talena would never joke about that. The tension had to be getting to her. "I don't understand. You are the perfect couple."

"He loves Melee."

Od stared at her. "You and Heath never even quarrel! And you get along so well with Melee. This doesn't make sense."

"I wish I had let him have her, instead of making her go with you. Then at least he would have had some joy of her before he got captured and lost the chance."

"Heath would never cheat on you!" he protested.

"That's right. He never would. That's why I had to make the decision, to make it possible. And I didn't. I was selfish. And now he's gone."

Od's head was spinning. He had never anticipated anything like this. "He can return after the war."

"By which time she may be dead."

Then he came at another aspect. "Are you saying I should not have married Melee? I thought we were agreed."

"We were. It was so convenient, to put the odd man with the odd woman, no pun. But we should have realized it was too pat."

"Melee is a fine woman! She—"

"Do you love her?"

"What kind of a question is that?"

"I'm not trying to insult you. As we know, you married her from friendship, and to take care of her, in memory of Dillon. None of us spoke of love."

"I think in time—she is the most exciting woman I've known."

"And Heath is the best man I've known. But he longs for Melee, and she longs for him."

"How can you know that?"

"We talked, she and I. And Avalanche."

"Even then? Before they died on the German front last year?"

"Even then. And now we have talked again. We have—similar marriages."

There was vastly more here than he could assimilate at the moment. "Are you saying that you should have broken your marriage, to give your husband to another woman?"

"That is what I am saying. I love Heath, and I want him to be happy. That would have done it."

"Talena, why are you saying this to me?"

She faced him for a moment, and he saw the tears on her face. "Because I made a mistake, out of misbegotten selfishness, and I should correct it if I ever have the chance. If Heath returns, I want to tell him to take Melee. But that affects you, obviously. I don't have the right to steal your woman for my man."

"She's really not my woman. I wouldn't try to tell her what to do." But he was shaken. Melee had filled in so well for Avalanche, even emulating some of her mannerisms, that sometimes he forgot about the intervening tragedy. "But she never said—never hinted—"

"She wouldn't cheat either. That's why you would have to release her."

"If she had ever spoken—"

"And if we freed them, you would be left with me. Could you stand that, Od?"

His amazement grew. "You are—you are offering yourself to me?"

"I suppose I am, Od. The true love is between Heath and Melee. We are the leftovers. I know you to be a fine man, and I think I would be as well off with you as with Heath. Setting aside the issue of love, which I seem destined not to have."

Od struggled to get the concept organized. "You are suggesting that we each release our spouses to be with the other. And that you and I become a couple. On the theory that neither of us is loved by our present partner, so we don't have much to lose."

"Yes. At least two people would be happy, instead of none."

"What of the children?"

"That's part of why I asked. They do come with the territory. I will not give them up."

"What would they think, if the couples realigned?"

"Heath is a fine man, and he does try, but the truth is, you are better with the children, Od. You have such a ready way with incidental information. You teach them while making them laugh. They would accept you. I would be completely candid with them. I think they would understand. The question is you. Is this a thing you can contemplate? Because if it isn't, I will neither do it nor bring it up again."

"Let me think," he said, disturbed.

She was silent, and he turned his mind to the problem, as if it were something apart from himself. Man B loved Woman A, but was married to Woman B. Could Man A accept Woman B? It seemed no more arbitrary than the original coupling of Man A and Woman A. Intellectually he could accept it. Woman A was a beautiful, passionate, dynamic creature, a joy to be with, but it was clear now that something was missing. Woman B was less lovely, but by no means unattractive, and had qualities to be admired. He had known her many years, and though he had never thought of her as a romantic possibility, she was an almost perfect friend.

But there was another question, and it was vital. "If you will bear with me, there is something I would like to do, and a question I must ask. Then perhaps I can answer."

She steered the car to the side of the road, in a section where no one was close. She turned to him. She had anticipated his thought. She knew him as well as he knew her.

He took her upper section in his arms as well as was feasible, and brought his face to hers. He kissed her.

And she kissed him back. Suddenly he was aware of her as a woman just as passionate as those he had known, and completely desirable. She was nobody's leftover.

The kiss was long, much longer than he had intended. It didn't want to be over. Finally he broke. "I think I have my answer."

"Yes, I could love you," she said, answering the unasked question. "In time."

"And I could love you. In less time."

"We are after all right for each other. In the long term."

"Yes. As other than friends."

She started the car and pulled back onto the street. "Thank you, Od. If Heath returns—"

"Yes. Tell him. But talk to Melee first."

"I have. She did not want to broach this with you. So we agreed that I would do it. To explore a possible realignment. But Heath also must be broached. Until then—"

"We are as we were. It must be agreed by all parties, before any action is taken."

"Agreed."

They reached the office building on Red Square. Talena stopped by the curb, and Od got out. "You have given me much to think about," he said.

"I have been thinking about it for a year," she said. "It is a relief to share it." Then she drove on, heading for her shopping.

He entered the building. He showed his papers, but the guard hardly glanced at them; Od was known by sight. He went upstairs almost unconsciously. What Talena had said—she had dropped a mortar shell on him, and he was only beginning to experience its fallout. To exchange partners—he had never thought of such a thing, yet it made eerie sense. He was well satisfied with Melee, but she had never said she loved him, and he had never said he loved her. Both were survivors of lost partners; they understood that about each other perfectly, and knew why they were together. Melee was a sexual delight, and excellent cook. But they had not yet even tried to form a long-term emotional commitment. Their losses were too close behind, and the war was too close ahead. He had thought that was the whole of it; now he knew it was barely the half of it.

Could he make it with Talena? He remembered when he had first seen her, a girl of thirteen but already nubile. She had gone after Heath even then, and gotten him despite her age. Now she was twenty-two, the same as Melee, whom he had known even longer. But Talena was a mother, many times over, and that provided her with a seeming maturity. He found that he liked the idea of sharing her family and her nights. She was a comfortable woman, and her daughters were well behaved. The eldest, Telita, better known as Lita, was a remarkably responsible eight-year-old. Yes, they were all familiar and nice. It was just the realignment of relationships that made him dizzy.

"Stalin has come to his senses," Nikita Khrushchev said as Od entered the office. "General Gordov has been demoted, and General Yeremenko is being given complete control of Stalingrad's defense. Get over there and see if he needs any help."

Od was actually a glorified messenger these days, because constant liaison was essential, and they trusted neither the phone system nor written messages. So Od passed back and forth between the offices, keeping this as constant as was feasible. He worked for Khrushchev, but had been on good terms with Yeremenko since Melee had served the general his first local meal. Regular personnel had taken over now, but Melee's radiance evidently still imbued Od in the general's eyes.

He got a car and driver, and took a circuitous route to the bunker. This was for two reasons: they did not want any more direct traffic there than necessary, lest German spies catch on and report the location for targeting for an enemy barrage; and it was best to survey the city regularly so as to know what was what. This time they looped through the western suburbs. The civilian population seemed confident and unafraid, perhaps because of its lack of accurate information. That was just as well, because panic would be no help at all. There were crude signs on trees and buildings promising DEATH TO THE INVADER.

But in the military, discipline and order were breaking down. Od could tell there was trouble just by driving the streets. The city garrison was in disorder, and military traffic was snarled and disorganized. Vehicles were wandering around as if lost, and an accident was blocking traffic.

Od stopped, and approached an NKVD "Green Hat." "Major Od, with Khrushchev," he said, showing his papers. "What's going on here?"

"Sir, the commander of the city garrison disappeared, and soldiers are deserting. They are fleeing across the Volga. We are doing our best, but we need better support."

"You shall have it," Od said. He got moving, cutting short his impromptu tour. The general needed to be informed about this.

General Yeremenko was indeed interested. "Things are falling apart," he muttered. "Too many leaks; too many troops back from the front who know better than the propaganda in the paper." He got on the phone, acting quickly to restore order and discipline to his command. Then he ordered a pontoon bridge to be built across the Volga, to speed up the process of reinforcement and supply.

The developments of the front were alarming. The German Sixth Army, commanded by General Paulus, was moving in from the west, ready to cross the river Don. But worse was the Fourth Panzer Army, under the aggressive General "Papa" Hoth. This force was moving along well-built roads, and had no rivers or rough terrain to cross. The units dug into the hills around Abganerovo were in short supply and had little heavy support. Already much of the Russian Sixty-Fourth Army was in retreat from the German tanks. Casualties were high, both from combat and fatigue. The troops were disillusioned and desperate, fighting among themselves for scraps of food and water.

Especially water. The Kalmucks, natives of the steppes south of the city, were ardent anti-Communists. They had poisoned most of the few water holes that existed in that arid countryside. Yeremenko arranged to send all the support he could muster, to slow the German advance. That was fifty-nine tanks. They were enough for nothing much other than a suicide attack. If they were lucky, it would delay the German advance one more day.

Od winced. Fifty-nine tanks and their crews sent to their doom, not with any hope of victory, but merely to slow the inevitable by a single day. The price of time was blood. Would the widows appreciate the need?

And the civilians were to be told nothing. There was no point in inciting panic in the streets. But how long could this go on, before further concealment was impossible?

It was a long day, and it was late when Od called home to be picked up. This time it was Melee who drove. "She said she talked to you," she said.

"She did." No need to ask who. Od re-oriented on the novel personal situation. Maybe it would ease the burden of his knowledge of the disaster closing in on the city. Life was becoming increasingly precious, as his awareness of its uncertainty intensified.

"She said you agreed."

"I said I would, if Heath does."

"He will."

"And if you do."

"I do. No offense to you, Od. If you decline, I will too. But I do want him."

Obviously so. "She surprised me. I had not had any idea."

"She surprised me too. I knew she knew, but I never thought she would give Heath up."

"It's just a notion for the future. You must talk with Heath."

"Od, we are at war. We don't have time. We have to do what we do when we can."

He glanced at her. "You act as if it has been decided."

"Will you let me go?"

"I never had any right to hold you. You have been wonderful, but—"

"You can have her tonight."

"What?"

"Let me go. Take her. If you are willing. She is."

"You really want this," he said, surprised despite what Talena had said, and what Melee had just said.

"Yes. I suppressed it before, thinking there was no chance. I was willing to try with you, Od. There has been no failure in you. You are the best of men. But now I know Talena is willing, I want it. I could love him."

"Then I will not stand in your way."

"I knew you wouldn't. But are you willing? I mean, not because of duty or decency, but because you might have a woman who is better for you than I am."

"That is hard to imagine. You have been a dream. But I always wanted more than beauty or passion. I wanted enduring love. I didn't have that with Avalanche, and couldn't have it with you. If Talena can give me that, she will be better for me."

"She can give you that."

"Regardless, you are free to do what you choose." He still found it hard to believe that the women had agreed to such a change.

Her mouth firmed. "Not until I know you are satisfied."

"But she is Heath's wife! I can't just—"

"And if he never returns?"

He pondered that. "I would be forsaking you for a widow. Making you the real widow. That hardly seems decent."

"Let me gamble on that. I want to take him the moment he returns. I know he will agree. He has always desired me. Free me. Take her tonight."

She was actually urging it on him. "I free you. I won't necessarily take her."

"They go together. If you are not in her bed, you must be in mine."

"She may not be ready." But again his awareness of the likely brevity of their life in Stalingrad influenced him. He wanted very much to be comforted and loved, this night. Melee was a great lover, but not a great comforter.

"She is ready."

"I feel as if I am on a truck being driven by a madman."

She smiled. "A car driven by a madwoman. Is it that you still desire me?"

"I'll always desire you, Melee. You are the world's most desirable woman. But it's the larger picture that concerns me. You must give me time."

"Then join her, and do no more than you wish. I will take care of the children."

"Agreed." That was a fair compromise, given the situation. He could sleep beside Talena and let her sleep.

They arrived home. "We talked," Melee said, and went to see about supper.

Talena looked at him.

"I will share the bedroom with you," Od said. "It need go no farther than that."

She nodded, and returned to the children.

One thing about this: it distracted him from the looming horror of the German advance.

When the children were asleep, Od went to join Talena. They lay beside each other in the darkness. "We agreed there would be nothing, until Heath returned," he said. "But Melee says she wants it settled before then, so she is free."

"Yes. Were he here, we could discuss it openly. But I know him. Once he knows the others agree, he will too. He would prefer that it be already decided, so that he has no complicity."

Od had had every intention of letting her be. But her very presence was compelling. He had known her so long as a friend, but never as a lover. He was rapidly coming to see her in that new light. "So it is between us. Do you wish me to touch you?"

He expected a demurral, or a counter question. But she answered directly. "Yes."

"Are you being honest with me?"

"I have seen a better course for us all, and want to confirm it. But I do need my sleep. I can't sleep until I know. Touch me."

He reached out and found her hand. Then he turned on his side, lifted his head, and kissed her lips. "What I want may not be what you care to provide."

"I can't be forward, the way she is," she said. "Tell me what you want."

He laughed uncomfortably. "I want to be at ease." That was an understatement. He wanted someone to cradle his head and reassure him that everything in the city would be all right, and make him believe it.

She laughed too. "All this time we have known each other, and it's as if we just met. We don't know what to do."

"Should we pretend we are two other people?"

"Heath and Melee!"

He liked that. "Hello, Melee."

"It's been decided. Od is with Talena. I'm with you now, Heath."

"But I know nothing of this!"

She turned into him and caught him with a fierce kiss. "You are mine at last, Heath!"

"But Melee—"

She pushed him down and straddled him with arms and legs. "I have stored up this passion for you for ten years. Now I will express it."

"But you were only twelve."

"If you had even looked at me, I would have done this." She kissed him, and ran her tongue into his mouth. "And this." She tore at his pajamas.

"But I wouldn't have dared do this." He slid his hands up under her nightie, finding her hanging breasts.

"And I wouldn't have dared do this." She slid a hand down and found his stiffening penis.

"But now you are not twelve, so it is all right for me to do this." He moved his hands down and around, cupping her buttocks and stroking her genital region.

"I am not twelve," she agreed, guiding his member into her. For a moment he was startled, because that was exactly the way Melee did do it, and the way Avalanche had done it. Evidently it was a trick all women knew, when they wished to facilitate things. And she did so wish, for she was warm and wet. He had seen the real Melee lubricate herself with saliva, and knew it was because she was not sexually excited. She did the job she meant to do, and did it well—very well!—but it was not desire. This time there was desire.

"Talena!" he said.

She lifted her head, and he felt her body stiffen. "Did I offend you? I'm sorry."

"No! It's that I want it to be you, not Melee. You and me only. No games."

"Of course." She did not relax.

He had to explain. "You truly desire me."

"Yes." She was still waiting for the rejection.

"You don't have to be anybody else. You don't have to justify it. I want—I want a woman who wants me."

Now she relaxed somewhat. "I want you."

"And I want you. Kiss me."

She pressed against him, all cotton and softness, and found his mouth with hers. No tongue, just lips and passion. He felt her vagina squeeze rhythmically, responsive to the kiss. He stroked her back with one hand, and her hair with the other, drawing her in closer, pressing her against him, feeling her breathing. He swelled and flowed into her, softly yet with the force of years of longing, and felt her yielding reception. She wanted so much to love and be loved, exactly as he did. How was it that they had never found each other before?

Finally they had to break the kiss, and come apart. "I think I must always have wanted you," he said. "But never thought to have you."

"I think I was a fool."

"No, Heath was a better prospect. That was always clear."

"What is clear is not always true."

He said it before he realized: "Talena, I love you."

She did not answer immediately. Then she said: "Let me wait until the light of day, to know for sure, before I reply. A decade's illusion is not cast off in an hour."

"I am not sure of that." For he had just done it.

"Neither am I. I think I know what I will say. But now—must we separate to sleep?"

"And you like to sleep close," he said, relishing the discovery. "Be forever close." He hesitated, then finally said it: "Comfort me." That was something Melee simply did not understand. Did Talena?

"In a moment." She rolled off him, and did some quick cleaning up. Then she returned, and he embraced her, and kissed her hair.

"You mean it?" she asked. "About comfort?"

"Oh, yes. Does that embarrass you?"

"Oh, no." She reached up and caught his head between her hands. She drew it in to her warm bosom.

He listened to the cadence of her gently beating heart, and drifted into a sleep that seemed like heaven.

❂

Talena woke as the telephone rang. Od got it; he was being routed out of sleep increasingly often, these recent days. Soon he returned to her in the darkness of the bedroom. "I must go in to the bunker. Hell is breaking loose."

"I'll take you," she said, scrambling up.

"Yes." He was getting efficiently dressed. They had all had to learn how to do such things without light, because of the blackouts.

Melee appeared, a dusky shadow. "Is it bad?"

"Keep the children close, and stay in range of the phone," he said tersely.

They bundled out to the car, and Talena took the wheel. The city traffic had diminished in the past week, and this early hour decreased it farther, which was a blessing. It meant that they could proceed fairly quickly.

"You aren't supposed to ask, and I'm not supposed to tell," Od said. "But I think you had better know. Promise not to spread this about."

"I promise." She was more than curious, because in the ten days since they had first made love and discovered love, he had grown increasingly nervous and harried, and she was sure it wasn't because of her. It had to be the war.

"The Germans have crossed the Don and are racing toward Stalingrad from the northwest, west, and south. They are within twenty-five miles of the city, executing a classic pincers movement. Hitler has decreed that the city must fall by August twenty-fifth."

"But that's the day after tomorrow!"

"General Paulus' Sixth Army is moving to block the Russian retreat, as tank columns bear south and the Fourth Panzer Army moves from the south. We probably can't stop them. We must either retreat immediately across the Volga, under the fire of the German guns and bombers, or try to stand and fight. Stalin will not allow retreat, so that's out. So we must prepare to defend the city block by block. We are trying to deploy our scant remaining forces along a thirty-one-mile perimeter to the northwest. These are internal security troops who lack heavy weapons, but they are all we have. When the Germans come, our best hope is that they aren't as good at street fighting as they are in open battle. But it will be ugly."

"And soon!" Talena said. "Two days!"

"Maybe longer. The fact that Hitler wants it doesn't mean Hitler will get it. But we can expect hell on earth here, as early as today. You must take the children and go. Take the ferry across the Volga. Don't speak to anyone else, just quietly go."

"But the neighbors! They must be warned."

He looked soberly at her. "Two things: if you tell, you will be breaking my word, making me eligible for court-martial. And the neighborhood will panic. They can't all evacuate today; there are not enough ferries. Maybe the pontoon bridge we are just now completing will help. But there is nothing but mischief in telling the neighbors."

She realized that it was true. "We will take the children and go. Better some than none."

"Better some than none," he agreed grimly.

But she hated it. "War is hell."

"I will check back on you if I can. But don't wait for me. You and Melee and the children must get out. I will contact you across the river, in due course. It may be days."

"I understand." They were arriving at the building.

"I love you, Talena."

She stopped at the curb. "I love you, Od." She leaned over to kiss him.

He got out, and she drove on. She had her orders.

But before she was halfway home, she bumped over a rough spot and the car's motor sputtered and died. Oh, no! Not this! Not now! She tried to start it again, but it was dead.

Od could have fixed it, as he was endlessly handy with all things mechanical. But she had no idea what to do. She would have to walk on home, and see if they could get a neighbor to work on it.

She got out and started walking. But this was not simple, because now people were appearing on the street, and she knew that she could not depend on civilized behavior. As a young woman alone, she could quickly get in trouble. So she detoured to take a street that was not much used, and detoured again when she saw anything suspicious. As a result, it took her much longer to get home than she liked.

Melee met her at the door. "What kept you?"

"The car broke down. We've got to get it fixed right away."

"For sure. Maybe Tourette's folks can help."

Talena considered. Tourette was a sixteen-year-old girl with an unfortunate behavioral syndrome, but she was a really nice person, and her family was competent. "I'll ask them."

"No. You're already tired from walking. Lita can go. It's not far, and she's a savvy girl."

Reluctantly, Talena agreed. She told her daughter where the car was, and what its symptoms were. "Tell them the matter is urgent," she said.

"I will!" Lita ran off, glad to be doing something useful.

"Now tell me what else you are so tight about," Melee said.

"It's secret. Od told me, but—"

"I understand. No broadcasting."

"The Germans are within twenty-five miles of the city, and coming fast. They mean to take it within two days. We've got to get out today, with the children, and we can't tell the neighbors."

Melee whistled. "I thought it was bad, but this is worse. Of all times for the car to go!" Then she thought of another aspect. "If Tourette's folks fix our car, we'll have to tell them."

She was right. They couldn't beg a life-saving favor of a neighbor, and leave that neighbor to the mercy of the Nazis. The Nazis made folk like Tourette disappear. "Them only."

They organized the children for an early departure. Whatever food they had was distributed in bags, so that if they missed a meal, the children would have something to eat. They were cautioned to stay in the house and be ready to get in the car promptly when it came. They behaved; it was clear that something extremely serious was afoot.

Lita came back with Tourette. Tourette was a rather pretty girl, brown of hair and eye, mature and discreet. Her malady had taught her discretion early. "My father knows about cars," she said. "But he's away on business. My mother Crenelle asks if she can help."

This wasn't good. "If she is handy with motors, yes. But it's not safe for a woman to be on the streets."

"They won't know," Tourette said. Now Talena realized that the girl was in baggy male overalls, with her long brown hair bound back and hidden under her cap. She was well developed, but at the moment she looked like a boy.

"Then I can take her there," Talena decided. "I'll change too."

The girls departed, and Talena got into some of Od's clothing. Fortunately she was thin enough in the derriere to jam in to his jeans. There was no problem with the heavy shirt; it was sufficiently loose on her.

Melee helped her fasten her hair back. "You look perfect, Mister Tal. Don't go ogling any pretty girls."

The girls and Crenelle, Tourette's mother, arrived. The woman carried a tool box and looked like a factory worker. "Tourette can stay in our house, if you wish," Talena said.

"No, I'm coming along," Tourette said.

"So am I!" Lita cried.

Talena opened her mouth, but the woman stayed her with a glance. "Please."

They were doing a favor; they deserved respect. "Stay out of mischief," Talena told her daughter.

"I will."

They started out. "We resemble three youths and a child," Crenelle said. "In case there is trouble, I must advise you that we are armed."

"Armed!"

"The city has bad elements, and order is breaking down. You are evacuating?"

"Yes. You must also. Today."

"But there has been no general evacuation order."

"I am not free to speak. But evacuate now."

"I understand." The woman knew that Od was a political officer, with sources of information.

They passed a man. He frowned disapprovingly, perhaps suspecting these juveniles of mischief, but walked on by.

They reached the car much more quickly than Talena had taken to reach the house, because they took no detours.

Crenelle immediately lifted the hood. She poked around the motor. "Now try it."

Talena tried the starter. The motor came to life. "You fixed it!" she cried, overjoyed.

"The distributor cap had been jogged loose. I had hoped it would be that. The description sounded like it."

They piled in, and Talena drove them back to the house, greatly relieved. "I don't know how I can ever thank you," she said.

"Oh, I think you have done so."

Talena thought of something. "Do you have a car?"

"My husband has it." And the woman had never hinted at the difficulty they faced, without transportation.

"Then you can't conveniently evacuate. You must come with us."

"That would be crowded."

The car held five adults. With the two of them, it would be ten people. The smaller children could double up, but it was still too much. "We'll make two trips to the ferry."

"Then we thank you, and will come."

"Get your things, and I will return for you and Lita." For Melee would have to go on the first trip, to handle the younger children. Talena would return alone.

They bundled Talena's five younger daughters and the little boy into the car. That was another thing they would have to work out: would Avan stay with Melee, or come to Talena? He was Od's son, and Od was changing families. At present he seemed to have two mothers, but that couldn't last forever. Well, it wasn't worth worrying about right now.

Talena drove, and Melee sat in back, holding Avan on her lap and half buried in four giggling little girls. The seven-year-old rode up front.

As they passed Red Square, the loudspeakers were blaring, warning of an air raid. They had done that often before, and nobody paid any attention. But this time, Talena knew, the wolf really was coming. Maybe not this hour or this day, but soon. She felt guilty, sneaking out of town like this, leaving others to suffer their fate. Yet she could not risk the children; that overrode all else.

She reached the river and looked out over the cliff to the water. They could see the new pontoon bridge. That would help a lot, as cars could drive right across it instead of having to wait for the ferry. They would soon be across, and she could return to tell the others the good news.

But as she made her way toward it, she found the road cordoned off. Military personnel were gesturing cars on by, denying the access to the turnoff to the bridge. "What's the matter?" Talena asked as she stopped.

"The pontoon bridge is being destroyed," the man informed her.

"But it was just finished!"

He rolled his eyes. "Don't I know it. The order came from General Yeremenko himself. It is to be destroyed unused."

Stunned, she drove on. "Why would they build it, and do that?" she asked.

"To keep it from falling into enemy hands," Melee said.

And that meant that the ten days it had taken to build the bridge had been too long. They expected the Germans to arrive at any moment, so didn't dare leave something they could use to forge on beyond the river. That was the most chilling signal yet.

She drove on to the ferry. "We'll wait for you," Melee said.

"No, don't wait! Cross as soon as you can. We'll take the next one."

Melee nodded. They could not say more, because of the children.

Talena watched the woman walking down to the ferry station, carrying one, leading the next youngest by the hand, and with the other four girls linking hands and following closely. There was something touching about the scene. A beautiful young woman with six children, going to the river.

But she couldn't dawdle. It was already late afternoon; somehow the day had passed unnoticed. She drove on back. She had to detour, because militia men wearing white armbands were blocking off some streets. They must be preparing for street resistance. This did not look good at all.

The loudspeakers in Red Square blared into life again. "Attention! Attention! Citizens, we have an air raid! We have an air raid!"

Talena drove as fast as she dared. But almost immediately the warning was followed by the loud bang of antiaircraft guns. People came out of their houses and stared at the sky, and Talena looked too. Where was the threat? Were German planes actually coming? All she could see were the gray puffs of the Russian flak.

But then, all too soon, came the lead group of German planes. She recognized the types, from long worried studies of the pictures. They were Stukas and JU-88s, flying in perfect V formations. The planes tipped sideways as they reached the downtown residential area, falling into their bombing dives. She saw the bombs falling, like tiny beads from the sky, as the planes zoomed on overhead and beyond.

She focused desperately on her driving. No bombs were falling on her street yet, but she heard the explosions as they struck other areas. Red Square, by the sound of it, and by the rising smoke. She had to get through while she could.

She reached her house and screeched to a stop. Tourette came out. She started to speak, as Talena got out of the car and hurried to the house, but didn't. Her face worked, and her arms twitched, but there was no sound.

Talena realized that the girl was having one of her fits. They could be triggered by tension, but usually passed quickly. She went up and put her arms around the girl, comforting her. She had always been good at that.

In a moment Tourette recovered control. "They are at our house. Lita wanted to help Mother, so I stayed here to watch for you. Then the bombs fell."

The bombs were still falling. "Get in the car," Talena said tersely. "We'll get them from there."

They got in and drove down along the block. And saw to their horror that Tourette's house had been hit. The front had collapsed, and dust and smoke were rising from it.

Appalled, they got out of the car and stood there staring.

Then Tourette spoke. "The front was hit. The back is intact. They could be there."

It was a straw well worth grasping. Talena stepped as close to the house as she dared. "Lita! Lita!"

Tourette went to the side. "Mother!"

There was a faint answer. It was Lita's shrill voice. "Mom!"

They oriented on the girl. She did indeed seem to be near the back. "Are you all right?"

"We are all right," Crenelle called. "But trapped. Debris fell across the hall."

They must have hidden in a closet or under a stout bed when they heard the bombs. That was just as well. "We'll get you out," Talena called.

They made their way around the house to the back door. It was intact, but there was debris beyond it. They pried and pulled at it, and heard the other two doing the same thing from beyond. It was nervous business, because they were afraid the fading bombers might return, and that the house might collapse worse because of their efforts. But before long they opened a twisted passage for the others to wriggle through.

They got into the car with their scant salvaged belongings, and Talena drove back across town. But now the roads were much worse, both because of the bombing and the desperate people coming out. They had to detour, and detour again, trying to pick their way through. As a result, a drive that should have been done in half an hour took over twice as long, and it was dark by the time they reached the ferry port.

There they found thousands of frightened civilians pressing impatiently against the lines of NKVD police who were trying to keep them under control. It was clear that many were leaving loved ones either dead or missing in the city; others, like themselves, were leaving family members in the militia or regular army. All of them were desperate to find space on the heavily loaded tugs and steamers being pressed into duty as evacuation craft. News of the proximity of the German front line might have been suppressed, but the bombing raid had gotten the message through: it was past time to leave the city.

Worse, there were German recognizance planes keeping tabs on them from above. The Germans knew exactly what was happening, and could strike at any moment.

They looked for Melee and the children, but couldn't see them. They walked among the refugees, inquiring, looking. They asked the NKVD personnel. Finally they found one who knew. "Beautiful woman with six children? She got the last ferry out."

She had made it! "Thank you, sir," Talena said.

"It's all right, lad." He turned away, distracted by some trouble farther along.

For a moment Talena was startled. Then she remembered that she was dressed as a male youth, as were Crenelle, Tourette, and Lita. Their struggle with the collapsed house had further mussed them. That was just as well, considering.

Now they just had to wait their turn. They walked away in the darkness, to find a private spot where they could squat and urinate. It would not be smart to advertise that they were four females ranging in age from eight to thirty-eight or so. Then they returned to the ferry port and settled down with the others to wait out the night. They nibbled on their limited food, not sharing it with strangers. That bothered Talena too, but not enough to override her common sense.

They slept on the ground below the cliff wall, on the level section between that and the river. They formed a square, each of them with her head on the lap of another. It was far from ideal, but better than nothing.

All night the boats came, picking up passengers. Talena could tell by their lights and sounds. The crowd of refugees shifted somewhat as each load went out, so that the remaining folk got closer to the front. But there were so many waiting that the boats seemed pitifully inadequate.

Talena realized that the boats were as heavily laden coming in as going out. They were bringing in reinforcements. That was encouraging. She heard some of the men grousing as they passed: it seemed they had expected to be deployed in the southern suburbs, but were instead being sent north to gird the lines around the northern factories. Naturally the brass cared more for the industry than the people! But at least they were defending the city.

In the morning there seemed to be just as many people as before, and more were arriving. But Talena, Crenelle, Tourette, and Lita were significantly farther toward the boats than they had been. They should make it out by the end of the day.

Then the German bombers reappeared. People screamed and fled as Stukas dropped bombs on the landing and launched strafing runs. The refugees were alternately driven against the cliff walls and toward the water as they tried to escape. The planes also targeted the boats, and managed to score on some. Talena saw blood and oil frothing in the churning waters of the river.

"This is no good," Crenelle said. "Even if we board a boat, it may be sunk."

Talena had to agree. Evacuation was no longer a feasible option.

They left, and made their way back to the parked car. They were lucky; it had not been touched. They got in and drove back across town. It was slow, of course, and Talena feared her petrol would run out, but they made it.

They entered the house, and Talena found something to eat. They fell into chairs and tried to relax. "You must remain here with us, of course," she told Crenelle. "I'm sorry we didn't get you evacuated."

"You tried. We have supplies we can bring and share. We girded for possible calamity long ago. Maybe the Germans will be turned back."

"Maybe." It was a forlorn hope, but they did not want the girls to be alarmed.

Then there was someone at the door. It was a man, with a large bag. "What is this?" Talena demanded.

"Get out of my way, boy. I'm cleaning out this house while I can."

"You're a looter!" she cried, outraged.

"Move!" He shoved her roughly against the wall.

"Get out!" Crenelle snapped.

The man paused. Then he backed away. "Yeah, sure, boy."

Amazed, Talena looked at the woman. She was holding a pistol. "I told you we were armed," she said.

So she had. "The girl too?"

Tourette opened her heavy shirt, showing a sheathed knife on one side, under her bra, and a small holstered pistol on the other side.

Talena took a deep breath. "Maybe you're right. Lita and I had better get weapons too."

"We have spare weapons at our house," Crenelle said. "We can show you how to conceal them."

They really *had* prepared for emergency! "Let's fetch them now. And spare food, if you have it. We may have to endure for some time."

"We may indeed," Crenelle agreed.

And what would they do when the Germans came? Talena hardly dared think about that.

❂

By the morning of August 23, the German forces were ready to resume their advance. The Russians had blown the bridge across the Don at Kalach, but now the pontoon bridge was complete, and the Germans controlled the west bank of the river and were rested and poised.

Heath knew when it started, because he heard the sound of the artillery and airplanes. Dr. Kohler also kept him informed, because where there was action, there would very soon be the call for medical support.

At 4:30 A.M. the push began. The Sixteenth Panzer Division, commanded by General Hans Rube, moved carefully across the bridge. The general was known as *Der Mensch*—"The Man"—to his troops. He had lost one arm in World War One, but it hadn't slowed him. Trucks laden with supplies, ammunition, and infantry followed close behind the tanks.

Russian artillery, alerted similarly by the noise, attempted suppressive fire, but it was ineffective. The Germans quickly secured their position as Stukas dived to attack isolated Russian artillery spotters. There was no effective resistance after that.

"We have got their goat," Dr. Kohler remarked with a smile.

To be sure. One of the officers of that Panzer force was Lieutenant Hans Oettl. He had found a goat wandering the steppe. He tied a red ribbon around the animal's neck and made a pet of it. It had been with him ever since. Now the goat was marching into battle, a mascot.

Behind the Panzer Division, the Third and Sixtieth Motorized Divisions struggled to keep the pace. Traffic patterns had become snarled, and trucks jammed the roads. Horns were honking with futility. Kohler's medical detachment was stalled; the Russians hadn't stopped it, but other military traffic had.

The doctor was in the truck just ahead of the one Heath rode in. Heath saw the man get out and walk down the side of the road. This was curious, because there were no injured soldiers here.

Then the thin doctor confronted a line of trucks that were in the way. He drew his pistol and pointed it at the driver of the first vehicle. "If you don't let us through, you'll get it right in the tires!" he screamed.

Daunted, the driver yielded. Dr. Kohler waved his detachment into the line of traffic. His truck hastily obeyed, leaving him behind. So Kohler jumped into the sidecar of a motorcycle and waved the cyclist forward, to keep pace with the trucks.

The driver, startled, gunned his engine. The motorcycle lurched ahead— and ran right into a hole. The doctor was thrown sideways. His head smashed against the driver's helmet. Ouch!

There was laughter from one of the trucks the doctor had stalled. But Heath was alarmed. That had been one hard hit! Heath peered out and back as his truck passed. He saw Kohler swig down some cognac and gesture ahead. He was going to stay with his detachment. But his face looked bad.

It was an hour before there was a pause in the momentum of the detachment. Heath jumped out and ran to find the doctor. "By your leave, sir," he said, putting his fingers to the man's swollen jaw. Sure enough: it was broken.

"I'll manage," the doctor snapped. "Just fetch me more cognac."

Bemused, Heath obeyed. The force hurtled on.

By 6 P.M. the Sixteenth Panzer had reached the Volga River, securing a position north of Stalingrad. But it had outrun its support. The Third Motorized had halted for the night twelve miles to the rear. The Sixtieth was another ten miles behind that. There was a danger in such swift progress: until the units could link up, they were isolated and vulnerable.

Dr. Kohler was not concerned about the details of the military situation, if he was even aware of them. He was living on cognac and chocolate. He set up his field hospital along a railroad siding. There were casualties to attend to.

"But you need attention yourself," Heath protested.

"Get me something to chew on," Kohler replied. He was obviously in pain, but would not relent.

Heath found a piece of cork from a spent bottle, and gave him that. Kohler put it in his mouth and clenched on it to keep his fractured jaw in place, then proceeded with surgery on a patient.

Heath got to work on his own patients. True to their agreement, he did his professional best for every injured man brought to him, without regard for his uniform. Most of them did not even know he was not German, since he spoke the language well.

Next day it continued. Battles brought an endless supply of patients. Suddenly a soldier burst through the doors. "The Russians have broken through!" he shouted.

Later, Heath would be able to assimilate the situation better. Because the German units had gotten strung out, the relatively weak Russian forces were able to attack. The Sixteenth Panzer was up against surprisingly effective militia units surrounding it, and General Hube had radioed questions about his tardy support divisions. But meanwhile the Third and Sixtieth Motorized were both being engaged on their flanks by a reckless assault of the Thirty-fifth Russian Guards Division. It was pouring into the gap between the German divisions, trying to prevent them from uniting. This was what the soldier's shout meant.

Kohler finished his surgery, then went to the door. He grabbed a pair of binoculars. Heath, still working, glanced past the doctor. Soviet tanks were squashing German vehicles, scarcely a hundred yards distant.

Kohler spat out his cork. "Load the wounded onto trucks!" he screamed.

The orderlies got to work. Heath went to join the doctor, uncertain of his place in such a situation. Suppose the Russians captured Dr. Kohler? Where would Heath's proper loyalty be in such a circumstance?

He had an answer: he would do his best to protect the doctor from mischief, for Kohler was a good man. To see that he was treated with respect, and perhaps given the same chance he had given Heath.

In front of the tanks there were hundreds of Russian troops. They were marching with their arms linked together and singing as they came across an open field toward the hospital.

Kohler's jaw dropped, making him wince. "What is this eerie parade?" he inquired. "Those men aren't even armed. Don't they know there's a war on?"

"I believe they are tramplers, sir," Heath said.

"What?"

"Conscripts from prisons and slums, and especially deserters, put into

uniform and used for the most menial or dangerous chores," Heath explained. "In this case, two tramp ahead of the tanks, to set off any mines
that may have been laid to take out the tanks. They are given plenty of
vodka to dull their awareness of the danger, and sent out with arms linked
to be sure that every section is treaded."

"Oh. I have heard of this, but never before seen it. I believe we normally
use prisoners for this purpose. Fortunately there are no mines." Kohler
climbed onto a manure pile to get a better view.

"Fortunately, sir?"

"If there were mines, they would blow up the men instead of the tanks,
and I would have to let you go to tend to your surviving countrymen. As it
is, those men are merely slowing the progress of the tanks, giving us more
time to evacuate."

A German officer drove up. "What's going on?" he demanded.

Kohler waved the man onto the pile. Somewhat gingerly, the officer acceded, his shiny boots a contrast to the dung they trod. The doctor handed
him the binoculars.

The officer put them to his eyes. *"Gott in Himmel!"* he swore in delight.
He shoved back the binoculars and ran back to his car. The tires screeched
as he sped off to an artillery command post.

Seconds later the whine of incoming artillery climaxed in rising geysers
of earth and blood. The officer had called in the coordinates, and the big
guns had virtually point-blank range. The song of the tramplers vanished
into the wind, replaced by the screams of the dying.

Kohler turned away in disgust. "At least they could have dropped the
first round short, as a warning," he muttered. "Or gone after the tanks
instead of the men." He pulled a fresh cork from his pocket and shoved
it into his mouth.

He glanced at Heath. "The attack is being rebuffed. Go tend the Russians. Send any who can walk, back to their own lines. Any you bring to
our lines become our prisoners. I will give our sharpshooters the order to
let the wounded go. But they will not let *you* go, you understand."

Heath nodded. "Thank you, doctor." That attack was indeed being
turned back, as the tanks fled the artillery barrage.

Kohler went back inside, to his operating table. Heath made sure his
medic's insignia showed clearly, and walked to the closest of the fallen
Russians.

There wasn't much he could do. The man's head had been blown off.
He cast about for others, amidst the debris of body parts, and a number
were alive but clearly unsalvageable. With instant access to a competent
hospital, and heroic measures, some might have survived with lost limbs.
But even if the German facilities were available to these men, they wouldn't
be enough. So he had to do triage, locating the walking wounded and
sending them back to their lines, and letting the others go. The whole
business was sickening.

In the end he sent perhaps a dozen back, brought three in for treatment and prisoner status, and left several hundred dead or inevitable. And returned to Dr. Kohler.

"We must move on to connect with the Sixteenth Panzer," the doctor said. "We must not remain separated, lest we be surrounded and destroyed. You saw how it was today; we may not always have artillery to call in at a moment's notice. The Luftwaffe will airdrop supplies. The Führer still insists that Stalingrad fall by tomorrow."

This time they got to ride in a command car. Dr. Kohler, still in pain from his fractured jaw, insisted that Heath ride with him in this relative comfort. "I need a distraction," he said.

So they rode in the back seat, and Kohler shared his chocolate and cognac with Heath. "What do you think of this war?"

"Sir, I am on the other side. You would not find my opinion compatible."

"Of course I won't! That's why I want to debate it. There's nothing like a good argument to distract the mind from incidental concerns."

Oh. Such as the broken jaw. "I feel that there could have been a certain lapse in judgment."

The doctor chewed on his cork. "Oh, come on, Heath! You can do better than that. Speak your mind."

"Naturally I think that Hitler should have left Russia alone. There was after all a mutual non-aggression pact."

Kohler considered. Then he leaned forward and tapped the driver on the shoulder. "My friend here is an enemy national, here under flag of truce. Do you think he is speaking his true mind?"

"No, sir," the driver responded dutifully.

"Perhaps he is afraid he will be executed for treason if he is too candid. So nothing of this dialogue will be reported elsewhere. Agreed?"

"Yes, sir."

"Because if it is, it just might be someone else on trial for treason. Understood?"

"Yes, sir." The driver's mouth would be shut. He would not want to cross the notorious doctor.

"Now try again, Heath. Speak perhaps as your Marshal Stalin would speak."

"You dogs invaded our peaceful meadowlands without cause," Heath said, smiling. "We will see your brutal leader cowering against the firing wall."

Kohler smiled. "Not with your present organization. Stalin is the most brutal leader on the continent. He has slain millions, consolidating his power. When we entered Russia, we were hailed as liberators."

"What do you expect, from civilians facing guns? Any who speak their true minds will be beaten, raped, tortured, or shot—and many have been. But they don't hail the German intrusion any more, after what your troops have done to civilians."

Kohler raised a finger. "A distinction, here, if you please. After what the Waffen SS troops have done, and the Gestapo." That was a section of the

German armed forces that won battles by taking enormous losses, and treated the losers with such brutality that it was said to revolt regular German army personnel. But the Waffen SS was in favor with Hitler because it got the job done when regular troops did not.

Heath nodded. "Distinction noted. I would have died fighting, rather than surrender, if I had faced Waffen thugs."

"Yet, setting aside the matter of civilized behavior, what of common sense? Your Stalin trumped up charges against most of your army's serious officers and had them exiled or executed, when everyone knew that they were good, competent, and loyal men. In two years he eliminated three of five marshals, thirteen of fifteen army commanders, eight of nine senior admirals, and the great majority of lesser commanders, commissars, and officers. That is why your army was unprepared to oppose any intrusion. Almost all of your trained officers were gone. And for what? To satisfy the political motives of a chronically insecure politician. No wonder you are unable to put up any effective resistance. No wonder your morale is lower than a pig's snout."

He had scored. Heath had seen the massive purges, and deplored them on both practical and moral grounds. But he wasn't free to say that. "I can not know exactly what was in our leader's mind. But when it comes to craziness, he can't compare to Hitler's confusions. Look at the foolish meddling that vegetarian is doing in your own army, so that your own stumbles slow you down as much as Russian resistance does."

Kohler smiled. "And did Stalin not change his mind frequently about the defense of Stalingrad? He was going to let it go, then decided to defend it at all costs once the military units were headed elsewhere. So we have no monopoly on crazy decisions."

"Which cost enormous loss of life and property, and set back the welfare of nations," Heath said.

"This debate is fading," the doctor said. "Now let me sleep."

Heath, too, settled back for a snooze. He suspected that Kohler had broken off the debate because he found himself in too much agreement with certain points, and that was not politically safe. The same went for Heath; Stalin had indeed been a monster when it came to purges of the military and certain civilian regions, and it was not safe to criticize any of that. The green helmets of the NKVD were everywhere, and it did not hesitate to act. So perhaps the two sides were not far apart in essential merit.

The Sixtieth Motorized moved to link up with the Sixteenth Panzer north of Stalingrad. Dr. Kohler set up his field hospital, and there was always business. The Russians kept attacking and being driven back, but each attack hurt, bringing increasing casualties. The fighting was a rough standoff, with neither side able to make substantial gains.

On August 25 the German Sixth Army tried to break into Stalingrad from the west. There was a constant stream of information, both official, which was not reliable, and unofficial, which was. Men who had been wounded in action could pinpoint where it had happened. A number of them were brought to Dr. Kohler's hospital when their own hospitals overflowed. The German tanks were halted by tanks and Russian infantry. Though the Germans had the superior force, they were not used to fighting within a city, and the Russians were using desperation measures that were surprisingly effective.

"We attacked with seventy tanks," a badly burned man said as Heath treated him. "We lost twenty-seven of them." He laughed bitterly. "And I thought the Molotov cocktail was a drink!"

Heath nodded. "It's a bottle of gasoline with a wick. Let a man get close enough to a tank to drop it in the hatch with the wick lighted, and that tank is done for."

"Now I know," the man agreed ruefully. "In the city streets, we could not orient our guns to bear on targets too high or low, and they took advantage of that to drop things on us from high windows. We were like muzzled dogs."

Heath hadn't thought of that. A tank in the open was almost invincible, but a city wasn't open. "What is it like in Stalingrad?" He had special reason to inquire.

"It is still burning from the fires started by the Luftwaffe bombing. The downtown district is a pile of rubble. I saw people wandering around dazed. They say that the insane asylum was opened, and the denizens let go, and they don't know what to do. It's pitiful."

"War is hell," Heath agreed. Privately he was wincing. If the city was like that, what of Talena and the children? They should have evacuated by now, but he would have to check the house to be sure they were gone. Suppose they were still there?

He spoke to Dr. Kohler. "When will you release me?"

"Heath, I want to. You have fulfilled your part of the bargain. But we are about to crush the resistance and take the city. I would be sending you into hell."

"But I fear for my family in that hell."

"They have not crossed the river?"

"I hope they have. But I can't be sure until I check the house."

Kohler considered. "I would much prefer to release you by the river, so you could cross to safety. But you will not go until you are sure about your family. Let us compromise: I will ask a friend, a Sixth Army officer, to check your house specifically when the city falls. And if they are there, to preempt it for his own use, protecting it and them from marauders. He is a decent man, not given to rapine or murder. But they will have to forswear partisan activity, and not try to kill him in his sleep. Can they be trusted as you can be?"

Heath considered. This was another excellent offer. But to what degree could he speak for the women? Talena was not a physical fighter, though what she would do if her children were threatened he didn't know. Melee, on the other hand, was indeed capable of fighting and killing. Still, she was a person of her word.

"My wife is Talena. She would give her word, and honor it, as long as our children are not threatened. But we share the house with another family, and the other woman would fight."

"Suppose he approached the house with a white flag?"

Heath smiled. "They would honor that."

"Then stay here until you have that report. Give me the address."

Heath gave him the address, and Kohler noted it down carefully. "My friend is Major Wilhelm, very intelligent and honorable. I am sure he will do it. But until the city falls, he will not be able to check."

"I understand." Thus simply had his tenure with the Germans been extended. He did not doubt the doctor's sincerity. He knew Kohler wanted his continued service as a surgeon, but also knew that the deal was fair. Kohler gave value for value received.

On August 29, General Hoth launched a new drive with the Fourth Panzer Army, from the south. The Russian opposition panicked, and thousands of troops were captured without a fight. Now the Germans planned to encircle the Russian Sixty-second and Sixty-fourth armies, with General Paulus attacking from the north while Hoth came from the south. But Paulus hesitated, feeling that his position was perilous; his forces were too strung out. When his position improved on September 2, he finally acted. The encirclement was perfect, but there was nothing inside the trap. The Russians had managed to withdraw just in time.

"It is like a game of chess," Kohler remarked. "Sometimes bold action is disastrous—and sometimes the lack of it is. But it is but a momentary setback. I hear that the morale of the Russians is extremely low, and that one commander lined up his troops and shot every tenth man. The pile of bodies was a warning to the others to stand fast."

"Maybe General Paulus should have been put in such a line," Heath said. "To encourage him to act before the fish escaped the net."

Kohler tried to contain his laughter, but didn't quite succeed. He was quite cynical about the ways of military personnel.

The Luftwaffe bombed again, and the artillery shelled again, and Stalingrad became one massive smoking ruin. Heath could see the smoke rising from beyond the horizon. *Talena, be not there!* he prayed.

Meanwhile news circulated that Stalin had brought in his most able commander, Marshal Zhukov, who was given the title Deputy Supreme Commander of the Red Army. He was now second in authority only to Stalin himself. General Yeremenko remained in charge of the action around Stalingrad.

"This Zhukov—who is he?" Kohler asked. "What does this mean on the front?"

"It means that you now face competence of a magnitude you haven't encountered before," Heath said seriously. "Zhukov is a master of strategy and tactics. This is where you are most likely to face defeat."

"But it requires troops and equipment to win battles, and we are the ones with those. Your marshal can't conjure these from the air."

"So the Japanese thought," Heath said. "Before he routed them."

"Well, we shall see. I still think you are safer here than there."

He was probably right. Heath was being well treated, and was in no immediate personal danger. Meanwhile, the retreating Russians were taking heavy losses, as any glance at the bodies on the battlefields showed.

On September 5 the Russians launched human wave assaults against the Germans' northern flanks, which meant many more casualties to the units served by Dr. Kohler. The attacks were not effective, but they kept coming, making the Germans nervous. General Paulus diverted some troops from the attack on the city to shore up this sector. Meanwhile, German tanks were again invading Stalingrad, and found the Russians dug in tightly amidst the rubble and cellars of the suburbs. Russian snipers and commandos were beginning to acquaint the Germans with a new type of warfare: guerrilla.

September 8, it turned out, General Yeremenko and Commissar Khrushchev retreated across the Volga River, setting up their headquarters at Yamy. That was another signal that the Russians believed that the city would soon be lost. The following day Paulus' mighty Sixth Army, 200,000 strong, prepared to deliver the final blow from the west, crushing the defenders against the river. The Russians hung on to the section closest to the river, twenty miles long and five miles deep. German intelligence indicated that the Russians had no more than 50,000 men and 100 tanks remaining.

"Their units are in tatters," Kohler said, relaxing with cognac after the latest emergency had been handled. "They will be destroyed." Then, aware of Heath's concern, he added: "I have told Wilhelm, and he has agreed. He will look for your house, and protect it. You will even be allowed to visit it, if you have reason. Then you will decide."

"Thank you, sir," Heath said, truly appreciative.

"You have earned it. You have saved many German lives, and eased my condition, especially considering my incapacity of jaw. I shall be sorry to see you go, and sorrier yet if I learn you have died. But your future is with your own. Perhaps we shall meet again, after the war."

"I hope so, sir."

Then another truckload of wounded arrived.

❂

General Yeremenko had crossed the river, but General Lopatin remained in charge on the west side. German artillery and mortar fire had constantly disrupted telephone lines to the command bunker.

"We can't continue this way," Lopatin said grimly. "We can't hold Stalingrad."

"But we still have troops, and solid emplacements," Od protested. As a political officer he had not participated in the actual combat, but morale was a significant aspect of his job.

"You think so? The Sixty-second army has been decimated in action. An infantry brigade now numbers only 666 men, only 200 of whom are qualified riflemen. A regiment that should have mustered 3,000 lists only 100 remaining. The division next to it, which is normally 10,000 strong, has a mere 1,500 troops. On the southern fringe of the city, the once formidable Thirty-fifth Guards Division now boasts only 250 combat-worthy infantry. And our commanders have withdrawn across the river. The situation is hopeless."

In the face of Stalin's order to hold the city at all costs, this comment was tantamount to treason, however realistic the assessment might be. Od did what he had to do. "Then perhaps you should inform General Yeremenko."

"He'll fire me."

"Yes, sir. Then you will be able to leave here."

"Like a rat deserting a sinking ship."

"I would not put it so unkindly, sir. But perhaps it is better to leave than to drown."

"Perhaps. See if you can get me a line."

Od struggled with the intermittent phone system, and in due course managed to get through. "General Lopatin for General Yeremenko," he said. When he had confirmation, he handed the receiver to the general and retreated.

It required only a few minutes. "General Chuikov will assume command," Lopatin said soberly. "You will remain to guide and familiarize him with this sector."

"Yes, sir."

In the next two days, September 10 and 11, Lopatin took the ferry across the river, the command bunker became untenable, and Chuikov arrived. Od barely had time to cross the city to see Talena and Lita. They were now sharing the house with the neighbors whose home had been destroyed: Crenelle and her pretty but awkward daughter Tourette. They had given up thought of evacuation, partly because it was simply too awkward and dangerous to manage. But partly, he knew, because Talena wanted to be with him, Od, as much as she could, fearing he might die before the siege of Stalingrad was done. He was deeply gratified by that, for her presence enabled him to withstand the rigors of exactly that threat. And partly, too, because Talena wanted to be where Heath could find her. So that she could tell him personally about the change in relations. She was not one to delegate what she felt was her responsibility, and this particular business was very much that. She had to free him to pursue his own love, now that she had found hers.

When the crunch came, any day now, and the Germans took over the city, Od would have to go with the Russian troops. Talena would have to take her chances with the Germans. She masqueraded as a boy, as did the others in the house, to avoid trouble on the street. With luck it would spare them what the Germans could do to women.

Had he had his choice, Od would have packed all four of them off across the river. But with the Germans strafing the evacuation boats by day, and the perils of lightless night crossings, he could not argue with their decision to remain in the city. If only this war would go away!

On September 11 a steamer brought General Chuikov to his new command post. Od had not known exactly when he was coming, so waited in the empty bunker. In due course a broad-shouldered, stocky man approached. His general appearance was slovenly, but that was common in this besieged city. He had a row of gold teeth, and that was uncommon. When he turned, and Od saw a general's star on his cap, he stepped out to salute. "I am Major Od, sir, here to show you where things are."

"First, the bunker."

"Yes, sir. But it has been abandoned. The lines simply aren't working, so nothing can be done from there. The new command center is on Mamaev Hill."

"Then take me there."

Od had the use of a car, for this purpose. He drove the general through the rubble-lined streets, following the route he knew.

"Do you know," the general remarked, "while I waited for the steamer to come, on the other side, I entered a first-aid station. I saw wounded men with blood-soaked bandages lying on the floor. They had been ignored for hours. They continually pleaded for water. I found a doctor and asked him why the men were suffering this neglect. He just shrugged. It seemed that the station didn't have the personnel or equipment to care for the number of wounded men inundating them. Of course I saw that water was brought. But it was an unkind introduction to the reality of Stalingrad."

"Yes, sir. It is similar on this side of the river. Many of our medical personnel were working in field hospitals near the front, and got captured by the Germans." He thought of Heath. Where was he now?

"War is hell." It was the all-purpose answer to the unanswerable.

"Yes, sir."

They reached the impromptu command post. It was a wide trench with a bench of packed earth along one wall, and a bed and table on the other side. The roof was made of brush, and covered with barely a foot of dirt. The antitank defenses were so flimsy as to be almost nonexistent. "This is pathetic," Chuikov said.

There were two people in the dugout: a female telephone operator, and a man. The man stepped forward to introduce himself. "I am General Krylov, your chief of staff," he said, saluting.

"We have a problem," Chuikov muttered almost inaudibly.

But he got right down to work, and the more Od saw of this, the greater his respect became. First he familiarized himself with the available forces, and he was a quick study. Then he worked on restoring morale. He assembled those officers and troops that were within range, and read rousing messages from Yeremenko and Khrushchev. Chuikov himself had a forceful and confident manner that tended to stiffen spines in its vicinity. But what really made the difference was the news he brought: reinforcements were on the way. Ten divisions, two armored corps, and eight armored brigades. "We have been promised ten thousand men and one thousand tons of supplies within the next three days," he announced, and cheering broke out. "You have done a great job; you will no longer be fighting alone."

That night Chuikov and his staff made plans for an offensive to secure the landing stages, for they were now within range of the German artillery. "I recognize three tendencies of the German army which I mean to exploit," he said. "It relies on the blitzkrieg, which makes the Panzers and infantry delay attacking until air support is present. It relies on tank strength, so the infantry is unwilling to advance unless the tanks are moving too. And the infantry prefers to avoid close combat. Well, we will force them to fight without their air support, and before their tanks get organized, and we will give them such close combat we'll be spitting out their eyeballs. Just as soon as those reinforcements arrive."

The staff loved it. They worked out the details, then spread the word for the troops to get all the rest they could. In three days, on September 14, they would give the Germans one awful surprise.

But the surprise was by the enemy. At 6:30 on the morning of September 13, the day before the planned Russian action, the Germans attacked. Od was already up and ready to drive his military car to the command post when the shelling began.

Talena flew to his embrace. "I love you!" she cried, as if this were the last time they would see each other. He kissed her and ran out to the car, trying to suppress a premonition that she was right.

He drove, and the city shook with the bombardment. It had the feel of a blitzkrieg. He hoped it was just his imagination.

He reached the command post. General Chuikov was for once somewhat at a loss. Explosions had severed his lines of communication, and he fumed as the repair crews hastened to restore them. But it seemed that as soon as one line was restored, another was knocked out. "We can't operate from this damned exposed trench!" he cried. But what was the alternative?

By mid-afternoon, the general was almost completely cut off from contact with his troops. "Pack up the command center and move it back to the Tsaritsa Gorge bunker!" he ordered. "At least we'll have decent cover there."

It was done. Reports came in, and the general stuck pins in a big map, getting the picture. The Germans had launched a two-pronged attack from the south and west. Mamaev Hill was one objective: where the command post had just been. Was that coincidence, or had the Germans known? The other objective was the ferry port.

It was indeed a blitzkrieg, the "lightning war." Luftwaffe fighter-bombers commanded the sky in groups of fifty or sixty, and the German advances were swift. Mamaev fell, and then that column turned toward Railroad Station Number One, seemingly unstoppable.

Chuikov got a connection to the other side of the river. "Where are those reinforcements?" he shouted into the phone. "We need them *now!* We are being torn up here." He listened, then hung up. "We are promised new troops to be ferried over in the night," he said. "But we must hold out until then."

The general summoned his last reserves of armor, nineteen tanks, and ordered them to guard the ferry landing. If that fell, the city was sure to follow.

Od could not go home, of course. His house was on the other side of Railroad Station Number One. That section was in immediate peril. "Oh, Talena," he murmured, pained.

That night the German lines came to within eight hundred yards of the command bunker, and half a mile from the Volga. Reports from the front indicated that the Germans thought that victory was at hand, and were relaxing their vigilance. They were drinking heavily and singing songs, lurching from corner to corner in the city streets.

That was not smart. Russian snipers took advantage of the situation, logging hundreds of kills. But it was spit in the wind; more German troops kept funneling into the center of the city.

In the morning of September 14, the promised Thirteenth Guard Division finally reached the east bank of the Volga River. One day late—and what a difference that made. They couldn't cross by day; the German aircraft would strafe them out of existence. They would have to cross that night. Which meant that the beleaguered Sixty-second, what was left of it, would have to hold out another day.

"Fetch Colonel Sarayev," Chuikov snapped to Od. That was the captain of the NKVD garrison.

The NKVD did not like working directly under the Army's orders, but Chuikov pressed the issue. "Do you want Stalingrad to be lost because you sat on your hands while the enemy took the ferry port and stopped our reinforcements from saving the day?"

Sarayev hemmed and hawed, but had to acquiesce. In this manner Chuikov obtained fresh troops. He promptly abandoned standard Red Army tactics and divided the NKVD forces into "storm groups" of ten to twenty men. "I will place these in strategic buildings throughout the downtown area, where they can act like breakwaters to funnel the German advance into approach roads that are already registered by Russian artillery. We can direct a withering fire there against their armor, while the storm groups can deal with the infantry that will be exposed by the absence of their armor. In addition, our small units will be mingled so closely to the German lines that the Luftwaffe bombers will be unable to drop their loads without risking their own ground forces."

"Yes, sir," Sarayev agreed wanly.

"Then make the assignments. I expect your men to show their mettle." The general went on to other business.

Colonel Sarayev got busy. He gathered his officers and others available and sent them to specific buildings. Od, conversant with downtown Stalingrad, was there to call out the most defensible and most strategic sites.

"And this?" the colonel asked, setting his forefinger on a large square just south of the Tsaritsa Gorge.

"That is a huge cement grain elevator," Od explained. "It is defensible and critical, for it still has much grain that either side can use. But it will take at least a hundred soldiers, because of its extent."

"We can spare only fifty," the colonel snapped. "So to make up for that, we shall give them especially competent command. Major, this is your mission."

Od felt as if he had suddenly been lined up before a firing wall. He wasn't a combat officer! But he realized that the colonel, angry about having his unit co-opted for gut fighting, was getting back at the general indirectly. There would be no appeal to reason. "Yes, sir."

He gathered the men, who were a motley group from several prior commands, briefed them, and led them to the grain elevator. It rose high on the plain, between the city and the river. It was in its way like a fortress, but it was so extensive that they would be lost if they tried to spread out across its every crevice. So he elected to occupy a limited section that could cover a broad approach. It was hardly ideal, but maybe the Germans wouldn't know the thinness of the defense. They would put on a bold show, anyway.

There was a corrugated metal side tower that had the height and position to oversee the main approach to the grain elevator. From this they could pick off any enemy soldiers who tried to get in, and could use their mortar to focus on any tank that dallied long enough for them to pinpoint. But it would be no picnic.

He assembled them within the tower. "Men, this will get difficult in short order," Od said, assuming his best combat-officer expression. "We shall have to be constantly alert. I know you are tired; so am I. So we'll divide into three sections, each of which will take a four-hour shift while the others rest. When we have to, we'll put two sections on duty, and finally three. Now assemble yourselves into compatible groups. You want to be fighting beside men you know will protect your life with their own." He glanced around, then pointed out the one other officer here. "Lieutenant, you will command Group A." He looked again. "Sergeant, you have Group B. I will take Group C. We must make the groups approximately even in size; if they are not, I will reassign men until they are. Now go and cluster around your choice of groups."

The men hesitated. Then one went to join the lieutenant, and two of his friends followed him. Another went to the sergeant, and several of his friends followed. Several who had been working with Od came to his group. Those at the end filled in to make the groups even; they evidently didn't much care which leader they had.

"Group A, take the first watch," Od said. "I think it will be a few hours yet before the Germans come, so if some of you wish to rest on duty, you may do so. But make sure that at least one man is constantly on watch at every checkpoint."

The lieutenant nodded, and made his assignments. The other two groups found places on the floor and disposed themselves for sleep. They knew that sleep would be in short supply once the action started. Some ate from their limited personal supplies, knowing that food, too, would probably be scarce.

That gave Od a notion. "Those who do not wish to rest yet, come with me," he said. "We're going to liberate some grain for personal use. Maybe we can make some decent gruel."

Several men came. "Sir," one said.

"Yes?"

"What about water?"

"Good thought! We'll probably have to dip it from the river. It will taste foul, but will have to do. Scavenge for containers; we'll need to stack all we can."

They found grain, and filled bags with it. Then six men took containers and went to the river. In the course of two hours they managed to bring a fair collection of pots and cans filled with water.

There was a man with experience as a mess worker; he became the cook. He made a small fire and boiled wheat, making batches of hot whole-grain cereal. They gave small servings to those who wanted them. There was no salt, sugar, or milk, but it was much better than nothing.

The sergeant approached quietly. "Some men were unsure of your leadership, sir," he murmured. "But they are reassured."

"Thanks," Od said, gratified. "But this is incidental. The test will come when the Germans attack."

"For sure, sir."

Od settled down and to get some sleep. He was lulled, ironically, by the sound of guns firing. They were still in the distance, and their progress was slow, as other defended buildings gave them pause. Most of the activity was to the south, as the Germans forged up toward the river. They would certainly pass this point, because they would want the grain, and this was on their way to the ferry port.

Could the elevator be held? He doubted it, but could never say that. *Talena,* he thought, and pictured her face. He had found true love late, but had no doubt of the fact. If he died tomorrow, he was glad he had had these few days in her arms. He hoped that as the Germans took over the residential sections of the city, they would spare the noncombatant civilians. He had agreed with Talena: she would surrender without resistance, and cooperate with whatever the Germans demanded, in the hope that they would have no reason to brutalize or kill her or the others. The *Wehrmacht* was a far cry from the *Waffen SS,* and they had pinned their hopes on that.

When he woke, Group B was on duty, and the men of Group A were relaxing and eating boiled wheat. Things were going well, so far. Men were drinking the water, and going out quietly to refill the containers, using the cover of night.

At dawn, it was Group C's turn. Reasonably refreshed, they took over the landings and slits that were the guard posts. Od felt tight, knowing that the Germans were most likely to attack by day, when they could see what they were doing. By the sound of it, they were now very close.

Too close. Od saw a German helmet down the street. "Enemy sighted," he announced calmly. "Let him get closer before firing; we want to take out as many as possible in the first volley. Those will be the only easy kills."

Soon the German soldier was joined by three others, walking warily toward the elevator. They were the advance scouts, the throwaways, there to trigger enemy fire so the tanks and artillery could orient on the resistance. The tramplers. But they could not be allowed to enter the building.

"Take aim at each soldier," Od directed. "The man farthest to the right, take out the German on the right. Next man, take the next, and so on. When I give the order, fire together, once, so there is no single source they can identify. If your shot wounds your target, don't fire again; casualties are more trouble to them than deaths."

When the four enemy soldiers were in comfortable range, he gave the order: "Fire."

There were four shots, almost together. Three Germans fell; the fourth staggered, then dropped to his knees. They let him suffer.

In a moment a tank appeared. It was of course invulnerable to their small arms fire, but not to their mortar. But the mortar needed a stationary target, and the tank kept moving. Its cannon oriented and fired. The shell struck the near wall of the grain elevator, knocking a hole in it.

"They don't know where we are," Od said, satisfied. "Don't fire until they send out more men."

Then the tank did something unusual. It raised a white flag of truce.

"Let it approach," Od said. "But orient the mortar on it. When they emerge to parley, do not fire. But if they try to return to the tank, destroy it." He walked toward their concealed exit. "Meanwhile, Lieutenant, you are in charge if I am lost." Od left the tower and ran silently around behind a wall, until he could emerge well clear of his true redoubt. Then he stepped out into plain sight.

The tank rolled slowly toward the elevator. It halted when it saw him, and its turret opened. An officer emerged, followed by an enlisted man. They came to stand about fifty feet from Od.

The officer spoke to the enlisted man, who then called out to Od in Russian. "Surrender to the heroic German Army."

"Go to hell!" Od called back, in Russian.

"We will spare you and your men if you surrender," the interpreter said.

"We will spare you and your men if you give us the tank," Od retorted.

The officer, receiving the interpretation, blinked in disbelief. "This is outrageous! We have three divisions here. One last chance: surrender, and save your lives."

"Walk away from the tank," Od replied evenly. "Then we will spare you and it."

The officer and translator turned and ran for the tank. But as they tried to jump into it, the mortar shell came down. The tank exploded. The officer, half stunned, stumbled back. They let him go.

But after that no truce was offered, and they knew that no quarter would be given. Od ducked back behind the wall and returned to the tower. He was immediately surrounded by his men. "That's telling them, sir!" one cried.

Now his knees felt weak. He had done what he had to do, but in retrospect it seemed suicidal. But at least he had won the respect of his men.

But at what price? The German officer had claimed they had three divisions in the area, and now it appeared he had spoken the truth. The enemy guns blasted the elevator and the tower day and night. The corrugated metal resisted the bullets and shells, refusing to fragment or crumble, but when a bullet came through and struck a man, that man was wounded or dead. Od's original fifty dropped to forty, and then to thirty, in the course of two days. Also, they could no longer go out to fetch in supplies. They had enough grain, especially considering that they had fewer mouths to feed now, but bullets had riddled several of their water cans, and they were getting nervously low on fluid.

Yet they held out, wreaking devastation on any German soldiers who ventured within range, and taking out another tank. That last had been a neat maneuver: the mortar had oriented on a particular spot on the street, and timed its fire to blast that spot just when a tank crossed it. The Germans thought it was spectacular sharp-shooting, and held their tanks back thereafter. But the Russians were running low on ammunition, and the Germans were massing. The end was drawing nigh.

Then they were reinforced by a platoon of marines, in their striped shirts and navy hats. Od had not thought much of that uniform before, but now it was beautiful. The marines brought supplies and ammunition, and gave them a chance to scramble for more water.

But the fight was hardly over. For the next three days German artillery fire pounded their stronghold, setting the grain on fire with incendiary shells, and riddling the outbuilding with high explosives. The enemy certainly knew where the Russians were now!

German infantry broke in and crept up the stairs. A man cried the alarm, and the Russians rallied to fight for their lives. They fell on the Germans with fists, knives, and small arms fire. They were used to the gloom of the interior, and were familiar with the tower's every crevice. The Germans were not, so were at a disadvantage. They were driven off in a savage fracas.

But the defenders were worn out, their ammunition was almost gone, and their water had run out the day before. Thirst alone would vanquish them if they didn't do something. So on the night of the twentieth Od roused himself to lead the men in a desperate search for water. His legs felt like deadwood, and he was bleary from lack of sleep, and knew he looked and smelled like a thug with his unshaven face and six-day-old uniform. But he was one with his men, and he had a job to do.

They sneaked out the door, crossed a field, went across a road, and into a gully. There they stumbled onto a German mortar battery. "Kill!" Od cried.

Desperation gave them strength. They waded into the enemy. The startled Germans, who must have been snoozing without a lookout (very bad form!), fled during the melee. Od's group had won the mortar position!

Better yet, the Germans had left behind gallons of cold water. Od and his men gulped it down gratefully.

But they had made a fatal mistake. They had been too dehydrated, and suddenly drank way too much water. The men started falling, suddenly sick. Od felt faint, and collapsed on the ground.

When he woke, he was in a dark cellar. He was missing his shirt and one shoe. His head felt light, and he could not move his arms or legs. He was lying on his side, bound hand and foot, and standing guard over him was a soldier of the German Fourteenth Panzer Division. The Germans were quickly putting out the flames and saving most of the grain. The elevator Od and his men had fought so hard to defend had passed thus quickly into enemy hands. Because they had been foolish about drinking water.

Forgive me, Talena, he thought. He had hoped to be a hero, and instead he was lost. He would never see her again.

Then he felt the metal poking into his bare back. It felt like shrapnel. Sharp edges.

He shifted slowly, heedless of the way the jagged metal cut his skin, while the guard peered out the window to watch the action at the elevator. He got his fingers on the shrapnel, and tried to work it around to cut the rope around his wrists. But he couldn't. So he bent his knees and brought it slowly to his ankles. He sawed, and sawed, interminably, scraping through one strand after another.

And in time he felt the rope ease, and loosen, and he was able to free his legs. Now could he use his feet to hold the shrapnel and free his hands? No, that just didn't work.

The guard came to check him, in the gloom. Od kicked up with his shoed foot, catching the man on the side of the head. He kicked again, aiming for the face, but hit the shoulder. He kept kicking, having no alternative, while the surprised German floundered. He hooked the man's legs with his other foot, making him stumble. Finally he scored on the chin, and the man dropped with a groan.

Od sat up, then lurched to his feet. He left the German and ran out the door. There would soon be pursuit, but if he could get outside, in the darkness, he could disappear. He ran up steps and out an open door. No one was watching.

Where were his men? He feared he knew. He had been spared because he was an officer, and they wanted him for interrogation. His men would have been dumped in a truck and shipped behind the lines to a compound, if they were lucky. Otherwise they simply would have been killed. They had caused the Germans a lot of trouble, stopping their advance for five days. In any event, they would not be sitting around waiting for him to lead them to safety.

So Od walked quietly away, toward the river. Now he was watching for Germans, and hiding at any sound. But the enemy was not looking for him, and he made it without trouble.

But his hands were still bound behind him. What could he do? He looked around, and found an old pier projecting into the water. Like most such structures, it had nails and hooks on its posts. He backed up to a hook, and set his knot on it. Bit by bit he worked the knot loose, untying it, until he had enough slack to draw one hand free. He had done it!

After that it was easy. He knew it was pointless to try to return to the command post; the Germans were thick between him and it. So he scrounged for planks, driftwood, and bits of rope, and fashioned himself a makeshift raft. He found a board to use as a paddle, and shoved off into the dark river.

It was no easy trip, even so, but he made it far enough across so that he was spotted by the Russians. They knew that no German would be crossing in such manner. They hauled him in and took him to the east bank. There he was given a ride to the refugee center.

A weary officer questioned him. Od started to explain about the grain elevator, but the man did not have time for details. "I believe you. Have you any family here?"

"Six children. And a lovely woman minding them. My wife." That was the truth, though reality was something else.

Soon he was dropped off at a house where several families with men in action were quartered. But they weren't entirely trusting. "Melee," a man said. When she appeared, the man flashed his light on Od's face. "Do you recognize this man?"

"My husband," she said instantly, running to embrace Od.

That was enough. "Take care of him; he's near dead on his feet." The man got back into his car and drove off.

Melee hauled him inside. The children screamed with glee when they saw him, and buried him in hugs and kisses. They seemed not to care at all about his horrible appearance.

Soon Melee was feeding him, and cleaning off his face and arms. "I'll give you one day to recover," she murmured. "Then you will take over here, and I'll go to war."

"But—"

"I have been going stir crazy, with you and Heath both gone, and Talena trapped. I must get into the action."

He saw that it was true. She was a fighting young woman, and it would take him at least a week to recover. "I will care for my children," he said. "And yours. You find Talena. And Heath, if he's there."

She kissed him. Then she put him to bed, alone. He did not protest. Their marriage was now in name only: a totally amicable separation.

❂

That morning Talena had seen Od off to work. That day the enemy forces rolled in. There was sporadic gunfire, but the Germans came in such numbers that it was clear they owned this section of the city. Talena watched apprehensively from her window. So it had after all come to this: they were to be captives of the Germans. Od would not be able to return to the house, even if given time to do so.

She saw the soldiers going from house to house, going inside, breaking down the doors if they were locked, and hauling out whatever they wanted. She saw them go to her neighbor Natasha's home. Natasha and her mother had been wounded by bomb fragments two days before, and Talena knew they were lying helpless inside. The men broke down their door and charged in with machine guns.

But soon the men emerged, carrying pots, pans, food, and bedding. Lita slipped out when the street was empty and went to inquire. Soon she was back with news: "They didn't pay any attention to Natasha or her mother. They just ransacked the house for what they wanted and went on. They are going to post their house for typhus, so the Germans will stay away."

"Clever notion," Talena agreed. Sure enough, soon a sign with TYPHUS scrawled was hammered to their door.

But hours later, a German medical detachment saw the sign. It acted promptly: it fired the house. The last thing the Germans wanted was that disease spreading to their troops. Natasha dragged her crippled mother into a backyard storage shack. There they huddled under a blanket on the concrete floor and prayed for rescue. Their ploy had cost them their house.

But no one came to Talena's house. The soldiers glanced at it and passed it by. What was going on?

Next day they learned the answer. A German infantry officer, a major, approached. He stepped up to the front door and knocked.

Talena stared at Crenelle. "Answer it," Crenelle said. "Otherwise he'll break it down."

"But what do I say to him?"

"The truth. We are at their mercy."

Talena went to the front and opened the door. "Yes?" she said.

"I am looking for the woman of the house," the officer said in passable Russian.

Talena realized that he had mistaken her for a boy. That was scarcely odd, because she was still masquerading as one. But this was the time for truth. "I am she."

The officer paused. "What is your name?"

"Talena."

"What is your husband's name?"

"Heath."

"What is his profession?"

"He is a doctor."

"What is your eldest child's name?"

"Telita. She is here."

The man smiled. "Then you are the one I seek. Will you give me your word to practice no evil against me, and to deceive me in no way?"

Talena nerved herself. "No."

"I am Major Wilhelm. Your husband is our captive. He is working with Dr. Kohler, as a surgeon. He is protected as long as he works loyally for us. He asked me to bring news of you, if you remained here. Since you are here, I am taking this house for my own residence, and will protect it and its residents from molestation. But you must give your word, for you are an enemy national. In return I will give you mine that you will not be abused in any way it is in my power to prevent."

Talena was astonished. "If I may—what did my husband say of me?"

The man considered. "Very little, actually. That you have six children, all girls. That he married you when you were just thirteen."

"Did he say he loved me?"

"I am sure he does. He was much concerned for your welfare."

"But did he say it?"

"I don't believe he did. But that would be a private thing."

It did sound like Heath. "I will give my word."

Surprised, he nodded. "Then please let me come in, for we must talk."

"We must talk," she agreed, opening the door wide.

He entered. He glanced around the sparse living room, selected a chair, and seated himself. "Please assemble all the occupants of this house."

"There are three others," Talena said. "My daughter Telita, who is eight years old." Lita emerged from the back room. "And my neighbor whose house was bombed, Crenelle and her daughter Tourette." The woman and girl emerged.

Wilhelm studied the three. "I think I would not have known you for women, had I passed you on the street." He glanced back at Tourette. "Except perhaps for you. I can see your beauty despite your camouflage."

"I think we must go," Crenelle said tersely.

Wilhelm held up a hand. "Do not be premature. I am not making any untoward suggestion. I am a family man. My daughter Faience is thirteen, which I judge to be about two years younger than you, Tourette. She will never be the beauty you will be, but she is bright and sociable, and I believe you would like her. I presume the name is not intended as a cruelty?"

"It is not," Crenelle said.

"In medieval times she would have been in danger as a witch. But we know better now. You are naturally very protective of her. You are of course armed."

Crenelle nodded, and Talena was impressed. This man was observant. Heath could not have told him of Crenelle and Tourette, because Heath had not known they would be here.

"I want your given word that those weapons will never be used against me or any member of the German occupation force."

"But we are enemies!" Crenelle protested.

"You are captives. I am offering you the freedom of this house, and to a degree this city, and protection from the Third Reich. Ordinary captives are to be deported to work camps in Germany. You may remain here, as my servants. You may keep your weapons, for you may be subject to attack by ruffians on the street. But you must give your word."

"What is your price?" Talena asked.

He returned his disquietingly sharp gaze to her. "Ah, you assume I wish the use of the women. But as I said, I am a family man, and my wife Fay would not understand. Yet it will have to be understood outside this house that I do have such use of both adult women, and that this is the price of your freedom from deportation. You will prostitute yourselves to protect your daughters and to remain here, where perhaps you have a better hope of survival and rescue. I control you by the threat to your children. So it must be believed. We will share a bedroom and a bed. Others need not know that the use occurs in shifts."

Talena exchanged a glance with Crenelle. Was this the first stage of a carefully choreographed seduction?

Crenelle shrugged. "Obviously you have the means to make such use of us real, if that is your intent. We don't have many options."

Wilhelm nodded. "Our relationship must be based on trust, for without it we shall be unable to cohabit in this house. But it seems evident that the four of you have reason to accept the agreement I offer, and that I can have the company and services of the group of you if I make this possible. I do miss my home life, with my wife and children. I will expect full maintenance of the house, cooking, laundry, errands, and social appearances at such time as I may entertain other officers. I should like to relax in the evenings with compatible dialogue, and to sleep without fear of betrayal. I believe we can do each other some good."

"Social appearances," Crenelle said. It was a question.

"One of you will dress in feminine style, attractively, and perform in the manner of a hostess. But you will not be subject to any sexual attention by any other man. It should be possible to make it seem that you are mine, without actually saying so. That is the best protection of that sort that I can offer." He paused, considering. "But should I be visited by a superior officer, and should he take an interest, I will not be able to deny him. You will in that event have to do what you must do, preserving the situation or destroying it. I can promise only that I will never try to arrange such a thing. But for this reason, I suggest that the girls remain as boys. They should never be part of any compromise of this nature."

Talena exchanged another glance with Crenelle. Perhaps she was indulging in foolish wish fulfillment, that this man was decent and would truly protect them. But there was no realistic alternative. "I agree."

"I agree," Crenelle echoed.

"Very good." Wilhelm drew an emblem from his pocket. "Put this on the front door. It signals that the house is reserved for an officer. Now conduct me to your bedroom, for I am tired."

Crenelle took the emblem. Talena showed him the bedroom. He lay on the bed and closed his eyes. She backed away and shut the door.

"I like him," Lita said.

"Stay clear of him," Talena said grimly. "Unless he commands you." She glanced at Tourette. "You especially."

The girls nodded. They had seen enough of war to know that the ordinary rules of behavior could be suspended, and that rape was not confined to grown women.

It settled in very quickly. Wilhelm gave them German money to purchase food, and they took turns going out to do it. They made meals as good as they were able, and took turns serving as hostess: dressing prettily and chatting in the evening as if they were Wilhelm's friends. He would dress informally, and they were supposed not to call him sir when he was out of uniform. It was a charade, yet it was satisfying too, for it made the war seem distant.

On the third day, Tourette insisted on taking a turn as hostess. Neither her mother nor Talena was easy about this, but the girl was mature for her age and extremely poised. It was her burgeoning beauty that bothered the adult women; a man could well take an interest, and that would be special mischief. She did, however, suffer a siege of her syndrome. Wilhelm simply looked away, ignoring it, as he did her loveliness. That was a relief in two respects.

They did rotate shifts, with Wilhelm storing his things in one section and having the bedroom from eleven in the evening until seven in the morning, Talena from seven to three in the afternoon, and Crenelle from three to eleven. It was understood that no one would open the door out of turn, and it worked well. It also meant that someone was always alert, and that was important. There could be hungry and brutal intruders who would be a threat to Russian and German alike. The girls shared the other bedroom, sleeping at night, and being quiet by day. Talena and Crenelle took turns tutoring them, and on occasion Wilhelm did also. "You may not approve," he said. "But at some point your survival could depend on your knowing some German words and culture. Always study your enemy, so that your decisions, when you have them, are based on a balanced picture. Now who was Johann Sebastian Bach?"

As the days passed, it became clear that the German officer was indeed honorable. He was out much of each day, active in his command, but relaxed when he returned for the nights. When Lita was confused about a German expression she had overheard when there was mischief on the street, he glanced at Talena, making sure she was paying attention, then explained to the girl.

"The literal translation is 'Thunder weather.' *Donnerwetter.* In other languages it refers to storms, but in German it is a swear word. Pretend you don't know it, as a lady who used it in company would be considered low grade."

Lita was delighted with the term, however. But she was careful not to use it audibly. Once when there was a storm, and there was a close crack of thunder, Talena heard her murmur "Donnerwetter."

Then Wilhelm announced company. "Please adjust your schedules, for I will be home tomorrow, and there will be a visitor. You, Talena, will serve as hostess. This is a very special occasion."

"When must I be ready?" Talena asked, apprehensive about this change in the routine.

"He will be here at ten in the morning."

"I could do it," Crenelle said, for that was the shift Talena normally slept.

"No." And that was that. Wilhelm's word was law. They had never known him to invoke it without reason, but neither did he always see fit to explain himself.

So Talena slept early, and dressed her best in the morning. She hoped the man did not turn out to be some grabby senior official.

Wilhelm dressed in full uniform. As the time approached, he explained a bit more. "The man wishes to meet you and Telita. She must wear a dress for this occasion. He will talk with you, but I must remain in the room. I regret this, but it is a condition of the meeting."

What was this? It didn't sound like an ordinary German officer. "Yes, sir."

"I will escort him in. You and your daughter will greet him as he enters. Then I will retreat to the background and be silent."

Not ordinary at all. What was expected of her? She would have to smile and socialize regardless, and hope that this did not bode ill for Lita.

Shortly before ten a vehicle approached. "Wait across the room," Wilhelm said. "The two of you together."

They stood together, facing the door, as he went out to greet the visitor. Talena heard their steps as they came to the house. They entered. The outlines of their bodies appeared in the doorway.

Lita screamed. "Daddy!" She flew across to hug him.

It was, indeed, Heath. He picked Lita up and swung her around, kissing her on the forehead. Then he turned to Talena.

She was in his arms and kissing him before she knew it. "Heath! You look so well! I was so afraid!"

"I was taken captive," he said. "I made a deal. I have been helping wounded German soldiers, in exchange for this reunion. They said the others evacuated."

"Yes. We—the car broke down, and we couldn't make it out. But we're all right."

Wilhelm cleared his throat. "You may use the bedroom, if you wish. I don't believe that will be a violation, if you promise not to speak of anything political or military."

"The bedroom," Heath said, amazed. "I never thought that would be allowed. Understand, Talena, I'm still a prisoner."

The bedroom. An aspect of reality dropped on her. "No."

Heath looked surprised. So did Wilhelm. "There is something?"

"Is there ever, Daddy," Lita said.

"Not—something didn't happen to the others?" Heath was abruptly looking nervous.

"Not exactly," Lita said.

Talena floundered, looking wildly around. Where was she to begin?

"I can tell him," Lita said.

Talena stifled hysterical laughter. "Maybe you had better, dear."

"Sit down, Daddy," Lita said. "This is wild."

They sat down. Wilhelm looked just as curious as Heath did.

"You are swapping partners," Lita said. "Mom's with Od, and you're with Melee."

Heath's jaw dropped. "I don't understand."

"We figured it out," Lita said proudly. "You always had the hots for Melee, and she did for you. So now you're switching. Mom's with Od now."

Heath looked at Talena. "I never touched Melee."

"I know, dear. But she has always been your desire. I concluded that I would rather see you happy with her, and look elsewhere for myself. So we agreed to exchange."

"I never asked you to do that. Our children—"

"Will be fine with Od," Talena said. It was getting easier, now that the ice had been broken. "Heath, we wanted to discuss it with you, but we couldn't, because you were gone. With the uncertainties of the war, we— we had to do as much as we could, when we could. So Od freed Melee, and I—I went with Od."

"*Went* with Od?"

"I love him, Heath. I was surprised, and so was he. But when we tried it, it was like a sudden realization. We are right for each other. As are you and Melee. I hope you understand."

Heath looked at Wilhelm. The German spread his hands. "I did not know. I thought all was well between you."

"All *was* well," Talena said. "Except that Heath couldn't love me. Now he can find love."

"But you have six children!" Wilhelm protested.

"And I'm the first," Lita said proudly. "But that was just sex. He wanted Melee."

"This Melee—what kind of a woman is she?"

"Oh, she's great," the girl said. "She cooks better than anybody, and she's the prettiest woman in the city. Except she's across the river with my sisters and brother."

"Brother?"

"Well, not exactly. But his mother died last year when the Germans— when you invaded, so they adopted him, and he lives with us."

"And she agreed to this exchange?" Wilhelm asked.

"Sure. She was all for it. She always liked Daddy, too, and now she can have him. It's great."

Wilhelm spoke to Heath. "I apologize for bringing you into this confusion, which should have been no business of mine. Can you accept their decision?"

"No!" Heath said. He stood. "I will return to Dr. Kohler now."

"Daddy!" Lita protested.

But Heath was already walking out. Wilhelm hurried to accompany him.

Blinded by tears, Talena didn't move. How could it have gone so wrong?

Crenelle and Tourette came from the kitchen, where they had been staying out of the way. They could not have helped overhearing. Crenelle sat on the arm of Talena's chair and drew her head to her bosom, wordlessly.

"But it's so good," Lita wailed. "Why did he walk out?"

"Sometimes men are like that," Tourette said, comforting the girl in a similar manner. "Their minds don't work the same way. Maybe when he thinks about it, it will be all right. This was sort of sudden."

Talena heard the car driving away. Then Wilhelm returned. "I'm sorry. I didn't know," he repeated.

"You're a man," Tourette said. "You must have a notion. Why did he do that?"

Wilhelm sat down again. "I think it was too much of a surprise. For more than a month he has been away, not knowing whether his wife and children were safe. Now he suddenly learns that they are safe—and that his wife has left him for his friend. If I returned to Germany to a reception like that, I would be devastated too."

"But if it is true that he always wanted the other woman—" Tourette said.

"I have on occasion seen lovely women, and have worked with them, passingly," Wilhelm said. "I might even have imagined how it might be to be with them. But I never had any wish or intention to leave my wife. I don't believe she ever wanted to leave me, either. It would be a considerable shock if she did."

Talena finally recovered enough to get into the dialogue that so directly concerned her. "But did your passing notice of other women ever prevent you from loving your wife?"

"No, of course not."

"Heath never loved me. He married me because he had to, after he lost his first wife. I thought he would come to love me, but he never did. He was a perfect husband, but he never loved me. Finally I realized that he never would. So it seemed to make sense to let him go to the one he could love."

Wilhelm shook his head. "You may have done too much. Had he initiated it, and you agreed, then perhaps it would have worked. But you did it without him. That may seem like betrayal to him."

"Oh, I never meant that! I thought he would be pleased."

Wilhelm considered. "This Melee—she really does want him?"

"Oh, yes."

"And she really is a good person? I mean, she would be good for him?"

"Yes, definitely."

"Then perhaps she should be the one to persuade him."

"But she's across the river, taking care of our children."

"But if he were freed to go to her—"

"He might not do it," Crenelle said. "Not if he rejects the idea, as he seems to."

"There is surely some guilt there," Wilhelm said. "He may feel that he drove you to this, by not loving you. He may feel that he should not have a reward for doing that."

Talena nodded. "That could be. He is a very moral man."

"But if this woman were to go to him—"

"Oh, she would convince him," Talena agreed. "She's a passionate tigress. She always held herself in check, out of respect for me. But now she doesn't have to. She would sweep him away like a tempest."

Wilhelm nodded. "Then if there should be the chance, she must be enabled to go to him. I feel a certain responsibility for this impasse, and wish to abate it if I can."

"You have no responsibility," Talena said. "You have been more than good to us already."

"Put it down to the vagaries of male perspective," he said, smiling. "If you should have any contact with Melee, let me know, and I will see what I can do. It may be as simple as arranging Heath's release, as Dr. Kohler has agreed to do, in a place and at a time when this woman can then intercept him. Then it will be up to her."

Talena got up, wiped away her tears, went to him, and kissed him. "I owe you more than I can pay," she said.

Wilhelm shrugged. "If ever a time comes when payment is feasible, then you can do it. Until such time, have no concern." But he seemed pleased.

Crenelle was less teary and more realistic. "If we have contact with Melee, it is apt to be because she has sneaked across enemy lines to rescue us. She will not be under the truce."

"But you are," Wilhelm reminded her. "She must accept it before she enters here."

Crenelle nodded. "But if she does, you must let her go again. I know this woman; she will not be a captive."

"This is the nature of a truce," he agreed. "She must bring no mischief to me, and I must bring none to her. But if she brings any mischief to the German Army while in the city, she will pay."

"If she comes here, no mischief," Talena agreed. "We will hold her to that. *If* she comes."

He smiled. "I rather hope she does make an appearance, if she is as beautiful as you say." He glanced around as if guilty. "No offense to anyone here."

The women and Tourette frowned, but then Lita laughed, and they couldn't hold the expression any longer. They knew that Wilhelm was joking, not really believing in Melee's power of appearance, but that Melee would make him a believer.

❂

Melee found space at the edge of a barge heading into Stalingrad. She wore slacks and an overcoat, and her fair hair was bound back under her cap, but she could not conceal the fact that she was a woman. It was the evening of September 23, and this barge filled with soldiers was the only one she had been able to approach. So she just had to take her chances with the men.

"Hey, beautiful, I have good vodka," a man called to her. "It has great warmth."

"Then it will keep you warm without me," she replied, making a joke of it. It worked; several men laughed.

She had always been noticed by men, though her family had tried to protect her. As a child she had worn ballet slippers and practiced pirouettes. Later, determined to be more than a calendar image, she had studied medicine. That was, she now realized, partly because Heath had become a doctor. When she married Dillon she had devoted herself to his support, but retained the dream. But when the Germans invaded Russia in 1941, and Dillon had been killed, she had abandoned any dream but vengeance. She had done her best for Od, supporting him and Avan fully, but her real desire had been to get out there and break sticks. She thought of the Germans as sticks of wood, to be broken, rather than as people being killed. Now at last she was free to break bundles of sticks. It would never be enough to assuage the loss of Dillon, but it might help. She was tired of being a gentle wife and mother; that was for Talena, who really liked it. Melee was a fighter.

She might have gone anywhere, to join the Resistance. But Talena had been caught in Stalingrad, and if she and Telita still lived, Melee had to help them escape. And Stalingrad was closest. So she would get there, and break sticks, and check on the house when she could. She knew it wouldn't be easy, but she would do it. In time.

The Germans had overrun the suburban areas of Stalingrad on September 13 and 14, but resistance had stiffened around the factories to the north, and along the river. It was the factories that counted, militarily; industrial capacity was the muscle of a nation. But the Germans were pressing hard, and Russian losses were bad, so replacements had to be supplied constantly. Morale wasn't good; deserters were constantly being shot by the NKVD and left lying in full view as a warning to others. It hadn't occurred to the authorities that anyone would try to sneak *in* to this action, which was why she had been able to. And of course the men did not object to the company of a young woman, however briefly.

She stood at the railing, gazing out across the dark water. She could see the flashes of guns firing, and hear the distant explosions. It was beautiful, in its ugly way, for it meant that not all of the city had fallen. The Germans had swept in, but had been slowed, and now their advance was more like a city block a day. Maybe the tide was turning, and soon it would be the Germans in retreat. She was here to help that happen.

The barge worked its way slowly toward a landing site near the Red October plant. The old landing site was no longer secure, so they couldn't use it, but the new position left them exposed on open water for a longer time. That made the trip nervous business, for the Germans knew about the reinforcements and were targeting any craft they spied.

"What brings you here?" a man inquired. Then, as he saw her wary reaction: "Don't worry; I'm fifty, and I have children your age. I'm not trying to get you under a blanket."

She could afford to trust him that far. After all, they were comrades in arms. "My husband was killed last year. I want vengeance."

A man about her own age joined the dialogue. "He must have been a lucky man—before he became unlucky."

"He was a fine man, and an officer. But he wouldn't leave his post when the sticks overran it, though he was wounded and ill."

The older man laughed. "Sticks! Very nice. We'll make a bonfire of them."

Then a German plane passed over them, so suddenly that it was as if it had come from nowhere. And it dropped a bomb directly in the center of the ship. Right where Melee would have been, if she had accepted the invitation for vodka. She and the two men were thrown over the railing.

Melee knew how to swim, of course, even in an overcoat. But it weighed her down too much, so she had to struggle quickly out of it, sacrificing her food and knife. She saw the two soldiers floundering near her. "Swim for shore!" she cried. "It's not far!"

She set the example, stroking for the west bank. The two men followed.

The current had not seemed strong when the barge was drifting, exposed to enemy fire. But now it seemed fierce, sweeping them farther downriver than their forward progress swimming. She was rapidly tiring. But she made it, reaching the sands of the west bank, gasping for breath.

In moments the two soldiers joined her, no better off. "Where are we?" the young one asked.

"I have no idea," Melee said. "We must be far downstream, well into German territory. It can't be safe."

"But we can't just walk north to join our unit," the older man said. "We'd have to cross the line of combat."

Melee realized that if there was to be any leadership here, she would have to provide it. She saw a light approaching them: surely a German patrol. "We have to get out of sight immediately," she said. "In here." She ducked into a nearby sewer outlet.

The two soldiers hardly hesitated before following her. It wasn't as if any of them had not discovered what the attention of the Germans meant. But the stench was horrible. Melee hadn't realized how bad it would be. But of course a sewer was a sewer; one did not expect roses.

They stood near the outlet, hoping that they could go back out on the open sand soon. But the flicker of the light just came closer. "They will see our footprints," the younger man said.

He was right. "Then we can't go back out," Melee decided. "They probably won't follow us far in, because of the smell. We'll have to follow the sewer until we can find an exit into friendly territory. If we go far enough north, that should be feasible."

"Good thinking," the older man said. "The tunnels should go to every part of the city."

Melee appreciated his concurrence. She thought of asking his name, but realized that they might be better off anonymous, so that if one got caught, he couldn't be made to tell the identities of the others. Also, exchanging names would personalize them for each other, making them acquaintances, bordering on friends. She wanted neither the implied obligations of friendship—how long before the younger man thought of sex?—nor the heartache of loss when one of them died. Because she knew that the chances of all of them escaping alive were small. They were lucky to have survived the bombing of the barge; for all she knew, they were the only survivors, because those others who had not been killed by the blast could have been stunned so that they would have drowned. Luck was a fickle lover; it could kill them as readily as it had spared them.

The deeper they got in the sewer tunnel, the darker it became, and the worse the air got. Excrement clung to their shoes and trousers. Melee had had a small flashlight, but had lost that with her jacket. So she just had to put her hand out front to feel the filthy wall, and trust that there was no hidden drop-off.

Something shoved her shoulder. She tensed, turning. It was the old man. "Sorry," he said. "I'm afraid I'm getting a bit dizzy. I can't breathe well."

She couldn't blame him. It was like sucking in a fog of feces. "We've got to keep going," she said tersely. "There's nothing to eat here, and we wouldn't want to drink what we're wading through."

"I know," he gasped. "I'll be all right."

They went on. But after a while the old man collapsed. "Hey, it's not sack time yet," the younger man said, trying for humor. But it wasn't funny; the older man had fainted.

"We can't leave him here," Melee said. "We'll have to drag him. Maybe there's an exit close ahead."

"Maybe," the young man agreed.

They caught the man under his arms and dragged him along. But the extra burden not only slowed them, it made them breathe harder. The air seemed to coat noxious slime on Melee's lungs, making her nauseous. She could tell by the young man's gasping and staggering that he was suffering similarly.

The old man woke. "You can't do this," he said. "You're wearing yourselves out. There's no sense all three of us dying. Leave me here. If you find help, send someone back for me."

Melee exchanged a glance with the dim outline of the younger man. "I hate this," she said. "But I'm exhausted. I think we'll have to do it."

"Until we meet again," the older man said, as they left him sitting there in the sludge.

"Until we meet again," Melee and the young man agreed, knowing it was a lie.

She didn't know how long they trudged on. Were they still going north? There had been curves in the tunnel, and branchings. She had lost all sense of direction.

She found herself holding on to the man. She realized that he hadn't grabbed her; she had become dizzy, just as the old man had. "Maybe you had better leave me, too," she said.

"I couldn't stand to be here alone," he said candidly. "We can rest, then go on."

She was far too tired to object. They sank down against the wall, and she slogged on into a troubled sleep. At least it was some relief from reality.

"I think it's morning," the man said, waking her.

Sure enough, there was a wan light showing from somewhere down the tunnel. Time had passed. "We've got to get out of here," Melee said. "I can't take any more of this."

They went toward the light. It was filtering down from a manhole cover. They stood under it and listened. There were no close sounds. So they braced under it and slowly pushed it up.

Fresh air wafted down, a blessing from heaven. Melee put her face to the slit and peered out. "Seems clear," she said.

They pushed it up the rest of the way, and scrambled out. Then they replaced the manhole cover. They hurried into the nearest alley, getting out of sight.

"Well, we're here," Melee said, perking up. The fresh air was doing wonders for her. "But where is here?"

Then a group of soldiers walked down the street, passing the alley. Their outfits were so dirty and ragged that it was hard to tell what nationality they were.

"Are we in the wrong section of town?" the man asked.

Melee considered. "Does it matter? We'll have to go out among them, until we can find our way to our own unit. We can pose as civilian workers. But I had better not look like a woman."

"Agreed." He faced her and helped her get her hair jammed back under her soiled cap. A button had been lost from the front of her shirt. She found a pin and used it to close the shirt up. "Slouch, and take small breaths," he recommended. Then: "I'd sure like to see you in a dress sometime."

She flashed him a smile. "Maybe if we make it back alive."

"Just in case—do you speak German? I don't. If they are the enemy, and question us—"

"Some. So I'll do the talking."

They walked boldly out into the street, as if they had a right to be there. Down the street, where the men had gone, a group of soldiers were lining up in front of a building.

"They have mess tins," the man said. "God, I'm famished!"

"So am I. So we'll join them."

"But those are soldiers! We don't know whether they're ours."

"And we're workers. Come on."

They joined the line. They didn't have any mess tins, but maybe they could borrow some. Melee nerved herself to bluff their way through.

A soldier next to them wrinkled his nose in disgust. "What in God's name is that smell?" he asked in German.

Melee's heart sank. They were after all in the wrong section. And the odor of the sewer clung to them, marking them distinctively. But she was too hungry to quit. So she decided to bluff. She held her place in line, ignoring the soldier's comment as if she had not heard it.

They made it into the mess hall. There were some spare mess kits, so they picked them up and took their servings. There was a Russian cook who peered hard at them, but did not speak. Melee thought feverishly: was this an ally, or an informer? She gambled, acting on intuition. She looked him in the eye, then turned her head and lifted her cap, giving him a glimpse of her bundled long hair, Russian style.

It worked. He gave her an extra portion.

They sat at a table, side by side with the German soldiers. Another sniffed and spoke up: "There's an awful stench here."

There was a murmur of agreement around the table. Melee wrinkled her nose too, pretending the smell came from somewhere else. Meanwhile, she gobbled down her food. It was so good to eat again!

Then a German officer passed the table. He took one look at Melee. "You're Russian!" he said.

"Nein," she said, knowing it was hopeless. They had been discovered. Was there even any point in trying to make a break for it? Without weapons, surrounded by the enemy—

Then the Russian cook she had halfway befriended rushed over to the table. "Sir, it is all right," he said in halting German. "These two are working for the Reich. Undercover work."

"They still stink to high heaven," the officer snapped. "Get them out of this hall."

"Yes, sir," the cook said. Then, to Melee, "I should have told you. You must eat separately. Not with the regular troops. Come with me."

Wordlessly, Melee and the young man rose and followed the cook to the kitchen, where he fed them well.

"You saved our lives," Melee murmured. "We are deeply grateful."

"When you get out of here, get across to the Russian lines," the cook said. "Don't waste any time, because if the officer investigates, he'll know I lied. Take the road north, out of the city; there's no action there at the moment, and you can get across at night."

Melee was about to thank him again, but at that point the German officer came into the kitchen. "You still stink," he said. "I don't care what kind of work you are doing, you're polluting the food. Get out of here now."

"Yes, sir," Melee said briskly. She stuffed a roll in her pocket, gulped down more water, and walked calmly out of the mess hall.

Only when they were safely away from the building, and out of sight around a corner, did she allow herself to react. "My knees feel like cooked noodles," she confessed.

"Mine too," the man said. "Thank God for that Russian cook!"

"He saved our lives," Melee agreed. "I could have kissed him. But I would have made him stink."

He laughed, perhaps more than the remark warranted. It was just such a relief to be alive and free.

Invigorated, they walked north. When they found a place to hide, they did so, and slept for several hours. Then they made their way at nightfall to the no-man's-land between the lines.

The moment they were through, Melee spoke up, loudly addressing the seemingly empty night alley. "We are Russians," she said. "We just crossed from the other side. Do not shoot us. I'm female."

They were immediately surrounded by soldiers. Light bathed them. Melee removed her cap and let her fair hair fall down across her shoulders. If there had been doubt before, it dissipated. Suddenly solicitous, the Russians conducted them farther behind the lines, gave them a drink, clean clothes, new rifles, and a chamber with a basin of water.

The young soldier hesitated. Melee knew why. "You have been a good companion," she said. "We may never see each other again. So I will give you a sight to remember. Just stand there and watch."

Then she stripped before him, and took the cloth and basin and washed herself completely. He neither spoke nor moved. He was riveted, as she had expected. She showed him everything, without being obvious about it. She had rewarded him for his constancy. Then she dressed in the new clothing. "I'm sorry I couldn't show you me in a dress. I hope you will survive the disappointment."

He tried to speak, but didn't seem able to. He did not, however, seem disappointed. "Now it is your turn. I will wait outside."

He nodded. She went outside the chamber. She had done him the additional favor of not embarrassing him by making him strip before her in an obvious state of sexual excitement. He would never forget her, though they had never exchanged names.

There was an officer outside. "Oh," Melee said, remembering. "There was a third member of our party. A man of about fifty. He fainted in the stifling sewer. We tried to drag him, but he made us stop. We had to leave him. We said we would send someone back for him, if possible."

"In the middle of German-occupied Stalingrad?" the officer demanded. "In an unmarked sewer?" Then he paused, noting Melee's expression. "We will do what we can."

"Thank you, sir." She gave him a smile. She knew they would not be able to do anything, but at least she had asked.

The line here was stable for the moment; they were content merely to hold the Germans off, as it was easier to shoot down an attacker from cover, than to do the attacking. They knew that their numbers were much smaller than those of the Germans, so a holding action was best, while they waited for significant reinforcements.

Melee had had some experience with rifles, but not enough, and this was serious. Nevertheless, she found that she was a pretty good shot, considering. She liked the contained explosion of the rifle, and the power of the shot as it struck a wall. This was much better than skulking through the sewer.

So she volunteered for sniping duty. They had set up a school for snipers in the Lazur Chemical Plant. She reported there with her rifle, not bothering to conceal her gender.

"But you're a woman!" the officer in charge protested.

She frowned as if confused. "What is your point, sir?"

Embarrassed, he brought her inside. On one wall of a long room they had painted helmets, observation slits, human outlines, and similar devices as targets. The room echoed with the reports of rifle fire as instructors hovered over their students, criticizing and improving their technique.

The officer brought her to an empty slot. "Fire at that pair of eyes," he said, indicating a crude sketch of a face with two big eyes.

She lifted her rifle and took aim. She fired. She saw the bullet strike to the right. She had missed.

"If you were in the field, the return shot would kill you," the officer said, disgusted.

That annoyed her. "Not if I had cover." She dropped to the floor, set an empty ammunition box in front of her, and poked the muzzle of the rifle just beyond it. She fired, this time missing to the left.

"I like your spirit," the officer said. "I will assign you a trainer. But if you don't get more accurate, you'll be out soon. We have too little ammunition to waste."

"Yes, sir!" she agreed enthusiastically.

She took turns firing all day, until her shoulder was numb from the shock of the recoils. But she was getting steadily more accurate as she responded to the advice of the instructor.

The man nodded approvingly. "You are learning well, and you respond well. I believe you can make a decent sniper. But you must understand, the work is dangerous."

"I want to break sticks," she said.

"Tomorrow, September twentieth, this school will be taken over by Vassili Zaitsev, a famous Russian sniper. He is arriving with the 284th Division. I will recommend you to him."

"Thank you."

The man hesitated. "He—he is said to have a taste for the women. You are a beautiful woman. If you do not wish—I mean no offense—"

"I will be other than beautiful tomorrow," she said. "Thank you for the warning."

As it happened, she was not the only woman in the sniping school. Three of the thirty students were female, and one of the others was well endowed. Melee kept her hair concealed, her shirt baggy, and rubbed some dirt on her face. Most Russian soldiers were unable to change clothing or wash frequently, looked chronically grubby, and suffered infestations of lice, so the appearance was not unusual. She resembled a boy. Even so, she was glad for the presence of the other woman, who was plainly flattered by the new instructor's interest.

Zaitsev did know his business. In short order he had winnowed out the poor shots and sharpened the good shots. Nervous when he first reviewed her, Melee missed her target, but hit it when he corrected her, and hit it dead center when he corrected her again. He could see exactly where she went wrong, and correct it with a few words. She was suddenly shooting better than ever before.

"But a target is one thing," he said. "A moving target is another. And a living person is another. Can you hit a man?"

"I can break a stick," she said. "Germans are sticks."

"You will do. Tomorrow I will teach you and the others the use of the sniperscope."

The training progressed rapidly. When Zaitsev was satisfied, he took a select group out to "No-Man's-Land," where they could get practice against actual German front line troops. They set up after dark, each behind carefully undisturbed rubble, and waited. Each was to cover an assigned section of the enemy line, and to wait for the proper opportunity. There was to be no random shooting; every shot was to be an attempted kill. Because, as Zaitsev made clear, each shot was a marker of the position of the sniper. If the kill was not made, the sniper quickly became a German target, for the enemy had snipers too. One shot, then hide.

After an hour of silence, during which her eyes became fully attuned to the darkness, Melee saw activity in her section. Was a stick about to foolishly show himself? Yes! A helmet was slowly rising from its cover. She waited, knowing it could be the oldest ruse in the business, a helmet on a stick. But it wasn't; it was a German solder who just couldn't resist looking at the enemy positions, thinking that because they were silent, they were inactive. She saw him more by the motion than the outline, a darkness against a darkness.

She let him stand, and turn, until he faced her directly. Then she squeezed off a single shot aimed at the center of the face. The rifle bucked, the head flung around, and the stick fell.

She ducked her head, keeping well out of sight. There was no return fire. But she was not fool enough to make herself a target. She knew the German snipers were looking for her, having a general notion where she was, but not a specific one. Because her shot had caught them by surprise, and the only one who might have seen the flash of her muzzle was dead.

She thought she might have been horrified, but instead she was exultant. Her first kill! She had come through. One trifling part of her vengeance against the Germans had been accomplished.

Later in the night, there was another shot, by one of the other snipers. The target fell, and there were return shots. But they were scattered; they did not have a specific target.

In the morning the snipers retreated. Zaitsev briefed them before they retired for sleep. "Congratulations, Melee!" he said. "You have graduated. But next time aim for the center, instead of for the left eye."

"Yes, sir," she agreed as the others laughed. They all knew that she couldn't have hit the left eye if she had aimed for it.

Then it was time for Zaitsev to break in a new batch of students, so the recent graduates had time off. Melee had special business, but she respected Zaitsev enough to clear it with him.

"You want to sneak alone across enemy lines?" he asked incredulously.

"I must check on my friend Talena," she said. "I need to know whether she and her daughter are safe."

"Do you know what the Germans will do to you, if they catch you?"

"They will rape my dead body," she said, touching the concealed dagger she wore. She would kill herself rather than submit to capture, because she knew they would torture her to death.

"That would be such a waste," he said. He had of course long since caught on to her real appearance, but also to her disinterest in having a more personal relationship with him. He knew that she had a man who was captive of the Germans.

"So may I go?"

"If your personal situation should ever change, remember this favor," he said, not compromising himself by giving open permission.

"Yes, sir." She was agreeing to consider him as her lover, if she lost the man she was after. In the circumstances, it was a fair exchange.

He produced a map. "Here, tonight, is safest." He touched a spot along the line of battle. "And here, tomorrow night, for the return. Do not get caught by either side."

Fair warning. He would cover for her absence, but would denounce her if she were caught. She nodded, and departed.

So, on the last day of September, Melee girded herself with dagger and pistol and went to the first crossing site. The line was in daily flux, with each side studying the position of the other, and at the moment this one was porous on the German side. Crossing was still dangerous, but her sniper training served her well; she could move silently, and spot sticks wherever they might be. She couldn't take her rifle along, but she should be able to avoid detection. She was wearing nondescript clothing that concealed both her nationality and her gender, though that would not save her if she got caught in no-man's-land.

She succeeded. By midnight she was across and moving southwest through the dark city. Before dawn she was watching Talena's house. It was occupied—but by whom? She could not afford to assume too much.

Just before dawn, a woman emerged from the back door. Melee recognized her: Crenelle, a neighbor.

She followed the woman, making sure no one else was watching. Crenelle went to her own house, which had been bombed. That explained why she had moved. But was that all?

Melee waited as the woman entered the wreckage. Then she approached, taking cover near the back door. When the woman emerged with a package, Melee addressed her.

"Crenelle."

Crenelle stopped immediately. "So it's you, Melee! I wondered."

Melee came out to meet her. "And you were ready," she said.

The woman shifted her package, revealing the pistol she was holding. "The streets are not necessarily safe at any time. What is your situation?"

"I am with the Russians on the front. But I had to check on Talena and Lita. What is their situation?"

"They are safe and well. Tourette and I share their house now. I have some supplies that help."

"The Germans didn't deport them?"

"We are protected by a German officer. Heath arranged for that. We serve the man, and he protects us."

"He lets you go armed?"

"Yes. We have a truce. We will not betray him."

"Well, I have no truce!"

"Then stay away, because we gave our word. He is a good man, and we need him."

"You prostitute yourselves for protection from deportation?"

"No. He does not ask that of us. But we would if we had to."

It was a fair answer. "What of Heath?"

"He works for a German doctor, under similar truce. But Melee—when Talena told him about the change, he did not accept it."

"Foolish masculine pride," Melee muttered. "Maybe I can seek him out and reason with him."

"No, that is too dangerous. But he could be summoned here. But you would have to join the truce. You would have to trust Wilhelm."

"Trust a stick ? I'd rather kill him!"

"You must not!" Crenelle said quickly.

Melee reconsidered. Crenelle was a tough woman who could be trusted. "Suppose I agree for an hour, so as to see Talena and Lita?"

"For an hour," Crenelle agreed.

She followed Crenelle, and they entered the house together. "I have a visitor," Crenelle announced, not loudly.

Lita appeared. "Melee!" she cried, hugging her.

Then Talena appeared, and did the same. "But where are the children?" she asked next.

"With Od. He had a rough session, and finally rafted across the river. So he took over there, and I came to fight. I'm a sniper now, in the factory zone. But I had to make sure you were all right."

"We are. But we're prisoners. You can't stay."

"So I thought. Crenelle said I would have to make truce for an hour, so I have done so. I just need to know how everything is with you, so I can tell Od and the children, or send word."

"But if Wilhelm sees you here, he'll have to report you," Talena said. "We're so glad to know you are safe, and so is Od. But you must go."

"Crenelle says I must trust your German officer."

"To meet Heath," Crenelle said.

Talena drew back. "Oh, I had forgotten! Yes. Heath—he—"

"Crenelle said. I said I could look for him, but she—"

"No, you would be caught and killed, and compromise him too. But he could come here, if you talked to Wilhelm. Then he could go with you, if he wanted."

"Do you expect me to believe a German officer would help two Russian nationals to meet, and to escape, without turning them in? This smells like bait for a trap."

"No!" Talena protested. "He is a man of honor. You must trust him."

Melee shook her head. "I don't think I can do that. I want to meet Heath, but it has to be my way. I will not trick him and me into betrayal and torture."

Talena clenched her hands. "Damn it, you're as bad as Heath is! You just can't accept something that runs counter to your prejudice."

That set Melee back. Talena had never before spoken to her like that. She looked at Crenelle.

"Believe her," Crenelle said.

She looked at Telita. "It's true," the girl said.

They all believed. Either this German was true, or he was the world's best deceiver. Melee would not accept it, except that her desire for Heath was so great as to imperil common sense. "You all swear that this German can be trusted?"

They all nodded.

Melee shook her head. "Then be it on your heads, if you are wrong. I will talk with him. But if he tries to kill me, or turn me in, I'll kill him first."

"He won't," Talena said. "He will honor the truce." She went to the bedroom door and knocked. Melee tensed, watching the door. "Sir."

"Yes." The voice was behind them.

They all whirled. There was a German officer in full uniform, with his

Luger drawn and pointed at Melee. He must have overheard them talking and climbed out the window, circled the house, and so caught them all off-guard. She had after all walked into the trap.

"But she is here under truce," Talena protested weakly.

"She spoke of killing me," the man said grimly.

"If you betrayed the truce. That is reasonable. She's not a prisoner."

"Lita has told me much of her," the officer said. "Even through her dull clothing, I can see her beauty." He smiled. "I think I can trust her honor. Now she will trust mine."

"Like hell!" Melee snapped.

Then he took the barrel of his gun in his left hand, let go with his right, and proffered it to Crenelle butt first. "Verify that this is loaded, and give it to her. Then I will summon her friend."

Crenelle, who clearly knew guns, checked the weapon, and brought it to Melee. "It is as he says. Do not act rashly."

Melee took the Luger and checked it herself. It had a full clip. She looked at the officer. He stood at ease. He had indeed forced the issue. He had given her the ultimate power in this house.

"Now I will make the call," he said. He walked to the telephone and spoke a series of numbers into it as Melee watched, holding the gun. The only way he could be sure of keeping his life was by playing it straight, because she could kill him before any German rescue could occur. Even if they surrounded the house with machine guns, she could take him out.

"Doctor Kohler," the officer said. "Wilhelm here. I have a message for Heath: Melee has come for you." He listened a moment, then hung up. "It may take two or three hours to get him cleaned up and routed here, but he will come. Now shall we relax." He walked to the easy chair and sat in it.

"Heath will come here?" Melee asked numbly.

"He will come here," the officer agreed. "Now we must plan strategy, or perhaps tactics. He may believe he must deny you, and that weapon will not win him over. Have you a better program?"

"But if he comes, the Germans will know," Melee said. "They will come too."

"No. Doctor Kohler has arranged to let him go, when the time comes. If you have a way to get him out of the city, you have only to persuade him to take it. There will be no pursuit." He fixed her with an eye turned steely. "And no word among the Russians of how he escaped. You understand why."

She did understand. There were Russian defectors as well as German defectors, so what was known in one camp was soon known in the other. Wilhelm could be betrayed by the Russians, and court-martialed by the Germans.

Melee realized that she had to trust Wilhelm. If she lost, it was only her life, which had been in constant peril in recent weeks anyway. If she won, she would have Heath. At last. "Agreed." Then she handed the gun back to Crenelle, who returned it to the man. He put it away without looking.

"You must change," Talena said. "One of my dresses can be altered for you."

They went into the bedroom and got busy selecting a dress and adjusting it to fit perfectly. They worked on her hair. They found suitable slippers. And makeup.

Within the hour Melee stepped out to the main room. "Perhaps the judgment of a man is best," she said. "Will this do?"

Wilhelm, seated in the chair, looked her up and down. "Ravishing," he said. Then he got businesslike. "When he comes, we can not go outside. You will have the bedroom, and we will not intrude. But if you let him leave this house without you, there will be no more I can do."

"Understood." Then Melee sat in a chair opposite him. "What is your price for this?"

"I have a wife and children in Germany. I want to return safely to them. If Germany wins the war, this will be feasible. But if Russia wins, it will be more difficult."

Melee nodded. "Give me Heath, and I will give you your family, if it is in any way in my power. If Russia wins, and I live."

He nodded. "We need say no more of this." For such a deal could imperil either of them with their own governments.

The six of them—for Crenelle's daughter Tourette appeared—talked amicably of general things, and Melee found herself coming to like Wilhelm. He had the sharpest mind she had encountered, and he was neither coward nor fool. She had to admit that not every German was a stick. She could see why the others had come to trust him, and to work with him.

Then a vehicle approached. "Perhaps you, Lita," Wilhelm said. "You have no adult agenda."

The girl nodded and went to the front door, then outside. "And perhaps you should make an entrance when summoned," he said to Melee. She agreed, and retreated to the kitchen.

Soon Lita returned with Heath. He was dressed in a reasonably clean civilian work uniform, and looked well. He stood at the doorway, looking at them all. "I had to come," he said. "To abate this nonsense. Is she really here?"

"She is really here," Wilhelm said. "Under truce. Will you go with her?"

"Of course not. My wife is Talena."

"In name only," Talena said. "Just talk with her, Heath. You owe us all that much."

"I will talk with her. Where is she?"

This was her cue. Melee stepped into plain view. She knew she was as striking as she had ever been. "Hello, Heath."

He looked at her, and paused. It had probably been months since he had seen any woman in a dress, and she was not just any woman.

In the silence, she walked on across to stand immediately before him. "I have come for you, Heath. After ten years, I have come at last."

He managed to speak. "You are Od's wife!"

"In much the manner you were Talena's husband. The motions are not the reality."

He looked around. "We can't have this discussion here."

"We'll have it in the bedroom," she said. She took him by the hand and led him there. No one else moved or spoke; they were like statues.

She closed the bedroom door. Then she embraced him and sought to kiss him. He averted his face.

"I know you have always wanted me," she said. "As I have wanted you. Why won't you take me?"

"This isn't a chess game, where pieces can be moved in honor of some grand design! This isn't right. We are married to others."

She decided to press the issue. "And all these years, you took poor Talena to bed but never gave her your love. Was that right?"

"I was always faithful to her."

"In spirit?"

"What do you want of me?"

"I want you to recognize reality. Come with me to the Russian lines. Rejoin your own people. Be my love."

"No."

She had intended to be alluring and persuasive, but suddenly she lost it. "Listen, you ingrate! We have risked our lives to fulfill your dream. You can't throw it away."

He turned, reaching for the door handle. She wrapped her arms around him and hauled him away. He tried again to reach it. She clung to him and wrapped her legs around him.

"Get off me, you bitch," he snapped.

"You turd!" she screamed. "I could have stayed safe across the river. I could have had another officer for a lover. I gave it all up, for the mere dream of you. And now you are rejecting me? You have no right!"

"I never sought the love of a twelve-year-old!" he said.

"So that's it! Well, I'm not twelve any more. And I'm going to prove it." She dropped her feet to the floor, braced herself, and hauled him stumbling to the bed. "Now get out of those clothes before I rip them off you."

"Don't act like a whore!"

"If you had the courage of your desire, I wouldn't have to!" she retorted.

"Sex has nothing to do with it. You have no right to break up my marriage to a fine woman."

"Talena's been bedding Od. Get it through your skull: those marriages are over."

He froze. Apparently on some level he had refused to recognize the relationship of Od and Talena. "That can't be."

"It can be, and it is. Now it's our turn." She backed him up against the bed and began unbuttoning his shirt.

He caught her hands. "Stop this, Melee. It's an ugly scene."

She went limp. "Do it with me this once, then go, if that's the way you really want it. Abolish the dream by realizing it."

He shook his head. "If I touch you, I'll never get free. You know that."

"Because you truly want me, and I want you."

"That's irrelevant." He let her go and turned away.

She realized with a shock that her all-out frontal attack was not working. He would not be seduced. She did not have the winning hand. It unnerved her; her power over men had always been unfailing. How could she fail with this most important one?

"Heath, tell me what you want of me. I love you. How can I be near you?"

He paused at the door. "I don't think it's right for you to be near me. I'm sorry." He opened the door.

She lay on the bed and buried her face in the pillow. She refused to cry, or to plead. She had been defeated, when she had never anticipated it. She had to let him go.

She heard the door close behind him. She did not move. She had lost the most important battle of her life.

She lay there for a brief eternity, stunned, knowing that when her feeling returned, the pain would be unbearable.

Then a hand touched her shoulder. She hadn't heard anyone come in. "I can't leave you, Melee," he said.

She lifted her head, not trusting herself to speak. Was this a dream, or a confusion?

"I crossed that room, and they were all looking at me," he said. "Every step I took was harder. I saw Talena crying." He paused. "I had to free her."

She nodded, still afraid to speak, lest it all puff away in smoke.

"I can't bear to see her cry. She's not like you."

Yes, Talena could express her pain. She could move him in a way Melee could not. Melee stared at him, dry-eyed.

He bowed his head. "I will go with you."

She found his hand, and brought it to her face, and kissed it. Then, suddenly, completely surprising her, the floodgates opened, and she was weeping.

He sat beside her and put his arm around her. "Melee, I'm sorry. I did not mean to be insensitive."

She still couldn't speak. She was afraid the tears would never stop, but then he was mopping her face, and it seemed unfair to keep wetting it down again, so she dried out.

Then she got up and changed back into her nondescript clothing. He sat on the bed and watched her without comment. When she was done, he stood, and they went together to the door.

The others remained as they had been, silent. They must have heard everything, and seen enough. It didn't matter.

"Thank you," Heath said to all of them. Then the two of them walked out the door.

Melee would have liked to say farewell to the others, but the present mood was too fragile to risk. They surely understood.

A car was waiting. Heath went to speak with the driver. "I will not be returning," he said. "Please thank Dr. Kohler."

The driver nodded, and drove away. Then they started walking north.

They avoided any Germans they saw, sometimes ducking into alleys or behind rubble. But as they approached the battle line there were too many. "We'll have to hide until nightfall," Melee said.

They found a bombed-out building with part of its second floor remaining. They crawled up into that, and lay waiting for the night.

"Shall we?" Heath inquired.

She kissed him. It was, she realized, the first time. Then slowly, gently, quietly, they made love. It wasn't at all the way she had imagined it, with roaring passion, but it, was infinitely more tender.

They slept, and it was beautiful, just being with him. He was indeed the man of her dreams. She just hadn't dreamed it correctly. How different reality was from expectation, yet also better.

In the night they resumed travel, and she led him through the secret route to the Russian lines. She was glad there was no trouble, because she would have hated to have to kill somebody while in this beatific mood.

She took him to her small chamber. "In the morning I'll introduce you," she said. He nodded, and they slept again, without sex.

The following day she introduced Heath to Zaitsev. "Good enough," the man said, as if this were routine. "We need another doctor."

Indeed, Heath was immediately busy tending to the Russian wounded.

Meanwhile there was important news on the sniping front. They learned that the Germans had sent for their own super sniper, Major Konings from Berlin. He had come to kill Zaitsev.

Far from being cowed, the Russian was satisfied. "It is a challenge," he said. "I must meet their champion and destroy him."

Melee was fascinated. Zaitsev was happy to acquaint her with the full significance and detail of the challenge. She knew this was because he hoped to persuade her to become his lover, despite her rescue of Heath, but she went along because she was truly interested.

Their first word of Konings's presence came from a prisoner, who revealed that the major was prowling the front lines. There was an immediate meeting of the Russian sniper group. Colonel Batyuk, commander of the 284th Division, was certain that the German sniper would be easy meat. Zaitsev agreed.

"But first I have to find him," he told Melee. "I have to understand his methods and habits."

Melee understood. Zaitsev had already killed several German sharpshooters, but only after days of watching their habits. It was relatively easy to kill a recruit who carelessly poked his head up to look around; she had done it herself. But a sharpshooter was another matter. He was hunter, not prey, and his weaknesses were subtle. So the special prey had to be studied, his spoor tracked, his water holes zeroed in, his sleeping and feeding patterns established. What was Koning's camouflage, his firing patterns, his ruses? Only then would Zaitsev end the hunt with a single perfectly placed shot.

"And I know that he is studying me as carefully," Zaitsev said. "He came here to get me. He will be reading leaflets describing our sniper techniques, and descriptions of my mannerisms. And of my girlfriends." He paused, but Melee did not comment. She did not care to offer him hope of success in that department, but neither did she want to discourage him prematurely. "Major Konings does not yet know the lay of the land. He needs to study the local terrain. He will not act until he is satisfied. That gives me time to prepare for him."

Melee paid close attention, because she aspired to be the best of snipers. It was a science in itself, with perhaps a week of work preceding the single second of the finish.

For several days she and the other snipers searched the ruins of Stalingrad through their field glasses, hoping to discover *the* prey. They came to Zaitsev with schemes to pull Konings out into the open, and some of them were fresh and novel. But Zaitsev rejected them all. "I will wait for my enemy to reveal himself," he said.

The duel began in earnest on October 7. Two Soviet snipers in the same area were taken out by single rifle shots. That had to be Konings's work. The field of battle was a stretch of no-man's-land between Maemev Hill and the Red October Plant. Zaitsev searched the familiar terrain. "Nothing unfamiliar," he muttered. "The trenches and bunkers are unchanged."

But they had learned one thing: the German had struck during daylight hours. He liked to sleep at night. So the duel had to be by day. Conditions were different, but Zaitsev was glad to oblige. One had to go where and when the quarry went.

Throughout the afternoon Zaitsev and a friend lay behind cover, running their field glasses back and forth, searching for a clue. Melee watched too, determined to contribute if she possibly could. Around them the constant bombardment of opposing armies faded into the background. At the moment it was a search for a single man. Melee and other snipers lay in better protected holes farther back, to observe and learn. They were too far away to be either good snipers or good targets, but they could see reasonably well.

As the sun dimmed, a helmet bobbed unevenly along a German trench. There he was! But Zaitsev did not raise his rifle and fire. Melee realized that it had probably been a ruse, a helmet on a stick or even an ignorant soldier sent out to draw fire, so that Konings could spot the location of the Russian sniper. Zaitsev had been too canny to fall for that.

When darkness was complete, the Russians crept back to their own bunker, arguing about Konings's strategy. The man had done nothing to reveal himself. Yet he could not hope to take out Zaitsev unless he joined battle. He had to be there, somewhere.

Before dawn the snipers were back in their holes, studying the battlefield again. Konings remained silent. When night came, they retreated to get some sleep. "I have to admire the man's skill and patience," Zaitsev said. "He took out two of mine, to get my attention. He knows I am watching. He knows I know that he will take out more of mine, if I don't get him." He glanced obliquely at Melee. "Perhaps even you, my dear." Again she remained, as it were, in her hole, not responding. If she gave him any opening, he would take her. "So I can not depart. He has me captive. Until I kill him."

The third morning began like the second. Then it changed. A political officer, whom she recognized as one of Od's associates, Danilov, came out to witness the contest. At first light the heavy guns began their normal barrage. Melee eyed the landscape, oblivious. It was as if the rest of the war did not exist, only this tense vigil.

Danilov suddenly stood, like an utter idiot, shouting "There he is! I'll point him out to you."

A single shot took him through the shoulder. The stretcher bearers came to take Danilov to the hospital. Zaitsev never moved. They couldn't even be sure it was him, and not some lesser sniper, for Danilov had been an easy target, and the shot had not been through the head.

Melee put her glasses back to the battlefield, concentrating on the on the sector in front of Zaitsev where she thought the shot had originated. On the left was a disabled tank. To the right was a pillbox. She hardly bothered with the tank, certain that no experienced sniper would use such an exposed target. The firing slit in the pilloox had been closed up. That wasn't a good prospect either. She saw a sheet of iron, and then a pile of bricks lying between the tank and the pillbox. Could that seemingly innocuous rubble be a hiding place? No, it seemed impossible.

Then Zaitsev used a simple trick, one that no self-respecting sniper would fall for. He raised a white glove on the end of a stick. As it showed above his parapet, a rifle cracked, and the glove was hurriedly pulled down. Melee knew it had been holed in the center. And she had seen the flash: Konings was under the sheet of iron.

But Zaitsev didn't fire at it. She knew why: there was no shot to be had. The iron would deflect the bullet, and a shot anywhere else would miss. The man had to actually show himself.

Night came, and the Russians retreated. "He's under the metal," Zaitsev said. "But I can't get a clear shot. Tomorrow I'll take a new position, one that will put the afternoon sun at my back." He glanced at Melee. "Pray that he doesn't change his hole."

"I supposed I could put on a skirt and dance over the metal," Melee said.

He laughed. "That would keep him there! But his jealous girlfriend would take you out with one shot through the knickers."

Melee didn't answer. Zaitsev was the one who wanted to get a shot at her knickers.

Next morning the Russian contingent was in its new nest. Konings's metal blind was to their southeast. Zaitsev's companion fired one blind shot, just to arouse their enemy's curiosity. Then they settled down to wait until late afternoon.

When their position was shrouded in shadow, and the sun was in the German's eyes, Melee knew that Zaitsev was raising his rifle into position and focusing through its telescopic sight. She saw a piece of glass glint once from the German's hiding place.

A helmet slowly lifted over the lip of the parapet. A shot cracked, and Zaitsev's companion jumped and screamed convincingly. For an instant Melee though he had been hit, before realizing the ruse.

Under the iron sheet, Konings lifted his head slightly, to make sure of his victim. It wasn't enough for any kind of target, but Zaitsev's shot took him between the eyes.

Heath just shook his head when she told him about it. "What you see as a great victory, I see as the sad death of one more man."

"But we have to win this war!" she protested. "We have to abolish the diabolical sticks!"

"They are not sticks! They are human beings, as we are."

"They are monsters!"

"They are human beings in a dreadful situation, as we are."

"How can you say that? You know the atrocities they have committed."

"I have seen the atrocities we have committed, too. There are good and bad men on either side."

She saw he would not be moved. She tried to end the difference by kissing him, but he would not bend to meet her. She realized, then, that their ideal love was nothing of the sort; she had brought him back, but they were still two different people. The perfection of the dream was not translating into reality. He had never said he loved her.

Was she to be like Talena, longing after a man who gave her lip service rather than love? She rejected the notion.

Melee was still in training, though she had a good grasp of the essentials. She was eager to do more, driven in part by her private personal frustration. So she was glad when she was sent on a special mission for the 284th Division. A captured prisoner had pinpointed the position of the German Army HQ. It was in a building between the Stalinski Flying School and the Red October Plant. She and five others were assigned to dynamite it.

Heath was one of the five. When she learned that, she went immediately to the commander. "What are you trying to do? Heath's not a fighter!"

"He asked to go," the commander said evenly. "Considering your relationship, I did not feel free to deny him."

Melee's protest died. Heath *did* care. But she hoped he didn't get his head blown off.

Still, she asked him why. "I thought I should get a better notion what you are doing," he said.

She had to be satisfied with that. "Just see that you don't get hurt."

At night they passed beyond Russian lines and crawled into German territory. They froze whenever they heard voices or saw a flare burst overhead; any motion could betray them. After a painstaking hour they reached their target: a half-destroyed apartment house. One entire wall was missing, revealing the tiers of its floors like a battered doll house.

The patrol slid into an intact stairwell. Melee was last. When they reached the second landing the others disappeared around a corner, but a noise distracted her. She whirled to see a German soldier emerging from behind a post.

"Hände hoch," he grunted, waving his pistol in her face.

The fool! He was telling her to arise her hands. He should simply have shot her. She lashed out with a boot, catching him in the groin. He doubled over, dropping his weapon. She grabbed his helmet and cracked his face into her knee. She needed to take him out silently, so as not to alert the Germans.

The man savagely bit her thumb. She knocked him down, twisting his right arm under his body. Then she took hold of his throat with both hands, choking him. He thrashed violently, but she held on. His helmet came off, and she saw that he had bright red hair. She leaned harder against his windpipe, and he gurgled horribly.

Then Heath appeared, looking for her. When he saw the situation, he pushed her away and smashed the German's head with his rifle butt. Then he paused. "What have I done?"

"You broke a stick," she said shortly, and ran on up the stairs, leaving him there. The others had put the dynamite in place.

It was time to light the fuse. "You do it," the sergeant told her.

She was glad to. She lit it, and saw it sparkle as it caught. At the sight, the others lost all caution. They ran down the stairs, careless of the noise. Scattered shots sounded behind them, but no one was hit.

Heath was below, tending to the red-haired German. "What's this?" she demanded.

"I am a healer, not a killer," he said.

"He tried to kill me!"

"No, you were trying to kill him."

She had no patience with this. "Come *on!*" She grabbed Heath's arm and hauled him along with her.

As they cleared the area, there was a shattering explosion. Light flared behind them. The German HQ building was destroyed. Later they learned that there had been no significant loss of personnel, but at least their mission had been accomplished.

Once they were safely back on their own side, she had at Heath. "You were trying to save that stick!"

"Yes."

"What am I to do with you?"

He looked soberly at her. "I think now I understand your appeal. You represent my dark side. I set out to be a healer, but there was that in me that desired the other face of the coin."

That cut right through her spirit. She could not deny it. Because his appeal for her was his healing. She was a killer. He was her bright side. "Oh, God, Heath! We are a match made in hell!"

He did not deny it.

In the last week of October the Germans assaulted the factories. They were being stupid about it. Had they focused their forces north and south of the city and driven wedges between the Russian defenders and the river, they could have cut off their supplies and starved them out. The way Od had been starved out of his building. Instead, the Germans were trying to use brute force in repeated frontal attacks, and taking heavy losses because of it. The snipers were a significant part of the defense.

Melee and several other student snipers took up positions in the top story of a tall building. They settled down behind piles of bricks to monitor enemy traffic. She saw German soldiers scurrying back and forth between trenches. She tracked their progress through her rifle scope. She was a student, but she was now a dead shot. It would be so easy to break those sticks!

But no one fired. Zaitsev had told them to wait for his permission before revealing their position. What a waste! She fidgeted at the window, furious at having to let so many sticks get away.

Then a column of German infantry suddenly burst into the open. She could stand it no longer. "Shoot!" she screamed.

The room blazed with rifle shots. Melee pumped bullet after bullet into the gray/green uniforms. When it was over, she counted seventeen dead men sprawled on the pavement.

They exchanged congratulations. They had struck a significant blow against the enemy, and registered many easy kills.

Then a succession of artillery shells exploded in the sniper's nest. Melee saw her friends being blown across the room. They were dead before they landed.

She fled the carnage and ran down and out the building. She escaped unscathed. But what bad luck to have the artillery strike just then.

But when she told Zaitsev her story, he slapped her violently across the face. "You fool!" he raged. "The artillery zeroed in on the source of the shots, exactly as countersnipers do. I told you not to reveal your position! Your stupidity alone is responsible for the deaths of your comrades."

Melee was stricken. He was right. She had been a fool, and her friends had reaped the consequence. She seldom cried, but now she did.

When she recovered full awareness, it was Heath who was comforting her. He said nothing about death or foolishness. He just held her. In that moment she loved him more than she had believed possible.

The siege was hard fought, but as October passed and November came, the balance was slowly shifting to favor the Russians. The stubborn defense had bogged down large numbers of German troops. The news was that a massive buildup of Russian troops was occurring beyond the Volga, enabled because the German attention was taken by Stalingrad. Melee was exhilarated. What they were doing here was paying off.

But there was a troubling development. Chunks of ice and sludge were drifting down the river, making it dangerous for supply boats to navigate. There would be little if any resupply until the Volga froze solid. Without adequate supplies, they could still be wiped out. Hungry and exhausted, they clung to their narrow strip of land along the west bank of the Volga, taking what strength they could from the fact that the Germans had not yet found the strength to complete their conquest of the city.

The news got worse. On November 7 special reinforcements arrived on the German side. These were the Pioneers, elite combat engineers. They were armed with flame throwers, machine pistols, satchel charges, and dynamite, and they were trained and experienced in urban combat. It was reported that they were confident that they would soon end the Russian resistance in Stalingrad.

Zaitsev was grim. "Hitherto we have been up against amateurs," he said. "These are professionals. Mere sharpshooting won't stop this crew. Still, we may have some surprises for them."

On November 9 the engineers made ready to assault the Russian strong points. Russian scouts had kept track, without being able to stop it. They knew that other troops had warned the engineers that here they were up against a different kind of war. The engineers shrugged this off.

Then they stumbled onto one of the surprises that Melee had helped set up. Just after midnight an explosion destroyed a room at the edge of a factory, killing eighteen Pioneers. They had triggered a booby trap.

But it didn't stop the attack. At 3:30 in the morning an artillery barrage signaled its beginning.

The Germans focused on two Russian strong points: a chemist shop, and the commissar's house. The first fell to them without trouble. But the commissar's house was another trap. Every opening had been sealed with debris, and Melee and others shot from tiny pigeonholes with deadly accuracy. One, two, three—she counted her kills as she picked off engineers. Maybe now the Germans appreciated what kind of war this was. The attackers were driven back with heavy losses.

But the engineers were tough. In the morning they managed to break into the house. The Russian defenders retreated into the cellars, but the Germans tore up the floors and threw down gasoline. "Get out!" Melee cried, realizing what was coming. They barely made it out before the Germans ignited the gasoline. The cellars were filled with fire. But the engineers didn't stop there. They lowered and set off satchel charges. Then they laid down smoke cartridges to blind anyone who might have survived the flames and explosions. They were indeed professionals.

Melee realized that the end was near. She and the others would continue fighting, of course, but it was clear that the engineers were going to take the remnant of the city that remained in Russian hands.

Within days of their arrival, the engineers had lost a third of their numbers. But the Russians had suffered worse, proportionately. Few of their troops remained, and Heath was working day and night to save the lives of those who had any hope of survival. The German assault on the factories had reduced Chuikov's HQ bunker to smoldering ruins, forcing him to relocate for the fourth time in seven weeks. No more supplies were arriving.

On November 15 the engineers turned right and left along the Volga, doing what should have been done at the outset. Melee and the others refused to be dislodged, but it seemed that any hour they would be wiped out.

That night two Soviet biplanes flew over at less than fifty feet altitude, hovering over the Russian position so as to mark it for a supply drop. The Russians lit bonfires, marking their position. But the canny Germans lit bonfires too, tricking the planes into dropping most of their supplies into German lines or the river. It just kept getting worse. Yet they hung on. What alternative was there?

One faint hope was that the Germans would misjudge the severity of the Russian winter, as they had in 1941. The hot dry extremes had held through October, but now were yielding to cold nights and drizzly mornings. The gray skies promised that the hard Russian winter was not far away. Melee, like all the others, knew the signs well. They might be short of food and ammunition and personnel, but they knew enough to be warmly dressed. If the Germans didn't, they might go the way of Napoleon.

But it turned out that the Germans had indeed learned the hard lessons from their campaign of 1941. Russian intelligence indicated that already German supply depots in the rear echelon had been established and stocked with winter gear.

That thought made Melee angry, because it reminded her that many of these depots drew part of their work force from Russian defectors. These "work volunteers" were dressed in German uniforms, given the same rations as soldiers, and paid for their labor. She hated them, of course, and would have killed any that came within her range.

"But what of the Russian cook who saved your life?" Heath asked. She hated questions like that, too, because they distorted her certainty. The matter of Wilhelm was similarly difficult, because he really did seem to be a good man. But for him, Talena and Lita would have been dead or in Germany long since, and Heath himself would still be working for that doctor. She would do her best to save Wilhelm, when the time came; she had given her word. But the matter left her with a knot in her emotion, where there should have been straight conviction.

Meanwhile, their desperate situation had its lighter moments. General Chuikov had a bunker under forty feet of earth, and thanks to his expertise and determination the Russians clung to the most critical ten per cent of the city: the industrial section. The general had thought to requisition twelve tons of chocolate before the ice floes made the Volga impassable. This wasn't foolish indulgence. Chuikov figured that if the river failed to freeze over soon, a ration of half a bar per day per man could allow them to hold out for two weeks longer. That could make all the difference.

There was a more serious wrangle over supplies. Every Russian soldier in the 284th Division in this area received a daily ration of three to four ounces of vodka. Most waited for it eagerly; very few declined. Even Heath accepted his ration, though he saved it to use as disinfectant in emergencies.

But Senior Lieutenant Ivan Bezditko, "Ivan the Terrible" to his men, had a prodigious thirst for alcohol. When troops from his mortar battalion died, he continued to report them "present" and pirated their daily rations for himself. Soon he had accumulated several gallons.

A supply major, in his warehouse on the Volga's bank, noticed the discrepancy in casualty reports. He phoned Bezditko to accuse him. "You thief! You are stealing from Russia. I'm going to report you. And I'm canceling your personal vodka ration."

Bezditko wasn't cowed. "If I don't get it, *you'll* get it!" he yelled.

The supply officer hung up, reported the transgression, and cut off the liquor ration. Nobody could bluff *him*.

Enraged, Bezditko contacted the firing point for his .122 millimeter mortar batteries and gave them precise coordinates. They fired, and the shells dropped with pinpoint accuracy. On the supply warehouse. Hundreds of bottles of vodka were shattered, and the startled supply officer was buffeted.

The incensed supply major called headquarters. But it brought him no relief: they needed those mortars. He was furious, but impotent. Within hours Ivan the Terrible's vodka ration was delivered, right on schedule.

Melee took heart in the story. To those in the trenches, the pursuit of vodka was serious business. Just a few days earlier some soldiers of the division had found several cisterns full of alcohol. They wasted no time: they drank the spirits so quickly and completely the cisterns were soon dry. Then they found another cistern brimming with spirits. They rose to the occasion and drank that one dry too. But that last cistern had held wood alcohol. Four men died and several others went blind. But the tragedy failed to daunt the soldiers' appetite for liquor. Many of them began drinking cologne to dull the horrors of life on the front.

Other troops of the unit found diversion in the company of two women who had set up housekeeping right on the battlefield. They had a cellar room twelve feet square whose only entrance was a door that lifted up from the ground. Inside was a mattress, about twenty pillows, a kerosene lamp, and a gramophone with several records. One was an Argentine tango they always played for visiting soldiers. One woman was a thirty-year-old brunette who had managed to find bright red lipstick, which she wore all the time. The other was a younger blonde who seemed pale and sickly. It seemed they were just waiting for the Germans to arrive. But they would entertain

any man for a few minutes in exchange for chocolate or vodka. Lines of
men braved shells and bullets to listen to that Argentine tango. Or so they
said. It seemed that a great deal of musical satisfaction could be had in
three minutes on a mattress. Melee didn't care for it, but at least it kept
the men from trying to grope her as much.

Even the squalor became a source of diversion. Lice were everywhere,
because of the men's inability to wash or change their uniforms. So some
men would go to a bare patch of ground and line their lice up to see who
could field the largest army of parasites. The greatest joy was word of relief,
which meant that a man could go to safety across the river, luxuriate in a
hot bath, be refitted with a clean uniform, white parka, and fur boots, and
then return to the lines. With luck and vigilance, it might be several days
before his condition reverted to normal. But of course the ice in the Volga
cut off that relief. Melee chafed as much as any; she loved sniping, but
hated being dirty and louse bitten.

So they endured, somehow, through November 18. Then on the nine-
teenth the Russians launched their counteroffensive. They struck at the
German lines north and south of Stalingrad, which were manned by Ru-
manians. Foul weather kept both air forces grounded. Morning fog gave
way to high winds and driving snow. The German reserves had trouble
moving through the snow to plug the opening gaps. The Russians, well
prepared, destroyed the resistance and moved on. The encirclement of the
German Sixth Army had begun.

Melee and the others celebrated. They knew that the Germans would
never take the factories now. They would be too busy defending their own
rear. So now it was just a matter of holding firm while the enemy grew
steadily more desperate. What would the Germans do when *their* supply
lines were cut?

Their holding strategy meant that there were fewer casualties, and they
were able to relax somewhat. Melee was able to spend more time with
Heath. She flung herself into sex with him, and he responded. But that
wedge between them remained. He was life; she was death. How could they
love each other?

"I would give you back to Talena, if I could," she said as they lay physically but not emotionally sated.

"She is better off with Od. He can give her the love I could not, and he
is a thoroughly deserving man."

"But you can't love me either," she said bitterly. "You can revel in my
body, but not my spirit."

He did not deny it. "It was my ten-year folly. The unattainable pasture
seemed greenest." He paused, considering. "But you could do better with
Vassili Zaitsev. He understands you, and has killed more Germans than you
have. I know he desires you."

"But I desire *you*," she said. "I always knew you for what you were, a
healer and a truly decent man. All that is decent in me yearns for you, and
that will never change."

He shook his head, bemused. "It is indeed an irony. I would never have visited this pain on you, had I not been foolishly blind to my own nature."

She got a glimmer of a strange idea. "I would not change you if I could. But could you change me? What would I have to be, to be loved by you?"

He sighed. "It is a fair question, but I fear it has no fair answer. I would not have you be gentle and supportive like Talena, because though I regard her as the finest of women, I never could love her as she deserved. You are her opposite, in that death is part of your makeup. Yet without that, your appeal for that aspect of me would be gone. I think I am defective, Melee. A puzzle that has no solution. I deeply regret that failure."

"No, you are perfect," she insisted. "I am the one who is wrong. I must change."

"I don't see how. I am attracted to that aspect of myself I hate."

That balked her search for a solution, so she let it go. For now she would take whatever aspect of him she could get.

In the following week they lived for news of the new front. The Russian armies slowly closed their pincers, but the Germans could still escape if they left Stalingrad and moved west in force. Yet, oddly, they did not. Instead they braced themselves within what they called *Der Kessel*, "The Cauldron," and did not move. It became apparent that Germany's Hitler, like their own Stalin, had decreed that there be no retreat. The Germans were caught not because they lacked the strength to escape, but because their leader refused to recognize reality. One German unit did try to break out, but the Russian forces destroyed it.

The enclosure was complete. The Russians had hoped to trap perhaps 100,000 German troops. Instead they had trapped nearly 300,000. What were they going to do with that many?

The Luftwaffe brought supplies in to the trapped Germans. But it was apparent that it was too little, and it would not continue, because a storm front was rolling in. The news from captured prisoners verified the obvious: the Germans were on less than half rations, and only a fifth of what they needed was coming in. They were, literally, beginning to starve. Time was destroying them.

"What of Talena?" Heath asked. "If the Germans starve, so will the Russians there."

"When I came for you, I talked to Crenelle. She has hidden supplies she is using to support them. She must have prepared well for such a siege. She's probably helping Wilhelm too, as long as he helps them."

"That is a relief," he said, and kissed her. "But we must help them, when we can."

The troops in the factory zone were not idle. They made increasingly bold thrusts against slowly fading German resistance. And on December 13, Soviet intelligence announced that it had pinpointed the German General Paulus' command bunker within the city. If they could take him out, German resistance might well collapse.

Zaitsev, Melee, and two others penetrated the lines in order to kill the general. One of the others was the girl whom Zaitsev had taken as a lover. Melee resented her, despite the knowledge that she could readily have taken Zaitsev herself, had she wanted to.

As they picked their way through the rubble, Melee tried to control her temper. The girl was immediately ahead of her, and she kept blundering and making too much noise. Why couldn't Zaitsev have left her back in his bed, safely out of the way, while the real warriors got the job done?

The girl made halting progress, and stumbled. "That cow!" Melee thought as she glared at the plump figure.

Then the cow stumbled again—and an explosion smashed Melee to the pavement. She had been hit in the stomach by shrapnel, and was bleeding into the gutter. *Oh, Heath!* she thought despairingly as her consciousness faded. Now she would never be able to change herself and win his love.

Her perception flickered, briefly. Zaitsev was carrying her back to Russian lines. She tried to protest, to tell him to leave her and get the mission done, but she was too weak even to maintain consciousness.

She touched awareness again, finding herself in a cellar hospital. Doctors were working furiously to control her bleeding. But what was the point? She would be better out of the picture.

At some point thereafter she heard, almost as if in a dream, two men talking. She recognized their voices. One was Heath.

"But I am a man of healing," Heath was saying. "How can I love a killer?"

The other laughed. It was Zaitsev. "That is no problem for me. I am another killer. But perhaps opposites do attract, for it is you she desires, not me. With that in mind, I would ask you this: predators are as much a part of the natural order as prey. Both need the other, if they are to prosper. Isn't the leopard as lovely in her way as the lamb? Isn't it possible to love the one as well as the other?"

"She is a leopard," Heath agreed thoughtfully. "I never thought of it that way before."

"I have heard she was gentle to her kitten."

"Her adopted son. Yes, she has been a good mother."

"And you were married to a lamb."

"And couldn't love her," Heath agreed. "I did crave the leopard."

There was a pause. Then Zaitsev spoke once more. "I think you can no longer postpone your decision."

Melee faded out again. She wasn't clear whether it was for an instant or an hour.

Then she became aware of someone's hand taking hers. She recognized that touch. It was Heath. She felt his breath at her ear as he whispered to her. "Melee! I can love you. But you must give me time. You must live to make it happen."

He had decided! He had chosen the leopard. Strength poured into her from somewhere. She smiled, and gathered her remaining resources for the effort of survival. She would break out of this siege. For the sake of what could be.

When she eventually regained full consciousness, Heath was there, loyally tending her. Her belly was bandaged and felt awful, but she was evidently surviving.

"What happened to the patrol?" she asked.

"The girl in front of you stumbled onto a mine," Heath said. "Fortunately she escaped with only minor injuries. You were the one who caught the brunt of it. Zaitsev abandoned the mission and carried you back."

"Abandoned the mission! But it was our chance to take out General Paulus!"

"No. It turns out that the intelligence report was incorrect. The pinpointed building was not his headquarters."

"You mean I almost lost my life for nothing? Because of a futile mission, and that damned cow?"

"Melee, I'm just glad that when your turn came, we were able to save you. Now you will be evacuated across the Volga, which is now blocking up with ice, forming a bridge. Your war is over."

"But the job isn't done! The sticks aren't gone from Stalingrad!"

"The ice bridge gives us access to the far bank. Our supply problems are over. And inside the Cauldron things are desperate. Their morale is suffering. Horses are being butchered. Guard dogs are as likely to be cooked as walked. They are done for. It is just a matter of time. Your job is to rest and recover. You almost died; now you must live."

"For you I will live," she agreed. "But we must rescue Talena. And her friends." By that token she included the German officer Wilhelm.

Heath had to remain, for there was severe need of his skills. But Melee was evacuated as soon as the route was secure. Heath kissed her as they bore her stretcher away. She smiled at him, hoping that this was not a long parting. She did not like being helpless.

They took her on a sled on the weird ice bridge across the Volga River. In due course she was back with Od and the children. They were solicitous, and though she felt she should get up and get back into the fray, she had lost a lot of blood, and there were infections to fight, and her recovery was slow. So she had to be satisfied with reports from the front. Each day that there was no report of injury or death to Heath was a relief.

It was a bleak Christmas season for the Russians, but worse for the Germans in the Cauldron. New Year's Eve Russian troops were entertained by musicians, actors, and ballerinas. Officers had parties for the entertainers. But one entertainer, the violinist Mikhail Goldstein, avoided the parties and went directly to the trenches to entertain. He serenaded them for hours. The work of German composers was forbidden, but he gambled that no one would report him, and played some Bach. The music was carried by loudspeakers, and reached the German lines. Suddenly all shooting stopped. When he finished, a loudspeaker in German territory carried a plea in halting Russian: "Play some more Bach. We won't shoot."

News came of Zaitsev: an exploding land mine had temporarily blinded him. He was out of the fray, after killing 242 Germans. But no word of Heath.

Offers were made to the Germans to treat the wounded and sick, and feed them full rations. But the Germans did not surrender. On January 10 the Russians attacked the city in force. Almost all German resistance faded under pressure. But still no surrender.

January 16 the Russians took a major airfield, leaving only one in German hands. Luftwaffe pilots soon refused to land at that last one, because it was unsafe and insufficiently managed. A few days later the Russians took that field too. News came back that word was spreading among the Germans that those who surrendered really were being treated well, not summarily executed. More than 100,000 German soldiers burrowed into the basements of Stalingrad to await the end.

January 31 General Paulus surrendered. The countersiege of Stalingrad was over.

Still no word of Heath. That had to be good news.

A few days later a military vehicle drove up to their house. Six figures got out and came to the door. Melee got up and went to see. She had been recovering for six weeks, and was doing better. She was alone at the moment; Od was out with the children.

Heath stood there. She extended her hands to him, yearning for his embrace. He enfolded her, gently. "I love you, leopard," he murmured in her ear.

"I love you, lamb," she whispered.

Then they got to business. "These five women need a place to stay," he said.

She looked past him, and saw Talena, thin but well. And Crenelle. The three others were shrouded. They would be the girls Tourette and Lita and—

"Five?" she asked.

"It may be years before German prisoners are released from internment, and we can't be sure of their treatment there," he said. "So we thought it better to bypass the process in this case. It was necessary to honor your promise."

"My promise?" she asked blankly.

The fifth figure in female clothing lifted the veil. Melee saw the somewhat embarrassed face of Wilhelm, the German officer who had protected Talena's house and brought Melee herself together with Heath and let them escape. One of those she had chosen to call sticks to be broken. Heath had seen to it that she honored her word, even to a stick.

Melee couldn't help it. She began laughing perhaps somewhat hysterically. Soon they all were laughing as they moved into the house.

Thus the German siege of Russian Stalingrad became the Russian siege of German Stalingrad, ironically. Because Hitler would not hear of retreat, 300,000 soldiers were sacrificed. It was arguably the turning point of the European theater of World War Two, for thereafter the Germans were retreating more than they were advancing. Severely weakened by its reverses on the Eastern Front, Germany thus in due course became vulnerable to the invasion by the allies across the English Channel.

Stories of personal heroism and dedication abounded, but were not always rewarded. One concerns Dr. Ottmar Kohler, who insisted that all aid stations should treat casualties within minutes of their wounding. He was certain that his method was saving lives. His patients often recovered from wounds that would have been fatal under the traditional methods. He was constantly receiving postcards from former patients, thanking him for his dedication and bravery.

Conditions at the end were truly desperate for the Germans. Dr. Kohler was rewarded early in December for his efforts with a ten-day leave in Germany to see his family. He tried to decline, but his superiors made it a direct order, and he went, promising to return. He could easily have feigned illness to avoid returning, but did not. Early in January the men of the Sixtieth Motorized enjoyed a special feast: the doctor had managed to bring thirty geese along in the Heinkel bomber that delivered him back to Stalingrad. Some of the patients in the hospital wept when they saw him come through the doors of the hospital.

Kohler was appalled by the condition of his patients. Many simply lay there and died without a struggle. No one professed to know what malady was responsible for this unusual plague. Convinced that he knew the underlying cause, he scheduled an autopsy on a thirty-year-old lieutenant to prove his case.

They laid the corpse open. There was a complete absence of subcutaneous fat. The verdict was obvious to the doctor. But the pathologist said "I cannot find any valid reason why this man is dead."

Kohler was stunned. "Shouldn't we at least offer an opinion among ourselves?" he shouted. "This man's heart has shrunken to that of a child. There's not a bit of fat on him. He starved to death."

There was only silence. During his absence, any mention of starvation as a factor contributing to death had been banned. The authorities did not want to admit that there was a supply problem. Disgusted, Kohler stormed out of the room.

On January 28, as the Soviets were retaking the city, Kohler had his hospital in the block across from the Tractor Plant. Wallowing in filth and blood, he operated in flickering lights and terrible cold. He had run out of morphine. Soldiers lined up outside the building, looking for a place to sleep. They were sent away, as there was no room in the hospital. In the morning they were still there. They had all died from hunger and exposure.

When the Germans surrendered, Dr. Kohler became a prisoner. Charges were trumped up against him, and he was imprisoned for eight years before finally being repatriated. It was another irony of war that a man so thoroughly dedicated to healing was punished for it. But he was just one tiny part of one minor unit involved in the siege of one city in one section of one theater of the greatest war of modern times. Who would notice him?

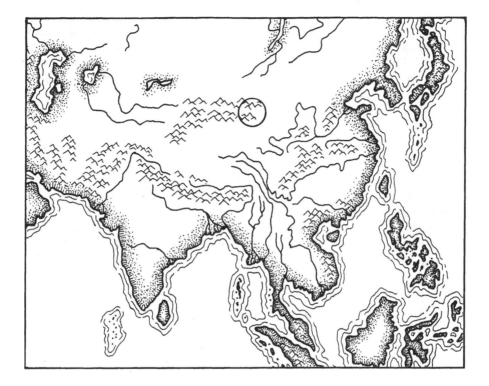

CHAPTER 13

DESTRUCTION

Mankind has always been violent, and though all the arts advanced with time, they have been paced by the art of destruction. The warfare between hominid species was brutal half a million years ago, and remains brutal today within our own species. Science, technology, and ingenuity have greatly increased the amount of damage a given war can accomplish in a short time. Finally, in the year A.D. *2024, it has become almost total. Fanatic cults have achieved the power and science to wreak utter havoc. Their problem has been to exterminate the unbelievers without being taken out with them. Thus World War Three started subtly, and was not quite perfect. The site is Tuva, and the language is Turkic, here rendered in approximate translation.*

Tuva is a small country, about 65,000 square miles, wedged between Russia and Mongolia, with a population expanding from about 300,000 late in the twentieth century to about one million in the first quarter of the twenty-first century. It was under the domination of the Mongols from the thirteenth to the eighteenth centuries, then ruled by China until 1911. Then it came under the sway of Russia, and was part of the Soviet Union until the dissolution of that empire in 1991. Thereafter it was nominally independent, but the expanding population and influence of China dominated first Mongolia, then Tuva, and about half its population became Chinese. Its capital city was Kyzyl, on the headwaters of the Jenisej River. Because Tuva was about as far from the centers of Eurasian power as it was possible to get, it was considered an ideal site to test special new technology.

TALENA was concerned. Od had been distracted for the past two weeks, and Melee confided that the same was true with Heath. Their two families shared a suite at the foot of what was colloquially called the Smog Nog, and the men shared an office in the Tower of Power. Things were chronically crowded all over, as it was believed though never spoken that the real population of China was now two billion people, and that this population was overwhelming all the neighbor states. The crowding brought the benefit of modern technology, providing excellent jobs and a high standard of living. So they weren't complaining. They had seen much worse times before.

Their small group had been close for years—closer than most others suspected—and they didn't mind sharing quarters. That way they didn't have to try to explain to others why their reality did not quite match the official relationships. Talena's nominal marriage was to Heath, and Melee's to Od, but that had become a fiction of the records. Similarly, her seven children, and Melee's two, were on the records as being from six families, and Talena cared for the nine as a foster parent, allowing both nominal parents in each other family to work full time. No one ever hinted otherwise; everyone knew how to get along despite the system, passing under and through the governmental rules.

"We must meet at the office today," Od said tersely. "Briefly, but all the children together."

"Od, what is it?" Talena asked.

"Nothing important," he said reassuringly. But his eyes flicked to the side, as if seeking the hidden monitor they knew was there. "A little party to celebrate the success of the Power Tower, which has been in operation a full six months today." But his eyes squinted; he wanted her to know he was lying for the benefit of the monitor.

"Oh, that's nice," she said, forcing the sound of delight. "I'll bring cake to surprise the children."

"And Melee can make party hats," he agreed. "But we must limit it to an hour, lest there be waste."

"Of course," she agreed, kissing him. The authorities had to know of their exchange of marriages, but didn't object, because it wasn't a political matter. If they ever got into political trouble, the matter of wife swapping (why was it never considered husband swapping?) would be exposed to ruin their reputations and justify their expulsion from society. So it was really a lever the state had to ensure their political correctness. Most families had similar liabilities; it was part of the system. So she made no in-house secret of her love for Od, and their friends and business associates never mentioned the matter.

But it was evident that something serious was afoot, for Od was not a man to cry wolf without reason. She would make sure to be there with all the children for the "party." And there they would learn what was bothering the men. The men would have a monitor-free section of the laboratory; that was the significance of the location of the party. The fact that they would not say what it was beforehand even to the women they loved indicated just how serious it was.

When Melee returned from grocery shopping, Talena mentioned it to her in the same manner as Od had: facing seemingly coincidentally away from the monitor and flicking her eyes as she spoke. "The men have set up a little party for the children at the office, in honor of six months' successful operation of the Power Tower. We'll take cake and party hats. But it must be limited to an hour, so as not to waste resources." The office was at the Power Tower, while the laboratory was here in the Smog Nog. Once the auxiliary work on the Tower had been completed, more would be done there. It was called the office mainly by courtesy; it had no electric power yet, and was a bare series of subterranean chambers. This was an irony, because the Power Tower itself was generating much of the power for the city.

"What a delightful idea," Melee agreed. "Let me make the makings, while you round up the children."

Talena nodded. She left the apartment, climbed stairs to the ground level, walked along the exit tunnel, was pushed by the cool six-mile-an-hour wind at her back, and stepped outside the building. She was near the center of Kyzyl, not far from the river. She stood by the street, signaling a ricksha. She knew most of the ricks, as she called them, and always got good service. Sure enough, one spied her and quickly came to pick her up.

"The school," she said, giving him a coin. He knew which one. She climbed into the covered rear portion and sat comfortably.

The young man pedaled his machine out onto the street and soon got up good speed. Talena gazed out across the cityscape, taking in the vertical signs and tall buildings. Even in her lifetime she had seen the massive presence of China intensify, until Kyzyl was arguably a Chinese city. There had been increasing local concern as the quiet invasion came, but this was mitigated by the improvement in the business climate. The Chinese had come bearing wealths of many kinds.

However, much of that wealth had gone into industrialization, and though that had brought jobs and money to the common folk, it had also brought pollution. This was the backwoods; it lacked sophisticated standards. That, it belatedly turned out, was much of its appeal for investors. Dirty industry was cheap and profitable. It had taken some time for the backlash to develop, with the struggle raging between jobs and breathing, but finally a special compromise had been worked out. The industry could stay, but the pollution would be addressed.

Now there was substantial development of a nature she suspected even the major centers of the world were not seeing. Such as the Smog Nog. She craned her head to glance back at it as the ricksha turned a corner. It was a massive translucent structure, six hundred feet high and almost five hundred feet in diameter. It was round, and hollow, so that it most resembled a giant drinking glass. It was in fact a pollution cleaner.

Its theory was simple: a circle of steel radio towers, each as tall as a sixty story building, was wrapped by a huge sheet of Teflon-coated fiberglass to make a single enormous chimney. Reclaimed waste water from a reservoir was pumped to the top of the structure and sprayed into the air above the glass as a fine mist. The mist evaporated and cooled the surrounding air. The moisture dissolved many of the pollutants in the air, which then rained down the chimney to be processed by the equipment below. The spent cool air flowed outward through a ring of apertures, cooling the vicinity. It displaced the hotter, polluted air in the vicinity, which rose up to be treated in turn as it crossed the structure. The downdraft also drove fan turbines that generated power to pump the water. Thus it was a smog cleaner that generated its own power and left the surrounding city cooler. The natives had viewed its construction with misgiving, but the decade it had been in operation had entirely persuaded them, and now the land around it was choice real estate. Cooler and cleaner air: what more could be asked?

After the success of Smog Nog, the design had spread to many other cities of China, and of the world. The air of the world was getting cleaner, and long-term pockets of pollution were being reduced. But the laboratories and scientists assembled for this first project had gone on to greater challenges. Such as the Power Tower.

But now they were arriving at the school. Talena was suddenly busy collecting nine children. By the time she had them assembled outside the school, the rick had whistled in a pedal wagon for her. Two strong men pedaled that, and there was room for all ten passengers.

Talena sat with her legs dangling over the edge, holding one baby, while nine-year-old Telita held the other. The remaining children sat around the rest of the edge, jostling each other and swinging their feet.

"Children," Talena announced, "we have a surprise today. We're having a party."

The children burst into applause. But Lita glanced sidelong at her, knowing that there had to be a reason. Lita had shared some rougher times with Talena than the others had, and was savvy for her age.

"It is to celebrate six months' operation of the Power Tower," Talena explained. "Your fathers worked so hard on that, and it has worked so well, that now we will all go to visit it."

There was more applause. They liked visiting the Power Tower. Talena could appreciate why. It was about as impressive a structure as mankind had built. And it bid fair to solve the power problem of the future.

They reached the Smog Nog. Melee was there with a package. She got on the wagon, and the peddlers set out for the Tower, having overheard the discussion.

"Who wants a party hat?" Melee inquired, opening her package. Of course there was a joyful chorus. She passed out the little paper bits, and she and Talena and Lita helped get them on the younger children.

Talena thought about Melee. She had adapted well to being a mother, after years of being siren and partisan. She had loved Heath, but discovered that he could not love her unless she curbed her killer instinct. Now she had her own baby, as well as the one they had adopted, and was learning to relate. And it looked as if Heath was responding. Talena knew Heath well, very well—she had after all borne him six children—and could see that it was working out with Melee at last. She was glad of that.

The Power Tower was out of town, but could be seen from a considerable distance. As they circled around a hill, it came into view, a thin spike on the horizon. That spike quickly grew as they moved toward it and the land leveled out. Its base was in a valley, so that it was taller than it looked from afar.

The children watched. They had seen it before, but were always awed by its sheer size. For it was the tallest man-made structure ever made, three thousand feet. It was not a lot wider than the Smog Nog, but was five times as high. It was made of stone and steel, with flying buttresses, and a network of guy wires. Even so, it looked precarious, because it was like a staff standing on its end, reaching far into the sky.

They reached the base of the tower. From here it was completely awesome as they craned their necks, trying to see the top through the buttresses and wires. There was a roaring sound from the wind that blasted out of the turbines at the base and swept across the landscape in dissipating channels. The ground shook with its constant force. Talena thought of a waterfall, only with air coursing along instead. The Tower was a mighty structure, with a feeling of enormous and barely contained power. She wondered perhaps irrelevantly what it would be like to make love in the Tower.

She approached the lead driver. "Please wait," she said, giving him more money. "We must return in an hour."

He nodded. He had probably taken officials here before, and waited for them.

They gathered in a group, wearing their party hats, and trooped to the entrance in the base. Talena and Melee carried the two babies, and Lita helped the youngest toddler to walk. Od came out to meet them, carrying metallic passes. Every person had to have a pass, for this was as yet restricted territory. Once everything was complete it was expected to become a major tourist attraction, because of its sheer size and its significance as the first of the future engines of power generation. But it would be another six months before the bureaucrats were sure it was safe.

The principle of operation was much the same as for the Smog Nog: tons of water were pumped up and sprayed from the top. It evaporated, cooling the air, making a fierce thirty-five-mile-per-hour downdraft within the tower that was used to generate enough electricity to power the city of Kyzyl and all its industry. The industry was not actually using it yet, because this first test year was in large part to establish the reliability of the system, but the capacity was plainly there. Towers like this, across the world, would make all other sources unnecessary. That was the dream, so close to being realized. Safe, free power!

Each child put on a pass. There was an electronic checkpoint at the door that beeped as each person passed through. Then they were inside the somber passage. The sound was diminished here, but the walls and floor vibrated with the power.

"Do you want to see the top?" Od asked the children.

There was another cheer, augmented by dancing and waving of arms. Talena was surprised, because hitherto only engineers and specialized workmen had been allowed aloft. Someone must have pulled rather forcefully on a string to obtain permission for this.

They crowded onto the service elevator and held on to the rail around its edge. It started up, accelerating swiftly to its ten-mile-an-hour cruising speed. Even so, it was three minutes before it stopped.

The door slid open, and they stepped out onto the giant rim. It was ten feet wide, but seemed precariously thin.

Heath was there. "Hello, leopard," he said, kissing Melee. But it was perfunctory, for they had serious business.

"Line up and look out across the landscape," Od said. "Like tourists. But listen carefully. Heath will give each of you an inoculation. It may make some of you feel a bit uncomfortable in a few hours, but it is necessary."

They lined up. There wasn't much of a view, actually, because the nozzles spraying water were making mist, and the incoming breeze was cloudy. But they could see way down the side of the tower, which was awesomely high. It fascinated the children.

"What is going on?" Talena asked. She knew that there were as yet no monitors up here, which was why they had come.

"A fanatic terrorist faction has started World War Three," Od said evenly. "They have developed a new variety of influenza that will kill perhaps ninety-five per cent of those it infects within five days of the onset of symptoms. It has no treatment, because it is designed to be resistant to all established remedies. The only way to avoid it is to be immunized against its carrier disease. This is another virus, a variant of the common cold. Heath could explain this in more precise detail—"

"Ballpark detail will do," Talena said tersely.

"The cold is typical and minor," Od said. "A few days of coughing and sneezing, and it passes. No fever, no lasting discomfort. Most victims can ignore it. But it carries a piggyback virus, a secondary infection, which has no immediate effect. It seems latent. Actually it is replicating itself, building up until it reaches its critical mass, as it were, when it overwhelms the host body."

This still needed simplification. "The cold spreads the flu," Talena said. "Then the flu kills you."

"Yes. The cold virus was released at the recent Olympic event, when athletes and officials from all the countries of the world were gathered in one city. Heath has been doing research on biological warfare, lest it be used against us, and noted the frequency of colds in those who returned from the Olympics. He studied samples, and discovered a mysterious complication. He notified the local medical authorities, but they demanded more solid evidence before acting. I notified the local political authorities, but they also saw no reason to react to an obscure suspicion. Nevertheless, we knew there was something, and it fit the pattern of a distribution device for a sneak attack of biological warfare. So Heath focused entirely on his laboratory cultures, while I focused on the political situation. I have not been able to isolate the particular faction responsible, but Heath did work out the nature of the flu. He developed a vaccine to prevent the flu from replicating farther."

"Farther? You mean we already have it?"

"We believe so. We caught those colds too. It would of course have been better to stop the cold, but we were too late for that."

Melee spoke. "The cold? But that's the harmless one!"

"In the same sense a gun is harmless," Od said grimly. "It is the bullet that kills. But the best prevention against the bullet is to deactivate the gun. The flu is spread initially only by its carrier virus, so if that is blocked, there is no contagion. But as I said, we were too late, by the time we learned, as the perpetrators surely intended. So we are acting against the flu. We can't abate it directly, but we can prevent it from growing beyond its present level in our bodies. That should keep it at subcritical levels and enable us to survive."

"And you are inoculating us against the bullet," Talena said, as Heath came to her with his little nozzle. He squirted a whiff into her nose, and it was done. "But once the flu appears, it will spread itself, won't it? So we'll be breathing in more of it anyway."

"Yes. And it might mutate. So we must move into the Power Tower before then, and remain isolated until it passes, just to be sure."

"How long?" Melee asked. "Before the flu starts?"

"It appears to have a delay of about two months," Od said. "Six weeks have passed since the Olympics, so our time is limited."

A typical understatement. Two weeks before the holocaust. But at least they had caught it.

"Why didn't they just distribute the straight flu?" Melee asked. "Instead of all this complication about a carrier disease."

"Because the key to global infection is global distribution," Od said. "If the flu started killing people immediately, its source would quickly be traced, and preventive measures would be taken before it spread widely. So there needs to be enough of a delay to allow it to spread across the world, and to be uncontainable. The two month period accomplishes that. Most people hardly notice and little remember a cold that passes; we didn't. So they fall naturally into the trap. Bureaucracies don't listen well, if at all, so nothing will be done. That is why we are saving ourselves; we can't do much more."

"But our friends!" Talena protested. "They will all die!"

"If we had enough vaccine for them all, we still wouldn't be able to use it," Od said evenly. "Because the moment we tried to do it in a monitored area, the authorities would sweep in and confiscate our supply, and probably imprison us for practicing illicit medicine. The bureaucracy may be slow to respond to a national or global threat, but any hint of untoward activity on the personal level will be obliterated. We must remain silent, and act in secrecy. If you are able to bring in any friends with their families, without alarming the populace, by all means do so."

Lita spoke up. "Does it matter if they get alarmed? Maybe then they would do something."

"Honey, they would riot," Od said. "And take us out with them. If only because they knew we were going to survive while they were not."

Lita considered, and nodded.

But Melee wasn't satisfied. "I've had some experience in combat. There will be riots anyway, when the nature of the flu becomes evident."

"Yes," Od agreed. "That's another reason we must get isolated."

"I mean international. Each country is going to blame its neighbors for the plague. They will go nuclear to eradicate what they think is the source."

"That too," Od said. "We hope that the depths of the foundation structure of the Power Tower will shield us from a nuclear blast, if it is not too close. The Tower itself is probably doomed, but its roots run extremely deep."

"You have thought this out," Melee said.

"Yes. We believe you should move the children in today; we have arranged for some supplies to be stored already. If you can get friends to come here quietly, we will accept them. But whatever is done, should be done within a week, to allow a margin of error. If we miscalculate the wrong way, we will get taken out with the others."

"Crenelle," Talena said. "Her family."

"Of course."

"Now we must descend," Heath said. "Before our hour is done. I suggest that you leave the children here; we will conduct them to the deep hidden bunker we have prepared. Wrap up your business and shut down the suite. We must be quietly gone."

"We can't leave the children here," Melee said. "The home monitors will note their absence, and know that we are up to something. We will be routed out before the mischief starts, and then we will be part of it."

The men exchanged a glance of chagrin. "She's right," Od said. "We overlooked the obvious. We must not do anything out of the ordinary, until the plague actually strikes."

Heath reluctantly nodded. "Then we must play it uncomfortably close. The Tower will be ready; we must be ready to move to it rapidly, on that day. But we can't discuss it or make any obvious preparations, at home."

"We know what we must do," Talena said grimly. "We will get it done."

"I can help you," Lita said. "Let me talk to Tourette. And Great-grandma Bata. No one will notice me."

Talena nodded. "That will be best." She acted as if this were routine, but her head was spinning with the amazing revelation. Biological warfare— and they were already victims. Except for the intercession of their savvy men.

They stepped back onto the elevator and started the brisk descent. Talena cautioned the children to silence about this. They had seen enough of war to understand.

The details were quietly accomplished. The key others were notified in hasty whispers at odd moments. But nothing overt was done. The children went to their day groups as usual, and the men worked in their office, and Talena and Melee did their work and home organization as they always had. But at night when Talena made love to Od, it was not endearments they whispered in each other's ears, but the details of their plan of action. There turned out to be a lot they needed to do, in very limited time.

They did it. As they organized for supper in the evening, Talena staged a dialogue with Melee for the benefit of the monitors: "Melee, remember last year when Lita and I were trapped with Crenelle and Tourette? We never really thanked them for their help. Let's invite them for a visit next week."

Melee considered. "That seems nice. But then what about William? If we want to have a reunion with those to whom we owe favors—"

Talena put on a look of surprise. "Why, you're right! But he's in Europe. He wouldn't want to leave his family."

"So invite the family too. I'd like to meet his wife and children."

Talena nodded. "He said Lita and Tourette would like his daughter Faience. But where would they stay? Local paid accommodations are too expensive."

"They can bunk on the floor of the office in the Power Tower, at night. We can move in some bedding for the occasion. It won't be plush, but I think they can stand it for a few days."

"Let's do it!" Talena agreed with girlish enthusiasm. "You call the men and warn them, and I'll call William now, before I realize how complicated this could be and change my fickle mind."

"I'll warn Crenelle too."

So Melee got on one line, and Talena on the other, placing the international call. She was in luck: six P.M. Tuva time was noon West Europe time, and his lunch hour. "Wilhelm!" she exclaimed in his language, using the current form of his name. "Do you remember when we exchanged favors last year, sharing a bedroom? Crenelle and I thought we'd like to do it again, for old times' sake. Melee wants to, also."

He was taken aback, understandably, but he was a very far cry from dull. He realized that she was speaking for the ubiquitous monitor as well as for him. She was implying intimacies they had not practiced, which meant she had something else on her mind. "I would like that, if the situation is similar. But I would not care to leave my family again."

"Then bring your family! We'd love to meet your wife, and children. So Lita and Tourette can meet Faience. Can you get time off from your work?"

"Perhaps next month. There are complications."

"Make it next week. In fact, make it *this* week, if you can. Our schedule is very tight, and next week may be too late. It means everything to us."

"If it is that important—"

"Believe me, William, it is. We want so much to see you, we just can't wait. Please say you will be here in the next few days."

"For a favor like that, we will do it," he agreed. "We shall make immediate arrangements."

"You're a lifesaver," she said brightly, again using a term that had a hidden literal meaning. "We will meet you at the rocket port."

She disconnected. "They'll come," she told Melee unnecessarily. "We must show them to Power Tower first thing."

Melee nodded. "They will be impressed." Especially with the news the men would give them along with immediate shots against the plague. Even one day before its outbreak would block it enough to save their lives.

Talena had cruelly mixed feelings. Suppose it didn't happen? That this was a false alarm, and they were disrupting their families for nothing, in the manner of end-of-the-world societies? Then they would look very foolish. Yet wouldn't that be better than what they believed would happen?

There were of course bureaucratic delays about scheduling, and it was six days before William and his family arrived. The time was very close, so Heath had to bring the immunizations to the house, concealed as a wad of handkerchief. Talena took them, and when she met them at the port, she embraced William, kissed him, and pressed the wad into his hand. "All of you," she whispered urgently into his ear. "Use these immediately."

"We are somewhat worn from the trip," he said. "Where is the public sanitary facility?"

She guided him to it, and the five of them entered. They would take the shots. Because the plague had not yet broken out, they were in time.

Soon they were riding a wagon to the apartment. William introduced his family: his wife Fae, fourteen-year-old daughter Faience, and eighteen-year-old son Bille, whose fifteen-year-old girlfriend Minne had also come along.

There were frantic greetings at the apartment, because Lita had brought

Crenelle and her husband and Tourette there to meet the visitors. But Lita also whispered grave news to Talena. "Mom, it's started."

It had started. Talena forced a smile. "We must show our visitors the Power Tower, where they can camp during their visit," she said. "Lita, get the pedal wagon we reserved."

But the girl shook her head. "The driver's sick."

"Then we must rent rickshas."

Lita and Tourette took Bille, Faience, and Minne out to round up rickshas. Talena faced the adults, her back to the monitor. "I know you can't wait to get settled. We won't waste any time." She made a small motion as of slicing across her throat, to indicate the seriousness of the situation.

They followed her out, carrying their small bags. And saw Bille hauling along a ricksha. "The rick is sick," Lita called to them. "We had to borrow it."

In a moment Tourette appeared with another. "We must maintain appearances as long as possible," Talena murmured to William. "So they don't realize where we're going. Within a couple of days, everyone will be terribly sick."

So William took his place in front and hauled the ricksha containing his wife and daughter and Minne, while Bille hauled the one holding the younger children. Talena, Crenelle, and Tourette walked beside, all of them secretly armed. Lita ran ahead, showing the way. Melee, who was in fine physical condition, followed, guarding the rear. They moved out into the city.

Chaos was commencing. The first sign of the plague was sudden fever and weakness—so sudden and severe that people were collapsing in the street. Others, realizing that something awful was developing, were desperate to get home. A man approached William's ricksha. "I'll take that," he said. "Unload your passengers."

William hesitated. Melee jogged up from behind. The man didn't notice. "Now!" he said, showing a knife.

Melee raised a small club that seemed to appear in her hand. She caught the man on the side of the head. He fell. William resumed motion.

After that, Crenelle and Tourette took up positions on either side of that rickshaw, and Melee and Talena went to the other one. There was no longer any doubt about the desperate nature of their situation. They had to get to the Tower as fast as possible, even if they had to kill to do it. "All sick people will die anyway," Talena said to William.

He nodded. Then he stumbled. He caught himself, but stopped walking. "I fear I received that medication too late," he murmured.

Oh, no! But she put the best face on it. "It should be effective, just not as much so, late. You may be sick, but will not die. Get on the other ricksha; the children can walk. They are just on it for appearance."

He nodded. He let go of the handles, removed the harness, and walked slowly to the ricksha. The children piled off, except for the smallest. Talena took the handles, but Melee came across. "I can do it better," she said, and she was surely right, because she ran miles each week for exercise.

They resumed motion. Another man tried to intervene, but Crenelle cut toward him with such an aspect of business that he fell back.

Then Bille faltered. They packed him onto the rickshaw in place of his mother, who walked, and Crenelle took up the job of hauling. They did not move at the speed the regular ricks did, but they were making suitable progress.

As Melee tired, Talena took her place. They were wearing themselves out, trying to go too fast for their abilities, yet their urgency was overpowering. Soon Crenelle tired, and Tourette took her place. They kept shifting off as required, rather than pausing to rest.

In due course they came into sight of the Power Tower—and were dismayed. There was a crowd of people around it. What was the meaning of this? Talena did not trust it.

"I'll find out!" Lita cried, and dashed ahead before Talena could stop her.

"I think we had better gird for defense," Crenelle said. Her daughter nodded, and so did Melee.

"There's a secret entrance," Talena said. "A construction tunnel the men salvaged as an emergency exit, just in case. It opens on a storage shack."

"Go there," Crenelle agreed tersely. "I don't think that crowd will let us through to the Tower."

Indeed, Lita was now running fleetly back, and several men were pursuing her. Talena felt a terrible thrill of apprehension. Her child was in danger!

"You get the others there," Crenelle said. "Let us handle this. We may not have much time."

Talena knew that this was best. She hauled on one ricksha, and two of the children pushed, moving William toward the key building. Melee did the same with the other rickshaw, bringing Bille, while Minne pushed.

Lita made it back. "They—they say the Tower," she gasped, and gulped for air. "The Power Tower brought the plague." She took another breath. "Mom—you and Melee—they recognize you."

That meant that the crazed people would try to take it out on them, as supposed agents of the horror. "Stay with me!" Talena cried. "We have a way in."

The first of the pursuing men arrived. Crenelle intercepted him. There was a plastic pistol in her hand. "Halt!" she cried.

But the man charged on in, ignoring her. His eyes were fixed on Lita.

Suddenly he stumbled and fell. Talena saw a wisp of vapor rising from Crenelle's pistol. It was a pressure gun, silent but deadly. The man had been shot to death.

"Everyone in that crowd will die anyway," Melee called. "It doesn't make any difference.

Talena remembered that it was so. Trying to spare crazed men who wanted to kill them was pointless.

Two more men came. Crenelle pointed the pistol warningly, but the men didn't stop. Crenelle didn't fire, and Talena realized why: the gun needed a couple of minutes between shots to recharge its pressure. But then the leading man fell. Tourette had shot him. As the second one charged Crenelle, she dodged aside, and clubbed him on the head as he passed, bringing him down.

But now Talena had to focus on her own business. They were at the storage shed, but the rickshas couldn't get inside. "Door inside, in back," she said, as she went to William and tried to help him get out of the ricksha. She caught his arm. It was burning with fever. "Lean on me! You must walk."

He tried, but could barely support his own weight. Then Lita came to help prop him on the other side, and they made an awkward trek into the shed. "Here," Talena said, spying the door, which looked like an ordinary exit. "Push on the center panel, and lift it up."

The children found the panel, pushed, and it depressed slightly. Then they slid it up into the door, and behind it was revealed a lever. They pushed that up, and the door catch released. The door swung toward them, opening onto a ramp going down into darkness.

There was noise behind them. Had the crowd followed? Then there came Melee's voice. "Go down. It's dark but clear, until the next door." She was telling Bille and Minne.

They careened down the ramp, the mass of the weak men propelling them. The children ran ahead, finding the second door, and opening it the same way. But William's increasingly awkward weight was bearing Talena down; she couldn't handle this much longer.

"This is just like old times," Melee gasped. Talena realized that she was thinking of her tour of the sewers the year before.

A light showed in the tunnel ahead. "Talena!" It was Od. He had come from the other direction. But he didn't take the burden of William. "Hold on; I must make sure all of ours are in."

Talena and Lita staggered on, while Od squeezed by and went to Melee's group. She heard him calling. "Crenelle! Tourette! Get in here now!"

"But more are coming!" Crenelle's voice came back. "We must hold them off while you escape."

"No! Just get on in. We mined the tunnel."

That made the point. Talena heard a woman scream, but it wasn't one of theirs. Then Crenelle and Tourette were in the tunnel, backing along it, watching for pursuit.

"All in?" Od asked.

"I think so," Crenelle answered. "We are the rear guard."

"Turn forward and brace," he said. "Cover your ears if you can."

Talena couldn't support William any more. They sank to the floor of the tunnel. "Hands over ears!" she hissed at him and Lita, and covered her own.

There was an impact of air, and a shuddering of ground. Dust swirled. Od had set off the mine, collapsing the tunnel near the shack. There would be nothing but rubble there.

After that it was easier. Od fetched a stretcher on rollers, and they hauled William along the length of the tunnel, and then Bille. Talena herself was hardly aware of the details, being too tired, and somewhat dazed by the explosion. But she knew they were getting it done.

In due course they were in the extensive subterranean network associated with the Power Tower; like a tree, it had as much of its structure below ground level as above, to ensure anchorage. Much of the labyrinth was unused and sealed off; it was in these depths that the men had hidden their retreat.

Other friends had made it in at different times by other routes. As Talena recovered full awareness, she took stock of their full complement. She wasn't sure how some had arrived, but was glad they had done so.

Crenelle and her husband were there, and Tourette and her boyfriend Bry, with his family. Bry's sister Lin was a very pretty girl, but she had six fingers on her left hand. William's family were there of course, with Minne; the girl had come down with the fever, but it was not as bad. And others, including specially ancient Bata, to whom they all owed so much. Like the Christians' Noah and his Ark, they had become a fair assemblage of bright and nice people, of several generations.

Then they waited. They had rigged a monitor system that tapped secretly into the State's Monitor network, so as to have comprehensive access to the world outside. Through it they could obtain news, entertainment, and critical data.

There wasn't much entertainment. All over Tuva and the world, people were stricken severely sick. What was evidently a terrible fever brought them low. The hospitals were crowded, but the nurses and doctors came down with it at the same time. Business, transportation, farming, and government crunched to a halt. Most made it home before the illness got too bad; some were caught on the way, as the rickshas stopped, and the motor vehicle drivers fell too ill to continue. So what they had seen during their rush to the Tower had been but a slice of the macrocosm, as they had thought. They had been right to fight their way there immediately.

Announcements were made: first, not to be alarmed. Then not to go out on the street. Then not to doubt that the perpetrators would be discovered and punished.

William and Bille began to improve. Their fever was declining. This was the proof of the vaccine: it had been effective, even only an hour before the outbreak. The virus had crested, and was not replicating further. But it would be some time before the men and Minne recovered.

The monitor system began to close down. It was largely automatic, but people had to operate the switches, and they were no longer doing so.

Power had to be routed through the region, to operate all of the systems. It stopped. The screen went blank.

Their own power remained, because it was tapped from the Power Tower itself. But without anyone overseeing it, soon it too shut down. Now they went to batteries. And to candles, which they had stocked substantially. The children enjoyed wandering around, each with a lit candle.

"Now comes the hard part," Od said. "We must wait without information at least a month, to be sure it is safe to emerge."

But in only one day they felt the terrible distant shaking of it, followed by much closer and worse: a nuclear blast had rocked the ground so hard that the Power Tower itself came down. Guy wires and flying buttresses could not hold it up when the ground itself rocked with such energy, and when an outflow of hurricane-force wind caught it.

After that, all was quiet. The war was over, in this section, and perhaps in the rest of the world. The angry victim nations had targeted anything suspicious, trying to be sure to get whoever had set loose the plague. The moment the first loosed a missile, others had too.

"Well, I hope they got the true perpetrators," Melee said.

"It seems likely," Od said. "Some nation's intelligence service should have had a notion, and they would have bombed all likely suspects. If any area of the world failed to come down with the plague, that region would be a target. Our region was a target because of its forward-looking technology. Fortunately for us they didn't attack the Power Tower directly."

"But we'll likely have some digging out to do," Heath said. "A number of passages near the surface will have collapsed."

"Which may save us from immediate nuclear fallout," Melee said.

"Our instruments show that the blast was close, but not critically close," Crenelle said. "If the normal weather pattern holds, the fallout will be away from us. This region may retain most of its vegetation."

That would be a blessing, because it would mean they could live on the surface, and begin to forage for fresh food. They could start farming, ensuring that they would not run out of food in the long term.

Talena knew that they would have to spend the month with candles and canned air, and would approach the surface with radiation counters. She knew that when they emerged there would be desolation. But there was substantial hope.

A few survived the plague by design. More survived by accident, in isolated villages to which the carrier cold had not spread. A number on missions on Antarctica and northern Greenland escaped. There were also those five per cent who endured the influenza and lived. Many of those were taken out by the nuclear fallout. Others died fighting for the diminishing spoils of a world no longer producing food. So the net survival was on the order of two per cent. Still, that was enough. Humanity had made it through its self-induced population crash.

Would it do better in the future? Only time would tell. But at least it had the chance.

F OR a quarter century I dreamed of the project that was to become this Geodyssey series. The first three novels essentially completed its essence: the history of our human species from dawn-man through the present. But the subject is so large that no one, or ten, or a thousand writers could ever complete it. It is my hope to continue exploring the bases and nuances of history as long as I live. How long that will be is uncertain; I am now in my sixties and my wife and I are considering whether to move to a retirement community. But I have hardly given up on living. Just before I started this novel, I bought a compound bow, and during the novel I learned to hit the target (never anything living) with increasing accuracy. I really hate losing or breaking five-dollar arrows! Just as I finished it, I bought a recumbent bicycle, and started learning how to pedal and move while lying almost on my back. Both of these relate to my continuing program of exercise, which together with a careful diet keep me about as healthy as I am able to be: good, but far from perfect. I also exercise my mind, which is why I learn new things, physically as well as mentally. This series illustrates much of the mental part.

At this writing, the next volume is just beginning to form in my mind: departing from prior conventions of the series, as this present volume does in some respects, it will follow several tribes or peoples through history, until they interact in the present. Such as the Alans, or the Basques, or the Maya. My researcher, whose work was invaluable for this and the prior volumes, should like the research on the Alans, for his name is Alan Riggs. But I was aware of the Alans long before I knew Alan. It should also address the problem of water. We need fresh water, and we are running out of it. It should also touch on other intriguing aspects of history, as I try to make them come alive for today's audience. History, as must be apparent, is totally fascinating for me, once it is gotten out of the schoolroom. Schools are the places that can make even sex boring, and certainly they do that for history, as students have to memorize the names and dates of lists of kings, as if that's reality. Well, when you start seeing novels like this one in the classroom along with the dry texts, you'll know that the schools are finally getting serious about teaching real history.

Every novel I do is its own adventure, and this one was typical in its atypicality. What seems to be straightforward in the planning stage can be diverted in many ways, as the Coriolis force of research and assimilation and greater understanding deflects my innocent notions into unexpected channels. Chapter by chapter, this one took its own course. I was going to start it at Chapter 3, the point at which the human species suffered reduction to a single region or tribe, accounting for the spread of the mitochondrial genes of "Eve," the common female ancestor. But I remembered that I had also wanted to stress the importance of the use of fire to our species, and that was well before that time. But it turned out that *Homo erectus* used fire too, so it was not a distinguishing trait. So then why and how did modern man diverge from his highly successful ancestral species? I pondered, and came up with a different answer. Thus the setting of the Great Rift mountains, and their special effect on that offshoot of Erectus that was driven there.

But I had always wanted to explore the reason for the development of extreme longevity in the human species, so had to add in another chapter. Thus my starting chapter was bumped to number three. I also wanted to address the start of farming. However there was also the story line to consider; I couldn't have just a series of essays. I had had this independent idea, really a daydream notion, of a young man coming to a fork in the path, and seeing down one side a pretty girl, and down the other an old hag, and taking the second one. What did this have to do with farming? Well, I struggled, and did manage to merge them, but the result was not quite what my prior fancy and foreseen. I had also wondered what would happen if a young, beautiful, strong-willed woman set out to seduce a man she knew was not allowed to touch her. So that, too, got merged, and changed in the process.

So it went, each historical notion merging imperfectly with each story notion, making a different novel than expected. I was also trying to unify it by addressing a number of the arts, because in my view it is the arts that truly define mankind and set it apart from all other species on Earth. But I had already done dancing, and painting, and music, and weaving, and other arts, so I looked for less obvious ones. These, too, meshed with my settings and stories in rather the way oil meshes with water; it was a continuing struggle.

Except when it came to Drama. For that I had the perfect example. One of my readers had sent me the Egyptian story of Osiris. Then when it came time to use it, I couldn't find the material she had sent, or her name. Evidently I had lost a folder, and I suspect it will reappear only after this novel is published. So the art that worked best nevertheless gave me the frustration of being unable to credit the one who put me on to it. Oh, I got the Osiris story itself; my researcher researched it in full in the library. Just not the credit. Gives an imperfect row of frowny faces. ☹☹☹☹☺

I wanted to explore the Olmec society, as that was the source of central American civilization. I thought there would be a good mass of political and economic detail through which I could thread my notion of a princess determined to subvert her guardian. No such luck; little turned out to be known of the Olmecs. Even the huge head statues that had intrigued me didn't work out; I couldn't find the article where I had read about them—all my other archaeological magazines were there except that one, so I must have put it elsewhere for safekeeping—and in any event, what kind of story could be told about the slow carving of a stone head? It would be like watching pigment parch. So I had little historical basis for my story. So what happened? It became a 45,000-word intense extended seduction that will probably be denatured by the editor.

Then there were the Celts, or Kelts. I wanted to explore this early European culture. But little of its actual history turned out to be known. The most definitive was in its interaction with the Romans. Thus this became a Roman story. Oh, I liked it; it just wasn't what I had been looking for. And Attila the Hun, a figure long maligned by irresponsible historians. But again, he was known mainly through his interaction with Rome. Another Roman story. Still, it's a historical interaction that deserves clarification, and I hope that my presentation helps my readers to better understand the real story, rather than the false one so widely propagated.

I felt it was time to explore the ancient civilization of Cambodia. But again, there turned out to be little actual historical information. One aspect was interesting, however: the settlement of disputes by confinement in towers. Those towers may have been rebuilt several times, and later the litigants were confined to covered platforms on the upper sections, but for my purpose small hollow towers worked best. I assume that the towers started simple, then got fancier as the process of celestial justice was refined. And the problem of longitude: perhaps one of the subtlest contributors to empire. Oh, I had my notions, and I wedged them in, but it was a constant challenge to make this collection into a unified novel.

I read that Napoleon encountered a Vietnam-like situation in southern Italy, presaging guerrilla warfare. Good enough; I sent my researcher into that recess of history. And he discovered that the case had been misrepresented. He does that; last novel, he found that the Great Wall of China didn't exist as a continuous whole, ruining my original notion. Before that, he found that a volcano I had depended on for excitement was inactive. Still, the backwaters of history are grist for my mill too; it is my contention that history is vastly larger and deeper than those lists of kings or the dates of significant events. Even if Napoleon didn't accomplish much in southern Italy, it was devastating for the local inhabitants. And so, in this desolate hinterland, three of my major characters died. That's the way it is, in real life. Great numbers of people expire not in glory, but in pointless incidental strife.

Then Stalingrad. That one proved out. Americans tend to think that World War Two consisted of two fronts: US vs. Japan in the Pacific, and US and some chance allies vs. Germany in Europe. It was more complicated than that, and much of the most brutal action didn't concern America at all. North America has never seen a campaign like that of the siege of Stalingrad, with its abundant ironies. Now you know.

I avoided World War Three in the prior novels of this series. I decided it was time to bring it onstage. But even that wasn't straightforward. What would quickly wipe out most of the human population of the world? My researcher and I discussed it, getting frequently balked. Nuclear detonations didn't seem sufficient, partly because whoever started it would surely want to survive the action. Selectively destroying the world, even in theory, turned out to be no easy task. So biological warfare seemed more promising. That could be selective, because of targeted inoculation, sparing the self-appointed Chosen while eradicating the vermin that are the rest of us. But how to spread it throughout the world before others caught on, researched to ascertain the true culprit, and struck back? That was tricky. We hashed it over, and concluded that a two-stage disease was best, one mild, the other deadly. How could my main characters survive it? Well, a doctor doing research in biological agents could catch on in time. So that's the way it was, but it wasn't very dramatic, because anyone out among the dying people is apt soon to be dead himself; they had to be protectively isolated. Not much excitement there. Thus it ended somewhat on a whimper rather than a bang. Realism makes for bad plotting. So I had to rework it to make the conclusion more chancy. After all, I'm writing a novel here, rather than actually destroying the world. The two endeavors have different objectives, whatever critics may say.

So writing this novel was like kayaking through the Grand Canyon, and I did get dumped often enough. But the essence remains: human global history is endlessly fascinating, and we could do much worse than study it. Not just for the lessons it has for the future, but for the insights into the nature of our species. I hope my readers found it worthwhile regardless.

There are a couple of credits. I notice unusual first names, having one myself, and it seems to be the ladies who have the greatest variety. When I think of something that would make a good name, I make a note, and this was the case with Avalanche and Melee. But sometimes I borrow from the names of my readers. One was Talena Klypak, who I think would have preferred to be named in Xanth, but GEODYSSEY was where I happened to need a name at the time. She was the same age as my character in Chapter 3, though both are older now. Talena the character had seven daughters, and perhaps more beyond this novel; she started young, and was very fertile, and her children were all healthy. Why? Because she is my characterization of the paleontological Eve, the mother of all present human beings. The evidence of her existence is present in the mitochondrial chromosomes of all of us, which are transmitted only by the woman. Similar evidence in the Y chromosome, transmitted by men, confirms the common ancestry we have. With each pairing, the mitochondria of only the woman are present in the child, and eventually those of one female ancestor spread throughout the species. Other traits of other people would have been passed along, so they were by no means extinct; it was just that this particular aspect stemmed from this one woman. It seemed to me more likely to have happened if she bore many daughters, because in this respect sons were wasted effort. I couldn't have the Talena of 250,000 years ago be that fertile, and not have the Talena of later years be less so, so she was always a prolific mother. What the Talena who contributed the name thinks of this I'm not sure. I dread receiving an un-fan letter fifteen years hence: "I was going to be the first female president, but thanks to you I had seven daughters instead."

Another reader name is Jilana, the eldest freewoman, from Jilana Conaway. She did not become a major character. It's a crapshoot, and most names go to incidental characters.

Normally in these novels, characters from prior volumes show up in the supporting cast. This has been the case here, too; those who watch closely will find several. But in one case some explanation is needed. Tourette was introduced in *Hope of Earth,* where her mother was not named. But there Tourette was named by Faience, as a private convention. Rather than have confusion, I had her keep the name here, though it is anachronistic, as this novel's first scene with her is earlier in time. However, each novel represents a different take on the larger history of the species, and one novel is not firmly bound by the portrayal in another. Details may differ, as they do between chapters in individual novels. All my characters are Everyman, Everywoman, and Everychild, appearing throughout time and geography in similar guises; that's part of the art of the series. So Tourette can be called that here. She will be called the same in the next novel, from the beginning, despite anachronism, where she and her family will be major characters.

I set up my characters to represent certain distinctive human traits, planning to illustrate these through the novel. But this too went wrong. Od represented Curiosity, and in time he was to become a scientist. But in prehistory science as such didn't exist, so he had to fill other roles. The later settings did not offer jobs for a scientist either. What do you do when you have a degree in science, and there are no positions open? You take what you can get. So my ambition for Od was frustrated, and he had to fill in whatever slots were available. The closest he came to science was in Chapter 10, when he explained the problem of Longitude to King George. In Stalingrad he had to be a political officer. Even in the final chapter, Heath pre-empted the laboratory science, so Od was still a political officer. Heath did get to be a doctor, in time. Talena was to be the creative story teller, and she did tell a couple of stories, but then the requirements of motherhood confined her mostly to the home. Avalanche was to illustrate the art of sex, and be a temple prostitute. But in my Egyptian setting they did not have temple prostitutes. She became more of a hostess, and later more of a call girl. Pul was to be a chronic bully, and he fit in well in the military life. Melee was to cover the domestic and culinary arts. But she was too wild and beautiful, and Talena had the children, therefore the home-making. So Melee finally got to indulge her appetite for violence, in Stalingrad. And Dillon was to be the arts of hunting and fighting—but Pul had taken the military life. So it all got garbled, just as things do in real life. Characters as Archetypes just didn't work out, but I couldn't scrap them once they had come alive. Then, after I had hammered it all out, my researcher read the novel and made notes, pointing out fallacies of history or logic, and I had to rework scenes. For instance, I had the families bringing food to the litigants in the Chapter 9 Tower Justice sequence; he pointed out that decisions were apt to come much more rapidly if food were denied, and that did make sense, and was probably the way they did it. So I had to rework that aspect. Thus I learned what not to do in the next novel, by struggling through unworkable notions in this one. Writing is a continuing education.

There are some deviations from the pattern set by the first three novels. Each of those was crafted for twenty chapters, with major settings at the quarter, half, and three quarter marks. This one is thirteen chapters, because I went for fewer and larger ones, and the major settings fell where they would. The next novel may have more; I'm freeing myself of the fixed framework. This makes for a less patterned effort, perhaps less artistic in form, but I hope still effective as a novel. In the prior novels, there were forenotes and endnotes for each chapter; in Chapter 8 of this one there were also some midnotes, to clarify the historical perspective. I thought about doing it in Chapter 12, but managed to avoid it. Of course Chapter 12, about the Siege of Stalingrad, was like a short novel in itself, 50,000 words long, with eight subsections as each character had two turns being the viewpoint person. The last one, Melee, was 15,000 words in itself, longer than many whole chapters elsewhere in the novel. But that wasn't the only difference. In the prior novels my characters have interacted with historical figures, as they do here, as Od does with Nikita Khrushchev (yes, the later Soviet premier was there, historically, as represented, except that he never had the pleasure of a peek into Melee's blouse) and Heath with Dr. Kohler, but never pre-empted them. This time Melee at one point takes over the role of a historical figure. She was Tania Chernova, age twenty. She was the one who caught the raft to Stalingrad, and traversed the sewer, and stank in the German mess hall. She was the one who broke eighty "sticks" before getting almost killed by a mine. She helped bomb the German HQ and shot the Germans in the street, drawing the return fire from the artillery that killed her companions. But the superimposition was not complete, for in real life Heath did not exist. Thus Tania did become super-sniper Zaitsev's lover. I wanted to show the Siege as it was, and Tania's adventures adapted readily. Od, too, pre-empted one person for one sequence: Lieutenant Khoyzyanov of the marines, at the grain elevator. But the real man did not escape after being captured. I pondered hard before allowing these character takeovers, not wanting to toy unfairly with history. But it seemed the best way to handle this particular situation. I felt that my readers would relate better if they knew the characters, and in any event, there was no other woman in the sewer with Tania, so Melee could not have been there as a separate character. But I do feel that the historical figures should be credited. They were the ones who were in that hell of war.

One of the differences between ambitious writing and unambitious writing is the artistry that exists apart from the story itself. The kind of thing that teachers of literature notice. This novel is not special in that regard, but there are spot aspects. The two longest chapters, 6 and 12, concern sieges: one of the emotion of a man, the other of a city. In each case, by the time the siege is won, it is reversed, and the besieger is besieged. Thus Melee wins Dillon, but he also wins her, while the Germans do take Stalingrad, but then are trapped within it. There is also a minor parallel between chapters 9 and 13, wherein understanding or salvation is found within towers. The last three chapters focus on the destruction of war, of increasing significance, as mankind plunges carelessly ahead and finally comes close to destroying himself. But I have to say that I didn't plan on these; they just happened. The things I planned on did not work out well, as already mentioned. Of course I don't place much stock in such things. GEODYSSEY is the most ambitious series of my career, as I try to learn about our species, and to fathom its interesting recesses, its delights and its follies.

So how did this come to be the second longest novel I've written? (*Tarot* was my longest, but it was broken into three volumes for initial publication.) Again, it just happened. I thought it was going to be 50,000 words shorter. Well, maybe next time.

But the overall series message remains: if we as a species don't change course, soon and significantly, we are going to pay an awesomely awful price. I show such prices in these novels, hoping that they will never actually come to pass.

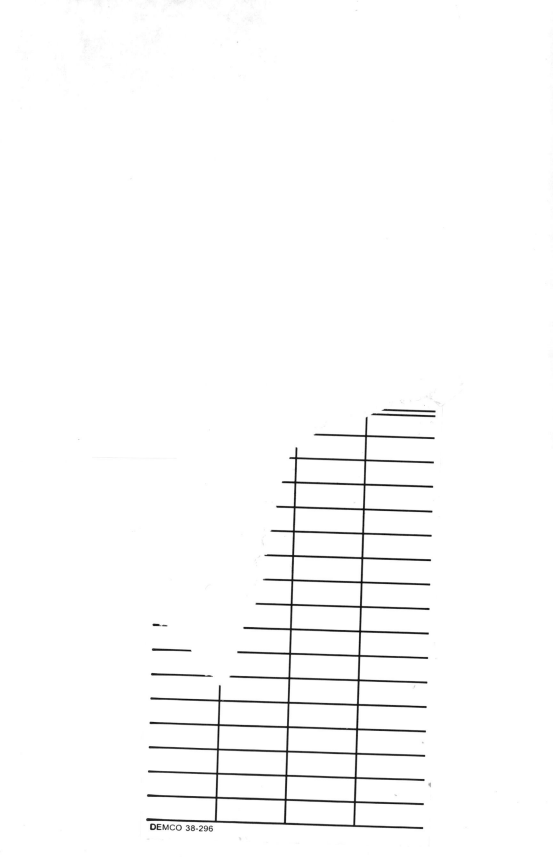

DEMCO 38-296